Library of America, a nonprofit organization,
champions our nation's cultural heritage
by publishing America's greatest writing in
authoritative new editions and providing resources
for readers to explore this rich, living legacy.

JEAN STAFFORD

JEAN STAFFORD

COMPLETE NOVELS

Boston Adventure

The Mountain Lion

The Catherine Wheel

Kathryn Davis, *editor*

THE LIBRARY OF AMERICA

This paper exceeds the requirements of
ANSI/NISO z39.48–1992 (Permanence of Paper).

Distributed to the trade in the United States
by Penguin Random House Inc.
and in Canada by Penguin Random House Canada Ltd.

Library of Congress Control Number: 2019936689
ISBN 978–1–59853–644–7

First Printing
The Library of America—324

Manufactured in the United States of America

Contents

BOSTON ADVENTURE

For Frank Parker

BOOK ONE
HOTEL BARSTOW

Chapter One

BECAUSE WE were very poor and could not buy another bed, I used to sleep on a pallet made of old coats and comforters in the same room with my mother and father. When I played wishing games or said "Star light, star bright," my first wish always was that I might have a room of my own, and the one I imagined was Miss Pride's at the Hotel Barstow which I some-times had to clean when my mother, the chambermaid, was not feeling well. I knew its details so thoroughly that I had only to say to myself the words "Miss Pride's room" and at once my feet stood on the tawny rug with its huge faded peonies, and before me was the window seat covered with flat, flowered cushions, at one end of which was a folded afghan, at the other, three big soft pillows on which cherubs floated amongst blue daisies, holding up in their dimpled hands a misty picture of a castle. And I could gaze through the windows which over-looked the bay. On a clear morning, looking across the green, excited water, littered with dories and lobster-pots and buoys, I could see Boston and its State House dome, gleaming like a golden blister.

Often at night, I pretended that I was sleeping in the big brass bed, under the fringed white counterpane, my head upon the inflexible bolster. Turning over, I imagined I could hear the rattling of the loose balls which decorated the foot-rail and which, when I tucked in the sheets, gave the Spartan bed, with its hard mattress and thin blankets, a kind of saucy vitality. Suddenly, as if it were borne on a wind, there came to me the fresh, acrid odor of Miss Pride's costly soap which she kept in a large carton under the bed. She was part owner of a soap factory, I had heard, and so, of course, it cost her nothing.

Some nights, though, my vanities were driven off, and I could not hold in my mind a picture of the room nor could I summon up the rich old lady. For on those nights, I lay terri-fied at the sound of my parents' quarreling voices. I mocked the deep breathing they expected of me, but the air would not go down into my lungs and was caught like a hiccough in my throat. There was a raw-edged blade of pain straight through my chest to my backbone as though fear had laid back the sheath of my nerves. Anxious for morning, I lay on my back staring at the invisible ceiling or cautiously I turned over on my side, making out the contours of the sagging bed where my mother and father were enormously sprawled out and humped up, hissing their fury at one another. Until I was about ten years old, though, my distress did not continue after their voices had ceased and, exhausted as much by being an audience as they were by being the actors, I would fall asleep at once. It was not until then, the summer of my tenth year, that I learned, in what terms of childhood I cannot remember, that peace was to be desired above all things. The upraised voices, the bitter blasphemies, the profound outcries of hatred carried through the day. If at the end of it there was a silent night, I lay awake for a long time waiting for the storm to break, and in the morning got up fretful for my vigil.

Our poverty was my mother's excuse for perpetuating the old anger. Although she had never been anything but poor, for her life in Russia before she married had been a tale of privation and suffering, still she had dreams of what it was like to be rich and, as she accused him, my father had promised her the finest of goods when he asked her to marry him. And what had she instead, she demanded. A two-room house in a fishermen's village where the sand seeped in the doorways and across the window sills, where the winter winds gained access through the cracks in the walls, and where in the summer time the heat descended from the low beaverboard ceilings in a steady, unmerciful blast. And had she to eat the fowl, the caviar, the strawberries and melons and pears he had promised? Our fare was no better than the poorest peasant's: day-old bread, *pokhlyobka*, side meat, and on great occasions, eggs. And did Shura Korf have a servant girl to go to the wine-cellar and fetch up champagne, Malaga, Rhine wines and Scotch whiskey, vodka and kümmel? Perhaps four times a year my father bought a bottle of corn whiskey from a bootlegger, and in the sordid kitchen they drank it in hot toddies which neither pleased their palates nor elevated their spirits and made them waken the following day with headaches, biliousness, and intermittent vertigo. Where were the yellow dresses, the summerhouse and the island in the lake, the solid silver samovar and the little black dog and the chestnut mare? What a brazen liar he had been! He was not the clever, ambitious man he had said he was when on the boat, caressing her as they leaned against the rail of the third-class deck, he had told her how he would have a great shoe business in the United States, selling only shoes made by hand and of the best leather money could buy. Why, he had declared he would have ten workmen under him! He would have commissions from the millionaires of New York City and Washington and Boston!

But see how it was instead: after ten years he was a nothing, a nobody. He *repaired* boots for the poor fishermen; he did not make them for the millionaires. He had not made a single pair for anyone but her, himself, and me.

My father, his pride lacerated, his shame festering would, at this point, retaliate. He would call on God as witness to his wife's failure to observe the laws of marriage: she did not honor him nor love him nor obey, but had made for herself a stifling little box of a life where she did nothing but slothfully brood and cry because she had no yellow dress. What man on earth would *want* to work for a creature like that?

I remember one of these quarrels especially well, not because it was different from any of the others, but because of what followed it on the next day. It was in September, the week before the Hotel Barstow was to close for the season, and I was awake, sorrowing that Miss Pride would soon go back to Boston and that all winter long I would have nothing to do but go to school. My father had gone off to the Coast Guard house where he often spent the summer evenings, playing checkers and drinking home-brew with the men off duty. I was always glad when he went, for usually it meant that my mother would be asleep by the time he came in. But tonight she was restless and several times she spoke to me, "I can't sleep. Sonia, are you awake, darling?" I did not answer and I heard her turn over, sigh, and murmur to herself, "Too hot." It was always either too hot or too cold for her, and not even in the spring or the autumn would she admit that the temperature was pleasant. She would present her perspiring face to my father, or, in December, would hold out her blue hands and say, "You want to kill me!"

For some time I had been living with Miss Pride, first in her room at the Hotel and then in her unknown Boston house and I was either half-asleep or else so preoccupied with my thoughts that I did not hear my father come in and it was only when I heard my mother whisper, "I hate you! Christ God, I hate you!" that I realized he had got into bed and that the close room was full of his breath.

"Let me alone," said my father. "I'm drunk."

But my mother repeated her malediction over and over as if neither he nor she would ever realize its full meaning. After a while, my father howled wearily, "Then go away, for the love of God!" He turned over and the bed springs gave a prolonged creak. My mother, though, knew that he was not asleep, and she began to talk in a monotone, marshaling the injustices she had suffered her whole life long until their perpetrators thronged the room. She began, as was her custom, with the beastliness at hand: "He tells his wife to go away. First he promises her he will be rich and give her a fur cape and French perfume and a hothouse with a gardener to grow white grapes. And then, in a little bit, he tells her to go away out by herself in America where she don't know how to talk to beg. He wants this wife of his to be a beggar! You wish it was winter, don't you, *mein herr*? So you could send me to the snow without shoes, me and my little girl. Well, sir, wait till the first cold weather and drive us out then. It won't be the first time for me. The child, she knows the words to beg with."

"You speak English," said my father.

She paid no attention. The past was advancing slowly upon her. I knew, because in the quiet I heard her sighing and I heard her rubbing her hands together as she always did when she was thinking of Russia. "It will not be the first time a man drove me into the snow."

"Shura!" implored my father. "Don't tell me again! I will go tomorrow to Boston for work if only you'll go to sleep now."

Heedless of him, she began. Under the night's still heat, her voice flowed like a deep, unbending river as for the millionth time, using the familiar words and images, she recounted the disasters of her childhood. It was a tale so fantastic that not even I, a little girl, could believe it. Yet it was one so horrible that to scoff at it would have been inhuman. In the pauses I listened but could not hear my father's breathing and I knew that he was wide awake, counting off each episode as it fell from her lips and calculating how many more were still to come before the end. As she mourned on, the heat was dispelled and the cold of Moscow's winter streets invaded the bedroom. As clearly as a few minutes before I had seen Miss Pride's afghan and pillows, now I could see nothing but crusted snow, a little cold, yellow sun, and the blue faces of poor people freezing in the gateways and the alleys.

When she was nine or ten years old, her mother died. Her father, who was a tailor and a libertine and a brute, commenced to drink heavily at the funeral dinner and continued to stay drunk for a week. It was in January and it was bitterly cold. The seven children, whom their father and his rioting friends drove away from the stove, kept warm only by hugging one another while the revelers, warm as toast with vodka and the stove heat, poked fun at the shivering little bodies and the chattering teeth and the bright red noses. One day, Constantin Ivanovitch Korf began to malign his dead wife, calling her in one breath a whore and a pious old crone, though she was neither but only a good hard-working creature who had come to the city from the farm and perhaps had died of years of homesickness.

Here came a hiatus in the narrative and I knew that my father, like myself, was mouthing the words that were to follow. She brought out: "The Russians are always homesick people." It was a minute or two before she went on, and in the firm enclosure of the silence, I seemed myself to ail like a Russian and a hot cloud grazed my eyelids.

"There was a yellow-haired German milliner who sat on his lap and pulled at his beard. *Fräulein* Lili, she called herself. I suppose she had no real parents and that was why she had no family names. She would sit there plucking the old goat's beard and call him, 'Constantin, my little bear.' Ah, it was sickening!"

His grief had flown away like a sparrow and he shouted for a song from *Fräulein* Lili. One of the children whimpered, whether from sorrow or shame or cold no one knew, but whatever its cause, the outburst was contagious and directly all the children were sobbing and wailing. You would have thought Constantin Ivanovitch would be too drunk to hear or care. But he flung the woman from his lap and stood up, his feet wide apart, shaking his fist at his sons and daughters. He shouted that he was through with his brats, they could freeze that night for all of him. Then he advanced and together they rose, holding up their little arms as if to thwart the blows from his hairy hands. They turned and made for the door as he followed, slapping their backsides until they were across the threshold. The door was shut. The bolt was drawn. Immediately the milliner began to sing:

> Till with age my hair starts graying,
> Till my locks have ceased to curl,
> Let me live in joy and gladness,
> Let me love a pretty girl!
> Let me live my life in joy and gladness,
> Let me love a pretty girl!

The children scattered, knowing that no one would take them all in together. Whether my mother wandered by herself for hours or for days, she was not sure, she said, for such cold as the cold of Moscow tyrannizes over the light and the dark; the sun is like one poor candle in a vast hall, or else, shining forth with a rowdy blaze, it burns and the kindled snow sears the eye. But at the end of whatever time it was, she was taken into the house of a witch, so-called because of her profession: for a price, she mutilated men who wished to escape military service. She cut off their fingers or their toes or broke the arches of their feet. This Luibka was a dried and wrinkled old prune of a woman with a cackling voice and a bright, shrewd eye and hands which, even in idleness, crooked as though they held a knife.

"*You* would have come to Luibka, Hermann Marburg," she accused my father. "*You* would be too lazy and cowardly to be a soldier."

"I served my time," he replied dully.

"In Germany, yes, where everything is soft. But you would have come to Luibka in Russia where the food is scarce and the soldiers' boots are no good."

The witch was not a bad woman, my mother insisted, but was only the innocent slave of the wicked men who patronized her. The customers might cuff and kick the little girl who washed the knives and handed up the cloths, but the old woman never raised a finger against her and never spoke so much as a single word of reproof. And still, though she had enough to eat and a dry place to sleep, there came a time when the witch's kindness was not enough to stop my mother's ears to the screams nor to close her eyes to the bloody blades and the anxious hound who sprang from his corner whenever a gobbet of flesh fell to the sawdust-covered floor. She was already a tall girl, about fourteen years old, when she left Luibka; and she was so comely that once she set about it, she had no trouble in finding work. She became a waitress in an officers' tavern. From two o'clock in the afternoon until two in the morning, she brought the gentlemen dinners and tea and suppers with champagne as well as the occasional glass of vodka and Löwenbräu beer, imported from Munich, the specialty of the house.

In many ways, my mother felt she had advanced considerably in the world for she was supplied with a pair of handsome uniforms and she was allowed to feed on delicacies, and her tips, because she was beautiful, were by no means trifling. And yet, with all her good fortune, there were times when she would sooner have been handmaiden to Luibka, for the officers made such impertinent overtures to her that she could scarcely sleep at night for shame. Once, in her second year, a cossack whose advances she had rebuffed slapped her face in a drunken fury and his companions jeered her and to him they cried, "*Touché!*" A few days later, she fell ill of a mysterious fever. She recalled that two old nuns, friends of the landlady of the tavern, came to see her sometimes in the afternoons and stroked her hot forehead with their cold white fingers. When she told them that her sickness had been brought on by a ruffian's spitefulness, they exchanged a glance and, smiling benignly down on her, they said perhaps God would call her to a convent.

All the officers were angry with Shura when she was well and went back to work, and as she served their dinners, they twisted her arms or dug their nails into her hands or stepped on her feet, and she was afraid to cry out lest she be discharged if the master learned how much his clients hated her. Once, as she was going home to her room a few streets away, a soldier followed and pushed her under the wheels of a cab; she was not hurt badly, but her face was cut and her whole body was one great bruise.

In her seventeenth year, she had saved enough money out of her tips and wages to set forth into the world. It was on the boat which brought her to America that she met my father. A week after they disembarked they were married. How great had been her hopes the day she left Moscow! Her fellow waitresses, clinging to her, sobbing with envy, had sworn that she would be rich. Disentangling herself and mounting the steps to the train she laughed and called to them over her shoulder, "Your turn will come. Come to a picnic on my island, my dears!" And how close to fulfillment had seemed those hopes when the fair-haired German boy, tall, well-dressed, smelling of expensive cologne, had promised her that fine house, that immense wardrobe, those journeys to Paris and to Shanghai and to the Panama Canal. Each night, as the old boat rocked and groaned through stormy water, he shouted his promises over the racket of the wind and the protesting timbers.

"What do I have?" she groaned. "Nothing. No dresses, nothing but slops to eat. Ah, Hermann Marburg, I hate you from the bottom of my soul!"

My father, now that the long, sad tale was done, had had enough. He laughed at her, and that laugh, made up of all the scorn of devils and all the resentment of the damned, made me half sick to death with fright and I was glad for the darkness so that I could not see his genial face askew and scarlet, for the sound could not help corrupting what it issued from.

"Hush!" said my mother. "You'll wake up Sonia."

But he only laughed the harder, gasping and choking as though this glee were a convulsion beyond his control. Then, quieted, in a solemn, even voice, he said, "The child should never have been born."

His words concluded the scene. Worn out, they went to sleep. Over and over, until my eyes closed, I imagined the day on which my parents would die and Miss Pride would come to take me to live at the Hotel, if they died in the summer, or in Boston, if in the winter. Or I watched the waves part and saw a dry path laid for me between the water's furniture and then I stepped forward off the beach and walked across to the first wharf in Boston harbor. I could hear the calm waves washing the rocks and the shore and although my mind was far away, I could hear their undertone, gentle and melancholy, reiterating endlessly my father's words: the child should never have been born.

2

On the following morning, both my parents slept late, and I was on edge, fearful that my mother would not be on time at the Hotel or that a customer would come to my father's cobbling shop at the rear of the house and finding the place closed would leave and not return. My worry made my fingers all impatient thumbs and the fire would not start for me. Through a shimmering veil of tears, particulars of the room, aglow with morning sunshine, were distorted in a dream-like beauty: the stains of the dark blue sink under the window were invisible and it appeared, with the glittering water-drops that depended from its brassy taps, patinated with green, like some old and precious vessel. The crimson geraniums on the sill above were blurred in a tropical splendor. As the kindling caught, my eyes cleared, winking away the transformation of the sink and seeing once again its preposterously graceful legs and its drainboard bristling with sodden splinters. I counted slowly to sixty before I lifted the stove-lid again to see the progress of the fire, and as I counted, stared at the two pictures which hung one above the other over the table. The lower one was a barn-yard scene of russet hens and two majestic roosters avidly pecking at the foot of a pile of manure while beyond them there loomed a red barn from which stared out a thoughtful cow. The higher picture represented two little girls in white dresses and white satin slippers playing with five white puppies under the supervision of the snow-white mother dog.

When the kindling had caught, I dropped in a few lumps of coal, then waited until I had counted two hundred before I closed the damper. I gazed at one object until I had counted fifty and then shifted my eyes to another. We had three hard chairs with imitation leather seats adorned with lions' heads in bas-relief; a bright red step-ladder; a footstool made of a cheese box; a pea-green washstand where stood a pitcher and bowl, discarded by the Hotel Barstow. Long ago, when he had bought the house, my father had put shelves up against one wall which were called "the book shelves" although they contained only a German translation of *Riders of the Purple Sage*, a Bible, my schoolbooks and a very old copy of *Harper's Magazine* in which I had one time read a bewildering advertisement: "Everyone wants a gold tooth. Now you too can have one by sending only ten cents (10¢) for a complete Dento-Kit." The shelves were crowded with pliers, hammers, Mason jars full of bacon grease as old as myself, an empty caviar can which my mother fondled now and again in memory of the day, ages ago, when she had eaten its contents; broken pipes, broken knives, shattered sea-shells, a landing net, a wooden snake, a gauze bag filled with venerable headache pills.

Just as I lifted the stove-lid for the third time, the door to the bedroom burst open and my parents tumbled out, shouting at me to put the kettle on for tea and to run unlock the shop and to run to the Hotel to say Mamma was not well today and I would do for her. These tousled, foolish creatures seemed not the same at all as those hobgoblins who had rollicked and bawled in their temper tantrum the night before. My father, while he rubbed his eyes with one hand, patted my cheek with the other and said, "*Good* morning, *Fräulein*. Look sharp, there. Today is the day we get rich all of a sudden, *ni't wahr?*" My mother did not hear him, for she was running water at the tap for her perfunctory toilet.

My father gave me then a purposeless wink and nodded toward the box of corn flakes on the table. "Esel von Hexensee hasn't eaten his hay yet." This was my favorite joke. Out in the shop, in the dark little room that smelled of pipe smoke and leather, he made up stories, pretending that I was a boy named Fritz or a donkey named Esel von Hexensee, and if I were the latter, he would fit a saddle to my back and two Concord grape baskets for panniers and drive me up the Zugspitz for some droll, pious purpose such as taking hot soup to Fritz who had fainted from the altitude. The games delighted me and when he was tired of playing, I would beg him to go on. "Na," he would say, suddenly sober. "I am stiff from beating that *dummkopf* Esel," and picking me up like a cat, he would put me out of the shop and bolt the door behind me.

I drank a cup of tea that had not brewed long enough, swallowed a few spoonfuls of corn flakes and ran out of the house towards the road leading to the Hotel. The fishermen were untying their boats and calling greetings to one another. Their wives stood on the doorsteps complaining to their neighbors that it looked like "another scorcher." Mrs. Henderson, who lived next door to us, cried something to me but I did not hear what she said and I ran on, flinging back, with no thought of its meaning, "I know it!"

We did not live far from the Hotel, perhaps no more than a quarter of a mile, but because after the cluster of fishermen's cottages there were no houses at all on either side of the curving white road, it seemed a long and tedious distance. Here there were no shade trees to interrupt the glare of the sand and the dry flowers that straggled half-heartedly along the road were too dwarfed even to cast a shadow. It was a relief to take a turning and then, from a slight rise, to see the big white frame Hotel with its bright flower beds and its verandas where hung baskets of fern and ivy.

The Hotel Barstow was the sort of place which never changes and then, with very age, it falls and the site is used for a new structure. Such a day was impossible to imagine. Anyone who had lived there assumed that the stuffed hoot-owls and the Wilson snipes and the herons would go on forever patiently standing on one leg in hoary moss or placidly sitting on unseen eggs behind their glass cases in the dining-room, that until the end of time the same old ladies, musty-smelling and enfeebled, would be offered cream-of-wheat as the first entrée on the evening menu. Forever, too, the same sort of pert, plump man would stand behind the curved desk in the lobby, fetching down keys and mail and inquiring after his guests' health.

Miss Pride, an early riser, was drilling on the beach, unwithered in spite of the sun which was already very warm. The clerk, Mr. Hagethorn, called from the veranda, "Well, Miss Pride, is it hot enough for you today?"

Unsmilingly she replied, "I observe no change from yesterday. Has the mercury risen?" Even in midsummer, she always wore black broadcloth suits and an olive beaver hat. She apparently suffered neither from the heat nor from the cold, for she did not shiver or perspire, and she was never heard to discuss the temperature.

I slackened my pace in order to hold her in my vision: straight as a gun-barrel, she carried her lengthy shadow up and down

the golden sand; or she rested it, squarely facing Boston, looking with her formidable eyes into the very conscience of her
care-taker who was probably loafing on the job. I had heard
someone say of my mother, "She is beautiful except in one
thing, her eyes are too large." I believed, therefore, that Miss
Pride was beautiful for hers were very small. They were eyes
more like a bird's than any other creature's: that is, such was
their intensity and their sharp change of direction (they never
wandered, but rather, disconnected their focus from one point
of concentration and abruptly fixed it upon the next) that they
gave the impression of being flat to the skull or slightly convex,
that they had a container more like a plate than a socket. They
were "on" her head rather than "in" it. I suppose in her pass-
port they were called "gray" or "hazel," but to me they were
"cold gold" and were like the yellow haze that followed sundown when the shine of the sand was gone.

I hesitated a moment in the hope that she might turn and
greet me. A sigh, involuntary and profound, ruffled up through
my lips and when it had passed, I ran to the back of the Hotel.
Without explaining to the head chambermaid that my mother
was ill, I snatched a mop and a broom and a dust-cloth from
the closet off the kitchen and ran up the backstairs two at a
time. For I wanted to repeat the strange experience I had once
had of regarding Miss Pride through the windows of her very
own bedroom. She was still on the beach when I stole to the
central window. Now a few bathers had come for an early dip
and Miss Pride was plowing up and down through the sand,
fixing them with her clear, indifferent eyes as though, without
loss of dignity to herself, her gaze could penetrate them to
their very giblets. As I watched her, taking in with admiration
each detail of her immaculate attire and her proud carriage,
I heard, from the adjoining room, embedded in a yawn, the
waking squeal of Mrs. McKenzie, a garrulous and motherly
old woman whom I had always disliked. Her room was no
pleasure to clean: her bed was strewn with corsets and short-
sleeved nightdresses, and on her bedside table, I often found
drying apple cores which I removed gingerly, having in my
mind an image of her with her sparse hair unpinned sitting up
in bed cropping with her large false teeth. Upon the bureau,

amongst sticky bottles of vile black syrups and tonics and jars of fetid salve, there lay her bunion plasters and her ropes of brown hair which she sometimes arranged in a lofty cone on top of her head. Usually she was in the room when I entered and she saluted me with disgusting moonshine as "mother's little helper" or asked me if my "beauteous mamma" was sick.

Now in Miss Pride's room, there was never anything amiss. Perhaps once or twice a summer, I found a bottle of imported wine or whiskey on her writing desk; this was the only medicine she took and she took it regularly in small quantities. On the bureau, the china hair receiver did not receive a wisp of hair, and there were neither spots nor foreign objects upon the white linen runner. A hatpin holder, sprouting long, knobbed needles, two cut-glass cologne bottles, and a black glove-box, shaped like a small casket, were reflected in the clear swinging mirror. Though I should have loved to dearly, I had not the courage to investigate the drawers which were always neatly shut, but I was sure that they were in scrupulous order. The other old ladies, almost without exception, allowed the feet of stockings and the straps of camisoles to stream from each gaping tier like so many dispirited banners.

As I watched, Miss Pride ascended the steps that led from the Hotel beach, and I knew that now she would enter the dining-room and, after she had eaten one boiled egg and one slice of toast, she would examine the newspaper over her coffee while all about her, her coevals would be prattling of their sound sleep or their insomnia, depending on how the dinner of the night before had affected them. It seemed to me that Miss Pride looked up and saw me even though my face was hidden by the marquisette curtains and my body was behind the heavy drapery. I backed away from the window and began to run the oiled mop over the edges of the floor which the rug did not cover. While I worked, I heard Mrs. McKenzie thrashing about in the bed and rise finally, stumbling over her shoes, bumping against the furniture and repeating her vociferous yawn. The sound of the bed rolling across the floor, as I pulled it out to make it, roused her to rap on the wall and cry, "Good morning, Mrs. Marburg! I've been a lazybones again today!"

I did not answer. There was something in the tone of her

voice, a quality of dampness—as though the words themselves were kisses from unminded lips—which embarrassed me. She called again, "Yoo, hoo, Mrs. Marburg!"

"It's Sonie," I grudgingly gave out.

"Oh. Well, Sonie, I'll be out of my room in three shakes of a lamb's tail and then you can come get me straight."

"Yes, ma'am."

"Get yourself a lemon drop, dear!"

Presently I heard her door open and close and heard her toil down the stairs, one dropsical foot at a time. I now worked rapidly, brushing my cloth over the bedside table, the writing desk, and the bureau, plumping up the cherub pillows and setting the bolster precisely at the head of the bed. When I had finished, I stood for a few minutes before the mirror and, as I had done many times before, pulled out the stoppers of the bottles and inhaled their clean, alcoholic fragrance. I opened the black box and gazed upon the white silk button gloves, the yellowing white kid and black chamois ones, amongst which were scattered single cuff-links, broken bone buttons, a mysterious, star-shaped brooch and three edible beads. My brief survey finished, I sat down before the desk and though I touched nothing, I took in everything: the brass letter opener with its carved wood scabbard, the matching ink-pot and pen and the dark green blotter in a brown leather holder, the calendar which gave the date, September 7, 1925. A week from today she would leave. All winter she would live in a house I had not seen and could not imagine, a house of which I knew nothing except that it was on the celebrated Beacon Hill, perhaps close by the luminous dome of the State House. My sorrow was reinforced when I saw a stamped letter, addressed in her careful hand to her niece, Miss Hopestill Mather, Camp Pocahontas, Southport, Maine. For, if I could not envisage the house which stole her away from me each autumn, I knew exactly what the little girl looked like who lived with her. Once, the summer before, when she was ten years old and I was nine, she had been brought by a small nervous woman, Mrs. Brooks, her second cousin, to have luncheon at the Hotel. She had been so self-assured, carried her head with such a grown-up dignity that she seemed advanced in her teens. I, who that day had been charged with filling the water glasses, stared from the sideboard at her bright red hair, caught at the left temple by a green ribbon and falling down her back, long and straight, over a white batiste dress, printed with tiny yellow flowers. As I passed by Miss Pride's table on my way to Mrs. Prather, I heard her say, "How absurd, Auntie! You ought to know the counselors are all stupid." And later, when I had returned to my post where, sick with envy of her voice and her cultured language I felt my face color and the pulse in my forehead leap, she signaled me with her white hand, calling, "Waitress! Water, please."

I could linger no more in Miss Pride's room, but cleverly I omitted to put clean towels on the rack beside the wash-stand in order that I might return after my other work was done, this afternoon when she had gone for a drive.

It was nearly luncheon time when I came into the lobby to dust the albums on the brocade covers of the round tables, and all the old ladies were sprily exercising the rocking chairs on the veranda, having a chat about relatives with diabetes and friends with Bright's Disease, and talking of their own improper pains, their bizarre sensations in the region of the gall-bladder, and their physicians who were either "very understanding" or obscurely "unsatisfactory."

"I love cucumbers," Mrs. Prather was saying, "but they don't love me."

Mrs. McKenzie replied, "I'm the same way with seedy things. They give me heart-burn and of course they clog the colon."

I drew back my hand with horror from the golden callosities of the "worked" covers on the albums for, smooth and round, they resembled human organs as I recalled them from the colored diagrams in my hygiene book.

A voice I did not know well inquired, "Has the Hotel Barstow always had a restricted clientele?"

"No, indeed!" cried Mrs. McKenzie. "About three years ago, a new manager came, a really vulgar person whom I'm perfectly certain was a Jew although his name was Mr. Watkins. And by the time I arrived—I came a little late that year—the Hotel was swarming with uninvestigated guests. I dare say we won't forget Mr. Johnson in a hurry, will we?"

The story of Mr. Johnson, one of the veranda favorites, was retold for the newcomer. From what walk of life he had come was impossible for anyone to tell. But he was no gentleman as a child could see in the first glance at his reversible silk shirts, his diamond tie-pin, his bright orange oxfords and his loud, checked jacket. He teased the old ladies by putting a bottle of bootleg whiskey on his table in the dining-room in imitation of their phials of medicine. "Oh, my hair hurts so," he would say and take a drink. He carried a walking stick, although he was neither a cripple nor a great walker, and the other guests thought it was probably hollow and contained a rapier.

"I've heard of such a thing, you know," said Mrs. McKenzie. "When my poor sister was in Wiesbaden taking the baths for her arthritis which nothing on earth would cure—how much money she spent I couldn't tell you and she must have suffered twenty years—there was a man living in a pension a block away who was proved beyond a shadow of a doubt to have a rapier in his stick."

"But now," pursued the unfamiliar voice, "now your manager is discreet?"

"Oh, Mr. Hagethorn is the soul of caution. He caters solely to those of us who have been coming here for at least twenty years. We call ourselves the Barstow family."

Mr. Hagethorn, pleased with the compliment that had come to his attentive pink ears, bawled in authority, "Sonie, clean up around the ferns there. Don't dawdle." The ferns and several potted palms made a little triangular garden in the far corner of the lobby, and as I made my way towards them, I perceived Miss Pride, sitting erect on a straight chair, half hidden by the foliage. This was her reading hour. Today she held *The Atlantic Monthly* directly in front of her. Her thin lips were set in concentration beneath her short, sharp nose with its contracted nares. She did not look up when I knelt down, three feet away from her and began to brush the fallen fronds into a dust-pan. I kept my eye on her and presently I saw a frown invade her high forehead. I did not know if she had come to a word she did not understand or if she were annoyed with the chatter that came through the screen door. Evidently the old ladies were now scrutinizing the fashionable young people on the beach who had drifted down from the smarter hotels and who were clad in bathing costumes that exposed long, sun-browned legs. "I just don't know," said someone, "I just don't know. Are

we advancing? Or are we going back to paganism? I don't say
it's immoral to expose the legs to the public eye: I say it's not
fastidious. Why, our chambermaid, Mrs. Marburg, has more
modesty than those young ladies out there who, you can rest
assured, either have come out or will come out at the Chilton
Club."

Even at this mention of my mother and although she must
have known that I was beside her, Miss Pride did not look at
me. Her frown deepened; reluctantly she closed her magazine
just as the only male guest of the Hotel, Mr. Brock, slipped
quietly through two pots of fern, carrying with him a folding chair which he set down beside hers. What impressed me
in that moment was that the frown, which had lasted two or
three minutes, showed that she had known of his approach
long before I either heard or saw him.

"Good morning! I hope I am not disturbing you at your
devotions?" The chuckle following his remark was not returned
and Miss Pride only said, "Good morning."

Mr. Brock was a soft-spoken and scholarly old man who,
although he had come from New York, called himself "a professional Bostonian." He was the victim of a delusion which he
propounded, whenever he had the opportunity, to myself, my
mother, the Mexican gardener, Gonzales, to Mr. Hagethorn,
to the waitresses. He believed that of all languages, only the
English was capable of vulgarity, and he claimed that bad
American books were transformed by translation into promising, if not brilliant, prose. He had made a collection of such
translations, having E. P. Roe, for example, rendered into
French and the Elsie Dinsmore books into Spanish. He had
given my father his copy of *Riders of the Purple Sage* and my
father, although he was totally indifferent to Mr. Brock's thesis,
so thoroughly enjoyed the book for its adventure that the old
man danced for joy, sure that this was the proof of the pudding.

Now he produced a leather-bound book from his brief-case
and handing it to Miss Pride, said, "I sought you out to show
you my latest find. This is *Bob, Son of Battle* in German or *Old
Bob, der graue hund von Kenmuir* and it is enchanting. Would
you care to read it?"

"No, Mr. Brock, I would not," said Miss Pride sternly. "I
do not share your enthusiasm for foreign languages. And as for

dog-books I had no use for them in my girlhood and feel quite sure I would find them even less to my taste now that I have passed beyond the age for juvenile literature."

He was not rebuffed. "I admire your linguistic singleness, Miss Pride, since in you I am sure it is the result of strong nationalistic convictions. Alas, we are not all by opinion or antecedents eligible for membership in the English Speaking Union."

"I am not a member of the English Speaking Union," she returned. "But in any case your remark is, to use a foreign phrase, a *non sequitur.*"

Mr. Brock, receiving the book which she extended, allowed his disappointment to show briefly in his foolish old face and then, catching sight of me, he cried, "Now here is someone whose father will appreciate the book." In a voice a little lower but not intended to be inaudible to me, he added, "Did you realize that this child's father is an educated man?"

"I believe I haven't had the pleasure of knowing him." Miss Pride took me in, perhaps for the first time since I had been coming to the Hotel, and I felt that in her rapid but comprehensive examination of my face and person she had discerned everything about me, that she knew I had once broken my collarbone, that I did poorly in arithmetic and singing and well in reading, and that brushing my teeth had not yet become habitual with me.

"Yes," Mr. Brock went on, "Hermann Marburg, the Chichester cobbler, is an educated man. A graduate of the *gymnasium* of Würzburg, Germany, and, except for an ineffaceable accent which I myself find appealing, has been completely bilingual since the age of eleven, and partially trilingual—his third language, of course, being French—since the age of fifteen."

Miss Pride did not seem impressed but rather than humiliate me, as I assumed, said nothing. "I have had several illuminating conversations with Mr. Marburg, sometimes in German, sometimes in English. I neglected to mention, by the way, that through his wife he has also picked up quite a considerable Russian vocabulary. Now a graduate of a *gymnasium*, Miss Pride, as you are perhaps not aware, is, if anything better educated than a candidate for an American baccalaureate degree. Yet the *gymnasium* is the counterpart of our preparatory school!"

"What do they learn?" inquired Miss Pride, frankly dubious.

"Having been something of a Latinist myself at Mr. Greenough's, naturally I admire Mr. Marburg's firm classical foundation. I must admit his Latin is less literary than ecclesiastical, for he was trained by the Franciscans, but it is, nevertheless, good, sound Latin. In addition he knows history. Oh, he knows his history *well*, Miss Pride! Roman and the French Revolution are his specialties. And then, although he's a modest man, I have no doubt in the world he could put many of our Harvard men to shame in the field of philosophy. Literature he is not so keen on although he did drop the remark that he had at one time been a great admirer of Goethe. Now there is a man who has the perspicacity to see what I mean when I say that in his language *Riders of the Purple Sage* is a superb piece of craftsmanship."

Miss Pride had had enough. She rose and her face, shaded by the wide brim of her hat, represented the pure substance of scorn. "You will forgive me, Mr. Brock, for finding your crotchet fantastic. It is my cantankerous opinion, sir, that you do not believe this nonsense yourself, but that you wish to disguise your appetite for rubbish. Not to put too fine a point on it, how could you, without the aid of some such camouflage, indulge yourself in Elsie Dinsmore at the age of seventy-two?"

Mortally wounded, he gave her a wan smile, "Your wit is all that it is said to be, ma'am."

Less coldly but with the same firmness she went on, "What interests me about this Mr. Marburg is, does he make his shoes well? Does he know *that* craft, Mr. Brock, as well as his Latin?"

"Oh, I have no idea. I never discuss business with him."

Miss Pride was looking at my feet, shod in a pair of white moccasins which my father had made. I was ashamed that they were so dirty and that my socks were ragged. She turned at the announcement of luncheon, but I did not fail to hear her say to Mr. Brock as they crossed the lobby, "I gather that he knows his business and has little of it."

After Audrey, the headwaitress, and I had set the tables for dinner, I went upstairs with Miss Pride's fresh towels. The corridor was quiet, for all the guests were napping. I could hear, through the wall by Miss Pride's bed, the faint popping of air in Mrs. McKenzie's nose as she slept deeply. Immediately I took my post at the windows and in about a quarter of an hour, I saw Miss Pride go down the wooden stairs of the porch, pinching the hand-rail with her gloved fingers. Then she waited on the lawn for her high, black limousine. Once I had seen in it vases for flowers on the sides, hanging like pictures in a house. I believed she had other decorative furnishings in the back seat as, perhaps, a needlepoint footstool and a writing board. What if she even had a tea table and at a suitable hour and place, ordered the car to be stopped and then served herself tea! I would dwell on this enchanting thought sometimes as long as half an hour, seeing with an overwhelming happiness the actual seeds of the strawberry jam.

Here came the car! Slipping round the corner of the Hotel, its long black snout caught the rays of the sun which shot fitfully into my eyes. It stopped and Mac, the chauffeur, stepped out. He was a thin, sharp, silvery young man who, in his gray livery, looked like an upright rat. He suffered from some strange distemper that caused his feet to swell, but though the valetudinarians of the veranda perpetually foretold Miss Pride's doom when the man while driving should die at the wheel (for they were enough acquainted with his symptoms to know that foot swelling indicated a rheumatic heart for which there was *no cure*), she kept him on and about twice a week was handed into the car by his lean, gray paws which, since they went out and withdrew so quickly, seemed to abhor their contact with the desiccated elbow that they briefly cupped.

"Well, Mac," came her voice, "I trust we are all in order. I must run in to Pinckney Street today."

So that was the name of it: Pinckney Street. I repeated the words to myself and the house where she lived all winter now seemed less strange because it was not merely in Boston but was in a specific street with a specific number of houses. Henceforth my daydreams would not begin with the vague condition, "When I live in Boston with Miss Pride," but with, "When I live on Pinckney Street."

"Oh, but before we go," she said, her foot on the running board, "I want you to take me to the shoemaker here. A Mr. Marburg."

The car drove off and I sank into the chair at the writing desk, faint with a conflict. For the joy I felt in Miss Pride's going to call on my father was scotched by my shame of our shabby shop, my father's untidiness, and my mother's loquacity. Nor did I know whether she was seeking him out as Mr. Brock did, because he was educated, or if she was going to him on business, to have him half-sole her Ground Grippers. If her intention were the latter, now, at this very moment, I must relinquish my ambition to be her young and well-beloved friend.

The letter to her niece was gone from the writing desk and in its place was one addressed to herself and postmarked London. I was less moved by the foreign stamp and the strange, thin paper of the envelope than I was by what next caught my eye: it was my own name, Marburg, written on a memorandum pad together with the legends: "Call Breckenridge at three" and "flue in the upstairs sitting-room." That meant, then, that there was also a *downstairs* sitting-room so that the house was surely big enough to accommodate me as well as Hopestill Mather and Miss Pride. Perhaps even now she was saying to my father that although she realized he was a good man and well educated, she believed he owed it to me to give me a better home which she herself was willing to provide.

While I was meditating, I was interrupted by Mrs. McKenzie. She took very short naps and I heard her suffocated scream. I was afraid she might sense my presence in the room next to hers and summon me to eat a lemon drop or send me to the village to fetch her a bottle of Moxie. I tiptoed out of the room and through the Hotel and then stood in the back yard hesitating. For I could not decide whether to go directly home and present myself in the shop where the interview would probably take place—unless my mother's curiosity were aroused at the sight of the black car and she insisted that they sit in the kitchen—or to go down to the Point and wait there until it should be over, passing the time in watching the sailboats and the barges going out from Boston harbor. But as I debated, I saw two old ladies round the corner of the Hotel with walking sticks and parasols, and I heard one of them say, "It's not far. The view is gorgeous and at this time of day, we'll have the whole Point to ourselves."

In order that my mother might not intercept me, I took the road on the bay side of the peninsula, approaching the shop from the rear. I stood on tiptoe outside the window and I saw, enveloped in the shadows, Miss Pride seated primly on a stool beside the wheels and shoe stands, while my father knelt, taking the measurements of her right foot. This foot, short and narrow, wore a tan silk stocking with heavy cotton reinforcements at the toe and heel, and I was momentarily shocked at the sight, for I had assumed that every article of her clothing, down to her underwear, would be black.

"I understand that you are a friend of one of my fellow-lodgers, Mr. Brock," she was saying.

"He comes sometimes. He is a scholar, I suppose."

Miss Pride smiled. They were both silent as he removed her other shoe and began to measure the left foot. I wondered what she thought of this large shaggy man who always looked unkempt and would have even if he had fastidiously groomed himself. He was the opposite, in this respect, of my mother who never looked dirty or untidy though she was both, and to a far greater degree than he. He was a tall man and the muscles of his youth had not yet been overlaid by flesh, but, at thirty-three, had begun to sag a little as though they were preparing themselves for a permanent relaxation. His thick, yellow hair looked like a palm thatch and now, as he bent over and it fell forward from his skull, I felt that I could lift up a flap of it and clip it at a single root like the midrib of a leaf. His face was broad and red and its hollows were scooped out cleanly so that, although it was full, the shape of the skeleton was clearly visible. His chin was cleft and his lips, whose usual attitude was one of curving downward, were quiet and contemplative and seemed not to belong to the chilled blue eyes which were those of a decisive man. Today, because of the heat, he was dressed like a boy and when he stood up to get something from the work table which required him to turn in my direction, I saw to my embarrassment that his white, short-sleeved shirt was torn at the shoulder, revealing a segment of skin, browned by the sun on the days he had gone bathing. His hair seemed fairer than usual and at the temples it was almost white.

Miss Pride, who had been leaning over his bent back, withdrew as he stood up, and she said, "I expect a good pair of shoes, Mr. Marburg. Your price is steep, but I have every confidence in German workmanship,"

He did not rise to her compliment but gave only the smile which politeness demanded. I fairly danced with impatience in the sand at his unresponsive face and at the impudence which had made him charge her a high price when he should, I thought, have done the work free and presented her as a gift the finest pair of shoes he could make. Ah, if she had come to call on *me*, not my father, how I would have entertained her! I would have made her a pot of tea and run to the village for a lemon and half a dozen jellied doughnuts. And I would have listened carefully to every word she said and nodded my head in constant agreement as she talked.

Although she saw that he was disinclined to talk (he could so easily, with the opening she had given him, explain that he had not always been a poor, shabby man, but that in Germany, he had been of a well-to-do family), she persevered. "You learned your trade in Germany, did you not?"

"Oh, yes!" In his voice, there was an impulsive note which, combined with my sudden apprehension of a half-empty whiskey bottle on the shelf over the door, alarmed me, and I was afraid that he might begin to calendar, not the events of his past life, but its errors. For when he had been drinking, he became neither rebellious nor self-pitying as did my mother, but he brooded, morosely accusing himself of heartless infidelities to the traditions of the Catholic church, of his family, and of his country. My mother believed herself to be persecuted by everyone she had ever known—with the exception of Luibka, myself, and a few neighbor women—but he knew, and was powerless to rectify the fault, that all his torture came from his own flabby will which swung him like a pendulum between apathy and fretful indecision. I could see through the clouded windowpane that he was preoccupied with some tangential thought as he wrote down the specifications of Miss Pride's feet in his notebook, and I was in mortal terror that he was going to tell her how long it had been since his last confession. When he did speak again, it was not in self-accusation, but it was from a point far removed from her question.

He said, "But even so, they don't know good shoes from bad here."

"If by 'here' you mean Chichester," returned Miss Pride, "I'm certain you're right. And while they might know skill when they saw it, these poor fishermen could not pay for it. But I beg to differ with you if by 'here' you mean something larger. Don't you think, Mr. Marburg, that in Boston, *we* know the real thing?"

The light which flickered in my father's face was quickly extinguished. "It's too late for *that*," he said.

"You are an obdurate man, sir. My father used to liken your countrymen to our own Puritans. Therein, he said, lay the greatness of the nation. I must confess Papa and I never saw eye to eye on your 'greatness' for even as a young lady, I was displeased with your romancing and your 'earth-spirit' but I can see that some of you are hard-headed. If you were not, how could you work so cleverly?" She paused, watching my father closely as though she were waiting for a reply or a confirmation, but neither was forthcoming. She went on. "If you came to Boston, you would be out of the doldrums. I recollect the governess to the child of one of my friends. When she came, poor *Fräulein* Ströck, she was timorous and wistful, for she had been for some time in an establishment in the middle west where her gifts—a little too Prussian for my liking—were not appreciated in the least. But she had not been with us, with Boston, that is, for a month before she had blossomed into what she had been born to be, a first-rate disciplinarian. I believe you will find we have our feet on the ground and that we need no divining rods to find our treasures."

My father, no more than I, did not know what to make of her lecture. Had I been inside with them, I would have inquired how many children were under Miss Ströck's charge or why it was that she was too Prussian to please Miss Pride entirely. My disappointment in my father's indifference and in the gesture he made of passing his hand before his face as if he were befogged, was converted into anger as I realized that he did not intend to make any sort of comment at all. Surely he, a grown-up man with an education so proudly advertised by Mr. Brock, could select something out of that subtle speech as a point of departure! How stupid and contrary of him not to ask, at least, if Miss Pride had ever been to Germany. Why, I, a little girl, could do that much!

But Miss Pride, to my astonishment, did not appear annoyed. With a grace which obviated the need for a transition, she said, "If I am pleased with my shoes, I shall want you to make more for me. I shall be anxious to put you in the way of further commissions. Surely you won't refuse."

"No," he said, but there was neither gratitude nor excitement in his voice. "If I am nothing else, I am a workman who does his work."

She stood up. "Now when the shoes are finished, you may mail them to me at this address." Taking a leather case from her handbag, she extracted a card from it. "I must say there is something about your shop I like. It strikes me as what I spoke of before: the real thing. Nothing is so close to my heart as that, sir: the real thing. And if you had known my father, you would see I came by my passion honestly."

"I hope you will be satisfied with the shoes," said my father. "But you must not expect too much. My hands are not as clever as they used to be. I am, you see, no longer a shoemaker, I am a shoe-fixer."

Miss Pride gave him her hand. "It's time you changed. Good-by."

He stood stupidly in the center of the room and did not open the door for her, did not, indeed, bid her good-by. When she had gone and the motor of her car started up, he sat down on the stool she had just occupied and putting his hands over his face, the fingers so tightly interlocked that their knuckles whitened, he groaned with some profound, enigmatic misery, and I stepped softly away from the window, perplexed that she who could cause me only happiness had caused him only pain. As I went toward the house, I was gradually infected by his terrible sorrow and felt my face grow feverish, recalling his words last night: the child should never have been born.

In the kitchen, I ran my fingers over the cold stove. My mother was sitting in a chair beside the sink and she drew me down to kiss me. "Who do you love, little Sonie girl?" she said, gazing at me with her great black eyes. And while I answered her as she desired me to, my mind was telling me the truth: "Miss Pride, not you, Mamma."

Chapter Two

D URING THE two years that my father supplied Miss Pride, her niece, and a couple of her friends with shoes, there were frequent conferences on the advisability of buying me a bed. But because the plans were always projected when my parents were drinking a bottle of whiskey and the morning found them oblivious of everything but their malaise, I continued to sleep on my pallet, made a little longer now to accommodate my increased height. Our prosperity was manifested in very little beyond a regular Saturday night pint of liquor. We did have a cerise rayon bedspread, a piebald linoleum for the kitchen floor, an eccentric shower-bath crowded into the minute closet we called the "bathroom," and I had a red coat with an astrakhan collar. But my mother had none of the things she longed for, and if my father, when he was drinking, offered to buy her a yellow dress, she refused, saying sadly that she did not want pretty clothes unless she had an estate with a lake where, on its island, she would be hostess at summer picnics. My father would commend her good sense and tell her, in a foxy whisper, as if for the first time, that he was "laying away a little something" and in a few years his savings would accomplish everything her heart desired.

When there was no whiskey to provide a recess in their old war, they sang two different tunes. My father cried that he was enslaved to Miss Pride whom he had come to detest, for he believed that her patronage of him was an alms-deed. "Four pairs of shoes in one winter for an ugly old woman!" he exploded. "Maybe she sells them at a profit. She can't wear out my shoes so quick!" He was displeased, too, that all his transactions with her were conducted by mail, as if she counted herself too good to come to his shop. When she ordered a new pair of shoes for her niece, she sent a careful drawing of the girl's feet together with the height of the arches. And when the sandals or the moccasins or the dancing pumps were delivered, he received a curt note of thanks which was folded around the check. Time and again he declared, "I will make no more for them." But he could never resist new, costly leather and he always took the work.

My mother, on the other hand, deplored his failure to exploit his Boston customers and said, with considerable truth, that if we moved across the bay to the city and opened up a shop there, we would really become rich. Then I could have as many pairs of shoes as Hopestill Mather and she could be driven about in a black car like Miss Pride's. But nothing could avail against my father's indolent pessimism, and he went on living in our poor little village precariously, like someone who, being exposed to the cold, finally quits the struggle to keep awake and sinks into what he knows is his last sleep.

For myself, I was torn between gratitude to Miss Pride for noticing us at all, for affixing her signature to letters to my father—letters bearing her address on Pinckney Street—and the knowledge that her relationship with us would never be anything but commercial. Nevertheless, my reveries of life in Boston persisted, became, indeed, as my experience widened, more specific and in a sense more real than my existence in Chichester. In the wintertime at school, I was known as a day-dreamer and often my teacher would hustle me out of Miss Pride's house with a mocking rebuke that made the whole class laugh: "Tell us what is so interesting that you can't remember the capital of Rhode Island, Sonie." At home, depending on the tempers of my parents, I was called "bright" or "stupid" or "silly" or "older than my age." Confined during the day by school-room walls where hung Sir Galahad and "The Stag at Eve," George Washington and President Wilson and Kipling's "If," plied by unanswerable questions, required to sing "I am a little *blue* bird" in reply to the teacher's full, contralto query, "Who is a little *blue* bird?", I would gradually float away, leaving my body behind, still sitting at the stained red desk. As I vanished, I would see the teacher jump to attention, gather her forces and in a moment overtake me, but not before I had slipped into Miss Pride's drawing-room, wearing a brown velvet dress and a yellow bone round-comb in my hair.

At night, bound by the narrow walls of our kitchen, I was not always absorbed in my book about girls at boarding school whose clever mothers had sewed for months before their depar-ture, making silk dresses and dark wool jumpers, warm wrap-pers, innumerable muslin guimpes, had crocheted fascinators and had bought blue merino stockings. Although I envied the fortunate creatures, my own life which I plotted in a variety of patterns was richer. My hair became blond; my name was Antoinette de la Mar. "Soon after Antoinette or Toni, as her chums called her, went to live in the Pride mansion on Pinckney Street, a handsome Harvard student named Andrew Eliot Cabot Lodge fell passionately in love with her. But as she had already decided not to marry anybody, she spurned him with a few kind but firm words. That night he shot himself, but he did not die and she nursed him back to health. She had many suitors but she lived only for Miss Pride who adored her and often had her do a toe-dance for her visitors who were often foreign kings and queens. They would say, 'I say, Antoinette de la Mar has it all over Denishawn. Why, Denishawn could never whirl on one toe that long.'"

My mother, who spent nearly every winter evening playing Patience (she always cheated, to my indignation, and as other disrespectful children in a fury curse their mothers, I would howl at mine, "You cheat at cards!"), would notice that for an hour I had not turned a page in my book. "Are you asleep, booby?" she would scold. "Are you asleep sitting up like a little cow?"

If my father raised his eyes from *Riders of the Purple Sage*, quaintly called *Das Gesetz der Mormonen*, to join our quarrel, perhaps to accuse me harshly of thinking of boys, my mother would instantly come to my defense and would commence to belabor him with vituperation. When they had finished the skirmish, my father would lift the red felt cozy off the white china coffee-pot and drink from a thick cup. He would then return to his book and my mother to her cards as she remarked, "*He* gets the fine pot for his coffee but Shura Korf has to keep her tea in a tin can." Perhaps he would ignore her, or would say, pointing to his chest, "The pot is *mine*. It is a *coffee* pot. Why don't you drink coffee?"

If she were in the mood for it, my mother would burst into tears and weep, "I hate you, ah, God, I hate you!" The real battle would then begin. They would threaten to kill each other or to kill themselves; they would wish damnation to each other's immortal souls; and each would blame the other for behaving badly in front of me. "*Lieber Gott!*" my father would groan, pressing the knuckles of his big red hands into his eyes. "What will become of my baby girl?"

My mother, clasping her hands together as if in prayer, would return, "She is safe with me! I will kill you if you hurt one single hair of her precious head!"

The outburst would be followed by a lamentation on my father's part as my mother sank into a brooding silence. He would draw me close to him and run his fingers through my hair and tell me he was sorry that he had neglected me. Sometimes he apologized because he had not reared me as a Catholic and he would go out to the shop, bringing back a catechism. But we made no progress. Our minds wandered from the questions, mine to Boston or to the last movie I had seen, and his to his boyhood. He would talk for a long time, but to himself. "Sonie, my patron is Bonaventure, but how I have forgotten him like all the other saints! It is the irony that he should be my saint because he hated idleness. Brother Sebastian, one of the friars who taught us, brought my brother up short and myself a few years later. For we did not like to be shoemakers like our father and our grandfather and our great grandfather. Friedrich would have nothing to do with the trade. He would go to Paris, to the Sorbonne, to study literature, he said, and philosophy. And I, I would go to Berlin to study the law. But Brother Sebastian knew it wasn't in us. He made us not ashamed of shoe-making. He would quote Saint Bonaventure: 'You, Friedrich, and you, Hermann, are amongst those to whom the Lord has given the grace to labor.' I would pray to my saint night and morning, to cure my sloth! It was a monstrous state. *Monstruosum quemdam statum inter contemplativam et activam.* See! It comes back."

In his excitement, he would take both my hands in his and cry, "My Latin is not gone, Sonie! I will teach you. Have we a book? A grammar? Well, then, tomorrow we must buy one."

But by the next day he would have forgotten. The catechism went back to the shop where for the next month it would lie untouched. Saint Bonaventure, Brother Sebastian, and indeed God, would be shelved like the little book. My father's face would resume its mask. While I, glad that I had escaped his instructions, happily pursued Miss de la Mar's career.

In my twelfth year, hardly a night passed from September until November that I was not unhinged from my sleep by my parents' voices. Something, I knew not what, had brewed between them a hotter rancor than ever before. I was propelled by their curses into consciousness and seemed driven into a socket in the dark from which there was no outlet. My bounded brain was as unalterable as a ball and it could neither veer in flight nor proceed to understanding: solid and of one material, terror, it lay in a minute cavern whose walls were fashioned from the rhetoric and the darkness. The daylight, freeing the sounds of boats and trains, the voices of fishermen and children, discovering the diverse landscape and the harmless countenances of my sleeping parents, repealed the fast laws that had held me to a rapt and aboriginal response and gave me the relief of wild tears. As soon as I had dressed, I would run to the porch of the Hotel Barstow as to a shrine and there, all alone and out of earshot of anyone, I cried until I could cry no more and until the reason for my grief had become obscured by the cold and my hunger. Often at this hour, the fog lay on Boston; I would be unable to see the State House dome and unable to visualize Pinckney Street. At last I would get up and start towards school, slowly at first because my legs were cramped, then faster until I was running through the mist. I usually arrived out of breath, a little late. Among the teachers it was a great joke that when I was asked why I had been crying, I would reply, "Oh, no, I wasn't crying. I didn't sleep well last night." They would say, "How imitative children are at this age! Don't you know exactly what has happened? One of her parents often says at breakfast, 'I didn't get a wink of sleep last night' and the child has picked it up."

On a morning in November, when the snow had fallen, I was crouched in a corner of the steps of the veranda, my face muffled in the harsh curls of my astrakhan collar. Today it was not foggy, but my view gave me no pleasure for the sky was leaden and the angry bay was deserted by all the boats. Last night my father had laughed, it must have been for half an hour and then, as if something had broken in him, shattered like a glass, he had begun to sob. I could hear his heavy body trembling on the creaking bed, and the weeping claw at his throat. And because each morning that was the way I cried, I knew his stomach ached and his nose was full. Not a sound came from my mother. In the intervals between the plunges of his agony, I could hear him whisper, "*Verzeihung!*" How far away he seemed! As I peered upward through the darkness at the dim white block which was the bed, I could not feel that the person weeping, as no man should do, was my father. Rather, it was the figure of a nightmare which crudely represented him. And yet I knew I was awake, for nothing was distorted as in a dream. Quaking upon the clattering springs, the figure was like a caged beast that had broken down in its futile struggle to escape. Downwards it plummeted into some unknown and pitch-black chasm of despair, but rose again in a brief respite to breathe that one word, "*Verzeihung!*" Twice, thinking I could stand it no longer, I started up to go to him and to lay my hand on his arm. But I thought then of how I was enraged at such a gesture when I was crying, and I lay back, mouthing the words, "Please don't cry, dear Papa." Why did my mother not comfort him? Once I heard her sigh and thought perhaps that was the prelude to some speech. But she said nothing and my father wept on, for hours it seemed to me.

The snow had begun to fall in the night and by morning it was thick on the ground. My father's face, in a deep sleep, was ashen and his eyelids were distended, the golden lashes stuck together. An arm was curled about his head. The woman who lay beside him, as motionless as he, appeared the soul of innocence as the gray light, filtering through the holes in the green blinds, exposed her white skin and her red lips and the black hair, unpinned and spread like a fan upon the pillow. She lay straight, her arms at her sides, as if she were dead.

This morning I did not and I could not cry. It was as though my father had done all the crying that could be done. Against my will, I continued to review his terrible collapse. What could it mean, I wondered, in a grown man? And would it happen again? Once he had broken the rules of a man's behavior, would he cry as often as I did?

I was startled at the sound of someone's boots on the gravel path at the side of the Hotel and before I could get to my feet, Gonzales, the gardener, was standing before me. He had always frightened me, for no reason that I could discover. He had the mildest of pink mouths under a thin, romantic mustache, and large bovine eyes beneath a low, protuberant brow. I disliked the way in the kitchen, in the summer time, he would steal up on me in his sneakers and put a soft finger on the back of my neck so suddenly that goose-flesh covered me and my heart pranced in surprise.

"What do I see?" he said, laughing, showing his teeth which were so small that the gum was visible above them. "What is the matter with *Señorita* Marburg? You tell Gonzales your troubles, honey."

He sat down on the step and put his arm around me. There was a strong assorted odor about him of something oily and something acrid, of garlic and of bootleg beer. He put his lips close to my ear, lifting up the edge of my tarn. "Tell, Gonzales, honey."

Too frightened to move or to cry out, I trembled in his embrace as he continued his unwelcome consolations. "There, there. If you don't watch out your face will freeze that way, sweetheart. Don't you want to tell your Uncle Jesus what's the trouble?"

"Is your name Jesus?" I asked him, my admiration for a moment making me forget both my misery and his rank smell.

He said "Yes," softly, like a lover, and hugged me closer to him. "If I was my own master like your daddy, I would make a lot of Novenas. But me, Jesus, I don't have the time."

In the summer, he always greeted me with some such pious announcement. He would remind me that my father was in a state of mortal sin because he had not been to confession or mass for seven or eight years, and he would ask me if I did not long to be baptized. He himself, with his eight children, received the Blessed Sacrament every morning at the six o'clock service and on Sundays entertained the priest, Father Mulcahy, at breakfast after the eleven o'clock mass. Once he had come to my father's shop, beseeching him to deliver himself up to the mercy of God. His big brown eyes had been full of tears. But my father had only confounded him by saying, "I know my own mind. I am no boy."

I said nothing in reply. He released me, lowered his head, and dangling his hands between his outspread knees, murmured, "Always remember, *Señorita*, that you and your poor father are in my prayers."

"Thank you, Mr. Gonzales," I said and slipped over on the step. "I've got to go to school now."

"Yes!" he cried, slapping his knee. "And I to work must go. I'm afraid to look in the pit. I'm as sure as my name is Jesus Francisco Gonzales that the hydrangeas were frozen last night." He stood up and started down the path, but pausing at the corner of the porch he faced me once more. "How is your mother, sweetheart?" I answered that she was well enough, only a little tired, for I was remembering how soundly she slept when I left the house.

The Mexican winked at me. "Tired of carrying the little one?"

"What?"

"I mean your little brother or sister or whichever it is Our Savior intends it to be."

"I don't know . . ." I began, but he cupped his hands round his plump lips and whispered loudly, "Your mother is going to have a baby, *muchacha*."

2

When I came home from school that afternoon, my mother was not in her accustomed place beside the stove, a most surprising fact, for she was a creature of tenacious habit, and had, since I could remember, taken up her place there an hour before sundown to idle over a glass of strong and bitter tea. She would rise, as I entered, and embrace me as if I were an intimate friend for whose visit she had been impatiently waiting, and then, drawing me to a chair beside hers, she would rub my cold hands between hers and say, "Oh, Sonie, how cold you are! Oh, the darling little hands all red!"

Often at this hour, I found neighbor women seated round about her, going over in exhaustive detail the difficulties of maintaining a household when there was no money to pay the high prices of food. I wondered if these women were as gloomy in their own houses as they were in ours, or if my mother's winter melancholy was contagious to them as it was to my father and myself. Strangely enough, when the heaviness of the bad weather skies had invaded our kitchen, she cast off the dark colors she had worn all summer and stepped forward, as lively as a bird, in a costume like a ballerina's. But her full skirt, the length of a peasant's dress, which was made of black challis and printed with bright pink flowers and fantastic pea-green leaves, her scarlet flannel blouse with tarnished German silver buttons, and her high blue leather boots, laced with tan hide, were not an antidote to her perverse mopes but seemed rather to be the excuse for them. Mrs. Henderson would come in and say, "How gay you look, Mrs. Marburg! Why, I can warm my hands at *you*." But my mother, in a voice bleaker than any winter wind along the beach, would answer, "It is the red that fools you. But look at the boots. Now *they're* the color my hands used to be all day long in Moscow, even in the house, and they were so stiff I couldn't hold so much as a wine glass by its little tiny stem." Sometimes, out of spite, she would then slip her arms into the sleeves of a blue Beacon-cloth bathrobe whose skirt hung to the floor; a high, pointed hood was attached to the back of the neck. It belonged to my father, and the sleeves were so long that the unfilled portions of them flapped like seals' flippers as she gestured with her invisible hands. Had it not been for her face, she would have looked like a monk of some outlandish order.

Softly I opened the door to the bedroom. She was lying there, either asleep or else so deep in thought that she did not hear me on the threshold. The dark green blinds were down, but the light of the sunset, coming through the holes and falling on her immobile face, gave it an even incandescence like that which comes through the hand when it is held up to a bright light. Her body was covered with an army blanket and though the room was cold, one bare white foot dangled over the side of the bed. I could see my breath. The windows did not anywhere quite fit their frames and we had failed to stop up many of the cracks in the walls, either through laziness or through the conviction that it would do no good.

There was only one other article of furniture in the room besides the bed, a tall combination wardrobe and bureau with a sliver of flawed mirror at the top, in a frame carved with the same ornate roses that decorated the feet. My father, I suppose because it was solid and perhaps reminded him of something at home, admired the *schrank* as he called it, and each spring he spent one entire day polishing it with salt and olive oil. Today, to my surprise, I saw that the two pots of geraniums stood on the top, blocking out the mirror. Their transfer from the sunny kitchen window was stranger to me even than the sight of my mother lying in bed before we had had our supper. Was she, I wondered, going to have the baby now?

Presently I tiptoed out and went to my father's shop. He was not working. He was sitting on the bench before the monkey stove, his head in his hands.

"Papa?"

He did not look up, but he thrust forth his long arm in welcome. "Hello, Sonie girl. Didn't you eat anything yet today?"

"I guess not."

"Why didn't you come home at noon?"

"Oh, I don't know. I guess I wasn't hungry, Papa. I guess I had an apple. What's the matter with Mamma?"

"She's tired maybe." Now he turned his face toward me and I saw that his blue eyes were troubled, but they showed no signs of their storm of last night. He smiled and with two hard fingers that smelled of tallow, he tweaked my nose. "I know what you want, Gretchen von Hexensee, you want to look at the tintypes."

They were not really tintypes, but the word amused him. I fetched the fat album from the high shelf above the window. It lay with his fat little *Messbuch* and a few fine leather-bound volumes of Schiller, Leibnitz, Cicero, Goethe, Mommsen, and Balzac. The books were not worn. Probably my father had never read them. They were mostly gifts from his schoolmates on the day of his commencement from the *gymnasium* and were inscribed in a bewildering handwriting, the same that I saw on the occasional letter which came to him from Würzburg.

Together we looked at the photographs in which my relatives genially smiled forth, all with my father's eyes. My grandparents sat side by side on a plush settle with a high, carved back. Their fat arms were intertwined and they stared directly into the camera. Their round faces were frank and innocent and benign; and their sober, old-fashioned clothes—my grandfather wore a long collar with a full ascot, a black coat with wide satin lapels and upon his knees he balanced a gleaming top hat, while my grandmother, with a black lace jabot at her stout old neck, was dressed in a striped jacket with leg-o'-mutton sleeves and a deep pointed bodice which met a black skirt—advertised them as people of respectability. Both of them were dead. One of the letters that had come to my father had been from his brother, Christian, announcing that they had died within half a year of one another.

My favorite picture was one of my cousin Peter taken when he was about five years old. His wide eyes stared at the photographer's incorporeal birdie and his lips were opened in perplexity. He was a bewitching little boy with fair hair, matted in curls tight to his skull, his solid body was encased in leather breeches, a jacket decorated with hearts, and tasseled socks. In his hands he ferociously clutched a hat with an improbably long feather.

"Some day, when we are rich," my father said, "we will go to see that boy. Shall we take our Packard car with us and honk outside of Fransiskanerstrasse *zwei und zwanzig*? Or should we not take it and walk from the station as calm as you please?"

I debated for a moment. "Let's take the Packard car," I said.

"I don't know when it would be that we would go."

"If Miss Pride keeps on buying shoes, we'll get rich."

"She only feels sorry for me, and I don't like that. No, in America they don't know a good boot from a bad."

"Then why don't we go to Germany, Pa?"

When he answered, he looked away from me. He moved to the window and stood looking out at the last glow of the sun on Boston. "I would be ashamed," he said. "How am I going to explain to my brothers and friends that I never had my child baptized?"

Whereas it embarrassed me to have Gonzales talk about his sins of omission, it frightened me to hear my father speak of them. Once, at Christmas time, he had made a *crèche* for me, carving out a youthful Mary and the doe-eyed animals and three Teutonic wise-men and the faceless Christ-child with a boyish rapture. I was delighted with it until, once it had been brought from the shop into the house, I saw that my mother had no interest in it and that my father had lost his. It was as if some ungovernable force in her was determined to extinguish every joy her husband might have. In his frustration and furious disappointment, he abruptly seized the platform and dashed it to the floor so that all the figures were broken and the frame was splintered. He stared down at the fragments, his hands hanging loosely at his sides. He said nothing, but in a moment he took his hat from the shelf and went out. Hours later, when he came back, totally drunk, he sat in the kitchen for a long time, laughing his inhuman laugh. In the morning I found him sleeping with his head on the table. For a week thereafter, whenever we were alone together, he invited me to look on him as the most obstinate of all sinners, and while I was not certain what he meant, I would rack my brains for a pretext to escape him, for I was mortally afraid.

He had pressed his cheek against the windowpane and when he spoke, a cloud formed on the glass. "Or how confess it to a priest?" he inquired. "Or anything else?"

There was no sound in the room but the spanking of a live coal against the purple sides of the monkey stove. And my father was motionless, with his eyes and his lips closed. Perhaps he had cried last night out of fear of his sins and the punishment God would deal to him. And what were his sins? He did not tell lies and he did not steal and he was not a murderer. It was true that he spent a good deal of time carousing with the Coast Guards, but so did the fishermen. What, then, had he done that tormented him so, even now when there were no outward signs of it beyond the pallid weariness of his face and the tension of his pose? I would have asked and my lips parted, but something hindered me from intruding upon his mysterious meditations and I said, my voice cracking, "I guess I better go help Mamma."

"*Ja*, you better," He sighed so that his whole lengthy frame shivered, and he turned to me with a willful smile which did not fool me, for the corners of his mouth twitched and would have turned down but for the effort he expended on their upward curve. "Don't you expect me for supper. I have some business." With this, he took down his sheep-lined mackinaw and his hunter's cap, put a pipe and tin of tobacco in his pocket and drew on a pair of mittens.

"Are you going to the Coast Guard?" I asked him.

"Curiosity killed the cat," he said waggishly but, like his smile, his jollity was forced and did not take me in.

"Where are you going, Pa?"

Suddenly irritated, he pushed me towards the door. "Shut up now," he snapped. "Go along to the house and mind your own business."

I watched from the kitchen windows until he had disappeared round the bend of the road, and then I stole out and followed. Over the crusted ruts for a mile I ran, ducking behind cottages and sheds when I feared he might turn around. At this hour the village was usually deserted save for the men going in and out of the pool hall in the splattered window of which a sign futilely proclaimed, "Ladies Invited." I had expected my father to turn in there, but he went on, passed the large, shadowy general store about which, even in winter and when the door was closed, there hung an odor of fish and fishermen and a rich, sweet smell which came either from raisins or chewing tobacco. I glanced across the street at the Bijou where the obfuscated films which wavered before our eyes like dispirited ectoplasm bore no more relationship to entertainment than the lusterless exterior bore to any jewel known to man. It was closed now and the torn sign advertising "Ben Hur" was streaked from melted snow. These, with a few churches, a little library, and a post-office made up our business district. On one side, overlooking the sea, was the Coast Guard house, on the other, overlooking the bay, was a small white hospital, enveloped for a quarter of a mile on all sides by a pall of mortal silence. Midway between the village and the hospital was the school, so newly built that its yellow-brick walls had not yet been relieved by shrubs and ivy. As I lingered in the doorway of the store until my father should be a safe distance ahead of me (he had paused to knock out his pipe), I was visited by a longing to see Marblehead, Salem, and Boston, and I was as weakened by the feeling as though I had seen them and something in the winter evening had made me nostalgic. And then I conceived the stubborn notion that the crisis which my father was passing through would end in a change of residence. Perhaps even now he was headed for the Marblehead bus stop and when he came home, he would have news of a house and a shop to which we would immediately move.

It was with a flush of anger that I saw, in a few minutes, what his destination was: the Catholic church, a small white building with a high green spire. It was called "The Chapel of the Little Flower." I followed him.

My schoolmates had told me, in frightened whispers, that Catholics prayed the dead out of Purgatory, whatever that might be, and I fancied my father kneeling before a High Necromancer, chanting in an unknown language. I had heard that priests were ghosts and since they had no substance, could never marry. Someone said they could change from one thing to another: "They can look like anything they want, like a billy goat if they want." There was something impressive to me in the sight of my father starting out to Mass on Sunday, wearing his suit and his polished boots, and carrying the *Messbuch* with its bright ribbons. Impressive and a little scandalous, even though I knew he never got as far as the church porch, but instead took another road which led to the Coast Guard house where he would spend an hour playing checkers.

A few parishioners were kneeling in the front pews of the darkened chapel, and now and again the door to the confessional swung open; I could hear the wicket slide and presently another penitent entered the box. There was a murmur, caught by a silence, and broken at last by the faint, sibilant Latin of the absolution. Those who had been cleansed slipped into the kneeling benches to say their penance, and as their lips mouthed the words of the prayers, their eyes were fixed upon a shining golden object on the altar: it looked like a child's drawing of the sun, for from the round white center, a thousand rays of gold shot out, glittering in the red light cast by the vigil lamp which swung very gently at the end of a long iron chain. My eyes grew accustomed to the shadows and I saw my father at the altar rail, far to one side, his head buried in his arms. Each time someone emerged from the confessional, I expected him to go in, but he did not stir. It was cold in the church and I shivered, leaned up against the side of the pew, and hugged my knees. It seemed to me a long time that I waited for the terrifying moment when my father would become a part of the esoteric game. At least five people went into the closet with their sins and came out purged of them. The last light of the day perished from the stained glass windows. Now only two people besides my father and myself remained.

Presently, the Irish priest came out, a tall, red-haired young

man, round-shouldered and near-sighted, with a face ravaged
by boredom and eczema, but not an unpleasant face and in no
way similar to my picture which had represented him as lithe
and swart, wearing a mustache and pointed beard over which
darted bright evil eyes. He passed close by my father as he went
into the vestry, but my father, deep in his prayer, did not look
up, and only after the door had closed behind the priest did
he rise and hasten out, looking straight ahead so that he did
not see me. But when the swinging doors had shut upon him,
I heard a voice in the vestibule intercept him. "Thank God,
man! You've come back by the grace of God! The new one
will have a better chance than Sonie." It was Gonzales. There
was the sound of a match being struck, and my father replied,
"You fool busybody." The outer door opened and banged to,
forcing a blast of cold air into the church. Gonzales went down
the central aisle, genuflected at the altar, and went to the right
where he knelt before a statue of a woman saint in a brown robe
who held roses in her hands. He crossed himself and began
to pray audibly. I ran from the church appalled, for there was
a presence there, not of God nor of angels, but of something
human, yet shockingly bodiless, and I felt as I had done the
time I had dreamed that I was dead and the only thing left of
me was the knowledge, suspended in a ball of solitude, that I
was dead.

The house was as it had been when I came in from school. My
father was not there and the shop was dark, and my mother,
still lying in bed, had not changed her position. I spread a piece
of bread with margarine and sprinkled it with sugar and I ate,
sitting on the floor by the stove, as in the light from the fire
through the isinglass I read a book lent to me by a schoolmate
called *Frances and the Irrepressibles at Buena Vista Farm*. The
thick pages were glossy and each one bore an actual photograph of a character or a whole group of them together, posing
in the costumes they had worn at a mock wedding or at the
minstrel show they had ingeniously produced. A child cannot
sustain his moods for long, and I, after a few minutes of inat-
tention, became completely absorbed in the adventures of these
wealthy, carefree, and urbane children. They were all upright
and considerate with the one exception of a rotten little boy

named Dickey Doolittle who one had no doubt would come all right in the end under the influence of his companions. They all lived in Wisconsin on a farm where fresh diversions presented themselves every day and where in the neighborhood, chicken thieves, Indian caves, buried treasure, and watermelon patches were to be had for the asking.

The door opened and my father, in an ugly temper, scolded me: "Now you'll go blind. What is the meaning of this, young lady?" When he found that the mantle of the Coleman lamp was burned out, he cursed savagely and ordered me to fetch a new one from the top shelf. As I did so, a pipe clattered to the floor and broke in two. It was one he never used, but he kept it as a curio, for its bowl was porcelain and baked into it was a picture of the cathedral at Worms.

"Now damn you!" he screamed. "Now give me the mantle from your damned butter fingers!"

He slapped me on the side of the head with his open hand and there was a sudden ache in my opposite ear. Then he turned away and as he adjusted the mantle, he growled, "What is the use? They make me come into a dark house and then they break my things. They should go to jail." When the white light flared up, I saw him move the red felt cozy and look at a heap of bits of white china, all that was left of his coffee pot.

"*I* didn't do it!" I cried. "I never did!"

"I know it," he said. "Your mother did it. She picked it up and threw it at the stove." Our eyes turned together and saw, beneath the oven door, two or three white glittering splinters amongst the ashes. I could not imagine so violent a gesture in my lazy mother. Her only weapon was her tireless voice. There must have been a quarrel of unprecedented savagery while I was at school, and I was glad that I had not come home at lunch time but instead had eaten an apple and a fig-Newton given to me by the Hendersons.

"Well?" shouted my father. "Well, where is my supper?"

"You said not to expect you, Papa. You said you weren't coming home."

"I did *not*." He spouted like a child and stamped his foot.

My mother did not come out, and my father was angry with me for cutting his bread too thin and burning the bacon, and when I asked him what I should put the coffee into now that

the pot was broken, he pounded the table with both his fists so
that the cutlery bounced, and then he put his head down until
his forehead was in his greasy plate and shouted, "*Confiteor Deo
omnipotenti, Beatae Mariae, semper Virgini . . .*" but he could
not go on. He rolled over until his face was pointed upward
to the ceiling and he wailed, "*Gott! Gott! Warum hast du mir
verlassen?*"

"Papa, do you want some cheese?"

"Cheese? Yes, that's the remedy! Give your father a spoonful
of cheese and that will get him out of hell!" He took me by
both arms and shook me until my dizzied eyes began to hurt.
"We're fit for nothing!" His eyes, afire and yet still as cold as
ice, looked upon me with such hatred and so terrible a threat
that I commenced to cry. My chin lifted and my eyes narrowed
and when he shook me again, the tears fell out. I could not stop
and though, when he released me, I covered my mouth with
my hand, the sound escaped me and the warm tears welled up
as freely as water from a drinking fountain. He let me go and
stepped back, aghast. Cruelly, yet out of the necessity to justify
myself, I sobbed, "I don't care! You cried last night!"

Twice he told me to be quiet and when I could not, being
now at the mercy of my gulping, he drove me into a corner of
the room, out of the circle of the lamplight and there, beside
the dark blue sink, I huddled against the wall, bawling softly
as my stopped-up nose bubbled and a faint interior disturbance
in my skull made me think my brains were rattling.

He pushed back the dishes and settled down at the table to
read, still so distracted that by mistake, he opened *Frances and
the Irrepressibles* and for some moments stared stupidly at the
pictures of little girls in hair ribbons and white party dresses
and high button shoes before he realized, with an outburst of
wounded dignity, that this was not *Riders of the Purple Sage.*

Just as he had thought I deliberately broke his pipe, now he
thought I had mischievously substituted my book for his, not
only to insult him with its childishness but to remind him that
he could not read English well and that I could. He strode
across the room and plucked me to my feet. "I've had enough
of your monkey business." He turned me around and hit me
four or five times on the backside. I did not cry out but my
tears continued to fall and I felt giddy as the blows stung me

through my thin skirt. The action satisfied him and he drew his chair to the fire and began to read. I collapsed once more into my corner, pondering how I could avenge myself.

Probably from his frequent readings of this book, my father longed to see the west and one time, some years before, when he had made a little extra money carrying trunks at the Hotel, he bought a fine yellow hide and made a pair of cowboy boots which he sometimes wore on Sunday. As he read, I could tell by the pleasure that illuminated his face and caused him now and then to chuckle deeply in his throat, that he was far away from me and that the world in which he rode a pinto cow-pony or a roan mare contained no blubbering, angry child nor any sullen, pregnant woman. Once he paused and swung an invisible lariat over his head, leaned forward on his horse's neck as to its flanks he pressed spurs with tied rowels. A little later, he whipped a revolver from his holster and aimed at the empty caviar can. Then, conscious once more of where he was, he kicked the stove in vexation and scratched his head.

As I crouched in my corner, I felt thin drafts of bitter air coming through the cracks in the wall and I thought of the hard, dirty snow outside and of the wind that came across the bay whipping granules of sand into the faces and onto the legs of walkers. I thought of my mother, when she was about my age, being cast out into the brutal night, and it came to me with a shock that that incredible man who dandled the German milliner on his knee was my own grandfather. I tried to imagine him and succeeded only in calling up an image of my father as he might be when he was old. This person I brought into the room and allowed to approach me and to send me away as he had sent away my mother and my aunts and uncles, and I tried to imagine what it would feel like to be exiled from one's own house. I was intent upon my painful fancy; I had closed my eyes and the cold from the window seemed more acute. The vision of my father-grandfather seemed actually to take on flesh and spirit.

A harsh and sudden voice spoke out: "Sonie, get to bed."

I had thought my father had forgotten that I was still in the room; his unexpected command, though its intention was disciplinary rather than unkind, thrilled me as if it were the completion of the scene behind my closed eyelids. For a moment I was not sure whether I had heard him say, "Get to bed," and not what I had expected the grandfather to say, "Get out." Whether it was the confusion in my mind or merely the shock of hearing words after so intense a silence, I do not know, but I burst into fresh tears, so stormily this time it was as though I had been storing them up and had only waited for a trifle to start the avalanche. My baffled father stood up and peered at me in my dark corner. He came towards me uncertainly, but I could not tell whether he was angry or remorseful. "Now, Sonie, now, girl. Come out of your corner." I did not stir.

"Come, *Mädchen*," he wheedled and I knew, because he used that tender word, that he was not cross. Perhaps he regretted his harshness and had realized my innocence. Still, I did not move, and he continued to come closer. He crouched down on the floor beside me. "There. There." He followed the dirty meanders of the tears on my cheeks with his forefinger. "Maybe they'll freeze there like icicles, *ni't*? The kids at school will call you a cry baby girl." Grieved at his mistake and not trying to make up for it by caresses, as my mother would have done, he had a dignity which I was bound to admire, and at last I smiled at him. "*Jawohl!*" he cried in genuine pleasure and then, in imitation of the friendly rancher of the Saturday night movies, he awkwardly offered me his hand and said, "Put 'er there, pardner!"

The cold from the windows laid metallic ribbons across my back. I was sickened to think of my aunts and uncles trudging, whimpering, in the Russian night, and in a glow of relief at my better fortune, I grasped the extended hand. In a meditative way, with his head bowed, my father began to finger my hand, pressing the ball of his into the hollow of my palm, lacing our fingers together, feeling the knuckles.

"Sonie," he said after a time. "What is it you want to do when you grow up?"

I could not tell him that my only ambition was to live with Miss Pride, for I did not want him to know that I preferred her to himself. But I said, "I guess I want to live in Boston."

"Boston? Is that all you want to do? Why, I thought you wanted to be a school teacher at least."

"Oh, no!"

"I guess I haven't done anything right. You should want to be a school teacher, I think. How far are you in your Latin now?"

"We don't start Latin till the eighth grade," I told him and then, because I saw how curiously he looked at me, I added, "I'm in the seventh now."

"It would be a comfort for a man to know what he used to know," he mused. Then, to include me he said with a spurt of good spirits, "I'll tell you what we'll do, Sonie, we'll go west some day to Cheyenne, Wyoming. Wouldn't you like to ride a little wild horse?"

I said I would in much sincerity, but because I was unschooled in both the scenery and the customs of the west, I did not immediately seat myself astride a horse or envisage Cheyenne, but instead, heard Miss Pride say to a friend, as I entered the drawing room, "*Here* is our cow girl. You know she and her father own several thousand wild roan stallions."

"I could make us some boots." He said that undoubtedly there was a place for a man like him who could make leather things. Cowboys were particular about their clothes, he had heard; that is, not dandified, but they liked expensive wool shirts and Stetson hats and since they hadn't for the most part any family to support, they could spend all their wages on clothes and *Schnaps*. He dwelt for a long time on their emancipation and prosperity; sometimes, for variety, he called them "the punchers" until I became quite breathless and pleaded to go at once.

I returned him from his rapture. He looked down at me through the sad gloom. "Well, now, *Mädchen*, when will you be ready to go?"

"Now!" It did not occur to me that we could not go the moment we had agreed on our destination, for, being altogether unacquainted with travel, I was not aware that it cost anything. I supposed, moreover, that if we needed money for our dinner on the train (I already saw myself eating a pork chop and as many bananas as I wanted) he, like Betty Brunson's father, the dentist, could "sell a bond." For this, I believed was the prerogative of a father. Whenever anyone said, "I wish I had a ukulele," or "I wish I had a solid gold barrette," Betty would reply, "Why don't you ask your father to sell a bond? Daddy always does." I had always had the vague idea that my father's bonds would be German and therefore less easily disposed of but that in an emergency he could market them.

"I am thinking," he said with a sigh, "that it might be better if I went on first and got things lined up, you might say, and then sent for you. By that time I would have the corral built and have you a nice little palomino horse. It's a long way out there. You would get sleepy."

"How far?"

"Maybe as far as two thousand miles. I expect it's five days or so on the train. A long, long way, Sonie girl."

"I want to go with you, Papa. Now."

He stiffened and stood up. My mother was standing in the doorway of the bedroom, her shadow so long it fell the length of the room and, making a right angle turn at the juncture, continued up the wall. She was pale and her staring eyes seemed uncommonly large. It seemed to me that they were never so beautiful as when she was angry. The whites of them were immaculate, not marked, as most eyes are, with shabby red tendrils, and the iris was so dark the pupil was nearly invisible, but in the sun or in the lamplight as tonight, an amber ray appeared intermittently in the iris, ending in the profound depths of that rich center. When my parents drank together, my father would gaze into her face and murmur, "*Die wunderschöne Augen! Die magische Augen!*" Tonight, in her sickness or in her despair or her fury, whatever it was that had driven her out to us, these eyes seemed, because of their wonderful and awful size, to be holding back their lids with effort.

Her black hair, pouched with white combs into a pompadour, hung to her waist and swung heavily with the movement of her body; it shone like a blue-jay's feathers. She stroked one hand with the other and in the hush we could hear the muted hissing of the skin being rubbed. On her tight forearm, I saw that there was a long scratch that had been painted with iodine.

My parents stood as if entranced, each waiting for the other to speak. If only they would now be merciful, embrace, speak softly! How could my mother, so beautiful a woman, create so much unhappiness for us all? For she was beautiful and her beauty was as holy a kind as that of the statue in the church before which Gonzales had been praying. Her rosiness, her clear skin, the sheen of her hair, her calm eyes, made the old ladies at the Hotel Barstow say of her, "She is the image of a saint." The line of the hair on her high forehead was almost straight as though a child, drawing a picture and unable to trace in it the actual irregularities of his model, had simplified, had tidied up. The planes of the face were clean and the silken flesh shrank shallowly beneath the cheekbone and became pallid or golden as the light struck it. She was a tall woman, with a graceful, lethargic carriage. Her hands were her only blemish, for they were always red and scaly with the cleaning powders she used in the summer to clean the bathtubs, and in the winter they were chapped. Her fingers were torn with cracks in the tips or hangnails or cuts from knives or gouges from bedsprings. They were always cold as though too much blood had flowed out of their rents, and I supposed that was why she continually rubbed them.

"It is no use, Shura," my father said at last. His voice was even and formal.

At his words, she bent her head down on her breast. The hair tumbled about her like a veil and at the base of her skull, the scalp was visible between cords of the hair heavily tossed forward. She moaned, "But you must not take Sonia away from me!" She flung back her head again and I saw that not even now was her face distorted by her feelings. Not even her mouth, filter of anger, bitterness, sorrow, became less charming, and the sweetness of its shape, the texture of its dark red flesh seemed to abate her passion, making it something strapped and aimless.

"If I go, I will take nothing but my body and my soul."

"Soul!" She spat on the floor before her bare feet. "Does a man have a soul that cuts his wife?" She held out her scratched arm. "Sonia, look! What do you think of a father like that, eh?"

"Why do you lie before the girl? She knows I never laid my hands on you. Tell her that you broke my china coffee pot and nagged me until I was crazy!"

"I hate you. Ah, I would hate any man that cried tears like a woman."

"And I hate you, Shura, with all my heart. You've ruined everything for me and I've had enough."

For the briefest moment, alarm showed in my mother's face, but then she smiled. "And so have I. If it weren't for Sonia . . ."

"Even for Sonie I've had enough now. From the beginning it is all wrong."

My mother's insistence flagged before the determination in his voice and she could not accuse him of any specific thing, but only said, complacently, "Thank God, she's a little girl. And by the grace of the Holy Ghost, there will be another little girl. I'll call her little Luibka."

"So, Luibka!" He laughed like a lunatic. "So we will call the witch's daughter after the old hell-cat. But what if the little whore in your belly turns out to be little Ivan instead? Little, little, little Russian woman, little God damn you to a little tiny Russian hell!"

"Hush! Before the child!"

His raging voice did not alter in pitch as, wheeling upon me, he commanded, "Pray for yourself, Sonie! Sonie . . ." He faltered and then, calmed, he took my mother's arm. "Put on your shoes, Shura, and come to the shop."

My jaws were sour and my mouth was full of saliva which escaped and wavered on my lips. When they had gone out, I moaned, and still, while my misery did not lessen, I saw myself slipping out of the house and running up the road to the Hotel. I would go through the basement and creep up the dark stairs and through the kitchen, the dining room, the lobby, up the staircase and through the corridor until I came to the door of Miss Pride's room. I would lie on the window seat with her afghan over me and my head in the plump pillows and there I would go to sleep. Perhaps I would find the furniture covered with ghost-clothes as I had once seen them so dressed in the lobby when I peered through the cracks of the boarding at the window. I would be delighted if the hat-pin holder were covered with a dust-shroud, and if the cherubs were dressed for winter. But I remembered, sadly, that there would be nothing in the room, for before she went away, Miss Pride always locked her belongings in the closet and handed the key to the manager. Well, then, what I must do was go to Mr. Henderson next door and ask him to take me across the bay in his boat. If I came to her, late at night, without a coat, she could not refuse to let me in. "I was expecting you," said Miss Pride to

Antoinette de la Mar as the latter sank down on the green velour davenport in the elegant drawing-room, "and so I have some sandwiches and a big pot of cocoa ready for you. Will you take one marshmallow or two?"

I was awakening for a long time, climbing the waves of my sleep and relapsing, dreaming and knowing that I dreamed. A cat had laid five hen's eggs which Betty Brunson advised me to name "Frances Irrepressible." The purr of the mother cat shaped into words, "Sonia, are you awake?" Beside me was my mother's lax, warm body, and through my half-opened eyes, I saw that her scratched arm lay across my chest. I was afraid she might kiss me and I pretended that I was still asleep.

"Sonia?" she inquired again.

The room was dark so that I was not sure it was day until through the thin walls I heard Mr. Henderson's voice. "Sarah!" he called. "*Oh*, Sarah! Bring me the gaff like a good girl," and I knew that he was going out to his lobster pots. Immediately afterward, the bells of the Catholic church rang eight o'clock and my mother sat up, as though the sound had alarmed her. She tested the temperature of the room by exhaling her breath in little puffs and saw, by the vapor issuing from her mouth, that it was keenly cold. Before she got out of bed, she shivered into her blue wrapper and drew on her stockings. I opened my eyes and asked, "Why am I in the bed, Mamma?"

She smiled. "Because your father went off somewhere last night. We are all alone, darling."

"Did he go in the *storm*?"

She nodded, but her thoughts were not on him. "You lie there till the fire is going," she said. "Maybe you won't go to school today? I'll make you a boiled egg for breakfast!" The prospect of so unusual a festivity brought a dancing light into her eyes, and with a liveliness I had never seen in her before, she moved about the room, stroking the velvety leaves of the geraniums which still stood on the bureau.

"He said he was going to put them into the stove because his pot got broken," she said as she took the flowers down. "But I hid them in time."

I lay still after she had left the room, listening to her shaking down the ashes and drawing water for the tea. I remembered, as from a dim former life, that some time in the night I had staggered, bloated with sleep, upon my mother's arm into the bedroom and I had flung out protesting arms and had muttered, "Leave me be," as she took off my middy blouse and undid the waist from my skirt.

I had never dreamed that the bed was so soft. The blankets and pillows were like loving, hugging arms, and I closed my eyes again, wishing that now I had it all to myself I might stay in it the whole morning. Directly I heard the Hendersons joining the Kadish children on the road to school. "Where's Sonie?" said one of them, and when there was no answer I was certain that they were whispering amongst themselves. Probably the Kadishes had heard the quarrel last night, for our houses were only a few yards apart. But I was not yet wide awake enough to be conscious of shame, and careless of all but this snug bed, I burrowed deeper into the blankets like a hibernating animal and thought of how, presently, I would break my boiled egg over a piece of bread and salt and pepper it while a cup of tea at the side of my plate steamed into my face.

Chapter Three

M Y FATHER had taken nothing with him: no clothes but those he wore, no tools, not even an extra pipe. Through the years of his absence, I used sometimes to wonder, as I looked at the kitchen shelves or at the traps in his shop, if he had not had time to collect his things together, if he had wanted to be on his way before the violence of his decision capitulated and left him still obliged to go but to go now without the desire; or if he had taken nothing in the intention of beginning anew, as unencumbered as possible, free both of the nuisance of carrying his belongings and of the reminders implicit in them of the life he had left behind.

His empty-handedness struck both my mother and me as evidence that he would come back, for he had a strong sense of possession, obvious from the clutter in his shop. He had brought from Germany four great boxes besides numerous small ones. These had never been opened because, being a poor man and unable to make new acquisitions, he did not want to wear out what he had. He saved everything for a "rainy day" but even when he was deluged with bursting clouds, he never so much as considered unlocking his treasures.

After we had had our breakfast, my mother, explaining to me that she was now in the fourth month of her pregnancy (sensing my disapproval she implored me, "Ah, good Christ, Sonia, you be nice to your poor mother!"), sent me to fetch Mrs. Henderson. She was feeling unwell and thought that the neighbor woman would prescribe something soothing to help her over the shock. She did look ill and weary and I was glad to shift the responsibility for her to someone else. Actually, I suppose, she was not in much discomfort, for as soon as Mrs. Henderson came, she brightened up and began to talk and eagerly to drink the tea into which had been poured a little rum. Mrs. Henderson was a large, good-natured woman, prematurely gray. Because of her hair and because she wore bifocal spectacles, I thought she was old, and at first had believed that she was the grandmother, not the mother of the children with whom I played. Plainly, she did not want to hear my mother's account of last evening, the preface to which greeted her the moment she stepped across the threshold. She asked me a great many questions about school, whether I was looking forward to the Christmas pageant, and if I liked Civics this year and if I did not agree that Miss Pickens, my teacher, was the sweetest woman on earth. My mother, who had no interest in my education, nodded her head now and then in bored courtesy until she could bear it no longer and wrested the conversation from us. She began to talk in a passionless monotone of what she called her "condition," and as she spoke of my father's disappearance only in relation to it, I could learn nothing new about what had happened after I fell asleep on the floor. Blushing, I went out to the shop.

For some time, I sat on the work bench gazing about me at the tools and the bottles of dye and polish and the hides hung along the walls. I intended to open my father's boxes, and it was as though I expected a new world to rise in primeval mist when I had lifted up their lids. For, knowing nothing but charm of Germany, I assumed that their contents would be charming. From my father, I had learned that castles were a natural part of the landscape of his country, that a faëry life as old as the earth whispered and flirted in the enchanted forests, that all families were large, rich and congenial and every Sunday afternoon went walking through the hills until they came to an inn tucked away in the chestnut trees. The father would point his stick and cry, "Listen, what do you say to a piece of cake, you, Hermann, you, Friedrich?" And they would all go in to drink some coffee or perhaps some red wine with a cherry *torte* or a plate of *lebkuchen*. I knew, moreover, that on the façade of my father's house in Würzburg, there were bas-reliefs of kings' heads, bunches of grapes, lyres, and goblets, and that within the house there was a big tile stove and all the sheets were pure linen.

Nearby the nail where the key of rings to the trunks hung, there was another nail from which dangled a black rosary with golden gauds, a present, he had told me, from his Aunt Therese, on the day of his confirmation. As the sheen of the beads caught my eye, I wondered if perhaps this afternoon, wherever he might be, he would go to confession. What would the father in the cubbyhole say to him? Would he tell him to come back to us? I was not sure yet that I wanted him to return. I had no feeling of loss thus far, and I could think only with joy that there would be no more quarrels at night. Perhaps now that he was gone, my mother would change, would emerge from her slovenly wrapper and her lazy ways, and would no longer spend all her time staring at the sea. (It happened that my father, from his windows, and I from Miss Pride's, looked toward Boston, but my mother, looking out the windows of our kitchen, could see only a long white stretch of sand and a few crags far off, and then the endless sea itself. It was an arresting landscape but one whose eternal monotony became maddening in time. But towards the sameness of her prospect, she was altogether indifferent.)

Into my life, moreover, my father's escape introduced a theme of mystery. Already he was, in my mind, an almost mythical figure, belonging to no category I had hitherto known outside the pages of books, for he was not merely a fugitive, he was also particularly my father whom, after a while when I was grown up, I might seek my whole life through, as I had seen daughters do at the Bijou, missing by a few minutes a reunion in a South American cabaret, a Peking tea house, an English garden party, our gondolas passing one another on the Grand Canal just as the moon was darkened by a cloud.

There were moments, to be sure, when I rebuked him for leaving us stranded with nothing but twenty-four dollars, which my high principled mother had tried, this morning, to put into the stove. But my prayers for our better fortune were today not directed towards him but towards some unknown benefactor. And when, as the day wore on, I began to miss him, I did not wish he were here with us, but wished that I were with him, as he walked along a road, smiling, his fair hair blowing, unconscious of everything but his freedom and the strength of his body.

I took the keys from their nail, pushed aside some cartons and heaps of kindling in front of one of the trunks, found the proper key and opened it. The lid resisted and the hinges faintly screeched. The odor of camphor balls rose strongly. Each article was wrapped separately in heavy brown paper. Everything was unused, but some of the cloth had rotted at the folds from lying there so long, and the paper of the brochures of cobblers' tools was brittle; the *Lederhosen* and the ski boots were stiff. I found cleated shoes, woolen underdrawers, skis, ski poles, ice skates, embroidered suspenders, hunting knives, and a rucksack. His clothes showed that he was not only a sportsman, but a gentleman as well, for amongst them were a dinner-jacket, a white silk ascot, a top hat, and a walking stick with a gold snake's head.

There were pictures of my grandparents taken at various times in their lives, tinted and contained in heavy gilt frames. Did these old people with their stern eyes and kindly mouths know, before they died, that they had a grandchild in America? Perhaps in the big shop in Würzburg, run now by my uncle Christian, there was a picture of Cousin Sonia tacked up on the wall. I could recall only one picture of myself, taken on an Easter day by Mr. Henderson. Together with his children I had posed, holding a calla lily in my hand like a scepter, and because the sun was in my eyes and I could not close my mouth for I had a cold in the head, my face drooped with stupidity. But I had worn new shoes, made by my father, and stood with one foot thrust forward; they were riding boots and at the tops, my initials, S.M., had been burnt into the leather. Perhaps even if my uncles and my Cousin Peter did not care for my face, they would see by the boots that I was their "kind."

My shoes, and nothing else, had always set me apart from other children, for they were of the finest leather and were most elegantly embellished. As I saw this morning how shabby my boots were, touched the thin spots on the soles that would soon be worn quite through, and remembered that I could no longer wear my summer sandals for my feet had grown too large, I was sorry that Papa had gone away. For if the other children had been surprised at this incongruous note in my raggedness, they had admired it. Even Betty Brunson, the wealthy dentist's daughter, had begged her mother for shoes like mine. And the band of horrid boys who, when I had pigtails, teased me for them and teased me even more when they were cut off and my ugly "bob" was fashioned to the uncompromising lines of a cereal bowl: they, too, had looked with envy on my red-brown boots of this year, laced with rough yellow thongs and equipped on the outside with pockets in which I carried a small, dull hunting knife, salvaged from the kitchen shelves, and an eight-inch celluloid ruler.

I looked again through Papa's effects, in the hope of finding some bauble that I had overlooked which would distinguish me as much as my shoes had done. There was nothing but the rosary, and although I was tempted to slip it around my neck, superstition checked me. In my ignorance, I thought its magic properties might operate to my destruction.

The sun was high and the piled snow was melting. I heard the Henderson children coming home for dinner, and I knew it was time for me to leave the shop which I already thought of as my own. I looked back one more time for a treasure, and now, not amongst the things spilled over the sides of the boxes, but on the work table, I saw a pair of slippers my father had made for Hopestill Mather. They were sandals with a strap up the center, through which passed another strap, fastened at the side with a gold buckle, and they had been dyed green, the color of the first leaves in the spring. One was unfinished: the sole had not been trimmed and jagged spears of thick leather stood out on all sides. But the sole of the other was so smooth and polished that it felt like satin to my cheek. I supposed she would have a green dress, made of taffeta or chiffon, and that in her hair she would wear a green ribbon like the one she had worn at luncheon that day with her aunt. I could see these little slippers dancing across a ballroom and I could smell the child who wore them: she would smell of Miss Pride's soap and of the sharp lily-of-the-valley cologne in the cut-glass bottle. I could see no one else at the party and even her partner was no more than a black mist. But the girl, with her yellow eyes and her white skin, her head flung back so that the bright hair fell far down, was as real as the soft sandals I held in my hands, and I hated her. I took off my boots and my lisle stockings and sat down to try on the finished shoe. It did not fit. My foot was too long and so broad that it would not even go into the vamp although I struggled and pulled until I was sweating. Angrily, I flung it into a corner of the room where, in the smudged shadows, it gleamed like a wet leaf. Her hands would be small too! Half the width, half the length of mine, white as her face, smooth as the sole of the slipper, her hands would be covered with rings and bracelets, set with green jewels. And her room in her aunt's house on Pinckney Street would have a green carpet and pale green walls and a green satin counterpane for the little green bed.

I ruined the slipper with the crude sole. Both straps I cut in two with a pair of heavy shears and I dipped my thumb in machine oil to deface the surface of the kid. I pulled off the buckle with a pair of pliers and I drove a long nail through the heel and into the wood of the work table so that it was pinned there. And then, leaving the contents of my father's boxes in disorder on the floor, I went out, glancing backwards once at Hopestill Mather's absurd shoe.

Mrs. Henderson had prepared a meal for us: a cabbage soup, made according to my mother's instructions, was simmering on the stove and beans were heating in the oven. She had brought a loaf of fresh brown bread, a glass of apple jelly, and a nicely colored pat of margarine. My mother had been asleep and she looked rosy and rested. When I helped her into the kitchen—for she said with entreaty in her eyes, "My condition makes me feel funny"—and put pillows at her back, brought the table near so that she would not have to stir about, I felt a momentary affection and kissed her lightly on the forehead. I told her that I thought we might sell my father's clothes and his ski equipment. Since they were foreign, I believed they would fetch a high price, and I fancied a sign which I would put up over the door of the shop: "Miss Sonia Marburg's Sports Goods Shoppe."

"Sell them? My God, you are talking crazy! He would kill you if you sold any of his trash. Kill you till there'd be nothing left of you."

"But perhaps he's not coming back," I said.

"I'll take another plate of *pokhlyobka*. Mrs. H. is a saint from head to toe." As she dawdled with the spoon, she went on, "He'll come back, you'll see, darling. I won't say when, not knowing where he went, but he'll come back and I know that. And if he finds his wool drawers sold, there's no telling what kind of way he'll kill us. I was saying to Mrs. Henderson that what I think he did was go to Boston to get a gun. For us, you know, sweetheart. And so tonight I am going to keep a lamp on and if they see it go out they'll hurry over to save us."

This transformation of my father into a murderer made me laugh aloud and when I covered up my giggle with a cough, she remembered that he had, she had always suspected, "sores on his lungs" because he coughed so much, and a pity it was he couldn't have kept his hands off me. Though my cough was purely voluntary and though I had never known my father to be ill, the remark distressed me and it was not for years after that that I was completely free of the notion that I had or might develop tuberculosis. She spoke of it from time to time, occasionally giving me garish accounts of his hemorrhages when his face turned blue and his eyes all but dropped from their sockets and blood spilled out from his lips as freely as wine from a bottle.

In vain I tried to convince her that it was only right we should sell the things in the shop. I said he would want us to, that, granted he was a bad man, he was not so bad as to want us to starve. After she had several times repeated in agitated whispers that he would be back that night to shoot us, she fell into her old, familiar placid grief, believed he would never return, and that I, poor, thin child, must make our living. "And the Hotel not open until summer time," she mourned, turning her eyes to the sand, the crags, and the ocean. "And Luibka coming. You must go to your teacher, darling, and tell her what a fix we're in." I asked her if I might have one of the dollars my father had left so that I could buy something at the store for our supper. She did not answer. Her elbow rested on the edge of the blue sink and she stared through the leaves of the geraniums, restored to their proper place.

2

On my way to school for the afternoon session, I thought considerably of my father. If he had left us at a different time of year, I think perhaps I would have been more casual. If it had been spring, the illimitable activities which the warm weather provided would have allowed me to set the catastrophe aside to think about when nothing appealed more strongly to me. For once April had come and my summer sandals were on my feet and my heavy sweater had been laid away with bags of tobacco to keep off the moths, I became a furious engine, liking to pursue, with an imaginary bow and arrow, an imaginary deer whose wild hooves carried me on a windy chase to the Point and back. In the fresh evenings, I played Run-Sheep-Run with the Henderson children and their cousins from Marblehead. Sometimes, hiding in a pack, feeling the hot breath of my fellows upon my neck and arms as we hunched up together under the shoulder of a rock or under the branches of a spreading bush, I would try to imagine another occupation: "What if I were doing arithmetic at home?" but the question would sink under my intentness and I could not, try as I might, conjure up a picture of myself in any other circumstances.

One spring, a disaster had befallen me. I had a pitiful little cat of which I was fond. It was ridden with fleas that it hunted with its sharp teeth, seizing bits of its hide ferociously enough to draw blood. And its ears were bald with mange which had also thinned the hair of its neck so that pink skin showed through. In its misery, it never purred, but under my petting turned up milky, half-shut eyes in a sort of stupid gratitude. It had been a charming kitten, though, and I hoped through some benevolence of nature it would be restored to its original state. And then, it was killed by Gonzales' bulldog when it still ailed. I saw the dreadful slaughter: the dog's eyes popping as he rent and strangled the creature, spittle mingling with blood, and I heard the cat's single wail of entreaty. Yet, although as a witness I was nauseated, once the cat was underground in a shoe box filled with petunias from Mrs. Henderson's flower boxes, my tears dried, my faintness passed and all that evening, as though nothing had happened, I exuberantly played Kick-the-Can. But then, months later, after the summer was over and the early evenings were too dark and cold for outdoor games, I felt my loss and besought my father to kill the bulldog and, for good measure, Gonzales too. He replied that it was "good riddance." Not only was my only companion for these winter nights gone from me forever, but my bereavement was mocked. My mother, hearing my lamentation, added to my sorrow such a weight of depressing generalizations on death and cruelty that the cat assumed a tragic stature and I thought I should never forget to mourn.

Now it was still winter when my father left, and in the desolation of the beach, I felt the desolation that would fall upon our house. The thought came to me that perhaps he would never walk along this road again and that he was therefore, in a sense, no longer alive, just as on foggy days when I could not see the State House dome, it was as though there were no Boston but that the city had dematerialized in the mist. A little wind, cold and wet with salt water, blew freshly into my face. I stooped to tighten the lace of my boot and as I did so, I felt that I had done this same thing before, but although I troubled my memory, I could not recall the other time. Afterwards and for many years, whenever I thought of my father, I saw him as though I were kneeling in the sand looking up at him on a gray winter day, our hair curling in the wind. Because my hands were cold and the lace was damp, the knot was not easy to tie. As I bent over, the smell of wetted leather came to me. When the odors, as distinct as on the day he left, came back at certain, sudden times throughout the years, with them always came the evasive feeling that every gesture I made and every particular in the landscape had been copied from some earlier day.

The fear that I might be taunted for my father's desertion rose to make me walk more slowly. I hoped to arrive after the others had already gone into the building. But immediately afterward, I quickened my pace at the thought of being stared at if I were tardy. I could hear the cries of children playing in the yard, mingled with the thud of balls being caught by the big boys of the eighth grade, and with the whizz and whine of swings where the younger children were pumping up. Then, when I had reached the gate and poked my head about one of the big cement columns which advertised the name, "Chichester Public School," and the date of erection of the building, and saw my boisterous schoolmates, I was urged forward by the desire to be hailed by them and was held back by the fear that I would not be and that my deficiencies, so mysterious to me and so apparent to them, would be more laughable today than ever. (I was always or nearly always the last to be chosen on a team, and I was convinced that the snub was directed against something less fundamental than simply my awkwardness in catching a ball or my inability to run without falling down on my face.) I expected to be greeted with a volley of catcalls which would proclaim my poor father's delinquency and would not spare my hair-cut. But my advance to the front door, although it was observed, did not disrupt the games.

Betty Brunson, who rarely addressed me, was embracing a young elm tree near the door and swinging round it, her head appearing now on one side, now on another. "Hi, Sonie Marburg, whatcha going to do this aft?"

"Oh, I don't know," I stammered.

"It so happens," she said, "that I happen to be going to New York. My father happens to be buying a car in New York City, New York."

A week ago, or yesterday, her voice would have been supercilious, for she would have been poking fun at me for being poor. But today, through a wonder of wonders to which I had no clue, she was *including* me as if her news and even her father's car were to be shared with me in the casual, communistic spirit that inspires the friendship of children. Heretofore, she had found space in the circle of her father's reflected glory for only two others, Esther and Ruby Beeler who were, strangely enough, even more impoverished than I. They, who had been pale, insipid waifs, bloomed under the patronage, became hearty extroverts with bold grins on their pinched little faces and roses in their cheeks which came, not from an amplified diet, but from happiness at being chosen. My first thought today was that they had offended Betty and that she was replacing them with the first person to come along. Her round face, with bright blue eyes and an obtuse nose, was framed by yellow, marcelled hair and the waves were held in place by tortoise-shell barrettes studded with rubies. She wore a coat of lambskin and a hat to match and from her pocket protruded fur-lined capeskin gloves. Without preamble, she began to relate the events of a "keen" Sunday she had recently spent with her highfaluting relatives in Boston. In the midst of her account, the Beelers came up. The three entwined their arms about one another and swayed round the elm tree with solemn faces as Betty listed the vegetables in the salad and the different designs on the coffee spoons. When she had finished, she said, turning to Ruby first and then to Esther, "We know a secret, don't we, Beelers?"

Her protegées said chorally, "We *sure* do."

Their solemnity reassured me. It was very likely no secret that my father had run away, for the Hendersons and the Kadishes would have conferred and brought the tale to school. There was, in the manner of the three girls and in the circumstances of the encounter, evidence that the secret bore a relation to myself and was not in the same category as the new automobile. I assumed that it was something from which I would make either a social or a material gain: I saw myself riding in Dr. Brunson's new car, going to a Valentine party at the Brunsons' house, receiving a box of candy, a charm bracelet, a round comb or a bottle of perfume from Betty, and, finally, achieving the summit of the improbable whose ascent is so easy when we are lifted up by the wings of our dreams, I imagined going to a "slumber party" at the house of Betty's surgeon uncle in Boston. Betty and Betty's life became the Alpha and Omega. I aspired to her small, snobbish sorority that fed on Tootsie Rolls and licorice wands, and whose insignia, provided by her father, was a Roi-Tan cigar label worn on the middle finger of the left hand.

The girls, or, as I now thought of them, "my friends" would not tell me, but continued to repeat in singsong, "We know a secret and we *sure* won't tell," until finally Betty, using her father's language nonchalantly, remarked, "Oh, by the by, old girl, I almost forgot. Pickens wants a word with you." Ruby, who was dazzled by her friend's recherché speech, but not too dazzled to follow with what, in her social stratum she believed was as debonair, said, "Ain't it the truth." Betty gave me a push, "Well, ta-ta till after school," she said and they retreated, walking backwards, their smiles giving way to brief glares of consternation as they almost lost their balance.

So Pickens (I dropped the "Miss" in my private thoughts, out of respect to Betty Brunson), I surmised, was in on the secret. This I did not relish, for it was to her that my mother had insisted I appeal for help. "Just tell her that your rascal papa left you and your mamma is in a condition. You beg her, Sonie, there's a good girl. You cry and say, 'Oh, Miss What-youmaycallit, I am *so* hungry, and we haven't no money, no food, nor fire and not a thing.'" Of course no child could say anything of the kind. I had made up my mind to speak to Miss

Pickens about customers for my sporting-goods shop, to make it clearly understood that I was launched already on a commercial enterprise of which the mechanism needed only the turn of a switch—the turn she would execute—to start producing a livelihood for me. In my determined independence, I thought of offering her a commission "per head" for any customer she brought me, a trick of business I had heard of through friends of my mother who paid taxi-drivers for touting rooms which they wished to let in the summer. My offer would demote Miss Pickens automatically from any position of benefactress. She was not a warm-hearted person but she was very sentimental and she viewed all successes as well as all misfortunes through tears which misted her spectacles but seldom acquired enough body to fall.

Miss Pickens was young but she already bore the marks of spinsterhood. Her fine chestnut hair was sparse at the temples and she vainly tried to hide her baldness with an absurd pompadour, bolstered up with a transformation, or, as we preferred, in our beastly way, to call it, a "rat" which sometimes became dislodged and hung spiritlessly down her cheek until she could repair herself in the teachers' rest-room. In her choice of clothes, she seemed to aim deliberately for the most unbecoming; she was perversely fond of chartreuse, mauve, and tan, which influenced and increased her sallowness. And so great was her belief in the ensemble that she wore everything to match exactly, including her stockings and gloves, even if she had to dye them, with the result that she resembled a caterpillar whose cocoon matches the leaf on which it is spun. Her medicine fetish was as persistent as any old lady's at the Hotel. During arithmetic in the morning, she ate a whole cake of yeast; at recess she measured out ten drops of belladonna from a bottle labeled "Poison!" and in the afternoon, stirred up a glass of psyllium seed which, mixed with water, looked like a thin brown mucus and repelled us all. No child had a crush on Miss Pickens, although I had at first been attracted by her cold, cultured voice and her elevated vocabulary which contained such words as "literally" and "intolerable" and "indefatigable," but her mannerisms quickly began to irritate me and I joined mine to the general growl, "Aw, she thinks she's smart." Her tear-clouded, octagonal glasses had given her the reputation of meaning well among the parents, who met all the teachers annually at the P.T.A. clambake. My mother was fond of relating how moved Miss Pickens had been when she told her of the time I broke my collarbone at the age of four by falling off the roof of the shop. "A person would think," my mother said, "that it was her own collarbone or her own child and happening right now instead of eight years ago." But really Miss Pickens' tears were trumped up. When Lottie Cummings' mother died, our teacher was blinded when she first interviewed the child but made no move to comfort her, only made her cry the harder by calling her "My poor, poor little girl." And after that, Lottie, who at the age of thirteen weighed 135 pounds, complained to her that the other children had commenced to tease her again now they felt the interval of mourning was over, but Miss Pickens did not restrain us in any way.

The building was empty save for a few teachers clustered about the radiator far down the corridor. As I opened the heavy storm doors and my nostrils were greeted by the familiar but always new odors of school—varnish, floor oil, felt erasers full of chalk—I experienced the feelings of light-headedness and pleasure I always did after I had been ill and then was well enough to go outdoors again. For it seemed ages ago, not yesterday, that I had entered here. I advanced, hunting signs of change, and found them everywhere: the old freckles on the drinking fountain I had never seen before, the ancient chains on the cloudy transoms, a green, crazed flower-pot which must have stood for fifteen years in the corner of a window sill above the stairs. And there was added to the heavy atmosphere a smell that was new to me, yet one I must have smelled daily for seven years: the smell of wet paper towels that filled the wastebasket beside the drinking fountain. It was so strong that the varnish, oil, and erasers were all but obliterated.

Miss Pickens, who had been humming "Comin' through the Rye" and supplying the percussion by tapping the gauge of the radiator with her long foot encased in a "health shoe," broke off her song and detached herself from the group of teachers to come toward me, her arms extended. I halted, suddenly trembling, like a person armed to defend himself against wild animals, but on meeting one face to face is immediately turned to stone. I quickly went into the seventh-grade room and scurried to my seat, laying my head on the desk, my arms folded on top, with the ostrich's belief that I was perfectly concealed, even though I could see her through an aperture of my intertwined arms, swaying through the aisle, the frolicsome tails of her beige chiffon scarf floating above the inkwells. She sat down in Rosalie Kadish's seat opposite me where there always hung an aura of onions which combined now with the teacher's smell of yeast, sachet, and a slight mildew.

"I understand," she said in her clear, uplifted voice, "that your father literally flew the coop. It was a naughty and intolerable thing to do. But every cloud has a . . . ?"

"Silver lining," I promptly supplied.

"Exactly, For one thing we won't ever drink beer at noon again and be sleepy in our sewing lesson, will we?"

Her sweetness curdled at the allusion. It was true. Whenever my father had the money, he brought home several bottles of beer from an old man who lived behind the Presbyterian church and carried on a paltry bootlegging business. I always begged for a glass, but my father, more through greed than prudence, refused me more than a cupful which he poured into my soup. However, this was enough, having it as I did in the middle of the day when I was already drowsy from the morning in school and the long walk home, and having it in combination with heavy food, to make me thick-witted and often Miss Pickens found me "*lite*rally asleep," a state at any time deplorable, but in my case magnified enormously since its cause was immoral, barbarous, and illegal. "To spoil good soup!" she fretted. Once, after I had committed some monstrous blunder in buttonholing, she called on my father and charged him with rearing me to be a drunkard. My father shrugged his shoulders and pretended not to understand her: "*Bitte, sprechen Sie Deutsch, gnädiges Fräulein?*" he said with a troubled face. She left, defeated and unfriendly, and had thereafter a chillness towards me which accounted, as much as my dreaminess, for my low grade in Deportment.

I said I supposed I would not drink beer again and the prospect saddened me. My teacher then laid a damp hand on mine and said, "There, there, it's hard, poor child, but we mustn't cry," and though she was not, of course, referring to the beer, I decided that my life would be unendurable without it. "We" had had until now no urge to cry, but her words, so mushy and stale and yet so tender and personal, started up a torrent of tears, and each time my inquisitive tongue received a drop, I was reminded, bitterly, of the way my father had put salt in his beer. I suffered her to lay her moist fingers on my head and arms and to come quite close to me in an embrace in which all the unhealthy odors she dispensed rose and eddied about me at the slightest movement on the part of either one of us.

"We must be *brave* and not be a burden to Mother who is bringing a baby into the world just for *us*," and then, to distract me, she said, in a fun-loving way, "I'll tell you what: I'll bet you a dollar to a doughnut it's a boy." When I agreed with a sobbing "Okay," she went on to tell me that as luck would have it, Betty Brunson's mother was also expecting the stork very soon, and she had been saying only the other day how much she would like to find a girl to help with the housework, and Miss Pickens had said to herself, "Why, I know just the girl. My Sonie Marburg is very capable and works at the Hotel in the summer so she must know how things are done, dishes and so on. I wouldn't be a bit surprised if she wouldn't love to work in that nice shiny new house where her chum Betty lives."

I lifted panic-stricken eyes to my teacher and dropped them at once. The shock had stopped my tears. I could not become a servant in Betty's house when she was about to admit me into her circle! Such a job, possible anywhere else and even attractive (for, in spite of my intention to refuse, I saw what I might gain in the way of petit larceny of sugar lumps and birthday candles and other staples which would never be missed), would cancel all those social engagements which had practically been proposed to me on the school ground just a few minutes ago. It was only after my stammered reply that my mother needed me at home, when Miss Pickens said, "Why, Betty thought it would be lovely. She'll be *so* disappointed," that I realized this was the secret. Everything had been ill-timed, and I, in my uncircumspect cockiness, had been caught in a trap.

Miss Pickens was stubborn and set before me arguments that I could not refute. I saw that the sooner I resigned myself the better, for my commercial pipe-dream could avail me nothing now that the teacher, essential to its working out, was set upon the new plan which, in her surpassing conventionality, she regarded as great good luck for me. She, being comfortably off herself, had no patience with pride in the poor as she often told us, apropos of tales she had read in the newspapers. Nevertheless, urged by desperation, I told her what I had intended to do.

Her befogged eyeglasses glared at me. "I'm surprised at you, Sonia. I didn't think you were a *silly* girl. You've been reading silly books instead of good books, suitable for your age group." ("Age group" was the sort of expression that had once fascinated me. She had learned her "Education" well and had not forgotten it, so that she sprinkled her speech with its vocabulary with a serene disregard for the class or age of her interlocutor. She had baffled Mr. Henderson by telling him that one of his children had no "community urge.") "Nothing, you poor silly child, could be less feasible than a sporting-goods shop in Chichester. There is only one sporting man in town so far as I know, that Dr. Galbraith at the hospital. And he, of course, goes in only for riding equipment. But I have a friend" (by a faint glow that simmered in her face I knew she meant a man friend) "who likes winter sports and if your father's skis are any good, it is quite possible I may be able to arrange a sale for you."

She obviously doubted the quality of my father's paraphernalia, and I said, "They're very expensive."

"Well, we'll see about that part of it. Don't you worry. I'll do my bit for you if you'll be sensible and go work for Mrs. Brunson."

I was gradually persuaded; rather, one self, already installed in the Brunson kitchen and reaching out a hand toward the sugar canister, was persuaded. Miss Pickens was pleased with my change of heart. "And now," she said, rising and plucking me by the shoulder, "now we must get rid of our tears, isn't that right? Hurry along, the bell's about to ring." And she hustled me down the corridor toward the teachers' rest-room. There was a recrudescence of my disappointment and I felt that I could not face Betty again today. I told Miss Pickens I felt a little sick and had a headache, couldn't I please go home?

"Certainly not," she said severely, but then, seeing how woebegone I was, she relented and in a burst of kindliness, even suggested that I wait in the lavatory until the other children had assembled in the classrooms so that I might leave the building without being seen. I was surprised that the teachers' rest-room smelled like ours and had the same gray enameled doors to the toilets. Only on great occasions of illness or accidents were children admitted to the room. Once, in the year before, some privileged little girl told us that as she was recovering from a nose-bleed, she had seen a cigarette butt on the floor, stained with lipstick. We tried to detect signs of guilt in all the teachers' faces, and could not, but the worldly Beelers said, "Oh, piffle, you dumb-bells. They *all* do it, but they flush them down the toilet."

I thought, as I sat on a backless couch, waiting to hear the last column of children march up the stairs and into the classrooms, that if only circumstances had not conspired against us, Betty and I, fast friends, might have taken up smoking.

3

To my mother, my father's desertion was like an eternally renewing spring from which she hourly drew accusations and complaints, and she shared her poisoned, enervating drink with anyone who would partake. Her companions in misery were poor neighbor women who, alternately pitying and envying, welcomed our misfortune as a distraction from their own worries. Mrs. Kadish, a thin, pinched, crotchety woman, the wife of a ferryboat engineer and the mother of six famished children, often came to call. She sat prissily erect, her hands folded tightly in her lap, nodding her long, hard head which was topped by a coil of graying hair. When she was not speaking, she pursed her lips in permanent displeasure, and when she did speak, it was in a high, nasal key, not loud, but like a distant scream.

As I came in one afternoon, she was saying, "I was on my feet at five A.M. this morning and I'm telling you, I've been on the go ever since. It's pick up! Wash up! Sew up! Rinse out! till a person could drop down senseless. You was saying, Mrs. Marburg, that it's hard if the man goes off and leaves the woman, but to my mind it's six of one and half a dozen of the other. If you don't have a grown man around, you don't have to cook so much and do up all them work shirts. Kadish could leave tomorrow and I wouldn't hardly notice only for the little dab of money he brings in."

"He hasn't left you yet, sweetheart," said my mother. "It's not the money. It's the *shame*. My God! You'd think this here wasn't his child not born yet and he went off to punish me. I know *you* don't think so, Mrs. Kadish, darling, nor Mrs. Henderson nor two or three other Chichester ladies, but what about the *other* people?"

Mrs. Kadish did not regard it a likely suspicion though it interested her. "You mean maybe they think you you-know? Oh, no, I don't *think* so. Why, Mrs. Marburg, nobody would say you was that type lady."

My mother began on a new tack: "Well, then, maybe they say *he* was the bad one and went off with one of those women from Marblehead, and maybe that's true, Mrs. Kadish, who knows? I'm no fool and I used to see them last summer wobbling down the beach by the gentlemen's house in dresses no longer than your camisole." The "gentlemen" were the Coast Guards, so known because one of them, five years before, had gone to Harvard.

"You're not telling me news," returned her friend. "But I wouldn't think that a family man like Mr. Marburg would take up with that type."

"Whatever people say—if they blame it on drink or on the other thing or something else besides—it's all a shame. But what can you do with Hermann Marburg? He is a *German*, dear."

Her voice fell upon the word "German" in such a way that the emphasis was ambiguous: either a German was infamous beyond pardon or pitiable beyond hope. Mrs. Kadish, after this statement, perused my face for a time. "German," she intoned. "And you, Mrs. Marburg, what was you saying was your nationality?"

"I am a Russian," said my mother without pride and without deprecation but with a kind of finality which set "Russian" distinctly apart from "German" as though it was perhaps not ultimately the best thing to be but was at least comprehensible. I could have corrected her: Russians, to the children at school, were utterly improbable though all that was known about them was that they had ludicrous names. A favorite sport was to tease me by saying: "Hisky, Sonivitch, have you got your geographysky home-workskivitch?" In a way, I was flattered by this, for it had replaced Pig-Latin and was known as Sonie-Latin. On the other hand, Germans were perfectly credible and, because of their reputation for cutting off the hands of sleeping children and of being sired by Kaiser Bill, they enjoyed a certain prestige. Sometimes, the three or four of us in the lower grades who knew a little German were bribed to sing, in a secret place, "*Stille Nacht, Heilige Nacht*" and the eyes of our audience grew more enraptured with each evil word.

"Rooshun," brooded Mrs. Kadish in her piercing voice. "So your kid is half Rooshun and half German—half Hun, as they say. Well, mine are bad enough: half Jew and half American. But not so bad as that." I felt a rush of shame which my distaste for her smelly children did not intercept. "But I don't doubt," she added in the same shrill note of lamentation, "but what she's a bright little slip."

"Bright!" cried my mother. "She's full of brains as big as an apple, that little thing is. And helpful, my God! Well, she's everything in the world you could want, Mrs. Kadish. Come here, Sonia girl, let me show Mrs. K. how long your eyelashes are," and she gathered me to her, pulling my hair as she held up my head for our neighbor's admiration.

"Tchk, tchk," said Mrs. Kadish. "She'll be pretty. She won't have no trouble getting herself a man, you know what I mean?"

"There's where you're wrong," replied my mother. "Not but she couldn't have any man in the world for the asking even now and only twelve going on thirteen, but what kind of a mother would I be to let an angel like her be treated the way my poor self has been?"

"You wait and see," warned Mrs. Kadish. "The time will come and whoosh! she's gone. But I wouldn't be thinking so far ahead, Mrs. Marburg. I must say I don't agree with you that she could get a man right now at her time of life. To my way of thinking she looks poorly. My Nathan might take her, along about sixteen or seventeen."

My mother gave a foolish laugh. "Your Nathan! Well, pardon *me*, Mrs. Kadish, but no thank you. I don't mean anything by that only I couldn't do without her." She pressed my head into her breast until I could scarcely breathe, but I had the strength to pull away from her and turn aside, my cheeks blazing. I did not know, indeed, what she would do without me, but I knew well enough what I would do without her. Right now, I thought bitterly, I would be *playing* with Betty Brunson instead of being on my way to her house to *work*. I murmured that I must go, that I would be late, for the sun was already going down.

"Poor baby," said my mother, stroking my hand. "She is her mother's staff of life."

"Would you mind telling me, Sonie," said Mrs. Kadish with a wily leer, "just what them Brunsons pay you?"

I told her they gave me three dollars a week. "Well, I'll be!" she exclaimed. "They're real free, ain't they? If you ask me, that's pure charity or pure show-off, I don't know which. Three dollars! And pretty soft, I expect?"

"Soft!" burst out my mother. "Soft! She slaves herself to the bone!"

Mrs. Kadish's curiosity was not satisfied. "You live high on three dollars a week now, and I'm not saying that isn't dandy, I'd just like to know how you do it. Now, me, I have close to ten a week and I can't hardly make both ends meet."

"We have a golden egg," said my mother proudly. "But we don't touch it only now and then."

"A golden egg?" queried the neighbor. "How's that?"

I was infuriated with my mother. She was talking about our "nest" egg as Miss Pickens had called it, the fifty dollars her friend had paid us for my father's skis, poles, boots, and leather shorts. I had wanted to keep our wealth a secret for I was sure it would be stolen as we had no good hiding place for it. Miss Pickens had advised me to take it to the bank in Marblehead, but I was afraid to go so far alone with that much money on my person, and we had put it between the leaves of my father's Bible, so close to Mrs. Kadish at this very moment that she could stretch out her hand without moving from her chair and take it all.

"You know the teacher, Miss Pickens?" whispered my mother. Her friend nodded, leaning forward. "She brought a man here and he bought all Hermann's trash for fifty dollars."

"No!" Mrs. Kadish's lips curled into a smile of disbelief. "May I inquire what this here trash was?"

I said, quoting the purchaser, a sickly young man who had resembled Miss Pickens and who had scarcely been able to contain himself at the sight of my father's belongings, "Four pairs of Bavarian skis and poles covered with plaited leather and four pairs of genuine Salzburg *Lederhosen* and galluses to match."

"Galluses?"

"I don't know the English word," I said.

The woman looked at me with respect. "Nathan knows some foreign words, too. Fifty dollars. I'm glad for you, I surely am. No telling what will happen. Sonie might get appendicitis and have to have them out. That fifty dollars would come in handy." She rose to leave and my mother extended her hand, fingers pointing downward as though she expected it to be kissed, "You come again, sweetheart, I'm always here in the afternoon."

"Some pregnant women crave dill pickles," said Mrs. Kadish. "I'll bring along four or five when I come next time. I was always crazy for them myself."

When she had gone I put out my mother's supper for her: a plate of cole slaw, a loaf of rye bread, a dish of Liederkranz, and a casserole of beans that had been heating. She looked with displeasure on the meal. "If only I could have one small cucumber in a dish of sour cream, I wouldn't ask for anything else in the world." We had been through the cucumber argument many times before.

"Oh, Mamma!" I cried. "You *know* they don't have them at this time of year."

But, as always before, she either did not hear or did not believe me. "A cucumber is a little thing to ask. If I could have just *one*, just a small withered one in just a little bit of sour cream, ah, ah, I could bear all the rest!"

She did not move from her chair beside the stove, and knowing that she would only eat when the notion struck her, I went out. But I did not go at once in the direction of the Brunsons' house where I had long since been due. Instead, I ran across to the Kadishes' house where a light was burning. Through the uncurtained window, I could see the children gathered about a round table in the kitchen, each of the six intent upon some project, piling up matches or painting with water colors or cleaning a comb, but not too absorbed to chatter now and then and to dart their black eyes about the table with a controlled ferocity as though they all hated one another but knew that they must stick together. All of them came from the same mold: the same crisp black hair glittered under the lamplight; their faces wore sharp, shrewd expressions, the upper half seeming to be drawn down by the weight of the nose, loosening then below the nostrils into soft lips and little chins.

Nathan, the oldest, a boy of fourteen, sat near the window reading, and as the lamp was directly shining upon him, brightly illuminating his face, I was able to study the birthmark on his cheek. It was probably because of this shocking purple disfigurement that he was so ill-tempered and also so precocious. He was as sensitive as if his mark were a raw sore, continually being rubbed against or hit. It extended from the cheekbone, over the eyelid and the low forehead, to the hairline, appearing the more brilliant because of the dead pallor it interrupted. His lips were pouted in profound misanthropy and he seemed, for all his concentration, to detest his book, for his forehead was drawn into a scowl and his erect body wore an air of unwillingness. I knew by hearsay as well as by the ever meditative look upon his face and by the constant presence of a book under his arm that he was learned. He did not read *The Boy Scouts in Arizona* or the *Motor Boat Boys*, but instead, lives of Napoleon and histories of Rome and the Waverley novels. He had greatly admired my father, and often on Sunday afternoons had come to the door, inviting him to take a walk. My father never refused him, and it was on these expeditions round Chichester that Nathan had learned the foreign words of which his mother was so proud. Tonight it was *Quo Vadis* that he had propped up against a sugar bowl.

I respected his scholarship, but in my lassitude felt no urge to emulate him. I sometimes wished that we were friends so that I might absorb his culture through our association. But I did nothing to make myself commendable to him, nor could I have, for he was a formidable critic of everyone and especially of girls. A foolish girl of his age had once cried out in derision, "Cranberry Kadish is my ideal of a perfect man, like fun!" "Her ideal," said Nathan with a contempt that far surpassed hers, "I suppose she means Platonic ideal because I wouldn't touch her with a ten-foot pole." The girl blushed and said, "You know what I *meant*. I meant 'idea.'" But her correction was too late and as she fretted over the failure of her arrow to kill, he regarded her with a triumphant sneer that twitched at his birthmark.

Tonight, made thoughtful by my mother's conversation with his mother, and, restless in my trap, I wished more than ever that Nathan were my "best friend" and that we took walks together in the evening, confiding in one another our sorrows and our ambitions. The desire for his companionship was tantamount to a betrayal of my mother who for so many years and so diligently had schooled me in the treacheries of men, although I believed she assumed that I would marry in spite of her warnings, would profit by none of her precepts, but by my experience would confirm what she had told me. And I, although it was my intention to remain unmarried (more in imitation of Miss Pride than to escape the pitfalls my mother had described to me), had a quite reasonable curiosity to know what were the manifestations of a man's descent from Satan. The marred Jewish boy, at his sullen labors, roused in me a strange new ravening and I all but tapped on the window glass as a sign that he was to come out to speak to me. As quickly, the impulse waned and I turned to go. But as I did so, I resolved hereafter to come each night about this time and take up my brief, secret vigil. I was light-headed as I went on my way and I felt a little sick. Each time his image returned to my mind, my throat thickened and my footsteps faltered. But though it was novel and mysterious, my disquietude made me happy and I began to sing one of my mother's songs:

> Far from where the men were reaping,
> Soon my weary self was sleeping;
> Slept and then waked—oh,
> Slept and then waked.
>
> Thus as I the time was whiling,
> Came a fellow, started smiling,
> Courting me, too—oh,
> Courting me, too.

Long my mother waited, wondered,
Long my sister waited, pondered
Where I might be—oh,
Where I might be.

Night came down upon the stubble.
Women have all kinds of trouble!
Woman's sad lot! Oh,
Woman's sad lot!

My installation in the Brunsons' house had been a disappointment, for I was in many ways farther removed from Betty than before. And so it was that I plucked the sting from my evenings there by silently communing with Nathan Kadish through the lamplit window.

At the Brunsons', as in my own house, the central figure was a pregnant woman, the very blazing personification of indecency, and Betty, quite unlike myself who found my mother daily more distasteful, adored hers increasingly, though I forgave her for she believed that her mother was going to a hospital to buy a baby from the supply kept there in a large ice-chest. The myth had been so fully developed in her mind that she was convinced the child had been specifically planned as a birthday present for her. It could not be a surprise since sometimes babies spoiled and you could never tell when there was to be a shortage. The Beelers, thoroughly sophisticated, left off their vain instructions when she told them sternly not to *dare* say anything nasty about her mother ever again. "But lookit how fat she's getting!" said Esther. "Look here," snapped Betty, "my Uncle Harry told my mother she *had* to get fatter, and if you don't like it, you can go jump in the lake."

The presence of the Beelers in the house was a sharp thorn in my side, for while I was confined to the kitchen, except when my chores took me into other rooms, they roamed at will throughout the house, obstreperous, dirty, and either through preoccupation with their absurd hilarity or through snobbery, they ignored me. I pondered how Betty, with her fastidious ways, could possibly find them preferable to me. They had warts and they did not wash. Yet, while I was paring vegetables, the three of them sat in the parlor playing Old Maid or came into the kitchen to blow soap bubbles or raced about in the upstairs, howling and giggling in some aimless game. I was not ashamed, though, as soon as they left the house. I was pleased to wear a starched white apron over a black sateen uniform when I brought in the soup and then served the dinner. The dark, round table glittered with silver and pink glass. The centerpiece was a bunch of crystal grapes on an oblong mirror. The Brunsons always ate by candlelight; the radio played soft "dinner music," "Roses of Picardy," "The Bells of Saint Mary's," and "The Blue Danube." They had elegant table manners, holding their left hands in their laps, breaking bread into small pieces before they buttered it, and making not a sound in their throats as they drank water.

My duties were very slight and Mrs. Kadish's accusation that I was overpaid was quite true. The reason was not, however, that Mrs. Brunson was a spendthrift, but that the cook, Maudie, shocked by my pallor and emaciation, did all my work while she kept me in the pantry eating beef sandwiches and doughnuts, and drinking eggnog. Maudie was not a native of New England, but had come here from Idaho because she had always wanted to see "the spreading chestnut tree and Plymouth rock and that old bridge where they disappointed the British." And so, when her husband was thrown by a "spooked" horse and died of a skull fracture, and her two sons had got married, she set out with her insurance money to see what she called "the old country." She was a horsy, red-cheeked, raw-boned woman, nearly six feet tall. On her day off, she lounged in a one-room house not far from the Brunsons', drinking whiskey and reading magazines called *Lariat*, *West*, and *Rio Grande Romances*. The combination of the liquor and literature produced in her a virulent homesickness which was contagious to her cronies—all men—so that her shack rocked with sighs toward evening when the men had gathered after work, as Maudie, in a plaintive, guttural voice, "My whiskey tenor," she called it, told anecdotes of horses, cattle, and bears, for all of whom she was lonesome. "Why don't you go back, Maudie?" the men would ask. "Oh, hell," she would reply, "it wouldn't be the same. My husband's dead and that dear old bench that throwed him is dead, and without them two Idaho'd be an ornery outfit. She was a little strawberry roan by the name of Skylark and she loved him like another horse and he loved her like another human. I often say it's good they went together." She would relapse into a dreamy silence. The men were deeply touched.

During the week she was never sad. She sang a great deal, but she had a very small repertoire. I think she knew only "Home on the Range," "I'll Build a Coffin of Pine," "Holy, Holy, Holy," and the obscene verses of "Frankie and Johnny," and she had only one tune to which she fitted all the words, like square pegs in round holes, as Dr. Brunson said. Finally she was asked to stop. She did, but the moment the kitchen door banged to and she was on her way home, her voice came thundering back to us.

She called onions "engerns" and told me to "pack them spuds to the dudes," and if Mrs. Brunson scolded her, she said with a laugh, "The old heifer's on the prod agin." I memorized her expressions and used them in imaginary conversations with men in ten-gallon hats as I rode the range or hog-tied the steers or branded the calves. Under the influence of Maudie's magazines, which I pored over far into the night after my mother had gone to bed, I began to write a story: "On a cold November morning," I wrote with a blue pencil on manila drawing paper, "you might have seen, if you had been on the sharp lookout, a shabbily dressed man standing in a dark doorway on the main street of Boise, Idaho. Over his left hip was a bulge and that was a shiny black single-action Colt .44 meant to kill Buck Johnson, steely blue-eyed foreman of the Lazy S 4 later in the day. The party in the doorway was a tough customer and his name was Scrub Maxwell. The men of Boise, who were every last one of them square-shooters, hated Scrub's innards, for he was a cattle rustler and a scalawag in more ways than one." There followed a series of unconnected adventures, including stampedes, the discovery of wolves in the chuck-wagon, the puncturing of the bellies of "five million head of pure-bred Hereford white-face cows and bulls as well as calves, heifers and steers that had the bloat off Indian paintbrush." Miss Pickens, to whom I unwisely showed my story, deplored this intellectual climate as much as she had my postprandial snoozes when my father had given me beer, and my compositions, all upon the same subject, that is, the heroism of the young sheriff, Sonny Marburn, came back marked in a vehement red pencil. And

when I wrote in an examination that "st." was the abbrevia-
tion for "steer" she held me up to the class as an outrageous
example of the idle mind.

Maudie left as soon as the Brunsons had begun their dessert
and I stayed on to serve the coffee and to wash the dishes. It
was strange, rather than embarrassing, to serve Betty and to
find her eyes always elsewhere than on me, and after dinner
to see her hidden behind a magazine in a corner of the sofa
while I cleared her parents' coffee cups away and brought in
the ice-water. But later, when I was washing the dishes, she
came into the kitchen and sat on a high green stool, talking
with me, telling me the plots of movies she had seen, reporting
on her Saturdays in Boston which were filled with visits to the
dentist ("My daddy wouldn't hurt me for the world," she said,
"so I have to go to Dr. Harrison on the Bay State Road."),
with music and dancing lessons, fittings at the dressmaker,
excursions to Schrafft's for hot chocolate with tons of whipped
cream, and visits to her Uncle Harry's house on Beacon Hill.
Or she told me about the decorations in her bedroom, as if I
had never seen them, had not, on Saturday when she was away
and it was my day to clean the upstairs, fondled and pawed the
porcelain shepherdesses that supported the lamps on her dressing table, their crooks bursting incongruously into parasols. I
had gazed, awed, at the glassy photographs lining the walls,
of Bebe Daniels, Clara Bow, Ramon Navarro, Janet Gaynor,
Richard Barthelmess, inscribed with grandiloquent scrawls to
"Betty." I had looked through the windows of the doll-house
where a whole family was engaged in ossified enterprises: a
baby with a rosy backside lay face down in a cradle; a fat old
grandmother stood in the bathroom, intently studying the tub
as if she wanted to make sure how things looked before she left
the house—she wore a hat and a fur-trimmed coat and carried
a folded umbrella in one hand and a knitting bag in the other.
A mother stood squarely in the center of the kitchen, a china
broom lying flat at her feet; and on the roof, the father of the
establishment was always emerging from the chimney where
he was presumably making repairs; his legs, up to the waist,
were invisible from the top but could be seen dangling through
the ceiling of the dining-room, his heels nearly touching the
rare roast beef (so life-like there were smudges of blood on the

platter) and the golden banana which dwarfed the meat, these two dishes being the sole fare of the family from the beginning of my acquaintance with them until the end of it. Two children, a boy and a girl, stood facing each other at opposite ends of the parlor, doing nothing. I was charmed by the tiny kitchen stove with a door that really opened, the delicate round gilt table in the vestibule which showed, through its glass top, a bright blue butterfly with folded wings resting on a shasta daisy, and with the perfect little Christmas tree that stood in the sun parlor, everlastingly green, its bangles and loops of tinsel and tiny Santas proclaiming that to this happy, paralyzed family, Christmas was every day.

I liked to look at Betty's collection of tortoise-shell round combs, her barrettes and her grosgrain hair-ribbons, her party dresses with artificial roses at the shoulder, her splendidly equipped writing desk with lavender and pink note paper, a brand new set of Prang's non-poisonous water-colors, red sealing wax, a gold pen and pencil engraved with her name, and a soft, white leather-bound New Testament with many colored place ribbons given her, it said on the flyleaf, by her loving mother two years before when she had been an angel in a Sunday School pageant. The inscription impressed me: "From your loving mother, Mrs. Robert Killigrew Brunson."

Occasionally, when I had washed the dish towels and had swept the kitchen floor, Mrs. Brunson would call out to her daughter, "Go on and make the popcorn if you want to, angel face." I would stay on then sometimes until ten o'clock if the Brunsons, absorbed in magazines, forgot to send Betty to bed, and as we ate the buttery popcorn (made in an electric drum with a wooden handle which one turned round and round) she might digress from her own affairs to talk about people and things that I knew.

Once she said, "I don't know how you stand living next to those awful Kadish simps, chum. Honestly, they're lousy. Cranberry makes me sick to the stomach to look at him. My mother wouldn't let me go with them for anything. Do you want to know something? They're *Jews*."

I was ashamed of my passion for Nathan and I said in defense, but meekly, "My father was a Catholic."

"Oh, that's different," she soothed me. "Daddy says you don't have to be a Catholic just because your daddy is. I mean, that's silly. I mean, well, after all, I'm not a Mason, am I, just because Daddy is?"

Despite her cordiality, there was a note of reserve in her voice as if my heritage had been discussed and rationalized and not merely accepted. "Anyhow," she went on, "Daddy has some good friends that are Catholics, but he won't have anything to do with a Jew."

A little later, on an evening when the Brunsons were entertaining, I learned how I was regarded in the household. Someone remarked on my extreme youth, and Mrs. Brunson replied, "But she's a jewel even so. You see, she was practically born in the pantry of the Hotel here and was trained before I got her." Dr. Brunson, a rash democrat, said, "She's good company for Betty, too." But his wife snapped irritably, "That's beside the point, Bob."

Betty, in our kitchen conversations, had not a trace of the haughtiness with which she had hitherto behaved towards me at school. At the same time, she gave me clearly to understand that our lives would never run parallel. She was to go to a finishing school and afterwards would come out in Boston at a double début with her cousin Frances Barker, the daughter of Mrs. Brunson's wealthy and successful surgeon brother.

One evening in March, Mrs. Brunson suddenly cried out during the salad course. We all—all but Betty—knew that her labor had begun several weeks before it should have. In their prudish way, her parents had planned to spare Betty any demonstrations like this and had hoped to have her installed in New York with a distant relative. In the tumult of getting Mrs. Brunson off to the hospital, the child was all but ignored, her father only casting instructions over his shoulder to Maudie to stay all night in the house and to me to keep Betty company as long as I could. Yet even in his agitation, he recollected her innocence and shouted loudly from the vestibule that he would telephone from Boston as soon as they had selected a baby. She was perplexed by the abrupt departure and a little annoyed since her mind had been made up to receive the baby after her trip to New York, but far from suspecting that she had been misled, she thought her mother had been informed (presumably by telepathy) that a particularly choice specimen was available and that if she wanted it she must make haste to be the first bidder. This delicacy was hard to understand, for in every other way the Brunsons were extremely common or, as they put it, "broad-minded." I, whose rearing had been far from gentle, had been told that it was unseemly to discuss any adventure remotely connected with the bathroom at the table, but any of the Brunsons might say, without a hint of embarrassment (although, because they always laughed, it was clear that they were somewhat self-conscious), "There isn't any more toilet paper."

Maudie, Betty, and I put up a card table in the parlor and Maudie taught us how to play five-draw, deuces wild. In the midst of the game, she brought us some hot chocolate and said, "Well, boys, let's lay off for five-ten minutes." Betty's mind had not been on the game and she was glad for the recess.

"Maudie," she said, "do you think Mummy is terribly beautiful?"

"Shucks. Of course she is. *You* know that and you're just fishing."

"I want to be just like her when I grow up."

"Don't you worry," said Maudie with a wry smile and a wink to me, "you will. You're the spittin' image of her now."

"I love her dresses!" cried her daughter in a rhapsody.

Mrs. Brunson dressed flamboyantly, even when she was pregnant, wearing, in the evening, flowered chiffon dresses that trailed the floor behind and barely covered her knees in front and black satin afternoon dresses touched up with rhinestone gimcracks. She always wore high heels. From her rather large, powdered ears depended tarnished bangles. Her blond hair, lighter than Betty's, dipped and rose in hard permanent waves that framed a puffy face with orange lips and an orange circle on either cheekbone, eyebrows like peaked black thread and a beak of a pink nose.

Maudie and I agreed that not only was she the handsomest, she was also the best dressed woman in Chichester.

"Mummy has style," said Betty smugly.

"Yeah," replied Maudie with a chuckle. "You mean the way she talks." Betty nodded. Her mother did have a certain style but it was not the kind that prejudiced anyone in her favor. Her everyday language was a mixture of slang and profanity. For years she said "for crying out loud" with an occasional variation, "for crying in the beer," and something that pleased her was "the cat's pajamas." But if she was annoyed with her husband, Maudie, a trades person or myself, she used a fastidious vocabulary and an elegantly sarcastic tone. "My good man, I scarcely mean to imply that *all* your meat is inferior," she said once over the telephone to the butcher, "but the cut you have sent me is *effroyable*," pronouncing the "effroy" to rhyme with "cloy."

Betty, after a moment's silence, inquired of the cook, "Maudie, when you got your boys, did they come right off the cake of ice or were they down on the shelves underneath?"

"Honey, I never got my boys that way. I got 'em like the cows git calves."

The little girl was startled. The Beelers had used dogs for illustration. She had believed that they were insulting her parents and indirectly calling them liars by stating as fact something contradictory to what she had been taught. Now she was disturbed in her ivory tower to find Maudie, an old woman and a mother, addicted to the same heresy. She asked for a fuller explanation.

"Well," Maudie began, "I ain't saying it's the same with everybody. Maybe we just tackle it this here way in Idaho." She talked with an impersonal candor as Betty's lips began to tremble and tears to falter from her eyes. When Maudie finished, "And I think it's a mighty shame you never knew about it before. Why, dearie, my boy Horace went to his first bulling when he was four years old," Betty burst into sobs and buried her face in the woman's bosom. "It spoils everything!" she cried. "*Everything!*"

"Now looky here," said Maudie, "you just quit that favoring yourself. Do you see Sonie Marburg bawling?"

But Betty sobbed on and on until finally she drooped with fatigue and Maudie carried her upstairs to bed.

The telephone did not ring that night, and it was only the next day that we learned what had happened. Dr. Brunson came back to Chichester and, harried, cruelly disappointed, he made no allowances for Betty's innocence, but announced forthrightly that the baby had been stillborn. A week or so later, Mrs. Brunson came home from the hospital and, quarrelsome in her convalescence, she discharged Maudie with the declaration, "This is an upper-class household, my good woman, and here we do not discuss certain facts, or, to put it in plain English, sex." But she was obliged to re-hire her when she could find no other cook. She made neither an explanation nor an apology to Betty; moreover, Dr. Brunson decided at the last moment that he could not take her with him to New York to buy the new automobile, and on her birthday she sat in the kitchen on the high green stool with Maudie and me, blowing out the candles and wistfully beseeching me to share my mother's baby with her.

Chapter Four

I HAD GROWN stiff from kneeling on the floor of the shop, my head pressed against the splintery work-bench. My hands were blue with cold for the fire in the monkey stove which I had built earlier had died. I must have been there a very long time. It was still some hours before dawn when my mother had jostled my arm and told me to run for Mrs. Henderson and now, from the looks of the shadows, it must be nearly noon. I had alternated a game of Patience with a prayer all morning long, for Mrs. Henderson, a pious woman, had enjoined me to implore of God my mother's safe delivery, and she must have known my mother very well for she had added that I should pray also that the baby be a girl. Now and then I had made a plea for myself, asking for the fulfillment of the wish I now wished every evening on the first star: "Let me go live on Pinckney Street." From time to time, carried away with speculations on the *décor* of Miss Pride's sitting room, I quit my devotions and went to the window, pretending that I saw there not the bay but the Charles River and that the ungainly dories were the sculls of Harvard crews whose existence I had learned of through Betty.

Hopestill Mather's slippers were where I had put them on the day my father disappeared: one, soiled now to a greenish gray, sat forlornly in the corner while the other was pinned to the work table. Miss Pride had written about them. I had opened the letter, addressed to "Hermann Marburg, Esq.," and read her request that the slippers be sent at once and that my father begin to make her a pair of "stout brown walking shoes." She expressed her surprise that my father was doing his work with less than his usual speed, but went on to say that his tardiness would be of no consequence if only the slippers were delivered on such and such a date. I assumed that on that day, a month before Christmas, Hopestill Mather would be going to a party. Several times I made an attempt to write to Miss Pride, explaining why they would never arrive, but I tore up each letter when I had finished it, and it was only after a second and much sharper note came from Pinckney Street that I at last sent off my apologies: "My father," I wrote, "has gone west and will never come back to Chichester again. He went to Cheyenne, Wyoming, to his cattle ranch. I am sorry about the dancing slippers, but he never finished them before he left and he said for me to tell you that he was sorry. He would have written you himself but at the last minute he had so much business to attend to that he did not have time. Yours truly, Sonia Marburg." A reply came by the return mail: "My dear Sonia: It was very thoughtful of you to write to me. I regret that your father has left Massachusetts. With best wishes, sincerely yours, Lucy Pride."

Even though the envelope had been addressed to me and this was the first letter I had ever received in my life, and even though its author was the one person whom I had never dared dream would write to me, I had been disquieted by it. It was not the brevity that disappointed me so much as it was the finality which was twofold in its implication: it told me that my father would never return (when I had written the word "never" to her, I had only half believed in it) and that now he was gone, she would have no further business with our household. And still, though her meaning was so clear it made my heart ache, so old and habitual were my aspirations that I did not cease to plan my life with her on Pinckney Street. And now, as I was awaiting the birth of my mother's baby, I was so far removed from the present time and Chichester that each moment of delay was a moment of bliss. A sound recalled me: I was still in tatters, the room was the reeking shack, the March wind through the cracks of the walls had set my teeth to clattering. Someone was tapping on the window and I turned.

"Come along, child, open the door!" It was Mrs. Henderson's sister from Marblehead who was visiting in Chichester that day. I unbolted the door and met her greedy face which nosed into mine, seeking my feelings. "Is it a girl?" I asked.

"It's not anything yet, sweetie, but it will be one or the other in a minute and your mother wants you there."

"I'll wait till it happens and then I'll come in," I said.

"No, you come along with me now. She's carrying on bad and wants you near."

Indeed, I could hear her carrying on, and while my feet were wooden, I knew at the same time that something must be done to hush her, and so I followed slowly, deliberately shutting off from my mind what was taking place in the house and instead calculating the number of steps from the shop to the back door. There were thirty-seven. I had never failed to count them when I went to the shop or when I returned and I never failed to forget how many there were.

Mrs. Henderson's sister ran her fingers through my hair as I opened the screen door for her. "How old are you?" she asked me. I told her that I was twelve. "Such pretty hair!" she said, but her face said, "To go through this and only twelve years old!"

The air in the kitchen was solid with heat and even the March cold we brought in with us was immediately absorbed. The stove raged and the ebullient pots danced on the iron lids; roasted and sealed into the atmosphere was the smell of carbolic acid and, I thought, of yeast. Seeking the sources of the odors, I saw in the wide window-ledge, beside the geraniums, a shallow bowl over the sides of which swelled an unbaked loaf of bread, and I wondered vaguely which of the two ladies had left my mother's side to make it.

The house was suddenly quiet. The door to the bedroom was closed, and beyond it I could hear nothing save the rustle of cloth and a splash of water. Mrs. Henderson's sister, her finger upon her lips, motioned me to the door, but I told her, "I'll go if she calls." The woman, who was not at all like her sister but was small and pretty and wore a velvety brown mole on her cheek like a beauty mark, hesitated and asked me if I were hungry. When I said I was not, she suggested that we play "Twenty Questions." I replied that I would rather just sit and wait. She felt then that she had done her duty and, relieved, hurried into the bedroom and its fascinating business.

My mother did not call for me, but now and then in the long hour when the obese and sweating dough held my gaze and my thoughts never came to life but labored futilely, I heard her groan and heard Mrs. Henderson speak kindly to her as she persuaded the child from its hull. Both the ladies had said to me when they arrived separately in the morning that they loved nothing so much as a tiny baby. I thought of Mrs. Brunson who still kept to her bed. Her pudgy fingers were always quarreling in a box of chocolate creams, trying to find one "fit to eat. My Gawd!" Now Betty, who had set her hopes on a baby, must content herself with her father's Packard sedan, with presents he had brought her from New York: a fire-opal ring, an angora cape, a rock garden in a glass sphere. For the least of these, I would have traded my mother's baby.

At last I heard the cry of a child, and I sprang to my feet. Mrs. Henderson was intently slapping the skinny backside of the wailing baby boy who looked like a brick-red fish and nothing human. His black hair did not grow from his skull but lay close like a mat pasted on, and his poor head which seemed all out of shape, curiously dented and noded, lolled over the midwife's wrist as though his neck had been wrung. When he was bathed and oiled and swaddled in a blanket, Mrs. Henderson carried him to the bedside and with a scoop of the blanket, framed the pitiful face from whose crimson mouth issued a ceaseless protest. My mother turned away with a groan. "Oh, take it away! Oh, leave me be!"

The neighbor woman, her kindly mouth half open with anxiety and surprise, whispered to her sister, "Poor dear, she's all worn out. Look, would you, he has his mother's hair and eyes," and she turned her bundle to me. I could see no eyes among the furrows of the ancient, vociferous face. But I pitied the improbable thing and against my will felt drawn toward it and asked if I might see its hands and feet, for I wondered if they, like the useless bud of a nose, had been executed as amateurishly. Indeed, no! Several authors had collaborated on the composition of this creature. The novice band that had created the nose which possessed only one property common to noses, that is, two large nostrils, had not been the same one which, with so grim and un-Christian a humor, had made the long, prehensile feet with all five toes the same length, flexing and straightening as though a jungle vine to swing on were just outside their reach.

"Somebody's pleased with her little brother, that's not hard to see," said Mrs. Henderson's sister with a giggle as she held out a finger for the gruesome foot to grip. Brother! I felt with this prodigy only the most general fraternity: we breathed and were flesh. And yet, immediately the words were out, a leaven commenced to resolve my wonder into the emotion the woman had assumed in me and my pity became protective. Almost as soon as my instinct to mother him matured, there came to me the more complicated feeling of love, so that I longed to hold him myself and to kiss his bawling, cockled face, and to bestow upon him all the tender services that were the right of anything so supremely helpless.

He was, said Mrs. Henderson to her sister, a "puny one," and the sister, feeling his feet and skinny legs, agreed, although she said she had seen punier. My mother, who lay with her eyes closed, scarcely moved her lips when she said, "If it's true he's puny like you say, maybe he won't live forever."

The midwife cried, "Oh, perhaps he's a little small, but he's healthy as you please. Just look at these fine hands and feet. Why, he has lovely bones, Mrs. Marburg!" But my mother had no wish to feel her son's well-shaped feet. Her hands curled as though protecting themselves from contact with the baby and only when he was taken from the room did her long, scarred fingers lie straight upon the coverlet.

Thinking she would fall asleep, I started to follow the women into the kitchen, but she called me back, piteously begging me not to leave her, and when I had gone to the bedside, she grasped my hand and would not let it go. From under the lids of her still closed eyes, a few tears seeped out. I was shocked at the sight of them and felt my throat grow thick.

"Come closer," she said softly. "I want to tell you something and I don't want the ladies to hear." I knelt at the side of the bed and she put her lips to my ear. "You're only a little girl," she whispered, "but you're not too little to learn something. Your papa won't come back now because somebody has taken his place. Listen to me: he prayed for a boy!"

"Oh, Mamma!" I cried. "It's just a little baby!"

The poor red parcel wailed in the kitchen and Mrs. Henderson cooed, "There, there. Isn't it a squirmer though!"

"Everybody's a baby once, darling," continued my mother. "That don't mean they don't get cruel by and by. I'm afraid of it, Sonia!"

But there was fear neither in her face nor in her voice as she lay back upon her pillows. I stood up. "Can't I open a window, Mamma?" I asked. "It's hot in here." It was not hot but it was close with a strange odor.

"Yes," she said with a sigh. "Open the window and let me get some air. Even though the sea air is bad for a person. I should live in the mountains."

I drew up the green blind, opened the window, and stood there breathing in the moist cold. The sun was bright as gold on the sand. My mother talked on. "There is nothing here but sand! In the mountains I would have a garden with melons and radishes and cucumbers. My God, I would have flowers! I love flowers, Sonia girl. Maybe you might buy me some? Fifty cents out of the golden egg wouldn't hurt, would it, to get your mother some *tsvetiki*?"

"I'll get you some," I said. "Maybe when Mr. Henderson goes to Marblehead he can bring them back. Is it violets you want, Mamma?"

"No, it's roses I want. Little yellow ones, Sonie." She stretched out her hands to me but withdrew them as I went to her. "Do you remember what was the name he said for a boy that night he left?"

I did remember. "Ivan."

"Yes, that was it. We'll call him that. Ivan." She pronounced it like a curse in order that without delay the child might shoulder the double burden of her hatred for him and her hatred for his father who had used the name to taunt her.

2

Until the Hotel Barstow opened and Miss Pride had come back and the Brunsons had gone to Provincetown, I was completely absorbed in my brother, and my daydreams of Boston came to me only at intervals. And still, though my love for him was so despotic that I could not imagine loving anyone else so much, I realized, the first time I saw Miss Pride at her regular place in the dining-room, that he had not, after all, won my whole heart. One of the waitresses had cut her finger, and I was sent in with the dessert, a bowl of canned peaches and a thin slice of chocolate cake. Miss Pride had been reading a letter but when I served her, she looked up.

"How d'you do, Sonia? Are you taking your mother's place today?"

"Yes, ma'am. I'll be here in her place all summer."

"Oh, indeed? Does she have other work?"

"No, ma'am. Mamma isn't very well this summer." Her eyes demanded the nature of my mother's illness, and I faltered, "She had a baby on the twenty-first of March."

"Mm." Then, as though she had given me as much time as she could spare, she turned again to her letter. I thought I had heard a note of disapproval in her voice and I regretted that I had not said my mother had broken her arm.

A few days later, she came into her room as I was dusting the bureau and, handing me a parcel wrapped in blue tissue paper, said, "I didn't know whether the baby was a boy or a girl, so I brought a little thing that would do for either." She left the room at once, before I had even time to thank her. My hands trembled as I untied the white satin ribbon around the little box. I was sure she had given Ivan a silver spoon. Instead, from a nest of white paper, I lifted out a bright yellow celluloid rattle made in the shape of a gourd. Still pasted to the neck was a sticker giving the name of a Marblehead novelty shop and the price, "15¢." My disappointment lay heavily on my heart until it was lightened by a remark my mother made when she looked at it. "Now that's what I call *lady*like," she said, shaking the rattle for her own amusement. "It shows she don't think we're poor or anyway she don't want us to know that she knows we're poor. If she had given us something useful, I would be mad." Mrs. Brunson, she went on to say, was not ladylike, because she frequently reminded me of my poverty by giving me Betty's outgrown dresses and sweaters. Until now I had not perceived the insult at the core of her generosity and had been only grateful. Mrs. Henderson, who was calling on my mother, eyed the rattle and said nothing. "Isn't that right, Mrs. Henderson?"

"I don't know but what it is, Mrs. Marburg," replied our neighbor in a voice of restraint. "As the saying is, it's not the gift but the spirit in which it is given."

During this summer of my thirteenth year, I was in the dining-room regularly, and because I often served Miss Pride's table and carefully attended whatever she said, I learned a great deal about her. I had been in the habit of thinking that she had come to the Hotel Barstow all her life, but I learned that a long time before she had spent every summer in Europe. Travel had left no mark upon her. When she spoke of France or Italy or Germany or England, it was to condemn the train service and the touts who "sprang out of the ground, especially in the Latin countries, selling everything regurgitated by the ocean and everything exported by the Japanese." She would say, "They hang too many pictures on one wall in the galleries. The Uffizi is a tiresome junk-shop." And I could see her marching through Europe without surprise, taken in by nothing.

Occasionally Miss Pride's lawyer, a Mr. Breckenridge, came to luncheon and I heard them talking of taxes and dividends. Once she said, "When you get back to town, I'd be obliged if you'd give Barton a ring and tell him I want to sell my Sears Roebuck. I'm going in for public utilities." I was deeply impressed by her State Street argot, a few phrases of which I had heard Dr. Brunson use to his friends. But Dr. Brunson could never have said, with such casual yet unfeigned interest, "By the way, what did the pound do in the Bourse yesterday?"

Even more than by her familiarity with high finance, I was stirred by her intellectual life. For years without fail, she had set aside two hours of each day, from eleven until one, when she sat erectly in a corner of the lobby reading *The Atlantic Monthly*, *Harper's Magazine*, and the novels of Trollope, Henry James, Thackeray, and William Dean Howells. When I was enchanted by a book and did not put it down for several hours together or when, in the winter time at school, I found myself in arithmetic lesson dreaming of being free to read, I was ashamed of my intemperance, remembering Miss Pride. I wondered if she would not be flattered if I dropped an intelligent remark now and again which would reveal that I had read what she had. Consequently I borrowed *The Awkward Age*, by Henry James, from the public library. The title appealed to me for I had heard Mrs. Henderson say of her daughter, Sarah, that she was at "the awkward age." After a tormenting evening of poring over the completely unintelligible sentences of the novel, I returned it early in the morning of the next day and I did not try again to read Miss Pride's favorite authors, but contented myself with attracting her attention in more modest ways. I made her a pen-wiper out of the top of a black cotton stocking and delivered it with a bunch of black-eyed Susans. She thanked me graciously. "You are very thoughtful," she said. "I will think of you every time I wipe my pen." Emboldened, I invited her to come see my little brother of whose appearance I was very proud, but she declined. "Some other day, my dear," she said. I never had the courage to ask her again, for I felt that she was not really interested in Ivan. I told her once that he had prickly heat. She shuddered, "Oh, mercy! How dreadful!" It had not seemed dreadful to me, but only uncomfortable for my little brother. Later on I realized that by "dreadful" she had meant "unattractive."

I was pained that summer by an episode in which she figured. Gonzales' little boy, Emmanuel, had clever hands and often painted water colors of flowers and waves and bright blue birds, and this year he had begun to carve things out of soap. One day he came proudly into the kitchen with a little madonna he had made. Everyone marveled at the folds of her gown, the delicacy of her halo, and the perfection of her tiny, snubbed nose. Audrey, the headwaitress, said that the figure must be exhibited in the dining-room to the guests at luncheon. Emmanuel's protests were taken as modesty, and so that day, the little Virgin was passed around from table to table and was universally admired. At last it was placed before Miss Pride who examined it carefully and did not smile; with a frown of annoyance, she lifted it to her nose and sniffed. "This is my soap," she said sharply. A silence fell upon the dining room and Audrey blushed as Miss Pride handed the figure back and waved her away. Some days later, I heard Mrs. McKenzie tell Mrs. Prather that Gonzales had paid Miss Pride ten cents for the cake of soap his son had stolen from the box under her bed.

The old ladies, with whom Miss Pride never associated, gossiped about her incessantly when she was out of the Hotel, and it was through them that I heard tales of Hopestill Mather, so discrediting that they afforded me the greatest joy. Mrs. McKenzie had heard from the mother of one of Hopestill's schoolmates that she had so hot a temper not one of the mistresses could discipline her, that she deliberately chewed gum in chapel, had spoken of God as "the old boy," and of the Apostles as "the whole gang." Miss Pride, it was said, obviously had no affection for her and only tolerated her in the house during the brief vacations at Christmas and Easter. In the summer, she was sent to camp in Maine.

"I pity the little thing," said Mrs. McKenzie in a low voice. "It can't be a natural life, you know. I've heard that her father wasn't all he should have been. Bad blood shows up, try as you may to conceal it. But fancy the high-spirited child spending her holidays in that gloomy old house on Pinckney Street! As I understand it, she hasn't any other close relatives. The line is dying out, and I do believe our friend is the last of the Prides."

If I were Hopestill Mather, I would never permit my dear aunt to send me away to boarding school. I would prevail upon her to let me go to a day-school in the neighborhood so that I might sit across from her each day at tea and on certain nights have dinner with her. On Sunday I would go, dressed soberly like her, to church. After the service (and I supposed we would sit in her own hired pew) we would walk around the basin of the Charles, no matter what the weather was, and then would lunch together at a long table, being sparing of our helpings.

Occasionally I heard Miss Pride speak of her niece to friends who came to the Hotel. I recollect one conversation I heard when Mrs. Brooks, who had brought Hopestill to the Hotel some years before, had come to spend the night. Miss Pride said, "I sometimes wish I had never seen the child, Josie. Yesterday I had a most unfavorable letter from one of the counselors. She's a born trouble-maker, you know. What will she be at twenty? It's not only bravado—one can't begrudge a child a measure of that. It's a deep rebelliousness against everything fitting and proper."

"You exaggerate, Lucy," replied Mrs. Brooks. "You can't get her father out of your mind. Amy says all the girls like her. Isn't that the important thing, after all, at her age?"

"I don't believe Amy said that, Josie," said Miss Pride, peering deeply into her cousin's skull. "Did she now, truly? No, I won't make you answer, for I know what's what. But anyhow, it's not what she does now that worries me, it is what she will do when she has, so to speak, reached the age of discretion. For I am as certain as I am that you are sitting here with me that with her it will be *in*discretion. The counselor wrote me that she had been caught smoking. At fifteen, Josie! And that she had tried to run off from camp in a baker's truck. I won't have you telling me that these are only a child's pranks. There is something loose in her character. Her holiday tantrums are blood-curdling! If she were not a child, she would have apoplexy, I'm quite sure—her face turns as blue as the sky."

Mrs. Brooks stretched out a consoling hand. "Lucy, you will never change. We can't all have your self-control, my dear! Why, Amy, your affectionate Amy Brooks, has her temper too. It's Hope's lovely red hair, as the superstition goes. But don't suppose I don't sympathize with you."

"I must confess her hair endears her to me."

"It should. She looks more like you every year."

As I was removing the plates, Miss Pride said, "By the way, Josie, remind me to show you the pen-wiper this child made for me. Isn't she clever to be a chambermaid and seamstress when she's only thirteen?"

Mrs. Brooks smiled at me and I noticed that her left eye twitched as she did so. "I should say! I expect my Amy and your Hope could learn a great many useful things from her. Is your father a fisherman?"

"Her father is a *fuyard*," said Miss Pride. She explained to me that she had told Mrs. Brooks that my father was a cobbler and added, "You don't know French, do you, Sonie? It's German you know, isn't it?"

"Yes, ma'am. In German it's *Schuhmacher*."

Whether Miss Pride appreciated my pen-wiper or whether she compared me, to my advantage, to her niece, I could not tell, but at any rate, she was increasingly cordial to me that summer. She sent me on errands to her room when she was waiting for Mac or settling down to her reading in the lobby. "Run upstairs and bring me a handkerchief, my dear," she would say, and the "my dear" or "my good child" made me think my case was not an altogether hopeless one. And when she left in September, she gave me a sealing wax kit in token of her approval of the way I made her bed. The wax was rather old and did not go on smoothly and the "S" of the seal was backwards. But I did not care. On the fly-leaf of each of my school books I dripped the blood-red taper and impressed my initials in the molten mound. So that just as each time Miss

Pride wiped her pen she remembered me, I remembered her whenever I opened a book.

3

My brother Ivan would have granted my mother's wish and died soon after his birth if it had not been for the constant ministrations of Mrs. Henderson, who was both a generous and a sharp-eyed woman. If her attitude had been preponderantly the first when the baby was born, it was the second that for five winters and summers kept her in daily communication with our household. For she was one of those people we call "good." There was in her not the impulse to intrude, but to embrace, not to scatter kindness but to mend with it, and to do so not in the light of this or that principle, but because love was her nature. Mrs. Henderson's reputation was widespread in Chichester and had even reached the Hotel Barstow. Once, in the third summer of Ivan's life, I heard Mrs. Prather saying to a young relative, "I'm far more tolerant of the Catholics than most of my friends, but I can't agree with them that everyone must go through Purgatory—oh, *I* shall, I'm a sinner, but I've known people so pure I'm certain it's the good Lord's intention they should go straight to Heaven."

The girl looked doubtful. "I don't believe you do know such a person—at any rate it can't be anyone I've ever seen in your house."

"No, she has never been in my house. But you know her if you've ever had any sewing or mending done when you've visited here. I mean Mrs. Henderson who lives on this road up about a quarter of a mile."

"Oh, yes, I've been there. But how do you know? Surely you haven't struck up a friendship with her!"

"There was no need. Her goodness is as plain as the nose on your face." And she went on to describe the serene household, equipped with children whose manners imitated their mother's and with a husband who, whatever he might be outside the house, behaved in that atmosphere as commendably as one of his own children.

The girl was still unsatisfied. "You have given me no proof. What has your seamstress *done*?" There was a silence. Mrs.

Henderson's advocate could not publish the chief reason for her immediate assumption into Heaven when I was near-by. But when, glancing back at the table from another part of the dining-room where my duties had carried me, I needed not to hear the words issuing so eagerly from her lips: she was, I knew, recounting our "story."

No doubt Mrs. Prather, who was a sentimental woman, exaggerated our benefactress's virtues. Mrs. Henderson was a "natural" and was to be envied and respected as are all people to whom being good seems the easiest part of life. A more sensitive person, one more dedicated to *doing* good, would have had, as I believe she did not, periods of despair at my mother's indifference to her services, Ivan's malicious ingratitude, and my own mercurial humors. She was as patient and dependable as a devoted dog who suffers his master to pull his tail and play all kinds of humiliating tricks on him without once growing angry. If, finding her at our house on my return from school, I saw that her finger was bound up with court plaster, I did not learn from her what the injury was, but rather from Ivan who had done the mischief himself with his sharp little teeth while she was fitting a new suit of clothes on him. And when he planted himself in her path as she was crossing over to our house with a plate of hot food and cried some unpleasantness which he put in the slang he had learned from me and the Kadishes, calling her a "lousy drip" or a "crazy dope" or a "dumb bunny," she only chuckled and with her powerful hands set him aside like a hurdle made of tissue paper.

She dressed my brother in the clothes her own children had outgrown and cut them down, taking great pains to make them fit his puny body properly. In the early years, she had been his faithful nursemaid, had, when she was too busy and I was at work or at school, charged her eldest daughter, Sarah, with his care. Between them they had fed and bathed and aired him and taught him to walk and talk. If they had failed to teach him manners (as my mother accused them—she had long since forgotten that she had any responsibility towards him herself), it was not their fault. They had tried to make him learn to say "thank you" and "please" but since in his own home there was no occasion for such delicacy, they had been unsuccessful.

If Mrs. Henderson deplored my mother's apathy, she never revealed it. Indeed, she treated her much as she did Ivan, receiving with composure the most outrageous insults, the most preposterous complaints with which my mother besieged her. She had once, soon after Ivan was born, made an appeal to her: "It's not my business, Mrs. Marburg, but I was wondering if you couldn't get a place now. There are jobs to be had for the asking in Marblehead and Lynn."

My mother stared uncomprehendingly. "And may I ask what Sonie would do if I was gone all day long and nobody was here to have a piping hot dinner for her?" Mrs. Henderson, who knew that I always prepared our evening meal before I reported at the Brunsons' in the winter and at the Hotel in the summer, sighed. "The child worries me. She don't look strong. I've a good mind to put her on Josephine's tonic."

Even though, since there was a shortage of help, my mother had been offered a slight raise in salary at the Hotel, she stead-fastly refused to go back. She spoke of her "disgrace" and said that she could never face respectable people again. "Respect-able people" became, in time, all the world but Mrs. Hender-son and myself. If another neighbor—Mrs. Kadish or Mrs. Radcliffe whose society she had heretofore enjoyed—came to call, she bolted the door and slipped into the bedroom where she stood trembling until the knocking stopped. But if she were surprised out of a daydream and looked up to find a caller outside the screen door, she put her finger to her lips and motioned towards the bedroom. "Sh! The child, he's sleeping." The visitor, who as likely as not had seen Sarah Henderson sitting with the baby on the beach, put down her offering—a pot of soup or a bowl of pudding—and smiled and went away and finally, wiser after a few more rebuffs, did not come back.

Although my mother had never particularly liked her neigh-bors and had rarely returned calls, she had always had sufficient relations with the women of Chichester to remain something like them, and had gone abroad enough to realize that the world was larger than her kitchen. Her walks now became shorter. She no longer, in the summer evenings, sat on the little step beside the door, star-gazing and dreaming of Moscow. Nothing would have induced her to go to the village, for she was afraid of being ridiculed. Once, when a Fuller brush man came and offered to give her, without charge, a toothbrush with black bristles, she believed that the whole community, in the person of this representative, was teasing her for not brushing her teeth. Thereafter, when peddlers came, she pretended to be a deaf-mute and gesticulated at them with a look of hopeless regret on her dreamy face. Her voluntary imprisonment gradually became complete, and for four years, after my brother's first birthday, she never crossed the sill of our door, save on a series of winter evenings in the last of those years.

One day, when my brother was about three, Mrs. Henderson came to sit awhile and as she sat, worked at some embroidery for a table runner. It represented a green straw basket from which radiated a bouquet of larkspur and daisies of unlikely colors, these being the satellites to a rose, three times their stature and as big as a plate in diameter. In the void of muslin on all sides of the design, single pansies, petunias, and bachelor's buttons came fortuitously to life under Mrs. Henderson's needle. My mother watched, entranced, and as the neighbor filled in a petunia's corolla, she bent over the work excitedly. "Oh, how magical!" she cried. "Could I ever make those beautiful posies?" Mrs. Henderson assured her that she could, and laying aside her table runner, she took up a piece of plain cloth and gave my mother a lesson in the elementals of fancy-work, demonstrating the "lazy daisy" and the French knot and the feather-stitch. My mother was impatient to try her own hand and when she had finally got a needle threaded and her hoops fitted together, began to copy the stitches. They came out all askew and unrelated; her French knots were rough burls and her draggle-tailed lazy daisies exposed their unkempt framework which should have been on the underside. But she was not in the least disheartened and long after Mrs. Henderson had gone, she continued to practice, admonishing herself, "Ah, Shura, you're clumsy. All thumbs and butter fingers."

The following morning, I found she had got up hours before me, had had her breakfast, and had even washed her dishes and now was back at work on her embroidery. I was sure she would be tired of it by afternoon, but as it turned out, I quite underestimated my mother's patience with herself. From that day onward she stuck to her late calling with the tenacity, the absorption, and the humility of an artist. When I could not buy cloth for her to embellish, she set to work on her own petticoat or on my winter underdrawers or on the kitchen curtains. Once, being without anything at all and having a great urge to execute some oak leaves and acorns, she ripped open one of our pillows, letting the feathers fly where they would, with the result that for weeks we inhaled down. The ticking, when it was re-stuffed, was still so roomy that what feathers I had salvaged assembled at one end or the other but never spread out evenly. She was so proud of the leaves and acorns which were, to be sure, done in remarkable verisimilitude but interested me less than almost any other of her creations, that she made a new pillow cover to protect them which had the same design, and as it turned out well—better, she felt, than the original—it too required a protector, also bearing the same design, and so on, until it appeared that our pillow was to have as many skins as an onion. And no doubt it would have if Mrs. Henderson had not providentially given us for Christmas a very elaborate pillow case, adorned with hollyhocks, which my mother felt was just the thing to cover all her precious acorns. She would gaze at the pillow and say, "You would never guess what's underneath!"

I thought that her activity should be functional and once suggested that we try to sell some of her work. She greeted the proposal with surprise but acquiesced and pulled out from under the bed one of the boxes that had contained skis and was now used as her treasure chest. She could not make a choice: this was the only spray of lilac she had ever made, that was her most successful poplar tree, the dish towel half-covered with a cerise posy had been made in honor of my birthday. She could not part with anything. As our house was becoming overcrowded with her heaps of decorated rags, I at length persuaded her to use the shop as a storeroom, and finding that once the things were out of sight she forgot about them, I advertised them at the Hotel the next summer among the help. Though I realized no money, I sometimes had the luck to exchange a pin-cushion bearing a Russian monogram in cross-stitch for a dozen eggs or a pot-holder in the form of a purple rooster for a pat of butter or a pair of old shoes. Some of her work I still have: a flour sack, smocked in scarlet silk which she gave me one Christmas. She could assign to it no purpose but said she knew I would like "the red." When this poor thing, its banal legend GOLDEN GRAIN showing through the smocking as GLDE RIN, turns up as I straighten my bureau drawers, Chichester's long winters return, sprouting their evergreen leaves and everlasting flowers in the snow and the wind.

After the first rapture of fancy-work had spent itself and she merely burned with a steady, sober flame which only now and again flared forth, as in the case of the oak leaves, she found several supplementary diversions which never lasted but which she undertook when she had nothing to embroider. Thus, on four evenings running one winter, I was commissioned to take dictation from her. I wrote long lists of all manner of things: the names of the guests at the Hotel as far back as she could remember, the nations of the world, kinds of flowers and fruit and fish, the days of the week, and the months of the year. And as she dictated, she drew from memory the designs she had worked in her colored thread, covering page after page of a composition book with likenesses of cosmos and bumblebees. She complained that her memory was bad and she wanted the names of things preserved for her. Even though she could not read my lists, the very paper was reassuring; looking at it, she said, she knew that she had the key to things, even though she could not find the door.

During the same winter that she employed me as amanuensis, she fell one day to musing on the wicker furniture on the Hotel porch, one piece of which, a rocking chair, had been given us by the manager when it had reached a state of total dilapidation. It was quite useless, but Mamma had dressed it up with a cushion and a tidy each saying "Hotel Barstow" which I had lettered for her and which she had filled in with lavender feather-stitching on yellow Indian-head. She inquired of me if the Hotel chairs were ever cleaned and when I told her I doubted it, at least that I had never been told to do anything with them except to move them into the sun or out of it, she was scandalized. Who knew but what that Mrs. McKenzie, who was always nibbling, had lodged an apple core or nutshells between the cushion and the frame? She began to explore the crevices of our rocking chair with a hairpin and brought up a quantity of lint and poked out to the floor a good deal of fine sand.

"There!" she cried triumphantly. "What did I tell you?"

All day she worked at the chair and when I came home from the Brunsons' that evening, I found a shocking monument of dirt on the floor which she had patiently dislodged. She was wearing a coat and a scarf on her head and she told me that she had a little business to attend to, would I accompany her and be so good as to find some candles? Since she was, I saw, bent on going and bent also on not divulging where or why or for how long, I agreed, and took Ivan to Mrs. Henderson's where he directly disrupted the tranquillity of the house with his evil howls, clinging to me as though I were the last familiar spar in that sea of piety and kindness. He bit my leg, at once to declare his ownership and his dependence. One of the little girls, Josephine, offered him a cookie which he threw to the floor in a fury. Unruffled, she picked it up and tried him with a balloon which pleased him slightly. "Now, then, aren't you ashamed of yourself!" I said and shook him by the elbow. But Mrs. Henderson pulled my brother to her and said soothingly, "Now you run along, Sonie. He's my boy for the evening. It wasn't a nice cookie and he had the good sense to see that."

It was a fine, cold night with surfaces that split under our feet and a bare sky furnished only with a few stark stars and an austere moon that pitched, in a thousand elliptical and gouty travesties of itself, amongst the waves and whose light resurrected from the shadows shafts of earth and the roofs of sheds and exposed completely a steep incline to the water which seemed, so regular it was, to have been paved by hand with smooth, round stones. We took the road that led to the Hotel and walked fast because of the cold. My mother, companionably holding me by the hand, walked erect and seemed herself, herself of days so long ago that now they had all but slipped from memory since there was so little in her now out of which to construct her as she had been.

It was the first time in years that we had gone out together and it was this phenomenon, coupled with the vigor of her movement and vivacity of her talk about most trifling matters of the village, and the inexplicable joy in her face, that unburied for me a Christmas Eve when I was four or five years old. My parents took me to a pageant in the Sunday School rooms of the Methodist church on such a night as this. Part of the

way I walked between them and part of the way my father
carried me, grumbling that I was too heavy. The Christmas
tree was as tall as the room and topped by a sugary star, and
onto its branches had been grafted incongruous fruits: crimson
bulbs and asbestos peaches and tongueless bells, all floured
with snow and illumined with a hundred candles whose flames
tossed whenever the door opened and closed. The people sang
carols, so simple and loud that I could catch all the words, and
my father, in a great tuneless voice, roared out the German to
the ones he knew. Each child was given a popcorn ball and a
glazed apple by a masked and padded Santa Claus. I was terrified, when I received my presents, to see, between his glove
and cuff half an inch of black skin! I told Rosalie Kadish the
next day and she, after conferring with her brother Nathan,
informed me that underneath his fine red suit, Santa Claus was
the pastor's Negro chauffeur.

All the way home from the party, my mother and father
drowned the sound of the waves with Russian and German
songs, interrupting one another and seeming to me, who rested
half asleep against my father's shoulder, more talented than
birds, for their repertoire was endless and their voices were the
loudest I had ever heard. I could scarcely keep my eyes open,
but I refused to be tucked into my pallet and sat in the kitchen
while they drank spiced wine that simmered on the stove,
giving off a fragrant steam from cloves and sticks of cinnamon.
A slice of lemon floated in their glasses. My mother blew on her
glass to cool it and my father suddenly seized her hand. "I wish
we were on the boat again, don't you?" My mother laughed
and flirted at him with her black eyes. "Go on!" she said. My
father mouthed at her the words "I love you," and then they
looked at me and smiled. "The sandman's got a certain party,"
said Mamma. I stumbled, dizzy with sleep, into the bedroom
and swayed as my mother took off my clothes. When I was
buried under the comforters and coats, they both knelt down
beside me, their arms entwined. The sweet odor of the mulled
wine was heavy on their breath. The last thing I recalled was
my father turning to kiss my mother on the mouth as though
their love had been refreshed by the songs, by the wine, and by
the sight of me, their child, going to sleep.

My brother would never have so pleasing a recollection as

this. I had tried to amuse him with the games my father played with me, but he was bored with Esel von Hexensee, and he detested Fritzie. If I read him a story, he would stamp his foot suddenly, stick his fingers in his ears and scream, "Shut *up*! I hate *Black Beauty*!" On rare occasions, if I brought him a stick of chewing gum or a jaw-breaker, he rewarded me with a pinched, reluctant smile, but an hour later, for no reason, would slip up behind me and give my hair a savage pull. He was so horrid and perverse and unresponsive that I think I should have lost my patience and whipped him if I had not known from experience and from Mrs. Henderson's tactful advice, that if I allowed my mother to see that he tormented me, her hatred would be dangerously magnified. Consequently, I suffered him to pinch and bite and scratch me, laughing if I could.

As I felt my mother's warm hand in mine, I was perplexed by the change that had come over her in the years since that happy Christmas Eve. Tonight, I found her lovable as she had been then, and as I had not found her for a long time. Each time I made a resolve to dedicate myself to loving her and making her happy, I was at once disheartened by the apathy in which I found her or, instead, by the senseless, fussy affection in which she buried me. These wards of mine were incorrigible. In both of them, the rare moments of joy and sanguine temper which I so greatly wished to protract forever, were accidental, and no matter what new order I introduced into our life, it would still be some short-lived genius of disorder that would galvanize them. Thus, for a week together, I might bring a new toy or sack of goodies each day to Ivan, sent by Maudie or Mrs. Brunson, and he would hate them all. Yet he would discover in my coat pocket a Luden's cough drop, fuzzy with lint. His eyes would dance with pleasure as he held it up to the light. "Let me have it, Sonie!" he would plead.

We were approaching the Hotel and my mother quickened her pace until she was nearly running. Reaching the porch, she went up the stairs two at a time. Then she held out her hands to me. "Why, they're not here, Sonie!" she cried. "Not one of them!"

"What aren't here?"

"The chairs, darling, all the dirty wicker chairs!"

"They're inside, in the lobby. They aren't left out during the winter, Mamma, you goose. Why, the rain and snow would ruin them."

"I suppose," she said sadly. "And I had looked forward so much . . ." She was peering through a crack in the boarding of the main door. "I can't see a thing," she said. "I don't believe they're in there." But another survey of the veranda convinced her that they were not outside. "Well, then," she went on, "the only thing to do is go in. A pretty pickle of fish."

I was about to object. My mother's absurd business might, if it were found out, cost me my job. How could we force a way into the Hotel without leaving traces? And would it not be guessed immediately that only crazy Mrs. Marburg would do such a thing, in the dead of winter, when even the most naïve burglar would realize that there would be slim pickings there? But I did not object, because I was curious about the way the Hotel looked, and had many times thought of doing just this myself, in those nights when my father was still with us, and most particularly the night he left. There was in my mother such a buoyancy, even after her first disappointment, that I was affected by it. We set about to find some entrance and at the back discovered a window with loose boards that yielded easily, and when we had rattled the frame awhile, we pushed it up and climbed inside the outer kitchen.

While from the outside, the building appeared impenetrable to light or air, within, drafts and moonlight, admitted through cracks, were everywhere. The old coal range, mammoth under a silvery hood, was lighted with a lackluster glow and it seemed, from the broken pane of its isinglass window and from the rim of its lids and its half-open damper, to expel cold air like needle-fine projectiles as we passed by. In the dining-room, the faithful birds stood obscurely behind their moonlit glass, waiting patiently through the long winter for the diners who, slowly through the years, had come to resemble them. Here was the owl that hung above the table where sat Mrs. Thompson, an obese, bedizened woman who had, in recent summers, abandoned her lorgnette as being both troublesome and ineffectual since she was half blind and vanity could hold out no longer. Now, upon her raptorial nose, she wore tremendous tortoise-shell glasses which, combined with the feathery, touched-up curls that beset her cheeks and the boned neck-piece of tawny lace that upheld her jowls, made her so like the staring owl above her that it would not have seemed altogether odd to hear a duet of solemn hoots proceeding from that corner of the room. And no less like her bird was Mrs. Holman whose table was beneath a blue heron, for she was lengthy and slim and she dressed in faded blue or gray; she swooped her grace-ful wings downward for the salt cellar or upward to arrest a slipping hairpin, as though she were always about to alight or about to fly off. Mrs. Prather, whose minute head, untidy as a nest, was an impudent joke upon her spreading, pyramidal body, was as ludicrous as her benumbed ptarmigan. Providen-tially, Miss Pride's table was in the center of the room and there was no feathered cartoon of her above her head.

There in the lobby crouched the chairs, their laps obliterated by diaphanous shouds of muslin. The covers of the round tables hung to the floor like skirts; I knew that the square humps atop the tables were the photograph albums and the paper weights in whose glass interiors were embedded pictures of a Sequoia redwood through which a man could walk, or a photogenic waterfall beneath an emerald sky, or a burro whose mouth released a balloon to hold the words: "Hee-haw! Howdy, Folks! You're looking at a Rocky Mountain Canary."

Our candles gave a gelid animation to the unshifting moon-light. The glass eyes of an antelope glinted darkly at us from above the desk and the shadow of the newel post on the main stairway swelled upon the wall like a jinn. My mother at once set to work. She uncovered a chair and set two candles on a cherry-wood milking stool, making stands of drippings. Her tools were a paring knife, a hairpin, and an awl from the shop. She was as intent as a surgeon. I watched her for a few minutes until she complained that I made her nervous and as the light was poor enough anyhow, she did not want my shadow inter-fering. "Run and play, sweetheart," she said. "You've made my hairpin slip through and now it's caught in a crack. Go away, do."

I glanced around, wondering if there had ever been a child who could obey her command, "Run and play" with any joy and frolic through this chilly company of ghosts without a backward glance. I lighted the third candle and proceeded to the stairway. My mother did not look up; she was humming faintly an old tune she had used to sing to me long ago.

Miss Pride's room was utterly bare. Even the mattress had been taken away and the skeleton of the bed rattled tinnily as I crossed the creaking floor. Its rug gone and its windows stripped, its cushions removed from its bare bones, the room was like a fowl plucked clean. There was no aperture in the boarding at the windows big enough for me to look through towards Boston, and in my disappointment, I tore at the wood and filled my fingers with splinters. The gesture was one almost of panic though my feeling had been disproportionate to it, but because my hands were so furious, I abruptly plunged into a welter of introspection, a train of incoherent moods. I had not thus indulged myself for a long time, for the simple reason that I had been too busy balancing my brother's humors to observe any lack in my own equilibrium.

Now, in her appalling summer room, my old longing to live with Miss Pride was revived in so weakening a way that I sank to my knees before the wooden barriers, feeling my face grow warm in spite of the cold and my eyes swell with tears that did not fall but clung to my lids. And when this first pain had gone—like the pain of a lover who visits an old rendezvous without his beloved—I dully recovered myself. The only gain there could possibly have been in this bizarre trip to the Hotel was a return of the joyous feelings I had had in the summer when I looked out these windows. And I had, without fully realizing it, expected an altogether novel sensation in seeing the dark, moon-tracked water from this hiding-place. For, although the years had brought me new and sometimes strong infatuations, knowledge had not abused the dream of my childhood. My perspective of all else might have changed, but Miss Pride and Miss Pride's room had remained unaltered, so that even now, when I was no longer a child, I had often in the summertime been healed of my anxieties over Ivan and Mamma the moment I stepped across the threshold of the room.

But tonight, in this cold nakedness, I was cheated out of my solace for I could not, with my eyes, burn a way to her in Boston. The uproar in me was brought on partly by the discrepancy between the placid vagary that was holding my mother's attention downstairs and my own tempestuous one upstairs, for, although they were equally profitless, mine had a kind of direction, and it seemed consistent with my bad luck that she was happy while I was so miserable, that she could sustain herself indefinitely on follies and unreal pageants and old woes. And my suffering was augmented when I reminded myself that I was nearly eighteen years old and in my last year of high-school and that the unplanned future was like a jumping-off place which I rapidly approached. My classmates talked confidently of college or business school or marriage and in all their talk, there was an implication that whatever they did, they would do it away from Chichester. The farther distant they set their next year's residence, the more unshakeable seemed their resolve so that I believed they would all be in Alabama or Oregon or New York and I alone would remain.

In truth, though, I had an indisposition towards all these careers. When I fumbled in my adolescent semi-sleep for what our teachers called "a way of life," there would come to me the image of Nathan Kadish who, of all the people I had ever known (excepting, of course, Miss Pride), commanded of me a profound respect. I had been in love with him for five years and all that time had carried with me a sharp recollection of the exact moment I had fallen in love, so that whenever I saw him, I could feel myself, a child, rise on tiptoe to look through the lighted window at his birthmark.

He had become, in his graceful, small-boned body and in his right profile, a coldly handsome boy. But because from one side he was beautiful, from the other, with its brilliant smear, he was more hideous even than he had been as a little boy. He had won a scholarship to Boston University where he was studying literature, but he came home for the week-ends and for holidays. Occasionally he came to call on me, late at night after my mother had gone to bed, and he talked to me with a grave, impersonal grandeur of his intellectual accomplishments.

In his Freshman year, in the first flush of rebellion against everything he had heretofore known or longed for, he had been a member of the Communist Party and had always carried with him his membership card with the alias, Stanley Finn. He made it clear to me each time he came to call that he would not have come if he had had anything better to do; our economic system was such that he had no money, he said, to go to Marblehead to get drunk; obviously he could not endure the atmosphere of his house where all aspirations were bent towards the impedimenta of a bourgeois life, the Philco radio sets, the Frigidaires, the upholstered parlor suites. There was nothing in his conversation or in the complete indifference of his countenance to indicate that he in the least enjoyed my companionship. I listened patiently to him, understanding almost nothing of what he said. As he talked, he concealed his birthmark with his long hand. But presently he would forget. His fingers would reach for a cigarette in the pocket of his sporty checked jacket and I could see the exciting monstrosity of his left profile. Feeling that I could no longer listen to his monologue, I would suggest that we drink some coffee, and as I busied myself with the stove and the water, he would continue, unperturbed, to analyze the villainies of liberals, but I would pay no attention. Instead, I would nurse the thrilling, secret glimpse I had had of his peeled cheek. He would be saying, "I'll tell you what. If you ever come to Boston, I'll take you to a meeting of the Party. You may be our type, as a matter of fact, though I can't be sure. The most sensible laborer often turns out to be a solid individualist. Some members of the Party used to be rich; they *know* that bath tubs and evening clothes are decadent. The rest of us have to take it on faith, and of course we do. But witness the perversity of human nature: here I am, a crusader of the Revolution, and do you know that even I sometimes would like to get dressed up in tails and go to the Ritz roof? Of course if that ever did happen, I'd snap out of it in pretty short order. I imagine I wouldn't be able to take their guff and would flash my C.P. card and land up in jail."

In this year, Nathan had withdrawn from the Party although he repeatedly told me that he still upheld its principles and had only stopped going to meetings because he had other things to do. Now he fancied himself not as revolutionist but as a literary person of Paris. His resolve had been made shortly after an evening we had spent together in my father's shop. He had asked if he might look at the books there, remembering from his boyhood that some handsome volumes had stood on the shelf above the door. He took down two, bound in red leather and heavily engraved with gold, and he said, "These are what he used to talk about. Your old man, I mean." They were *Wilhelm Meister* and *Werthers Leiden*. After that, whenever he came to see me, his manner was strangely gallant, his voice was softer, and he often used German words, uttering them with surpassing tenderness. He would go to the window and say, "*Ach, der Abendstern!*" Or he would fall into long, melancholy silences and occasionally would leave the house without a word.

Only the last Sunday he had brought me a book to read. It was called *Confessions of a Young Man*. I had not read much of it yet, but its effect on me was already marked, and I was anxious for the next week-end to come so that I might tell Nathan that I understood why it was he wanted to go to Paris. Shivering in the icy room, I thought of the book and wished that I were a young man, queer enough to keep a tame python, clever enough to educate myself at the Nouvelle Athènes where the painters and poets gathered nightly as a learned and bibulous academy. I thought how simple my actions would be if I were a great, confident pagan egoist like George Moore. Would I not, if I were a young man, leave Chichester and my foolish mother? But I was not fitted for such a life, not only because I was a girl, but because I was an ignoramus. I nearly cried aloud thinking of the sloth of all these past years that had prevented me from reading less than a tenth of what Nathan had read. Here, only two years older than I, he was a storehouse full of books. Even at my own game, he surpassed me, for he spoke and read German with twice my facility. To be educated was the privilege of our class, he had told me. That was the weapon whereby we could conquer the bourgeoisie. I did not know precisely what he meant. Whenever I dwelt upon his words, I could only imagine myself dazzling Miss Pride with my culture; I had no desire to overthrow her, only to make her welcome me.

All plans were as cold as my quaking shoulder-blades. I stood up and stamped awake a sleeping foot. Opening the door, I heard my mother caroling happily at her excavations. I called, "We've got to go now, Mamma. I'm nearly frozen."

"Why, we just got here, silly. I've only begun. Flap your arms."

When I went down, I found that she had finished one chair and was beginning on a magazine rack. She said, "If you'll help me, we'll get through faster. But it's not easy work and you're not used to it, so perhaps you'd better just sit there quiet and watch Mamma." She had, for years, spoken to me as if I were still ten years old. I watched her for a while. She had stopped singing and her lips were parted in concentration. Her eyes sparkled in the candlelight and when she withdrew a long, matted strand of lint she laughed for joy and cried, "Goody!" At last I could hold out no longer and begged for a hairpin. It was good fun and when I, too, extracted a rope of lint, I felt the same brief glow of achievement that I did when I won a game of Patience. But my enthusiasm for the business quickly died and I grumbled that I would leave Mamma alone there if she did not come home at once.

On the way back my mother enumerated the varieties of filth she had brought to light. She planned her schedule for the next night's work. With industry she believed she could finish all the chairs in less than a month. She found me quiet and suspected that I did not care. Very well, I needn't go back. She would go alone if I preferred to stay at home idling with that little black beast of a boy.

Knowing perfectly well how angry she would be if I did not mollify her, I still could not bring myself to speak. For after my fretting in Miss Pride's eviscerated room and after I had become disgusted with the explorations of my hairpin, I had concluded that my predominant feeling towards my mother was boredom. I was surprised because always before I had thought it was a mixture of rebelliousness and loyalty. I was suddenly impervious to her and did not care if she burst into tears and cried for days. I even smiled smugly in my brutal silence.

The pitch of her voice never changed, but its volume increased so that halfway between the Hotel and the Hendersons' house, she was howling abuses, not at me, for as always her madness showed its method, but at my father whose bad treatment had made me lazy, dull-witted, completely insensitive to important things. She railed to the wind for I steadfastly held my tongue. I was closer to my father because her racket had brought back those nights when she had quarreled with him. If I had broken my silence, it would have been to imitate his laugh, provoked by the devil that had taken up permanent residence in her and, anxious for a wider acquaintance, sought admission also to me.

From a little rise, we could see the Christmas tree alight in the village square, a bright triangular scar in the darkened town, and to me, a mockery of that other one, that charming, dressed-up fir whose needles' fragrance lingered still in my memory and seemed even to cling to my mother's hair as she spluttered beside me. She, too, saw the tree and stopped talking, ending a sentence with a smile. She touched my arm. "Now isn't that pretty?" she said. "It would make a nice Kodak picture."

"I was thinking I would get Ivan a Christmas tree, Mamma," I said. "Do you remember the one in the Sunday School rooms a long time ago?"

"That must have been when Hermann Marburg was still here. He used to pinch your little toes and I would tell him what a terrible thing it was to do but he would never stop."

My anger flared forth. "You mean *you* pinch Ivan's toes!" I cried.

"Sonie, you stop it. I don't know what's come over you. Did you ever *see* me pinch him?"

"Yes! No, oh, I don't know and I don't *care*!" I took her firmly by the elbow. "Look here, you've got to stop being mean to poor little Ivan. Do you hear?"

She did not answer but tried to wrest herself away and looked at me with widened, terrified eyes. "Damn you!" I cried. Because I had never cursed her before and the sensation was intoxicating, I repeated it twice until she, stricken speechless, loosed from my grasp, hurried on ahead of me. On the instant I saw her disappear from view I felt released from my responsibility to her and it occurred to me that if she were walking out of my range of vision forever, I would not have the slightest remorse.

Yet my emancipation vanished when I had reached the Henderson house. Ivan, being part and parcel of my duty towards her, required my care, and while it was too late to reform her, he was not yet damned. I must continue as before. Sarah Henderson opened the door for me. In her face, calm had been replaced by solemnity and the gesture she made of extending her hand and laying it upon mine, so gently I knew she meant me to be quiet, made me sense that disaster had befallen someone.

We entered and I saw my brother asleep on the leather sofa. At the first sight of him, I thought I had been mistaken at the door and Sarah had only intended me not to disturb his sleep. But then I saw the signature of agony in the blotches of red on his white cheeks and the blood on his lips, the saliva that bubbled up with each deep, sighing breath. The pose of his body was not like a child's but like an adult person's, drugged or unconscious. Simultaneously, I heard the voice of my heart consenting to the appeal of his collapsed flesh, and heard Mrs. Henderson telling me that he had been "seized" while he was playing. He had been in a temper that I was so slow in coming and had flung himself to the floor and kicked his heels, had been so convulsed in his rage that he was doubled up and frothing at the mouth and muttering all manner of strange things. Finally Mr. Henderson had gone for Dr. Galbraith and the doctor had said the child was epileptic.

"Will it happen again?" I asked Mrs. Henderson.

"Yes! Yes!" cried Sarah, beside herself, unmindful of her manners and of the charity in which she had been schooled by her mother. "You must take him away and never bring him here again! It's too awful!" And she ran from the room weeping. I was unnerved by the change in her and knew that what she had seen must truly have been "too awful" if it had disrupted her serenity.

Mrs. Henderson and I faced each other over the sleeping child. "If he's not excited, he won't have the fits. It's temper brings them on. Don't you mind Sarah."

Mr. Henderson, a small, sandy man, usually as easy-going as his wife, shifted his chair beside the fireplace and said, "Well, I mind Sarah and I mind my other children, and God save you, Sonie, but you mustn't let us see this again."

"Hush, Ross," said his wife. "Pity the poor girl and boy."

"I do! I do! Lord knows I do, but I'll do nothing more than that."

He pronounced the ultimatum without rancor, but I knew he would never retract it. He kicked the hearth and commenced to pare an apple. A curl of red skin coiled into the coal scuttle and at last the globe of fruit was naked and white. He quartered it, leaned back, and began to eat, surveying his domain but never once permitting my brother and me to enter his ken. I stared at him with envy. There was a look of satisfaction in his stark, rusty face as though he were in command of his squads once again after an undisciplined excursion. His house, with its long-waisted, uncomfortable chairs, and the sturdy tables, more hewn than built, and the useful gimcracks—the basket for firewood, the cast-iron hearth accessories, a dun-colored cushion or two, a braided rug—the house and his sleeping children were like a standing army at its post, not hostile but prepared for hostilities, on guard at all times against intrusion. At a distance he might pity the enemy but he would fight to the death if they tried to impose their outlandish ways on his world.

He finished the apple and spat into the dying fire. "Well, tomorrow's another day," he said, and as though he shut a book, he closed his face for the night, locking in its changes of expression and its few words. Presently he left the room.

"I'm sorry," I said to Mrs. Henderson. I could think of nothing else.

She put her large arms about me. "There," she said. "You don't pay any attention. You pray, child."

4

For five successive nights my mother went alone to the Hotel and each time stayed past midnight. She did not know until the sixth day what had happened at the Hendersons', for Mr. Henderson and I had carried Ivan home after Mamma was asleep and in the morning, except for a clot of blood on his lip, he appeared normal. But on the sixth day, Sarah Henderson came to bring some bread to us while I was at school. Probably still under the influence of her terror and knowing too little of my mother's aversion to Ivan, she told the whole story and heightened some of the details. She was fascinated in spite of herself and was drawn to us with a morbid curiosity. If we met on the street, she paled and would have turned into the nearest shop to avoid me had she not longed to know the answer to the question she asked me each time, "Has he had another one yet?" Her myopic eyes behind rimless spectacles registered her disappointment when I told her no.

By evening of the day on which my mother first heard of Ivan's affliction, she was convinced that she had seen the fit and she described it to me in such accurate detail that I was half convinced myself. She told me how his face had turned purple and his eyes had started from his head and his voice had sounded strangled. There was a frightening eagerness in her face as she talked and when Ivan came in from the bedroom, she stretched out her arms to him and said, "Come, sweet baby boy, come, darling, come kiss your mother." Ivan stuck out his tongue and Mamma laughed as if nothing had ever pleased her half so much.

Later that evening I was studying my lessons and she was at work on a stamped bureau runner I had brought her from town in the hope that she would give up her sprees in the Hotel lobby. Ivan was quietly playing on the floor with a toy truck Mrs. Henderson had sent. Absorbed, I was not watching them, though now and again I was aware of them, for I would come to a word in *Macbeth* which I was obliged to look up in the glossary. The interruption caused my mind to slip back into the ordinary world and I looked up, taking in my surroundings with detachment. They constituted, with their other occupants, a prison escapable only through some such occupation as I was just now engaged in. My dog-eared book, bound in maroon cloth, bandaged with adhesive tape where it had been pulled apart by careless hands, was called *Literature and Life.* I had never fathomed the title.

It may have been a sound or it may have been intuition that made me turn and see my two companions hypnotically attached, their gazes joined, their large eyes directly focused and mirrored as though the reflection could burn through to the brain and destroy it, gazes of equal strength, age meaning nothing. Hatred and desperation freighted all the black eyes. But age gained. As I watched, Ivan screamed, throwing back his head which languished on its stem while his live mouth travailed in calling my name, "Sonie! Sonie!" He was purple when I reached him and gripped by a vise I could not pry apart. His teeth were clenched and his fists were clenched and his head, which the second before had been horribly agitated, was turned to one side as though fixed there forever. But before I had really taken in this petrifaction, he was violently released from it and his head, his arms, his eyelids, his legs twitched, and over his busy lips poured blood-stained foam such as I had seen drool from the jaws of the bull-dog that had killed my kitten.

"The beast!" shrieked my mother, and in her face and body, a sympathetic disquiet began, aping his, until she rose from her chair and went to the window where she stood sobbing with her forehead pressed against the glass.

He *was* a beast, the very repository of all bestiality, composed of filth and evil, as though his interior life, in the cavern of that rocking skull, were one of utter nastiness. In a moment, he passed into the third phase of the fit, a coma so profound that I might have thought him dead if I had not seen him like this at the Hendersons'. I carried him to the bedroom and put him on the army cot I had bought for him the year before. While I bathed his face, I heard the sobbing of my mother in the other room, like the sad cries of certain birds or the collision of breakers with the sand. I sat down on the floor beside the little boy, feeling no longer any disgust now that he was relaxed. In a little while my mother came in, bringing another lamp. She had unpinned her hair which rippled to her waist and glowed in the light and upon her face there was, as I saw so often, the beauty of a saint which flowers through the perpetual renewal of mercy.

"My God! What shall we do, Sonia?"

"He'll be all right in the morning," I said.

"Will he do it again?"

"He won't unless . . ." I was on the point of saying, "unless you scare him again," but I changed the syntax to the passive voice, "unless he's scared."

"But he wasn't scared tonight. How could he have been scared?" Her direct, innocent gaze did not prevent me from hearing the guile in her voice.

The next morning, before school, I took Ivan out to the shop on the pretext of giving him a present and I told him that if Mamma ever frightened him, he must run out of the house and either bolt himself into the shop or else walk down the beach and wait for me to come home from school. But he must not go to the Hendersons'.

"She don't scare me," he said sullenly. "*You* scare me, you lousy old girl," and he gave me a kick on the shin that made me wish to thrash him.

My warnings for a long time were useless. He remembered nothing of what had happened before the fit, but only that he fell asleep and awoke, inexplicably sick at the stomach, his lips and tongue sorely bitten. Gradually he began to attach these feelings to me, for I was always the first thing he saw when he came out of his coma, and he developed such a repugnance to me that when he saw me coming home in the afternoon, he hid under the bed, and it was only my gift of candy or a new lead pencil that induced him to come out. Again and again, I begged him to leave my mother when he felt nervous, and at last, after a particularly severe attack when he had emerged from the coma only to repeat the frightful process two or three times, he told me that he remembered something Mamma had done: she had been looking at him although he had his back turned to her, and when he faced her, he was afraid, he did not know why.

Then, instead of me, he began to avoid her, and sometimes he followed me all the way to the Brunsons' like a little dog and sat in the pantry without moving or making a sound until I was ready to go home. Nearly every afternoon I met him on the road, his overcoat buttoned up wrong, his pilot's helmet pulled down so far over his face that he could barely see where he was going. He refused to go to the shop, for he said Mamma came after him and looked in the windows and he could not look away when her eyes were on him.

5

On a Friday afternoon, early in January, a snowstorm came up. The snow fell in swift spirals, floating like gulls into the tree branches in the school-yard. The soft, circling petals smoothed away the harsh outlines of buildings and bony trees and transformed the light in the study hall. By the time school was out, the snow was several inches deep and was still falling. Mrs. Brunson was having a dinner party and had asked that I come to work immediately instead of going home as I usually did to prepare supper for my mother and Ivan. I enjoyed the evenings when the Brunsons entertained: the overheated house, immaculately clean, was redolent with the perfume of cut flowers delivered that morning from Boston, with the smell of roasting beef or turkey, of whiskey, and of cigars. Latterly, much of the management of the dinner parties had fallen to my lot since Maudie had begun to drink more and more and at the same time had lost her ability to hold her liquor. As a consequence, she often forgot essential dishes on the menu and ruined others.

The guests lingered a long time over their drinks. When the Brunsons drank, it was neither in the manner of my father and mother who had been maudlin or gay by turns, nor in the manner of Miss Pride whose indulgence at specified hours was less for pleasure than for the observation of custom. With them, it was a ritual which employed its own argot and its own paraphernalia. They drank whiskey high-balls made with ginger-ale, out of glasses decorated on the outside by a horse's head which, on the inside, underwent a sly metamorphosis into a naked woman. At the end of the third drink, Dr. Brunson would say, "Well, I guess this one can't be told in mixed company. No, no, I can't do it." But he was quickly persuaded that the ladies were not so easily embarrassed, that they themselves could tell much worse, and he would tell a story, usually with a medical background. I, passing the canapés, could not understand it, but I could not have been more shocked, for the laughter that exploded at its conclusion was as brazen and knowing as the look on the face of a small boy who has just chalked an obscene expletive on the sidewalk.

Tonight, in addition to drinks beforehand, the guests were served wine at dinner and they dallied at the table an unconscionable time. Maudie had complained early in the evening, "Somebody keeps spiking that grape juice I have to drink to keep my strength up. Why, Momma dear, that there's so all-fired potent, like the feller says, you could float a sledgehammer on top of it," and she had staggered out of the house the moment the dessert was served. It was after ten o'clock when I got home, and I was surprised to see the light still burning in the kitchen, but more surprised, when I entered, to find my mother idle for the first time since she had taken up fancy-work. She looked up, smiling.

"What kind of soup did they have, darling?"

"Chicken," I said, warming my hands at the stove. "It's cold, Mamma. You've let the fire go nearly out."

"It snowed hard, didn't it? A big deep snow, wasn't it? And did they have a salad?"

"Yes, and chocolate soufflé and two kinds of wine."

"Ah," said my mother. "Ah, how nice! But tell me, Sonia, sweetheart, how *deep* is the snow?"

"It's terribly deep. In some places it was up to my knees and there's a terrible wind."

"It's funny that you came home alone."

"Why? Did you expect someone?"

"Oh, no."

I was taking off my galoshes when she said, "Ivan went to meet you. It was snowing, but he didn't care about that. He only thought about seeing his precious Sonie."

"When did he go?" I cried.

"Oh, a long time ago. Just after the storm began. Here, have a little tea. You look tired."

"Which way did he go?" Though I knew I must find him at once, I could not leave for my amazement at the way she sat there, offering me a cup of tea. What would she be able to say to herself if I found him dead? And I knew, without believing it, that if I did, she would not feel the least necessity of making excuses to anyone, certainly not to herself.

She laughed uncertainly. "I don't know which way he went, but he went fast." And then, reaching out her hand to me she whispered desperately, "Let him go, for God's sake, Sonia, let him go!"

I did not answer but ran out of the house. The snow, which had let up for a little while around dinner time, was falling more thickly than ever and the loud wind drowned my voice as I stumbled down the road toward the village, calling to Ivan. Twice I thought I had found him and when I discovered that what I had seen in the distance was only a rock, I sank down with weariness and grief and would have stayed there but for the image of my brother as he might be suffering that drew me to my feet again. The versatile wind enclosed me in a live, round cloud and the next moment flattened me against a moving wall and then withdrew, leaving me in a noiseless little space where the snow fell gently and straight down. From time to time, I felt warmth slowly returning, but it never reached my feet or fingers because the wind halted it again and exploded charges of snow into my face or beleaguered me with unremitting blasts. Sometimes I plunged up to my knees in drifts as soft as pudding. I was trying to go in the direction of the Brunsons', thinking he might have found his way there, but I could distinguish no landmark to set me right. In a brief lull of the wind, I heard the angry ocean and the next moment slipped and fell into a deep pit which I recognized as being a few hundred yards from the Coast Guard house. I rested a moment and closed my eyes to the wet snowflakes and then struggled up the steep bank. A sharp stone cut into the palm of my hand and I could feel blood seeping through my rent wool mitten. I called, "Halloo! Halloo!" hoping that one of the Coast Guards would hear me. I went on, bent nearly double against the blast. Now I had lost all sense of direction: when the wind paused, I listened for the ocean but the sound came now from one place, now from another. I did not know whether I was hearing the bay or the sea. I rose up straight to call again and saw through the snow, near by, a lighted doorway, and I ran on shouting. As I drew closer I saw that the figure framed in the yellow block of light was Mrs. Henderson, shaking out a tablecloth.

"Ivan is lost!" I cried.

"Lord have mercy! Sarah, Ross, Jack, Josephine, get on your overshoes! The little Marburg boy is lost in the snow!"

The three children and the father were ready at once, as if they had been awaiting the alarm, and with no more account of the catastrophe than they had heard through the open door to the dining-room where they had been sitting round the table playing Lotto, they hurtled out the back door and into the storm while Mrs. Henderson filled a glass with rum and told me to drink it before I went out again.

"You're soaking wet," she scolded me. "You should have come here first." She tied a scarf about her head and went out after the others.

I started after her but halfway to the door shivered with

mortal cold and turned back to drink the rum. It had an immediate effect on me. A bone-deep drowsiness made me nod and
shake myself. I stared into the dining room from my place at
the kitchen table and saw the scattered Lotto cards, the chairs
pushed back, the upturned ash-tray on the floor. The alarm
clock in the window sill above the sink, ticking off the minutes
of my brother's absence in the furious snow, attracted my eyes
and I watched the minute hand creeping so slowly it seemed
not to move at all. I closed my eyes, but the measured tick-tock
stayed with me. It must have been for the briefest moment that
I half fell asleep while I still heard the tinny seconds clicking
into the past, and when I opened my eyes again I knew that I
had dreamed of being in Miss Pride's drawing-room where I
had seen a box of ferns like that in the seventh-grade room at
school. I had been alone. I felt I had just come in off the street,
for cold enveloped me like a loose cloak. It was the selfishness
of my dream that made me leap to my feet and run out the
door, but just as I reached the bottom step, I heard voices near
and Mr. Henderson came into sight, carrying Ivan's insensible
body.

"The poor little duffer," said the man. "He was lying in the
pastor's garden."

We kept him there that night, though Sarah and her father
protested, sure he would have a fit immediately on regaining
consciousness. I said I thought we should have a doctor, but
Mrs. Henderson assured me that a doctor could do nothing
that she could not do for the time being and that we would
call one tomorrow if it were necessary. She made a bed for
him on the sofa in the parlor and we sat up all night, for he
was feverish and tossed so violently that he would have hurled
himself to the floor if we had not been there to hold him back.
Mrs. Henderson took up her knitting and worked nimbly at
the heel of a sock. The room was unbearably hot and smelled
of the camphor-oil on Ivan's chest.

"Why don't you sleep a little, Sonie?" said Mrs. Henderson.

But I refused. I felt I must be vigilant now since I had abandoned him this afternoon. "I love Ivan," I said.

"I know you do," replied the woman. "I'm sure of it."

"I couldn't bear it if anything happened to him! Do you
believe me, Mrs. Henderson?"

"Indeed I do, Sonie. You mustn't feel bad about staying away this afternoon. He'll be all right, you'll see. Sonie, over there you'll find some magazines. Don't you want to look at them? I think we oughtn't talk too much for fear of waking the little boy."

Toward morning he was more peaceful and his forehead was cool. At sun-up we carried him home. My mother had been waiting up all night for me, and she was melancholy. She said nothing, only stared as we lowered Ivan to his cot.

He improved during the day although he developed a cough that troubled us and when in the afternoon he seemed to be choking with it, Mrs. Henderson sent me to the hospital for Dr. Galbraith. "Be clear with him, Sonie," she said. "It's sometimes hard for the doctor to follow what a person's saying, you know."

It was not because he was stupid but because he was an alcoholic that Dr. Galbraith could not follow. His quick speech, hampered by a hasty stammer, was deceptive. He spoke so rapidly he concealed the degeneration of his mind and appeared to be a man whose energy outdistanced his tongue, whose attention at any moment was subdivided many times, giving to each focus a degree of concentration varying with its importance. Breathless with the long run through the cold, I stood beside the desk in his sterile cell, while the doctor nervously twisted a fountain pen round and round between his plump fingers and interrupted me.

"Just a minute, you must try, you must try to control yourself."

I sensed in his voice an agitation that surpassed my own. And while he kept me there with his trivial questions which he brought out with a great struggle (he even asked my age) he only made me wilder and himself more confused, so that, in the end, when he did come, he was not in the least prepared for what he found. I had identified Ivan as the child he had seen at the Hendersons' and he thought he was being summoned to another epileptic fit. For a moment I was not sure that he would come at all. He sat staring at me, moving his lips. He had a repulsive face, flabby, blotched, and dissolute. The crescents of dark flesh under his eyes were distended and the eyes themselves were bloodshot, filmy, and of a color akin to auburn. His lips, tumid and wet, worked slowly over what his eyes saw as if, once the object were removed, he would still be able to recall it by running his tongue over his lips which had mouthed it and shaped its secret formula. He had had, I had heard, several attacks of jaundice and his skin was permanently stained to so dark a color that it resembled sunburn.

At last he rose with a convulsive jerk. "Will I need my stethoscope?"

Thinking he spoke to me, I said, "Why, I should think so, sir!"

He laughed self-consciously. "I talk to myself. It is the privilege of an old man." And abruptly he pinched my chin between his thumb and forefinger.

Ivan's illness was diagnosed as bronchitis. The doctor prescribed mustard poultices and a benzoin kettle. "Keep him well covered up and put on the mustard as hot as he can stand it. It's not a bad attack and the fever isn't high. Call me if he seems to fail, but he won't, he'll be all right, quite all right."

He left some sleeping powders with us and these we gave Ivan every eight hours so that for several days we kept him asleep save when we woke him to pour a little water or broth down his parched throat. We made a tent of an old sheet and kept a pot of benzoin bubbling on a kerosene stove beside his bed. He was never himself but muttered and groaned and stared at us without recognition. His bright cheeks blazed under my fingers as I tried to stroke away the illness that racked him, hooped his body with a cough and cast it down, gasping.

My mother remained in the kitchen, sleeping on the floor occasionally, but for the most part making feather-stitched pot-holders. As she worked, she sang Fräulein Lili's song in a soft but penetrating voice, over and over again until I begged her, bursting into tears, to cease. And when she did not, Mrs. Henderson laid her hand on mine and shook her head.

When I came home at noon and later after school and then in the evening, I could hear her before I had left the road to turn into the lane:

> Well they know without my telling
> Where she lives, for whom I long.
> Round their hoofs the snow is swirling.

> Loud the coachman sings his song.
> Round their flying hoofs the snow is swirling.
> Loud the coachman sings his song.

Or, in the night, half asleep but alert to every noise, I could hear her sorrowing, for she had changed the gay tune into a dirge:

> Hurry, horses, faster, faster!
> Quick, my flying hawks, away!
> Days and hours like these are golden—
> We must seize them while we may.
> Golden days are these and golden minutes—
> We must seize them while we may.

She never spoke to me. She might look me full in the face as if she were about to say something. Then, if I spoke, she drowned out my words with another verse of her song or, instead, repeated one line again and again with a passionate monotony:

> Hurry, horses, faster, faster!
> Hurry, horses, faster, faster!
> Hurry, horses, faster, faster!

But my little brother heard nothing. His fever was coy; each time it went down, Mrs. Henderson and I were comforted, but only for an hour or so. On the fourth day, there was no diminishing of it at all. On the contrary, it went steadily higher until it had reached 106 degrees. Mrs. Henderson said he should be taken to the hospital at once and she called out the window to Sarah to run to the village and telephone the doctor. It was late in the afternoon and I had been home from school for an hour or so. Terrified as I was by the anxious tone of the woman's voice, I was so weary that when she advised me to go into the kitchen to rest for a few minutes until the doctor came, I agreed.

My mother, her head bent over her work, was singing through smiling lips. The sun was going down. The red light glowed on her face and hair with a softness and subtlety that made it seem a property of her own being, an interior light which, passing through the many filters of her body, the tissues, bones, and muscles, was revealed, at its mellowest, upon her skin so that her face did not reflect the sunset but resembled it. Through the window I could see the sky, striped with stratus clouds of pink and deeper shades of pink, separating here and there to disclose a streak or patch of green like pale shoots and leaves amongst flowers.

Each day, I wished to prolong this hour so that I might have time to do in it all the things that were suggested to me. I wished to walk down the road to the Hotel Barstow to see the rows and rows of windows shining like solid blocks of wine-red ice, giving to the old-fashioned, quasi-baroque façade an interest which was lacking at any other time. The whole aspect of the building would be improved, for this was a benevolent kind of light which enriched the shadows with the same ruddy color it infused into the surfaces, but in such a way that there were no abrupt contrasts, only a deepening and reinforcement. It was quite unlike the light earlier in the afternoon which, cold and white, accented the dirtiness of the old paint and brutally discovered all the vulgarity of the building, the whimsical fenestration following the roof line, the tedious repetition of egg-and-dart, the ogees of the veranda, the festoons of roses looped and ribboned over the doors and windows. I should have liked, too, to look at the State House dome from Miss Pride's belvedere and to accompany with my eyes the snail-paced approach of coal-boats to Boston harbor; or to watch, from the topmost of the rocks at the Point, the fearful, reddened water which now in the winter supported few fishing and no sailboats, as if it had devoured them all but still in hunger thrashed many tails and snarled for something more to swallow.

I could not even choose between the sky and my mother's face, and my eyes roamed heavily from one to the other. Her chant, toneless, and yet indescribably sweet, went on:

> Till with age my hair starts graying,
> Till my locks have ceased to curl,
> Let me live in joy and gladness,
> Let me love a pretty girl!

> Let me live my life in joy and gladness,
> Let me love a pretty girl!

I felt that I had all the time in the world. In various versions, I posed myself the question: Is she mad? Can she sing really as carelessly as this when her son is dying? Or is it that the song hides her feelings? Her needle's movement followed the pattern of the rhythm of her voice; at the end of a line or at a rest, she would gracefully and deliberately draw out her green silk thread and let it hang in the air a moment like a sunbeam. I could not tell, afterwards, if it was one or several minutes before I realized that she was silent and had looked up from her fancy-work. She rose and crossed directly to the bedroom door. I followed her.

She went to the cot and said in a whisper, not to me nor to Mrs. Henderson but to herself, "I think he's going to die." She touched the little boy's forehead lightly with her finger-tips. A shudder coursed through Ivan's thin body under the bedclothes, and my mother drew back in alarm. His stifled breathing seemed to stop and then began again, a rattling, wheezing inspiration. Forgetful of my duty towards him and even of my love, I could only look on him with horror, but I was impelled to his side where I knelt down, taking his tiny wrist between my fingers. The pulse raced under by untutored touch. His sharp little face was distorted and blue; the red lips hung and the cheeks drew in. I heard someone come to the door and, thinking it was the doctor, turned in relief, but it was only Sarah. "He advised another poultice and he's coming in half an hour."

"Oh, Lord!" cried her mother. "I don't know what to do. His poor little chest is raw where they've been." But, although she was certain that the doctor was wrong, she was obedient to his professional orders, and went to the stove to heat the mat. I followed and opened a new shaker of mustard. The sharp smell stung my nostrils; in this one whiff seemed to be embodied all the others that I had taken in in these four long days. I lunged heavily against the stove in my sudden fatigue and burned my wrist. Instinctively, I put the hurt place to my tongue and as I did so, my mother called from the bedroom, "Sonia! Hurry! I think he's dead."

As I dropped his hand, thin as a bird's foot, and turned to my mother I thought I saw, passing like a light across her face, a look of pity and regret; but perhaps I only imagined it for immediately she smiled and said, "See how peaceful he is."

Mrs. Henderson covered his face with the sheet and, turning, hid my face from him in an embrace. I could feel her bosom rising and falling tranquilly as she murmured, "There, there, the little fellow's better off now God has taken him. Just you rest a little, pet, and then you go over to my house and stay until I come." But in the other room, while she was comforting me, my mother was admitting Dr. Galbraith and I heard his voice, curiously cleared of its stammer: "What charming work you're holding there, ma'am. I had no idea my little patient's mother was an artist."

"My son is dead."

"Oh, I didn't know! It must have been only a few minutes ago."

"In there," she said. "I was just making a poultice—you see I had everything ready, when suddenly he cried out and I went to him. He died in my arms."

"God bless you."

My mother began to cry softly. "I tried!"

I did not ponder then what she meant. I leaned against Mrs. Henderson and breathed in, with the sweet, herbal odor of the benzoin, still bubbling futilely, the smell of her freshly ironed cotton dress.

"You run along, Sonie. Get Sarah to make you some lemon verbena. It'll rest you."

I did not want to leave her, for I was protected by her kindly, corseted body in its pale blue dress printed with little white flowers. The moment I released myself, I would see Ivan and know that he was dead. I was broken suddenly and I sobbed against the cotton, "Oh, Mrs. Henderson, my wrist hurts where I burned it!"

Chapter Five

OVER THE place where Ivan's cot had been and where now there was nothing but a rag rug with four square indentations, the smell of benzoin still hovered faintly. The snow from the storm had melted and a dense fog enveloped Chichester. All day, from early morning, we had heard the solemn foghorns. My mother and I sat silent before the stove in the afternoon. Her face was overcast and I believed that when she had wailed to Dr. Galbraith, "I tried!" she had meant, "I tried to love him." For in the night, sleepless for both of us, she had murmured, "My tears are all gone, Sonie," as though all the springs of her being, save her love for me, had been drained, perhaps long before his birth.

Mr. Greeley, the undertaker, had come to take my brother's body away when I was still at the Hendersons' house. He was a man of dreadful stature and horrifying countenance which consisted of a pair of lifeless eyes set in deep, dark pits, a long nose which had deviated markedly to the left, and a set of long and murky teeth behind a walrus mustache. He relished his profession. His parlors were situated in isolation on the road towards the hospital. The yard behind his sprawling, tacky yellow house was planted with tombstones, for he was a merchant as well as an undertaker and a licensed embalmer. When Mr. Greeley learned that we had no money and that Ivan was to be buried as a pauper, he could not conceal his disapproval from my mother and Mrs. Henderson. "For a child," he reproached them, "I have such a nice choice: one sandstone group of angel, lamb, two doves, another along classical lines in which the lily *motif* is used. My real prize is waiting for a little child, a granite headstone with an all-over design of cast-iron roses." He went on to complain that a child should not be sealed into the ground without the services of either Father Mulcahy or Pastor Ferguson. The grave would be unmarked, he said, and we would never know where my brother lay.

Mrs. Henderson, repeating his words to me, assured me that he was not an unkind man but only tactless in his disappointment at being cheated out of a ceremony. But she deplored his effect upon my mother, who had become almost hysterical, had declared that she would die of shame if she could not buy the cast-iron roses for her son. And she had implored the undertaker to wait a few days before he buried the child, for we would surely be able to find some way to have a decent and proper funeral.

Exhausted, my grief still tightly coiled as the kernel to my shock at seeing him die, I was vexed and said heartlessly to the neighbor woman, "Oh, why *can't* Mamma leave well enough alone!" for I felt that now I could not bear to hear her lamentations, which I knew would be forthcoming if the gravestone had become, as I believed it had, a fixed idea.

Mrs. Henderson replied, "She will forget, Sonie. Never you fear. She's upset, poor thing, but she'll get over it."

"You don't know Mamma," I said irritably.

"Oh, I'm not so sure. Here, you take her this bit of upside-down cake and see if you can't get her to take a little nourishment."

To my surprise, my mother did not mention the funeral that evening, and in the morning when she spoke of it, I was sufficiently relaxed to feel my loneliness and to think she was right in wanting something better for Ivan than an anonymous grave in a potter's field.

We had been shown great kindness by the townspeople: they had sent us flowers and notes of sympathy and someone had brought a book of funeral hymns. Dr. Brunson, with well-meaning generosity, had personally delivered a bottle of imported brandy and had said bluffly, "I think at times like this you ought to think of the living." My mother had wanted to open the bottle at once but I had dissuaded her. These tokens of commiseration offered us only a spiritual crutch, and there was not one name signed upon the cards that I could call out and ask its owner for the price of a headstone. Not even Gonzales who, although he had neither called on us nor given us flowers, had sent one of his children with a note informing us that he would offer his mass each day that week for the repose of Ivan's soul.

That morning, I had gone to the store for a box of matches. The hush which greeted my entrance and passage between the long, brown counters was more than the ordinary respect paid to the bereft. Accompanied by intense stares and a coloring of cheeks and a withdrawal away from the aisle, it had in it an edge of doubt. And when Mr. Bennett, the store-keeper, said to me, "How is your poor mother?" and without realizing that his question was elliptical and expanded would have been, "How is your poor mother bearing up?" I replied, "Oh, she's awfully well, thank you," a murmur of voices rose behind me. I knew, although I could not catch a word of what they said, that the story of Ivan's illness was known and that this self-appointed jury which convened whenever the population of Chichester was reduced or added to was putting down his death as "peculiar."

Set into the counter there were bins of dried foods and in the glass door of one, I caught the tilted reflection of my face. I saw, to a shame that made me cringe away, that upon my lips there was a light and careless smile! Then, as though to show my judges that my sorrow had not left me so indecently soon, I turned to face them and as I did so, saw Sarah Henderson and her father at the center of a knot of people in the back of the store. Mr. Henderson averted his gaze as I looked in their direction, but Sarah met me coldly with her enlarged, near-sighted eyes. Then Mr. Henderson looked up. Encircled by the marks of sleeplessness, his eyes accused me, I thought, of bringing trouble to his household, and when, in a voice I could not control so that it was cracked and breathless, I said, "Good morning, Mr. Henderson," he did not answer. Later, remembering his silence, as wounding as ice to the bare skin, I told myself I cared nothing for his opinion. But my urgent indifference did not heal me.

A change had come over Sarah Henderson which alarmed her father and herself, and indeed her whole family, and which had begun shortly after Ivan's first fit. Whether the shock of what she had seen that night wakened what had been merely dormant, or whether her strangeness would have come about anyhow, I cannot say. At any rate, she had begun to walk in her sleep, and while she never wandered farther than the back porch, she was in dread lest she should walk down to the sea and be drowned before she could master herself. She had headaches and bad dreams and she was ill-humored. Mrs. Henderson thought new glasses would cure her headaches, and that her bad dreams came from eating indigestible sandwiches and pickles before she went to bed. And if Sarah would take a little more exercise, her disposition would improve. She had been out of school for several years and had never been able to find work; she had no talents, no interests, and no beaux. Mrs. Henderson said, "You're bound to get notions if you're idle."

But Mr. Henderson blamed Ivan. He also blamed his wife who, he thought, in going so often to our house, brought back with her some contagious and powerful virus. At last he saw nothing for it but to move away and had got a job in Maine. He was already making his preparations, and this morning in the store he had piled up several pasteboard cartons. Now I have no doubt that we did not drive him away and that the removal to Maine promised the family far more than they had ever had in Chichester. But my self-consciousness dyed everything to match its own color, and for a long time I believed that I had uprooted Mr. Henderson and had unbalanced Sarah.

The villagers recovered their voices as I stepped away from the counter with my matches. As though by way of apology to me for their silence or to indicate that they had not yet heard the news, they began to talk of things which bore no relation to the death. They commented on the fog and listed its attendant injuries to motorists and mariners, and they prophesied the immediate ruin of the United States under its existing government, exchanged receipts for salt-rising bread, and told jokes involving a judge and a colored man named Rastus. But the lively tone was betrayed by a slackening of pace as I went down the aisle toward the door, feeling the eyes of everyone upon me.

And yet, when I had been at home only a few minutes, the flowers began to arrive and the notes, composed laboriously in an embarrassment that concealed itself behind phrases like "the dear departed" and "passed on to a better world," so that I thought I had misconstrued the silence in the store, for the names of some of the people who had been there were on the cards.

We sat among the sweet carnations and daffodils and roses whose fragrance and chaste petals, some of them made even lovelier by the whorls of steam rising from our teacups, softened the edges of our predicament.

It was my mother who spoke first. "If it was summer, the ladies at the Hotel would get us a nice coffin and a pretty tombstone. Miss Pride would give us the money if it was only summer. Don't you have anything left of the golden egg?"

The golden egg had been used up years ago, but my mother could never believe it and now and again she sought it in my father's Bible, tearing the thin pages in her impatience.

I had thought of Miss Pride, but I had hoped my mother would not. The temptation to send her a letter had been strong until I remembered that often I had heard her talking to her friends of the impertinent requests she received through the mail. A young man who described himself as a "would-be writer," after paying Miss Pride and her deceased father (neither of whom he had ever known) three pages of fulsome compliments, asked her to forward him a Remington typewriter at her earliest convenience. It was his specifying the make of the machine that most appalled her, and she had sent him a lead-pencil with the note, "I regret that I cannot supply you with a Remington typewriter and hope that you will instead accept, with my best wishes, this Ticonderoga lead-pencil." But, on the other hand, I had heard that she had sent two deserving young men, of good but impoverished families, through Harvard. I thought of how, when I was a little girl, I used to dream of her coming to our house, wearing black silk gloves and carrying a funeral wreath for my dead parents. I said aloud, "I wonder if she *would*."

Pretending that I was going for a walk, I went out of the house, but instead, crossed over to the shop. It was here before Ivan's epilepsy that I had done all my reading and studying, for in the house I could never be free of interruptions. I had made my father's work table into a desk, its principal feature being a German silver inkwell embossed with doves which I had found in one of the boxes. The room was dark from the fog and I lighted a candle by whose unsteady flame I composed my letter to Miss Pride. I stated my case formally, saluting her "Dear Madam" and offering her, in exchange for the fulfillment of my "novel request" my services in the humblest part of her establishment for the rest of my life. I asked her to telegraph her reply. But if she were disinclined to forward me the money, I begged her to forget my importunity and to regard me still as her "obedient servant, Sonia Marburg."

The moment I had dropped the envelope through the brass

lips of the box in the post-office, I burned with shame and had I not dreaded the curiosity of the postmaster, would have begged him to return it to me. The text of the letter now seemed at once flippant and turgid. I had been tricked into my pomposity by the corpulent silver inkwell as though its original owner had left his nineteenth-century clichés behind to mingle with the ink.

Dr. Galbraith was fitting the key to his post-box and as he withdrew a packet of mail and glanced through it, he was the object of the scrutiny of the postmaster who, leaning forward against his bars, remarked, "Well, Doc, I sure did fill your box this morning, but I guess it's mostly ads and them journals."

"Oh, yes, yes," said the doctor in his pestered way. "Thank you. It's a very interesting collection," though he was shuffling the envelopes so rapidly that he could not possibly have told where they had come from.

"You been riding a horse, Doc?"

To the doctor's fuscous cheeks arose a blush as he looked down at his clothes and then at the postmaster, who had not been in Chichester long.

"Uh, no, no, as a matter of fact, I haven't."

The doctor's innumerable costumes were all spectacular and meticulously tailored, and they gave him the air of a "sporting gentleman" of a bygone era. One thought of his "cravats," not of his neckties, and remembered their large, loose knots in the French style. He very often wore riding clothes as he did this morning, and it was said that he had once been an excellent horseman, just as it was said that he had once been an insatiable student of literature and had once "performed creditably" on the violin. Now, the only reminders of those talents were his dashing habits, his immense, unhandled library (presided over, I had heard, by busts of Dante, Pericles, Shakespeare, and Vergil under whose staring eyes he drank each night to a point of stupefaction), and the recollection of Mrs. Prather who had heard him play the solo of Dr. Joachim's Hungarian Concerto.

With his russet breeches, which descended over his handsome legs into boots so lustrous and pliant I longed to touch and crush them in my hands, he wore a checked and belted red-brown jacket and a maroon silk ascot, and upon his head, a green hat grizzled with silvery veins and proclaiming its continental origin by a *gamsbart* sportively stuck in the band. It was no wonder that the old ladies at the Hotel Barstow, too old to be the object of his lascivious eyes, found him charming and said he "cut a fine figure." They admired his apparel and said that too often a physician tends to resemble his successor, the mortician. His other suits were of fine materials, all double-breasted and of a cut which did not vary through the years, yet always seemed to be at the peak of fashion. And while the colors and the patterns of the stripes or checks were conservative, the accessory trappings were of the liveliest declensions, being the racing lifeblood of the subdued carcass: neckties (or cravats) of orange silk and crimson wool, printed challis, dotted China silk, pongee, fortified linen, diapered or imprinted with arabesques or stripes or hexagons. His handkerchief and his muffler, if he wore one, matched or complemented the tie as did his socks and the band in his hat. And carrying to its uttermost his nice feeling for detail, he even had alternative spectacles which today, to go with his riding togs, were horn-rimmed, but tomorrow, with blue serge would be rimless octagons, and the next day, if the fancy struck him to dress for dinner and go into Boston, would be a pince-nez with a black ribbon and mother-of-pearl nose pieces.

Dr. Galbraith did not seem to recognize me, though once or twice he looked in my direction as I lingered in the room, studying the announcements of Civil Service examinations and the photographs of coarse, unshaven rascals with prices on their heads for the robbery of banks or the kidnapping of children. I wished to speak with him but hesitated in the presence of the postmaster who was still regarding him with the frankest inquisitiveness.

He was about to leave and I prepared to follow him, but the postmaster, perhaps in the intention of keeping him there a little longer so that he might continue his investigation, bawled, "Doctor, what can a person do for the bloat? Seems like every meal I get all bloated up afterward."

The doctor wheeled about. "What a thing to say," he spluttered, "in front of a lady," and he motioned toward me, "whose brother has just died."

The man gaped stupidly behind his bars. "Well, bless your heart, hasn't she ever heard of the bloat? I'm real sorry to hear the bad news, but I don't see I gave her any reason to be peeved."

"Come, Miss Henderson," said Dr. Galbraith and held the door open, adding, as we passed into the fog, "What the devil is your name?"

"Marburg. The Hendersons live next door to us. Dr. Galbraith, I wonder if Mr. Greeley would let us have another day . . . you know, about my brother. My mother doesn't want him to be buried like a pauper, and I thought if you spoke to him, he might give us some more time so that we can try to find some money."

We were walking so close together that our arms kept brushing and each time I moved away from him, his hand groped out towards me for support.

"Just a minute. I can't seem to think in a fog."

We could see no more than ten feet in any direction, and I felt as if I were suspended in a gaseous sphere, for the blindness of the air made my locomotion seem rotary and almost effortless, and when the doctor softly collided with me, it seemed even more that we were going round and round in a circle, he overstepping the bounds of the outer ring while I, with difficulty, maintained my footing in the inner one.

I repeated my question to him. "Well, I don't know . . ." he said.

Beyond us, we could now and again hear voices and the distant foghorns which only isolated us the more since there could be no proof, until someone entered our shortened range of vision, that the experience was not unique for us, just as it is said that perhaps a tree, falling in a forest, makes no sound if no one hears it.

The doctor stopped me and sighed deeply. "Look here, Miss Martin, I don't believe . . . I'm not certain, but the fact is that when a cor . . . someone is buried in this way it is not . . . well, frankly, it is not embalmed. I . . . no, I regret very much that it really is an impossibility." He clasped my arm tightly with his trembling fingers.

"But we will know by noon tomorrow and it could be embalmed then, couldn't it?"

"I wouldn't worry about that if I were you, my dear. These things are . . . my poor girl, there is no *shame* in being a pauper! But if you should know by noon tomorrow, I daresay something could be arranged. I'll speak to Mr. Greeley."

I thanked him and prepared to take leave. "How is your mother?" he asked me.

"Very well, thank you, though she's terribly upset to think we may not have a funeral."

"Ah, yes, yes, it's too bad. She is an, ah, an admirable woman. What is her name again?"

"Mrs. Marburg."

"Oh, yes. She is very handsome. She isn't an American?"

"No, she's a Russian."

"Fascinating!" he cried. "She looks like a painting I used to be fond of. A madonna, you know, something of that sort, very likely by a Russian painter. Will you give her my regards?"

"Yes, Dr. Galbraith, and thank you for all you've done."

"It's nothing, my dear, nothing at all," and he grasped my arm again before I could escape our hollow ball and get into another where I was alone. When I had gone some yards beyond him, I heard him call, "Morgan, is it, or Martin? What the devil is the name again?" But I did not answer.

My mother was embroidering when I got home. Upon the chest of Ivan's outing-flannel nightshirt, she had made an enormous rose in black cotton and was now sketching a wreath of smaller roses to encircle it.

"The shroud," she explained.

I would have snatched my brother's pitiful nightshirt from her hands, but I knew, by the diligence with which she bent over her work, that if I did, I would be subjected to an endless tirade. I only said, "Listen, Mamma, you mustn't count too much on the funeral."

She looked up innocently. "But you promised the cast-iron roses, darling! Why, Sonia, I wouldn't have gone to all this trouble to make the shroud if you hadn't promised me!"

"Mamma . . ." I began, but words were useless. I drew a chair to the fire and sat brooding, my eyes fixed upon the oven door where the word "Enterprise" was elaborately printed in blue. "For God's sake, Miss Pride, help me," I thought. "If she doesn't get the cast-iron roses, what will I do?"

The fog continued into the next day so that when we got up, it was only the clock, not the appearance of the world, that told us it was morning. From six until noon, I waited for the telegram. I was no longer ashamed of my letter. I was conscious of nothing but the hours ascending to their climax, three o'clock, which was the hour Mr. Greeley had told me he would "dispose" of the body. One of the hours dragged by so slowly that each second of it was a lifetime, but the next was swiftly gone. Because, in my impatience for the message, I could not bear my mother's humming and smiling as she patiently filled in those gruesome black roses, I had gone to the shop soon after breakfast where I fidgeted with the playing cards and dreamed over *Ethan Frome*. Each time I heard a voice calling another name, not mine, I bent my head over my desk and closed my eyes in a total blankness of disappointment. Hopestill Mather's time-blackened slippers, which had remained all these years where I had put them on the day my father went away, infuriated me as they had not done in a long while. I would have slashed to ribbons what was left of them if my father's tools had not been rusted beyond use. Now, at this very moment, when grief and terror were consuming me, Hopestill was probably laughing, with her handsome head flung back, her bright mind far from death or poverty. What would she do, I wondered, on a slow, gray day like this? She would still be in bed, under a light green eiderdown. Or perhaps she was having her breakfast on a tray and in a little while would lazily get out of bed for a long, perfumed bath. Why, her allowance for a month would pay for my brother's headstone!

The time was so deliberate that I could fix my attention on nothing save the knocking at our kitchen door and even my desire for what the telegraph boy would bring became vague. My necessity was so pressing that several times I was sure I heard my mother call to me. At last, indeed, I did hear her, and I ran out. As I crossed the yard I heard, like an insistent warning, the long-held note of a foghorn which was answered on the other side of the tongue of land by another, the two echoing and re-echoing. Then they subsided and there was a silence until a still more remote bleat sounded up the coast.

My mother was smiling radiantly and I smiled in response, sure the telegram had arrived. "It's all right, darling," she said. "You sit down and I'll tell you about it."

I glanced round the room for a yellow envelope, but I saw none. I observed that my mother had laid aside Ivan's nightshirt and was now making a basket in cross-stitch on a pot-holder.

"We have been stupid," she said. "Why, Sonie girl, the thing to do is to give our little boy an ocean burial the way the sailors do."

"In the water, do you mean, Mamma?" I cried.

"Yes. It's clean out there, and, oh, so much better than to be buried like a poor person!" She leaned forward eagerly and took my hand, saying in a whisper, "After dark, we can go tonight. No one will see us."

"But we would have to have a boat. Oh, no! No, Mamma, I can't bury little Ivan that way."

She tried to persuade me. Softly and affectionately, she described the dignity of such an act, told me how the bells and the waves would be eternal mourners for the little boy. She said the strange things that grew at the bottom of the sea would be fine flowers for his grave. If we must go out in a boat, would not Mr. Henderson take us? We three would go out, dressed in black, early in the evening. It would be ever so much nicer even than the cast-iron flowers.

Hearing once again the inconsolable moan of the foghorns, I was almost won but I did not speak.

"You run ask Mrs. Henderson," she coaxed, "and then go to the man who took him away. You fix it for me, sweetheart."

Mrs. Henderson had toward the sea the animadversion common to all the wives of Chichester mariners and fishermen. She personified it as a treacherous siren, forever discontent with her partial government over the men and striving with all manner of clever devices like storms and fog, to win full sovereignty over them. Thus, when I told her of my mother's proposal her bland face was disordered with revulsion. She recovered her voice and told me she was very sure so irregular a procedure was quite illegal, but as she was by no means an authority, we would go together to inquire of Mr. Greeley, and we set out through the fog.

It was a little after two when we were admitted to the mortuary parlors by a disheveled and grumpy housekeeper who, having been so long in the society of cadavers, seemed to have lost the use of her voice and addressed to us a solitary grunt, presumably intended as a command to us to follow her. We waited for Mr. Greeley in a small, cold room, immoderately decorated with rubber plants which had grown to a disquieting height, and furnished with seedy leather rocking-chairs. Perhaps I only imagined it, but it seemed to me that under the smell of disinfectant that pervaded the house, there was the rank odor of putrefaction, and I whispered to Mrs. Henderson, "Oh, let's go home! I'm frightened!" But the undertaker had entered the room. He greeted us with as warm a smile as his parody of a face could muster and said, "Ah, ah, then you have found a way to get the little boy a headstone. Well, I'm glad, indeed I am. I hope you'll take my jewel, my roses. He will sleep better beneath it."

"No, sir," I said. "We can't have a funeral after all. But there is something else . . . Mrs. Henderson, *you* tell him."

The woman told him my mother's plan, and as she talked he pulled the ends of his mustache, exclaiming softly, "Ridiculous! Fantastic! What on earth!" And when she had finished, he rose to his full, improbable height and declared, "One may not cast a body into the street or into a running stream, or into a hole in the ground, or make any disposition of it that might be regarded as creating a nuisance or be injurious to the health of the community. This is the law, Madam. And 'running stream' can, in this instance, refer to the water of the bay or of the ocean. Do you think that I care to be apprehended by the Boston Harbor Police? Do you think that *you* have the authority to do what you wish with this body?"

I could feel the large and abundant tears crawling down my cheeks at his impressionistic yet graphic picture of my brother's corruption. Seeing my misery, he was gentler when he spoke again and even laid his hairy hand, which wore a Masonic ring, on my jerking shoulder.

"Look here, young lady," he said, "you let me bury him now as I planned and if you get some money some day, we will disinter the body and start all over again. All right?"

I nodded my head, for I could not speak. I heard Mrs. Henderson inquire if she might at least supervise the dressing of the child for whom she had had so great an affection and heard the undertaker refuse. She took me by the elbow and I rose. "God bless him," she said, and as we left the room, Mr. Greeley's voice came to us in a clatter of enthusiasm. "I hope you will be able to get my rose piece! The best of luck to you!"

"You mustn't mind him," said Mrs. Henderson as we started home. "It's his job, and a thankless one."

"Oh, I don't blame him! I only don't want to have to tell Mamma."

"Well, then, we won't tell Mamma," said Mrs. Henderson with a trace of annoyance. "I suppose there's nothing against a white lie to give *you* a little peace of mind, Sonie."

"But she'd want to go to the grave sometime."

"Not if she thought he was buried at sea, dear."

"But she wants to go out in the boat herself, Mrs. Henderson!"

"Oh, we could change her mind with a hot toddy, I think. You mustn't suppose I don't know your mother," she said grimly. "And since we're going off to Maine directly, I'd like to think I left you without too many worries. Let her come down to the wharf, yes, and let her see you get into the boat with Ross. He'll take you out a little piece and she'll never know the difference. If she wants the poor lad to be down with the seaweed, let her think that's where he is." She was very angry. With an outraged, "I declare!" she fell silent for so long a time that I thought she had not been in earnest. The plan was, I saw, ideal, but I dared not hope it could ever be realized, for I was certain Mr. Henderson would not agree to so romantic an enterprise.

We had reached our cottage before the neighbor woman spoke again. "Sonie, you mustn't ever think I was being harsh with you a while back there. I was out of sorts with your mother for a minute, thinking as I was how you're nothing but a child yourself and put up with all these carryings-on. I'll serve my time for those mean thoughts about poor Mrs. Marburg. I do think it's best to humor her. We'll do what I said now. I'll step across to your place after supper."

That evening, about seven o'clock, my mother and Mrs. Henderson and I were waiting on the beach by the wharf. Although we could not see them, we could hear the dories dip and sway at their sodden moorings. Someone passed behind us and we could hear the hiss of his slicker and dimly we saw his lantern. My mother, wearing her bright winter dress covered with an old, rusty black cape, stood erect beside me. I was surprised to see that she was a little taller than I. Her arm was linked in mine, and through the mist I could see her long fingers on my coat sleeve. Mrs. Henderson stood on the other side of us. None of us spoke, but there was something in my mother's stance and in the way her hand, seemingly relaxed, was firm on my arm, which told me that she was profoundly excited and a stealthy glance at her parted, upward curving lips, informed me that her excitement did not come from grief. My glance, shifting, met Mrs. Henderson, who had likewise been looking at my mother, and it seemed to me that her eyes, behind her faintly glimmering spectacles, would be cold and unforgiving.

"A nice night," said my mother after a time. "Don't you think it's nice, Mrs. Henderson?"

"A little chilly," replied the woman. "I'm worried about you, Mrs. Marburg. I don't think you're dressed warm enough. As soon as he comes, we must hustle back to the house."

"Oh, yes," cried my mother. "Oh, of course we must! Did Sonia tell you what that good man said when he brought the brandy? He said, 'I think at times like these, you ought to think of the living.'"

It was some minutes before we heard Mr. Henderson call out to us. "Ready!" he cried. "Can you see, Sonie? Come straight to the end of the wharf."

I stepped forward, the two women following me until we reached the wharf, which seemed no more than a long, insubstantial shadow. Mrs. Henderson squeezed my hand, and my mother, who had already withdrawn, called, "Dear Sonia! Dear little girl!"

"Mamma!" I cried in an abrupt, inexplicable desperation. "Mamma! Mamma! Where are you?"

"Hush!" said Mrs. Henderson.

"Are you lost?" came Mr. Henderson's imperative voice.

"She's coming, Ross!" returned his wife.

I lingered for a moment at Mrs. Henderson's side. We were both motionless. We heard my mother's feet lightly running over the wet sand, and in a little while, an eerie voice singing in the distance. Then I ran to the end of the wharf, my head down, scuffing my rubber soles to keep from falling on the slippery boards. I went down the ramp to the float where the boat was moored. As Mr. Henderson stretched out his hand to help me, a phrase of my mother's song came swelling towards us on a little wind.

"Mr. Henderson, I'm sorry . . ." I began.

But his calloused hand was full of sympathy and he muttered, "Rich or poor, a person must stand by another person."

The dories softly plopping in the water made a sound sadder even than the horns. "We'll go round the Point and out a bit," said Mr. Henderson. "I like a fog myself."

The whirr of the motor prohibited talk, and the foghorns were all but obliterated save when they were very near. To our right, until we rounded the Point, were the lights of Boston, blurred into one long line which shifted with the movement of the boat. Miss Pride and her niece would be just sitting down to dinner. I could hear Miss Pride say crisply, "I had another of those beastly begging letters today. Do they think we're made of money?"

The water was choppy around the Point and I was filled with a mixture of terror and exultation when I considered that not far from here were the high seas in whose tumultous bowels lay the bones of the dead and the timbers of shattered ships. The fog was a little lighter. Far away were dimly visible a bunch of lights and I knew that it was the steamer to New York proceeding to the Cape Cod Canal. What worlds there were on this side of Chichester! On the bay side, there was Boston, single and supreme. But here: the furious cemetery, over the residents of which one plowed in a massive ship to Europe; the fabulous New York; and to the west of New York, that variegated land so tediously described in the geography books. I supposed that bizarre as its name was, even Nebraska was real. The feeling and the taste of the spray were unaccountably thrilling, and I, forgetting the absurdity of our errand, wished that we might all night long cut through the water, our motor as loud as gunshot in our ears, and all about us the danger of death. And I knew then why Mr. Henderson had been so amenable to his wife's suggestion: he, I was sure, enjoyed the outing as much as I.

Suspended in my excitement so that for that brief time my life was one dimensional, I could not tell how long it was before Mr. Henderson cried at the top of his voice, "Now, girl, it's time to turn back!" Then I wished my brother's body *were* in the boat. Here, out at sea, I would push it into the water and the waves would move him miles away The putrid smell, in its thick envelope of formaldehyde, which I had detected in the mortuary, returned to me and I retched as I did whenever I smelled ether. I would rather have Ivan in this vast natural grave than in the unmarked, communal earth where lay the unclaimed bodies washed upon the beaches.

I bent my head in my hands and cried because the child was dead, and I did not look up again until I knew we were going through the narrow shoals at the Point. I could see the sharp, glistening rocks and could hear the gulping of the water against their base. Since I could remember, I had been afraid of this place, for here, in a storm, a fisherman's dory had been dashed against the crags and his two children's bodies had never been found. We entered the dense fog again and made for the wharf. As he shut the motor off, Mr. Henderson said, "Well, Sonie, well, you had your ride."

I said, "Mr. Henderson, I am very grateful. I hope you don't think I'm crazy."

"You? No, I don't think you're crazy, Sonie." He was searching for something in the bottom of the boat. "Look out you don't lose your way in the fog."

"Well," I said. "Good-night, then."

"Good-night." I moved on up the ramp. "Was that your mother singing?"

"I guess so," I said.

"I never heard a thing like that before."

Though his words had perished, I now, as I reached the float, apprehended the note of fear in his voice.

I had just passed the great shadow of the Hotel when I heard footsteps somewhere near me. "Where are you?" cried a man's voice.

"Here!" I called. "Are you lost?"

We approached each other, crying out at intervals, my invisible companion saying he had lost his way. We met then, and I was able to make out the indistinct contours of Nathan Kadish whose voice had been in no way familiar.

"What a hell of a thing," he said angrily. "I can't even find my way home."

"I'll lead you." We took hold of one another's hands and moved forward through the murk, he with his other hand thrust out before him as though he were brushing branches aside.

"I went to see you and your mother told me where you were. Listen, Sonie, I'm sorry."

We groped in silence. I did not know whether to tell him that the journey in the boat had been a ruse to fool my eccentric mother or to allow him to think that I had buried Ivan so that he would not know we were now technically known as paupers.

Suddenly, when our feet told us we had reached the road, he stopped and seized me. His mouth waspishly raged over my face with kisses while he held me in an embrace so disabling I could not breathe or defend myself. "Isn't it queer like this in the fog?" he whispered.

"Let me go, Nathan," I gasped.

"Come back this way. Let's sit on the Hotel porch."

We walked far apart, the fog rearing a barrier between us; we found the path leading to the Hotel, fumbled up to the top step, and sat down side by side.

"I suppose you think it's funny that I picked tonight of all nights to start making love to you. I didn't do it accidentally. I was waiting for a sign and tonight I got it when your mother said that Henderson was taking you out in his boat."

"What kind of a sign was that?" I asked him.

"Oh, that you're deep."

"But it wasn't my idea," I protested, immediately regretting my honesty. "It was Mrs. Henderson's."

"Hell," he brooded. "But you *are* deep. I couldn't be in love with a woman who wasn't. If I could, I would have been in love with your mother for her looks."

I laughed. "In love with Mamma? Why, she's middle-aged!"

"She's thirty-four, as you told me yourself."

"But, Nathan! You're nineteen."

"That doesn't cut any ice. I happen not to be in love with your mother. My interest in women does not lie entirely in their accidents but in their substance, and the substance of your mother appeals to me about as much as the substance of Mrs. Gonzales. However, the point is not that I am not in love with

Shura Korf, but that I *could* be if I wanted to. I might add that I at one time conceived a major passion for a woman of forty and discontinued the affair only when she talked of divorcing her husband, a beauty-parlor operator, in order to marry me. And mind you, it was not her age that made such a marriage unappetizing to me. I am, and I acknowledge it without false modesty, extremely precocious and I have known for many years that marriage precludes love."

Recognizing the source of his position, I said, "Oh, I forgot to tell you. I've been reading *Confessions of a Young Man.*"

"By that I assume you mean to imply that I picked up my ideas about matrimony from George Moore," he said with a sneer. "The presentation of your charge is grotesquely naïve. My integrity obliges me to correct you: I am, to be sure, very similar to Moore, but the similarity antedated my reading of the *Confessions.* I have *always* been a citizen of the world, a pagan, an iconoclast, and from time immemorial my motto has been *Ars longa est.*"

"Are you going to be a writer, Nathan?"

"Of course," he replied simply and his voice was surprised that I should ask the question. "I am a satirist."

"What are you going to write? Poetry?"

"I will not choose my form until my soul is ready. My knowledge is vast but inchoate. At the moment, I am collecting experience. That is why I sought you out tonight. You interest me and when I say I love you, I am not using the word in its conventional sense. In a way, the word is almost synonymous with *curious.* I am curious to know what sort of person has emerged from that amazing combination, Hermann Marburg and Shura Korf."

"Have you found out?"

"No, but I have a clue."

I remembered, from long ago, the words of this boy's mother: "So your kid is half Rooshun and half German, half Hun as they say." I said, "Do you think I'm more like Mamma or like my father?"

"I can't tell yet. If you got to be like your father, I'd want you to live with me—for a while at least. He was the most sensitive man I ever knew."

"Did you know my father very well?"

"I know him better now than I did then, of course, because when we used to take those walks together, I didn't know as much as I do now about what had soured him. But looking back, I can see that he was crucified. Why, God! His conscience was hammering the nails in every minute of his life, and because he couldn't reason well—he didn't have much mind, you know—he figured that that eminent monument to filthy lies, the Roman Catholic Church, was right and he was wrong."

"I wonder if he ever went to confession after he left us."

I began to muse upon my father. How immediate before me were his crude bones, refined by the sunburned flesh! How directly did the wintry eyes advance! The face retired, and instead, I saw myself kneeling in the road to tie my boot lace. My loneliness was spatial and atmospheric, implanting in my heart a sadness which had not been there when the fact of his leaving stood alone. And as I saw that figure of myself in the uninhabited landscape where, in the leaden sky, the sun seemed slowly to fade rather than to sink, like a light-globe with weakening filaments, there came again that disturbing half memory which had eluded me as I knelt down and felt the salty breeze in my face.

"And that is why I love you," Nathan was saying and I realized with a start that I had not been listening to him.

"Why?"

He looked me full in the face. His eyes alone were distinct in the misty darkness. "Which one of them were you thinking about? Your father or Ivan?"

As he spoke, six horns, one after the other, lamented Ivan with a single, prolonged moan. Nathan took my hand as the sound died. "How wonderful it is in the fog," he said, "when you can't see Chichester and you can't see Boston and *ergo*, if you have any gifts, you are, as I said, a citizen of the world."

"I'd rather be a citizen of Boston."

"You're not that stupid." His head hovered over mine, swaying down and withdrawing as if, preoccupied with his thoughts, he had started to kiss me and then had forgotten. "Really, you're not that stupid, Sonie. Don't you know you don't fit into the pattern?"

"I don't know what the pattern is."

"I don't know either, but you don't fit into *any* pattern, not any more than I do."

"Oh, but I'm not intellectual like you, Nathan."

"I should say you're not. Still, that doesn't keep you from being intelligent, does it? For instance, you don't have to know the theology of the Catholic Church to know that your father was persecuted, do you? And you don't have to know psychology to know that your mother is . . . well, to know what your mother is like."

"What did you start to say about her?"

"Nothing." But his arm pressed hard against my shoulders. "Freedom is the first thing you've got to get. Think of the *Confessions.* That was the primary requisite for him, and it's the same thing for us."

I was seduced by the memory of the Parisian apartment and in that moment, when Nathan's proximity lent me strength and when, moreover, Boston was visible only as a line of murky lights, I promised myself that I would have the best, whether that was to be had across the bay or across the ocean. I said to Nathan, "Now I know what you mean."

"Do you?" he cried. "If you do, I'm mad with joy! But you must know independently of me, you see, Sonie."

"Oh, I do. I see it quite apart from you."

And I did, because in that vague but luminous and intricate future, that tree-filled and fragrant garden, I did not see Nathan more clearly than I saw any other of the witty and sensitive and handsome people. What I saw was myself, that activating principle which set my feet upon a boulevard, and simultaneously made me love, sense loss, hear, now in Chichester, a final foghorn, that law or theorem of nature for which the term "Sonia" and its variant "Sonie" had arbitrarily been chosen.

Nathan stood up. "What happens next," he said bitterly, "is that we do what everybody else does. We fall in love and then it goes bad, but that can't be helped. You are in love with me, aren't you?"

"Yes."

He ran down the steps. I could hear his feet quickly crunching the sand as he withdrew into the fog. I sat still a little while.

His kisses, like echoes, were repeated on my skin. From the points where his lips had touched, sensation rayed out until my whole face throbbed. But although I felt as brilliantly branded as he was himself, I was aware, not so much of the maturation of my love for him as I was for the achievement of knowledge: the knowledge that my father had deserted me forever and that forever Ivan would be dead.

2

The fog was dispelled on the next day; all traces of the snow were gone save for small pyramidal drifts in the corners of steps and in the crotches of leafless vines on the wall of the Catholic church. And the sun, in the vivid sky, warmed the wind, disclosed again the waves and the broad, shining shingle. It was one of those days that come as a surprise in the middle of winter, like a gift sent on no anniversary, so that the pleasure takes us unaware.

Early in the morning, hunger had awakened me. But as I dressed, my desire for food faded and I felt a little sick, for I remembered, seeing the empty space where Ivan's bed had been, that last evening I had been unfaithful to him by greedily snatching at Nathan's praise and affection. I made myself a cup of tea and as I sat down to drink it, I heard the Kadishes' door slam and through the window saw my lover running, hatless, his shirt tail streaming out behind him, with a book in one hand and a cinnamon roll in the other. He did not seem ludicrous. I half rose to call out to him, but remorse arrested me, and I deliberately looked away, whispering my brother's name as I bent my bead: "Oh, Ivan, Ivan, Ivan," but the invocation was futile.

My mother kept to her bed all the morning and in the early afternoon she called me in. At first, when I sat down on the edge of the bed, she only stared at me. In these past months, her eyes had made me uncomfortable; I was afraid when a look from her demanded one directly from me, for it was as if she spun out a thread connecting with me which some vague superstition prevented me from breaking. If I came in from school and found her huddled into the old wrapper, staring at the oven door or gazing out the window, removed in a world as private as sleep, yet obliged by habit to make a transition back to the world that contained my presence, she would carry her stare to my face and, after a time, would see me. "I didn't hear you," she would say, for her senses were confused. Actually, she had heard me, but the sound of the door and of my footsteps were only now related to the sight of me. So now she regarded me for long minutes before she spoke. Her eyes, in another setting, might have made her look perpetually feverish, but because of her high color, they were the domestic and innocent eyes of a healthy animal. And yet there was something added to them; they, like the lines of her face, had been touched up, refined, perhaps by some ancient drop of Oriental blood. It was not hard for me to understand, seeing her this morning, how Nathan could be in love with her.

"He's drowned," she said. "You can't imagine what it looks like when they take it out of the water."

"Hush, Mamma, you go to sleep now."

But she would not be quieted. She gave me a sly smile. "Let me tell you what happened to me once, Sonie. Okay?"

"No! I don't want to hear."

"Please! It's not about Luibka, darling." Knowing that if I did not hear the story now I would be obliged to later, I sat down. She held both my hands tightly and her eyes never left my face.

On a feast day, when the summer was at its hottest, she had gone in the evening with four friends to the river to swim. They had to pass by the cemetery at the Devitschiepol convent where tents had been pitched for the feast and where *kwass* was sold at little pavilions along the paths. Each of the five girls carried a white sheet to wrap herself in when she came out of the water. On the way they had been joking, calling them their shrouds and winding sheets.

A group of Cossacks, a little drunk, were standing beside a booth, listening to a fair-haired Pole who, in a piercing, sorrowful voice, was singing this song:

> They shout the loud alarm,
> My war steed paws the ground;
> I hear him neigh,
> O, let me go!

One of his companions cried out, "And what does the girl say to that, eh?" And so he sang again:

> Let others rush to death
> Too young and gentle, thou
>> Shalt yet watch o'er our cottage home;
>> Thou must not pass the Don.

Laughing, the girls went on, and one of them paraphrased the last line of the soldier's song, "Thou must not swim the Moskva." Already they could feel the cool water on their hot, dusty bodies and they hastened on through the crowds into a quiet lane that led to the river bank. One by one, as silently as fish, they slipped under the still, black surface. How good the water felt when they floated on their backs, letting their unbound hair be soaked to the roots! They called to one another: "Isn't it splendid, Dounia?" "Are you cool yet, Varenka?" "Look at Shura! She is going under the water!"

Afterwards, they sat for a while, wrapped up in their sheets, listening to the remote, enchanting voices from behind them in the town. Across the river they could see the fires of night fishermen. A trout leaped like a silver tongue. Someone began to sing the Cossack's song, but all at once broke off and cried, "We're not all here! Shura? Marfa? Dounia? It is Varenka who is missing!"

With the tails of their sheets flying behind them, they ran in their bare feet up and down the grassy bank, calling to their friend, but there was no answer save for the sleepy murmur of the river and the bumbling of the city. They called for half an hour until their throats were sore and then, crying, clutching at one another, they fled back the way they had come. The festival was as lively as ever, and the Polish soldier, drunker than he had been before so that his voice was deeper, slower, and more melancholy, was singing still as if he had never left off;

> Let others rush to death
> Too young and gentle, thou
>> Shalt yet watch o'er our cottage home;
>> Thou must not pass the Don.

The girls, half naked, their bare legs showing through the folds of their white wrappings, shivered though it was a hot night, ran into the church of the Virgin of Smolensk, and after they had told two nuns of the catastrophe, fell on their knees and prayed.

Days later, the body was found in shallow water and brought in by a boatman. Varenka's companions were summoned to identify the sodden, bloated parody of a human being. Faceless, livid, softened, it was a horrid spectacle. Of all the girls, Varenka had been the gayest. Only two days before, her grandfather, a rich merchant in St. Petersburg, had sent her a pair of Torjeck-leather boots and a blue silk blouse with a thousand tiny pleats. How Dounia, Marfa, Shura, Manetchka prayed for her! And yet, not one of them could remember how she had been when she was one of them, but only how she had lain dead on the counter, swollen like a fat fish and like the fish, white, shapeless as if the bones themselves had been worn thin by the water and were no stronger than those of a halibut.

"If you had touched her, your finger would have gone in like dough, Sonie. Oh, you can't imagine!"

I was dazed, not by her dreadful story, but by the realization that she had hated Ivan so much that she had tried to make his burial the most loathesome she could conceive. It occurred to me to tell her the truth, but I was afraid of the cunning in her face.

"If I could forget about *him*. But his head keeps floating up at me. Oh, so white and ugly!"

In my astonished face, she laughed! She was laughing not with humor but with joy, like a young girl in love who can find no other expression for her rapture. And then it came to me with a shock that the song she had been singing last night as she went through the fog was the same one she had sung me this morning when she told me the story of Varenka, so that I knew it had all been planned and she had not just now recollected her friend.

I looked upon my mother with sheer fright. It was as if I looked upon naked evil in the person of that woman whose beauty so far surpassed any other I had ever seen that it was almost divine, as if she had come directly from the hand of

God, but had, immediately afterward, been inhabited by a ravenous and indefatigable fiend. Or perhaps she was not alive with wickedness but was dead with it: an empty vessel, or an excellent hull holding a withered fruit. I wondered how deep she was and if my own depths of which Nathan had spoken were the same.

There was a familiar expression in her face which had taken on repose after her fit of laughing, and seeking, at last I redeemed the day Ivan had been born when her strength had rallied to give him a name. I had wondered why she had called him Ivan rather than Hermann since the latter had come to be a generic term of opprobrium to her. It was that her eccentricity, her madness, call it what you would, was shrewd. Hermann would have been too much. I had known that even in her stupor then she had hated my brother and, later throughout his lifetime, I had sometimes wondered why she had not hated him as she carried him before his birth and why she had not hated me. She had not, because she had fortified herself, long, long before, with the conviction that men were all villains and women were their innocent victims.

She had closed her eyes. "Leave me alone now, Sonia," she said wearily. "It is all over."

I stood looking down at her for a moment and I exulted in the trick Mr. Henderson and I had played upon her. Saddening as it was not to know where Ivan was buried, I was consoled by the fact that he lay in the dry ground.

Just as I closed the door behind me, I heard a car stop on the road beside our house, and stepping to the window, I saw that it was Miss Pride's and Mac was handing her out. Rattled as I was, I collected myself sufficiently to realize that it would not do to receive her in the house, for my mother might repeat to her the story of Varenka's death. I went out to meet her. She was carrying a fuchsia-colored cyclamen planted in a little white pot. When she caught sight of me, she said, "My dear, am I too late?" vesting her cold voice with a gentleness I had not heard in it before, and looking at me with a genuine compassion.

"We buried him yesterday," I said.

She took my hand. "I only got your letter this morning and I came immediately."

The word "immediately" made me see her leaving her breakfast half eaten and her mail unopened and not waiting even to
cancel her engagements for the day. Had I observed my picture
carefully, I would have seen it was full of errors, for it was
already afternoon and if she had got my letter in the morning
post, she would have had ample time not only to finish her
breakfast but her luncheon as well. Neither did it occur to me
at once that she was not telling the truth and that she must
have got my letter the day before.

"It's very kind of you, ma'am," I said. "But I'm sorry that I
troubled you."

"What kind of friend would I be if you weren't free to
trouble me?"

Twice as electrifying was this second shock, this designation
of herself as my "friend." But strangely, my first reaction was
not one of pleasure, but almost of disgust as for a few seconds
she stood before me, not as that grand Bostonian to whose
slightest favor I had aspired, but as a selfish old woman who,
as a sop to her conscience, had brought me a potted plant.
It seemed to me that she had aged remarkably since the past
summer. Probably no change had taken place in her at all.
It is difficult, in a wrinkled face, to compute how many new
wrinkles have appeared in a year's time, or to see, in white
hair, all the stages of its purification. It was, rather, that I
had changed and my altered feelings had turned a spotlight
upon the arthritic stiffening of her fingers from which she had
removed the white gloves, the desiccation and the yellow hue
of her creased skin, the protuberation of her veins, the liverish
patches on her wrists, the aridity of her thin lips. But a censor
in me checked me before I had disarrayed her features beyond
repair, and as from her small, brisk person there emanated the
sharp odor of her expensive soap, she recovered her familiar
and beloved shape.

She said, "If you're not needed here, won't you drive to
Boston with me and have a cup of tea? Mac will have you back
in time for dinner."

I told her I must be at the Brunsons' by four o'clock. "Nonsense. No one would make you work today. What Brunson is
it?" And when I told her Dr. Brunson's name, she said, "Oh,

then he must be the Brunson brother-in-law of Harry Barker. I dare say he's not such an ogre that I can't beard him in his den. I'll just run on and tell him you won't be there while you're getting your things and we'll pick you up afterwards."

It struck me, as I went into the house to get my "things" (a large blue tam and a shabby leather jacket the sight of which, hanging listlessly on a nail behind the kitchen door, made me wish I had not accepted the invitation) that it was odd she had gone to the dentist and not to Mrs. Brunson. I concluded that she was afraid she might be trapped into a conversation with my mistress if she called upon her and such a conversation, entertaining as I conceived it, would cause Miss Pride severe discomfort.

My mother had fallen asleep. I put the cyclamen on the high bureau, predicting as I did so that when Mamma learned where it came from, she would remind me, as she had often done in the past, of Miss Pride's gracious gift of the rattle. (I was not disappointed. That evening when I came home, she was drinking a glass of the dentist's brandy and tenderly cupping one of the blossoms in her hand. "It's just like that man said, a person ought to think of the living. I think that Miss Pride's sweet.")

Warmed by a lap robe as soft as fur and lulled by the steady speed of the automobile, I looked through the windows with careless eyes, not paying the close attention I had always planned, to every feature of the road and the villages through which we drove. And yet I repeated to myself, "At last I am going to Boston," and the wonder of it was reinforced when Miss Pride marveled that in eighteen years I had not been farther away than Salem. Had she known, she said, she would have come to fetch me long ago. Sometime this spring she would come for me and would show me the Public Gardens when the tulips were blooming and the children were riding the swan-boats.

She inquired if I had heard recently from my father and when I told her I had heard nothing since he left, five years before, she shook her head with some unexpressed disapproval and said, "You have been very brave, my dear child."

I could not reply to the compliment and I had no wish to deny it. I said, "Did Dr. Brunson say it was all right?"

"Oh, perfectly. He's a very good-natured man. I was amused to see a placard hanging prominently in his office which read 'Terms Strictly Cash.' He appears to be more prosperous than most men of his profession in small towns."

"He has a practice in Marblehead too," I threw out.

"As a matter of fact, I have met him before and his wife, too, on several occasions. And isn't there a girl about your age? I met them under circumstances which makes it more convenient for me to be unable to place them clearly."

Inspirited by my curiosity, I asked, "Was it here or in Boston that you met them?"

"Why, it was in my own house, Sonia. They came uninvited to my open house on Christmas Eve two or three years running, and each time I was so muddled by the throngs of people, all of whom appear at those affairs more or less familiar, that I said to Dr. Barker, with whom I have a nodding acquaintance, 'One does see such remarkable people in one's own drawing-room on these Christmas Eves of ours. Can you tell me, for instance, who that blonde woman is over there by the buffet with the identical daughter? Perhaps they are friends of the accommodator.' And of course, as you've already guessed, the woman was Harry Barker's sister. But what an unconscionable snob the doctor is! He did not enlighten me. He allowed me, each year, to make the same mistake. This past year, someone standing near-by jostled my arm and led me away to inform me of my *faux pas*. I was at first outraged with Dr. Barker for disclaiming any connection with his relatives. It's not the sort of thing one does. But on second thoughts—and on looking for a second time at your employer—I forgave him, but could not resist the temptation to apologize for my mistake. I fear I made the poor man quite miserable. He greets me most perfunctorily on the street now." She smiled at her triumph, effaced the look of amusement, and said, "You are disloyal. You should not have allowed me to tell you that unfortunate story. As penalty, you must now tell me *your* opinion of Chichester's leading citizens."

"Why, they have been very good to me, ma'am."

"You speak the language that befits the grateful servant. But it was my intention today to give you a little vacation from your servitude. I wanted to have a long talk with you about that very charming man, your father, and what you remember of him, and what you think has become of him. And I wanted, even more, to know something about *you*." Placing her hand lightly on my wrist, she said, "I admired your letter. Its restraint, its language gave more pleasure to me than anything that has come in the mails in thirty years."

"Thank you, ma'am."

"Now, Sonia, for the rest of the afternoon, *do* call me not 'ma'am' but 'Miss Pride.' As I was saying—you must forgive me; I am an old woman and apt to shoot off on a tangent at any moment—this is your holiday. I want you not to speak as a servant. I want to know something about you and therefore, I wish you to begin with your opinion of the dentist's family."

I thought for a moment. "They are rather money-minded, I think. And Dr. Barker won't come to their house, although they invite him all the time. It's as though he were ashamed of them. I don't know why he should be unless it's that Mrs. Brunson wears an awful lot of lipstick and she's too fat for her dresses and for the high-heeled shoes she wears."

My companion's face showed nothing. I did not know whether her objective had been the one she had stated to me, or if she had wanted, out of sheer malice, to hear ill spoken of people so far her inferior that I was surprised she even troubled herself with thinking of them. She questioned me not only about the Brunsons' reading habits and their friends and their political and religious opinions, but also about my own, and when she had exhausted my information, said, "Now that I have your *dossier*, let me ask a final question: Would you really come to work for me without any wages?"

"Indeed I would, ma'am."

"Miss Pride, please. You don't think you could do better? You don't think you have any other talents?"

"Oh, no, I have no talents, Miss Pride. I'm very poor in school. I won't be given any honors at commencement."

She smiled. "Nor was I given any honors. But I wasn't thinking of that kind of talent. I mean the talent of character which hasn't much to do with braininess. With brains, yes, but not with braininess. That, you may as well know, I can't abide. It isn't useful to a woman and I'm not altogether sure it's useful to a man. Dr. Philip McAllister is a brainy man and he's not as sensible as he might be. Do you know him?"

I said I did not, that I had only heard his name. He was one of the house physicians at the Chichester hospital.

"He's one of my niece's beaux and a charmer. But brainy, as I say. I suppose you had Dr. Galbraith for the little boy? Between you and me, Sonia, he's a rascal. He's killed as many patients as he's cured, but then, as I often say to Philip, they all do. I am my own physician. I ventilate my house well and I take a walk every day. As a result, I'm never ill. I don't believe in any of these fads, these vitamins, allergies, neuroses. I am the most old-fashioned woman in Boston."

I told her—because I could think of nothing else to say—that I was never ill, and that I believed I had made up my mind never to be ill when I was a child and was offended by the medicine bottles of the Hotel guests. And then, when she said nothing, I asked her pointlessly if she were coming back this summer. "What made you think I would not? No, *I* don't change."

There was a momentary silence. Twice she parted her lips but thought the better of it. Then she plunged in. "You have read more than I thought you had. Not more than I should have expected you to, but more than I really like. At your age, you should concentrate on manners, my dear, not on ideas. But that can be remedied later. Will you be satisfied with a very simple explanation of why I have fetched you out of Chichester? Can you believe it is no more than that I am interested in human nature and see in you an interesting juxtaposition of class—whatever that absurd term may mean—possible only in a democracy in an advanced stage of decomposition? I mean by that: my family, on my mother's side, was established in this country by an indentured servant whose master settled in Virginia. The descendants of my ancestor, having acquired their freedom, worked north to Massachusetts. In those days, to be sure, such servitude was often little more than a convenient way to get passage to the colonies. A servant had not necessarily been a servant. In the case of my family, I don't know, for the records are full of gaps. But for the sake of argument, let us say that servants' blood runs in my veins. Yet I am, for all practical purposes, a member of the oldest American aristocracy."

Her glittering golden eyes, full on my face, commanded me to keep my mind on what she was saying, and I listened intently, nodding now and again as I did in Plane Geometry class when I did not understand a word of the instructions.

"You're no servant, Sonia. You belong to a class which no longer exists in this country, that is, the artisan class. And since so august a body of society has been demolished you must, so to speak, skip a grade. I may as well tell you that your father is the only specimen of his lamented genus I have ever had the good fortune to know, and it was a bitter day when I heard he had left us. For he left *me* as well as you and your mother, my child. I felt, 'So long as Hermann Marburg makes my shoes, I will be in touch with the reality of the past.' Ah, he did not realize his responsibility!"

As she spoke, she lifted the hem of her long coat. "You see what I wear now. Painful, hideous, expensive, flimsy! And look at your poor feet, those poor feet I used to see when you were a little girl. Then they wore shoes that had been *wrought* with devotion. I hope for your good father that he went back to his family in Würzburg."

"I hope so too, Miss Pride. But he said that night when he left that he was going out west."

"Perhaps you'll meet once again. You must forgive me if I am I blunt: he was a fool. He took the indifference—they were poor, how could they help it?—of the fishermen as an index to all Americans towards good leather-work. He was like the visitor who sees only New York and carries away the impression that the United States is a hodgepodge of skyscrapers and horrible racket. Actually, if he had come to Boston as I begged him to do time and again, he would have prospered."

"I guess so. But he didn't have any energy, you know."

I was thinking of how he would brood on the winter evenings because Saint Bonaventure had failed him or he had failed the saint, he was not sure which. He was not altogether dead, for, corruptible as were his vows to go to Mass, they must have sprung from a recognition of his sloth which, by the creed of his hard-working family as well as by that of the church, was a deadly sin. And the fact that his reaction was overt, even though incompleted, suggested a residue, at least of the talent of remorse. Paradoxically, this very filament of remorse had served as the central thread in a great fabric of mortal sin, for, stirring him out of his house on Sunday morning, setting his feet on the road to the chapel, it languished; his contrition melted and, his mind reflecting, his will consenting, he went no further, took the other road leading to the Coast Guard house. But it had not occurred to me until now, hearing Miss Pride praise his talents, remembering how Nathan had admired his sensibilities, that my father was not a man whose misery could be mitigated by a change of environment or an increase of worldly goods or an establishment in a society. He was a robbed man, and the robber of what Miss Pride had esteemed was the very thing Nathan had loved: his sensibility, refined by what influence I could only conjecture. And this sensibility had led him away from the traditions of his religion and his work and neither the one nor the other could stand alone.

"Energy?" queried Miss Pride.

"I don't know how to say it. I only mean that I'm not sure he would have been happy just to thrive in Boston."

"Why, on the contrary, I think he would have. He was, after all, not a very complicated person. I daresay if he had just had his beer and *Wienerschnitzel* and had been able to hold up his head amongst his neighbors, he would have been completely happy."

Although I did not disagree with her, I did not, reflecting on him, think that my father had been so naïve a man, nor had he been so much the conventional comic-strip German. Miss Pride was either forgetting or ignoring my mother who was the author of a good deal of the tumult in him. Quite different, for example, from the rough kindness he showed me in the shop had been the nature I saw in the house when all the mild amusement at our jokes had faded from his face, as if he stepped from the sunlight into the shade, or as if his skin, obedient to the affections of his soul, darkened with his entering into the gloom which enveloped my mother and all she touched. Just as, at other times, in his shop, he would be gazing out the window at the bay and his heart could not fail to impart to his face some of the joy he felt in seeing the clean white sails under the blue sky and on the blue water. The impressions, altered by his heart into a desire for a life inclusive of such things, would be altered once again until in his eyes and lips there would be indications that he was deep in a radiant dream of being already part of such a life, being free, I suppose, not only of his duty towards my mother and me, but free even of the memory of it. How inevitable it seems that happiness will be the next state we come to if only we are once rid of our present sorrow! Our troubles seem to have but one axis: we forget that even though our love were returned, our debts would not willy-nilly take themselves off; that even though the headaches which plague us were cured, we should still suffer from a broken heart. Could my father, who had cried like a child and sobbed that despairing word, *Verzeihung*, be content ever with what Miss Pride imagined for him? His sin of omission, because it seemed imposed upon him by some external evil, angered him, for he had gone so far in his transgressions against the law of the church that he could no longer bear his terror of the consequences and temporarily substituted another emotion. Just so, the dipsomaniac wrests himself from the fear of his desire by changing the name of it to "need," thus to tolerate his destruction as if it were no fault of his own. It was this reasoning in hallucinations whose existence he felt obliged to prove to others that made him say, if I asked him why he had not gone to church, "Something I can't account for held me back."

Miss Pride was asking me a question. "You're finding the approach to Boston distasteful, aren't you?"

I quickly looked out. We were going through the merry slums where wanton cats sprawled full-length on the sidewalk and dirty, murderous children shot pop-guns at one another and hideously howled against the exasperated clang of the trolley-car. Bleak tenements nudged a pallid sky where Chichester's sun did not shine. Dark cafés, sunk like black eyes into the walls, advertised with winking, blood-red lights, "Beer . . . Schlitz . . . Beer . . . Schlitz." Some distance ahead of us I saw the white column of the Customs House, and I realized with disappointment that all the way, the State House dome had been invisible, and that, because of the detours we had made, my original impression of it as dwarfing all the other buildings on the mainland, would be altered, would be perhaps forever lost. I asked Miss Pride if we drove past it.

"Oh, you shall see it, never fear. I see you've been properly brought up to respect Boston." Her voice was ironic. "But I'll let you in on a secret—I think the State House is a perfect fright."

She said there was no time today to acquaint me with Boston's points of interest (dashed by her contempt for the State House, I was just as glad) but she would show me the one thing which she had always felt was the jewel of the city. She would not care about the destruction of everything else, the First Church or the gardens or King's Chapel, if only the Granary Burying Ground were preserved.

We entered its iron-bound precincts and advanced down the central path between the splitting gravestones that tilted backwards toward the austere obelisk of Franklin and the eroded sarcophagi. The several trees of the yard, black-trunked, thickly burled, and leafless now, and the naïve death's-heads, sprouting angels' wings on the decaying wafers of rock, were dextrous accidents, for they, and the wind we heard when the noise of traffic was briefly suspended contrived to give the place an air so formidable and esoteric that I felt death, at his most facetious unsightliness, walking beside me. I understood why she had said this was the heart of the city. Walled on one side by the Athenaeum through whose back windows a solitary old Bostonian, withered and hewn, was gravely regarding us, the sparse and lowly graves of the harsh garden testified to the city's conviction of its rightness and its adamant resistance to change.

Miss Pride confessed that she was partial to graveyards and often spent a full day in the one in Concord where the famous authors were buried, and of which she was particularly fond since it accommodated many of her ancestors. She spoke of others in New Hampshire and in Maine but declared that this small antique plot where we moseyed was her "first love."

"I don't know why it is nowhere but in New England do you find a well-turned cemetery. In France, they're nondescript. There is one other graveyard that took my fancy. When I was a young lady, I one time went to New Orleans and took a side trip to a little town where some sort of pioneers, German, I believe, had been buried. (My ignorance about the rest of this country, my dear, will shock you. I'm like the woman who said she went to Los Angeles by way of Charles River Village.) It was in a grove of oaks, dripping with Spanish moss which made everything most gloomy, most Doré. I found it creepy, I must admit, but it *was* handsome."

I admired the darling of her heart but asked her why she preferred it to all the others, and she said, "Well, in some of them, the newer ones, the horticulture is rather too much and the epitaphs have certainly gone downhill. But the fact is, that the names in the others are second-rate. That is, even Mr. Emerson can't compete with Revere or Otis. Don't misunderstand me. Some of my best friends are named Emerson."

She had sent Mac on and we walked to her house down the street past the State House to which I found myself indifferent. And at the moment I released my long-cherished impression of it, I realized that my desire for Boston had never been so real as it was now as, grimy, tattered, large for my age, I strode beside this clean, tart woman, so certain of her good blood, her wit, her wealth, her position in society (so *au courant* with her ancestral history that she could call a Cabot inferior to a Prescott, like a Howard running down the House of Windsor) that she could appear on the streets of her city in any company without the slightest risk of censure. Earlier, I had told her that I was not properly dressed to go to tea. "Dressed?" she had said. "Do you call me dressed? You may be more formal in Chichester at tea time than we are in Boston, but you look dressed enough to me. The important thing is, are you warm enough?"

"Now, we turn here," she said, "and then we start going down. Our Hill is a real hill. I always say it's really much steeper than the Great Blue Hill." Indeed, with a push, one could go hurtling down the brick-paved sidewalk and never stop, but shoot into the Charles which was visible, far below, as a wedge of chilly blue, crossed now and then by a white sail. Miss Pride, sure-footed as a burro, marched briskly down, and I, joyously regarding her from the corner of my eye, kept as close to the houses as I could in order not to bump clumsily into her. Her house was not far; its front windows faced Louisburg Square and here, as if it were an oasis chosen to delight the eyes of some favored heavenly power, the sun, hidden elsewhere by the city's smoke, shone brilliantly on white doorways and their brass trimmings.

Tea was served to us in the library, a lofty room at the back of the house, chilled and dark. Through the drawn, dark red curtains, the late afternoon light barely penetrated. Miss Pride asked me if I would like to have the lamps turned on and when I replied that I liked the dimness (it was not true; I would have liked to look at everything under a searchlight), she said, "It seemed a little *triste* to me, but you, of course, are feeling a little *triste*." She had thought to have a fire today but it had turned out so warm we would only be uncomfortable—she found the room stuffy as it was. I agreed, although the damp coolness of the place filtered through the layers of my skin and set my bones to dancing.

When she went out for a moment to speak to a servant, I made a tour of the room. The middle sections of the end walls were recessed for twin fire-places with black marble frames; in either was a bed of solid, tawny ashes, the careful accumulation of years. The hearths were flanked with bookshelves reaching to the ceiling and in a far corner, near the windows, stood ladders which might be attached to a track at the baseboard and to an upper shelf so that one might investigate the high books. I was more impressed by these appurtenances than by any other in the room, for they suggested a most serious purpose and I had never dreamed of seeing anything like them in an establishment other than a public library or a shoe store. The outer wall was taken up by two long casements between which stood a Governor Winthrop secretary. On the wall above, a gentleman forthrightly speculated on the tall cabinet opposite him through whose glass doors were visible silver loving cups and brass placques standing upright in a narrow trough. I say "gentleman" because I knew at once that he could have been nothing else. The edges of his gray waistcoat were piped in white and his cutaway, the warm color of a dove's back, was striped with fine silver threads. He was a lean man and in his severe face, age had peeled the flesh almost to the skeleton, but it was evident, in the bright, flat eyes (uncannily perceptive either through the painter's skill or his model's power to project his character into the canvas) that age had not deprived the brain of its faculties; they almost spoke. He was, I knew, some relative of Miss Pride's, and I believed he was her father, for the eyes were exactly like hers and, for the sake of experiment, endowing them with life, I observed that from numerous angles, they, too, seemed to stare suddenly first at one thing and then at another. They did not *follow* me, but waited until I had reached my new destination before they apprehended me again. I was standing near the cabinet when Miss Pride came back into the room. Before me was a small table on which stood a satinwood chess-board and ivory men. Two chairs had been drawn up in readiness for a game and upon a little glass-topped stand, a decanter had been placed with two inhalers.

"Oh, do you play?" asked Miss Pride. I said I did not. "You should learn. It is the best of all games, the greatest test of intelligence. Bridge, I have no use for. My father, whom you see up there above the desk, was the foremost chess-player of Beacon Hill in his time. This room, in a sense, is dedicated to his pastimes. For in addition to being a past-master at chess, he was a great reader, as you can see from the size of his library. And here, in this cabinet are his yachting trophies. But I have tried to make the place cozy, not too much like a museum, you know, not too much like a mausoleum. After all, we have graveyards to take care of the dead, we needn't keep their ghosts in our houses."

I was curious to know who the chess-game had been set up for, and presently she enlightened me. "I must confess to a degree of vanity over my own game. My friends were corrupted some years ago by that humdrum Oriental importation, Mah Jong, and have never since been able to keep their wits about them at the chess-board. Consequently, for a long time I have had to be satisfied with playing against myself. Occasionally I get wind of a young man at Harvard College who knows a smattering and I do enjoy the combat. But a young man against an old woman is not quite pleasing. They're always anxious to finish the game so that they can start reforming me." The word "reforming" she whispered, drawing out the second syllable with an intentionally comic puckering of her lips that made me laugh and ask her what their mission was.

"My dear," she said, leading me to a fat, short sofa, upholstered in red velour which had faded in some places to a rusty pink, "don't ask me that until I have had a cup of tea." The tea had arrived just then, and I was disappointed to see that the refreshments were only rye bread spread with sweet butter and thin slices of fruit cake to which I had always had an aversion. "Will you have sugar and lemon or sugar and cream?" she asked. I told her I took nothing in my tea and I refused anything to eat. My abstention seemed to please her for she remarked, "Why, you're a perfect guest. I think it's foolish to stuff oneself at tea time on strawberry tarts and all sorts of sandwiches. In some houses it's become a regular meal. I feel we carry our Anglophilia too far sometimes, don't you? Or perhaps you think we don't go far enough?"

I had no idea what she meant. There was nothing patronizing in her voice, nothing in the least supercilious and I concluded that any young lady should be able to specify at once, and with reasons for her choice, the camp to which she belonged on the question of the American imitation of British customs (I was at least, through the help of my reading, able to grasp the meaning of the word). I was tongue-tied, but at length, when I saw her hand poised over the teapot as she waited for my answer and realized that she did not introduce subjects of conversation that one might take or leave, I brought out, "I have never been to England." The faintest of smiles pinched the corners of her eyes, and she changed the subject to literature which I had told her, on the way in, was my principal interest.

I learned that she regarded literature as utilitarian, as essential to good breeding. It was an ingredient of life like religion, and just as one believed in God and invoked Him but trafficked only with the minister, so one believed in Shakespeare but depended on *The Atlantic Monthly*. Instinctively she felt learning to be a masculine province, even though she was an advocate of equal rights. She told me how well-read her father had been, how he had been instructed by all these books that lined the walls, whether they were poetry or fiction or history, and she rather raised her voice on "poetry" as though it were remarkable that he had found it useful, and admirable that he had renounced the temptation to enjoy it, had solemnly been "instructed." In the last years of his life, he had taken up Oriental languages and for this she had the deepest respect. "Now the mastery of a language I can understand. It is as thrilling as chess, and it is useful, although poor Papa never benefited from his Japanese as he only learned it when he was too old to travel. But he had the illusion, at least, that he was getting somewhere, don't you see." Hastily, as an afterthought, she added, "My dear, you must not think for a minute I'm like that quixotic Mr. Brock at the Barstow. A foreign language is useful in a foreign country, and I suppose that if one were cast on to a desert island and had nothing to read but a French translation of Mr. Emerson, one would be justified in reading it."

The mission of the young men who played chess with her was, it appeared, to induce her to read modern poetry. She had no patience with these eccentric cubs who had demolished tradition, and she found particularly infuriating certain New Englanders who had seen fit to poke fun at their countrymen. "I see nothing intrinsically humorous in the name, *The Boston Evening Transcript*," she said in temper, "and much as the author of its contumely is respected, I think he writes doggerel. I have never quite got his connections clear. All I know of him is that he was born in Saint Louis, even though he really was an Eliot. Times change. In the old days the people we claimed as our literary men were born in Concord or Cambridge." I asked her if she had known Amy Lowell well and she replied, "The less said about Amy Lowell, the better," so that I supposed—because I was sure Miss Pride had the pick of all Boston society—that the two had had a disagreement in which, of course, Miss Pride had been in the right. And later when she said, reverting to an earlier subject, that literary people were often "brainy" and that she did not enjoy brains when she was relaxing at her tea-table ("All things," she said, "in their places."), I decided that Miss Lowell had perhaps never been invited to the house and that their meetings had only taken place in the Athenaeum.

Poetry frankly made her uncomfortable. She had not the same aversion to music or painting, perhaps because the media of the composer and the painter were foreign to her and she did not see their creations in the context of their lives. Not so with a poet who laid his very heart at her feet, tracing upon it as upon a contour map, his unbridled passions. Some young person, child of an old friend, had one day come to tea and had brought with him the Holy Sonnets of John Donne, and in spite of her protests, had managed to read one aloud to her. It was a particularly passionate one (Miss Pride, disliking

such words as "passionate" said "fantastic") ending with the
couplet:

> Except you' enthrall me, never shall be free,
> Nor ever chaste, except you ravish me.

The same young man had, she understood, taken to writing
poems himself, much in the insolent tone of the mocker of *The
Boston Evening Transcript*, and had composed some vicious
lines on the Granary Burying Ground. The young man's
"case" was a mystery to her because he had not only come from
a perfectly dignified family and had gone straight to Harvard
from Groton and was going into the law, but also because
he was directly descended from at least two of the illustrious
skeletons in the yard.

I was in love with that young man who had perhaps sat on
this very sofa, resplendent in a long coat and trousers of a different cloth and thick-soled shoes and a bean-shave, reading
poetry in the accents of Beacon Hill's Olympians. Magnificent
creature, that intellectual aristocrat, pausing between crew
practice and an evening at the Porcellian Club to exhibit, in
an old lady's fusty house, the fullness of his life! I at once
hoped that I should one day see him here in all his gentlemanly
regalia and that he had been forbidden to come again for his
importunity. For equally in love was I with Miss Pride whose
small, dour world was governed by one and only one principle,
a principle that varied neither in time nor place, a law which
forbade riot to follow on the heels of chance: John Donne
might once in her house pose as a forward woman, begging,
in so many words, to be seduced, but he would not behave so
twice. Between those two astronomies, the young man's whose
earth was plural, and Miss Pride's whose solitary world was
Boston, round which the trifling planets revolved at a respectful distance, I could not choose, for both were true.

We had finished our tea. Miss Pride rose and as she moved
about the room turning on the lamps, she said, "Your letter so
charmed me. And as I read it—let me say that I was impressed
by your calligraphy which has the purity without the flourishes
of the Spencerian hand—I said to myself, 'Here is *one* person of
the new generation who preserves the ideals of my own. I will,

indeed, come to her aid.' I cannot tell you how much it grieves me that I was too late. My little flower, I'm afraid, was hardly a substitute. Yet, without me, you solved your problem, you were not stumped. Oh, you'll be all right! I will say quite candidly that it flatters me to think I have perhaps had some influence on the development of your character. I have, although you have perhaps not been aware of it, been closely observant of you for several years and had thought, from time to time, of making the proposition to you which you set forth in your letter, that is, that you enter my service. But when you wrote me, I knew then that that was not the ticket. My dear child, what talents you have! And a chambermaid!"

I had nothing to say in reply, but cast my eyes down at the carpet as she went on, "I was saying to my niece that if she had only kept her eyes and ears open as you have done, she would have been a singular young woman. Now I know nothing of your circumstances and little of your capacities, but I shall not lose my interest in you and since I should like to do a little something, in return for the rare pleasure your letter gave me, I have ordered *The Atlantic Monthly* for you and in the next few days will send you a box of books which I am sure you'll find profitable."

"That's very good of you, Miss Pride," I said. "I like to read."

She asked me then if I knew stenography. "What a pity," she said. "I thought they taught you that sort of thing in the public schools. I was about to say that I shall presently be looking for a secretary. The fact is, my dear, which I hope you won't breathe, that I have been thinking of writing my memoirs. Now you'll think me outrageously pretentious. I haven't a scrap of talent, as I'm quite aware, but I feel it my duty to preserve certain things, certain recollections of my father, a most praiseworthy man. But there's no time to tell you about Papa. Perhaps you wouldn't care for that sort of work anyhow."

"Oh, on the contrary," I cried. "I should like nothing better. But of course I could not leave my mother."

"No, I suppose not. One's first duty, after all, is to one's mother, or to one's father, as in my case. Well, we shall see."

The chiming of an unseen clock warned me that I must leave. Miss Pride led the way to the drawing-room to show me her Copley which she had mentioned earlier. As she opened the door, I saw, seated before the fire on a low bench, a girl with long red hair. She did not turn at the sound of the door but said, "Auntie?"

Miss Pride turned to me. "Some other day you shall see the Copley. Good-by." And without shaking hands with me, she disappeared into the drawing-room, closing the door behind her.

The word "drawing-room" had fascinated me for many years. When I first learned that Miss Pride's house was equipped with such a place, I furnished it with an erratic ensemble, elements of which I borrowed from every interior I had known or read about. It contained, among other things, a box of ferns like the one in the sixth-grade room at school. I had at first interpreted the meaning of the word as "a room where people draw pictures"; but this I rejected when I heard the expression "to draw out," and I thought that a drawing-room would be the setting for skillful conversation. When at last I learned that the word had been truncated and was actually "withdrawing," I envisaged a group of ladies cringing through a door as brutal men advanced, much in the manner of "The Rape of the Sabine Women," a brown, stained print of which hung in the classroom of the Latin and French teacher.

Today, seeing my first drawing-room, I was deeply shocked, for in that brief glimpse, I was able to take in everything. It was no larger than the library and because it was well-lighted and the other had been dark, seemed even a little smaller. It was dominated by three large rival "units": a bay window equipped with a long seat and a great many pots of foliage, a grand piano draped with a Spanish shawl, and a fire-place. Amongst, between, around those three behemoths, crouched chairs, to each of which had been assigned a companion, if not a table, at least a footstool or a standing lamp. The impression I got from the threshold was that if one wanted to reach the bay window, for example, he would have to "thread" his way through the furniture as in a crowded restaurant where the only vacant table is at the farthest end from the door.

As for a moment I stood where she had left me, I tried, quite frankly, to hear what was being said beyond the double doors. I caught only one sentence, spoken by the girl: "No, Aunt Lucy, it isn't that *you* depress me, it's the house. Otherwise, I would have dinner in tonight."

I tiptoed across the hall. I did not know what to do. My jacket and tam were nowhere to be seen, and for a terrible moment I thought Miss Pride had forgotten to tell Mac to drive me home and that I should either be obliged to wait until she came out of the drawing-room, displeased to find me still here after she had told me good-by, or that I would have to find my way back to Chichester on foot, through the evil purlieus of the city. Near-by me, I saw a table on which lay a silver plate containing calling cards. The magic names sprang forth from their immaculate plaques in the dim light of the hall: Cabot, Frothingham, Coolidge, Hunnewell, Adams, Heminway. I could feel the very breath of her eminent callers who dropped, as though it were nothing, their venerable surnames in her vestibule.

A door behind me opened and, startled, I wheeled about, still holding a card that bore the name Apthorp. I thrilled to the recollection of having seen the name in *The Education of Henry Adams* which I had read by mistake for Civics class instead of *The Americanization of Edward Bok*. To be caught thus snooping in the calling cards gave me the same feeling of terror that I had felt in grammar school when I was apprehended in the act of passing or receiving a note, and for a second, being unable to make out who was in the hall with me (for I was so confused that I saw a white apron without realizing it), I was sure that I would be turned out of the house in disgrace. But it was only the servant girl with my things to inform me that Mac was waiting.

3

My mother had been ill for a long time with stubborn influenza, complicated with bronchitis. For two months, with a few brief intervals, she had been stupefied by fever and by the enervating sweats which came on when her temperature fell. Her sleep was disturbed by nightmares and she would call out to me in a terror that did not leave even when I had wakened her or when she had told me her dream and I had talked soothingly to her. The dreams pursued her even in her lucid moments and she would fall to weeping because the room had taken on the appearance of the cave she had seen last night or because, superimposed upon my face, was a word of Russian written in huge black letters, or because the bed was intolerably filthy to her since a few hours ago, two colossal tomcats had relieved themselves there. I suppose her dreams tarried exceptionally long because of the fever which could construct a complete hallucination from the barest materials: a piece of lint on the counterpane could swell and shape itself into the mammoth cats, or, vice versa, the cats of the dream could be reduced to a piece of lint. Her whole life was a fantasy, whether she was awake or asleep. If by chance her mind cleared and the objects about her righted themselves, it was not because she had recovered her senses, but that pain had driven the delusions away. Then she lay gasping, pressing her hand against the place in her chest that ached and burned from her shattering cough, and what she saw then: the bleak features of her impoverished room, my face ashen from the glare of the snow-light, the snow itself outside the uncurtained windows, these things were worse than her imagined tormentors and she would tell me to draw the blinds and light a lamp, do anything to change the scene of her suffering, to divert her for a few minutes at least.

Chief of her nightmares was one in which Ivan appeared to her. Often, when I wakened her, she would mistake me for him. She would shrink away and breathe, "You're dead!" Invariably, after this exclamation, she would be seized with a violent attack of coughing which even her syrup would not soothe. I could hear the tortured rasping of her breath between the barks, and if any ease came at all, she used it up in moaning, "Oh, God! I can't breathe!" It was no doubt only coincidence that made her suffer particularly after dreaming of Ivan, but I believed, half superstitiously, that she was being punished in her own heart. She often spoke of him and of Varenka, and whenever she heard the foghorns, every muscle in her body tensed and between clenched teeth she said, "It is down where *they* are, wrapped in seaweed." Who "they" were she could not or would not tell me. And she thought his hair had grown long and that his nails had pierced through his shroud. "I can see him, Sonie," she mourned. "His little body, swish, swish with the waves, just like Varenka. Oh, Merciful Mother! Oh, *mertvoye ditya*!" The Russian words, "the dead child," were uttered with an elegiac languor, implicit in the syllables themselves.

It was partly because I was sure she would not believe me that I did not tell her where the dead child really was. Even more, though, it was because I took a cruel and perverse pleasure in what I was sure was the remorse of her inner soul. His death seemed newly accomplished each day and gradually, while at first my grief had been intermittent and like a tide had washed over me only at intervals, now it became a constant and a profound pain, reaching to the farthest corners of my heart, delivering an unpredicted blow to every delight, whether or not I had been reminded of him. Flirting, in a band of girls with a company of boys, I abruptly ceased my giggles; the isolated moment silenced the flattering insults. I could smell the strange rankness of Mr. Greeley's waiting room, could see the black roses on the little nightshirt, and I could feel in my temples the vibrations of Mr. Henderson's boat as we passed through the shoals, where the water had a sinister, subterranean rhythm. Or I would waken in the night and leap from the bed, thinking he had called out. Confronted by the emptiness, my being screamed at the knowledge that he was dead.

Dr. Galbraith came once or twice a week to see my mother, although I had never summoned him. The excuse he gave me, jocularly as though I had no connection either with her or with Ivan, was that he did not want to lose another patient in our house. He gave her, I thought, too much sympathy, so that as she grew a little stronger, she declared that she was growing weaker, and when for a whole day her temperature was normal, the next day it had soared, by the aid of hot tea, to 103 degrees. Beguiled by the idea that she might have consumption, she told the doctor that her mother and father had both died of it, and she was delighted when he promised that as soon as she was well enough to go to the hospital, x-rays would be taken of her chest. In the beginning, I believed that he was deliberately leading her on and that he hoped to cure her psychotic mind as well as her infected bronchial tubes. Thus, one day when he left her bedroom, after a cursory examination and a long talk, I walked out to his car with him on the pretext of asking him how her chest sounded. But instead I told him of her cunning trick of elevating the mercury in the thermometer by immersing it in her tea. "I don't want Mamma to become a hypochondriac, sir!" I said. "Can't you help me?"

But he missed the point entirely. "The temperature may be absent altogether in a case like this," he said. "It's the sound of the râles that tells the story."

"Oh, I don't deny that she's ill," I replied. "But, Dr. Galbraith, she shouldn't put the thermometer in her tea!"

"No, she shouldn't." He laughed. "Be sure you don't give her very hot tea or the thermometer will break into smithereens and you'll have to buy a new one. Good-by! I'll drop around in four or five days. In the meantime, just follow my directions."

When even her authentic abnormal temperatures had subsided and her cough had gone almost entirely and by her color and her returning flesh I knew that she was nearly well, the doctor still did not discontinue his visits. He came only in the evenings, and sometimes called for me at the Brunsons' to drive me home, a courtesy that never suited me since he was not the kind of man who could inspire young people to chatter, and if he asked a question, the answer was always too simple, and I would reply in a monosyllable. He would inquire, for instance, if I liked Latin, and because, in his voice, Latin acquired a colossal unimportance, I could say no more than "Yes" or "No," depending on how well I had translated that day. A gluttonous boredom resided in him and its appetite was insatiable. He might look at the full moon whose reflection floated on the dark blue water and he would sigh with a vast ennui. Occasionally, he exhaled the piney odor of gin and at these times he was more animated, but he looked at me so lecherously and his talk tottered so perilously on the brink of obscenity, that I preferred his other mood. "I bet you're the kind of girl that keeps the boys at arm's length, aren't you?" Or, "What do you young people do after the picture show? You don't go home and you don't study. Or do you study nature, that is, *human* nature down at the Point?"

Some people, among them the charitable but mawkish Gonzales, declared that Dr. Galbraith had only taken to drink after his wife's death. But others, like the Hendersons, said he had always "gone pretty heavy on the bottle." He was known to have women just as he was known to be a drunkard, but he took great pains never to be seen in the company of the women and never to be seen drinking. Thus, his depravity, never demonstrated as sordid, was surrounded by an appealing aura and no one identified so dapper a "professional man" with a "drunk" or visualized him with a fancy woman. Through a wonderful stroke of luck for him, the old ladies at the Hotel knew nothing of his reputation as a voluptuary, and if they had been told that his eccentric color came from jaundice which had been brought on by many years of copious, solitary drinking, they would have said confidently, "Oh, you're quite mistaken. He goes every year to Florida and somehow manages to keep his tan twelve months at a time."

My Latin teacher, a scholarly man named Mr. Sylvester, thinking that Dr. Galbraith was a friend of my mother's (for he, like the rest of the village, had heard of these visits, but had not troubled to acquaint himself with my mother's social position so that for all he knew she could have been a well-bred woman who had seen better days) told me that I should value his society since he was a man of rare talents and had written more than a dozen musical compositions, chiefly string quartets. The information had come to Mr. Sylvester in a round-about way and he could not even recall whether he had heard it from anyone of taste, but he was under the impression that the doctor had been first-rate. "But he gave it up for some reason, and one wonders why," said the teacher. Accordingly, partly to satisfy my curiosity and partly to stave off his discomforting badinage, I told the doctor one night what I had heard.

"Yes, as a matter of fact, I did make up two or three little things. I hadn't thought of them for years. I haven't played my fiddle since my wife died. Who told you about that?"

"Mr. Sylvester, my Latin teacher."

"Apropos of what?"

"Nothing. I suppose he knew you were taking care of Mamma."

"Oh, yes, of course. I suppose you told him your Mamma was sick and that I was bringing her prescriptions and what not? Well, will you give my regards to Mr. Stuyvesant and tell him that my music is a dead soldier?" He had stopped his car beside our house and turning his fuddled face away from me, said into the fresh, windy April air, "You have brought up the past to me by what you've just said. When you are my age and can look back as many years as I can, you will remember this evening and say, 'Ah, at last I know what Dr. Galbraith felt.' Miss Moffatt, I had the most beautiful wife in the world. She was French and she was religious. My house is full of sacred objects that she bought in the by-streets of France and Italy. I have a *prie-dieu*. A Spanish crucifix dating from the thirteenth century, set in a tabernacle of Carrara marble. On my desk, a *memento mori*, a small skull carved of bone. I could never replace the least thing." He faced me again. "You forgive an old man his reminiscences, don't you?" He leaned across me to open the door, and as I stepped out, he said under his breath, "The odd thing is I have forgotten every word of French. *Madeleine*, there, I pronounce even *it* the English way."

The wistful note had left his voice and the sorrowing smile his lips by the time we had entered the house. "I'll just have a look-see at my patient," he said heartily. "She is, ah, she's valiantly combatting this pestiferous bug." Because I knew as well as he did that the combat was over and that if she wished she could get up any time and resume a normal life, I looked away from him in embarrassment. He sensed it and he said, "The peril of this kind of thing is the relapse, you know. There's the danger of tuberculosis." The last word he said in a whisper, stretching up on tiptoe as if to carry the sound completely out of reach of my mother in the next room.

"Sonia!" came her voice. "Sonia, darling, is the doctor there? I coughed some blood up this afternoon."

Dr. Galbraith's face twisted in a faked consternation.

"I don't believe it," I said sulkily.

"Coming, Mrs. Morgan!" cried the doctor. "Oh, by the way, I forgot the bouquet I brought your mother. It's still in the car. My garden is, so to speak, overflowing, and I thought I would like to share it with someone. I don't know what it will be . . . my man just snipped a few things for me. Would you be so kind as to fetch them?" He went into the bedroom, leaving the door wide open. As I left the house I heard him say, "We'll get the better of those darned old bugs yet and put some roses in your cheeks."

I was out of the house for only a few minutes, but when I came back, I found the door closed although, because the lock was defective, it had fallen slightly ajar. I heard a conversation about my mother's fancy-work. In her convalescence, she had begun to make fir trees, the decorative possibilities of which she had heretofore overlooked, and extraordinary birds which never pleased her. She would say, "I've left out something," and puzzle over the creatures, turning her hoops now to one side and now to another and never seeing that each one of their plump behinds was destitute of tail feathers. But the doctor, blind with infatuation, assured her that they were beautiful, that she was a "regular ornithologist."

"I like to see these homely virtues in a woman," he was saying in a voice that had borrowed some of the nocturnal quality of my mother's. "My own wife was a great hand at dressmaking. I still have some of her gowns in an old trunk in my attic."

"Did she die or did she light out one fine day?" asked my mother.

Shocked by her expression, he did not immediately reply. "She died," he said at last. "It makes one lonely."

"Lonely! After my Hermann went away I used to cry myself to sleep every night of the world. But that was nothing to what it's been like since little Ivan died."

"I know, I know."

"You was saying you have some of your wife's clothes. I wish to God I had some of Hermann's. But my little girl sold them all as soon as he was gone."

"We can't expect children to understand these things."

There was a long pause. I had put the flowers in a jar and thought to take them in to Mamma, but as I approached the door, I was urged by a powerful curiosity to know what was taking place in the bedroom, and I crept along the wall to peer between the hinges of the door. The doctor was bent forward, his hands palm upward lying on the counterpane. Their skin was even darker than his face and the nails were a corpse-white. The fingers were short and swollen, the skin stretched so tight it seemed about to split like the skin of a sausage as it is being cooked. These clean, brassy hands played the supernumeraries in the drama of the eyes and lips, and as I watched, they curled into cups as slowly as a flower closes. Then the thumbs moved over the nails of the index fingers with voluptuous deliberation as though the contact with the smooth surface were exquisite.

The left hand was raised. The man carried the source of the sensation to his mouth, passed the nail several times over the sensitive area under his lower lip.

My mother's eyes were cast down but her lashes coquettishly flickered. Her fancy-work lay at her side. The doctor wiped his shining lips with a purple handkerchief (This evening he was dressed in a gray suit and his accessories were purple. He smelled, as well, of lavender water.) as if he had been eating the face before him and its flavor had been so delicious that in his gorging he had been too enthusiastic to mind his lips. But he was not making love. In a moment, although he whispered it, he said, "Let me listen again to that right lung." I saw him push her nightdress down and explore her breast with his stethoscope, his head bent down so low he seemed to strain not to lay his face on her naked flesh. "Oh, that's so-so," he said with a laugh. "I must keep you here another week," and gazing, deeply stricken, into her eyes, he took her pulse and announced, as if it were a declaration of love, that it was still a little rapid. My mother made no response, but picked up her embroidery hoops across which, this time, was stretched a branch of honeysuckle to which a deformed humming-bird was paying a visit. Dr. Galbraith glanced down and cried, "Charming! How I would like to have some of those things in my house! Would you . . . could I . . . my dear Mrs. Marburg, would you do some table runners for me?"

"Just at present I'm rather busy," said my mother. "But perhaps I could do a few later."

"Excellent! I'm going to New York next week. I'll just pick up some stamped things there."

"My hoops are cracking."

"I'll buy you some new hoops! I'll buy you some ivory ones inlaid with gold. I dare say they have such things?"

"Why, certainly they have," said my mother. "Once I had a pair of solid gold ones with diamonds set in. That was just one of the things Hermann carried off with him." She coughed a little and the doctor bent closer to her.

"What you really need," he said with such terrible excitement that the stethoscope shook in his hand, "is mountain air. Don't you know anyone in the White Mountains or the Adirondacks that could put you up for a few weeks?"

"Ah, doctor, that's just what I've always said! The sea air is bad for me. But no, no, I don't know nobody in the mountains. I'll just die here like the child."

"Yes, yes, well, that's neither here nor there. I have made up my mind that you *must* have mountain air. I will see what I can do—come to think of it, *I* have a friend in the Adirondacks who might very well let me, that is, let you have the use of his cabin. Charming place, set in a grove of fir trees with a lake near by. The problem, of course, would be finding someone to take care of you."

"Oh, Sonie's a good mother's helper. She's a dreamy girl and goes off a little crazy now and then, but she's a sweet nurse all the same."

"I don't doubt that," said the doctor. Frustrated, unable for a moment to find his way to the fulfillment of his obvious scheme, he swore softly under his breath, apologized, and said he had just remembered an important engagement he had not kept that afternoon. Then he continued, "I don't wish to interfere in the upbringing of your daughter, Mrs. Marburg, but it seems to me that this is a very important time of her life . . . that is, in school. That is to say, from my point of view, it would be actually *dangerous* to take her out of school now, just a few months before commencement. Why, she might not get her diploma! Where would she be then? No, I think you ought to let her finish the year out. I will find you a companion myself."

My mother's eyes shone at the prospect of the mountains. It was the first time, to my knowledge, that she had ever earnestly wished to leave Chichester. I have never known anyone in whom wanderlust was so completely lacking. Perhaps she was incapable of imagining a place in America other than this seaside village, but tonight she was granted second sight. As if she were already listening to the wind through the fir trees, she murmured, "I love the mountains. They don't smell of clams."

"True, true! And not only that but they're healthful. Why, you'll be a new woman in a month or so. I'll just send my friend a telegram. You leave it up to me, Mrs. Marshall, I'll arrange the whole thing."

My mother did not thank him, for, completely egocentric, she was never aware that the betterment of her fortunes initiated in anyone but herself. Yet for his reward, the doctor got a flashing smile of joy which so enlivened her pale face that he could not resist the temptation to touch her and he lifted her hand which still held the hoops and yarn and kissed it. I nearly cried out, for I was not only surprised at the doctor's premature and uncircumspect advances, but I was afraid my mother would be shocked out of her placid daydream of the mountain cabin and would realize what his motives were. But either through greenness or complacency, she did not object to his caress. Barely conscious of it, in fact, she allowed her hand to lie in his until she was urged to go on with her humming bird.

The doctor rose and as he did so, his greedy eyes suddenly widened with horror as he realized that they had been talking loud enough for me to hear. "I completely forgot! I brought you some flowers. The girl went out to my car to get them . . . it's strange I didn't hear her come in."

"She came in all right," said my mother. "She'll be out there doing her lessons. She wants to be a school teacher, doctor. Won't that be a feather in my cap?"

"It certainly will!" he cried passionately. "She's a fine girl. Now I must be running along. *Au revoir.*"

I slipped back to my place at the table and opened *Literature and Life* at random; the pages fell back at *The Deserted Village.* I pretended to be so engrossed that I did not hear the doctor come up behind me and jumped, startled, when he said, "Well, now that's a coincidence. I was about to tell you that the village of Chichester is soon to be deserted by its gracious citizen, your mother. I have been thinking for some time that she needed mountain air to dry up those little scoundrels in her bronchial tubes, and I've got her consent to send her off to the Adirondacks."

"That's awfully kind of you," I said. "But we have no money even to pay her railroad fare, and I shouldn't like to let her go alone anyhow."

"But she wouldn't be alone. I would . . . that is, I intend to get a companion for her, a sort of nurse person, you know. I'll pick up someone or other in New York."

"But the money . . . we haven't any money at all."

"In questions of life and death, we cannot consider money. I understand that you intend to be a school teacher. Very well, then, when you have your post you can pay back the money

I intend to advance you. No!" He raised his hand for silence. "I won't hear any objections. I *owe* this to you. I have few pleasures in life. I am a lonely man, a widower, and where I can spread happiness, I *will*. Let me, I implore you, let me send your mother to the Adirondacks in memory of my wife."

He did not look at me as he spoke but gazed about the room and finally, his eye lighting on Dr. Brunson's brandy, he seized his hat and cried, "I must get on at once. Now, Miss Marburg, I'm not taking 'no' for an answer. I'm going to drive your mother down myself. Doesn't that reassure you? I've got to run on to New York anyhow in a week or so and it will fit in perfectly. Good-by for the present. I'll look in tomorrow."

My mother was delighted with the flowers and buried her face in them. She was still flushed with her thoughts of the mountains and she talked ecstatically. "My stars, darling, imagine it! It was fate that made me start doing the fir trees. Oh, how happy I am! I've been so unhappy! You don't know how unhappy a person can be, baby girl."

"Mamma, don't go away," I said sadly. "I would be so lonesome without you."

"There! She's cross that I'm happy! She doesn't care if her mother dies. Oh, Sonia, I never thought you'd turn against me, I never did!" Tears started to her eyes and she drew up a pathetic cough. "All right, I won't go. I'll just die here. I suppose it was a whole cup of blood that came up this afternoon, but it don't matter." She caught her breath. "Give me the syrup . . . No, no, don't give it to me. I'll just go on and die now."

"Don't talk like that, Mamma," I said. "Wouldn't you like a cup of tea?" But she refused. I sat down on the edge of the bed and pulled her fancy-work toward me. "Oh, what a lovely humming-bird! You're so clever, Mamma."

Pleased, instantly reconciled to me, she caught my hand and kissed it quickly. "Do you like it, darling? What do you say I do some of them around the hem of your voile dress?"

"Well, I don't know . . . "

"No, I don't either. It might make the other little girls jealous. It might hurt their feelings. Oh, you're good, dearie, always thinking of others. You're my baby girl, aren't you?"

"Yes, Mamma. Shall I turn out the lamp now or do you want to work a little longer?"

"I'll work a bit. I'll tell you what, when I get my ivory hoops, I'll make you a blouse with tulips on it!"

As I studied, unable to concentrate, I heard her talking to herself. I thought that perhaps it was the approach of sleep that made her mutterings more and more incoherent. Several times I looked in, but she was wide awake, still multiplying the blossoms of the honeysuckle. At first she talked of the mountains and the fir trees, inquired of herself if she thought the snow would still be on the ground, said, "Yes, it will be a good thing for her. Shura, even as a child, didn't like the smell of fish. She was real unusual about it, Mrs. Henderson." She proceeded then to her work. "It's not as easy as rolling off a log to do a sandpiper, Sonie, darling. Naturally it looks easy as pie to somebody that don't know the first thing about needlework, but all the same I'm willing to make them. Do you want two on each side of the collar or just one? No, the sandpiper is not my favorite bird. Best I like peacocks, next best parrots, third best bluebird. Sandpiper is way down the list, maybe last."

Then she ceased to make sentences and though she did not raise her voice, it became intense as she uttered single nouns or strung together a group of unrelated verbs: "Run and swim and holler." After a moment, "Mrs. Purple Grackle?" she inquired. "No, Mr. Humming-bird. *Mister?* Or *Doctor* Humming-bird?"

I paid little attention to her. Gradually I forgot about the doctor's visit and I read hard at *Ode on Intimations of Immortality*, my next day's assignment. My interpretation of the poem, nevertheless, was influenced by the childish prattle that issued from the bedroom and a part of my mind (the same shallow part that put into my mouth most preposterous errors when I was translating Latin at sight, making me read "In the midst of its boughs and yearly arms spread the opaque elm tree, huge, where sat Sleep vulgarly," for "*In medio ramos annosaque brachia pandit Ulmus opaca, ingens, quam sedem Somnia vulgo*"), obeying the advice of my English teacher to bring literature into my life and vice versa, suggested to me that my mother was returning to her childhood and if her mood lasted, she might go even further and briefly visit her heavenly home.

She talked continuously, then sang a little, then imitated a drunk, "They're flying *all* around thish room. Get thosh boids out of thish room." Something clattered to the floor. "Sonie!"

she screamed. "Come quick!" I ran into the bedroom. She had flung off the bedding and was sitting up straight, her hands over her face.

"Mamma!" I scolded her. "Put the covers over you. You'll catch cold again."

"There were birds in here, Sonie!"

"No, no, you only dreamed there were." I put the back of my hand to her cheek. It was blazing. "There, now, you've got yourself worked up into a fever again," I said and put the thermometer into her mouth. Troubled, I wondered if she had actually coughed blood that afternoon. I looked around for signs but saw none. Gently I drew the blankets up about her again but she cast them off, mumbling around the thermometer that I was trying to suffocate her. She did have a fever, higher than it had been since the last acute phase of her illness, but I told her that her temperature was normal. "You're just tired, Mamma. It is a little warm, I guess. Would you like a sleeping powder now?"

"Yes. And you come to bed, do, darling. I know there were birds in here. You keep watch for two hours and then wake me up and I'll keep watch. I don't want them to get tangled up in my hair. They do that! Especially the kind that are part mouse, you know the kind I mean."

"Bats?"

"Yes. I wish I had a nightcap. I know, let me wear the little boy's stocking cap."

I took the little red and white cap out of the bureau drawer. "It won't fit," I said. But she reached out her hand for it and set it on top of her head. She pulled at it but when she had let go, it immediately contracted, skimmed to the top of her head and sat there precariously. But she was satisfied: "It looks like a nightcap, anyway, don't it? It's like not letting a dog know that you're afraid and he won't bite you. I suppose it's the same with bats."

She was still restless and insisted that I sit with her a little while. First the lamp, then the darkness after I had turned it out, harried her and she turned her head this way and that, groaning and sighing until at last she fell asleep and I went to bed on the pallet. Because I was exhausted and slept dreamlessly, I was sure I had only just closed my eyes when a cock's crow and my mother's shriek came simultaneously to my mummified mind and I awoke to the grisly light of early dawn and to my mother, kneeling at my side. She had had a nightmare. She was in the house of the witch who was no longer a woman but a man; a semicircle of people stood round about an ancient hag dressed in black who writhed in death-throes on the floor. The onlookers were solemnly interested but made no move to help the woman who had been poisoned by the witch. My mother was accosted by Ivan, grown into a tall young man, and he said, "That is my Mamma. We knew it would happen at the Reds of Easter. When is it your turn?" Suddenly, looking at her hands, she saw that they were covered with a crumbling brown incrustation, green in spots with mold, and the witch, who stood near her, touched her bare foot so that more of the crusty scabs appeared. He touched her at various other places until her whole body was infected; she could not get away from him although he was not holding her; her feet were rooted to the floor. A hideous scream came from the throats of the people who watched. At last, when she was entirely covered with the vile stuff, he seized her by the arms and kissed her lips until the blood streamed from them, soaking her blouse. She saw then that he intended to lift her up and carry her to a couch, set in a vast bowl of water through which swam goldfish with enormous human eyes that devilishly winked at her. In shame and fear she begged to be released, and as he laughed at her protest and lifted her up, she screamed and wakened.

I got up and led her back to bed. She was crying now with horror at the memory of her loathesome skin and yet with relief that it had only been a dream. Her skin was cool and in spite of her tears she looked rested. I would have liked to go back to bed, for my head was throbbing from insufficient sleep and my eyes were hot, but my mother declared that she could not close her eyes again for fear the dream would go on to its dreadful climax. She asked for a lamp and while I was getting her breakfast, she commenced to work again on the proboscis of her humming-bird. "Talk to me, Sonie. You know, talk a blue streak so I'll know you're still there."

Sleepy and cross, impatient with her fancies, I talked, with an intended irony which missed its mark, of my stolid mistress, Mrs. Brunson, who slept until ten every morning, never had nightmares, was never ill, and did not depend upon her daughter for her amusement. I did not, it was true, have the slightest respect for her. She was growing stouter as the result of over-indulgence in chocolate creams and alcohol and although it never occurred to her to reduce her consumption of either, she had become extremely touchy on the subject of her expanding hips. If someone paid her the compliment, "How well you're looking, Dorothy," she interpreted it as meaning "How fat you're getting," and she would reply testily, "Same to you." I had at no time envied Betty her mother, but this morning, as I waited for the tea to brew, I wished my own mother's silliness were more like hers which did not rouse the household out of sound sleep and did not, even when she was drunk, conceive the notion that birds were flying about her bed. Moreover, Mrs. Brunson's dreams, which she was fond of telling at the dinner table since her best ones came during her afternoon nap, were of the most pedestrian variety, as banal as her speech.

"And Betty writes to her mother once a week from boarding school," I was saying, "and every time says, please send me a white bengaline evening dress or please send me twenty-five dollars to have my picture taken. And Mrs. Brunson just says okay. She's the most unselfish mother I ever knew. Mamma, are you listening?"

"Sure. That Mrs. Brunson must be lazy. Why, I wouldn't feel I was worth my weight in gold if I didn't get up till ten o'clock."

"Do you by any chance mean worth your weight in *salt*?"

"Toot toot toot toot toot! Somebody got out of the wrong side of bed this morning, it seems to me."

I went on with my narrative. The tempo of the Brunsons' lives slowed down as I talked until, by the time the tea was ready, the dentist and his wife had become as inactive and unfeeling as the china family in Betty's doll house.

"I can't wait all day for my breakfast," called my mother.

"It's only five-thirty. The fire won't get hot. Oh, Christmas, Mamma! Why can't you be like *other* people?" I had not intended to be harsh, but I had burned my fingers on the metal teapot as I lifted it from the stove and since I was vexed already, the little injury enraged me. No reply came from the bedroom. When I took in her tray, my mother did not look up but stared at the back of her hands. "In the dream, the bones right there felt like they were broken under the sores. It was awful! I don't know if I can eat anything, thinking about them."

Nevertheless, she lifted the teacup and drank a little. "Listen," she said, "it wasn't Luibka in the dream at all. It was a man, like I said, and he wasn't a stranger either, but for the life of me I can't think who it was. Not your father. Not Gonzales. Not Mr. Kadish. Who in the world was the nasty dog?" She named the men she knew: doddering old Mr. Brock at the Hotel, Mr. Henderson, the Fuller brush man who had given her the black tooth-brush, Mr. Greeley, her father, Nathan Kadish. The doctor did not cross her mind.

I thought of going to the hospital after school to tell the doctor that my mother could not see him that evening, and yet I reasoned that I could give him no proper excuse, that I might offend him by appearing to be suspicious of him when perhaps he was only acting out of the goodness of his heart. All day I was anxious. I could feel my forehead wrinkle into a frown that did not come from my diligent following of the text of the *Aeneid* or the *Ode*. I did not hear my name called out in the Algebra class roll and I elicited from my teacher the remark, "I must be having a hallucination. I could swear someone was sitting in Sonie Marburg's seat."

All the day I was thinking the word "insane." In telling my mother that morning of the daily life of the Brunsons, I had recalled a recent conversation between the dentist and Dr. Roberts, the only other physician of the town besides Dr. Galbraith. The doctor had just been reading of new surgery which was now employed in some cases of insanity. "The cure, to my way of thinking, is as bad as the disease. To be sure, they don't take after you with butcher knives and so on, but they become inhuman, have no feelings. The optic thalamus is put out of whack. Tell them somebody died and they'll laugh their heads off. Tell them a rattlesnake is behind their chair and they'll just grin. I'm an old-fashioned man. I believe in the good old-fashioned insane asylum." Mrs. Brunson who, when she had had too much to drink, tried always to ask intelligent questions—perhaps to prove that she could still follow the talk even though she could not hold her fork in her hand and spilled water in her lap as she lifted her glass to her lips—said, "But that would be used only for violent cases, wouldn't it? Not for the people that just say strange things and think they see pink elephants and so on?" The doctor, a man who in all things saw black or white, replied shortly, "I may be wrong, but personally, I think people who see pink elephants—unless they're stuffing you—are insane. We all have our off moments, but I don't think a healthy mind is ever off enough to see a pink elephant."

Had my mother actually seen the birds last night, I asked myself, or was she only teasing me? Perhaps it was the fever that had made her talk so strangely, so much more strangely on reflecting today than it had seemed last night. Moreover, I wondered why she had forgotten the mountain air and the pine trees in the Adirondacks this morning when she had been so enraptured at the thought of them last night. I did not want her to go! I was sure she did not need mountain air—the doctor himself, at the beginning of her illness, had told me that the idea that climate had anything to do with pulmonary diseases was nonsense— and I believed that on the contrary what she needed most, and what she would always need, was my pampering, for she was a very young child. And while I pitied Dr. Galbraith, I was not willing to sacrifice my mother to his loneliness, not even in the memory of his devout French Madeleine. Nor, on the other hand, was I any more willing to sacrifice him, poor gallant goose, to the persecutions to which Mamma had subjected my father.

Briefly I desired to tell Dr. Galbraith how she had literally driven Papa away, and when school was out, I started down the road toward the hospital. But I turned back, realizing what such a revelation would imply. It would be the grossest impertinence on my part to tell him, a physician, and presumably acquainted with mental as well as physical disorders, that my mother was insane. It struck me that perhaps I had been wrong all along, that he had no improper designs on her, that in reality the cabin in the Adirondacks was a sanitarium. I planned to talk with him that night and to beg him not to take her away.

The doctor did not call for me at the Brunsons', and as there were guests at dinner and the cocktail shaker had been refilled so often that I did not begin to serve until nearly eight, I was late in leaving for home. Maudie had gone sometime before, inviting me, as she did almost every night, to drop in "for a snort." For the first time I had been tempted. I was very fond of Maudie, even though she was tiresome, and my spirits never failed to rise in her presence so that even my boredom was curiously exuberant. I did not want to go home; there was something gruesome about the doctor, and I kept thinking of the *memento mori* on his desk in the library where he drank alone, as his servants reported in the village. And I thought of the marble tabernacle for the crucifix. When I visualized the latter, I was simultaneously reminded of the shoals, I cannot possibly say why except that the word "marble" suggested something chilled and ghostly and "tabernacle" made me think of the dark-room at school where the physics teacher developed films and where, because of the structure of the room or its position in the building, the acoustics were peculiar and the sound of feet in the hallway above was like the surge of waves.

I thought perhaps he would not come tonight or that he would have left by the time I got home. Consoled a little, as I passed by Maudie's cottage I was glad I had decided not to go to her, for from the open door, brightly lighted with a Coleman lamp, came the sound of her loud, untrue contralto harmonizing with two masculine voices in obscene excerpts from "Frankie and Johnny." The rest of the way home, I reiterated a telepathic message to the doctor, "Go home, Dr. Galbraith, go home."

But his car was beside the house. The kitchen was mobbed with flowers as though a garden had magically been planted there since I had been gone. Branches of lilac drooped over the sides of the blue sink; the table was piled with jonquils and iris; on the chairs, wrapped in wet newspapers, were sprays of syringa, forsythia, and Japanese quince. Old marmalade jars and jelly glasses were filled with lilies-of-the-valley whose little ivory bells trailed down or nestled close to their broad caressing leaves. I stood on the threshold, breathing in the sweet air. A breeze blew through the kitchen window and carried to me the whole essence of the lilac with which it had been charged as it traversed the sink. For a moment, overjoyed with his bountiful gift, I was remorseful that I had been suspicious of the doctor. His flowers showed that our pleasure was his purpose.

From the bedroom, as usual, came the voices. They were

laughing tonight over some private joke and I gathered that it had to do with the cabin in the Adirondacks, for I heard the isolated words "lake" and "firewood" and "chipmunks." Evidently they had not heard me for they continued to talk as I walked about the kitchen from one group of flowers to another. Shortly the door opened and the doctor came out.

"Good evening," I said. "How lovely your flowers are!"

The doctor grinned obscenely at me and leaned against the table for support. One foot, handsomely shod in a half-boot, moved in an uncertain circle on the linoleum. The bright bronze hands tossed fretfully from their limp junctures as he said thickly and in a masterful imitation of my mother's accent, "I am *so* glad you like them, dear. They are all from my garden and they are *all* for you." His sweet breath came to me in gusts, mingling with the flowers' fragrance. Abruptly, his hands and feet were stilled and he rose to his full height, rocking slightly but apparently in command of himself again. "It's close in the bedroom," he said, still thickly but now without the accent. "I felt a little giddy for a moment. I was just about to examine your mother. It wouldn't do to fold up in the midst of that, would it? Give a patient a bad idea, make her say, 'Physician, heal thyself.'" Suspecting that he had a mission of delicacy in coming away from my mother, I asked him if he would like to wash his hands before he made his examination, and although the door to our "bathroom" was open and revealed only the toilet, its sole article of furniture besides the shower, he thanked me, said that was what he had come out for, and went in.

After I had kissed my mother in the dim bedroom—for instead of her lamp, only a single candle burned on the stool at her side—I went to open the window at her request. Just as I turned back into the room, Dr. Galbraith entered and resumed his seat at the side of the bed. I saw that more of his flowers were strewn on the floor and my mother clutched a spray of lilies-of-the-valley in her hand. She had not been working on her embroidery; there were signs of no activity at all, and to my relief, I saw that there were also no signs that the doctor had been drinking here. Beside the window was our clothes closet—a rod across which had been stretched a cretonne curtain—and I stepped back into the large shadow it cast, less out of the desire to spy than out of reluctance to pass the doctor and be required to speak to him again.

"All righty," he said. "We'll just have a look at this clogged-up ventilator and then I'll be running along. Will you just slip your nightie down over your shoulder, please?"

My mother obeyed docilely, gazing the while at her nosegay. "Isn't it sweet," she murmured, "just like little darling bells."

Dr. Galbraith ran his hand over the smooth round of her shoulder and a look of alarm fled over her face as she glanced up at him. Almost shyly he looked away and fumbled at the clasp of his stethoscope case. But he did not complete the business. "Oh, Shura!" he cried. "Let's not pretend any longer!" He slipped his arm under my mother's shoulders and drew her up to him, covering her face with long kisses as his whole body shuddered.

My mother struggled and screamed, her head flung back and her eyes dilating as the stubborn man continued to kiss her neck. "Sonia! God Almighty!" I stepped forward into the weak light but the doctor was oblivious of me. "Darling, forgive me, I frightened you." His forehead glimmered with drops of sweat which he wiped off with the back of his hand. My mother, whimpering, could not take her fascinated eyes from him while he, as if he were paralyzed, hovered over her, afraid to kiss her again, yet afraid to move lest he break the enchantment cast by her unworldly eyes.

I touched him on the shoulder, feeling nothing but the deepest commiseration for him, and he drew back from the bed. But still he could not rise and, relapsing into his violent desire for her, he grasped her stiffened hands as she shrieked again, quivering pitiably like a baffled mole dislodged from his safe tunnel. "The sores!" she howled. "Oh, oh, God! They're all over me!" He stood up and perceiving that I was beside her and that she was free of him at last, my mother turned away from us and buried her head in the pillows, and there lay murmuring.

"What the devil is she saying?"

"She's talking in Russian. She does that when she's upset."

"My God!" He strode in fury out the door and I followed him. "Well?"

"My mother has always been a little strange, Dr. Galbraith," I said, "ever since my father went away. Even before that I guess." He stood with his arms at the sides of his long gray tweed coat. He was staring bleakly at the barnyard scene above the table. "Dr. Galbraith," I went on, "there is no way I can pay you. I'm very grateful, really."

"I had never considered a fee. A doctor assumes responsibility for a patient without thinking of the money," he said impatiently.

"I'm so sorry about it all, sir! You see, I think my mother is insane."

It was the first time I had said the word aloud and it shocked me almost as much as it did him. He stared at me, absorbing the words after the sound was gone. "Insane?" he repeated. "Why, of course she is insane, but, I must confess, she hides her symptoms well. I swear, Miss Marburg, I had no proof of it until tonight."

"What shall I do?" I asked him, for it was natural for me to appeal to him since he shared my knowledge. His expression changed from disgraced rage to anxiety. "Come to my office tomorrow afternoon," he said, "and we'll discuss it. She shouldn't hear us, you know, in her excitable state. Tomorrow, promptly at four." He hurried out, businesslike, professional, hiding beneath his manner the relief he must have felt in knowing that my mother had not "rejected" him since she was incapable of doing so.

When I had heard his car drive away and I went in to her, I saw the marks of her real madness in her glazed eyes that looked at me without recognition and did not move as I moved but continued to focus in the place I had just quit, and in her rigid pose which broke only when she tore the petals languidly from the doctor's flowers, and in the steady monologue in Russian that ended at last in a fitful sleep. And when, in the morning, there was no change in her and she would not eat, but pushed the tray aside, spilling the tea on the counterpane and watching it spread, I thought there was no hope. "Mamma?" I tested her, but she would not look up. I should perhaps stay with her, I thought, lest she conceive some devilish desire to hurt herself or to wander to the village in her nightdress. But because she was no longer recognizable as my mother, but was only an inhuman parody of her, I was frightened and did not want to remain in the house. A little faint, because I could not eat my breakfast, I took up my schoolbooks, locked the door behind me and started down the road.

It was a fine day; as green as leaves, the water was bifurcated by the yellow spear of the land. Our little white house and the Kadishes' blue one sagged on their shallow foundations, hiding from my backward view the Boston shore-line. Just ahead of me, Father Mulcahy sauntered slowly, reading his breviary. As I passed him, looking sideways into his raw-boned face that years in Chichester had not filled out or sweetened, it occurred to me with a wild, obscene humor that I might ask him to come exorcise my mother. I was so close to him for a moment that I could smell the wine on his mumbling lips and by leaning a little towards him could read, at the top of his book: "Die 28 Apr.—S. Pauli a Cruce." He jerked his head like a rooster and said, "God's warning."

"What? What did you say?"

"I said good morning." He looked curiously at me.

"Oh! Good morning, Father. I thought you said . . ." And I ran on, strangely exhilarated by the priest's odor, with which the air still seemed saturated, though I knew that was impossible and what I smelled now was the perfume of the lilacs blooming in all the yards.

Chapter Six

D R. GALBRAITH was not in his office at four on the next afternoon, and I was told that he was ill. I did not believe it, but felt sure he was avoiding me. Nor was he there on the next day, and the nurse, refusing to tell me when he might be back, suggested that I go to Dr. Roberts. On the fourth day, having resolved that this would be the last time I should inquire for him (I thought the nurse had been given my description with the orders that on no account was I to be admitted to his office) and should then go to the other doctor, I was informed that he had died that morning, a little before noon, of a heart attack. Upon the words "heart attack" the nurse ever so discreetly placed a stress which told me that he had perhaps died of what he said but that its cause was a prolonged debauch.

The nurse behind the circular counter wheeled her swivel chair back into place before her typewriter and began sorting large yellow cards. I wanted to ask her more, but I could not think of a way to frame my questions. To be sure, the doctor's death was no more than coincidence and my mother, who all day long talked tenderly to herself in Russian and one by one ripped the petals from his fading flowers, was no more to blame for it than I, or than this imperturbable woman in the starched white cap. Though I had cared nothing for this stammering dandy and had many times wished him out of the way, I had wished him no harm, "out of the way" having meant only "out of our house." But I was shaken with something simulating the grief I had felt when I dropped my brother's hand, and my knees went weak, as I remembered that I had sometimes pitied the man. I had pictured him in his library, perfectly groomed, as if his loving toilet had been made for some honored guest, though no one ever called on him, and he sat alone, sunk in his jejune thoughts that the whiskey enshrouded. Gossip ran that in this room, the shrine of his dead wife's sacred objects, there was a bar concealed in the paneling which opened at the pressure of a button, so that in the evenings Dr. Galbraith could dispense with the services of his butler who was allowed to enter the room only in the morning to clear away the evidences of his master's lonesome spree before the parlor-maid came in to clean. I wished to ask the nurse if he had died there. Once he had told me that two malachite urns stood on his mantelpiece and that the draperies were ruby-colored brocade. Perhaps he had chosen as his shroud one of his Scotch tweed suits in which the brown was enriched with red and with it he had worn green socks and a green cravat.

"When is the funeral?" I asked, although I did not really want to know.

"I haven't the least idea," replied the nurse without looking up. "You might ask his housekeeper. All I know is that he is to be cremated."

I felt that if I moved from the counter where I rested my elbows, I would fall in my weakness. An interne who had been watching me absent-mindedly as he whirled a piece of rubber tubing round and round, pocketed his plaything and stepped to my side. Out of a mechanical kindness, he placed his hand on my shoulder and said, "Take it easy." I burst into tears, inexplicable to myself, and stumbled through the sunlit lobby, my legs enfeebled, my mind a blank. The scene detached itself from its aseptic smell and the white entourage of nurses and internes: its properties receded and I, hurtling up the road, was too alone to measure the degree of my loneliness, for I did not know where to turn for advice.

Yet, on the day following the doctor's funeral in Cambridge, I was receiving counsel from young Dr. McAllister in the same office where I had first seen Dr. Galbraith. That other day, the hygienic glare of gray walls and white wainscoting had combined with the blue shadows of snow-filled trees beyond the windows into a hard, glacial light. The old man's skin had been green as if its natural yellow hue had been mixed with the blue shadows, and his eyes, pillowed by their pendulous sacs, had ambled sensually over me while his addled brain danced in bewilderment. The tall, bony elms of the hospital courtyard had whined and rattled and then, when the wind died, a company of discursive sparrows raised their voices in the hush. The only other sign of animation to be seen from the window was a solitary pigeon promenading over the slate roof of an adjacent ward about whose red chimney wound the steam from two small exhausts.

The new occupant sat before the open windows through

which, gentle and billowing, came the May day's limbering
breezes and edgeless light. The world beyond was spacious
and subtly illuminated; the landscape, perhaps as much as the
young doctor's adroit kindness, loosed the strictures of my
terror, and after my first ferocious declaration that my mother
was insane, I was able to speak without a stutter.

Dr. McAllister was somewhere between twenty-five and
thirty; he was spare and angular and erect and his obvious
good health recommended him, whereas Dr. Galbraith's diseased complexion and unstrung manner had made him seem,
from the very beginning, an uncertain ally. The tone of the
young man's voice was restorative, for he was at once casual
so that my story seemed automatically less calamitous than I
had thought, and authoritative so that I knew I could depend
upon him.

I had come to him because I had not wanted to consult Dr.
Roberts, who, being a good friend of Dr. Brunson, might,
despite his professional ethics, drop a few hints to the dentist. I
wished, so far as possible, to keep secret this new excitement of
our household. To be sure, everyone in Chichester had said for
years that my mother was mad, and the children who had used
to come to play up towards our house no longer came. The
villagers and the shopkeepers had, after Ivan's death, stopped
inquiring about her. But still, they had no proof.

It had not been easy to gain an audience with Dr. McAllister,
who was a house-physician and not allowed to have private
cases, and so I had written him a note, saying that Miss Pride
had asked me to look him up. He had sent back the reply that
he would be delighted to meet me at such-and-such an hour
on Sunday afternoon at a tea-room in Marblehead. It was the
hasty note of a busy man who, aware of his duty towards his
friends, parcels out his leisure time with no sign of the irritation he feels that he can keep no part of his life to himself. I
would have let the matter rest there had I not, on returning to
my mother, found her up and dressed, carrying a basket on her
arm with the intention, I was afraid, of going to the village. I
had urged her to go back to bed, but my entreaties were futile
for she understood nothing but Russian. I had then given her a
glass of brandy (she had at least not forgotten brandy) in which
I had dissolved one of the sleeping powders left over from her

illness. I must say here that this ingenious trick afforded me the only amusement I had in ten days. I could not help smiling, as I pulverized the pill, at the grave necessity that had driven me to practical joking, and when she began to droop, after no more than a quarter of an hour, I laughed outright. I had then locked her in and run back to the hospital where, on a sheet torn from my loose-leaf notebook, I wrote Dr. McAllister that I had an urgent message for him from Miss Pride. A cold, dubious answer came back at once saying that he would see me in his office in a few minutes.

The doctor had been reading. When I came in, he took off his horn-rimmed spectacles, uncovering eyes which were a blue resembling the flame from certain kinds of wood or oil, a color simultaneously fierce and smoky. In his face there was a union of austerity and simplicity, coming partly from its actual architecture: the defined planes of the jaw and cheek and forehead, the thin lips, the narrow nose, and partly from his expression as he intelligently and nobly appraised me, trying to adjust me to my note.

"You have a message for me?" he said, smiling and motioning me toward a chair. "You must be a friend of Miss Pride's."

"I am, in a way," I said. "But I am really here under false pretenses, for I have no message for you. I had to see you. It's about my mother."

"I don't have a private practice," he said. "Our head, Dr. Galbraith, recently died, as perhaps you know, and his place has not yet been filled. But Dr. Roberts is in town, I'm quite sure." As though to clinch his dismissal, he withdrew his spectacles from the pocket of his white coat and opened them.

"I know that," I said. "But I don't want to go to Dr. Roberts." He waited for me to go on, but I could find no more words, and as I kept my eyes averted from him, seeing the green felt under the glass top of his desk with the harried realization that I had no idea what I was looking at, I knew what his next question was going to be, but as in the dream when our benumbed throats will not let pass a cry for help, I could summon nothing to stave it off, and when he spoke, I heard him as though his voice came from a phonograph record whose revolutions I did not know how to stop: "Look here, I don't know who you are but I don't believe you are Miss Pride's friend. All this mystery doesn't ring true. Are you quite sure it's your mother who is ill? I don't want to sound unkind, but tell me frankly, isn't it instead that you've committed an indiscretion and, to use the common expression, have got yourself knocked up?"

Because I had known that that was the way he would interpret my timidity and my lie about the message, I could not be angry with him for anything but the vulgarity of his phrase, which he had used in the intention of lowering himself to my level, but at the same time had uttered in almost audible quotation marks to assure me that he would have nothing to do with the matter, that I had come to the wrong person for an abortion.

I found my voice and said, "Oh, no, it's not that at all. It's that I think my mother is insane."

"You should have said so at once. Please forgive me, but your coming here was so unusual. Why do you think your mother is insane?"

I told him her history. As I talked, his attentive blue eyes showed me that he was marshaling recollections that my presence and my story disinterred, was giving the skeletons flesh and blood, yet was keeping me, my "case," separate like the solo part of a concerto which is enriched and surrounded by the ritornelle. To ease me, to divert me from the horror of what I told him—for one's sin or sorrow is most intolerable at the moment of confession even when we know that we are soon to be absolved or comforted—he halted me now and again with seemingly inconsequential questions or observations. He had, for example, been to Würzburg and as he spoke of it, pleased that I had caused him to remember the hotel where he had stayed which had formerly been a Franciscan monastery and still preserved an atmosphere of asceticism, he canceled out the distaste and aloofness that had been in his voice when he thought I was pregnant, and without deviating from his purpose as a physician, elevated me to his own plane as at first he had descended to mine. He was, I could tell, profoundly moved by Ivan's death and burial. He said, "Your story *is* a Russian one," and asked me if I had read Dostoievsky. I said I had not, but he led me to the place from which he surveyed the geography of my mother's mind so that I saw her not as my mother, but as a type, as the embodiment of the traits he had read about. We looked together from our vantage point and, lighted by the stories and the novels from whose context he extracted what was applicable to my mother, I saw her, for a little while, as he did.

When I had finished my account and he began to speak, he did not offer me any solution and he said he could not counsel me until he had seen my mother and had judged for himself whether her symptoms corresponded to my report of them. It was easy enough, he said, even for an experienced person to confuse hysteria with insanity, and while he did not say so, he implied that possibly because of my concern over Ivan, my own hysteria had made me exaggerate her eccentricities. "She is perhaps best off at home," he said, "where she can be guarded against excitement. If, that is, she's curable, and the chances are that she is."

"But where else could she be?"

"Perhaps I have misunderstood you." He looked away from me and briefly examined the scene from his window as though he were trying to integrate all its essentials, its colors and its forms, as if he hoped to find there the way to put his words best. "That is, I assumed in your coming to me that you wanted more than a listener. I thought you had been debating whether or not to send her to an asylum."

Chiefly, I suppose, because there was none near Chichester and I had, therefore, no actual impression of the appearance of such an establishment, an asylum had never once occurred to me. My mother's madness had been clearly separated from any other madness. And I said to Dr. McAllister. "Oh, but she isn't violent! She couldn't be put into a strait-jacket."

He laughed. "You're behind the times. We're not going to put your mother into a strait-jacket. Why, mental hospitals are no worse than this these days." He motioned toward the silent corridor. "But we needn't talk about that any more. I'll look around some evening soon, as though I were paying a call on you, and see what's what." He glanced down at the blue card on which he had been making notes, to refresh his memory of my name. "We've covered everything now, haven't we, Miss

Marburg? I would like, though, to ask you one more question. Why was it you used Miss Pride's name instead of another? You know, you could have said Dr. Brunson sent you."

"She spoke of you to me. I connected your name with her and with her niece, for she said you were friends. You see, last February, when my brother died, Miss Pride came to see me and took me into Boston. I had tea with her . . . in the library." I had heard no more from her. She did not come to fetch me to see the Public Gardens, as she had promised, nor had she sent me the box of books although *The Atlantic Monthly* came regularly. Boston had receded a little farther each day until now, the sea again seemed the only road to the State House whose glittering dome had once more recovered its pure shape after my new impressions of it had shuffled off into the past. I had thought my afternoon with Miss Pride was engraved indelibly on my mind, but at last I remembered clearly only the horny black trunks of the trees in the Park Street cemetery, only the names Franklin and Revere, and only the metallic voice of the girl saying "Auntie?"

But the proximity of this man, to whom having tea with Miss Pride was probably the most ordinary occurrence, brought back the objects of our common knowledge: the portrait, the chess table, the silver platter for the calling cards. And with the objects came my hostess's warm, albeit noncommittal, compliments. On an impulse, I said, "Perhaps you could tell me why she invited me to come to tea?"

"Miss Pride is a very generous woman," he said with the simplicity but lack of conviction with which, in speaking of the people we do not like, we acknowledge their virtues that are good in themselves but can serve no purpose to us. "She is known, I believe," he continued, "as one of the *most* generous women in Boston. Last year, for example, she gave five thousand dollars to the Community Chest."

"I have admired her ever since I can remember," I told him.

"Really? Well, then, perhaps that's one of the reasons she was, as you say, so 'kind' to you. I have never had the honor to be at tea with her alone . . . and never in the library."

I could not grasp his irony. Did he mean that I *had* been singularly honored? Or had she, by shutting me up in the library, merely been taking precautions against my being seen by a chance visitor? I rose to go, dissatisfied with what the doctor had said and liking him a little less for not praising Miss Pride with the passion that I had believed must reside in the breast of anyone who knew her. He came around the desk and I observed that when he walked, his body did not bend in the slightest; his back was as straight, as inflexible as Ivan's had been a few hours after his death.

"You can count on me. But the next time you want to crash a gate, make sure you have the right password. You wouldn't have got in today if I hadn't had an inkling that your 'message' was nothing but a leg-pull."

I knew, by the pink eastern sky showing through the leafy chestnut trees, that it was time for me to be at the Brunsons'. Since my mother had been ill, I had been allowed to come an hour later but had made up for the lost time by working all day on Sunday. Mrs. Brunson was displeased with me, for I had been distracted and had done my work carelessly. Still, she had made a tentative promise to promote me to Maudie's place in the fall. Maudie had by now completely lost control of her appetite for whiskey and twice had watered Dr. Brunson's Vat 69 to his humiliation, on the second occasion, before a guest who, sipping a cocktail made from the expurgated bottle, remarked, "They certainly don't put any teeth in their whiskey any more, do they?"

In spite of knowing that I would get a dressing-down, I dallied along the way. This garden-filled and springtime world through which I moved was perfumed with the closely clustered lilac blossoms in the yards I passed, roofed over by a coral, turquoise, and violet sky. The heard, but unseen, white skirts of the sea fluttered sweetly against its boundaries. Just as Nathan's kisses in the fog had warmed my sorrow to its bloom, and my love, though contiguous, had only served to enhance its somber colors, so the young physician's accidental exhumation of Boston had, immediately afterwards, caused me to see the loveliness of Chichester to which for several months I had been indifferent. And now, stopping to bury my face in a branch of lilac in a sudden infiltration of an unobjectified but passionate happiness, the purpose of my interview seemed to me to be but a tenth part of what had been accomplished, and the least important part, as if my fear that Mamma was insane had been only an excuse to know Dr. McAllister and had been, in a sense, almost as trumped up as my "message" from Miss Pride.

He had said, "We should not rush ahead to conclusions, but you should think this over. Let us say you keep her at home, protect her for the better part of your life so that you don't marry or don't realize whatever your ambition is. Would the martyrdom be worth all that? It's the question you must answer for yourself, for salvation for one soul is perdition for another and what might send me to hell would give you grace." His lofty terms, *martyrdom*, *salvation*, *perdition*, *grace*, were no longer the mere names of abstract states over which I had carelessly slid my eye on the printed page, but were the components of my own future, and I said "grace" aloud, my lips stopped by the dense purple trumpets of the flower I had pressed against them. My happiness confounded me. As though it were as perishable as the crisp lilac, I allowed no thought to come near it and refused to listen to the voices within the house behind the hedge which, organ of their owners' uncertainty, talked back and forth of the likelihood of rain. But the footsteps which I heard coming behind me, I did allow to intrude upon my mind, thinking perhaps they belonged to the doctor on his way home—his home? I questioned, but could see him only behind the desk in Dr. Galbraith's office where the white marquisette curtains were inflated by the breeze. The footsteps were quick and the heel-taps rang brashly on the sidewalk. Someone called my name, but there was no need to turn, for Nathan Kadish was beside me and had put his shoulder behind mine. When I saw his face, it was the good side at which I looked.

"What have you got there?" he asked me, although all I had, as he saw perfectly well, was the branch of lilac that I had bent down to smell, but love is a child at language, speaks nonsense, asks stupid questions, makes insipid replies—"Don't you know a lilac when you see one?"—and means to convey just the opposite of impertinence.

"You don't seem surprised to see me," he said. Rather he whispered, so close to my ear that his lips almost touched me, for the voices on the porch reminded us that we were not alone here as we had been in the fog. "I never can remember," said a woman, "whether it's feed a cold and starve a fever or the other way around just like I can't remember whether a ring around the moon means good weather or a storm."

"I guess I was thinking about you," I said, although this was not true. I had been thinking not of him, but of myself in whom the blood had defecated its black humors and had left only love but love as an envelope that was as yet empty.

"You're not sore, then?" He meant: Was I not angry, then, that my last glimpse of him until now had been when, shirt-tail out, he hotfooted it for the bus to Boston without a backward glance and had not written me a letter? No, I could tell him honestly, I had not been angry. I *had* been sore; my heart had been skinned by his silence. I had learned from his mother (who believed, for the simple reason that we were neighbors and about the same age, that Nathan and I were friends, but never dreamed that when she uttered his name my skin erupted into goose-flesh) that he would not be home again until the end of the term for he had got a job working in the Brookline Economy Store and all his leisure time was occupied. But I had not failed to call at the post-office once a day for two months in the hope of some word from him. The soreness had gradually disappeared, like a headache, and though I was not conscious of my relief, I was able now to pass the post-office with indifference. But just as the headache has not really gone but has been hidden under sleep and requires only a sharp noise to cast off its covering and meddle with our nerves again, so Nathan's appearance—weeks before I had expected him—reminded me of the shame of his neglect, renewed the sensation of his kisses, and made me, as before, stretch upwards as if I stood on tiptoe to scrutinize his birthmark, sudden through the lighted window. And I knew I had not ceased to love him, that the wrappings in which I had laid away my hopes were not winding sheets, were only masquerade, out of which they came now with their sweet, young faces.

The dense branch swung back to the bush from my relaxed hand as five o'clock rang out from the Catholic church. "Golly, I'm late," I said.

Nathan stepped to one side and with a gallant gesture offered me the outside of the walk. He said, "I know you think it's impolite of me to walk on the inside. I do it intentionally because I do not believe in bourgeois etiquette. Probably you want to hurry because you are afraid of the bawling-out you'll get from that bourgeois ignoramus who has the egregious impudence to call you her 'servant.' I have no doubt that if I invited you to stop in at Red's café for a Budweiser draft, you would refuse. I'm not reproaching you. You're merely victimized, a helpless cog in the machinery of social corruption."

"I would stop at Red's," I said, "but it's so late already and I promised to be on time tonight. They're having company."

Nathan's full lips curled in a sneer. "Don't go into detail, I can get the picture. I can just *see* their company. Does that illiterate trollop, the daughter of the house, still infect the atmosphere with her noisome presence?"

I told him that Betty was at school in New York. "As it should be," he said, nodding gravely. "There she will learn the elegant antics of the capitalistic prostitute. Oh, lofty ideal!"

He was lagging, coming to a full stop occasionally to convey his italics or exclamation marks by kicking a paling of the white fence, and if I quickened my pace, he pulled me back by the elbow, saying, "Where's the fire? Courage!"

I was nervous and bewildered by his talk, and although when his fingers closed over my arm as he detained me, the contact softened my bones and caused me to float without exertion, I could not help being disappointed that we dwelt in worlds so far apart. "Nathan, are you a Communist again?" I asked him.

"Again? When was I not? Oh, wait a second. Do you mean am I a member of the Communist Party? Or do you mean am I a dialectical materialist? Am I a Marxist, is that what you're asking me?"

I could only shake my head at his terms.

"No, I belong to no party, faction, or school of thought. But I hate the bourgeoisie because they are the enemies of freedom. I am a revolutionist, yes; I am a nonconformist, yes. But no, I am not a Communist, I am a cosmopolitan. Sonie"—he turned to me with a serious stare—"I am going to Paris."

"When?" I asked.

"Typical," he said irritably. "Typical of an unimaginative woman to try to pin me down about *when*. Next you'll ask me where I propose to get the money and if I intend to live in the thirteenth *arrondissement*."

His irritation was transmitted to me. I was angry that from our conversation had been deleted any reference to ourselves except as we figured in the grim farce of existing Society, by the denunciation of which he made me cherish my desire to know what it was before it was annihilated utterly by the revolution. The word "society," even though I was sophisticated enough to realize that he used it in its larger sense, was reflected on my mind as "Boston Society." But while Nathan had no doubt that if, in his life-scheme, he decided to include me he could convince me of the truth of his cosmopolitanism, so I believed he would sacrifice his crotchets to my own. Each of us regarded the other as a child; each smiled inwardly and with indulgence at the other's self-deceptions. And when I said, partly to tease him, that I still admired Miss Pride, he patted my hand comfortingly as if to say all was not lost, that he himself would remove the scales from my eyes.

Now and again, I was exhilarated by what he said of Paris. "My genius will bloom in a shabby *bistro*," he said. "In the beginning, I will have only friends, rum, *bock*, and market girls. But later, having fame, I will, if I want her, have a bonafide Faubourg *duchesse*."

Without realizing that the source of my rage was jealousy of that imaginary duchess, I blurted out, "Oh, I'm *sick* of George Moore."

"Give me three reasons," he demanded.

"I'm not interested. But no one with that much conceit can be decent."

"Decent? What language they teach them in school nowadays! I suppose you think an artist ought to be a humble worm? Humble, like you? You, Sonia Marburgovna, are the most self-conceited baggage I have ever known."

"I?"

"Yes, you," he mocked me. "For example, on the night you made that melodramatic, also fraudulent, also imbecilic Lady-of-the-Lake voyage around the Point to deposit an imaginary corpse in the Atlantic Ocean, did you not later lap up for flattery what was intended as advice? Did you not, when I absent-mindedly exaggerated your nature and called you deep, believe that you really were deep?"

I blushed and did not reply. We had turned into the street

where the Brunsons lived, and Nathan stopped. "I won't go any farther. As it is, I'm close enough to smell the putrefaction. Since you won't—or as you are deluded into thinking, you *can't*—go to Red's now, would you like to after you have finished cleaning up their swill?"

I had not drunk beer since my father went away, and I was curious to know what it tasted like and what its effect would be. I was elated at the thought of the evening we might spend in the dark, disreputable saloon that advertised tables for ladies. Encouraged by the beer (and bock beer was in now), perhaps we would be able to revive the mood in the fog. But when Nathan added, "Shall I call for you here or at home?" the image of my home and its drugged occupant made me catch my breath as I realized with abject shame that I had not thought of my mother since the moment Dr. McAllister, changing the subject, had asked me why I had used Miss Pride's name.

"No, I'm sorry, I can't." Too late I saw I should have said, "I can't *tonight*," but the pressure of the immediate future when my mother should awaken made me unable to look further ahead into an evening when I might be free to drink beer. I think Nathan acted not out of embarrassment but at the command of a reflex when, before I had uttered the last word of my refusal, he put his hand to the left side of his face and leaned into the shade of the elm tree under which we stood. His unilateral smile of twisted lips and one bright, malicious eye measured the altitude of his anger whose heights he had instantaneously scaled. With his right hand he tipped an imaginary hat and said, "I *beg* your pardon, moddam. No offense intended, merely a case of mistaken identity."

I started to explain to him why I could not go with him, but he raised his hand for silence. "No, really, I'm not in the least interested. I was under the impression that we had a tacit understanding, commonly known as 'friendship,' but I see I was wrong. It is just as well. Momentarily, under the influence of certain romantic symbols, I forgot that I must burn the midnight oil tonight over the misguided but well-meaning Thomas More. Please overlook my brief collapse."

"Oh, Nathan!" I cried, hoping by the tender tone of my voice to convey my despair so that he would forgive me and I might then tell him about Mamma. But I did not achieve my aim. The long white fingers of his left hand stole downwards and revealed, bit by bit, his garish cheek. "It was all right in the fog where nobody could see you, wasn't it? But it's a horse of a different color—rather, to be more exact, a *freak* of a different color—in the clear public light of our respectable village *bistro*. Come off it, lovey, you call me Cranberry behind my back, don't you?"

I was possessed by the deliberate unveiling of the birthmark and in a voice that came not from my conscious self but from the fanatical rapture with which I had secretly stared at it when I was ten years old, I said, "No, I love your birthmark."

He had not expected me even to say the word, spoken perhaps for the first time in his presence since he was a child and was the target for his contemporaries' downright jokes. My beastly declaration, a maudlin lie as he believed, brought a flush to the uncolored side of his face. As if confronting me with the tool of my crime to watch as my guilt blanched and shook me, he slowly turned his head so that his right profile was concealed by the trunk of the tree and from the dull ember which ran from his hair to his chin, the diabolical eye winked its purple lid. His limber lips were drawn to this side and from them issued a laugh in which mirth was not even pretended but which was the distance-muted entreaty of a wounded animal.

"That's a hot one," he said. "*Very* funny. Your wit, if you must know, surpasses your beauty. Let me say, however, that I have always been attracted by your hair. I observed the redolence of its natural oils in the fog. It reminded me, I don't know why, of the interior of a water-logged tennis ball. I trust you will never cut its pristine grease with that decadent commodity manufactured by your Heroine of the Barstow, that is, soap. Well, I must go home. Hark! Do I hear my doting mother calling Cranberry! *Oh*, Cranberry!"

Jauntily, his arms swinging and his metal heel-taps clicking pertly on the sidewalk, he went back down the street, but at the corner turned and called, "I say, be an old dear and burn up those letters of mine, will you?"

"What letters?" I cried.

"Oh, curses on my absent-mindedness. Here I was thinking you were Josephine." And he was gone, around the corner, his footsteps audible for a few seconds.

I reasoned, as I lingered in a breathless sickness, that if he had loved me, he would have sensed that I was in trouble, would have reviewed my words and noticed that there had been an inexplicable change between the time we met and the time we parted, and that the love so obvious in my voice when I had spoken through the flowers could not have perished within the space of ten minutes. And yet, when I considered what our relations might be after he had begged my pardon (for I had gradually progressed from a state of dazed helplessness to one of indignation and desired not to make an apology but to be tendered one by him), I was not sure that my love had not begun to wane a little after all. I was almost certain of it later, at the Brunsons', when I heard Dr. Roberts remark, "We couldn't hope to get a prize like young McAllister for this town. He's cut out for a metropolitan practice. He'll be one of your fifty-dollar-a-house-call society doctors. He's got the style all right," I had just gone through the swinging door into the kitchen to bring more wine from the ice-chest. When I heard the young man's name mentioned, my cheeks warmed and I cooled them at the rush of frosty air from the opened door as I withdrew the bottle of sauterne.

In the following weeks, I did not become indifferent. The turbulence that stormed about my memories of Nathan did not subside but I moved, so to speak, out of range of its danger by promising that I would not make the first step towards our reconciliation. And in time the cool-headedness that I feigned became actual, and once more when I looked toward Boston, the city which I imagined stretching out behind the State House did not go beyond that part of the Charles visible from the top of Pinckney Street, did not include Boston University or the Brookline Economy Store.

2

Dr. McAllister, after he had seen my mother two or three times, said that for the present she was well enough off at home. The first time he came, a few days after my talk with him, she was still in a state of total lethargy, but she had begun to speak English again. She was under the impression that the doctor had come to see her fancy-work and she exhibited it to him with the boredom and hauteur of a great lady who has at last summoned up the energy to pay a duty call on a dowdy friend and dispenses her good manners with an effort of will. "Thank you," she said when he complimented her on a set of table mats embroidered with yellow tulips. "It don't show up in this light but it's done well if you like tulips." Dr. McAllister said he was very fond of tulips and was surprised at my mother's indifference to them. She smiled with some lofty, secret knowledge of the flower's faults which she did not impart to us. Soon afterwards, in what I later recognized as a gauche breach of taste, I invited the doctor to drink a glass of brandy. My mother allowed her daft eyes to rove from one to the other of us. "Brandy?" she queried. "I don't know what you're talking about, Sonia. You must forgive my daughter, Mr. Whatyoumaycallit, she's always been a dreamy girl." I started to point to the shelf where the bottle stood, still half full, but the doctor shook his head at me, and my mother went on, "I had a little money here years ago and this silly child can't believe it's all used up. Mamma, where is the golden egg? she'll ask me and look in the Bible where we used to keep it. But she's a treasure all the same."

She would have gone on in an interminable eulogy of my abilities, my eyelashes, my character, had she not been silenced and rendered immobile by the returning torpor which immediately extinguished the light in her eyes and fixed her mouth. She sank to a chair and did not change her position for the half hour that the doctor lingered. Her hand, resting on the table covered with her fancy-work, could have been made of marble.

On his later visits, Dr. McAllister saw her alone, in the bedroom, and I could sometimes hear him interrupting her in the midst of what I knew, though I could not distinguish the words, was a tale of persecution. "Now, wait a minute, Mrs. Marburg, I haven't got the scene clear in my mind. Tell me what the place *looked* like." She would begin again, her voice sailing the calmed waters of her perpetual woe.

He told me that it was possible she was posing, that she was cleverer than I thought, but when I asked him what it was she could gain hereby, he could not answer to my satisfaction. "I don't know. Maybe she's afraid that now you are nearly grown you will leave her. But that mustn't alarm you, for I don't think she'd ever do anything drastic to keep you with her."

"Drastic? Why, she would never harm a hair of my head."

And he replied, "Certainly not," but his tone was so positive that paradoxically it was suspicious and a week later, when I went to the hospital to see him, I said, "The other day when you said my mother would never do anything 'drastic' to me, did you mean it?"

"I knew you would be troubled by that and I regret I said it. But the fact is that insane people—and mind you, I'm not saying she's insane—can turn against anything if they feel they're driven to a wall. For instance, when your mother discovers that you lock her in, she may be furious. That's why we must decide about the asylum soon because you won't be able to deceive her indefinitely. And that's why—that and because even suicide is not an impossibility—you'd better get rid of anything she might use against you or against herself, knives and so on."

"I can't believe it," I said. "Why, now she's not much different from what she's been for years. Now that she's started to speak English again."

"I don't doubt that. But has it ever occurred to you that for years you have been in exactly the same danger that you are now? You don't think, do you, that this has come on her overnight?"

"Oh, no," I said. "I guess I've known it for a long time. I always just thought she was queer and never was afraid until that night Dr. Galbraith came."

I could hardly bear to be in the room with her, not because I was afraid of what she might do to me, for, despite the doctor's ominous warning I remained convinced that, as I had told him, she would not "harm a hair of my head," but because she trusted me and did not know that at any moment I might lock her up behind high walls whose corridors rang with maniacal laughter and groans of the hopeless damned souls of this hell on earth. And when Dr. McAllister one day gave the place, which hitherto had existed in my mind merely as the word "asylum," a name and said we would send her to Wolfburg, it seemed to me that evening that she must be able to read my mind, obsessed with its hypocrisy. For heretofore *the* asylum had been as remote in space as her admittance there had been in time. But the articulation of the name and, further, the articulation of one that was not unfamiliar to me, forced me to open my eyes to its masonry, its approach, its gates, for this was a tangible destination. Thus, we could no longer use the conventional formula, "if she is taken somewhere," but now must say, "if she is taken to Wolfburg." Moreover, Dr. McAllister had this time used the active rather than the passive voice, had said, "We will take her," not "She will be taken," making personal the escort which had formerly been an abstract force. The doctor said, "Wolfburg has beautiful gardens, kept by some of the inmates." I wondered that he, in his kindness, should have built me so cruelly real a picture, going even so far as to name a particular feature of the lunatics' industry, an herb garden rivaling the famous one in Concord. But his intention was not tactless; it was just because of his frequent references to Wolfburg in the weeks that followed that I was able, when I first saw it, to enter the gate with composure and to admire that very horticulture, the first mention of which had unnerved me.

Miss Pride, either through Dr. McAllister with whom I saw she was on very good terms (even though he was too "brainy" for her liking and though his liking of her had certain reservations which he had taken no pains to conceal from me) or through her sharp eyes, knew that something was troubling me, and from the first day of her return to the Hotel, I felt her observant gaze upon me, missing nothing, as I served in the dining-room. Forbearing to make any comment when I confessed that I had not read anything in *The Atlantic Monthly* but the stories and the poems, she gave me a look so discerning that I felt any explanation was unnecessary since she apparently already understood why I had not been able to study out the essays. I was careful to wear an imperturbable countenance whenever she was near-by. If it happened that during the night I had slept badly and had dreamed of Ivan and had wakened to my mother's presence beside me in the bed, then had been unable to burst from the infrangible circle of my anxiety over her, I was still not so forgetful in the morning as to allow my face to relax into its natural weariness, but instead smiled and walked briskly as I took Miss Pride's dropped egg in from the kitchen. The effort that went into keeping myself upright and my eyes wide open perhaps imparted to my appearance the very rigidity I had strived for.

It was my misfortune, however, to be caught off guard several times by other guests. Mrs. Prather, for example, a woman of what are called "good intentions," had come to call on my mother at the very first of the season, for she had heard of Ivan's death through Gonzales. She was, as are all those with good intentions, democratic, as I had often heard her say. "I do not feel toward my servants as many people do," she would remark on the veranda. "I think of them as human beings, every bit as good as I am." In her humanitarian ardor, she called on us one Sunday on her way home from church, crept to the door with a soundlessness which may very likely have been calculated in spite of her charity. She caught me in tears, their cause being vague in my mind now, for I could have been brooding either over Nathan or over my mother. But I explained them to Mrs. Prather as being brought on by headaches from which I was never free. She refused to accept my reason and, offering me a handkerchief which she carried in a tatted pouch and smelled faintly of scent and, as if I were five years old, producing a lemon drop from a paper bag in her pocket, she begged me to tell her "all about it." I stuck to my guns and she asked then to see my mother, but I replied that she was in mourning and did not wish to speak with anyone.

After this visit, I sometimes overheard my name spoken on the veranda and I was said to be "looking badly." The voices were lowered as the ladies explained why I did. Some believed that I was anemic; others thought that my mother was ill and that my pallor came from staying up with her at night. No one suspected her of being mad, but they delighted in talking about Ivan whose epilepsy had been reported to them in as much detail as he could recollect, by Gonzales when he drove them from the station. A number of them said that the disease was hereditary and either through loyalty to their sex or through expostulation of my father whom they had never ceased to discuss, they designated him as its transmitter. They were opposed by the group who maintained that epilepsy was acquired after a blow on the head or an attack of scarlet fever.

Miss Pride, of course, took no part in these discussions, but possibly in the intention of showing the other guests that she had an interest in me far more generous than theirs, which was merely clinical, conversed with me as I served her. Far from elevating her in their estimation, her gesture was deprecated as bad taste and disservice to myself. "She won't go to heaven by bending over backwards to that child, pretending to be a Little Sister of the Poor, when she wouldn't part with a red cent of her precious money," it was said vindictively. "My word! You can't get credit for *talk!*" The old ladies were more displeased with Miss Pride this summer than ever, for the young Dr. McAllister was a frequent guest at her table and it was so arranged that it was never possible for anyone else to engage him in conversation. What if he *was* a personal friend of hers? Were not physicians, in a sense, public property? Consequently, since Dr. Galbraith, whose death was long and solemnly lamented, could not be consulted over the soup and since his successor never came to the Hotel for meals, Miss Pride's monopoly of the market was found intolerable. Finally someone hit upon the hypothesis that she had paid for his education and had offered to set him up in practice, the bribery being motivated by her desire to marry off her troublesome niece to him.

It was quite true that the chief interest in common between Miss Pride and Philip McAllister was Hopestill, proof of which required only the most casual eavesdropping. But it was also true that Miss Pride had known the young man's family for many years and had moved in the same feminine circles as his mother, who had gone that summer to London, and his grandmother. Dr. McAllister's father, a retired Unitarian minister, used sometimes to come to see his son and always made a point of lunching at the Hotel. I took pains to stay as near them as possible so that I might not miss any of their talk. The Reverend McAllister was withered and singed and clad from head to toe in decent black. All that relieved his funereal attire was a gold watch chain across his convex middle from which hung a Phi Beta Kappa key. He was a dabbler in oddities. He knew, for instance, that the armadillo always bore identical quadruplets; he offered this news with a brief, factual account of the duck-billed platypus, but he went no further, although Mrs. McKenzie, who overheard him, was enchanted and pressed him for details. Or he would trace at length the development of spiritism, but far from discussing it in the light of his religious tenets, he merely presented the case as though it had no bearing on anything else. Gravely he would imitate the Fox sisters, "Ho, Mr. Slipfoot, are you there?" Or, if he were invited to express his opinion of Christian Science, he would repeat an anecdote he had heard about Mrs. Eddy which was perhaps illustrative of his feeling but which suggested, to his discredit, that that was all he knew about Christian Science. He was, as his son remarked of him once, the kind of man who came out ahead in pen and pencil games.

Miss Pride did not particularly like "the Reverend" though she respected him, for she had been taught that it was improper not to respect the cloth. She said in a low voice to a friend who had come to dine with her, "He is a very good Christian, I grant you, but he's a frightful bore."

The friend, a woman with a broad, innocent face, said, "I can't believe he's a bore, Lucy, though I've only met him once or twice. Why, I was dumfounded, when I dined at his house once, at the size of his theological library. And the books were so worn, so obviously *studied*. No, indeed, a man who has read that much can't be a bore."

"I don't think Reverend McAllister *has* read them all," said Miss Pride with a malicious glint in her eyes. "As for their being worn, my dear, haven't you heard of second-hand shops? But I'm not singling him out. I think the clergy has fallen into the sere and yellow leaf where learning is concerned. Last New Year's Eve, I went to Estelle Hornblower's at home and was literally forced by Lincoln Nephews to go into the little white parlor where six ministers were sitting about like a plenary council. Lincoln had said, 'Lucy, I want to show you something straight out of Trollope.' Three of the creatures were Anglo-Catholics and were, I do believe, the poorest Latinists I have ever seen. They were talking about *On the Sublime and the Beautiful* by Theophrastus! Well, the Reverend was there. 'Hold on,' says he, 'Theophrastus isn't your man. He wrote those little vignettes you call *characters*.' 'Nonsense,' said one of the Anglicans, 'I'm not so rusty on my English as not to know those little things—sometimes I believe they're called hornbooks—were a seventeenth-century invention. But if Theophrastus didn't write *On the Sublime and the Beautiful*, who did, pray?' Do you know not one of them knew and Lincoln Nephews had to set them right?"

"Well, *I* wouldn't have known," said Miss Pride's friend. "I'm so ignorant I would never be able to criticize the clergy in that way. But in case I'm some time asked, who *did* write it?"

There was an imperceptible pause. "Why, Lucretius," said Miss Pride. "I thought everyone took that in with his mother's milk." But a little later on, she interrupted an anecdote her friend was telling to say, "You'll tell me that people who live in glass houses shouldn't throw stones. Didn't I just say Lucretius wrote *On the Sublime and the Beautiful*? I must have been asleep, for as I perfectly well know it was Longinus."

However much she deprecated in private his want of education, she was so cordial to the minister when he took a meal with her that I began to wonder if the old ladies' conjecture had not been in part correct, that is, that she was anxious to make a match between her niece and his son. For it was only in the presence of these two men that she had nothing but good to say of the girl. Hopestill's defiance of convention was transformed at these luncheons into her "high spirits, her vigor." Her beauty, ordinarily spoken of as "something about her that her extreme clothes brings out which I find very strange," was alluded to with respect. She became "intelligent" instead of "foxy." But the Reverend was deaf to all these virtues of Miss Mather because he wanted to inform the company that some things had not changed with the times at all, that in reading Emerson's letters he had discovered that the train fare from Concord to Boston was exactly the same in 1860 as it was today. The young man, to whom Hope's graces were not news, as soon as possible effected a transition to another subject, less, I thought out of embarrassment than annoyance because he knew Miss Pride spoke with shameless insincerity. Usually, he would inquire of her how she was progressing with her memoirs. "Hush!" she would say in real consternation. "You must not broadcast that. I'd be the laughing-stock of Boston if anyone knew. But since you ask, I'll tell you quite frankly that at times I despair. There is more to writing even of this sort than meets the eye. If I had a secretary, I feel that I could simply fly through them. The difficulty is that my sentences look so undistinguished when I see them in my own handwriting." She would glance at me as though to say that she had not forgotten our conversation in her library, and the young doctor, following her eyes, would briefly ponder me.

It was a midsummer night, cool after a sultry day. Gonzales had picked a bouquet of tea-roses and bridal wreath for my mother and I was taking them home, after work about nine o'clock. My mother, her face streaming with perspiration, was sitting beside the stove in which she had built up a raging fire that roared through the open damper. For further warmth she was wearing the old hooded wrapper and my sheep-lined slippers.

"Why, Mamma, why have you built a fire? It's like a furnace in here!"

I saw that despite her dripping face she was shivering and her teeth chattered between her words as she said, "Maybe you don't feel the cold if you're full of brandy. Not everybody has the good luck to have a little something to warm them up on the inside." The steady accusation in her eyes did not waver, and then I observed that the kitchen was in disorder. The shelves had been ransacked and half their useless objects had been thrown down so that broken glass and monkey wrenches and empty cans lay in a nondescript heap on the floor. Weeks before, at Dr. McAllister's injunction, I had taken the bottle of brandy to the shop. I said nothing.

"I suppose fairies drank it," said my mother. "I suppose the same little fairies that stole the golden egg so a person couldn't buy so much as a thimbleful of wine when they were dying of the cold. I guess they locked the door so a sick woman couldn't get a breath of fresh air if she needed it. It couldn't have been the invalid's daughter, oh, no."

I had often rehearsed my speech but as it issued, it sounded flat and false. My unsteady voice belied the words: "Yes, Mamma, I did lock the door. I didn't want to worry you and so I didn't tell you. A lot of houses have been robbed this last week and I didn't want the burglars to come here. You know how you lose yourself in your work and sometimes don't even hear me when I come in. I didn't want you to be taken by surprise."

She rolled her head crazily round and round, stopped, grinned at me, and rolled it again, repeating in what I suppose she thought was an imitation of my father, "*Ja, ja, ja, ja, ja, ja!*" Though the effort of moving in this inferno was exhausting, I started to clear the table, for usually at this hour we had a glass of lemonade and a sandwich of sardines or cheese. "Don't touch my belongings!" cried my mother. "Don't you dare!"

"Oh, Mamma!" I said, hoping to hide my alarm under impatience. "Don't be silly, Mamma. I'm not going to do anything to your lovely table-runners. I'm only going to fix us a little supper."

"Come here a minute, Sonie," she wheedled. "Come over by my chair. I want to tell you a secret." I advanced with dread and knelt down when she touched my shoulder. "Closer, sweetheart. There." She pushed back my hair and pressed her lips to my ear. "I hate you!"

I tried to rise, but she had put her arm around my shoulders, holding me against her with prodigious strength and I felt that she had barely tapped her resources, that if she desired, she could crush my bones. And as she had used to do when my father was her victim, she repeated her words half a dozen times in a monotone but with a crescendo which was meant less to convince me than herself. Sweat poured from our close faces and I felt its tickling rivulets down my back inside my dress. I begged my mother to release me, but she was not sure that we both understood yet and she continued to reiterate her declaration until, like my father, I cried, "Then leave me alone! Let me go!"

She did let me go. She jerked me to my feet with her superhuman strength and, like a skilled wrestler, hurled me to the floor. My head struck the leg of the sink and dazed me for a minute as she stood looking down. I implored her to believe that I had not locked the door to torment her, that the brandy was all gone, that the golden egg had been spent years before. At each of my attempts at speech, she again rolled her eyes round and round and hooted, "*Ja, ja, ja, ja!*" She drew her chair to the sink and sat down, daring me to try to stir. I lay still. In a few minutes, I could feel the sweat spreading in a pool all about me. My mother leaned across to the table and turned down the lamp, but by the starlight from the window I could still see her glistening face, beatified in the repose that had settled for a time on her lips and in her eyes. If I rose up on my elbow or stretched my legs or rubbed my head which still ached, her crazy skull commenced its revolutions and the "*ja, ja!*" came forth like the rasping of an imperfect machine.

The heat made me drowsy and though I fought off sleep I surrendered to it for brief, troubled fractions of the hours my mother guarded me. Then I awoke, my head throbbing, my flesh swollen and drenched to see her shining eyes which, so far as I could tell, had not left me for a second. Each time, I heard a loud popping or dripping somewhere outside the house, like water falling drop by drop on metal or like a sheet of tin cracking with expansion. Confused, I imagined it to be hot outdoors and I dreaded the morning and the progress of the day towards noon, that debilitating hour of fire when the heat shimmered in visible undulations over the grass and the sun, the tyrant of the bright blue skies, roasted one like a sucking pig, unstuck the pores of the body so that the sweat poured forth like water from a tap, slackened the senses, and benumbed the mind. It was as if the streaming of my flesh was in anticipation of that hour. Then my mind cleared; I remembered that there was a fire in the stove. I heard the ocean and longed to bathe my scorched body in it; my throat was parched; I conceived the sound as the slow leak of an ice-cold spring. Once I murmured, "Mamma, can I have a glass of water?" but my plea evinced only her derisive grimace and her absurd "*ja, ja!*"

A little while after the church bells struck midnight, my mother fell asleep in her chair, her head resting against the corner of the sink. I sat up slowly lest I rouse her, took off my shoes and then I crept, inch by inch, backwards to the door. As I passed the stove, its dying but still ferocious fire made me feel faint and ill. I gained the door and stood up; I could see her still in the light from the window. She had not stirred. I slid back the bolt and went out, brought the outer key from my pocket and locked my mother in, and then, revived by the salt breeze, I ran in my bare feet over the sandy path to the shop. The shop was cool and damp and I shivered with the sweet change. I put a piece of smooth leather to my cheek, then pressed my forehead against the windowpane, then coiled the cold rosary into my hand. Coolest was the bottle of brandy which I held in the crook of my arm. I did not go to sleep again for fear my mother, waking up, would find some way out of the house. I remembered how Ivan had told me that if he ran to the shop to escape her, she came to the window and peered in at him. I sat at my desk playing Patience by candlelight. Maudie had taught me half a dozen variations and I played them all, winning often and easily. The dawn was an eternity in coming and yet it was not four o'clock when the gray impinged upon the black shadows and I could see the dim outlines of the Boston water front where lights still burned. In another hour the lobster men set forth; I saw their green dories and their small, white motor boats and heard their terse greetings to one another. But the signs of normal human activity and the faithful daylight did not, as they used to do when I was a little girl, rout my fear. My legs were bruised where I had fallen, and my head ached, no longer from its blow against the sink but from the beginning of a cold. I sneezed and wished for a handkerchief. I knew that I must leave the shop before it was any lighter, for I did not want my mother, waking, to see me through the window, but afraid that she was already awake, I lingered a little longer in indecision.

At the first flush of the sun I slipped out, stooped down low as I passed the house, then ran till the wind whistled in my ears, in the direction of the hospital. My bare feet stung and my temples throbbed, but now that I was actually escaping her I was conscious of nothing but my terror, and if I had paused, it would not have been to stop my little pains, but to look back to make sure that she was not coming. I flew down the street where Nathan and I had dallied by the lilac bushes and noticed that the dead flowers were rusty among the green leaves, but just beyond them on lattices or against the walls of the houses, morning glories had opened up their bright blue horns. Taking the short-cut, I ran past Mr. Greeley's mortuary where a green neon sign burned still in the front window: "Chichester Funeral Parlor." In a moment, when I had turned

a corner, I saw the hospital at the end of its concrete driveway
and to my relief, saw that the operating room on the top floor
was illuminated with a livid blue light. I remembered that Dr.
McAllister was the anesthetist. Uppermost in my mind then
was my need for a handkerchief before I presented myself to
him.

3

Dr. McAllister called for me every Sunday morning to drive me
to Wolfburg. West and south of Boston, the asylum was not
far from a farm where his aunt, with a large staff of gardeners
and farmers, grew apples, roses, wheat, cows, and guinea hens.
She, her nephew told me, would have liked to believe that she
pitched hay, milked cows, churned butter, and cooked for the
harvest men. Although the young man freely joked about her
to me, almost a complete stranger, he was very fond of her and
told me that he would not miss his Sunday luncheon with her
for the world. I had not believed him at first, thinking that the
aunt was apocryphal and manufactured to allow me to accept
his charity. But Miss Pride, who knew of our expeditions, said,
"I dare say Philip McAllister likes having company when he
goes to see his aunt. You must ask him sometime to drive you
past her place. Her roses are so splendid that I have often said
she should go into the florist business."

While the drive to Wolfburg was either tedious (if I wished
the visit to be over quickly) or too swift (if I particularly
dreaded this day with my mother), the drive back was delightful. It was the late afternoon when the air was unburdening
itself of the weighty heat and the tight sky was split with pink
clouds. I would have liked to walk a little way into the groves
we passed, where twisting avenues, flowery and humid, opened
sometimes in a delta at the highway. But the desire was a lazy
one and equal to it was the wish that I might go along this
way hours longer, my obligations behind me, and all about me
the embracing summer, most tranquil at this cooling hour,
gentlest on this kind of road where the sheen upon the leaves
proclaimed the heat and the shade between the tree-trunks
proclaimed its compensation. The opulent overflow of verdure,
berries, flowers, was arrested like the subject of a picture.

When we reached Chichester, it had been dark half an hour and Boston was alight. I stood on the steps of our house, watching the doctor drive away, and stood a little longer looking up at the Barstow where Miss Pride's three front windows were rosy with the light that came through her striped curtains. It was then, when I entered the house that I realized more clearly than when I had been with her that my mother was no longer here, but in the vast, labyrinthine asylum where she was known by number and species. The mustard-yellow enameled walls of the main corridor were lined with hard benches where we, the visitors, sat bolt upright with cold, fixed faces as if we wished it clearly understood that we had no desire to sympathize or compare notes with one another. The blatant squawk of the girl at the address microphone came through ubiquitous concealed outlets: "Dr. Sho-ort." Or, in nasal ridicule, "Dr. *Fink*elstein." I could tell by the impatience with which they sometimes flung down their magazines that the other visitors detested the bodiless parrot as I did, and I wondered if they, too, desired to talk back to it, or, even better, to seek it out in its vociferous den and, if necessary, strangle it. One by one we were summoned to the gray cubicles where the jovial doctors in charge of our "case" glanced through a manila folder at typewritten sheets, the slowly accumulating history, the record of the arduous battle. As I passed down the corridor in the wake of a matron, silent with ill-nature or boredom or perhaps with the mere consciousness that she was sane, I peeped through the open doors of the offices and saw that all the other doctors looked like mine: their broad, red faces glowed with health; rimless spectacles sat on their neat tan noses; their grandiose condescension gave their voices a vast range of pitch, from a high amiability to a deep-toned expression of totally indifferent regret.

But it was neither the waiting nor the short visit with my mother that distressed me. It was the knowledge, after I had lighted the lamp in the house where she had always lived, that I had left her behind and that perhaps at this very moment she was imagining what I was doing. It was usually an hour before I was quieted, and then I began to read. Later, if the memory of her empty, staring eyes or her incoherent words came to me, I rationalized, said that she did not suffer as much as I since she was barely aware of her surroundings. I repeated to myself the doctor's exhortation that I must not feel guilty. His advice called him forth to replace my mother, and I searched the conversation we had just concluded for clues of how he felt towards me, if I were anything more to him than an element of a case that had been foisted upon him.

I had been nervous, on the first of these drives to Wolfburg, recalling that Miss Pride had said the young man was "brainy" and I feared that he would discover that I was ignorant, that he would report his finding to Miss Pride, and that I would fall from favor. Consequently, I spent the Saturday evening before the trip poring over the several copies of *The Atlantic Monthly* which had come and memorized certain facts about Russia, about overproduction, about co-operatives. But my preparation was unnecessary. Dr. McAllister shaped the conversation to suit himself and I was relieved of any responsibility. He was principally interested, I found, in religion, but I was never sure whether he was religious or merely inquisitive. When he spoke of the survival of the churches in the Soviet Union and said he longed to go to Russia to see how religion accomplished its ends under official atheism, he spoke as someone might who wished to visit Heidelberg to hear medieval drinking songs in a country where only German was spoken, or to see pagan rites in Christian Mexico. I had told him once that my father was a Catholic and he questioned me in detail on fasting, confession, and holy days of obligation. Only occasionally could I give him an answer, and he marveled at my want of knowledge but marveled even more at my father's neglect of my spiritual education. He had heard (again his information was a tourist's) that no nation had bred a more devout species of Roman Catholics than Germany. And he observed, "If you had been brought up a Catholic, you'd know how to feel toward your mother, I dare say. You'd know so much better than I, a doctor, that you'd have no need of the advice I've given you." On another occasion, he asked me if I had ever heard my father speak of the Cistercians. "If I were a monk, that would be the order I would choose. I sometimes think there would be nothing pleasanter than a vow of silence."

I had noticed on my first visit to him in the hospital that his posture made one think his bones were of an unbending substance and when I observed over a period of time that he never relaxed, I inquired of Miss Pride if she did not admire his carriage. "Not at all," she returned, "but I do admire his fortitude." She told me then that, afflicted as a child with infantile paralysis, he had been able to assume only two positions, that one perfectly erect, the other bent nearly double at the waist. When he settled upon medicine as a career, he wished to be a surgeon and subjected himself to an operation of great delicacy which, if it were successful, would allow him to move freely. A surgeon could not be limited to a perpendicular position and a forty-five degree angle. The operation, involving the replacement of some of the atrophied spine, was followed by a period of twelve months in a cast from which he was released, totally unbenefited. He had had then to abandon his ambition. He did not reveal his disappointment to anyone, said Miss Pride, and refused to recognize his "handicap" or to refer in any way to what he might have been if his luck had been better. I think he endured a great deal of pain, at times, and I pictured him when he was alone, giving in to the agony that he had reined in all day just as I, on Sundays, delivered myself to the dejection that had been engrafted in me by the visit to the asylum earlier in the day. And as this gloom seemed to await me in my house, like a devilish creature that I had promised myself to on the condition that it would not come out into the light when I was still with my friend, so I thought that Dr. McAllister unleashed his tormentors in his room and permitted them to do as they liked with him for the season of his solitude.

Unlike Nathan whose disfigurement had given him a morbid appetite for abuse—turned either against himself or against those who he imagined laughed at him—Dr. McAllister had taken his much greater deformity almost as a gift of Providence, for, forced by the needs of his body into frequent hours of leisure, he had had the time to read extensively. But the leisure was work and if he relaxed his sickened muscles, he allowed his mind no rest. He slept no more than four hours, originally for the sake of discipline and later because his strict self-denial produced in him a habitual insomnia. He had told me, when I came to the hospital at five in the morning, that he had only just been preparing for bed when he was summoned to the operating room at four o'clock. The evening, he said, he had spent in studying a Russian grammar, suggested to him by the inconsequential babblings of my mother.

It was perhaps because he knew the whole of my story and had even lived through a chapter of it himself that he took an interest in me which was disproportionate to any offering I was capable of making him. Or it might have been, instead, that the Sunday drives were a prolonged but unconscious apology for his unjustified rebuke on the occasion of my first visit to his office when he thought I was seeking an abortionist. No mention was made of his mistake again, not, I am sure, because a review of the incident would have caused him any embarrassment, but because he had forgotten it when I ceased in his mind to be the kind of young woman liable to the charge. He thought that the principle of my being was a fanatical filial piety, carried to a degree that necessarily excluded the sort of selfish attachment which could terminate in so sordid a dilemma as an illegitimate pregnancy. His misconstruction, his over-simplification of my relationship with Mamma made me suspect, sometimes, that he had not the insight into people which is, we are told, the prerequisite of the successful physician. Now neither had Dr. Galbraith understood our household but for a different reason. He had been a blind man leading the blind. But Philip McAllister, through an intellectual, an almost literary faith in the perfectability of human nature, believed that had I not been completely devoted to my mother, I should long ago have run away from home. Thus, assigning to me the sanguine humor in distinction to the bilious or the choleric, he neglected to take into account the fourth, that is, the phlegmatic, which made up at least half of my composition. But whatever his motive was, he succeeded in my gradual reformation. By respecting my loyalty to my mother, he unwittingly shamed me into a real loyalty whose articulation was my faithful weekly visit to the asylum which came, in time, to be essential to my life. Although nothing was accomplished and frequently I was not allowed to see her (For she had seasons of bitter hatred for me as the cruellest of all her persecutors. These came when something sharpened her senses and she realized where she was.), I was determined to regain her love just as the sometimes uncertain communicant is determined to learn faith through his reception of the holy wafer and his prayers.

Yet I sometimes confessed to myself that I was exactly the opposite of the altruist. The renascence of her love would gain more for me than for her; mine was a craven peace-making. I was further hypocritical in that I acted for the young doctor's applause. Just as I had concealed from Miss Pride the marks of sleepless, undisciplined nights, in the doctor's presence I feigned joy at seeing my mother again after seven days' separation, and, on the return, grief at her unhappiness. We can be over-scrupulous, beg our confessors to double our punishment since they, we declare, have been too innocent to grasp the magnitude of our sin. We can, in love, doubt that we really love and suspect that we have bluffed our lover into the passion which will at any moment perish when he sees we have won him with half lies; or, brooding over a slip of the tongue, a misstatement, we can convince ourselves that our minds are really stupid and that all our words are fraudulent. Our conscience is speaking to us in parables. Thus, my desire to become once more the center of my mother's life was earnest. What was contemptible was my publication of it to the doctor as if it could not stand alone, or as if since it could engender no reward for me I must seek his praise for compensation.

His education of me had its more practical specialties. Where I had heretofore read at Miss Pride's prescription and had felt false to her standards if I had chosen something not primarily useful, I now, at the doctor's advice, followed my own inclinations, and was even persuaded that the writers she most admired, that is, James Russell Lowell and Emerson, were by no means inviolable and that the mortar of her ivory tower was chauvinism, not knowledge or taste. For observe, Dr. McAllister counseled me, she was uncritical of style and uninterested in a writer's conception of truth, but if he had been buried in the Sleepy Hollow Cemetery at Concord or lay in a less illustrious but still New England graveyard, he was a great man. She believed neither in Emerson's oversoul nor in Thoreau's religion of blueberries and Walden Pond; she was unimpressed by Henry Adams' genius, had even remarked once that he was a little too long-winded for her liking. I was not disillusioned by this exposé, but on the contrary delighted in her consistency, deplored by her demigod as the hobgoblin of little minds.

But at the same time, I was liberated from the tyranny of *The Atlantic* and of Harriet Martineau's peregrinations.

It was towards the end of the summer that Dr. McAllister first asked me what I proposed to do after the Hotel had closed. I told him that Mrs. Brunson had invited me to be Maudie's successor. (Maudie had gone to Idaho as soon as the Brunsons left for Provincetown. She went by bus, taking with her a quart bottle of whiskey and parting from me with a hearty handclasp and the exclamation, "Idaho, here I come! It's round-up time for this here old bench.") The doctor said, "Is that what you want to do?" As if I were speaking to him in his professional capacity and telling him the symptoms of a disease which I knew to be incurable, I told him that since I could remember my goal had been Boston, that the only career I had imagined for myself was serving Miss Pride as her housemaid or her laundress or her lady-in-waiting.

"I dare say that could be arranged," he said. "She spoke to me the other day of getting a secretary and I'm under the impression that she had been thinking of you. She is very fond of you, you know."

I was not so pleased as I felt I should have been. It was as if she had sent the doctor as her ambassador for some obscure purpose of which even he did not know. And I was invaded by the same doubt of her that I had felt when she brought the cyclamen after Ivan's death and I had seen her in the winter sunlight for the briefest moment as an old, ugly woman inspired by a tenuous and urbane evil. But the doctor's blue eyes, in which were registered many thoughts in no way connected with me, were so ingenuous that I was convinced he spoke the truth and that she was, indeed, fond of me.

"That was good of her," I said. "But it doesn't help me, because I have no qualifications to be her secretary."

"But even that is of no importance. I've told you, I think, that she's thought to be one of the most generous women in Boston and there is no reason why she shouldn't send you to a business college."

On an impulse that I regretted and in which I heard myself speaking with Nathan's irascible and naïve resentment of wealth, I told the doctor how Miss Pride had conveniently arrived in Chichester the day after Ivan was buried in the potter's field, although I was certain she had got my letter sometime before. He answered with a laugh, "You don't understand the first article in the philanthropist's code which is that one never takes suggestions but always hunts on his own hook for the places where his money will do good. If it weren't for that, I would have suggested myself that she send you to a business school. As it is, we must simply wait and see if it occurs to her. And if it doesn't, that still won't mean you can't go to Boston. I'm a native of the place too and have ways of getting young ladies jobs. I might even hire you as my receptionist, though you wouldn't like that."

Our conversation took place on the last Sunday he drove me to Wolfburg. In the middle of the next week he was leaving Chichester for a vacation in Manchester where, as I knew, Hopestill Mather was spending the summer. Afterwards, he was going back to Boston to begin his practice in an office, outfitted by his doting mother with glass brick partitions, a costly imitation Kashmir, lucite magazine tables where would lie what she called "the leading periodicals" and the alumnus bulletins of Groton and Harvard. He had described the appointments of his office with what I felt was an unwarranted sarcasm and had told me that if I were ever ill, after I had come to Boston to live, I must allow him to examine me with his Shreve, Crump, and Low stethoscope kept in a Mark Cross case.

He shook my hand when he had stopped before my house and said, "Good luck. Perhaps we'll meet again in Boston." But I felt no promise in his words. I felt that he was already absorbed in the mainland while I was re-dedicated to my insularity and as, from the corner of my eye, I saw the lighted window at the Kadishes' and the shadow of Nathan's younger brother, I read the doctor's optimistic sentence as the epilogue to my long, feverish dream. A few hours later, reasoning that actually I had never been closer, that he was a more persuasive advocate than I could ever have been myself, I realized that I had not felt my isolation from the house on Pinckney Street confirmed forever, but that I had known I should never navigate the space between his planet and mine. The acceptance, without the least titillation, of the window which had once enshrined my first lover's birthmark, on reflection brought me, like a slow-working liquor, to a luxurious intoxication and I knew that for a second time I was in love.

My house was cool and it smelled of oranges that had faintly rotted in the window-sill. I wished that I had asked Philip McAllister to come in to drink some brandy so that in the course of an hour I might feed upon his mobile face and his rich voice. I went no further in my demands, but I knew that so long as I remembered him, the light from the window next door would have no power to make me regret or desire or stew in anger.

On the Sunday after Dr. McAllister left, Miss Pride came to my house, catching me, to my consternation, reading the comic strips instead of, as we would have both preferred, finding me ensconced behind the last issue of *The Atlantic Monthly* or Mr. Emerson's *Self Reliance*. I had been lying on the floor, moreover, on my belly and had been breakfasting, as I read, on a banana and a jellied doughnut. When I sprang to my feet at the sight of her standing primly at my kitchen door, I put the inflated doughnut, oozing out its raspberry heart, on the shelf amongst the pipes and tools and empty jars. My guest had never been in the house before (or anything like it, I suspected) and as we talked, she examined everything, not overlooking the remains of my disgraceful meal, with extreme care as if she were trying to find one object less dreadful than the rest. With a candor that was both brutal and complimentary, since it assumed that my taste was akin to her own, she asked me if I did not find the two pictures above the table appalling. I agreed and she said, "I knew you wouldn't mind my speaking plainly. It is one of the privileges of age." Now I had some years before acquired an animadversion to the little girls and the springer spaniels and to the barnyard and, because I idealized him, I could not imagine what had possessed my father to buy them. But I concealed the identity of their purchaser by saying, "They were in the house when my father came. He always hated them but my mother was fond of them." She ignored this false and cowardly aspersion on my mother and stated the purpose of her visit.

"I thought, since Sunday is not one of my motoring days, that perhaps I could lend you Mac and my car for your trips. I told Dr. McAllister that he was rude not to warn me sooner that he was leaving. It only occurred to me this morning when I was served by the substitute waitress. I had forgotten it was Sunday."

I thanked her, not without noting privately that she herself was leaving Chichester a week from today. But she went on, "And something else came to my mind at the same time. Perhaps I mentioned the memoirs I hope to write this winter? And didn't I tell you I needed a secretary to do the 'dirty work'? I know you haven't the qualifications but after all you could go to a school of some sort to learn, couldn't you? The fact is that my niece who, as you know, has been living with me, is going to New York for the winter and I shall quite rattle about by myself in my house. I would like to offer you your lodgings as well as the trifling gift of your tuition. Would you be interested?"

She rose and drew on her gloves as if the matter had been settled and her question had only been rhetorical. I stammered, "Oh, Miss Pride, you are very kind to me!"

She glanced at the floor where my rainbow funny papers lay and I was not sure that she would not retract her invitation. But she said, looking up at me again, "Not at all. Now Mac is right outside and I'm going to walk back to the Hotel so you can start out to see your mother." She started to the door but turned. "My dear, you won't bring your pictures to my house, will you?"

BOOK TWO
PINCKNEY STREET

Chapter One

THE BACK BAY Business College was a morose establishment in a once fine house on Dartmouth Street, now infested with tongue-tied girls who seemed always on the verge of tears under the persistent scoldings of the mistress, a vulpine woman in her forties who regarded herself as an educator. Had we been a little younger, I am sure Mrs. Hinkel would have rapped our bungling fingers with a ruler, for incompetence inspired in her the most ardent displeasure. At the very beginning, she had singled me out for especially lusty maledictions, insisting that I was wasting my money and her time, for I would never in a thousand years learn to operate a typewriter with any more skill than a dog. What aggrieved her the most in me was the "reach stroke" of my right fourth finger for which she held a marveling contempt: "Class, gather and observe! Observe the fantastic reach stroke Miss Marburg deludes herself into thinking is the *proper* reach stroke. Learn by this example if you ever hope to make an asterisk visible to the naked eye!" In other branches of my commercial education, I was somewhat abler, being at the top of the class in Business English (because I could immediately distinguish between the nominative and the subjective cases and because the subjunctive mood did not baffle me) and being known as a "good worker" in the shorthand class.

The student body strikingly resembled the staff. They were all torpid and bird-like by turns and their humor consisted in such expressions as "I see, said the blind man," and "Well, laugh, I thought I'd die." I ate my lunch at a drug-store with five or six of my classmates who discussed silk stockings and serials in the *Ladies' Home Journal.* They could talk for three quarters of an hour, without any waning of interest, about the confections peculiar to the Boylston Street Schrafft's. The intimacy of the group (they referred to one another's sisters by their given names and inquired after mothers and fathers and aunts) made me suppose that they were old friends and had gone to school together and I felt, therefore, that my exclusion from their talk was not my own fault. I learned in time, however, that they had never met before the first day of classes at what they jokingly called "dear old Back Bay." The discovery made me feel immature and when I could, I avoided these womanly lunch hours, not through snobbery, but through a sense of maladjustment.

I detested the business college, but at the same time it afforded me a contrast to the rest of my life without which I might have come to regard as habitual those things which gave me keen pleasure. I enjoyed the retreat I made each day from the gray plaster walls, the methodical accent of the typewriters, and Mrs. Hinkel's dour face in which her acerbity was coagulated in a large, asymmetrical, nose. I went slowly through the Public Gardens at the hour of the exodus of the nursemaids who wheeled out the infant Cabots and the recalcitrant Chandlers. I crossed Charles Street and in traversing the asphalt boundary, entered dissimilar territory: the Common where orators and their satellites and their hecklers yelped and gestured with impotent passion. My own latchkey, fitted to the burnished lock of the white door, admitted me to the silent vestibule, in the dim light of which the mahogany tables, identical and facing one another, gleamed smoothly. Not a sound greeted me. As I pushed open the door to the empty drawing-room, I heard the crackling fire that had just been started. In another hour and a half, this room would be the scene of the comings and goings of Miss Pride's callers whose voices were carried up the stairwell and into my room.

Some afternoons, I stepped across the threshold and wandered about the drawing-room for a quarter of an hour, musing on how it would be when it was occupied by Miss Pride's friends. At first I had thought of the room as altogether Victorian, but after a few investigations, I saw that its objects were disparate and that the only really Victorian part of the room was the bay-window, furnished with an uncushioned love-seat of some stony black wood, the arms carved and embossed and curled; the feet of a stunted lion had been calcified and grafted on to the slender ankles of the seat's well-developed legs. On either side, stationed on the floor where presumably they got the morning light, were a variety of house-plants, no one of which laid claim to beauty. They were kept there and were replaced when they died (this happened rarely, their chief virtue being longevity) because they had been there forever just as a Pride or a tributary to the family had always lived in the house. Miss Pride detested them but would not have dreamed of having them removed; she was especially offended by one species which had large flat dusky leaves chased with pink striations. She did not know its name but called it after a kind of cookie it reminded her of, "Aunt Alice's Birthday Trifle" which had figured in her childhood. Evidently some former owner of the house had been a Francophile and another had fancied Oriental handiwork, for upon the ormolu top of a tulip-wood commode there sat a golden Buddha and above him on the white New England wall hung two Japanese prints of long ladies, long herons, and long sprays of wistaria. Yet at the Buddha's feet, as if to confirm the nationality of the commode, lay aimlessly an ivory-handled dagger of which the blade was inlaid with slate-blue *fleur-de-lis*. The sofas, high and stuffed with an inelastic substance, and the slipper chairs, low, velvety, resilient, had, like Aunt Alice's Birthday Trifle, grown up with the house and their removal was unthinkable although even Miss Pride admitted that they were hideous. Cluttered and inarticulate as it was, I preferred this room to the library, for it was lighter, being at the front of the house and carpeted with a buff rug sprinkled with rich, blue flowers, and its anachronisms imparted to it an atmosphere of geniality as if each heir had accepted the vagaries of the one who preceded him with good will and added his own in the same spirit. The library, on the other hand, was a formidable, masculine province, dominated by Mr. Pride and by several umbrageous ancestral portraits. The furniture was plain, solid, useful. Miss Pride had told me that on Christmas Eve when the revelers and carolers thronged Beacon Hill and one's door-bell rang a hundred times whether or not one had intended to hold open house, her father had read aloud to the servants from the Gospel according to Saint Matthew while in the drawing-room his daring wife, trembling with fear at her own importunity, served sillabub and *lebkuchen* to the visitors. In the library, too, President Eliot had been in the habit of spending two or three evenings a month playing chess with Mr. Pride. His daughter described to me one such evening, "My mother sent me down to ask Papa if they would have some Brazil nuts with their sherry. She was never content to let well enough alone. She was a regular doter. The gentlemen were in the midst of their game and my father, very much annoyed at the disturbance, put his finger to his lips and motioned to me not to move a step nearer the table. President Eliot looked up and through me; my father finished a play and said, 'Sir, for your sake, I regret the brilliance of my rook's performance, for it has won the game for me.' 'You apologized too soon, sir,' said Mr. Eliot and bending forward with a smile like the Cheshire cat's, he captured the rook and checkmated Papa. Then, without any further talk, they set up the men again and to my question would they like some Brazil nuts with their sherry, Papa curtly replied, 'No.' But President Eliot, without looking at me though he glared at my father, said, 'Speak for yourself, Mr. Pride. I, for my part, would relish Brazil nuts as a reward for my triumph.'"

After I had heard this story, I never went into the library without being intimidated by the ghosts of the scholarly chess-players, for their sturdy square table and the board and men remained beside the fireplace, and a decanter of sherry with two glasses stood waiting on a cabinet. At first I thought the preparations were a memorial, as important in the history of the family as the silver christening cups and the yachting trophies on display behind the glass doors of the cabinet, and that in time, when the house became a museum, a copper plate, attached to the table, would inform tourists that President Eliot had played chess there. But I was quite wrong: the table was in readiness for Miss Pride who, with a manual of famous gambits, worked through game after game by herself every Sunday morning before church, and the sherry, too, was kept there for her when, having defeated the white men with Phili-dor's Defense, she took her own reward and, braced, went off to King's Chapel. Occasionally she would play a game with one of her friends, but these trifling conquests took place in the upstairs sitting-room, for the namby-pamby stratagems of the amateurs would have desecrated the ivory and ebony men of the library who had been in the service of brilliant generals.

The contrast between the drawing-room and the library was not, of course, accidental. Their distinct gender dated from the time the house was built and the drawing-room was still the "withdrawing room" to which the ladies repaired after dinner. The curious thing to me was that Miss Pride, being without a master for her parties, played both rôles. One morning she asked me to fetch her an aspirin tablet for she had a headache as the result of "combining spirits." The evening before she had been detained in the drawing-room by a boring nobody so long that when she finally arrived in the library to unlock the liquor cabinet for the gentlemen's brandy and whiskey (she would never in the world have allowed her servants to perform this duty), they were quite languishing and the delay made them drink twice as much as they would have ordinarily, to her appreciable financial loss. And she, although she had already had her Cointreau with the ladies, was so loath to go back to the tiresome guest (she was one of those creatures who late in life had become domestic and on Thursdays experimented in the kitchen with such materials as junket and peanut butter, and on all the other days tired out her friends with forcing her barbarous receipts upon them) that she "took a breather" with the men.

Each day, I saw the first tea guests arriving, for when the sun began to set, I took up my post at the window of my bedroom and did not leave it until the momentary yellow light just preceding darkness had made all the leaves of Pinckney Street declamatory. I longed to see from the outside these windows through which I looked, but I could not relinquish the prospect I had of Louisburg Square, its dead grass and dumpy statues enlivened by the rich light while the iron palings reasserted their dead, absorbent blackness. At this hour, the letter-slots and knockers blazed; the marble lintels seemed as cool and old as something from an ancient palace. Long and lean, the houses deepened into purple with the decline of the sun. Far up the street, forming the background to a pattern of golden elm leaves, was a bright blue door. From time to time, a man in a derby and a black Chesterfield would briskly cross the square to our house, and in a moment I would hear the door-bell. Or a chauffeur would hand out a lady from a gleaming automobile. Talk and laughter presently surged up the stairs.

When the arc lights came on, I left the window and turned on the lamp beside my bed. My room sprang forth, enlarged, entirely changed by the light. The ceiling seemed immensely higher, the wide, polished doors as tall as a castle's portals. Even my single bed with its lace counterpane and folded puff was more luxurious. To the left of my double windows was a

massive, flat-topped writing desk with deep drawers on either
side which had been filled with watermarked paper, yellow
second sheets, onion skin and carbon paper. Its surface was
furnished with silver tools: letter openers, penknives, scissors,
boxes of paper clips and rubber bands, and postage stamps.
In a small upper drawer, there was pale green stationery with
our address embossed in small white letters. The typewriter
on which I practiced my home-work had its own stand at the
right corner of the desk so that I had only to turn my chair to
be facing it.

The joy my room gave me was, each day when I switched on
the lamp, so intense that my being required its articulation and
sometimes I could not see the deep mole-colored carpet and
the silvery draperies at the windows for my tears. Again, the
Breughel and the Vermeer and the Rembrandt prints, hanging on the ivory walls in double frames, could make me smile
smugly. As large as a room, my clothes-closet was equipped
with shelves for my expensive shoes, with padded hangers for
my evening dresses, and with a ceiling light so that I could see
to choose my costume. My bathroom was not adjoined but
was down the hall a little way. Six thick, white towels, monogrammed "L P" hung about the gleaming tub. The medicine
chest was filled with bottles of cologne, Miss Pride's soap, with
a tooth-powder made up by a Dartmouth Street pharmacist,
and with cans of faintly scented talcum powder.

On the left wall of my bedroom, near the fireplace, was a
locked door leading to Hopestill Mather's sitting-room. And
the windows above my bathtub gave on to a shaft across which
I could see the windows that corresponded to mine above her
bathtub. It was not until I had been in the house ten days
or more that I saw her apartment. A maid was preparing it
for her return from Manchester, and as I passed through the
hall, I stopped to ask the girl some needless question about
my laundry. I saw that it was true, just as I had imagined it,
that the room and the one beyond it to which the door stood
ajar was carpeted with green. In the generous bay-window was
a wine-colored *chaise-longue*. The fireplace was in the same
position as the one in the drawing-room, and in Miss Pride's
room directly below this. Over it hung a portrait of Hopestill
as a child. She wore a full-skirted white dress, ballet slippers,

and a green hair ribbon in her red hair. It was so striking a likeness that I could hear her voice calling across the dining-room, "Waitress! Water, please." On either side of the hearth were wing chairs upholstered in green and wine-red stripes. Beside each was a table underneath whose glass top showed bright Italian tiles and upon which stood *cloisonné* cigarette boxes, match-holders and ash-trays. Against the wall opposite the windows stood a delicate Victorian writing desk, flanked on either side by low shelves filled with books still wearing their glossy, gaudy jackets. Through the distant door, I caught sight of a mahogany highboy and the corner of a four-poster bed.

An hour after the tea guests had gone, I would join Miss Pride in the upstairs sitting-room where we had a glass of sherry and a light conversation, after which we went down to dinner. Sometimes she repeated an anecdote she had heard during the day or summarized a colloquy that had struck her fancy. Usually, though, she questioned me about my attitudes, interspersing her interrogation with pointers on conduct. One Friday night she requested me to come downstairs at tea time the following afternoon to be, as she said, "broken in," an unfortunate phrase since it was also the one she used in speaking of servants whom she had trained. I was never, she admonished me, to regard myself as a servant. But at this phase of my career, when I had learned little more at the commercial school than which were the "home keys" on the typewriter, she could not truthfully call me her secretary. Moreover, being a woman completely sufficient unto herself, she could not introduce me as her "companion" without discrediting herself or making her friends suspect that her eyesight was failing. Nor could she pretend that I was a distant relative or the daughter of an old friend who until now had been in boarding school in Switzerland, for it would take no more than one conversation for anyone to know that I had no connections with Boston and therefore none with herself. What I was, in point of fact, was her "case" or her "project" or whatever the word was that was then in fashion to describe the beneficiary of that allotment in a rich woman's budget called "Miscellany." But wishing to spare my feelings (and also because practicing charity under one's roof was seldom "done" unless the recipient was the orphan of a friend or relative who had been left with no money), she did not fancy my presentation in these terms. At first, it had been her intention to keep me imprisoned while she tutored me in etiquette and until I was able to operate a typewriter, but this plan soon appeared impracticable owing to the fact that my residence in the house had leaked out, presumably through the servants.

She had hit upon a solution at last. Until I should be qualified as a secretary and until she saw fit to admit publicly that she was going to write her memoirs, she gave me to understand that I was to offer no unsolicited information, but if I were pressed I was to say, quite truthfully, that I was studying to become the amanuensis of a writer whose name I was not at liberty to give, that she and I had met through Dr. McAllister and she had invited me to share her house which, in Hopestill's absence, would be too lonely even for her. I was permitted to say I was from Chichester but almost all the rest of my background was to be obliterated from my memory. Quite understandably she did not want it known that my mother was in an asylum. No more did I. There was little danger of the fact coming to light, for the summer residents of Chichester did not move in Miss Pride's circles nor anywhere near them, and the only link presenting any danger was Dr. Barker, who not only had a bad memory for names but was also opposed to gossip and would certainly never dream of repeating anything so banal as his sister's report of Chichester's insane woman.

Having set the hour for my début in her drawing-room, Miss Pride went on frankly to clarify her plans for me. I say "frankly," but the word is inexact, for her confessions were so subtly put and she displayed so ambiguous a wit that it was only after I had left her and had gone to my own room after dinner that I realized how stark had been her projection of the future. She was mortally afraid of growing old; if she were to dodder into half-crazed and ludicrous senility, as both her father and her mother had done, she wanted a caretaker to silence her, to dissuade her from both the crabbed and the maudlin antics of old age. She feared blindness (she, whose eyes at seventy had never been fitted with glasses) and dreaded being deprived of reading and of walking. "I don't fancy taking up phonograph records to amuse me at my age," she said scornfully. She was not sure I was the right custodian for her; that, only time could

tell, but she wished me to consider whether I should like to
think of myself as permanently installed in her house, and she
implied that I would not be forgotten in her will. I was grateful and happy at the prospect, even though it was impossible
for me to imagine her so changed as to need the services of
what amounted to a nursemaid. I told her that and she replied
grimly, "My dear, we're all fools before we're fetched by the
pale rider."

She dismissed me with that, but as I was passing through the
door, she said, "Hope returns tomorrow. I fancy she'll come
in about tea time."

"I am anxious to meet her."

Miss Pride looked directly into my eyes. "I am sure you
are," she said. "I have the feeling that you have a preconceived
notion of my niece."

"I saw her once, you know. She came to the Hotel some years
ago. Perhaps you don't remember."

"My life has not been so helter-skelter that I do not remember its events, Sonie," she replied. "Nor have I forgotten
Hopestill's dancing slippers."

A blush raced to the roots of my hair and my voice broke as
I said, "My father didn't finish them."

She smiled wryly. "Hope refused to go to the party without
them. I dare say if you had known that she spent that evening
in her room, howling for her slippers, you would have sent
them on." But while she twisted her dagger in me, her smile
changed to one of great friendliness and she added, "The battle
must begin early in our lives if we are to be victorious, isn't
that right?"

2

I had dressed with care, but although I had been leisurely, I
had a full hour before I could go down. Miss Pride had told me
that she had no intention of "presenting" me, that I was merely
to appear and "take things as they came." It would be better,
she told me, not to be too prompt. I moved impatiently about
my room, sat at my desk awhile and read one sentence over and
over in *The Rise of Silas Lapham* without ever comprehending
its meaning. Moving to the window, I sat for a while on the

ledge, shivering at the icy air that came through the cracks, and stared at a boy, dressed like a Harvard student, loping up Mount Vernon Street across the square. Something in his carriage reminded me of Nathan. Without any transitional thought, I turned back into my room and standing, one arm on the foot rail of my bed, I opened *The Confessions of a Young Man*. When I had promised myself, on the night Nathan and I sat in the fog on the steps of the Hotel Barstow, that I would have the best, I had allowed destiny to choose the circumstances for me. I had at no time doubted that the choice of Boston by my guardian angel had been supreme wisdom, that this was the soil in which my gifts, whatever they were, would fructify. And thus, when I read George Moore, and I read him constantly, I did so out of the desire to prove to myself that the "best" Nathan had wanted for himself and for me was in reality only second best. My talents were not artistic, not creative. I felt that they were assimilative and analytical, that what I saw in Boston, what I had seen in Chichester I understood, but that I could not reassemble my impressions into something artful. I could not ennoble fact. It was experience of the most complex order that I desired, and while there were times when, exploring the narrow streets of the back side of the Hill, I wished my knowledge to include the cafés and *ateliers* and the quays of George Moore's Paris, the wish was diluted as I turned toward home and thought of my room, of Miss Pride, and of our conversation over the sherry glasses. She, I thought, was worth all the freedom and all the abandon, worth, indeed, all triumphs.

I closed the book. Opening the door, I heard many voices rising up, and I knew it was time.

A dozen people were already drinking tea when I went into the drawing-room and were deep in conversation so that my entrance passed unnoticed save by an elderly gentleman, seated upon an ottoman though his years should have got him an easy chair. He rose at once and came toward me, fumbling in his coat pocket. "Hello, there!" he cried. When he had got midway and had put his eyeglasses on, he halted and said, "Oh, I thought you were Hope."

"No, sir, I'm Sonie Marburg."

He murmured something like "Well, that's nice," or "Well, I declare," but kindly offered me his hand anyhow, though he did not come nearer and I was obliged to go after it. I should have liked to prolong our handclasp since his plump fingers were warm, and I was chilled to the bone after this first day of cold weather in the Spartan temperature of Miss Pride's house. As I had come down the stairs just now where drafts blew out of the very walls, I had had to stop several times to rub my stiffening fingers together and to check the clatter of my teeth. But the weatherproof Bostonians, seated in the drawing-room which was not perceptibly warmer than the upper floors, were not only comfortable so that their bright cheeks glowed with excellent circulation, indeed, they had even suffered someone to "crack" a window through which came an unflagging blast of late fall air.

The old man's fingers abandoned mine too soon. He introduced himself as Admiral Nephews and then returned to his ottoman, leaving me where I had been intercepted, still faced with the problem of what to do with myself. I felt that I was undergoing a radical physical transformation and was sure that if I could look at my feet (I was prevented by the unshakeable rigidity of my neck) I would find them twice their normal size and that my hands, pendulous at my sides, had likewise doubled their proportions, while my neck and face were suffused with a rashy red. I was further certain that if I were called upon to speak, my voice would issue either croaking or inaudible. I was rescued by a sign from Miss Pride who, lifting neither a finger nor an eyebrow nor speaking my name, commanded me to come directly to the tea-table where she was officiating. So peremptory was her aspect which alone had beckoned me, as it had done in the dining-room of the Barstow, that had I been in the middle of a sentence or had someone been in the middle of one addressed to me, I should instantly have obeyed her.

"Take charge for a while," she said when I came to her. "I must speak to someone." Then, bending over as if to inspect the plate of lemon slices, she said in a much lower voice, "I think you should be more sparing of lip rouge." This was by no means the first reproof I had received since I had been in Boston. She had taken it upon herself to civilize me, or, as she called it, to "caulk" me, for, she said, not even the sturdiest vessel could weather such storms as I had without some damage. The "storms" were not so much the facts of my father's desertion, my brother's death, my mother's calamity, as they were the omissions in my upbringing. She had sent me out when I first arrived to buy my winter wardrobe and when I had returned with what had struck my fancy, she had at once sent for her car, taken me and all my purchases back to the shops and chosen my clothes herself. For, although I had bought four pairs of gloves, I had not bought a hat, and although the coat I had picked out was a formal Chesterfield, my shoes were all flat-heeled oxfords.

Out of sorts with the cold, terrified by the roomful of people, I might have risen at her criticism—not from resentment but from despair—and left the house had not Miss Pride immediately retired, placing in my hands the custody of the tea-table, and allowing me, by her quick departure, no time to worry my smart into a real state of mind. I was quite bewildered by the array of shining vessels before me and especially nonplussed at the sight of three pots of about the same size, any one of which might contain tea. Before I had time to lift up their lids to determine what was inside, the old man who had mistaken me for Hope Mather tottered up and extended his cup, winking so broadly that one whole side of his face was stitched up, and saying in a humorous stage whisper, "It's my fourth! I thought I'd get my refill when Lucy wasn't here, what?" I chose the wrong pot and filled his cup with hot water.

"Here, here!" he cried, laughing and turning away from me. "I say, Lucy! Did you tell this young lady here to give me water if I asked for any more tea? That's a good one! It's like the orderly I had on the *California*. He liked his gin, that chap. Well, ma'am, he drank so much of it that towards the end of an evening, his mates used to slip a bottle of water in front of him and if he said it tasted queer, those rascals told him his taste buds were paralyzed!"

By the sparse but indulgent laughter that followed the mild little anecdote, recited loud enough for anyone to hear, I judged that it was not a new one, and that the interest which lighted up the eyes of all the guests was not in the story-teller, but in myself who had been discovered, as if by accident, within the Admiral's orbit. Miss Pride alone did not laugh. She stood by the door to the dining-room, and it was only after she had transfixed me with a gaze of exasperation for my mistake, that she attended to what she had gone for and rang the bell for a servant. The others resumed their talk, but now and then stole a tactful look at me, pretending to be glancing at the portrait on the wall behind the sofa where I sat or to be merely making sure that the Admiral was still there.

"I beg your pardon," I said to him. "I really didn't intend to do it." I filled a new cup with tea and handed it up but neglected to offer him any accessories. "Oh, come, dear girl," he said, "you're treating me shabbily. I take two of sugar and *copious* cream. You youngsters these days don't believe much in tea, what? It's all cocktails for you, what? I remember, ma'am, that when I was a boy I had carving lessons and my sisters had lessons in the technique of the tea-table. Don't they teach that any more?"

"I don't know, sir."

"Where did you go to school, mademoiselle?"

"In Chichester."

"I didn't know there *was* a school in Chichester. I didn't know there was anything in Chichester except those humdinger cherry-stones and that scuttled hotel Miss Lucy Pride risks her life in every summer. Was it day or boarding?"

"It was a public school," I said apologetically.

"Oh!" said Admiral Nephews, drawing up a chair. "I dare say you wouldn't get anything fancy there. Perhaps it's just as well. Perhaps we all learned folderol, who knows? I expect you had practical things like manual training and geology, what?"

"Why, no, I think we had the usual things."

"Latin, I suppose. I guess *Arma virumque cano* isn't Greek to you!" He chuckled, wrinkling up his pleasant, rosy face. "And French. Everyone does a good deal of French. *I* did. It's a good thing. One goes to Paris after all and doesn't want to look like a booby. And English? You're up on your English, I wager. Let's test you. Now I'll give you a fleet of quotations and you tell me what they're from. Ready? First:

> Shall I compare thee to a Summer's day?
> Thou art more lovely and more temperate.

Well?"

"Shakespeare," I said, but in a voice that shook with dread of his more difficult questions. "It's the beginning of one of the sonnets."

"Good! Second:

> When in disgrace with fortune and men's eyes,
> I all alone beweep my outcast state."

"That's Shakespeare, too," I said.

"Where do the lines occur?"

"In a sonnet, sir!"

"Good! Good! Excellent! Once more:

> That time of year thou may'st in me behold
> When yellow leaves, or none, or few do hang."

"Shakespeare!" I cried, hoping he did not intend to go through the whole sequence.

"I'll give you *E* for excellence, young lady. But now I think I may be able to stump you. Try this one:

> She shall be sportive as the fawn
> That wild with glee across the lawn
> Or up the mountain springs:
> And hers shall be the breathing balm
> And hers the silence and the calm
> Of mute, insensate things."

My luck continued, for in the year past I had learned my English from an effusive woman whose adoration of Wordsworth had made her give all the rest of literature nothing more than a lick and a promise while upon her exegesis of *Ode on Intimations of Immortality* and *The Prelude* she had spent nearly six months.

"Bravo!" cried the Admiral, putting his hand on my knee and continuing confidentially, "Do you know that I committed every line of those Lucy poems to memory in honor of Miss Pride? Perhaps she'll tell you some time how I recited them to her in this very room on the occasion of her twenty-fifth birthday. You may not see this in her, but I still think of her as just what the poem says, 'as sportive as the fawn.'"

The garrulous creature's eyes were dewy and I wondered if he had been a rejected suitor, for I was sure that if he *had* been a suitor, Miss Pride would have rejected him straightaway after his recitation of the Lucy poems. She must have been born hard-headed, I thought, and at the substantial age of twenty-five would have given anyone what-for who compared her to a "sportive fawn." The fawn herself was moving in and out amongst her guests and there was in her carriage such a vigorous uprightness, and in her face, from which her exasperation with me was not altogether obliterated, so formidable an aloofness that I was on the point of laughing out loud at the old man's metaphor. As she halted before each of the little groups, I observed that she treated her friends with very little more warmth than she did me or her chauffeur. She did not bend towards them, but stood erect, looking down upon the interrupted talkers and perhaps rewarding them with a cool smile. Her smile had about it the same economy that had her speech and her eating habits and her apparel. I do not mean that she lacked either cordiality or humor and no doubt she was genuinely fond of many of the people gathered here. But she was never, so to speak, surprised into a smile, and she allowed her smile to last only so long as it was justified by the nature of its provocation. I noticed, however, that she was not the only one who husbanded her responses, for often one of her guests cracked open and resealed his mouth as perfunctorily as she. I admired their abstention, regarding it as a kind of hallmark of the Puritans, like the haemophilia of the Bourbons. I had noticed, from the beginning, that Miss Pride was extremely frugal of her laughter. Now and again, she was amused enough to emit two muted barks of the same volume and duration, as if she were actually saying "Ha! ha!"

As Admiral Nephews followed her course with his nautical eyes, I warmed towards him for no other reason than that he admired her, and had not the very nature of my own admiration insisted upon discipline as its principal component, I would have exclaimed, "Isn't she wonderful!" in order to hear his corroboration. She was, in truth, more wonderful today than she had ever been. Although her guests were as pedigreed as she, and no doubt owned the famous names I had read on the calling cards, she outshone them all just as she had outshone Mrs. Prather and Mrs. McKenzie. Her preeminence came partly from the mere fact that she was the hostess and therefore the star performer, but even more from the *noblesse oblige* with which she had turned me loose in her drawing-room despite my over-painted lips. A lesser lady would have sent me back to my bedroom to remove the rouge lest my bad taste reflect upon herself.

The Admiral, having satisfied himself that I was tolerably educated, did not inquire further into my background but after congratulating both me and himself on our learning (for he found it as remarkable that he, an officer of the navy, was versed in poetry as that I, educated at a public school, was) said, "Hope Mather would have known them all, too. She's a clever one! I heard she was coming home today. Where is she?"

I told him she was riding horseback in Concord where she had spent the night, having only just come back from Manchester. Thus far, I had not seen her.

"Now there's a girl that can ride a horse. I suppose she's the best horsewoman I know barring Mrs. Nephews, who was perhaps a shade more prudent. I well recollect when Spencer Mather's daughter was no higher than a table, she managed a two-year-old that Mr. Apthorp had in Bedford. She was a caution! She had a way with the groom, that little spitfire had, and she got him to saddle the horse that wasn't really broken yet, and before a fellow could say Jack Robinson, milady was on the horse and out of the stable, riding him into the ring. We were just coming back to tea—I expect we had ridden to Carlisle that day—and what did we see but that red-headed baggage putting the colt through his paces. When he frisked too much for her taste, she gave him his comeuppance with a whack over the nose with her little crop no longer than my forearm. She sat like a lady! Well, ma'am, while Spencer Mather was giving the groom a piece of his mind, the governess was leading Hope away and I believe" (the Admiral, overcome with laughter, could not go on for a moment), "I believe she must have been *living* in the stables for the vocabulary she used on that poor little Parisian spinster. It was too funny, you know!

Hope swearing to beat the band while the little mademoiselle was crossing herself. I dare say Hope doesn't remember those words now!"

After a few concluding chuckles, he sobered and went on to list Hope's further accomplishments. I gathered that she not only "sat a horse well" and "knew a good mount" when she saw one and had numerous other equestrian talents, but that she was an excellent swimmer (the statistics of the length of time she could stay under water, the distances she had swum, and the sensational dives she had executed, were quite lost to me who could not swim), could not be defeated on the tennis court, and was a girl who could jibe her boat into a sixty-mile-an-hour breeze with the skill of a veteran mariner. Indeed, what the girl could not do, he, for one, didn't know. "Why, she could milk a cow if she was asked to!"

Since he apparently knew her family well, I wanted to inquire of him whether Hopestill was descended from the famous Mathers, but I had no opportunity, for his praise of her athletic exploits led him to tell me about his grandson who was a lieutenant commander, stationed in Hawaii and who was also "no slouch" on a horse. It was the Admiral's dream that through this young man, Hope might be annexed to the Nephews family. "But neither party," he said with a sigh, "seems to want my will to be done."

I said, "Perhaps that's because they're so far separated?"

He replied, "No, no. It's a case of 'east is east and west is west and never the twain shall meet.'"

I was to learn that the Admiral could not get through a day without using at least one quotation and that because he had given up reading poetry some ten years before and now took his entire supply from Bartlett's, half the time his tags had nothing to do with the context of the conversation. But he was known in Miss Pride's circle as having a colorful and individual speech, the flavor of which derived partly from his literary allusions and partly from his use of polite address which, to ladies, included "*Fräulein*," "*Señora*," "*Madame*," as well as "Ma'am," "Miss," and "Madam."

I thought Miss Pride must find his gabbling ludicrous and I was astonished when she came up to us and greeted him most affectionately: "Lincoln Nephews, you're too old to be flirting with this young lady. Now tell me what you've been up to. Evelyn Frothingham just told me you had been to a dance at the Country Club. What an old beau you are!"

"I was and I had a thumping good time. So often the Country Club is stodgy, but this time, ma'am, it was superb. Why, Lucy, I tripped the light fantastic until two o'clock in the morning."

I could not think what criterion of stodginess old Lincoln had set up, any better than I could imagine him "tripping the light fantastic," since all three words were so peculiarly inapplicable to his embonpoint. It gave me great pleasure to hear of "the Country Club," "the Chilton Club," and "St. Botolph," as though I were peeping through the windows of those chaste establishments where, in the libraries and the ballrooms and the parlors, the thoroughbreds of Back Bay and Beacon Hill were engaged in fashionable diversions, the nature of which was still unknown to me, though I pictured the Admiral nursing a breather of brandy in the company of his pink-faced and bald coevals, while Miss Pride and members of her "reading circle" traced genealogies over their tea. On the Saturday before this, when Miss Pride was lunching at the Chilton Club, I had received a telephone message from her which obliged me to go round there to deliver her calling cards which she had left behind. When the door had closed upon me and I was actually on the premises of this sanctum sanctorum, I could not have been more stirred if it had been the residence of queens and princesses, though I saw only the vestibule with its cloak booth, presided over by a matronly woman in spectacles and a starched white cap and apron who, with her cultivated speech and her remote manner, could have been a member of the club herself. Through the half-open door directly in front of me and at the end of the hall, I saw the edge of a dining-table and a thick gray rug and half a portrait of a lady. From the room issued talk and laughter so that I knew the ladies were still at lunch and I would not, therefore, be allowed to hand Miss Pride her cards, but must entrust them to the custodian of the wraps. A waiter, as distinguished in his swallowtails as an ambassador and having a foreign accent, said he would have someone remind Miss Pride in "Meesis Saltonstall's party" that a parcel was waiting for her, and he went off to elect a responsible member of his staff to bear these tidings to my mistress. Afterwards, as I walked home along Commonwealth Avenue where the bright early afternoon sun displayed to their advantage the genuine and the false violet windowpanes, I chose the houses where she might go that afternoon to drop her card when Mrs. Saltonstall's party, like a courtly banquet, had been adjourned. Until then she would be inaccessible to everyone but those whose lineage entitled them to push open the door in the Chilton Club and pass between the portals into the dining-room.

Miss Pride and Admiral Nephews briefly and malevolently discussed the Evelyn Frothingham who had informed Miss Pride of her friend's revels and was, I gathered, still in the room and possibly within earshot. Miss Pride said she was resembling a toad more closely each day and the Admiral agreed, adding that her model was an especially unsightly specimen. Having demolished the poor woman, they proceeded then to what I soon discovered was the favorite topic of their generation in Boston: namely, the Irish politicians who had "taken over" the city, and were an even greater menace in Cambridge. Today Miss Pride had the openers: she had heard that afternoon that a young lawyer, distinguished for his illustrious family connections, for his irreproachable court record, for his manners and his charm, had suddenly taken it into his head to campaign for the mayor of Cambridge, and had been seen, only the night before, at a roadhouse near Weston in the company of six Irish politicians. And the same unnamed source had informed her that far from being ill at ease in their midst, the renegade from the Republican party whose name was Carew or Carey, I could not tell which, was in his element, was actually the ring-leader and was so disheveled from drinking and shouting and lolling about that he was barely recognizable.

The Admiral had a counter: another man, of Mr. Carew's (or Carey's) generation and kidney had recently, to curry favor with these same Irish politicians of Cambridge, been overheard panegyrizing the Roman Catholic Church in the presence of certain notorious gossips who were sure to spread the word.

"What would our great grandfathers have thought if they had known Boston was to become a Popish stronghold?" said Miss Pride, appalled at this "case."

"Well," replied the Admiral, "I don't know the answer to that one as I never had the pleasure of knowing my great grandfather. But I know that my grandfather would have said aplenty in strong words, ma'am, after the ladies had retired. My grandfather, you know, used to be acquainted with Matthew Arnold's mother, and when he learned that she turned all the pictures to the wall Sunday, when he came back from Oxford and had children of his own, he did the same thing. He was an exceedingly pious man and I dassen't imagine the way he would have scored the Catholics. In those days, of course, they hadn't become a problem. The old order changeth."

I stopped listening to the conversation, and while I was still digesting the fact that Admiral Nephews' grandfather had known Matthew Arnold's mother, I heard a sharp-faced, diminutive woman, who was sitting near-by, say to a young man, "Oh, a man and his books are quite separate things *I* think. I never knew anyone more charming and affectionate than Henry James and he was always one of my dearest friends, but I can't abide his books."

I could not evaluate accurately the aspects of this select world: whether the personal connection of these people with the immortals, or their poised arrogance in regard to such issues as the contemptible political machine of Boston, or their stylish language, or their blueblooded ugliness was the more impressive. The roots of Miss Pride's guests were so deep and tough that I thought they were eternal, and the word "decadent" that Dr. McAllister, a traitor to his intended destiny, had used so often in speaking of Boston when he was trying to depress my expectations, was misleading. Decay must come from within and I could imagine nothing but an external calamity, a social revolution that could eradicate this solid society. Perhaps that was the aim of the ultra-montane newcomers. It was not, I concluded, that what they said and the judgments they passed were of any profundity or of any insight (on the contrary, they often sprang from a primitive and passionate ignorance of the opinions of the rest of the world but which, despite their egotism, contained a measure of self-distrust) but that the manner of these pilgrims' heirs was so fearless and direct that one was not struck with their fatuity. The woman who had been fond of Henry James spoke, a little later on, to the woman I identified as Mrs. Frothingham (she was, as her critics had described her, a reptilian, puckered, misshapen person), of her opinion of people who experimented with flowers. "Really, I do feel," she said, "that this craving for a *tulipe noire* is ridiculous. It debases nature." I believed her implicitly, though this was a subject I had never before pondered. Immediately thereafter I was won to the side of her adversary who, with as forthright a tone, rejoined, "I can't agree, of course. One might just as well say that formal gardens are a debasement of nature. Or that grapefruit is."

"I think grapefruit *is*. I don't care for it at all."

"But not formal gardens?" inquired Mrs. Frothingham drily.

"Ah, you have me there, you clever woman," laughed Henry James' friend, and I gathered that she had a formal garden. "I'll 'bone up' on that poser as my little Stephen says and tell you my answer Thursday at Sarah Cushman's."

"Shall you be there too?" said the other in surprise.

"Certainly. We have declared a most just armistice. I dare say it's in our blood, and no doubt we'll be far more battle-scarred than we are now before we die. But for the time being the white flag is up."

I was intrigued by this feud, so publicly alluded to, and was disappointed when later on I learned that the two warriors were sisters. Mrs. Frothingham and her friend, having shelved their differences on flowers and grapefruit, now exchanged views and reminiscences, having in their retinue a regiment of names as they traversed miles of drawing-rooms, summer residences, and the parks of foreign cities, dignifying the most trifling detail with a judicious and clear-voiced appraisal that made life and the world singularly leveled down and homogeneous. The small, sharp woman hated the new Pompeii for the same reasons (though these reasons were not stated, were, she said, "self-evident" so that I, who could not discover them, felt stupid) that she hated *tulipes noires* and grapefruit. Mrs. Frothingham maintained that these same mysterious reasons, which she readily apprehended and despised, were meaningless and that exactly the opposite was, in each case, true.

3

I rose, intending to make my way to the bay-window and try covertly to close it for I was suffering acutely from the cold. Miss Pride detained me. "I want you to talk with Amy Brooks, who is over there by the fire. She's about your age and a very suitable person."

"She's literary, ain't she?" asked the Admiral.

"No, she paints. But she's about Miss Marburg's age."

She indicated a person whom I had noticed before and had taken to be about forty-five. Now I subtracted a few years, but could not believe she was any less than thirty-eight. She had been in conversation with a stout old woman who now got up and was about to leave. I heard her, in parting, say, "I wish I had been half so clever as you when I was your age, Amy. You must come to me soon and bring some of the thingumabobs you were telling me about." With this, refusing assistance though she was very lame, she began a labored journey with her cane towards Miss Pride, and as I observed her, waiting a moment out of respect for her age before I took her place beside Amy Brooks, I recollected a scene that each fall repeated itself in Chichester. In the afternoon, it had rained, but the air had cleared by evening. As I walked home from the Hotel after dark, ahead of me I heard the steady, three-legged walk of old ladies with sticks over the wet gravel road, and voices, strangely sweetened by the waves or by my distance from them, deliberating the further necessity for umbrellas, even though they did not stray far from the veranda and could immediately have got to shelter if the rain began again. Children of the village, playing Run Sheep Run, passed me and overtook the strollers, scampered through the weak circle that the flashlight of one cast on the ground, and ran on, giggling.

I stood aside to let the old lady, who was dressed in mourning, pass. She gazed at me with dreamy, half-blind eyes and gave me a smile, the sincerity and sweetness of which momentarily disrobed her of the concealments of age and revealed her as she once had been. "How d'you do?" she said. "I know all about you, my dear." But before I could reply, she had taken the Admiral's arm and was being eased into a chair beside Miss Pride.

My appointed interlocutor was ruinously plain, wanting both an adequate nose and chin, but having, for compensation, large square glossy teeth and hyperthyroid eyes. She was small and nervous and given to giggling as well as to sudden fits of seriousness when her whole organism tensed to apparently agonizing statements like, "I have been reading Eugene O'Neill!" or "Last week I went to T Wharf and spent an afternoon sketching!" Then for a few seconds she would stare at me with her high, blue, mammiform eyes.

I said, "Were you sketching boats?"

"Yes! All kinds. Even a dear little Chinese junk! Not from China, of course. It belongs to some arty people, I think, but that doesn't keep it from being cunning, does it? Do you sketch?" I regretted that I did not. "Oh, but you should! There's really nothing like the satisfaction it gives one. Don't you think one ought to have an outlet? I do! I think it's so important these days, especially. I don't pretend to be an artist, you know!" She was visited again, distractingly, by giggles which delayed her. She continued, "I mean, I think it's so necessary to be in touch with art, don't you?"

I supposed that it was, but I could not expatiate for I was tongue-tied before this ebullient spinster whose upbringing had taught her to say the most platitudinous things to a complete stranger but to say them so firmly and courteously that they sounded indisputable. Her zest—she said in a few minutes that the reason she sketched was that she wished people to know what she thought of life—was a consistent style, plagiarized and monotonous and eminently respectable.

Sorrowfully from Miss Pride and admiringly from Dr. McAllister, I had heard that Hopestill Mather filled her leisure time with none of the mild artistic enterprises commonly undertaken by young ladies who had been "out" for sometime, the water colors, the humorous poetry, the informal essays, the sculpturing in plasticine, the rendition of Chopin. Yet, although she had repudiated the conventional patois and honestly acknowledging that she had not even the mildest of gifts, her opinions were by no means poles apart from those of Miss Brooks as I realized, recalling the doctor's further comments. For I had been told that Hope did not want to "lose touch" with art and desired to be one of its patronesses. Dr. McAllister's irony came to me only now, for I had not perceived that this innocently overbearing notion was not unique in the girl I had set out to dislike. Art, to the Misses Brooks and Mather, was a custom: one "kept up" with the newspapers and fashions, was on the alert for word of engagements, marriages, births, débuts, and similarly, one did not like to "lose touch" with art.

Miss Brooks informed me that her stepmother, the Countess von Happel, had done a great deal towards bringing good exhibits to Boston. "Don't you think Europeans have more *feeling* for art than we do?" she said. "My stepmother is Viennese. She may be here later on today." Nor had the Countess neglected contemporary artists, struggling in Boston and New York; she visited their studios and hung their paintings in her dining-room and very often sold one, for a small sum, to a guest who admired it. "It might be only fifteen dollars, but you know even fifteen dollars will give an artist a lift. Oh, I think it's wonderful the way they keep on in their horrid little studios!" "They," a grubby and deserving species, sounded like prisoners serving a term for a felony they had not committed, to whom a gift of cigarettes or chocolate bars meant a new lease on life. I said I had heard Hopestill Mather was another good Samaritan, interested in the artist's welfare, though no doubt not on such a grand scale.

"Well, with Hope, it's different," said Miss Brooks. "She's more *Bohemian* about it. I mean, Hope is almost more interested in the artists themselves than in their work. You know! She's interested in *people*. We call her the 'psychologist.' She wants to find out what makes an artist and not what an artist makes. It all depends on one's point of view. Now the Countess is a great admirer of Van Gogh, but she doesn't care a bit for all those scandalous stories about his ear and so on. But how Hope loves them! Art is my stepmother's life, art," she added, "*and* dinner parties." This last was offered with a freshet of giggles which I took to mean that the Countess' predilection for dinner parties was of notorious proportions.

This girl, so inferior to my ideal conception of a Bostonian, and yet, with all her cordiality, so aloof, unwilling even to inquire what my business might be in that drawing-room (For how could she have failed to sense immediately that I was an outsider?) had, when she began to speak of Hopestill Mather, changed her tone from nervousness to calm, as if she were held in check by a powerful emotion which had put a stop to the vertigo of her introspection and had made her temporarily critical. I said, "Do you know Miss Mather well?"

"Oh, of course," she replied. "She's my cousin."

In the course of that day, I discovered a Bostonian general principle: namely, that everyone was related to everyone else, or if blood kinship did not obtain, something else almost as binding did; people had gone to dancing school together or their fathers had been law-partners or their mothers had been Red Cross nurses in the same village in France. But this kinship, even that of blood (perhaps actually it was true more of this than of the other kind) was so taken for granted that it was almost uninteresting. It was important to know who had married into what family and who were the forebears of the bride and groom and whether the bride's mother were the Martha Endicott who had gone to Winsor School with Priscilla Bradley but had married into Philadelphia. All of this was of vital concern, but half the time, the performers of that drama, coiled about itself innumerable times, were known most vaguely to their commentators. And the relation of twigs to the trees had become so complicated that no one could straighten it out immediately: the whole rigamarole must be gone through each time. Cousins were not appreciably more kindred than friends, and friends never knew when they would discover that they were really cousins, the fact being established only by an accidental remark dropped by a former Bostonian, who now lived in London, and relayed home in a casual letter by her visitor. Thus, Miss Pride had not told me that Amy Brooks was Hopestill Mather's cousin and Miss Brooks herself had supplied me with the information almost as an afterthought, really only to explain why she knew Hopestill as if their being cousins (since obviously they were not friends) was the only thing that would induce them to know one another.

Still, she had not spoken disloyally of Hopestill—perhaps, again, because her etiquette, the guardian angel of people in society, directed her, not her feeling—but she had spoken coolly and appraisingly as of a slight acquaintance and one whose "philosophy of life" was opposed to her own. But I suspected that there were other grounds, less intellectual, for the enmity, and that the divergence of their paths toward art was merely symbolic. It struck me that this poor ill-favored, twitching girl envied her cousin's good looks, or that she would really have liked to mingle with the Bohemians as Hopestill did but, being spurned by them, had to cloak her disappointment in an indifference to the "psychology" of the artist.

I said, "Perhaps Miss Mather spreads the word about her artists just as your stepmother does."

"Oh, certainly!" she cried vigorously. "You mustn't misunderstand me. Hope doesn't trifle with them. She *believes* in them, you know. It's her catering to them that I don't see."

"Her catering?"

"Yes! Literally! She takes them strong cheese and rye bread and marinated herring and beer. And don't think for a moment she does her shopping in any usual place like Pierce's! No, she must have the shabbiest delicatessen on Revere Street! Oh, Hope is all of a piece."

This time I joined in Amy Brooks' laughter and when we had finished, I looked up to find that we were being approached by a pair of extraordinary young men, introduced to me as Mr. James and Mr. Pingrey. They appeared to have been turned out on the same wheel and in the same proportions and differed only in their decorations, like "basic" vases which may be painted appropriately for a particular décor. They were the tallest men I had ever seen and, though they must have been no less than twenty-five years old, were still unused to their height, as if they had shot up overnight and had not learned how to steer themselves. Their knees were in a perpetual state of semi-genuflection and they thrust their heads forward and afterwards tossed them back in an agony of clumsiness. One was dark and a little bald, sallow, thin, strained, but the other was blindingly fair, as shining as a Swede and having the color of new apples splashed recklessly about his broad, bony face. I had not witnessed their arrival and the shock of seeing them suddenly before us unnerved me: it was as if, like genii, they had vapored forth through the floor.

Miss Brooks, when she had presented her friends to me, travailed again in the mirth of her nervous system, and Mr. James and Mr. Pingrey were sympathetically infected, twisted and turned and bent their knees like two damaged snakes as between their giggles they all three reviewed some esoteric anecdote of their last meeting which, as nearly as I could make out, had been at a masquerade ball given by the Countess von Happel. I could not help thinking that the most elaborate costumes would fail to disguise any of these freaks in the slightest.

"And what have you been doing since?" said Mr. Pingrey, the fair young man.

"I was just telling Miss Marburg that I have been sketching. I was at T Wharf last week, Edward, and do you know there was actually a *Chinese junk* there?"

"I don't believe it! Truly I don't believe it! I must have proof! You must show me a picture of it!"

"*Do* come to see it. I value your criticism, you know. Come to tea soon, you will, won't you? And you tell me what *you've* been doing since that disgraceful party."

Edward Pingrey drew up a chair as Mr. James goggled uncertainly at me, not sure whether the *tête-à-tête* which was about to be launched between Miss Brooks and his companion would exclude us and necessitate a separate conversation. He also drew up a chair, to my side of the sofa, prepared for the worst. But Mr. Pingrey, though he bent toward Amy quite intimately and now and again emphasized a point by laying a huge, spatulate forefinger on the arm of the sofa within an inch of her hand, and addressed her solely, did not lower his voice and even glanced at us occasionally as he talked as though to make sure we were listening.

"Well, I've been doing something perfectly delicious, Amy. I have become intrigued with politics, of all things! You would never guess, would you, that a confirmed old ivory towerite like me would ever get involved in politics, but I have, my dear, up to the neck!"

"But what kind of politics, Edward?"

"By no means the usual kind! Not these tedious" (he pronounced "tedious" with a "j") "municipal squabbles. Don't misunderstand me: I realize the appalling state the city is in, of course, but there are so much bigger things! Such universal problems! I've joined an extraordinary group called '*Les Chevaliers de la legion de Lafayette*' which will eventually be *the* international party. We wear red shirts, and I just wish you could have seen us, sixteen of us, marching through the Mill Dam in Concord the day we were formally sworn in. Amy, they're bright red, really scarlet!"

Miss Brooks laughed. "I can't take you seriously, Edward. I don't believe for a minute you marched down the Mill Dam. They wouldn't *let* you in Concord!"

"Oh, wouldn't they though! You can never guess who is the leader of our group. Guess!"

"Someone proper? Someone I know?"

"No one but your esteemed Uncle Arthur Hornblower!"

I burst into laughter, an attack which came upon me quite unawares like a disease that strikes without preliminary symptoms. Until I heard Mr. Pingrey say "your esteemed Uncle Arthur Hornblower," as if "your esteemed Uncle Arthur" were his given name to match his absurd surname which came directly out of the *dramatis personae* of an Elizabethan comedy, I had not altogether been aware that Mr. Pingrey and his sallow shadow, Mr. James and Amy Brooks were three superb, natural clowns. Now I was shaken to the soul with the circus and felt that if I heard again a mention of its patron, Youresteeemedunclearthurhornblower, I would roar uncontrollably. The three performers stared at me in amazement. I was silenced. At last I said, "I beg your pardon. I was only thinking I used to know a terribly peculiar person named Hornblower." But as I uttered the name again, I was overcome.

Mr. James bent a reproachful gaze upon me. "It's not at all a common name," he said.

At that moment I was saved, for I saw Dr. McAllister coming into the room. He paused on the threshold and surveyed the guests and when he saw me, smiled. He gestured toward Miss Pride to indicate that he would join me when he had spoken to her. I rose from the sofa. "I'm very sorry I interrupted you, Mr. Pingrey. I was ever so interested."

The two lengthy young men stood up and bowed gravely. Miss Brooks giggled and said, "I think Uncle Arthur *is* comic, for that matter. It's been so nice to talk with you, Miss Marburg. We must have another nice long chat about sketching." And she extended to me a smooth, dead hand.

4

In the earlier part of the afternoon when, each time the door opened, I thought Dr. McAllister would surely enter now, I believed that he would be distant, no longer interested in me since he was in the center of a web woven about him by metropolitan society. For while in Chichester he could combine the offices of friend and counselor, here, I thought, his science would be separate from his social manner and that still unable to see me in any rôle but that of factor in "the Marburg case" he would shun me, not uncharitably, but to spare me the repercussions of a chance remark that might be dropped by one of us and apprehended by some stranger who happened to be within earshot. But his smile, which was transmitted to me like a message in code, intended for only my perusal, assured me that his generosity had not been modified. On the heels of this sense of security, and at the moment when, deliberately turning his back toward me, he sat down beside Miss Pride and the Admiral, came a searing jealousy of the dozen people in the room who one by one broke from their conversations to cry out their delight at seeing him again or to go directly up to him with the request that they be allowed to "have" him next. For I had failed, in my portrait of him, to particularize the background, having painted it before I had studied him in all kinds of light and from all angles. I had been literal and knowing him out of his *milieu* had been blind to the fact that he belonged to a type from which he could never extricate himself though he might denounce it. As he himself had told me, among the idiosyncrasies of this type was a simultaneous craving for and aversion to society, so that a complete break could never be effected. These were not merely the habits of a lifetime, he had said, but were the habits of two and a half centuries. In the renegade who has extirpated his New England accent and has espoused the life of the new frontiers, there is still the Puritan within his unalterable bones: a forward young lady at a house party in Winnetka, Illinois, importunately makes eyes at him, and if he recovers from his surprise sufficiently to make love to her, his performance will be cold, utilitarian, and intemperate.

At the same time, I should have disliked it if, after his brief salutation to Miss Pride and the old lady in mourning, he had come at once to greet me, for I passionately desired to have evidence that he "belonged." Yet, because I believed myself to be in love with him, I was nettled to discover that he was a great favorite. Thus, at the same time that I admired him as an aristocrat (the critical "I" did this, the I who was not in love), I wanted him to be a superior plebeian, a sort of polished edition of Nathan Kadish. Now, on the other hand, I had no desire to emend Miss Pride; her text did not bewilder me, and I was confident that I could imitate her style. In order, however, to meet the demands the doctor would make upon me if that extra-professional friendship I so coveted were ever to mature, I would have either to add something original to my translation of the old woman (I knew that he privately deplored my choice of model) or practice a certain dishonesty in deleting the elements in her that especially annoyed him. I wished to do neither, and it was for this reason that I hoped he might shoulder the responsibility himself and discover to me a strain in himself which matched my own.

It was ten minutes before he glanced towards me again and even then he did not come to my isolated place in the bay-window. Attentively and with a charming smile or as charming a look of commiseration, he listened to gossip, complaints and reminiscences, making no distinctions, as far as one could judge from his facial expressions, between youth and age or between old friends and slight acquaintances. As his tour (as impartial as his visits to ward patients) brought him closer to me, I could hear his replies to remarks addressed to him.

"Why, all I know of Germans is that in general their anatomy is similar to the American variety. That's all I'm required to know in my profession," he said to a woman who had just returned from a Bavarian watering place and confessed, with mock caution, that she had great faith in the Nazis (she pronounced the word with a scrupulous *tset*) as the liberators of the nation from her post-Versailles quandary. Now, in fact, I knew that the doctor had very strong opinions of the Nazis, but he refused to discuss the subject with this frivolous Germanophile who chose to esteem in the new system its most obvious, most spectacular, and most ambiguous virtues: the superbly trained Storm Troopers, the powerful health of the children in the youth movements, the touting of Wagner. He had deliberately made his reply as stupid as her observation, but if he hoped thereby to make her own words echo to her shame in her ears, he was disappointed, for she said, "Do you know I don't really believe you? I think there is some secret of strength in the German body that exists in no other. Why, half of them, I should say, eat oleomargarine and have for years, and yet they're the healthiest people in the world."

Not because he was in the least interested in the conversation, but because it was his moral duty, imposed upon him by his knowledge, to correct her, he replied, "Not only is margarine not unhealthful to anyone, but you would find if you cared to make a survey that an enormous percentage of the American people never use butter at all."

Vexed, the woman dropped the subject of the German physique and said, by way of dismissal, "At any rate, I think we all must recognize eventually that they are the leaders of the world." Further infuriated by a remote, ironic smile on the young man's face, she abruptly turned to her neighbor and shouted venomously, "What is the shocking tale I hear about your nephew and the Communists in Cambridge?" Dr. McAllister made his escape and came to the love-seat.

"I've expected to see you here long before this," he said genially. "I thought you looked forward to tea-parties."

I explained that I had not stayed away by choice but that Miss Pride had been educating me up to this afternoon. I intended no disloyalty because, far from being indignant, I was grateful for my preparation: had I not had it, the discomfort I had felt when I first entered the drawing-room would have continued and my talk with the Admiral would have fared much worse. But the doctor was contemptuous. "She drives a hard bargain," he said. He inquired about my business training and he asked me if I had found Boston up to my expectations. I told him I could have asked for nothing better.

"And Miss Pride? She's teaching you the useful arts, I trust?"

"Oh, indeed!" I said. I told him of the early morning conferences at which I was present. We took our breakfast together in the dining-room (Miss Pride was never tempted to be served in bed, a practice almost universal amongst her friends who, she told me, took as much care in selecting their bed-jackets as they did in selecting their dinner dresses) and at the end of it, Mary, the cook, was summoned from the cellar. Miss Pride was like a general previewing, with his aide, the campaign about to be started, the ammunition being money aimed where it would do the most damage to the enemy, for the Messrs. Pierce, Anderson, Rhodes, and the anonymous gentlemen entrenched in Hood's Dairy, Lewando's Cleaners, and the Megansett Fish Market were, to use her own expression, "to be watched untiringly." The flattering telephone voice of Mr. Campbell of Rhodes' might win someone off his guard to buy oranges at eighty cents a dozen by describing the properties of the fruit with such a wealth of mouth-watering adjectives that one might believe it was cheap at double the price.

Miss Pride had requested my presence at the meetings of the economists because she thought I should learn to run a house. If I proved to have any common sense, she might in time confer upon me the high honor of running *her* house. She had long been desirous of some such assistance, for her other affairs kept her busy. These other "affairs" included not only her extensive social life (I had been agreeably surprised that she dined out so often and went to so many concerts and luncheon parties, for I had supposed that she was as ascetic in this department as in any other) but also with a great many negotiations with her lawyer over her real estate, with her affiliation with divers philanthropic organizations interested in women's prisons and in Christmas dinners for underprivileged children (whose fathers, no doubt, were those impassioned speech-makers in the Common who were after the blood of Miss Pride and her kind). She had recently, also, been in collaboration with the widow of a Harvard professor, preparing his correspondence and lectures for publication, and this took her to Cambridge for one full day each week.

When I mentioned the work in progress, Dr. McAllister interrupted me. "Have you heard that the correspondence has become a thorn in her side and she only does it now out of a sense of duty?"

"Why, no, you're quite wrong. It's exactly the sort of thing that suits her, she tells me."

"She tells you very little. But she tells me very much. She took umbrage last week when she found a reference to herself in one of the early letters. She copied it down and it was so priceless I learned it by heart. But I won't tell you."

"Why not?"

"Because you'd be furious."

My curiosity made me promise that I would keep my temper. But as he quoted the letter, my skin tingled with rage. It read, "Several of us dined two nights ago at Mr. Everett Pride's who, as you know has one of the most elegant houses on our fair Hill. His treasures include a superb Copley, an indifferent Badger, three Homers that they tell me are fine (you know I never get anything from him but *mal de mer*!) and an excruciating creation of his own, his daughter Lucy. Awful to look at, tormenting to hear, she reminds me of nothing so much as a curlew."

"What a fool he was," I said, "to write that down!"

"I will say for Miss Pride," said the doctor, "that her wit is always ready. She told me what she had said to the widow after she had run across the passage. She said, 'Bosworth was pretty damned gawky himself, Mildred.'" He laughed at the sally which I found less amusing than I would have liked, and then asked me, "What do you think of Admiral Nephews? He says you're a pippin."

"I liked him. Is he . . . Nothing."

"Come, is he what?"

I flushed but plunged in. "I was going to say, is he fashionable?"

"The most fashionable you could find in his generation," returned the doctor with a smile. "Not in the one just after him, though—he's a Unitarian."

Because most of my information about Boston came from schoolbooks, I did not know, until Philip McAllister told me, that Unitarianism had been out of style for more than half a century. Most of its present-day supporters remained in the fold because that was the environment to which they had been, as the psychologists say, "conditioned." The Admiral, who was by nature a sensualist, would far rather have gone on Sunday to the Episcopal Church, the higher, the better. But an atavistic conscience held him in check and he made only a minor concession to his idiosyncrasy: he attended services at

King's Chapel where, despite its dedication to that doctrine indigenous to Boston, retained still a Royalist flavor, and old Lincoln Nephews could listen without shame to the organ, choice of Handel for King George, and fancy himself in the presence of ecclesiastical pomp.

I was about to ask another question about the Admiral, but the doctor diverted my attention to a miniature which he had picked up from the table near us. Handing it to me, he said, "Boston *was* something in those days." The faded miniature in its napless, maroon velvet frame presented a solemn, forthright girl. The central part in her straight hair was as precise as a clean wound. It was a face that made no compromises and in which no rounded lines appeared save those essential to the cheeks; her eyebrows were straight, her lips were straight, her nose was like a blade. The painter's colors seemed artificial, for one thought that the original had been a study in black and white. The high, round collar was pinned with an oval brooch, and the invisible ears terminated in smaller matching ornaments. She was an Endicott, he told me, related distantly to Miss Mather's father. He meant that Boston was something in the days when hell was immediate, altruism was ruthless, and justice was Mosaic. Now, cured of its chills and fevers, its blood watered down, it was no longer exciting. Still puritanical, it tried to imitate Sodoms and Gomorrahs in their decenter fashions, but the result was only dowdiness. Consider the Admiral, my friend commanded me, who had sunk in his rosy obesity upon a sofa and was telling the old woman dressed in widow's weeds a joke at which neither laughed aloud although the exertion both of the telling and of the listening made all four wattles wag and the two heads nod. He was no cavalier! His cavorting at the Country Club was so respectable, so circumspect! His affectation of French phrases and his Latin, employed to give him a cosmopolitan piquancy, so marked him as a citizen of Boston!

"I find him charming," I said.

"So do I," replied the doctor. "But preposterous. That's my grandmother, by the way, whom he's regaling. She and Miss Pride are currently enemies."

I asked him why this was and he said, "Chiefly because my grandmother is a possessive old woman and next to her house in Concord, I am her favorite possession—her only grandchild, you see."

"But surely Miss Pride has no designs on you!"

"Oh, but she has. When you meet Hope, you'll see her aunt is barking up the wrong tree though. She wouldn't have a dozen of my kind."

At that moment, there appeared before us an anxious little man like a caricature of Terror, for his feline green eyes were immensely magnified by a pair of very thick lenses and his small mouth trembled beneath the insufficient ambush of a sandy mustache. He was a newcomer and said hastily that he intended to run right along as soon as he had spoken to the doctor whom he drew aside and talked with in a whisper for a few minutes.

The room was less densely crowded now for it was a quarter past six according to the delicate china clock on the mantel which, after it had made a sound like the last quiet purr of a cat before it goes to sleep, gave forth a single, bell-like chime, sustained and questioning. I had not noticed the clock before as it was dwarfed by the tremendous Copley incongruously placed above the narrow marble mantel. I discovered that I had not been conscious of the room at all until now, had not observed, as I had always intended to do, its transformation when it was occupied by guests. Now, at this late hour, dimly lighted, its walls pink from the fire in the hearth, it seemed surpassingly feminine and agreeable. I looked towards Miss Pride, handling her dainty Bavarian tea china and deftly replenishing the hot water in the silver tea-pot, conversing the while with her friends, so much the lady that both processes were carried on without any interference to each other. It came to me, so deliciously that I wanted to clap my hands together and crow, that I had never seen Miss Pride in the library without her green beaver hat: thus she had given me my tea there on the first day I had been in her house and thus she was, ready for church, every Sunday morning when I went in to pay my respects as she was playing chess against herself. I recalled the way my father had always worn his hat in the shop but left it there when he went into the house. While I knew that Miss Pride had been bareheaded the night she joined the gentlemen in their brandy, I was sure some other appurtenance, conversational perhaps, had disguised her feminine nature so that the bequests of her male ancestors were more apparent than those handed down from the mothers of her line.

Dr. McAllister's alarmed little man scurried away, looking straight ahead as though he were afraid of being trapped. He was like a rabbit running through a clearing. He did not make it, for Miss Pride caught sight of him and cried, "There he is now! Stop, Otis Whitney!" Obediently and out of breath he trotted to her side. My friend sat down beside me on the love-seat and watched the scene: Mr. Otis Whitney had been pushed by a thin but powerful forefinger into a chair beside the tea-table and was undergoing an inquisition about the health of his son who was under Dr. McAllister's care.

Abstractedly the doctor said, "By the way, I told my grand-mother a little about you. Nothing you wouldn't want known, but she's a kindly old soul and you might like to visit her some-time when you want country air."

Just as I glanced toward her, there came a lull in the conver-sation of the group that sat between us and the tea-table and I heard old Mrs. McAllister say to the Admiral, "The report from Manchester this year is the same as ever. Hope Mather had all the beaux. Isn't she a heart-breaker! But you know she comes by it honestly."

The Admiral, not only to flatter Miss Pride who had half turned away from Otis Whitney, but also because he believed it, replied, "Indeed she does that. Why, the only young lady who could hold a candle to Lucy Pride was her sister."

But the old lady, with the sure touch of malice, said, "I quite agree, but actually I was thinking of Spencer Mather at that moment more than of his wife."

I knew already the basis of the slanderous remark, and Dr. McAllister filled in some of the details for me. Hopestill's father had been a notorious libertine, had married Charity Pride for her money, had flaunted in her face his philanderings with common women, and had died most disgracefully at a house party when, drunk, he had been thrown by a spirited horse that he could barely have managed sober. His wife died shortly afterwards of humiliation, it was believed. The doctor pointed to the grand piano at the left of the love-seat. "Miss Pride keeps this, mind you, not in memory of her sister who was quite accomplished but in memory of Spencer Mather's brutality. It has a dummy keyboard. He was extremely sensitive to noises and could not bear to hear scales. After he got her this travesty—and she was so mild she didn't protest—he used to say, 'Look at poor Charity. She plays all day long and never gets anywhere.'"

In reply to my suggestion that the ill-will between Miss Pride and her niece stemmed from the former's dislike of Spencer Mather, Dr. McAllister said with a smile, "We don't speak of 'ill-will' between them, my dear. To use my grandmother's phrase, we say they are both 'strong characters.' But, yes, that is perhaps why they don't get on. That and the fact that Hope is said to resemble her aunt as she was at twenty—don't ask me why the similarity annoys her. One would think she'd feel the opposite when people say of Hope, 'She's the image of you, Lucy.'"

Miss Pride had leaned over the diminutive and still fidgeting form of Otis Whitney and was saying to Mrs. McAllister, "I heard you mention Manchester. I understand the summer was, as they say, a 'dud.' Hope wrote that if it hadn't been for your Philip's little visit the whole season would have been a total loss."

"Don't flatter me, Lucy," laughed the old lady and, turning to the Admiral, said, "Isn't she the purest Christian to compliment me on that no-account grandson of mine! There's nothing I'd rather believe. Why, I would be overjoyed if I could think that wild young rascal occupied the least place in Miss Hopestill Mather's heart! No, Lucy, my dear, *I* know and *you* know that she's a sensible girl. Look at him"—she pointed to my companion and at the same time sent him a conniving and adoring smile to indicate that she was merely playing a game, merely looking out for his interests—"he's barely civil! And I see he has already victimized the youngest lady in the room. I give you my word of honor, he has been boring her with some awful descriptions of his interminable 'cases.' Really now, Lucy, admit he's not nice."

Philip flushed and shook his head at his grandmother like a reproving parent. His gesture was unfortunate for she cried, "Now he's signaling me to hush! You see, he has a bad conscience. Admiral Nephews, what would you do with such a rogue?"

Miss Pride, who knew perfectly well that Philip was the apple of his grandmother's eye and who took as an insult to her intelligence this deprecation of him—so false that the voice with which she ran him down was brimming over with love—said, "I can't say I see eye to eye with you. What you say of Philip applies much more to Hope. Perhaps we're both right, though, and in that case . . . well, birds of a feather flock together."

The old lady was outwitted, for she could not admit that what Miss Pride said was precisely what she meant, that Hopestill was the unruly, fickle egotist that for the sake of her campaign against their marriage she had pretended her grandson was. She rose, fumbled for her stick, and said in a voice audible to everyone in the room, "Perly, Amy Brooks is coming to dinner with me next Tuesday. Can I expect you too? We can't get along without you if we play 'I am a famous man.'" And to Miss Pride, she added, "I dare say I couldn't engage Hope for that evening, could I?"

"On the contrary," rejoined Miss Pride, "she likes nothing better than to go to your house. Shall I give her a message?"

"I thought she was going to New York immediately," said the foiled grandmother.

"Not until next week." Then, with a slight sharpening of her expression, for evidently she had changed her tactics and had decided that it was better for the time being not to expose her niece to the determined old woman, she said, "But she will be occupied with packing. No, perhaps I'd better not mention it to her, for she would want to come and she really wouldn't have the time."

Mrs. McAllister sighed with relief, blew her grandson a kiss, and hobbled from the room on the Admiral's arm. Her place was filled at once by Mrs. Frothingham who asked for another cup of tea and said, "I'm lingering disgracefully long. I want to see Hope and hear all about what she's planning to do in New York. I do think she's too clever to go off all by herself. Can she really be serious about studying psychology?"

"You must ask her, Evelyn, for I'm too ignorant of the subject to know. Can anyone be serious about it? I must confess *I* can't. I have no more faith in dreams and the like than I have in Sally Hornblower's spirits. By the way, have you heard her latest? She swears that at a séance not long ago a Japanese girl was present and asked to be connected with some departed relative and, my dear, not only did the connection go through but the medium gave the message in colloquial Japanese!"

"Odd as that is," said Mrs. Frothingham in a lowered voice, "it's no worse than the way Arthur Hornblower has been cutting up. Have you heard . . ." But Miss Pride put her finger to her lips and motioned toward Mr. Pingrey who was still talking excitedly to Miss Brooks. "Is he . . . ?" queried Mrs. Frothingham. Miss Pride nodded and I caught the whispered words, "Berthe and I are campaigning in that sector."

Philip McAllister covered his smiling lips with his hand and then, on the pretext of examining a pot of philodendron, murmured to me, "My grandmother would like me to marry Amy Brooks. As you've probably deduced by now, our free will is purely relative. My mother had first say about where I was to go to school—there was a great to-do about it, I've been told, when I was two hours old—and my grandmother agreed on Groton instead of St. George only on the condition that I marry Amy who was then sixteen months old."

"And you don't like her?" I asked.

He did not answer. In less time than it had taken for the sound of my voice to carry to him, he had moved into a world poles apart from mine. I knew by the eager light that suffused his pale face, until this moment drawn and mask-like with fatigue, and by the tensing of his fingers from which arose a hygienic odor, that what had galvanized him and was still invisible to my eyes was some private shock. I had heard the front door open and a feminine voice say, "Good afternoon, Ethel." The interval between the salutation and the appearance of the guest in the doorway—during which I identified the voice as the same one I had heard in this room when Miss Pride had left me in the vestibule—was an ordeal for both of us and in order to hide, on the one hand his impatience as a lover, and on the other, my curiosity, we began to exchange views on the probable success of Miss Pride's memoirs as if it were the subject we had wanted to bring up all along but had been prevented by the intrusion of gossip which we could not help overhearing. And when Hopestill entered, even though nothing could have torn his eyes away from her, my friend, in an untroubled voice, was telling me that he liked nothing so much for bedtime reading as personal reminiscences and hoped Miss Pride would take Saint-Simon as her model.

Hopestill Mather, whose autumnal hair I remembered from the day at the Hotel, paused at the door like an actress over-doing her entrance in the fear that the audience would not applaud. And then she pressed forward, leisurely, through the assembly of guests and bandy-legged slipper-chairs. Her eyes were astray as she murmured courtesies which marked her as a person of poise and breeding, as though she were ambling through an art gallery, untouched by what she saw but know-ing, with a firm, sure, aristocratic knowledge, that what she saw was right: that the Ruebensesque woman, who had been seated all afternoon beside the fire-place in conversation with a distinguished middle-aged man, was not to her esthetic taste, but that she recognized genius in the composition; that her cousin Amy Brooks belonged to an eminent school though she lacked the characteristic color that marked even the lesser works of Rembrandt. Though she might despise her aunt and her aunt's friends, she seemed not to question their essential mettle: they were the authors and the stewards of reality. For the time being, I had gathered, she had chosen to visit other worlds, both real and unreal, by which she had been remem-bered in the last will of a larger order than New England. Between these greetings (the uniform warmth and urbanity of which, exactly like that I had observed in Dr. McAllister, made me see, with a pang of envy, that to start with they had a funda-mental fraternity), as she held up her manners like the emblem of a secret cult, she showed by a smile in our direction that she was sorry to be detained in her progress to us who were, she promised, to receive the whole heart of her vivacity and not merely these pulsations which she allowed to the others.

Even from this distance and unable to distinguish her voice from those chattering others, or to see, because of the dim light, what sort of body encased the person I had envied for so many years, even so I had a feeling of that allurement that had been hinted to me in various ways, for though she was not beautiful (there was enough light for me to see that) she emanated a terrible femininity, like a soporific perfume, so that the men, while they rose promptly to their feet, allowed her to speak first as if they needed time in which to collect their wits.

She bent down to kiss her aunt as Admiral Nephews stood up. "I'm next," he cried. "Hope, you outshine yourself. When are you going to have dinner with me?"

The girl turned up her smiling face to him and received his kiss. "You name the night, Admiral Nephews. For you, I'm always free, sir." She sat down beside her aunt and they began to talk so amiably that I doubted if, after all, they really were enemies. But they spoke formally as if, while they were good friends, they were not altogether intimate. Hopestill complimented her aunt on the sandwiches and Miss Pride congratulated her on her costume, even though she had once told me in disgust that the girl spent nine-tenths of her time and all of her money on clothes, an indulgence shocking to a woman whose wardrobe consisted of four identical black broadcloth suits and two dark red evening dresses, one made of velvet and the other of crêpe. Her niece had converted a simple yellow dress into a "costume" by the addition of an Indian belt made of great silver conches. Her arms were laden with bracelets and her fingers with turquoise rings. Her long hair hung as straight as rain, an angelic, down-burning fire that parted for her small, perfect face which disdained the pastes and pigments of the cosmeticians, but was pale where God intended it to be and shone where He had burnished it. She was tanned from the seashore sun and from her ride this afternoon, retained the last glow of rosiness in her cheeks. She was tropical like the surcharged parrot; one felt that her flesh was hot to the touch and that her small feet, shod in white buckskin moccasins, were furnished with velvet pads like a cat's. When I first took her in, I did not recognize her belt as Indian or her yellow dress as being of a particular cut and fashion: it was rather as though she were clothed in some natural, unpurchased habiliments like a leopard or a Luna moth.

"Oh, please don't third-degree me," she said, laughing, to Mrs. Frothingham. "I don't know anything about psychology. I'm taking it up because I've soured on painters after this summer. It would shock Auntie if I told you why."

"Shock isn't the right word, my dear," said Miss Pride. "The nonsense of Wainright Lowe hasn't shocked me for years, but no one bores me more to hear about."

"Hope!" cried Mrs. Frothingham. "Don't tell me you picked *him* up!"

"How was I to know? Of course I *did* know the moment I stepped into his studio. But I simply couldn't shake him."

"He paints his pictures in half an hour," said Miss Pride. "As a matter of fact, I think I could do them in fifteen minutes."

The Admiral said, "I must confess, Hope, that I'm glad you've gone in for something besides all this painting hanky-panky. Psychology is a little too new-fangled for me, but still . . ." He rose and kissed Miss Pride's proffered hand. "As always, I've enjoyed it, ma'am, and unless I'm dead before then, I wager I'll show up again next week. I'm well pleased you've got yourself a companion for the winter since this intellectual young lady insists on going off to Babylon." The whole group at the tea-table glanced toward me and the Admiral said, "We talk the same language, Miss Marburg and I. I'm going to steal her some afternoon for a walk around Fresh Pond. Far from the madding crowd's ignoble strife, we'll revel in the English poets. Good-by, Lucy, good-by, Hope, good-by, Evelyn. Good-by, you three graces!"

Mr. Otis Whitney, who for the past few moments had been invisible, being blocked out by the Admiral's bulk, stood up and implored, "Lincoln, if you've got your car, would you be so good as to drop me?" But Miss Pride pulled him by the coattails and said rather sharply, "You only just came, Otis. You haven't told me a thing about Frank. Now do begin from the beginning. Where did he get that disgusting disease?"

Hopestill excused herself from her aunt and Mrs. Froth-ingham and came to us. The doctor rose and, erect as he was because of his deformed back, gave the appearance of leaning forward. The hand he offered shook and the voice with which he greeted her was unnaturally high and diffident. He was not used to her yet, I thought, and his eyes had not accustomed themselves to her ferocious radiance. Oblivious to all save this ignited tulip, he raised his hand and touched her hair. I sighed without meaning to, as if the inhalation were the vehicle for this strange scene. The doctor introduced us and, sensible of my presence for the first time since he had heard the front door open, reinstated me as his friend. "Sonie will be glad you've arrived at last. She's been here a month and this is her first public appearance."

"How do you do?" said the girl, smiling warmly at me. "I'm sure it's been awfully dull for you, and I haven't a doubt that Philip hasn't lifted a finger to amuse you."

The doctor made the lame excuse that he had been busy, although, had he thought back, he would have known that I—who until this moment had not resented his neglect—could hardly swallow it since he had intimated that he had come to tea here several times when he expressed surprise that he had not seen me before. But I was more embarrassed by Hopestill's scolding than he, feeling that he found me a bore or that he had avoided me because he pitied my misfortunes or dreaded my complaints.

Hopestill looked restlessly about the room. "Five minutes of this sort of thing and I'm at the end of my tether. Don't you think we should have cocktails?"

There was a good deal of Miss Pride in her, I saw. Her eyes were similar, small and nacreous like painted ornaments. She had been allotted less than her share of flesh and it was as dry as paper, and so pale her mechanism seemed to run by something other than blood or else in her the blood was really blue. And her voice, which her cold spirit permitted to be merely tinged with cordiality, had the same metallic opacity, lacking resonance and melody but having instead a vast range of pitch.

"I would be delighted," said Philip. "But doesn't your aunt belong to the school of thought of my sainted grandmother which holds you mustn't drink for pleasure but for the sake of your appetite?"

Hopestill smiled vaguely. "If they're similar in that respect, they wouldn't admit it, would they? Why, if Auntie knew that, she'd either turn teetotaller or dipsomaniac."

"Or else tell everyone that Grandma got the idea from her and was secretly an old soak."

"I need a drink." She had been toying with the foliage as she sat on an ottoman. She was dismembering a spray of fern. "I hate this hair-like vegetation, don't you, Miss Marburg? It fits though. My horse threw me twice today in the ring, in the mud. My trousers were ruined. I beat hell out of him. *That* I enjoyed."

A pained silence followed her confession of sadism. To consolidate our awkward triangle and to change the subject, I said, "I met your cousin and her two tall beaux this afternoon." And then, because she seemed to think I had something more to say, I told her of the predicament I had been entangled in by Your Esteemed Uncle Arthur Hornblower. Her face, instead of reflecting the amusement I had expected, hardened against me and anger brightened the flare of her eyes. I learned my lesson in the silence that followed my joke's collapse, but sick with humiliation, thought my experience would never benefit me, that this defender of her relatives whom she could not, nevertheless, abide, would refuse to have me any longer in the house. She looked away from me. "Have you heard the marvelous thing Uncle Arthur did? He changed his will last summer and left something like a hundred thousand to Vanzetti's sister. Isn't that really *good* of him?"

The doctor, perhaps not realizing that her chief purpose had been to reproach me, said, "Why, what a turncoat you are! I thought you were the most rabid supporter of the Committee's decision. Don't tell me you've got some inside information about their innocence!"

"On the contrary, I'm perfectly sure and always will be sure that they were guilty, but that doesn't mean Vanzetti's sister was. And Uncle Arthur, after all, could be prompted simply by generosity, couldn't he?"

"No," said the doctor with a smile. "But I say, about those drinks? Does she keep the makings in the library?"

"We'll have to have second best and that's in the pantry. Look, there comes the Happel. What a pity she has just missed seeing Amy flanked on each side by a tall beau!"

The scorn of her remark, far surpassing the acidity of mine, was deliberately aimed at me, and by it she gave me to understand that she was at liberty to say what she liked about her dowdy cousin, but that it would behoove any outsider to keep a civil tongue in his head. I was distressed when Dr. McAllister left us to confer with Miss Pride, for, since she had imposed upon my conversation a prohibition that applied to the only thing we had in common, that is, the guests, I had nothing to say to Hopestill. But she realized that it was her duty to select a subject for us and she gave me a sociable smile which only made me uncomfortable because it showed that she had now put me in my place and, confident that she would have no further trouble with me, could proceed.

"Aunt Lucy's house isn't the gayest in the world, is it? Has she sent up Mercy to keep you company?"

"Mercy?"

"She's my aunt's cat. Since her last accouchement, she's been rather peckish. Even so, I'm surprised Aunt Lucy hasn't introduced you. Do you like our house?"

I answered abstractedly, so overcome was I at the idea of Miss Pride's cat. There was something perplexing and a little unpleasant in her concealment of it. (When, on the following morning at breakfast, I confronted her with my knowledge, saying that I would like to see Mercy, she said, "She is nervous. Perhaps in time she'll be up to society again," quite matter-of-factly as if the person in question were a friend for whom a long sea voyage had been too much. I said it was strange that I had never heard the cat cry. "Oh, no," answered Miss Pride, "she's not much of a talker. She's well satisfied with her bedroom just off mine.")

"I'm sorry I must go on to New York so soon," said Hopestill. "Tell me, do you think you'll be able to stick it out?"

"Stick it out?"

"Yes, I mean it's rather a grim prospect, I should think, to be shut up in this gloomy old house where the ghost of my blue-nosed grandpa walks every night. Or perhaps you have friends in Boston?"

"A few," I replied warily.

"In that case, then, you won't be lonely. Where are you from, by the way? Auntie told me, but I have a rotten memory."

"Chichester," I said.

"Oh, of course. I know nothing about the place. I haven't been there since I was a very little girl." She paused and looked closely into my face, and then went on, "Chichester has produced a very objectionable person by the name of Betty Brunson."

"I know her."

"She turns up on Christmas Eve, at places she'd never be invited, with an entourage of horrible boys from New York. She's exactly like a guide and says, 'Now this is typical of Boston,' or 'You'd never find this outside Massachusetts,' and all in the world she's pointing out is someone's Cape Cod lighter or a Currier and Ives."

I was so panic-stricken at the thought that I might some time encounter Betty Brunson in Boston that I could make no comment. Hopestill gave me a second of her searching looks.

"Have we met before?"

"No," I replied firmly.

"Your face is so familiar. Were you at the Porcellian dance last spring?"

"No. I'm sure we haven't met. I would remember you."

"I couldn't forget *you*. We *have* met, Miss Marburg. It was ages ago, wasn't it?"

Again I denied it. But she pursued. "Perhaps you were in Chichester one time, a hundred years ago, when I had a nasty meal with Aunt Lucy and Cousin Josie."

"Perhaps," I grudgingly allowed.

"Look here," she said, "I must get this straight. Auntie has been so damned mysterious about you. I know you're going to do the famous memoirs but what else? Are you somebody incognito? As they say, scratch a Russian waitress and you find an archduchess. I suppose it works the other way too, scratch an archduchess and you find an upstairs maid."

Taken off my guard by her unconsciously shrewd guess, I made a slip of the tongue which, had her attention not at that moment been diverted, would have let her know instantly all she needed to know about me, for I said, "No, ma'am, I'm not either of those."

"Look, Philip has seduced my aunt. What a perfect butler posture! There—I've shocked you." She laid her hand on my arm. "*So* sorry."

The girl was aboriginal and had eaten the whole apple. A pagan priestess in her yellow vestments, she moved her supple arms and torso as if in an abortive dance, turning now to the infatuated doctor who was bringing the drinks like sacrificial libations, and now to me, her face a plastic substance that alternately showed derision or aggrieved boredom, or, if she had a moment before glanced at her aunt, a profound and muddled rebellion. In order to lower the tone of our conversation I said, "Do you sketch, Miss Mather?"

"No. Neither do I write nor take part in amateur theatricals. But I *am* literate. I'm what my long-suffering aunt calls 'advanced.'"

My question had been a happy one and she talked for some time, even after we had been interrupted by the arrival of the drinks, with a real enthusiasm which made me think she had, after all, some sort of inner life and that her interest in dress and horses was no more than a trifling avocation. She had recently "discovered" psychology and now felt she had wasted her whole life on trivialities. "The pious doctor calls me heathen because I believe in dreams and the *anima mundi*. You know, don't you, that identical twins have been known to have the exact same thought at the same moment even though they have been miles apart?"

The moment she had excitedly uttered the statement, her interest vanished. She sighed and said through a vapor of ennui, "Of course that sort of thing is trimming. What I'm interested in is the good of psychology, that is, the advertised good: no one, they tell me, needs to be neurotic."

"I quite agree. I wish you would tell that to your friend Pope," said the Countess von Happel who, with another woman, crowded into our little recess. Hopestill introduced me to the large, fragrant Viennese and to the other, Mrs. Choate. The Countess, speaking to her friend and to me, explained, "Pope is a surrealist, ladies, but I call him a fool. Hope, he brought me a gouache called 'When Lilacs Last in the Dooryard Bloom'd' though it was just a great gray study of nothing at all. If you turned it upside down, you got a sort of feeling that a goose was squatting on a picket fence. I asked him why on earth he had picked the title and he said that the rhythm matched the 'color cadences' but, my dears, there was no color in it!" Fashionably dressed and set with colossal jewels, the Countess reached across to squeeze Hope's hand and with an equine laugh cried, "Admit it's a damned fraud."

"Oh, Berthe, *don't* let's have that all over again. You know

I'm *quite* able to see the virtue of your Davids and Rembrandts and Bellinis. You just judge them and modern painting on different psychological levels."

"That's the fraud! Psychological levels indeed! But, darling, let me tell you the rest of the story about Mr. Pope. He came to my last Friday wearing bathing trunks, galoshes, a figured waistcoat and an enormous tam-o'-shanter. Naturally we ignored him. We're not amused by such clowns, at least not in a small music room."

"He was pulling your leg," said Hope.

"Well, my soul, don't you suppose I knew that? But he got no satisfaction out of his performance and he's ruined himself so far as I'm concerned. I shouldn't dream of letting him come again. Annaliese Speyer was quite faint when she saw him. Really, she was! I had to send for aromatics."

The Countess resembled photographs I had seen of Empress Augusta Victoria. Blond bangs, arranged beneath a little green velvet hat, imperfectly concealed a high, wide forehead which, as the conventional sign of intelligence, was enhanced by a pair of large blue eyes, half-closed with a superciliousness which also infected the well-shaped, slightly curving mouth. Dominating the whole was a noble nose, too large, but soundly and handsomely built, and that this eminent organ, in which all the pomp of her history was centralized, might be displayed to its fullest advantage, she carried her head at a backward tilt. Less fine than the elevated nose but more commanding was the Germanic bosom of which the velvet covering was like the hull of some fictitious fruit. The voice, initiated in some other region, traveled through the buried core and was flavored with a stout sweetness as though her words were sopped in rich, old wine. I should have guessed that she had been a singer from the massive bust, the voice, and the carriage. I did not, but she told me. She took the cocktail I handed to her and with her free arm encircled my waist so that I was gently drawn to her.

"You make me think of a pupil I once had in Vienna. Do you like Schubert?" I said I could not distinguish one composer from another and that I much regretted my bad ear. "Well, then, we'll train that ear. No one in Boston has a better gramophone or more gramophone records than I. You come to see me always."

The word "gramophone" misled me: I imagined a small box with a black enameled horn, shaped like a morning glory. Such an instrument had been kept in a far corner of the lobby at the Hotel Barstow, and occasionally in the afternoon when the guests had had their naps and had gone out for a brief "constitutional," I put on "*Der Tannenbaum*" or "*Ich Liebe Dich*" or "Drink to Me Only with Thine Eyes" sung in a sad, rippling tremulo which brought tears to my eyes. I told the Countess I was grateful, but this was a lie: her loving gesture, though it was only a part of her patronizing, impersonal manner, had made me think of my mother and had returned me directly, by no détours of specific memory, to the horror of womanly affection which I thought I had outgrown. As in a long moment when I rested against the firm pouch of her bust and inhaled the odor of lilac, as fresh and springlike as if it came from the living bloom, and my only thought was how best to disengage myself from her embrace, Dr. McAllister, from across the room where he had taken a cocktail to Miss Pride and Mr. Whitney, shot me a look of warning or disapproval and simultaneously I felt the Countess' strong arm tighten about my waist. Before my mind's eye, like the immobile tableau of a dream, she and I appeared in this fond attitude, alone, before the sorrowing tin morning-glory in a dim, overheated room. I said in haste, "But I'm not often free. I'm studying stenography and my classes last all day!"

She let me go and laughing on one rich, contralto note, chided me, "Go on then, dissembler! You don't regret a bit that you can't tell Bach from Offenbach."

Everyone laughed at her play on words. Miss Pride smiled and said to me, "You mustn't miss an opportunity like that, Sonia. Not everyone is admitted to that famous salon." Horribly embarrassed by my blunder as well as by my egotistical assumption that this resplendent personage had an ulterior motive in her cuddling, I protested, and the hearty woman, speeding me on with a resounding smack on my backside, forgave and engaged me to come two weeks hence to a *Kaffeeklatsch* where I would find other people "in the same boat" with myself.

Miss Pride at last released Mr. Whitney, who for the past half hour had been fussing on the very edge of the sofa, so anxious to return to the hospital bedside of his son to congratulate him on the good tidings he had received from Dr. McAllister. He had, being at the end of his patience and ready to scream with vexation, finally risen and squeaked like a schoolboy, "Lucy, I *have* to go!" Clutching his hat, which he had refused to give up when he came in, in the hope that he would be able to make a flying visit, he dashed from the room. Miss Pride left her post and came over to speak to the Countess.

"I hoped you would come in," she said. "I rang you up earlier to make sure, but you weren't home. I have a bit of news for you. You know what I mean. I had a telephone call from New York this morning."

"Indeed!" cried the Countess and a flush of excitement illuminated her already well-lighted face. "Well, darling, can't we step over there?"

They moved off arm in arm toward the tulip-wood commode and stood there talking gravely for some time. I thought it singular that these two should have a secret. Hopestill, perhaps sensing my curiosity, enlightened me. Both of them, being shrewd business women, were in the habit of exchanging tips on the stock market, but did so out of earshot of everyone else, partly because they knew their passion for finance (which they had managed to dissociate from "cash" and "money" and approached as a pure science) would be considered in bad taste, and partly because they were frankly unwilling to share with anyone else the precious information that their Wall Street brokers periodically hissed over the wires. They were subscribers to the daily forecast of the Dow-Jones averages and to Barrons, and when they met, if it were at a dinner party, in Stearn's department store, or in Mrs. Gardner's palace, they instantly locked arms and conversed in whispers, comparing notes on the vagaries of the Greyhound Bus Company, like doctors consulting on a difficult case.

Mrs. Choate, stranded with the three young survivors of the tea-party, glanced from one to another of us and chose me to receive her first remark. "I know you must be a capable young woman. Just fancy learning stenography! Why, it's ever so much cleverer than my little avocation!"

She studied me brightly. Hopestill and Philip, refusing to

come to my aid, began a private conversation and I was obliged to inquire what Mrs. Choate's avocation was.

"I have taken up cookery. You know I'm a southerner and though I've been here for many years, I've never got used to Irish servants. I simply can't manage them! My cooks won't cook as I tell them to. And last year, I had gone without hoe-cake as long as I could bear it, so I simply went to the kitchen one Thursday and made myself hoe-cake. Ever since then, I've spent every Thursday experimenting. I'm always saying to Hopestill that she ought to take it up."

The woman gave Hope a humorous wink which missed fire and received no response. She went on, "Of course *no* one north of the Mason-Dixon Line knows how to cook."

Hopestill's voice was suddenly raised and I had the feeling that what she said had no part in her conversation with Philip but was merely thrown out as a bait. "It's a nuisance finding a restaurant when one's dining with a Negro."

The doctor, taking up her game, maliciously replied, "An awful nuisance. It's simpler just to dine at home."

Mrs. Choate paled. But though her face, a large and youthful one, wore a hurt, quizzical look, she said determinedly to me, "Perhaps you'll come to me some Thursday for a meal of greens and spareribs. My soups and desserts are not strictly southern, for I invent things, but the main course is always authentic."

"I had a splendid time at his apartment in Harlem . . ." Hope was saying.

Rebuffed, Mrs. Choate rose. "I'm going to interrupt that conference of the experts over there. I want to tell Miss Pride my latest discovery. I have invented a divine egg, poached in thinned tomato paste."

Hope grimaced, composed her features, and said to the outsider, "Oh, Mrs. Choate, I hear you've turned cook. I'm fascinated. Do you really make corn-pone and all those amazing things?"

But the woman was on her guard. "It is nice to see you looking so well, Hope," she said. "Philip, how is your dear mother?"

"Mother is very well," he replied. "She has almost lost her British accent."

Mrs. Choate smiled sickly and took her leave.

"She isn't southern at all," explained Hopestill to me in a whisper. "She's just a terrible fake. You'd think she'd been born with a mint julep in her hand and a fine old southern grudge against the damned Yankees that did in her grand-daddy's plantation. My Aunt Lucy, who can't stomach her and couldn't from the very first, found out that she lived in New Orleans for ten years before coming here but before that lived in California! But did we sound too beastly?"

They had, indeed, sounded beastly to me and I had suffered as much discomfiture as Mrs. Choate. I could not answer but instead inquired, "Is she the Countess' friend, then?"

"She's nobody's friend. She either just shows up at tea time and manages to walk in with someone else, or she makes every-one come to perfectly horrible parties—she uses marshmallows in her salads and starts off with hot wine and I'm sure none of *that* rot is southern—so that she has to be asked back."

Miss Pride had observed the approach of the bore and quickly guided the Countess along to meet her, then seized Mrs. Choate and marched her back to us. "Of course I think," said Hopestill, "that the Negroes are the coming race."

The Countess leaned over and embraced Hopestill. "To use that word you're so fond of, Cousin Hope, you're too 'advanced' for me. So I'm going to leave before I hear why you think the Negroes are the coming race. You have frightened me enough already with your threat that Dali and Chirico will come into their own and reign forever. I couldn't bear to have the blackamoors reigning too! I love you! Good-by! Come along, Mrs. Choate, I'll drop you."

Miss Pride, to my astonishment, murmured to me, "From the top of a high building, I hope."

Our hostess went out with the ladies and from the vestibule, we heard her say, "Mrs. Choate, there is an article on New Orleans in a recent issue of *The Atlantic* that ought to interest you."

"Really? I never read *The Atlantic*. I just skim it the way I do the Bible." The Countess chuckled, but Miss Pride said coldly, "Some other day I must ask you to explain that provocative remark." There were brief adieux and afterwards Miss Pride went upstairs to dress.

The emptied room seemed smaller, for it was now quite dark at the windows and the pale lamps revealed only their immediate environs. We moved toward the fire. I knew that I should leave Hopestill and the doctor, but the cocktails had made me careless and drowsy. I did not want to lose my warmth by going up to my room where the fire had probably died.

"Sonia—that's all right, isn't it?—made a conquest of the Countess, Perly."

"That's only Berthe's way."

"You mean she loves *all* young girls?" said Hopestill with a laugh. "Tell me: How did you find us?"

"Oh, Hope!" protested the doctor.

"Don't be absurd, Philip! She didn't miss anything. Haven't I the right to know the total impression she's got?"

"I had a pleasant afternoon," I said. I could have added that this termination of it was as disagreeable as anything I had ever encountered.

Hopestill extended me her small hand which, in my clasp, was as lifeless as the hand of a sawdust doll. "It's been so nice to meet you, Sonia. The best of luck."

I had not expected to be dismissed so soon and, clumsy in my surprise, I knocked over an ash-tray on a small table by the hearth. I bent to pick up the cigarette stubs but Hopestill said, "Oh, for goodness' sake, don't bother about that."

Reddening furiously, I started to the door. The doctor walked across the room with me. "I wanted to ask you," he said, "if you still go every Sunday?"

"Of course," I replied.

"That's right. You're awfully good. By the way, don't think we're giving you the cold shoulder. The fact is I . . . we haven't seen one another for quite sometime. We're *very* old friends, you know."

"Yes," I said, but my voice was unconvincing and he must have known that I was offended.

"Believe me," he said anxiously, "you *are* a good girl."

The door closed behind me. My goodness remained in the library with its advocate while I put my eye to the keyhole. The doctor was kissing Hopestill's neck. She paid no attention to him but poked the fire and at last, lifting up her head to address the Copley, "Great God, it's just like dancing school except that then you didn't have that ramrod down your back! Perly, Sonia is just the girl for you and the battle is half won because she's obviously mad about you." She flung back her head so that her hair reached to the middle of her back and laughed heartily.

"Hush!" said Dr. McAllister. "She may be in the hall."

I stood up quickly and went to the stairs, but I heard Hope-still pause in her laughter to say, "I meant absolutely no harm. I'm just a little giddy, and she was so *incredibly* solemn!" And then, as solemn as I had been, she added, "Imagine Aunt Lucy not telling her she had a cat! I swear I think the woman's mad."

Chapter Two

I N ORDER to make my appearance at the Countess von Happel's *Kaffeeklatsch*, an attention to her I felt imperative since it was my first invitation in Boston, I had been obliged to negotiate with Mrs. Hinkel so that I could be excused from the last class, Business English. (The Countess kept European hours, serving her afternoon refreshments at four instead of five, a custom Miss Pride regarded as so novel that she almost never went there to tea.) Mrs. Hinkel was furious at the presumption of her "laziest would-be professional woman" and said, "I suppose you think you know all about correct usage! I have not been headmistress of this college for fifteen years without observing, Miss Marburg, that the graduates of public schools, with the exception of those from the Latin schools, know next to nothing in regard to grammar. You may think now that dangling participles and 'due to' and prepositional phrases are the least of your worries, but the time will come when you will ask me for a recommendation and I will have to say, 'The candidate under consideration left much to be desired in her work in Business English.' However, as the useless expenditure of my time and your money doesn't bother you, run, amuse yourself, go to the movies, go to the beauty parlor! Respecting your language, don't worry! Don't let business interfere with pleasure!" She dispatched me to my debauchery with a military salute and returned, secretly delighted with the rhetoric of her diatribe, to the book she had been reading called *Hints to Commercial School Teachers and Administrators*.

I would have liked to explain to her that the prospect of a musical afternoon afforded me no pleasure, that I could far better endure the boredom of the class in Business English (in which, as she perfectly well knew, I was the only literate pupil) than the snares I was bound to fall into at the Countess'. But I knew that I would only enrage her further, and I held my tongue. My hand was on the door knob when she burst forth again. "I may as well tell you, Miss, that I am so displeased with your work here, and feel so strongly that this expenditure of *my* time and *your* money is useless that unless I am informed of marked improvement in your attitude, I shall have to ask you to leave. My time is simply too valuable to be wasted." The threat was purest nonsense, for she would not have dreamed of parting with my money which came in regularly each week, but she was a great believer in intimidation as an academic principle, and having very soon discovered that I received her recriminations with just the degree of terror she needed to nourish her sense of power, she never let a day pass without summoning me to her office or cornering me in the corridor to remind me, exultantly, that my ignorance and lassitude were eating up her time.

I was on the point of tears, not so much from her scolding as from what was in store for me as I left the building and closed the outer door behind me, massive, black, embossed with a wreath. I was not only convinced that what Mrs. Hinkel had said was true, but also that the whole of my Boston enterprise was a fiasco. But just at the moment when I was wishing myself back in Chichester, I saw, mincing uncertainly down Dartmouth Street, a figure so familiar, so instantaneously reminiscent of the stuffed birds, the rocking chairs, and the chilled farina pudding at Friday luncheon, that its appearance was like an ominous symbol, and for a second or two I thought it had no substance or else belonged to a stranger and not, as I had at first thought, to Mrs. Prather. There was no turning back, for she walked quickly and was upon me before I could contrive an escape.

"Of all things," said Mrs. Prather, taking both my hands. "What on earth are you doing so far away from home? Do you and Mother live in Boston now? Around *here*?" I replied that I lived here, but by myself. Her weak eyes begot two tears and she squeezed my hands. "I'm the limit! Imagine not recalling that sad, sad story. Now, child, don't tell me a thing, I can read it in your face: you want work."

She opened her handbag which contained, I saw, an apple, a Hershey bar, and a great many loose lozenges, and withdrew a calling card on which she begged me to write my address so that when she heard of something she might get in touch with me.

"But I don't need work," I protested, making no move to take the proffered pencil.

She was surprised and, for the first time taking in my new, expensive clothes, she said forgivingly, "Dearie, it doesn't need to be all over for you. You write down the address and I won't hold it against you. We'll get you out of there just as quick as we can and no one will be the wiser. I would take you straight to Arlington this minute rather than have you spend another night in one of those places, but for the time being, I'm crowded for space."

Without mentioning Miss Pride, I made it clear to her that I was not living in a brothel. She was greatly relieved and said that in that case I might come to call on her some day and tell her "all about it." "Whenever you get tired of your present place, I know just the house for you. A dear friend of mine has never had a good second maid and I know she would take you in a minute if I recommended you to her. You would have a room to yourself, I happen to know, and two afternoons off not counting Sunday."

I was anxious to be off for I had just heard the bells at Trinity chiming a quarter past four, but Mrs. Prather held me another five minutes, describing the excellent treatment I would receive at the hands of her friend who, at last it appeared, was an invalid and in spite of suffering horribly from one of the digestive disturbances for which the Hotel guests had such an affection, had the "sweetest nature in the world." In parting, she tried to give me her Hershey bar which I refused, but not liking to seem rude, I asked if I might have one of the horehound lozenges. She then released me. "Good-by, good-by. I'm glad it's not what I thought. Now remember me and when you need me, come to Arlington. I'm in the phone book. I expect it's time for Cinderella to run home to her pots and pans. You know, the French people have an expression when they take leave of one another. Instead of saying 'good-by,' they say *au revoir* which means 'till we meet again.' So that's what I will say to my little Chichester friend, *au revoir*."

I did not stop running until I was two blocks from the Countess' house, and it was only then that I tasted the full flavor of the bitter, not unpleasant horehound. It was a taste that belonged exclusively to Chichester and the summertime, and it made me a little nostalgic. Although I realized that I had

had a narrow escape and that I must henceforth be troubled
by the knowledge that I might meet Mrs. Prather again round
any corner and the next time might not be alone, this return of
the past through the candy, despite my homesickness, restored
my eagerness to continue the present time, and I was grateful
for the old lady's errand that had carried her down Dartmouth
Street in time to save me from a craven retreat.

The meeting had rendered me a service by taking my
thoughts off the entrance I was about to make into a strange
house, so that when I opened the street door, I rang the bell
at once without having to wait for courage to lift my finger to
the button. I was admitted by a manservant into a vast lobby
lighted by three iron candelabra and a number of sconces
placed at intervals like arc lights. I had heard of the Countess'
prejudice against electricity, the effect of which, she claimed,
was to destroy shadows, and shadows, like echoes and like the
aftertaste of Moselle wine, were sources of inspiration to her.
She had succeeded in creating with her candles a theatrical
effect, and through some optical illusion made by the long
shadows against the walls, which a highlight here and there
revealed as lustrous and would have shone under electricity, the
hall seemed much larger than it actually was and the ceilings
loftier. I was guided over a Persian carpet and past "occasional"
groups of high-backed chairs and console tables upon which
stood vases of yellow rosebuds whose outer petals were ruffling
into full maturity. Then, as though entering a bay from an
estuary, we turned to the right into a wide, square room, dominated on the left by a staircase, illuminated like the entry with
sconces, and on the opposite side by a portrait of the Countess
in a double frame. She sat at a spinet in a pale blue Empire dress
with her golden hair piled high, her head held well back to set
off her nose. It was impossible to tell whether she were about
to play or had just finished, for her musicianly hands rested in
her lap, and the expression on her face gave no clue since all
the other features were tyrannized over by the nose, sufficient
unto itself. Just as the candlelight, perhaps intentionally, hinted
that the owner conserved imported customs, older than the
old Boston house, older than her own experience, dating from
times before the fall of princes and the commercialization of
palaces, and by its metamorphosis of the hall, otherwise so like

all other halls on Beacon Hill, sharply designated the mistress as a member of a different species, so the portrait, pompous with the self-importance of the ruling class, gave those who viewed it to understand that an even further distinction was to be made between the Countess and her neighbors: that in that species she was a unique specimen, for she was not only aristocratic, but she was beautiful and talented as well, and, implied the station of the picture, according to standards that were not local, the *most* beautiful and *most* talented woman in Boston.

As we reached the foot of the stairs, the manservant spoke for the first time. "The name, please?" When I had told him, he repeated my name, putting an interrogation mark after the "Miss?" not in contradistinction to "Mrs." but to "Princess" or "Baroness," as if he were not in the habit of announcing the untitled bourgeoisie. I took a dislike to him partly because of his tone and partly because of his impassive, coarse, cunning face in which I seemed to read condescension as if he had divined that until recently (or perhaps even now) I had been "in the service" like himself. I said sharply, "I am expected."

"Certainly," he said, a flicker of a smile adding, "Don't be so naïve as to think I will take your word for it," and he indicated a divan, wide as a bed and upholstered in yellow satin, where I might wait, and left me, sending his dignified shadow ahead of him between the misshapen parodies of the balustrades on the uncarpeted marble stairs.

The yellow sofa was so placed that from it one could look nowhere but at the portrait of the Countess; and so, in my enforced contemplation of it, I was amused to see that upon the spinet there stood a vase of yellow rosebuds, the duplicates of which were set in such fresh profusion upon the tables in the entry. But a second discovery was even more amusing: I had been struck by the radiance of the canvas because the nearest sconce to it was several feet away, and now I perceived that craftily concealed under the inner frame at the top was a long, fluorescent tube sending a smooth shower of light over the whole surface! This in a Puritan house! In the hall of a great lady so sensitive she could not abide electricity! It occurred to me that other people had not seen what I had but had simply taken for granted, or had not noticed at all, the extraordinary visibility of this one object in the shadowy lobby, for Miss

Pride or Hopestill, when they had told me of the candelabra, would surely have told me of this inconsistency if they had ever observed it. For, although they were both fond of her as were their friends, they found Berthe von Happel irritating and would most likely have been delighted to learn that at least in one particular she was a fraud. "I don't mean to criticize Berthe's taste," Miss Pride had said, "because on one level it is superb taste, but I must say that there is something *malentendu* in the way she has turned poor Ralph Brooks' house into a museum. And not to put too fine a point on it, frankly, when I go there and the last thing I have seen is the Common, if I'm coming from Pierce's, or General Hooker, if I'm coming from Goodspeed's, I feel very much as if I were going into Loew's Orpheum."

The butler was gone so long that I began to think I had come on the wrong day or that the Countess was offended by my tardiness, or, worst of all, that she had not really meant her invitation, could not remember any Miss Marburg, and would instruct the servant to turn me out, a commission that would delight him. The first time I reproduced the scene in Miss Pride's drawing-room, the date and the hour of the engagement were perfectly clear, "Friday week at four o'clock," but, as minutes passed and the porter of my banal name did not reappear and I again and again rehearsed the Countess' words in an effort to determine who was to blame for my mistake, I became so confused that had not the word *Kaffeeklatsch*, which I had never before heard spoken, been audible in each revision I made, I would have believed that the invitation was imaginary. Presently I heard the door-bell and stood up, thinking that the butler would come down to answer it and on his way would inform me of my verdict, and indeed, in a moment there came to me the sound of music as if a door had suddenly been opened on a floor above. Still, he did not appear. Yet I heard voices in the entry and immediately the treacherous butler, who had evidently come down another way in order to tease me, came into sight but vanished as soon as the visitor had turned toward the stairs. The visitor appeared tremendous, for he was magnified by the shadows: his pale hair, which might have been blond or white, lost and then regained its glow as he passed the first sconce. I stepped forward, still in the shadow, intending to ask him if this were the day for the *Kaffeeklatsch*. He wheeled, startled, and peered through the dimness.

"*Doch, ist's so spät?*" he said.

"*Nein, es ist früh, glaub' ich.*"

"*Warum denn . . . ?*" He came closer. "Oh," he said, "oh, forgive me. I thought you were my daughter, Annaliese. It's so dim here. I expect I'll find her upstairs. Excuse me!"

"*Ich bin auch deutsche.*"

"*So?*" Impatient to be off, his eyes wandered up the stairs.

"I mean, sir," I said, "that for a moment I, too, was confused and I thought you were my father. But I see now that your dueling scar is not the same."

He gave a short, unamused laugh. "That's the way to tell, *nicht?*" And he ran up the stairs two at a time.

I had not, of course, mistaken him even though he did, in a general way, resemble my father, but I had been seized by a terrible longing to speak German and to be allowed to enter the upstairs room from which the music issued and which I conceived of as a world separate from Boston, the one to which I belonged and the only one in which I should ever be happy. But it was not only the man, apparitional and fugitive, that snatched me from the present time and Boston which I had hoped would be as familiar to me as a native habitat, it was, even more than him, the music. It was of a sort and played upon an instrument which I had never heard before: its academic precision was so intellectual, belonged so much to that altitude where mathematical progressions and retrogressions were animated by imaginative genius that, just as one cannot look directly at the sun, so I could not submit the part of the mind that hears without the protection of the part that sees. Thus, my pleasure came to me attended by memory of scenes or objects, my mother's face, the beach at Chichester, my father's rosary hanging in his shop, the summer drives to Wolfburg, so that the passage of the music to my heart was insulated, roundabout, enriched. And I saw, as though I stood upon it and not upon the costly Persian rug, the sweating sand at Chichester, pawed by the surf on a glaring August day, where my father and I had stopped to watch a plover. The amber-clear, archaic notes, plucked from the siccative strings of the instrument I did not know, and the stranger's voice, and the somnolent waves cast out and entrapped my father's exclamation: "*Ein Regenpfeifer! Still!*" My longing to speak German was then elaborately if minutely satisfied by the redemption of "*Regenpfeifer*," a word I had heard only that one time, twelve years before.

The cessation of the music reminded me that I had been waiting an unconscionable time and was no closer to the Countess von Happel than this romantic representation of her, larger than life size. I wondered if, by hanging it here, she had meant to tantalize as well as impress visitors who, unknown in the house, were not allowed to go at once into her presence. It was a mistake, if this had been her purpose, and an insulting one to prolong their suspense, for, like the magazines in the busy dentist's office, it became an unendurable bore, and one's temptation was to leave and come back on another day. The postponement of a disagreeable affair and the self-righteousness in which it has had its genesis afford as much relief as if the pain or the embarrassment has been undergone, is finished, and can be forgotten. But just as we throw down the magazine, so trashy it seems like a calculated insult to our intelligence, and prepare to announce cuttingly to the secretary that our time is precious, we had assumed, when we made the appointment for four, that we would be attended to at that time, the door opens and the dentist emerges smiling, disarming us with a genial apology and a word of sympathy about the suffering our wisdom tooth is causing us. I had reached the turn in the hallway and had just annexed a new feature to my grievance, for I was hungry and my vitals informed me that it was past the hour when it was my secret and shameful custom to eat two crullers and drink a cup of coffee in a small, steamy café at the top of Pinckney Street, an indulgence into which I had been forced by the meager fare at Miss Pride's tea-table. The butler, coming through a door at my right, which I had not noticed, stopped me, and said that I might go up now, that Madam had been playing and he had been unable to announce me at once. Then, by way of apologizing for his suspicions, he said flatteringly, like the dentist, "Madam is waiting for you."

2

"How d'ye do?" said the Countess who stood in the doorway and drew my arm through hers, the vegetative softness and fragrance of her person and the intense heat of the small room making me think of summertime. "It's a pity you had to wait. Tell me, how did you like that little likeness of me in the hall? Did you notice it?" She turned her profile to me, waiting for my answer, and when I gave it, saying that I had been charmed, she continued to pose a moment longer in imitation of the "little likeness" as if she were not in the least concerned with my opinion, the anticipation of which, in fact, had set every nerve in her body tingling. Then, pressing my arm against her, she said, "It's an excellent painting, even if you don't like the subject, isn't it? I debated with myself a long time before I hung it at all: Will people want to look at poor me? I said to myself. But what nonsense! The painting is the thing, you goose, people won't even recognize you, you're simply incidental to the composition." I agreed that the painting was excellent (for all I knew it was, but it had struck me as being remarkably dull), but that she was wrong in thinking people would not recognize her, for she, not the composition, was its *raison d'être*. She could not deny my praise, but brought up from her interior an exultant purr: "Did you look at the hands? They are divine!"

This toll was levied upon every newcomer; some, less green than myself, added a gratuity to the set fee. Twice during that afternoon and many times thereafter, I observed the transaction carried out on the part of the Countess with a sort of childlike poise which made one feel that she was not so much vain as honestly amazed at her endowments. And when she had made her concluding remark, to one person about the hands, to another about the throat or the eyes, in a lowered voice as though she were praising someone within earshot, she became an amiable, solicitous hostess dedicated to the wants of her guests. Like the hypodermic injection of adrenalin that instantaneously relieves the asthmatic, the Countess' hospitality at once made me forget my annoyance and my hunger. She now allowed me to pass through into a small, bare room which in no way conformed to the speculations I had made about it when I was half submerged in the yellow satin sofa. It was an ascetic's cell on the top floor and at the back of the house, presenting a view from the uncurtained dormer windows of chimney pots and blind brick walls. Central in the room and, unlike the portrait, requiring no contingents to play up its merits, stood a rosewood harpsichord from which had been plucked the brilliant, incisive tones I had heard downstairs. The owner's seal, a silver pitcher full of yellow roses, had been placed on the wing directly in the player's line of vision. The other decorations of the room were testimonial: uncolored photographs of Mozart, Bach, Haydn, Handel, with perukes and lacy jabots, hung in a row upon one wall and opposite, between two bookcases, a deep square frame preserved a letter signed "Franz Liszt." Here and there stood high-backed, uninviting chairs without arms or cushions. The music, the wild log fire, and the table of refreshments were the only provisions for comfort. A few of the chairs were occupied, and several people stood around the table by the windows where they helped themselves to coffee and cakes.

The Countess, leading me to the table, said, "You must have been late, for I began sharp at four. There's no point in coming at all if you miss the music."

"I'm very sorry," I told her. "I met someone on the way. But there will be more, won't there?"

"More?" she repeated incredulously. "Well, you *are* a baby!" But she patted my hand kindly and chuckled. "No, after I've played one opus I'm through, for I won't mix composers and I won't overindulge in one. But you didn't know. All's forgiven. Next time you'll know better and not let yourself be waylaid."

"Then I may come again?"

"If you don't, I won't forgive you. Now let me get you started and I'll come back to you later on. Just now I must speak to *Herr* Speyer and his adorable daughter. I'm losing them. They're sailing for Germany, naughty deserters!"

The Countess plucked a boy by the sleeve. "I want you to meet this unfortunate young lady who got here late and 'sat out' the whole of the minuet."

The boy, a tall, frail Jew with a womanly grace in his long, supple fingers and a transparency of skin, turned eagerly at the sound of her voice, but not to meet me. "Oh, Berthe, you were wonderful today! When I closed my eyes, I could have sworn it was Landowska playing. I was overcome!" He was, in truth, dumfounded and gazed at her with famished, radiant eyes. The Countess puckered her brow in annoyance. "You're a trifler, Gerhardt, but you don't take me in. I'm improving, yes, but I'm still a greenhorn. Now be good and give Miss Marburg a cup of coffee." His eyes implored her retreating figure to come back, but simultaneously he said to me, "Will you have cream and sugar?"

I was surprised at the Countess' treatment of *Herr* Preis who was obviously head over heels in love with her. And being certain, from my own observation as well as from remarks dropped by Hopestill and Dr. McAllister, that vanity was the principle of her being, I could not understand why she had taken his compliment with so much displeasure. I thought perhaps he knew nothing of music and, being devoted to it almost as much as she was to herself, she could not accept homage to one and not to the other. But then I learned, in our ensuing conversation, that the unhappy boy had himself taught her how to play the harpsichord.

Because the room was small, it seemed crowded with people. There were, in fact, less than a dozen. They had not gathered into groups but wandered with their coffee cups to examine the letter from Liszt or the unrewarding view from the windows or to smell the roses on the harpsichord. A hush prevailed like that in an art gallery. The Countess, engrossed in a whispered conversation with *Herr* and *Fräulein* Speyer, made no attempt to remedy her guests' unease. I had no choice but to remain with Gerhardt Preis who would have liked to leave me, like a wounded animal, to nurse his hurts in solitude. Feeling that for the time being at least, he was incapable of talk, I made the opening remark myself, expressing my surprise that the guests were not, as I had expected them to be, in the midst of a spirited discussion of music. I had supposed, I said, that the company would be made up of experts and of ambitious amateurs.

Preis gave me a pained smile. "Berthe does not allow us to talk music here. Why should she? What more can be said than she says when she plays?"

"But surely," I said, "she must like to talk shop. I thought all artists did."

He shook his head. "Not the Countess von Happel. She's above it."

"Well, then, I'm more comfortable. I thought, when I came, that the talk would be too intellectual for me to follow."

"Intellectual!" he exclaimed to himself and for a moment drank in his own scorn. Then facing me with a civil smile, he changed the subject. "Your name is the name of my father's town. Do you know it?" I told him I had never been to Germany. "I shall never be in Germany again. No doubt you guessed that I am a Jew. I was born in Marburg, but I have no memory of it, for my mother took me to Paris when I was very small and we only visited Germany in the springtime. My father was a manufacturer of surgical instruments and as you Americans say, he 'made a fortune.' I'm therefore of that species Berthe finds so odd. She's completely above money, you know." I smiled, recalling her parleys with Miss Pride.

The young man continued. "Have you heard about the time she met the millionaire department store owner from Chicago? It's the most *Happelisch* story in the whole Berthe *Sammlung*. This Croesus was house-guest of someone she had invited to one of her Saturdays and he had to be brought along. As they were starting in to dinner, she said to him, 'You must go first, for I understand that you are a "merchant prince" and my only other noble guest this evening is nothing but a poor little Russian baron.'"

A pretty, dark-haired girl beside us took a step closer and frowned at Preis. "I was at the dinner-party. It was appalling, because, you see, Mr. Bruce was my mother's guest and it was very trying to us. For he was by no means a stupid man and he perfectly well knew he had been horribly insulted. You know, she ought to inquire into people's histories before she plays such a joke as that. We all think he is a fine man and not at all coarsened by his money. And anyhow, he came from Boston in the first place and went to Harvard. I think the Countess goes too far."

"I disagree," returned the young man sourly and his tone implied that the girl had taken far greater liberties than their hostess had done with Mr. Bruce. "It's of no use to criticize Berthe. She's unique."

"You forget that this is Boston," said his adversary. "To be quite blunt, Mr. Preis, what I mean is that we New England-ers were here a great many years before you refugees started arriving."

Immediately she regretted her tantrum since, though she had enjoyed it, it had been a breach of manners. But instead of apologizing, she simply left us and vanished from the room without telling the Countess good-by. I remarked to Mr. Preis that she seemed to have had enough of the salon.

"No, she hasn't had enough at all, and unless Berthe over-hears her sometime, she'll be back every Friday all winter long. No one refuses invitations to this house. Berthe shouldn't live in Boston, of course, for it's very bad for her. She only does it because she's fond of the way she's done her house, though I've told her a thousand times she could have done a better one in New York. She's made for a Central Park penthouse. I hope you appreciate her, as I see you're not a native. If you have the good fortune to be asked often, I *beg* you to see how adorable she is. I'm afraid this is my last afternoon here! I've offended her somehow. She's as sensitive as the princess who could feel the pea."

His misery was so acute that he clasped his head in his hands and did not stir but sorrowed behind the handsome façade of his Hebraic face, his eyes closed, his full red lips parted as if in illness. I was deeply touched. "Perhaps things will come all right in the end," I said.

"Oh, you don't know her at all or you wouldn't talk about things coming all right in the end. No, when she's through, she's through once and for all. I could no more get her to forgive me than you could get her to play again this afternoon."

"But what have you *done*, Mr. Preis?"

"I fell in love with her, and that's against the rules. You can remember me as the first exile from Berthe von Happel's Fri-days you ever knew. It's no consolation to me to know that you will see a good many more like myself in the course of time."

The Countess had gone to the door with the Speyers and allowed *Herr* Speyer to kiss her hand. Then, drawing Annaliese to her, she kissed the girl on the cheeks and on the lips and cried, "Don't change a particle while you are gone. I shall die of a broken heart if you cut off that golden tail about your head! Good-by! I love you!"

Above the heads of the embracing women, there appeared the face of a young man which, as the girl submitted to a final kiss upon her mouth, registered a virile horror, a response that the scene did not elicit in my companion who had not taken his eyes off the Countess for a second. The Speyers left and the head which had materialized out of the shadows in the hall acquired a body. The Countess smiled radiantly and had already forgotten her grief at the farewells. She told the young man she was sorry he had been kept waiting, that she supposed he had got sick and tired of her "little likeness" in the lobby. I turned my head in embarrassment at the repetition of her welcoming speech and told Mr. Preis that I would like to look at the view from the windows.

"Well, I shan't go with you. As for myself, I find that kind of view uninspiring. Do you really like to look at dirty chimney pots? Anyhow, I must speak to this low character."

The low character, having acquitted himself of his debt, hastened to greet his friend. "You're still here, then. I must talk to you. Can't we go now?" He started, seeing me. "Oh, I'm sorry. I didn't know I was interrupting."

"I was just leaving."

"Don't on my account, please." His bashful smile, as he blushed, so delighted me that although I should have left him at once to his confidences which he was perishing to impart to his friend, I did not move aside. He looked no older than a schoolboy and I could scarcely believe Preis when he introduced us, describing Mr. Garvin as a Harvard graduate student of philology, and went on, to the boy's discomfort, to tell me that his formal study of language was not enough, but that he was now about to tackle Japanese.

I said, "I am living now with the daughter of a Sinologist, or so I've been told he was. He had a large library of Japanese books too."

The two young men laughed and Gerhardt whispered to me, "He wants only a *speaking* knowledge of it, Miss Marburg."

"That's what I wanted to tell you about," said the other. "He's beat my time, just as we predicted."

"Who? Kadish?"

"Who else? He ran her down yesterday. And mind you, he had just left me five minutes before."

I could not help my outcry of surprise, but having no wish at that moment to acknowledge my acquaintance with Nathan, I turned abruptly and filled my cup from the large silver urn on the refreshment table. But I did not move out of earshot of the young men who, pausing for a moment after my ejaculation, continued their talk.

"And let me tell you what else he's done," said Garvin. "He is contracted to teach one Harry Morgan of Park Avenue, Long Island, Beverly Hills, and Sun Valley enough German to get him through the course he flunked last year. Where the hell did he get the German is what I want to know."

"Oh, he knows German," said Preis. "He speaks it like a native."

"Are you pulling my leg? I didn't know he knew a word of it."

"There's a lot you don't know about him. And a lot I don't know. But tell me how he got the *Japanerin*."

"Not here. Later."

"But how with that . . . Oh, all right. We'll go in a minute. Let me stay just that long since it's the last time I'll be here."

Gerhardt's face had lighted as he saw the Countess bearing down on us, sending her resonant laugh ahead of her. "Come along, Preis, you can't accomplish any more here than you can at Jacob Wirth's," whispered Garvin.

The Countess, without glancing at Gerhardt, took me by the arm and as she led me away, called over her shoulder to Garvin, "Come next Friday, won't you?" Then, in a lowered voice to me, "I didn't ask him to come for the music as I'm sure he hasn't got an ear. I'm trying to drop the other one, and I thought I might get his friend to take him away with him. I'm sure he won't show up again next week."

I said, "I'm sure I shouldn't want to 'drop' anyone who admired me so much as Mr. Preis does you."

The Countess shuddered. "Ugh! I can't bear it. Really, give a refugee an inch and he'll take an ell. You understand, I hope, that I am not a refugee?" I took her question as meaning, "You don't think for a moment that I have Jewish blood, do you?" or else as implying that she had come here of her own free will from a society that was not in the least threatened by the upstart revolutionists who had played the devil with people of Gerhardt's class, definitely inferior to her own.

I flattered her a little on her excellent English and asked her then how long she had been in America. I listened to her voluble reply with only half my mind while the other turned over the remarkable mention of Nathan Kadish's name. I had been titillated at the sound of it, but without immediately being jealous of the Japanese girl whom he had "run down" I devoutly hoped I would not see him. With a coldness that startled and even alarmed me, I knew that at this juncture in my life, other things—indeed, *all* other things—were more important to me than being in love and, particularly, in love with Nathan.

The Countess was saying, "I have been here seven years and I've been a widow five, so you see I've had to make my own way like all the immigrants. How precious you are to praise my English! It's all right for ordinary chatter, but you'd never guess how it fails me when I'm confronted with a conversation about music: I can't understand a word. And consequently, much to my sorrow, I've had to avoid friendships with my fellow-artists. You can imagine how painful that has been."

The Countess puzzled me and from time to time the thought flashed across my mind that she was a fraud. Yet, I had it on what was probably good authority, that her talent was prodigious. Miss Pride had told me that before her divorce from Count von Happel and her marriage to Ralph Brooks, she had enjoyed a brilliant reputation in Vienna both as a singer and as a pianist. Hopestill Mather believed that her practice of filling her salon with people ignorant of music was sheerest snobbery, that she was the victim of the common European delusion that Americans had no taste and no artistic principles. And still, as Miss Pride pointed out, she had, with the sagacity of good breeding, made several concessions to Boston. True, she had remained aloof from its musical enterprises (tyros, asking her opinion of Koussevitsky, received the damning faint praise, "He's all right, though by continental standards, these conductors in America are a society of mountebanks.") but had gone in whole-heartedly for its art. Rather too effusively for her fellow-citizens who knew better, she declared that the Fine

Arts Museum was superior to the Luxembourg. Miss Pride said that her concessions reminded her of the Greek who had set up the statue of Aristides in Louisburg Square and then to conciliate the rest of the community had faced it with one of Christopher Columbus. "Two negatives don't, in that case, make a positive," she said. "If we *must* have Aristides, whoever he may be, why can't we at least have Daniel Webster?"

I was curious to know why the Countess had left her Viennese husband, but nothing she said enlightened me. Except for brief interruptions when she told her guests good-by, that she loved them (this was her unvarying epilogue as the reference to her portrait was her opening gambit), she would not let me go but for three-quarters of an hour interrogated me minutely. She appeared disposed to regard my candidacy to her salon with favor. To my relief, she was incurious about my background and when, in connection with something she said about a room at the Chilton Club, I told her that I had never been there for I did not belong to society, she laughed and squeezed me closer to her.

"American society! The nobility is made up of 'cattle kings' and 'wool barons' and 'merchant princes' and between you and me, you're just as good as the rest of 'em, whoever you may be. I must confess a great weakness for New England, but try as I may I cannot take any stock in its society. Why, my people, when they are calculating time reckon in centuries, not in decades. It so amuses me to see Lucy Pride (I love her dearly and I hope you do too) show off her tea service which belonged to some governor or other in the eighteenth century. I don't call it 'old,' though I do call it pretty. I brought very little with me from Austria, only a few knickknacks, among them a set of tankards that have been in my family since the thirteenth century. I think them fairly antique. I'm going to tell you a story on myself before you hear it from someone else who might make me sound brutal. I had only been in this country a few years and I had heard so much about the 'wool barons' and so on that I thought perhaps the government *had* established a peerage. You're laughing at my innocence and I don't blame you! Well, a man named Mr. Puce (I have to chuckle at the name because it reminds me of the gloves I have always had my chauffeurs wear) came to dinner here and the person who brought him introduced him as 'the Chicago merchant prince.' How should I know any better? American names are so exotic, you know, to a foreigner, that it's not a bit strange to think of a 'king of Wyoming' or a 'grand duke of Iowa' or 'prince of Chicago,' so poor me! I had him go in first to dinner. He was flattered half to death, and the only reason the Baron Kalenkoff didn't leave at once in a fury was that he thought I was playing a joke!"

I could make no counter to this, and instead went back to the beginning of her anecdote. "I would like to see your tankards, Countess."

She laughed richly. "I'm no collector, darling! I'm not interested in *things*. Art is *my* life. Make me happy and tell me that it's yours too!"

"But I'm very green," I told her. "I would like to make you happy, but I'm afraid all I can do is read."

"Oh, but that's marvelous! I hope you aren't so modern that you will find what I like *démodé*, as Hope Mather does. I can still cry at *Père Goriot*. As for modern novels, they don't touch me. Either they're cold or gross. And *need* they be so difficult?"

I could not resist the temptation to advance myself with the Countess. "Balzac is sublime," I said. "He has touched all passions and given the commonplace the stature of tragedy. I cannot feel that Shakespeare is any greater." I was quoting from George Moore, a passage which had at first captivated Nathan with its audacity and then had filled him with derision. Since I had read very little of Balzac and worshipped Shakespeare with the fine rapture of adolescence, I visualized inverted commas about my words, but my voice did not convey them to the Countess who cried, "Lucy said you were clever, but she didn't prepare me for this! What an addition to Boston you are!"

My voice shook with shame as I replied, "Oh, I have only a few tags."

"By the way, I don't understand your name, Sonie. Is it short for Euphrosyne?" Through a misreading of the word, she had metathesized the vowels and pronounced it "Euphrysone." I explained that Sonie was my own childish corruption of Sonia. "What a pity," she said. "Not that I don't love Sonia for you, but it would have been so delightful if you *had* been named

for the goddess of Mirth. Your eyes are so merry." She held
me off at arm's length. With a supreme effort I obliged her by
grinning, hoping to infect my eyes with the merriness I put
into my lips. "There! Isn't it the image of Euphrysone!"

A woman and her daughter came up to us at that moment
to say good-by. "Amelia and I have so enjoyed the afternoon,
Berthe. I love your nest and your cunning little harpsichord.
You're like a sirocco to warm our cold New England."

The Countess glowed. "You're a fibber," she said, rising and
taking both hands of her guest. "But you must come and tell
me the same sweet-sounding fibs every Friday you possibly can.
Next week I'm going to play the Haydn Opus 21 in D Major."

"I don't believe I know it," said the woman who did not,
in that sense, *know* any music. "But if you will let us, we will
come, won't we, Amelia? Amelia is wild about music, aren't
you, Amelia?"

Amelia, fourteen years old, a gawky girl with long legs and
knobby knees who was, obviously, at this stage of her life, an
enemy to music and to mankind, nodded in agreement and
said in a high, rushing voice as if she had got it by heart, "Yes,
I am, Countess von Happel. I don't know anything about it,
but I know what I like."

The Countess took them to the door, kissed them and
proclaimed her love to the furiously blushing and twitching
Amelia. She returned and settled down beside me again to
resume her inquisition. But at that moment, she perceived that
Garvin was edging toward the door, leaving Gerhardt Preis still
standing by the refreshment table. "Well," she said resolutely,
"I may as well do it now, make it quite clear he can't come
again. Lou," she called to a girl who was reading the titles in
the collection of record-albums and turned at the sound of her
name, "will you come meet Miss Sonia Marburg?"

Lou, who did not supply her surname, sat down beside me
and laughed softly. "She's had to take steps at last, poor Berthe.
You're new here, aren't you?" When I told her that I was, she
asked frankly, "May I ask how you met the Countess?"

"At Miss Pride's, at tea the other day. Do you know Miss
Pride?"

"Oh, gracious yes, though I haven't seen her in a month of
Sundays. Has Hope gone on to New York yet?"

"She left on Tuesday, but she'll be back tonight. She's going to spend week-ends here."

The girl laughed. "I dare say that was her Aunt Lucy's idea. Poor girl, she does hate Boston so. You didn't know she hated it? She has a perfect complex on the subject."

"I can't understand that. I've seen very little of it, but that has seemed charming."

"You mean you've never been to Boston before? But where . . ."

The Countess had dispatched Mr. Preis and returned to us. "I heard you tell Sonie that Hope has a complex. This child hasn't been here long enough to know all our complexes and reflexes and prefixes, Lou, and I don't want you to let our cat out of the bag. She'll detest us and run away."

"Berthe, you're priceless! Why, that's what makes us so interesting."

"Do you know what Amy and I think? We think Hope is going to change her tune and fall in love with Boston after all."

"Why that prediction?"

"Don't *you* think she'll marry Philip McAllister?"

"I'm sure I haven't the least idea," returned the girl coldly and rose. "Berthe, I've had a wonderful time. May I come again next week?"

"But, darling, don't go yet! I want your opinion. You know he went to Manchester for his holiday this year. Don't you think *that* indicates something?"

The girl merely smiled and drew on her gloves. "Will you ask Amy to ring me up? I want her to do Monadnock for me from the top of Prospect Hill. No, don't get up. Good-by."

When she had gone, the Countess put her arm about my waist. "Now I have you all to myself. Tell me, don't you think we're right about Cousin Hope and that nice young man?"

"I don't know Hope at all well. She seems a little . . ."

"A little highly seasoned for Philip? Of course we all think that, but that's precisely the reason we think he'll pursue her to the end. His mother and grandmother are so opposed, you know. Everyone talks about it *ad infinitum* so I'm not telling tales out of school. Haven't we got mean little minds?"

A hysterical laugh from the doorway announced Amy Brooks' breathless arrival. "Berthe, *darling*!" she cried and skipped across the room to kiss her stepmother. "I was so engrossed in doing the Oyster House that I completely forgot it was Friday. Mr. Pingrey was along and we've already had our tea. Do you forgive me?"

"I don't mind anything you do so long as Mr. Pingrey is your chaperon. We were just making a match between Hope and Dr. McAllister, and I was also on the very point of saying I'm betting on another marriage of a certain young lady not a thousand miles away to a young man whose name begins with P."

Amy Brooks collapsed in shaking laughter, her eyes brimming with tears, and I got up, unnerved by the spectacle and aware suddenly that we three were alone. The Countess permitted me to go only after she had got my solemn promise that I would come to her every Friday for the rest of my natural days. "And now, good-by, come back to me. I love you!"

3

Dinner was served punctually at seven, and nothing would have induced Miss Pride to delay it by a minute. She regarded tardiness at mealtime as the same sort of self-indulgence as illness. But as she insisted that I dress each night (she did not herself, but thought that I should "learn how to manage an evening frock against an evil day," the evil day presumably being the one on which I should be invited out somewhere) I could not help being late, and she had finished her soup when I entered the dining-room. "We dine at seven, Sonie," she said, laying down her spoon. "You shouldn't have changed."

"I thought you wouldn't like it if I didn't."

"When two rules conflict, the important one is the one that should be obeyed. It is commendable in you to remember to dress, but punctuality is infinitely more important. I understand that you were late to Berthe's today." She leaned forward so that her face was framed by the white candles as she confronted me with this astonishing information. Was I so simple that my very actions could be read in my face? I dared not question her and for some minutes she pursued the subject without hinting at the identity of the scout who had lurked about the doorway on Beacon Street to time me. But she was not angry. She smiled. "It was a mistake. Berthe is rather lax about everything except her Fridays. I suppose it meant you didn't hear the music and that never sets well with her. But she wasn't offended. She telephoned me the minute you left the house to say how pleased she had been with you. She referred to you by some foreign nickname that I did not catch. I was rather surprised you were already on such intimate terms."

I explained how she had come to call me Euphrosyne (rather, Euphrysone) and while Miss Pride said nothing, I was sure she was taking in every word in order to repeat it the next time Berthe's name was brought up amongst her friends. I went on then to tell her that I had been delayed because I had encountered Mrs. Prather on Dartmouth Street.

"Who is Mrs. Prather?"

"Why, you must remember her. She has come to the Barstow every summer for years. At least as long as you have. She sits under the ptarmigan in the dining-room."

"Oh, yes, I remember. For a long time I thought her name was 'Mather' and wondered if she were a relative of Hopestill's. I did not inquire. I don't understand why you should have been late on account of her, though. She's simply the kind of fright one stares through if one's in a hurry, ain't she?" In a sense, she had forgotten who I was and that I could not possibly have cut Mrs. Prather. I went on to tell her of my conversation with the stupid but kindly old soul who believed I had become a prostitute. Miss Pride was vexed, not because of Mrs. Prather's delusion, but because I had spoken unguardedly in front of the maid. She rebuked me while the girl was still in the room. Upon her mischievous Irish face appeared a grin of malicious pleasure, so that I knew the scene would be reproduced in the cellar as soon as we had left the dining-room. "For a moment I couldn't place Mrs. Prather," she said. "But now I recall that she is a woman of great breeding, and if she thought you were pursuing the oldest profession as it were, she probably had good reason. I have often warned you, as you can't deny, that the excessive rouge you use on your lips is far from good taste. And I should remind you that in scorning Mrs. Prather's offer to recommend you as an upstairs maid may, in time, prove to be the greatest folly. If I were you, I would not be at all sure that I would not end up as an upstairs maid or even as a 'useful' servant."

She had never spoken so harshly before. In my agitation I took far more meat than I could use and it occupied so much space on my plate that when Emma came round with the vegetables I had to push it to one side and in doing so pushed it off onto the table altogether. Miss Pride, whose avian eyes had not rested for a moment in their barrage of killing looks on me, said, "Oh, my soul! Emma, bring a clean mat for Miss Marburg." The girl, nearly overcome, rushed to the pantry and banged the door shut, there, as I imagined, to giggle at my bungling. But when she returned with a clean napkin, the scolding was over and Miss Pride was genially telling me of her morning which she had spent with her Cambridge friend, the widow of the Harvard professor, in the Concord burying ground.

"And that reminds me that Philip McAllister called this afternoon and said that his grandmother would like to have you and Hopestill come to tea tomorrow. He'll drive you up. If you have time, do take a stroll through Sleepy Hollow. But don't put it off until after tea. Laura McAllister is such a chatterbox you won't get away before dinnertime." (Later that evening, she said, "When I spoke of Mrs. McAllister l didn't mean anything unfriendly by calling her a chatterbox. She's a charming woman, and it would displease me to hear that you had repeated what I said." With an antediluvian notion that marriages could still be made by families rather than by individuals, she was anxious to stay on the right side of Philip's grandmother.)

The account of her day amongst the graves alleviated only the suffering she had inflicted by humiliating me in the presence of a servant, but the other suffering that came from the fear that this was to be only the first of such occasions lingered as a dull but obtrusive ache. And because it was a symptom common to many diseases, there was no way immediately to identify it. It was inchoate fear, the first sign of all those irascible emotions that include hatred, contempt, despair, and so on. And after dinner, as we sat for an hour, according to our custom in the upstairs sitting-room and twice Miss Pride

corrected my pronunciation of a word in the article I was reading to her from *Harper's Magazine*, the pain became acute for
a moment and when it had gone I felt the vague nausea that
accompanies shock.

We did not have our coffee until I had finished reading, at
eighty-thirty. It came up then on the dumb-waiter and Miss
Pride established herself behind *The Boston Evening Transcript*
while I filled the cups and brought a bottle of Benedictine
from a closet in the "office." My mistress was proud of saying
that she took no medicines but "vinous and spiritous liquors"
which she called "the medicaments of Nature," and while she
drank very little at a time, she had a glass of something at
regular intervals throughout the day: at eleven in the mornings
of week-days, she had a glass of port, but on Sundays, after her
chess game, she had dry sherry. Before luncheon and dinner,
she had two glasses of sherry and in the evening with her coffee
a liqueur or a measure of rum which she took neat. The best of
her liquor was kept in the den just off the upstairs sitting-room,
and this was reserved for her own use. Less excellent whiskeys,
brandies, liqueurs, and wines were kept in the library and given
to guests when she entertained formally. The pantry and the
cellar were stocked for the rank and file with domestic dry
wines, low-priced Bourbon, and gallon jars of gin. I was not
invited to pour myself a glass of Benedictine, but invariably
she said, as she folded the newspaper but continued to read it
and as I handed her the tiny green bowl on a thin gold stem,
"Perhaps you'd like a glass of sherry. I won't offer you any of
this, for I'm sure you wouldn't care for it, and it's so dear I
can't allow it to be wasted."

Tonight, drowsy with the rich wine, out of touch with Miss
Pride since she never spoke once she had begun to read the
financial page, I felt simultaneously dissatisfied and proud.
The dissatisfaction I erroneously (and perhaps intentionally)
set down to the sherry, the effect of which had been to usher
in a memory of the beer my father had used to pour into my
soup. I conjured up his youthful face, so like that of *Herr*
Speyer, and wondered at its incongruity in this rich woman's
parlor, and felt that I had betrayed him since my own presence
here was no longer incongruous. It was as if I had supplied his
attributes, plagiarizing those my creator had conferred upon

me; or, conversely, that *I* was the chimera, the reflection in the flawed looking glass, the misquoted doctrine, and he the paradigm. His presence became as palpable as that of Miss Pride. The *du* of *Herr* Speyer's remark, that intimate address, lay like a ghostly hand upon my cheek. Like a pilgrim, used to sleeping out of doors and claustrophobic in a house, I inhaled jerkily as if the air within this silent, genteel room were poisonous to my lungs, as though, if I could, I would escape the carnivorous flowers and come again among the harmless edelweiss my father's fancies had picked for me as I sat hearing his stories in the shop in Chichester.

I rose. "I believe I'll change and take a little walk, Miss Pride."

She did not look up. "I hurt your feelings at dinner, did I not?" But there was nothing in her voice to indicate whether she were sorry or if she intended me to apologize for my milksop sensitiveness.

"No, ma'am."

"I've told you not to call me 'ma'am.' 'Sir' is all very well, but 'ma'am' I cannot tolerate. You mustn't take me seriously when I'm crotchety. I wouldn't let you be an upstairs maid for a dowager duchess, let alone for one of Mrs. Prather's hypochondriac friends. No, indeed, I don't intend to turn you out. Stick by me, Sonie, won't you, and put up with my flip tongue? My father used to tell me I wouldn't have a friend in the world by the time I was thirty. Perhaps he was right and the only reason people come to see me is that they're after the rum cakes on my tea-table."

"Really, Miss Pride," I protested, "I wasn't in the least offended. I thought perhaps you had been annoyed by something earlier and were just out of sorts a little."

"You guessed it perfectly. Now don't put a false construction on this, for on second thoughts I realized that I was quite wrong. I was annoyed by the way Philip McAllister asked for you on the telephone this afternoon. I had the disagreeable feeling that if you had answered, he would have asked you to meet him for tea, and I said to myself, 'Surely that child can't be having rendezvous with Philip who is virtually Hopestill's fiancé.'"

Until now she had been talking to me behind the rustling

screen of the *Transcript*, but now she lowered it and as I earnestly denied that I had seen Philip at all except in her own
drawing-room, I winced at the firm set of her jaw and the
suspicious, narrowed eyes. Though what I said was true, I did
not feel that I had been absolved of my guilt, but that she
was reading my mind in which my sporadic infatuation with
the doctor was trying in vain to flutter out of reach of her
superhuman intuition. Her gaze was like a magnet that drew
towards it my will-less secret. Five minutes before, I had not
been conscious of my love which, at best, when I was not with
him, was like the exhilaration the novice feels from drinking,
not like the somnolent pleasure of the addict. But now I felt
feverish and giddy. Thus, the innocent man on trial, under the
skillful bombardment of the prosecution grows hot and quivers
and finds his voice distant and shrill as if a subtler faculty than
his conscious mind has been besieged and he is no longer sure
that he did not commit the crime.

"Poor girl," said Miss Pride, "it's not easy for you. You're
homesick, I expect, not lovesick. I'm not up on my psychology, as Hope would say. Tell me, did you meet any interesting
young people at Berthe's today?"

I told her of Gerhardt Preis whom she had met and had not
cared for. "When I was your age, I deplored race prejudice.
To my dear, single-minded Papa's chagrin, I used to seek out
your Israels and Rachels, the bigger the nose the better. But
at last I admitted to myself that I was just like everyone else. I
didn't get on with them . . . their aggressiveness distressed me
in public and their money mania at last got the better of my
idealism. Now, while I say 'live and let live' I must confess I
sympathize with that particular of Hitler's program. Did you
meet anyone else?"

With relief I spoke of Mr. Garvin—relief because I did
not share Miss Pride's prejudice and while neither did I feel
strongly partisan towards Jews, the subject always embarrassed
me because, not being able to detect Hebraic blood at once
except in a most obvious face, I was afraid that someone's toes
were being trod on. And even here in Miss Pride's sitting-room
where there was no one to be offended (unless I myself were
partly Jewish, a not unlikely possibility), I disliked the open-
ness of the attack because, by my ambiguous silence I was no

doubt giving her the impression that I subscribed to her view, and later on, when a Jew was present, she might call upon me to confirm some anti-Semitic statement.

She was inordinately interested in what I told her of Mr. Garvin because, through my desire to hasten from the Jewish question, I exaggerated the scraps of information I had gathered about him through his conversation with Preis, and told her that he was a student of Japanese even though I had been corrected by the boy himself. "What a small world we have," said Miss Pride, beaming with pleasure. "To think that one of your first acquaintances in Boston should have the same inspiration that my father had. Perhaps he would like to look over the books here. Is he a presentable young man or is he one of those brainy people, like Hope's artists who don't wash very well?" On the contrary, I told her, Garvin was, if anything, overwashed. His tanned, freshly shaved face had been as clean as a baby's; his dark blue suit and his white shirt, his blue cashmere tie and matching socks were so fresh from the cleaner and the laundress that he could have posed, with no subsequent touching-up on the part of the photographer, for an advertisement of Miss Pride's White Cloud soap. "And what is his background?" she asked me next, but I could not satisfy her. "Berthe will know, I suppose. We might ask him to dine with us some evening. I don't want to deprive you of all society, you know, but at the same time I don't want you to drift away from me."

"Oh, I can assure you," I laughed, "that Mr. Garvin and I didn't strike up an acquaintance at all." Actually I did hope that I would see the young man again but only because I was inquisitive to know what sort of friends Nathan had.

"The Countess gave me a surprising piece of news. She says you're sharp as a tack on the subject of French literature. How in the world did you come by that?"

"She's quite mistaken. I know nothing about it . . . I . . ."

Miss Pride rolled her eyes in a way that was at once so omniscient and so repulsive that I had to look away from her. "You're quite right, my dear child, most of us are credulous geese. To be candid with you, I'd rather have you like this than have you be a real but bumptious intellectual."

"Like this?" I repeated, feeling that I ought to defend myself.

"I said *most* of us are credulous geese. But *I* know what you know. All I ask is that you don't take your game seriously."

I saw nothing for it but to confess that I had, indeed, been bluffing at the Countess' and to my relief she dropped the subject.

"Am I right in assuming that this restlessness of yours—this wanting to go for a walk in the middle of the night—is just that same homesickness we were talking about earlier? And that you're not growing tired of your life here?"

I assured her that I had no different ambitions than to keep her company, but there flashed across my mind, set off by her uncertainty of me, a sense of power over her that allowed me to make a private reservation. I would stay with her *so long* as she upheld her part of the bargain and did not deprive me of my freedom in those hours which were not dedicated to her. For it had occurred to me that as she grew older she might become more demanding of my time. Indeed, she had prepared me for that in our conversation the night before my first tea-party when she had said, "I don't want you to make up your mind yet, for you may find me too exacting. It will not be my fault, for I pride myself on respecting other people's privacy in their leisure hours, but it will be the fault of senility, that wretched Mr. Hyde I shall become in my last days." I had then disbelieved her completely, even though a few days later, I heard Hopestill say to someone, "Auntie is so improvident in her choice of fixed ideas. She surely *will* dodder into crabbed old age if she keeps thinking of it."

Tonight, like a subterranean river, a senile complaint slipped through her words and it did not, at last, seem unlikely that in a while the undertone would become the minor key in which were played the jeremiads of those whose only future is eternity.

Laughing, when she spoke of the humiliating possibility of a wheel chair, I said, "Miss Pride, you should bone up on those Thibetans who claim they know how to live two centuries or so." I was recalling a photograph I had seen in a newspaper of a Hindu, said to have been born in 1786, making him a century and a half old. The broad, bald skull had looked like a death's-head and the drooping eyes had been tenantless, mere vacant openings in round pits of black shadows. The long dark lips were stretched in a hideous grimace, not of scorn for the photographer but of a corrupt delight in the pyrrhic victory of flesh over time. The caption had read, "Says He Will Live Till 2000 or After."

"I should hope not!" she exclaimed. "Do you think I want to see Boston turned into a hive of Customs Houses and aeroplanes replacing automobiles? No, thank you. I don't fancy myself rocketing about in the air with Mac at the controls. A century is too long for anyone to live. To go beyond *that* is my idea of anticipating Judgment Day. Tomorrow afternoon at Mrs. McAllister's, you will possibly meet a Mr. Childreth who is the oldest living graduate of Harvard College. He was of the class of '67. Although he still has his own teeth—they're no beauties, however—he has quite lost his reason and reads books written for children. It always strikes me as ironical that on Commencement Day he marches at the head of the Harvard procession when he barely knows his A.B.C.'s."

"But *you* won't be like that, Miss Pride."

"I'm not at all sure. If I am, though, I hope you'll have the goodness to lock me up. Even my father, a most sensible man, got notions toward the end. He confused me with my sister Charity and believed that neither of us was his daughter but that our surname was Fleet. 'Charity Fleet,' he would say to me, 'I want you to take my green bag which is full of peanuts and go feed the squirrels in the Common.' He had never fed a squirrel in his life, and until he was in his dotage always referred to them as 'the Common rodents.' And of course his bag hadn't so much as a peanut shell in it, but only his rice-paper books."

She fell silent, thinking perhaps of her father, and I started toward the door to leave her to her reverie, but she looked up. "I don't know how I started on that digression. We were talking about your friends, or rather, your friends-to-be. I dare say it isn't my place to say this as it's the duty of one's mother, but since yours is not accessible, I must look upon myself as your guardian. To put it bluntly, Sonia, you don't consider marrying, do you?"

"I don't know. I suppose I've never thought much about it. Perhaps I shall want to after . . . that is, when I'm older."

"But, my dear child, don't you see? Hasn't Dr. McAllister ever discussed the matter with you? I think it's a pity he's your doctor. He's a perfect scamp in many ways and has *always* been a heart-breaker, but that's beside the point. He ought at least to guide you, knowing what he does."

"Do you mean that I shouldn't marry because of my bad heredity? Because, why, yes, he has talked to me about it and has told me I shouldn't think of such things." This was not quite true. He had one time compared me to himself and had said our misfortunes could be turned to good account if we looked upon them as symbols, perhaps of original sin or of mortality, like Dr. Galbraith's *memento mori*. However, this had been in one of his religious moods when he was gathering all manner of disparate elements into his train of thought. He had never actually spoken to me of marriage and I, who seldom thought of it, had not solicited his advice.

"Times change. Nowadays children aren't spanked, don't learn Latin, don't respect their elders. And I haven't a doubt it's thought old-fashioned to be wary of insanity in the family. But, Sonie, there have been *two* instances of it in your lifetime, very close to you. I must say it would give *me* pause."

Had Miss Pride been able at that moment to read my mind, she would have been convinced that my mother's idiosyncrasies were already cropping up in me, for as I listened to her, I lost my identity. I was invaded by the strange feeling that I was not myself, or rather, that this was a phantom of myself, projected into Boston by my real being, still in Chichester. I had had this sort of experience before: in the winter just past when the days were at their shortest, I had waked once at four o'clock but had had no way of knowing whether it was four in the morning or four in the afternoon. Even though my mother was still asleep beside me and though no sounds of life came from outdoors, I concluded that it was afternoon, that we had slept through the whole day, and I rose in haste, ashamed of my sloth. As I shook down the stove, live coals fell into the ash box and I knew that it was morning or no fire would be left. Although I was wide awake, I had the sudden feeling that I was still in bed and that the person or the thing that held the cold stove shaker was not a dreamed-up aspect of myself but was a clever imitation. It was not so much Miss Pride's wounding, though perhaps sensible, counsel that made me take refuge in this fantasy—for I suppose the psychologists would say that my lapse was in effect an "escape from reality"—as it was that it did not seem to be the first time she had spoken thus. On one level, that of my conscious memory, I knew that this scene had not been played before, but on a secondary plane, her speech, down to the very syntax of her sentences, was so familiar that I knew, or thought I knew, exactly what was coming next. And for that short space, I believed that I was in my bed at home, enacting a daydream. The fact that restored me—in itself absurd, far from conclusive, but nevertheless as quick-acting as the cock's crow that hurtles ghosts and goblins back to hell—was the chiming of the clock on the mantelpiece marking ten. Or rather, I heard only the tenth stroke but knew that I had heard all the others as well and that Miss Pride's "Times change" had been uttered just as the first note sounded.

"I'm so glad to be here!" I cried.

"That's a *non sequitur*," smiled Miss Pride. "But I take it as a compliment, and also as a sly hint that you've had enough of my sermonizing. Very well, you win. I shan't mention it again. Let your conscience be your guide."

I ran up the stairs and locked the door to my bedroom. Standing in the pitch darkness, I imagined what I would see when I snapped on the light. For this was one of the moments, most delicious because they came so seldom, that I realized I was in Boston. My eyes grew accustomed to the darkness, and I could see across Louisburg Square to Mount Vernon Street where a house was lighted up for guests who came and went with singsong greetings and farewells. Amongst them, perhaps, were the Countess von Happel, the girl named Lou, Philip McAllister. Immediately above a chimney there shone a star so large that I thought at first it was a light. Automatically, I said, "Star light, star bright, first star I've seen tonight; wish I may, wish I might have the wish I wish tonight. I wish that:" But I had got my wish and could find no other. The room was here and my signature was on it: my own pajamas and dark blue wrapper would be lying on the turned-down bed.

I groped for the switch. The instantaneous flood of light broke my tension. But the order of things, deranged by two chance encounters, first with Mrs. Prather and then with *Herr* Speyer, and by Miss Pride's admonitions, was set right again. The mechanism would not be so tight for the repair, would henceforth be more liable to collapse, but for all practical purposes, it would serve. I was engulfed by a wave of love for Miss Pride, and gone with the dissatisfaction I had felt earlier was the spontaneous and perverse desire to marry that had not occurred to me until she had implored me not to.

Again, I so strongly disbelieved that she would grow old I wished to run downstairs to assure her. How could she? She who, the day before, had walked to Pinckney Street from Harvard Square and showing less fatigue than I who had strolled slowly home from Dartmouth Street, a tenth the distance, had taken me to King's Chapel where for an hour we had admired the shabby gravestones in the burying ground, smirched with the droppings of impartial pigeons. She had looked at her man's pocket-watch which she carried in her handbag and said, "Oh, we have half an hour before tea. I suggest we take a walk to Trinity and back." I had lagged behind sometimes, but she pressed on, her ruthless pace diminishing at no time, not even at street crossings. As she often said, she had been a pedestrian long before automobiles had been thought of, and she was not one to give them the right of way. The light on Arlington Street had just turned red and cars were commencing to move along against us, but Miss Pride did not stop. A truck-driver, halted by her formidable approach, leaned from the cab of his monstrous machine and said, with certain awe, "Look at that damned old bird." The old bird gave vent to one of her rare laughs and said to me, "He's only envious. The great thing has lost the use of his legs from running that juggernaut. Come along, we must work up an appetite for tea, you know."

Rejoicing in my success at the Countess' and in my secure position in this house, I could not fix my attention on my shorthand exercises. I must have been daydreaming for some time when I became aware of voices in the room below me, that is, an unoccupied guest room where, as Miss Pride told me, she was sketching her memoirs. I opened my door and stood in the hall listening. I could hear nothing but an unintelligible murmur and was just returning to my room when a door downstairs was opened and Hopestill's voice came up to me. "But how peculiar you are about it, Auntie! Why isn't it possible that I saw her in Chichester?"

"She wasn't there that summer. But it's not of the slightest consequence whether her face is familiar to you, Hope. The important thing about Sonie is that she's contracted to me."

I could fairly see the girl shrug her shoulders as she replied, "I understand, dear. I shall keep my hands off."

"You do not become less vulgar. Good-night."

I slipped back into my room. Lying face downward on my bed, I could hear the eccentric fury of my heart-beat.

Chapter Three

HOPESTILL MATHER, when she came home from New York for the week-ends, was so disarmingly attentive to me that I came to think of her as an ally though I would have preferred to look on her as an enemy. On certain evenings, usually Friday, when she stayed at home, she invited me to come to her room where she served me hot buttered rum which she prepared with water kept steaming in a silver pot under a cozy. Frankly impressed by the way the Countess had been struck with me (To my blushing delight she said once, "Aunt Lucy is going to give Berthe what-for one of these days if she doesn't stop telling everyone that *she* found you."), she was endeavoring, I thought, to discover for herself what it was that had so rapidly elevated me to a place of honor in the salon. It was not, she warned me, a very high distinction, for the Countess was a little too hyperbolical to be taken quite seriously. She was bound in conscience, moreover, to point out to me that I had arrived on the scene just at the moment that Annaliese Speyer's departure had, so to speak, left a vacancy. At the same time, she expressed her congratulations and told me that if I "handled" the Viennese properly I would find her a faithful friend. She had never been urged to entrench herself in the little society of the music room, possibly because, knowing too much about the Countess, she had never paid her the homage strictly required if one were to become a habitué.

Having gone this far, Hopestill decided to continue to the end and refilling my mustache cup with rum presented me with the bare and slightly scandalous facts about her cousin by marriage.

The Countess was a "natural," she said, having been blessed with a perfect ear and with perfect taste. But through an inertia, deeply hidden under nervous energy and physical tirelessness, she had never supplemented her native and very considerable gifts with any study, was and always had been totally ignorant of the science, the history, the criticism of music. And, although she had no intellect, she had the intelligence to realize that if she were to be happy in the kind of musical circles to membership in which she was entitled, she must learn to think about her art and how to talk about it. The task was too enormous and it did not occur to her guileless mind to bluff her way through, though she was not above setting herself up as an expert amongst people whom she knew to be worse informed than she. Thus, in Vienna, her peers and her admirers were never permitted to make her acquaintance. At the same time, because she had been born self-conceited, she craved to be spoiled by something more personal than the press and more objective than her husband the Count, her doting family, her aristocratic but inartistic friends. She was ambitious for a following of innocent people. Consequently, she had divorced the Count and married the New Englander (whose name, for obvious reasons, she did not take) and immediately on coming to America, instituted these little musical afternoons to which, as a rule, only young people ("preferably tone deaf," said Hopestill spitefully) were invited. And now, if she were threatened by one of her guests who was disobeying the rules and learning something about music, she could take refuge in her difficulty with the English language. The audacious guest was shortly dropped.

I asked Hopestill if this, then, accounted for her treatment of Gerhardt Preis. "In a way, yes," she replied. "But there's more to it than that. That part of Berthe is more complicated." She told me that the Countess had deliberately made the young man fall in love with her while he was teaching her the harpsichord, for, it was generally assumed, she far preferred his enraptured looks and his mash notes sent with the yellow roses he showered upon her to any formal discussions of the music she was studying, and because Preis spoke German she could not pretend not to understand him. Then, having extracted his usefulness from him and far outstripping him in her management of the instrument, she got rid of him. Here the second of her peculiarities entered in. Apparently it would have been simple enough to keep him on tenterhooks indefinitely, to make his lips always the vehicle of nothing more dangerous than professions of love. And it would have seemed that keeping him by her would be greatly to her advantage since everyone knew that his virtuosity promised him an eminent career. Why not, then, since his sting was removed, save him as an ornament for her salon? The fact was that she disliked men.

I must have shown by my face how shocked I was at this revelation, for Hopestill hastened on to assure me that her cousin
was not a Lesbian, was probably not even conscious that she
preferred women to men. (It had not, of course, occurred to
me that she might be perverted in this way. What alarmed me
was the thought that she might prove similar to my mother.)
She did not fear them, but she recoiled from them in a frigid,
old-maidish way, and unlike Miss Pride who could join the
gentlemen almost as a gentleman herself, she was ill at ease in
their company, embarrassed, often rude, because her vanity
warned her that they would make love to her. The third gift of
her fairy godmother (the first two being talent and self-esteem)
was a stern, intuitive moral nature which kept her so under control that none but the most astute observer suspected anything
irregular about her, but which allowed her to surround herself
with girls, to caress them chastely, to send them presents, and
to write them affectionate letters, indulgences permissible since
they could have no consequences. I asked how her second husband had figured in this intricate pattern.

"Oh, poor Cousin Ralph was baffled by her, but he was
grateful because she was so sweet to Amy. Aside from that,
the marriage was a dud. She treated him like a butler—always
called him 'Brooks'—and wouldn't speak to him before four in
the afternoon when she was certain of having callers."

"Do you think she's taken me up because she's certain I'll
never know the first thing about music?"

"She's not *that* naïve," returned Hopestill with a laugh.
"Why, the Countess is certain of nothing, but she has her high
hopes."

"And did my predecessor keep her part of the bargain?"

"To the letter."

The Friday evening conversations became, after a few
months, an established institution. Hopestill told me frankly
that she far preferred to hear my bulletin on the afternoon
in the music room to going to parties. I obliged her, partly
because I would not have known how to refuse, and partly
because it was flattering to have so eager a listener and so open
an admirer of what she called my "faithful eye."

We who put in a regular appearance at the Fridays were all
girls. Occasionally there turned up a pedigreed young man from

Harvard or a European man engaged in some enterprise far afield from art. The girls were second- or third-year débutantes, girls in that interval between the coming out and the wedding. They waited charmingly and passively for the materialization of a husband. They made no effort to shorten the period of their retirement, concealing, as nuns conceal their bodies, the aspirations that fluttered in their hearts, but showed, by deferential questions and mild, general compliments to the correct young men that, as it was proper in society girls, they respected men as a superior breed in whose eyes they did, indeed, wish to find favor, but neither hastily nor through their own maneuverings. Perhaps it was their modesty that made them aloof, eclipsed their individual history, lined them up alongside one another like those rows of bathing beauties whose real names have been changed to place names such as "Miss Rhode Island" or "Miss Great Lakes." Perhaps the modesty was their strategic principle and the one whereby they were the most successful because its employment was so unself-conscious. I sometimes reflected that they were like their ancestresses whose names and probably whose noses and eyes they retained, of whom we know through historical, sociological, even psychological studies as "the New England woman," and whose personal style, whose distinctive behavior have been leavened by time so that we see as sisters and coevals and identical specimens Priscilla Alden and Mary Chilton and Margaret Winthrop, all dressed alike in blue-gray homespun dresses with white berthas, seated before a spinning wheel, all combining in equal proportions in their characters the virtues in whose names Pilgrim daughters were christened: charity, prudence, hope, faith, patience, from which admixture emanated dignity, loyalty, thrift. Now in these twentieth-century women, there remained all those traits but to no end (rather, to no end of which they themselves were aware) like the appendix in our bodies that no longer serves us. They were like ancient vessels the archaeologists disinter which have been revised by time and the earth's chemicals so that the luster has been obfuscated by a patina, a marine green-blue encrustation, here and there punctured, as by a star, by a minute gleam of the metal underneath.

I had no communication with them. They behaved towards me with a warmth, a sincere interest which for many months deceived and flattered me so that I was at a loss to explain why they not only did not invite me to their own houses, when they were so cordial—even to the point of seeking me out in the music room—but that also, when I met them on the street, as likely as not they cut me dead. It was the very lack of condescension, the tactful omission from their conversation of anything which might remind me, to my embarrassment, that I was not of the sisterhood that finally enraged me. It was no ordinary snobbishness which inspired them, on meeting me, to acquire a burning interest in an object across the street, and, indeed, it was perhaps not any kind of snobbishness but merely another aspect of prudence, resident in them all, that like a fog concealed the roads branching off from the one they traveled which, because they traveled it in homogeneous company and had been set upon it by their parents whom they had no reason to distrust was, they knew, the right one. Prudence lighted them and made the pitfalls solid; prudence, like a composition teacher, assigned them "topics" to beguile the tedium of the journey; and prudence, like a duenna, supervised their romances. A palmer like myself, straying by chance and for a brief season across their path, was not invited, as a rule, to travel onwards, for they had been warned, as children are warned against accepting candy from strangers, that appearances are deceptive and one can no more be sure of the probity of a slight acquaintance than one can be sure of the purity of the substance under the chocolate coating.

They dressed well and without taste as if the caution of their forebears lingered yet. They had let modern fashion shorten their skirts in the daytime and lower them again in the evening, but had stayed the hands that would cut too daringly, would drape them too caressingly. So, at the Countess' dinner parties (her "Saturdays," as they were known) they appeared in evening gowns which were not memorable; pleasing, they might be, or quaint, or festive (which boneless adjectives Hopestill, if she were present, employed in her compliments to them). Their tremulous chiffons and pale crêpes, enlivened but unrewarded by a locket or a brace of gardenias, passed muster and no one noticed them.

Similarly, their conversation was lacking in excitement, though it was grammatical and scrupulously took into account the interests and prejudices, so far as could be determined, of their interlocutors. They had no affectations, aired no scandals, and had no discoverable attitudes save those they had inherited, like their noses or their jewelry. Their differences of opinion gave rise to no choler when they found themselves beside the heir of a different type of estate. "Oh, I forgot you subscribed to the New Deal," would say the daughter of a laissez-faire liberal. "Don't tread on me and I won't tread on you." Or the devoted sister of a young man, who wrote abstruse poems, would reply blandly to the boy who had attacked the "cult of unintelligibility" in *The Harvard Advocate*, "*De gustibus*. I refuse to quarrel with you on that score."

I had acquired, through no endeavor of my own, the reputation of being "literary," and almost every Friday, I was approached by a Miss Hornblower or Coolidge (who the day before had failed to recognize me as we passed one another on the stairs of the Public Library) who would say, "I've been hearing the most interesting things about you. My mother, who is a dear friend of Miss Pride's, was telling me that you want to be a writer. Do tell me what you're writing, for I'm dying to hear." The notion, actually, was Miss Pride's own and was derived from an innocent statement I had once made to Admiral Nephews. He, because when I first met him I had recognized the passages of poetry he quoted, thought that I had the same taste in literature as his own, and he used to bring me, the moment he had finished with them, the novels he had borrowed from a lending library, and which I was obliged to read out of respect for his thoughtfulness. I had at last grown tired of pretending to share his enthusiasm for books that were barely plausible and were certainly not distinguished, and said of one I had just read, "No, sir, I do not think it is excellent. I could write a better one myself." This was not true, to be sure, and I did not say it with any intention of proving it, but the Admiral misconstrued my boast and acquired the conviction that I was secretly engaged in writing a book. He reported his suspicion to Miss Pride who did not bother to ascertain its truth and who henceforward told everyone that I was anxious to be a writer and even supported the fiction by such statements as, "But I know Sonie well enough to know that it won't go to her head. She's much too sensible to become one of your peculiar Bohemians." I felt like the person—the person we all are at some moment in our lives—who is asked to play the piano and who protests he does not know how, cannot tell one note from another, and who has never depressed a single key, but who is accused of false modesty and begged to run off just some simple piece. In vain the defendant repeats that he is ignorant, is let off with the threat: "Very well, but you won't get off so easily next time." To the girl who was dying to hear about my writing, I replied that she was mistaken, that I had no such lofty opinion of myself, and she would say, exactly like the hostess who swears she has often heard us play, "You writers are all alike. I suppose you won't even tell me where you publish your stories?"

The Countess, making the most of my imaginary calling, directed our conversation, during coffee, into literary channels and I sometimes found myself being posed a staggering question about French poetry, for example, on which I was said by our hostess to be an expert.

I was genuinely fond of the Countess and suffered considerable remorse after I had joined in Hopestill's laughter at her expense, just as I did when I listened, without protest, to trenchant comments on her aunt and on Philip McAllister. Nor had I any reason to suppose that I was not myself the object of that merciless judge of her peers, but on the contrary could fairly hear her say of me to Amy Brooks (as she had said of Amy Brooks to me), "She's such a *deliberate* fright." It was perhaps because of this sharp tongue that Hopestill did not get on well with other girls, like those, for instance, who came to the Countess'. She was not well liked and never had been. At school, she had broken rules, had been slovenly and disrespectful, and so lazy a student that she had failed to be graduated. At her début, one of the most lavish ever held at the Country Club (her grandfather had left twenty thousand dollars for this specific purpose), she had drunk so much champagne that she could remember no one's name, could barely dance in time to the music, and had been insufferably rude to several older people. She was, moreover, thought something of a slacker, because she had never sacrificed any of her time to "good works" and long after all the other girls, who had come out in the same season that she had, had dedicated themselves to nursing or visiting the poor or reading to blind old women, Hopestill continued to fritter away her time with all the indolent pleasures of the débutante. It had particularly annoyed her friends that she had steadfastly refused to take any part in canvassing for the Community Chest Fund but instead had "done her bit" by contributing a large check to the drive and putting the whole thing out of her mind.

Declaring that she found me a "relief" (I would have preferred to be a little more stimulating), she included me in most of her plans over the week-ends and shortly after our first meeting she proposed that she teach me how to ride. I had hesitated, fearful of the ludicrous figure I would cut on a horse, but she had been persistent and Miss Pride had welcomed the project with enthusiasm, for, as she said, "Anyone with your constitutional aversion to exercise must be *made* to exercise." And consequently we went to Concord each Saturday afternoon where I was slightly more competent than I had hoped. Philip had been as ardent a promoter of the lessons as Miss Pride to my slight resentment for I thought he regarded them as a therapeutic measure to distract me from thinking of my mother, something which I rarely did save on Sunday when I paid her my weekly visit. As a result of his interest, he arranged to have us change into our riding clothes at his grandmother's house and to have tea there when we came back from the stables. He nearly always joined us and drove us back to town.

The young man's gallantry was impartial even in Hopestill's presence and while I knew by the heightening of his color as he first caught sight of her that he was in love, he was no more attentive to her than he was to me. And I, having just come back from an expedition in which my performance had been at best tolerable and in which hers had been brilliant, was more nettled than if he had ignored me entirely. It was as if, on these occasions, he looked on me as an appendage to her. Curiously enough, I was conscious of being in love with him only when Hopestill came back to Boston. So long as she was in New York, I could hear his name spoken or even see him on the street or at tea without the slightest discomfort, but the moment Hopestill stepped into the house late Friday afernoon I was ignited with jealousy, made the more obstreperous because I knew she was not in the least in love with him. Particularly excruciating to me were some evenings when, Hopestill being otherwise engaged, he was asked to take me to the Countess' "Saturday" and while I had spent the whole afternoon in a state of tremulous anticipation, my pleasure ended as soon as he called for me. He was either too absent-minded to hear my answers to his questions or he assumed an avuncular manner, offering me the most banal and unwanted advice on how to converse with my mother. In either rôle, I sensed his dissatisfaction at not being with Hopestill.

On one clear February day, Hopestill persuaded the riding master to let us go alone. "I'll pay you double," she said. The man looked dubiously at me, one of his least accomplished customers, but Hopestill snapped, "What difference would it make if that wreck you foist off on my friend *did* break a leg? Besides, she doesn't go in for jumping." He reluctantly agreed and we set off. Ducking our heads, we cantered through the brushy bridle paths and then came out into the open russet fields. Hopestill ran her sorrel mare over a rise and down and out of sight; presently, far off, I saw her hair, sharp as a scream and sudden as a flame, fling up along the ridge and for a space it flew, bodiless and horseless like a burning bird. I sat on a flat rock under a wine-glass elm tree watching her, while my horse stood near-by with a languidly drooping head, as disinclined for exercise as I. This was the first time we had ridden since early in December for it had been too cold. Today there was sun and air as gentle as spring. It was like the day the year before when Miss Pride had come to take me in to Boston. There was little essential difference, I thought, between that version of myself who, shabby and with grimy fingernails, had sat bewildered in the gloomy library and this one, pranked out in costly jodhpurs, waiting in a cramped and uncomfortable position for my skillful friend to ride back. There was a gross and disquieting discrepancy between my expensive clothes and my luxurious pastime and my little brother's unmarked grave.

As I thought of Ivan, there returned to me the mood that had followed immediately on his death. It was a recollection, rather than a memory, a poetic farsight, a distillation of a feeling which was not watered down by physical details but was the dense experience of comprehending death. I did not envisage myself standing beside his cot nor did I, as I usually did when

I thought of the scene, redeem the odor of the benzoin. It can be said that memory is a sort of *entrepôt* serving the busy traffic of the unreflective mind, and that its stores, behind an unlocked door, may be rummaged through and plundered at any time; thus I had found the footsteps of the old ladies walking in the sand at Chichester to match the lameness of Philip's grandmother in Miss Pride's drawing-room, and thus, also, confused by the music and by the stranger in the Countess' lobby, had brushed off the dust from a forgotten incident and by a misapplication of the styles of sensation, compared the music to the sunlight of that past day, and remembered *Regenpfeifer* because I had been addressed in German. But recollection, on the other hand, is in more formal custody, can be seen only at certain hours and those being far apart, the time of day or month or season being rarely, or not at all, repeated. Thus we say of people who were once in love that they cannot "recapture" their joy and the words "I was in love with that person" are an historical statement which may be attended by illustrations: a café visited by the lovers when they were in love, a railway carriage where they sat with arms entwined, a shop where they met one day by chance. So also, when one says, "I was ill at that time," memory shows him the mercury of the thermometer at 104 degrees, but neither the rapture nor the fever is revived. The essential has been extirpated, whereas it is the essential and only the essential that recollection values. Severe in its gleanings, it seeks to preserve our continuity: the old man recollects though his memory, we say, has failed.

With useless greed I tried to detain this temporary wisdom, this growing pain even when I heard the rush of Hopestill's horse's feet returning. But the sense of death was instantly annihilated by the sound. At the same time, the power that had generated the intense and total knowledge had not been all used up, and being unable, because the thing was finished, to repeat the process that had transported me to the past, I directed the residue towards an envious hatred of the girl who had now ridden into sight. It had occurred to me that if I were not obliged each week to compare myself to her, to my disadvantage in every particular, I would be appreciably more urbane than the chambermaid from the Barstow who had not known what to say when she was asked if she were an

Anglophile. I could tell myself that Hopestill and I belonged to different species and should not, therefore, be judged by the same standards. But this was cold comfort. As she dismounted, I indulged myself in a feast of torment, taking in her green suède waistcoat under a silvery gabardine jacket, her slender legs in black breeches, her eloquent hair disordered by her ride to its benefit. I hated her the more for her good manners when she said, "I don't blame you for not coming. That bag of bones would drop dead of the shock if you made him run," because she perfectly well knew that I was afraid. We sat in silence for a few minutes. Hopestill lighted a cigarette and meditated the smoke.

"Are you going to Berthe's tonight?"

"Yes. Are you?"

She shook her head. "I'm going dancing."

I did not look forward to the evening. At the bottom of the Countess' invitation, a square of mellow vellum headed by a coat of arms instead of an address, the calligraphy of which was so elegant that the only decipherable symbols were the date and the hour (one could not possibly tell whether the guest of honor was to be a Belgian brain surgeon, an Italian poet, a Danish architect, or a Canadian bishop), she had written—this in a legible hand—"Nicholas Doman, charming, from Budapest, will call for you." I was tired of the young foreigners she "dug up" for me. Their difficulty with the language discouraged and then annoyed me as did the *Weltschmerz* that was a property common to all their eyes. Or, if they could speak well, I was irritated by another quality in them, one which I could not properly define: it was a staleness or a frustrated sensuality or a womanly tenderness, or perhaps all three that sounded in their voices, as if they were visiting an invalid surrounded by flowers that had withered but had not yet lost their fragrance. In the cushiony cocktail lounge of the Lincolnshire, over the yellow, arid popcorn and the dubonnet, rich, beautiful Gerhardt Preis, whom I had met by chance in the Public Gardens, confided one afternoon in me that his ambitions were to live forever as a celibate (because he could not have Berthe von Happel) in a hotel in Paris and to write a book (he would give up music, inseparable from her) which would be the modern counterpart of Amiel's *Journal*. From his homeless, continental Jewish face emanated the odor of pomade. In the vestibule of Miss Pride's house, he kissed my hand and then withdrew into the dusk, stealing on his suave feet past Louisburg Square under the spiritless rain that had begun to fall. I was certain that Nicholas Doman from Budapest would not be as charming as the Countess testified. He would very likely be addicted, as most of her hangers-on were, to telling anecdotes in French.

I told Hopestill my dilemma. "Oh, well," she said, "you won't have to be stuck with him the whole evening. That's the beautiful thing about Berthe's parties, you can take your pick after dinner. Anyhow Philip will be there."

"Will he? After dinner you mean?" I said.

"Yes. Why, Sonie, you're blushing!"

I was not blushing. I had been too taken up with a plan to escape the Hungarian to care whether Philip came, but her accusation immediately elevated the temperature of my skin and my eyes began to smart.

"If you say so, I suppose I am," I said.

She laughed. "Why don't you skip dinner and go afterwards with him and avoid the Hungarian altogether?"

"I couldn't do that. But I'm very glad he's coming. At least he speaks English."

"And he's very fond of you, too." It was a serious statement and I could detect no ridicule in her voice. She put out her cigarette on the trunk of the tree. "You know, somebody like you would be good for Philip McAllister. He's a monkish bloke."

"Well, I'm not," I replied testily.

"Of course you are. If you weren't, would you have chosen to be buried alive in my Aunt Lucy's house?" And after a moment, as if to herself, "Jesus Christ! How you could do it I shall never know!"

"I'm satisfied," I told her.

"Oh, I know. And so is my aunt. Poor creature, she deserves someone like you after me. Have you noticed, by the way, how much we would like to murder each other these days?"

I had, indeed, noticed that the girl and her aunt had found it difficult to be anything more than civil. Arguments arose at the dinner table over such trifling matters as the advisability of giving the Countess a set of artichoke plates for her birthday which Miss Pride thought would be welcome, or an onyx deer that had caught Hopestill's eye. Or they railed at each other over the season of some cousin's marriage or another's début. Or Hopestill would contend that her aunt's salad dressing was unpalatable because it was made with lemon instead of wine vinegar. Often I was called upon to settle a dispute. Invariably I agreed with Miss Pride out of cowardice, and while she readily used me as a court of appeal, she sometimes forgot, in her periodic scoldings, that I had settled an argument which otherwise might have gone on indefinitely, and she told me that she was by no means flattered at my constant agreement with her opinions. "I am an old woman," she said once, "and it has taken me many years to develop my prejudices and my affinities. It is nothing short of impertinence in you to adopt them without doing any of the work." Now on the other hand, Hopestill frequently expressed her gratitude: "If you hadn't settled on the artichoke plates, we would have gone on quibbling for weeks."

"We've disliked each other more since you came," continued Hopestill. "But I suppose that's reasonable. Do you know what is making my aunt's blood boil now? She's afraid Philip is interested in you and she's perfectly wild that I'm not doing anything about it."

"Oh, drop it," I cried and got to my feet.

"As you say," she agreed, shrugging her shoulders. But she was not content to remain silent long and when we had got back to the bridle path, she said, "Really, I was quite serious when I said some one like you would be good for McAllister." Her use of his surname unaccountably put me at my ease and I asked her why. "Well, I'm sure I don't know if you're religious in the least, but you have a nice sort of tranquillity about you that might turn into piety. Philip's bound to get religion sooner or later and I'd be the worst kind of wet blanket. I'm like Aunt Lucy: I think of God as a great big man."

I laughed aloud for what she said was so absurdly precise. It was quite true that Miss Pride thought of God as a big man who had, in misty times, drawn up the Ten Commandments, and about Whom it was in bad taste as well as half sacrilegious to talk. She had towards Him the same attitude as she had towards the figures of literature, save those who had died in her lifetime. They wore the same antediluvian halo which, if seen in the cold light of Boston, would have struck one as pretentious. And so, although it was fitting for one to have an acquaintance with God and with Milton, it was not proper to display more than the merest courtesy towards them. It was acceptable to discuss a literary person (or a religious one) to whose name could be affixed the title "Mr." Thus, Miss Pride spoke of "Mr. James" whom she had met several times and of "Mr. Emerson" and "Mr. Lowell" (she had caught a glimpse of these latter two when she was seven years old); but as no one knew anything about "Mr. Dryden" or "Mr. Goldsmith" it was best not to speak too cordially of them. God was no more adaptable. With no intention of disparaging her, I presented this observation to Hopestill and she agreed with an amiable laugh.

"Yes, God and Shakespeare frighten her half to death. I think that's why she's so bent on making you out a literary person. She can't ignore literature but wants it homemade and by someone she can eat dinner with. She tried very hard once to know Amy Lowell, but she never succeeded."

My disappointment at this statement was less than my surprise, for I had conceived Boston society as so closely knit that it was as strange that two members of it were not acquainted as it would have been if La Grande Mademoiselle had not known Madame de Maintenon.

By the time we had reached the elder Mrs. McAllister's house, I had recovered from my choleric attack and could look on Hopestill with equanimity. Fortified also with the knowledge that I could not possibly fare too ill at the Countess' that evening since Philip would be there by himself, I was almost buoyant.

The old lady always kept us waiting for at least a quarter of an hour in the library after we had been announced. Then, the rustle of her black skirts and the tap of her cane apprised us of her arrival and we stood up as she, after a formal, "Good afternoon, young ladies. I hope you enjoyed your ride," sat down in a chintz wing chair under a portrait of her husband for whom she still wore mourning, though he had been dead for twenty years. She had no sooner put her feet on the chair's matching stool than she said, as if it had just occurred to her, "What do you say to a cup of tea? Perhaps they'll have something in the dining-room for us. My grandson promised to call on me this afternoon and I must have tea for him, you know."

Philip's grandfather had one time been headmaster of a school so imitative of Eton and Harrow that the whole house spoke with a British accent. It had been Mrs. McAllister's custom, in his lifetime, to have a "day" for chosen boys and because often as many as forty had dropped in, she had entertained them at an immensely long table in the dining room. Although now there were never more than half a dozen people to be served, twenty chairs were in readiness and as many cups stood before the tea urn. We were fed the simple food the boys had been fed: gingerbread squares, small sweet buns, and English muffins. On the preposterous plea that she could not handle "them all" by herself, she always placed Hopestill at the opposite end of the table so that the poor exile's voice barely carried to us, while I was seated on her right ("I never have time to get really acquainted with this young lady") and Philip on her left ("So that he can fetch and carry for me.").

Hopestill spoke of the old lady's "closed door" policy while the one employed by her daughter, Philip's mother, was the "open trap." The younger Mrs. McAllister joined us today a few minutes after we had taken our places. Her pretty, submissive face was framed with white hair, the overnight acquisition at the time her son fell ill of infantile paralysis. After kissing her mother and nodding politely to me, she went at once to Hopestill whose two hands she clasped as she cried, "How glad I am to see you! Here, let me feast on that exquisite frock. Who but Hope Mather would think of bottle-green velveteen this year when the rest of us are all in navy blue?"

Hope, complimenting her in turn on her hat, exchanged an amused glance with Philip while his grandmother said, "Bottle-green is very nice. Marian, would you look at this child's nautical costume. I swear she robbed Admiral Nephews for her buttons. Why, they're the real thing."

Her daughter nodded and turned again to Hopestill. "When are you going to let me have the honor of supplying you with a dressing room? I do think you're unkind to give my mother *all* the pleasure. I have three rooms that are never in use, and if you'd only consent I could have more than these five-minute glimpses of you. I'll tell you frankly that if I once got you, I'd kidnap you for a whole week-end."

Philip, knowing that his mother would make use of such an opportunity to satisfy so completely any curiosity the girl might have about him that she would never want to hear his name mentioned again, hastily interposed, "But, Mother, they would have to be driven from the station then, for they couldn't possibly walk to our house and the walk to Grandma's, as I understand it, is part of the expedition." Both Hope and I confirmed him, but his mother was stubborn.

"Does anyone have a more selfish son?" she cried. "Really, Philip, one would think you were afraid I intended to blacken your character." This, of course, was precisely what she would have done, by going into his inconstancy, his hypersensitivity about his back, his egotism, his carelessness, by exhibiting his ugly baby pictures, by telling damning anecdotes, by resurrecting instances of his devotion to herself and attempting, in the light of the latter, to make Hopestill realize that she must play second fiddle to her if the marriage ever came off.

The conversation, passing beyond the skirmish of wits, became general. Philip, casting a studious glance upon me who did not participate, said, "You must have given Sonie a run for her money today, Hope. She's got the wind knocked out of her."

"Oh, on the contrary," she replied with a laugh, "she gave me a run for mine." And she began to praise my horsemanship and to deplore my horse, inventing a fantastically untrue account of my bold jumping and running which I was too dumfounded to deny. Old Mrs. McAllister patted my hand, said she could tell by my appearance that I could manage any horse, called upon her grandson to agree that I was the very picture of a healthy athlete, hoping to embarrass Hopestill who, though she was sound as a dollar, looked frail, and had chosen, instead of normal pleasures, the ugly affectation of the bluestocking. "I think you're very wise, Sonia," she said. "Why on earth our Hopestill wants to waste her youth and ruin her complexion investigating people's nightmares I will never understand. And as for 'repressions' and 'sublimations' and so on, I think the least said about them the better. Goodness only knows we have serpents enough in our gardens without importing any more."

The iciness of Hopestill's smile was lost on her half blind hostess as she replied, "But, Mrs. McAllister, all of us are not so fortunate as you. My own garden was swarming with serpents when I first stepped into it."

Philip's mother, leaning toward her, cried, "You clever thing! You know how to get the better of my mother! Tell me, Hope, what sort of thing do you *do*?"

"Oh, I . . ." For the first time since I had known her, I saw Hopestill hesitate. Momentarily she averted her eyes as she jerkily returned her teacup to its saucer. Then, with a smile, she explained, "I'm not studying formally, you see, but with a psychiatrist. I see his patients and study their case histories and so on."

"What kind of patients are they, Hope?" pursued the woman. "I'm really ever so interested."

"Well, my man is rather fashionable and most of his patients are idle women who don't like their husbands for one reason or another or else don't have husbands and think they'll go off the deep end if they keep on living alone."

Old Mrs. McAllister snorted gustily. "And what's the cure, eh?"

"They're analyzed, of course, and Dr. Ragsdale gives them things to distract them. Ice-skating, knitting, growing herbs in the kitchen window."

Philip's grandmother was silent with disgust and then, in order to hear no more of Hopestill's nonsense which she was pouring out by request to her companion, she turned to Philip and said loudly, "I want you to give your father a talking-to, Perly. He's set on selling the Bedford Road house. I would as soon cut off my hand as see it taken over by a stranger."

"And so would I," said the young man in sincere alarm. "What gave him that idea?"

"I can't imagine," returned the old lady. "But between ourselves, I have never felt your father had much sense of history." Philip whispered, "You have never felt he had much sense of any kind, have you, Grandma?" But Mrs. McAllister was not going to agree to such a judgment of her son in my presence, and she went on. "I have always wanted *you* to have the house when you marry. Did you see the enchanting little water-color Amy Brooks did of it for me last autumn?" Then, turning to me, "You must make Philip take you to see it some day this spring. You will not find a more charming place in all New England."

The conversation at the far end of the table was lagging. Hopestill, getting up, said, "We must go to see the house some afternoon. It's my aunt Lucy's favorite next to her own on Pinckney." She directed to me an ambiguous smile which I took to mean that she had not quite made up her mind to relinquish Philip altogether, but that she would let me know in good time if I might go alone with him to inspect the house.

"You three," said the younger Mrs. McAllister, "you three are inseparable, aren't you?" I knew by her tone and by the look of injury on her turned-down lips that she liked me no better than she did Hopestill.

"We are separating now," said Hope. "But Philip and Sonie will meet again at the Countess'."

As I was taking leave of my hostesses, Philip and Hopestill went into the hallway to get our coats. When I started out to join them, lingering at the door a moment to receive a final compliment upon my robust health from the old lady, I heard Philip saying, "I don't need a procuress."

2

The Countess' "Saturday" was a formal dinner party for rarely more than ten, followed by a soirée at which one met chiefly Germans and Austrians who had had the foresight to leave (and in some instances, to leave with their money) in the early days of Hitler's regime. There were, in addition, titled personages from other parts of the world: a Korean prince, a Russian baron, a Polish count. The Bostonians who came were either charmed by the illustrious company or outraged, the latter group maintaining that "these refugees" were impertinent and arrogant because they had the crust to criticize the United States and even, with supreme bad manners, to imply that it was only through luck, not through wisdom, that we were not ourselves ruled by a Hitler or a Stalin.

The dinner, consisting of many courses, was served by two fat, frowning Alsatian matrons, while the wines were poured by a little Hawaiian houseboy, employed, the Countess acknowledged, because he was decorative. Otherwise, he had almost no qualifications and cried a good deal for a female monkey named Lilioukalani whom he had had to leave behind. Three bitches, a schnauzer, a Doberman, and a boxer, paced the floor beneath the table or stood between two chairs, gazing first at one guest until her wish was granted and he threw her a morsel from his plate, and then at the other until he likewise succumbed to the plea in the piteous eyes. Miss Pride who, characteristically enough, liked dogs "in their place" almost never accepted an invitation to dine with the Countess, but if she did, she overlooked the dogs as one would overlook a foreign object in the dessert. Unfortunately they were particularly attracted to her because she carried with her the odor of her cat, Mercy, and during the soup, when they had no pressing business in other quarters, the three of them clustered about her legs sniffing. Her aplomb was admirable: as she drank her soup, crumbled her bread, and listened to the man from the Rhineland who was interested in guilds, it was not apparent that a debate was going on within her, whether to kick the brutes once and for all or to endure.

As soon as the gentlemen joined us, the door-bell commenced to ring and rang at intervals until well past eleven o'clock, bringing to us fortunate ten, a varied assortment of entertainers. Our hostess, immense and blazing in a diamond tiara and a cloth-of-gold gown which sheathed her ample flesh like hide and of which the central interest was a green orchid growing out of her mountainly bust, stirred her guests about, dispatching me to a Norwegian painter, Edward Pingrey to a cloth merchant from Berlin, Mrs. Hornblower to a young Puerto Rican of ambassadorial connections whom, unfortunately, it was easy to confuse with the houseboy. We were not allowed to remain long on any assignment. The Norwegian woman and I would just be establishing a communication of sorts after several false beginnings, when the Countess would descend: "You two charmers mustn't monopolize each other! Sonie, go speak to that woman over there, the dark one, Frau Gross. She's perishing to meet you. You're much alike—imaginative, *spirituelle*. She's a little deaf." Frau Gross, more like her name than the Countess' description of her, had not wanted to meet me, did not know my name, had not, in fact, ever seen me before and could hear nothing of what I said. In this enforced rotation one could hear conversations on German air-power, on French food, on Roman relics in England, on American politics, on European and tropical diseases, on coin collections, on train travel in the interior of China.

If one flatly refused to talk, being stricken tonight with one of those moods of taciturnity that visit us all, the Countess suggested cards in the library. It was not too happy a substitute, for she forbade such banal games as bridge or hearts, allowed only recondite or obsolescent ones like omber, loo, piquet. It was nearly always my bad luck, if I were sent to "make up a table," to find Baron Kalenkoff and one other person preparing a deck for omber, the most bewildering of all the games. The Baron, a handsome, well-tailored man in his thirties, a cosmopolitan and sycophant of wealthy women, was, as someone said, a "rattlesnake" at cards. He had, in addition to that acumen known as "card sense," such perennial luck that his adversaries regarded him with suspicion, not as a shark, for he was clearly a gentleman, but as the darling of some prodigal goddess whose invisible fingers distributed the cards in such a way as to make him invariably win. Now the only two people who had mastered the rules of omber were the Baron and the Countess and of course the latter did not play on her Saturdays. Consequently, the two of us who were obliging the Russian floundered in terminology without having the slightest idea of the procedure and lost all our money, sometimes a very considerable amount as the Baron liked high stakes. I might learn the "basto" and the "spadille" and the "matadors" of one trump by the end of a hand, but my knowledge was useless in the next when a different trump was named. It did not bore the Baron at all to play with fuddled opponents. On one occasion the nightmare lasted three hours and a half and was only concluded because supper was announced.

After that calamitous evening (poor Mr. Pingrey and I each lost fifteen dollars and I had to borrow money from the Countess), I did not go any more to the library, no matter how indisposed I was to chat with the Korean prince who had acquired the remarkable notion that I was an ardent student of pre-dynastic Chinese bone inscriptions, on which he was an expert.

I remained in the large drawing-room, the setting for our ballet. It was furnished with the gleaming surfaces and floral furbelows of Louis Quinze, whimsically repeating the colors and the materials of the costume of the *première danseuse*: if she had chosen pale blue, it was to set off the chairs upholstered in azure satin or the skies in the murals inspired by Boucher and executed by a young relative whom she had sent home at once as soon as he had finished. Another night, as if the looped draperies at the wide bay-window had not been admired enough, the Countess appeared in a dress of olive velvet and remarked, "I got the idea from my windows, as you see." There was a profusion of bare marble infants attached by their umbilica to the central support of gilt tables, or sprouting from the center of their curly heads bronze candelabra with a dozen sockets, or standing in pairs on the tops of cabinets bathing one another or posing as if for leap-frog or simply peeking at space with their stone eyes. It particularly irritated Miss Pride that two spurious Watteaus hung on either side of the fireplace where formerly, when the first Mrs. Brooks had been alive, there had been a genuine Trumbull on the right and on the left a stuffed twelve-pound trout from New Brunswick, caught by Ralph Brooks at the age of nine.

This evening, Baron Kalenkoff at once set about to recruit five gulls for loo, among them Nicholas Doman who offered me effusive apologies in several Continental tongues. Out of the corner of my eye, I observed the approach of the Korean prince and fearing that if I were cornered by him, I would miss Dr. McAllister I cast about for an escape. To my relief, I saw Miss Pride entering with a young man whom I had seen here several times before, and I hastened to her.

"Your admirer is downcast," she said, nodding in the direction of the prince. (She had no use for any race but the Caucasian and she believed that no one these days was a prince and that no one would be until a son was born to the English king.) "Where Berthe finds them all one will never know."

The young Jew at her side gazed about the room with a supercilious detachment. "From an employment agency, no doubt," he said.

Miss Pride, regarding his witticism as inappropriate, gave him a lacerating stare. "And what is it you do, sir?" she inquired.

Several times I had been seated next to the boy at dinner and each time had experienced a pleasurable shock at the resemblance he bore to Nathan Kadish. He was intelligent and insolent, and his voice had in it the same overstimulated quickness that had my friend's. But I had always found in him something lacking but which I could not name. He seemed, despite his carefully composed effrontery, entirely innocent, like a hornet that has been disarmed. Tonight, a trifle not only showed me why I had never struck up more than the most formal acquaintance with him, but restored a scene in Chichester just as earlier in the day I had recovered Ivan's death. A girl passed by and a breath of her lilac scent loitered in the air. The fragrance brought to my mind the last time I had seen Nathan and what I had said to him: "I love your birthmark," but the words reverberated now with a new undertone and with the addition of two other words which had been elided, that is, "I love *you for* your birthmark." And I knew then that all that had fascinated me in Nathan was his disfigurement, solely that, for I had never felt protective of him, had desired more than anything else to touch, examine, and discuss what was taboo. This self-revelation so appalled me that with a rudeness equivalent to that of Miss Pride's companion, I abruptly turned as he was in the middle of a sentence addressed to me, and offering no explanation, walked away to a deserted corner of the room, where I stood, faking a brown study so that I would not be disturbed, as horrified at my sinister nature as if I had found the marks of a vampire on my throat. (On the following day, Miss Pride, never dreaming of the reason why I had gone away, congratulated me on my resolute principles—for she assumed that I had been offended by his insolence which, in her fervor, she believed was incarnate in all Jews—saying, "I would have done the same. Courtesy to a discourteous Jew is beating one's head against a stone wall. And yet I, despite my strong feelings, could never have done what you did.") And I

wondered if I would have coveted Philip McAllister if he had
not been deformed. Dizzied by this symptom of an abnormal
and somewhat repulsive nature in myself, I felt the need to be
reassured, but paradoxically, the only person who could reassure me was Philip himself. The moment I had formulated the
speech I would make to him when I asked his advice, I realized
that I was really not in the least troubled by my perverse taste
in men, that I had only been seeking an excuse to occupy his
attention with my problems. I suppose that I was determined
to be in love at whatever cost.

The Countess was surrounded by her guests who were pleading with her to play for them. The Korean prince had attached
himself to Miss Pride and was no doubt lecturing her on bone
inscriptions. No one noticed me as I left the room, picking up
as I went out, a "fine" edition of Heine's poems, the sort of
book to be found all over the house, expensive, delightful to
the touch, kept pliable and burnished by a man who came to
oil them twice a year. Reconnoitering at the foot of the stairs,
I heard nothing save the voices above me, muffled into one,
monotonous and fluid, and the occasional chime of metal from
the subterranean kitchen. Then I sat primly down on the yellow
sofa, letting the book fall open where a red ribbon marked a
former reader's place. It was then that I was ashamed of coming
down so frankly to waylay Philip, for, although I could not
understand the poem, certain phrases, ironic, overharsh out of
their context, stood out and served to dismantle me and the
room of our reality, so that the lurching shadows, brandished
by the candles, the histrionic portrait, the off-beat of my heart
like a mis-set metronome became the properties of something
third-rate and sentimental: I was like the hoydenish girl growing into womanhood who finds the foretaste of maturity cloying, drives back her unwilling body, partially relaxed in the bud
of the bloom, to tomboy pranks. I wanted to get up from the
sofa and go back to the drawing-room, but I did not move and
told myself that it was absurd to regret what had not happened,
that in all likelihood I would do nothing regrettable, but that
it would be a test of my strength to remain.

The door-bell rang. I heard the butler pad out of the dining-
room and his "Good evening, Dr. McAllister. You'll find them
in the drawing-room." I had risen and could see, along the

wall, his unaccompanied shadow advancing toward the turn in the lobby. My self-denial, in the half-second before we were face to face, held me poised, but when he had stepped around the corner, my resolve collapsed because the thought that came to me was not, "He has come at last," but "He has come alone for the first time," and I was less conscious of his presence than I was of Hopestill's absence. Thus, when I stepped forward, my gesture was annihilatory, was the action of jealousy so unreasonable and eyeless that neither love for him nor hate for her entered as items in its muddled contents. I stood, an awkward girl of nineteen, with one hand holding the book opened to "Enfant Perdu" and the other grasping the young man's shoulder, and I imprinted on his mouth a lightning-paced and pastoral kiss. There was not, as I wished, a pit of impenetrable darkness to receive me. I tottered back a step and let my hand fall from Philip's shoulder. As if to steady me, he took my hand and I was again propelled towards him while, by way of recognition, he spoke my name, or as by way of prelude, admonitory or consoling, of the kiss with whose ruthless luxury he sought to shake the flesh from my bones. Its abrupt urgency was unmodified, but, like a sudden shaft of blinding light cast by a random luminary, it revealed to us both a principle, a basic form as simple, as abstract as the line between two points. We stepped apart, prepared to partition and bury the sheer serpent. He continued to hold my dry and bloodless hand.

Neither of us spoke, and I, glad that the incident was over and taking his silence as a token that what had just passed between us was not to be incorporated into our relationship (that, being an accident, it deserved neither apology nor analysis), started toward the stairs. But Philip detained me. "We'll go in together," he said.

"Oh, I think we shouldn't," I replied. "Miss Pride is here tonight."

"She doesn't own you. She certainly doesn't own me."

I was uneasy when we entered the drawing-room together, certain that the hubbub in my mind would be visible in my face. Miss Pride, still listening courteously to the Korean, missed nothing, but turned upon us those yellow and accomplished eyes which accused me of committing an outrage. I looked away but Philip returned her stare and said to me, "The effect was just what I wanted."

Miss Pride, scrupulously faithful to her word, did not deprive me of companionship. From time to time, she summoned to dinner a group of people near my own age who, although they were well-born and well-educated, did not belong, and never would, to her sphere, but to a frustrated imitation of it. The young men, who showed by their faces and their manners that they came from good families, revealed by their clothes that they were not well off, while the girls, students for the most part from Radcliffe, had sublimated their natural longings for dress and parties into a defiant intellectuality, terrifying to someone like myself. The dinner parties were formal and while we were having our cocktails and elaborate canapes in the drawing-room, Miss Pride, grouping us together, attempted to break down the barriers between herself and them and between them and me. And if she succeeded at all and with the help of the Martinis we were talking with a minimum of restraint, our discomfort immediately returned when she, our only leaven, set down her glass and announced, "And now I'm going to leave you to yourselves. You won't want to be bored by an old woman. As my father used to say, no Utopia can destroy the aristocracy of years and the older one grows the more inferior one's caste. Good evening, I must hurry on to my fellow plebeians." She left us. A quarter of an hour elapsed before dinner was served and the cocktail shaker was empty. As she had not commissioned me to refill it, I dared not go back to the pantry in the fear that the vermouth and gin had already been put away and that I would return empty-handed, unable to explain my failure to my guests. A hush then fell upon us and continued through dinner. The young men joined us before half past nine and by ten everyone had gone home. Ashamed, disconcerted by the erudition of the college women who had been discussing Hegel's antinomies, the *Faerie Queen*, and *La Grande Jatte*, I went up to my room to drug myself with typewriter practice.

But because I did not wish to appear ungrateful or incapable of acting as a hostess, I said nothing when Miss Pride planned another of these exhausting fiascos. And since she was a friend of their families, her recruits rarely failed to accept her invitations, usually issued over the telephone to their mothers. Certain that she had pleased me and furthered my interests, she remarked once to the Admiral who had inquired how I put in my time, "Why, she keeps a regular salon to which only the cream of the intelligentsia is bidden. I don't stay among them, they're so formidable, so I always arrange to have other fish to fry. I wouldn't like them to find out what a dunce I am."

It was difficult to reconcile her selection of my friends with her antipathy to "braininess" for these young people had nothing if they had not that. And if she hoped to launch me on a social career which would not interfere with her other plans for me but would satisfy the natural demands of my youth, she was doomed to failure. They were all too busy, too ambitious, and too learned to seek me out, but it did not seem to occur to Miss Pride that it was strange I never received a return invitation.

I easily divined that the principal reason for her supervision of my social life was that she wished to distract me from thinking about Philip. She was not, of course, protecting me from disappointment but was looking out for Hopestill's interests, or rather, for the interests she devoutly desired the girl to have. I had heard from the Countess that the doctor had the reputation of being not only fickle but catholic in his love affairs, and just the year before had been all but engaged to a nurse from Nova Scotia in the Salem hospital whom he had boldly introduced in Boston even though she had, said the Countess, "the table manners of a Bavarian, the opinions of a barbarian, and the looks of a Paphian." It was true that she had been only a passing fancy and as soon as he had broken with her, Philip had fallen in love with Hope all over again as he had done each time he had strayed away. Just as he had often threatened to abandon medicine and become an astronomer or a carpenter or a Trappist monk but always returned to his profession with renewed enthusiasm, so he had invariably come back to Hope after an excursion in another quarter. While it was Miss Pride's belief (relayed to me by the Countess who did not dream, of course, that I had more than the merest interest in the doctor) that he would never marry unless he married her niece, she viewed with trepidation any symptoms in him of infatuation with another girl.

Although she did not mention his name to me and made no comment on the incident at the Countess', her campaign was perfectly apparent. She made a point of never inviting Philip to her house unless Hopestill was there, of always going to the Countess' when he was my partner and on such occasions of taking me home in her own car, of taking any telephone messages from him to me, even though I was at home, on the pretext that I was busy studying my bookkeeping or my shorthand. He, on his part, was delighted to have a chance to tease her and all during the spring telephoned me almost every day, requesting her to tell me that he would meet me "as usual" at the Lincolnshire or that he would pick me up the following day at Mrs. Hinkel's. The messages were never delivered and he, of course, had not meant them seriously, but Miss Pride arranged to have me run an errand at the hour he had named and, in order to make sure that I was obeying her, telephoned my destination to give me a further commission.

I could have told her that her precautions were needless. We did meet surreptitiously but it was only their secrecy that made our evenings together more entertaining than those I spent with Miss Pride's academicians. We met once every two weeks in the Union Oyster House where, in an atmosphere of sawdust and the acrid rot of crustaceans' shells, Philip was by turns courtly and brusque, but neither the one nor the other to any degree that would have told me how he thought of me. Nor did I, indeed, know how I thought of him. It was as if both of us were engaged in a pursuit of phantoms. We parted formally at the door of Miss Pride's house, but in our short lingering there was a mutual inquiry as if we had seen for an instant that which we desired but which distrust immediately obliterated. We were like blind men who, through some somatic perspicacity, can accurately judge spatial relationships and sense the presence of someone in the room but cannot, without the assistance of their hearing or their touch, know who it is. So we were at once the blind men and were the coy creatures who would not speak and would not offer up their faces or their hands for the expert, identifying touch. Or we were amateurs after nightfall in a terrain we did not know, hearing the hounds bay their triumph; to our untrained ears the sound of these fanatics might come from any direction, and we stumbled, parting company, running this way and that, encouraged by the near-ness of the sound which in the next moment was miles away. At last we were to find the captive in its dog-rimmed tree, the coon peering suddenly with its owlish eyes, the clever possum faking sleep; we had known this was the quarry, this quaint and useless beast, but we were disappointed, resented our fatigue and chill, wondered why hunters and dogs night after night returned to the woods for the absurd quest. But going back the way we came, we did not voice our foolish grief, merely com-mented on the sky and its omens for the next day's weather.

I would afterwards lie sleepless for hours in the double enve-lope of darkness and quiet. Sometimes my thoughts wandered to other things, but they returned to what most tantalized them, bringing back from the impersonal world, prosaic crusts by which to compare their banquet. I would consider Miss Pride, asleep on the floor below me, as stark as an effigy while Mercy, whom I had never seen, toured the room on consider-ately noiseless feet. Or I stared at the grove of sharp iron spikes outside my window to keep the pigeons away, like a full quiver in the arc light. Hearing the impatient whistle of a train about to depart, I thought of how, if it were leaving from the North Station, it would pass by Walden Pond and Concord. If it were leaving from the South Station, it would go towards New York, that unimaginable foreign country from which Hopestill dutifully returned each week-end. And I would ponder her in whom there was at work a ferment which neither Philip nor I could analyze. It was more, he said, than a love affair. She would not come back to Boston so faithfully every Friday afternoon if it were only that. Her whole life there was a secret she guarded so jealously that she had refused even to list her address in the *Social Register*. She gave no apparent signs of restlessness. We continued to go to Concord to ride and she as adroitly tortured the McAllister ladies as she had always done. The altercations between her and her aunt were a little more frequent but not much fiercer. But I knew, from our vague and slightly drunken conversations on Friday nights and from our sparse talk on the train back from Concord that she was on bad terms with herself. For there was no longer the camaraderie between us which had allowed us to gossip, to communicate on the same level. The Countess' musical afternoons did not amuse her, nor did she welcome any of my observations on her aunt's friends which heretofore she had relished, saying, "It takes an outlander to trap us alive." We talked now and again of a book, or in a desultory way Hope would tell me of an encounter in a Harlem night-club. There was thus apparently no more between us than between two people whiling away an hour in a train by means of a spotty conversation. At the same time, there was a bond of sorts between us which, although she did not know it, went back to the day when I, a little girl, had first learned that she lived in this house. Sometimes, against my will, my eyes were drawn to the portrait of her as a child. Once, seeing my contemplation of its delicate and sentimental color, she said, "I was really a nasty little proposition although I look so winsome there. But what child wouldn't be nasty who grew up in this place?"

I was infected both by Hopestill's furtive trouble and by Philip's capriciousness and had it not been for Miss Pride's reliably unchanging manner, would have probably given way to a dangerous dissatisfaction. She, I was sure, had no idea that my life did not satisfy me in every particular. She herself was so pleased with my progress that she invited me to live with her again the following year. Indeed, she declared, she hoped I would take up permanent residence on Pinckney Street. She regretted that she could not offer me her hospitality for the summer, but could instead provide me with a splendid opportunity to put into practice my stenographic training. I was to work in her soap factory in Cambridge, an arrangement which everyone except myself regarded with the greatest enthusiasm. The plan was generally thought to be my own idea and Miss Pride would say to her friends, "Sonie is the cleverest person here. No summer stupor for her: she has got herself a job, mind you, and while the rest of us are loafing, she will be earning money." Only the Admiral expressed doubts. "Why, child," he said, "won't you be lonesome?"

I was extremely lonesome. Philip had gone back to Chichester, and all the people I had met at Miss Pride's or at the Countess' had left for the Cape or the North Shore. It was too hot to read. My furnished bedroom on Kirkland Street was under the roof and the air was motionless all night. I lay naked on the bare floor, the sweat tickling my legs and back like flies' feet and, stupefied, I thought of nothing. It was, in this season, almost a pleasure to visit my mother. Although the trip was complicated, including three stages, by bus, by subway, and again by bus, I made it with a sort of martyred delight. As I sat in the crowded subway train, nudged by people carrying fading flowers and boxes of cake to their Sunday hostesses, or fanning their streaming faces with the Boston *Globe*, or swaying half asleep from the heat, I was more at ease than I had ever been in Miss Pride's house. At ease, even though at the end of the torpid journey there was neither rest nor entertainment, but the disinfected madhouse where I sat with Mamma, bored, sleepy but required to be on my guard each moment.

On the few unseasonable evenings when a languid breeze stirred the papers on my writing table and my pores stopped gushing, I wrote letters to Philip and to Hopestill and to Miss Pride, but only the last did I ever mail. On the way home from the letter box, I would stop and buy a bottle of sherry and once again in my characterless room would steep myself in the harsh, unpalatable wine and stare gloomily at the crabbed, complaining lines I had written to the people I could not fathom, yet could not ignore.

3

The second autumn in Boston differed from the first only in that we had begun the memoirs. We worked each morning except Sunday from the time our consultation with the servants ended until luncheon was announced, but for all our diligence we proceeded at such a snail's pace that I saw we had before us a labor of many years, and I wondered if the final product would be worth it. For Miss Pride, shrewd, witty, and fluent in conversation, was inarticulate when she began to write. The juvenility of her diction and the crudity of her syntax surprised me, for her few letters to me had been as elegant as her speech. After floundering for some months with no success, we at last hit upon a plan. She would write me a letter, very carefully in the style of Horace Walpole, of whom she was an assiduous student, which begged me to set down in "sound English" the anecdote which she then wrote out in her tumid language. As her calligraphy was obscure (not intentionally, as the Countess von Happel's was, but because she wrote in the heat of passion), it often took me a full morning to decipher a single sentence and in a short time my desk bore a formidable sheaf of manuscript which I had not transcribed or edited. Thus, all morning we worked facing one another at two long desks which had been pushed together.

Hopestill came home less often than she had done the year before and when she did come, I rarely saw her. We discontinued our evenings in her room and our rides in Concord. She was apparently so uninterested in anyone in Boston that she preferred her own society and during her visits kept to her room, emerging only for meals. Gradually she became for me no more than a ghost, one belonging in a way to Chichester, and I was free at last of any envy of her. Her clothes, if they were more spectacular, were no more expensive than mine; if I did not have Philip McAllister's whole heart, as she had had it at various times in her life, I had his constant companionship which even Miss Pride had been forced to recognize and tolerate. In my good fortune, I could afford to pity her for her misanthropy, and for the solitude in which she inexplicably had immersed herself. It was therefore the more startling that we again came together without warning and with most savage intimacy.

Philip had not waited even long enough for a cup of tea, but had only come to arrange to call for me at dinner-time. We were going later to the Countess'. The business had been transacted within earshot of Miss Pride intentionally, and while she made no alternative suggestion, she said with great displeasure, "I hoped you would have dinner with me. Now I shall be all alone." Philip gave her a smile. "She needs a change of air every now and again, you know."

The younger Mrs. McAllister had been Christmas shopping and declared when she came in that the only thing which had relieved the tedium of the task was the prospect of a "reviving chat with Lucy Pride." She had, however, after a perfunctory, albeit effusive, salutation to her hostess, immediately sought out Amy Brooks and the two of them had sat, heads together, on the sofa where Amy was in the habit of holding court for

Mr. James and Mr. Pingrey. Philip paid his brief compliments to his mother and left the room. I went to the window and saw him for a moment hesitating before he went down the street. I was surprised to see that he was wearing a bowler today and that he carried a stick, for usually his dress was of the most casual. I experienced a moment of peculiar distaste for him as I watched his grotesquely military bearing in which, it seemed to me, I had sensed a new element.

Half an hour after he had gone, Hopestill made an entrance into the drawing-room, pausing as she had done the first time I saw her, at the tulip wood commode to reconnoiter and to determine which of the guests after her aunt deserved her first greeting. She was dressed in green moiré, the severity of which did not check her flaming beauty but struggled with it in a magnificent combat, so that her sudden appearance in the doorway, unexpected, was like a chivalric, plangent war brought to our quiet gathering.

"Why, Hope!" cried Miss Pride. "I didn't expect you for ten days."

"I know," laughed her niece. "It was to be a surprise, Auntie. You're glad, I trust?"

Because she had never before "surprised" her aunt with a visit, the old lady looked questioningly at her, but smiled and said, "Delighted."

When she had kissed Miss Pride and the Admiral, Hopestill crossed the room to Philip's mother who, on seeing her, cried out, "Oh, how glad I am I dropped in today! I never dreamed you'd be here. Philip will be wild when he knows he missed you. He just this minute left."

"It's nice of you to say that he'll be 'wild,' Mrs. McAllister. But since Amy was here I imagine he had quite a full enough afternoon without me."

Mrs. McAllister bit her lip in vexation. Philip had only nodded to Amy. Moreover, Amy had dropped a few remarks that had intimated at a romantic attachment to Edward Pingrey. I had heard Mrs. McAllister say, "But, Amy, he's not really your sort of person, do you think so? I'm extremely taken with Edward, as we all are, but he has never really belonged to your set . . . to yours and Philip's, that is." Amy ingenuously replied, "Why, Philip and I don't belong to the same set at all. I believe he thinks I'm unconventional." Her giggles commenced and drowned out the older woman's next speech.

Now, unwittingly nettling Mrs. McAllister, she said to Hopestill, "He snubbed me completely. He only came to make a rendezvous with Sonie."

"Ah," said Hope, glancing in my direction. But she turned again to her cousin. "I like your dress, Amy." She could not suppress a smile for Amy, who had no judgment about clothes, was wearing bright red wool, most unbecoming to her colorless face to which she had clumsily applied orange lip rouge and excessive mascara.

"It's terribly red, isn't it?" cried Amy, beside herself with her strange nervousness. "Edward likes it! Hope! I have read Freud since I saw you last!"

Hopestill smiled condescendingly and turned to Philip's mother. "I hope your mother will still let me dress at her house."

"Will you ride in this weather?" cried Mrs. McAllister.

"It's just the kind I like. The colder, the better."

"Well, you know you're always welcome, my dear. You haven't changed your mind about coming to my house instead? But perhaps you wouldn't like to feel indebted to Philip for I should give you his old playroom and he's most sentimental about it. I don't blame you: I shouldn't like to owe that young man a thing. Tell me truthfully, Hope, don't you think he has a heartless nature?"

"Indeed I do," replied the girl. "And that's the reason we've always got on so famously, for I'm heartless too."

"What a fib! No one has a warmer heart than you."

Hopestill, outraged because Mrs. McAllister had raised her voice so that everyone in the room could hear her, took her leave but not before she had said icily, "It's kind of you to compliment me so, but I'm bound to disappoint you if you really think I'm warm-hearted."

They embraced tenderly and the older woman said, "You could never disappoint me, Hopestill Mather."

I had been on the point of going upstairs for I had a few letters to type out for Miss Pride, but Hopestill intercepted me and taking me by the arm, led me back to the love-seat in the bay window. As we sat down, I saw that she was shock-ingly altered from the last time she had been here: the violet glades were deep beneath her glaring eyes and as deep were the new hollows in her pale cheeks which had lost their luster and had the gray opacity of fatigue. And as she talked, hysteria expanded her nostrils and shook her lips.

"Where did Philip go? To the hospital?"

I told her I thought he had gone home to dress for dinner.

"I'll telephone him then. I'm awfully anxious to see him. I don't suppose he told you what his plans were for the evening?"

"Why, yes. I'm having dinner with him and afterwards we're going to the Countess'."

She raised her eyebrows in a faked surprise. "Oh! I didn't know you actually dined with him."

"Yes. I often do."

She repeated, "I didn't know you actually dined with him. But it's of no importance. I dare say he didn't know I was coming on today. I wrote but perhaps the letter was delayed. I should have wired."

"You wrote?" My alarmed question was involuntary. Then, flustered by her lofty imperturbability, I said, "I've got some letters to go off. I'd better go up now."

"Will you look in on me when you've dressed, Sonie?"

I rose and started across the room as Hopestill went to sit beside Admiral Nephews. Miss Pride, who had left the room just after her niece arrived, was returning and I confronted her in the hall. "I trust you're going back to the letters. They're urgent and must go off tonight by air." I promised that I would not fail to get them in the post and moved past her. "One thing more, Sonie," she said, laying her hand on my arm. "I cannot condone—and I certainly cannot overlook—your behavior with Dr. McAllister. Two people remarked to me today that you seemed to be flirting with him. For your sake, I denied the accusation though I regret to say that in doing so I was also denying the evidence my eyes furnished me. I speak only for your own good, believe me, Sonie. I don't blame *you*. What was more natural than for you to go to Berthe von Happel's little parties with him? But it shouldn't have gone beyond *that*, my dear. It's been imprudent of Philip to encourage you in this infatuation. If I had been he and saw what was coming over you, I would have left you strictly alone. Why, Sonie, you're too sensible a girl to hitch your wagon to a star like that. Surely you must have heard what sort of person he is—one can't count the girls he's trifled with."

"Oh, you needn't worry about me, Miss Pride," I told her. "I have my feet on the ground."

"That's the way to talk! I knew you had good sense. Well, we all must take our foolish holidays, mustn't we? But now, since you know people have talked—unjustly I do believe—you'll take care not to let them talk again, won't you? Run along now and don't forget the letters. Isn't it nice that Hopestill came back just in time?"

"In time for what?" I inquired dully.

"Why, in time for Berthe's party. This is her most elaborate one of the year."

It was still early when I went to Hopestill's room, but she was already dressed and was seated before her fire engaged in wrapping a Christmas present. Her small sitting-room was confused with suitcases and unopened parcels and in the window stood a locked wardrobe trunk. "As you see," she said, following my eyes, "I've come back for good. When I've tied this knot, let's have a glass of sherry. Can you believe it, I had the fortitude to take a bottle of Aunt Lucy's private stock." I said I would have none. "Oh, do!" She dropped her package and took hold of my wrist, digging her enameled talons into my skin, as if my abstention from the stolen sherry threatened a catastrophe. She filled two glasses and gave me one. "Here, take it. You've never tasted anything like it."

She took a sip from her glass and picking up the fallen ribbon and the shears, turned to her work again. "Sonie," she said, "would you mind awfully if I went to dinner tonight with Philip?"

I drank before I answered her. "Did your aunt tell you to ask me?"

"Auntie? Of course she didn't. What business would it be of hers?"

"I only wondered."

"Well, she didn't. It was my own idea. I knew you wouldn't mind and you don't, do you? Did he by any chance," she said, looking up from her package, "send you those camellias you're wearing?"

I said he had. "They're lovely on your dress and what a lovely dress it is, too." I could not return her smile. She went on matter-of-factly, "Look here, Sonie, you're not in love with him, are you? Because if you are, I'm devilishly sorry. I'm afraid I rather put ideas in your head."

"Oh, I assure you you didn't."

"Sonie, I simply couldn't stick New York any longer!" she burst out. "I don't think I'll ever leave Boston again. It's more than flesh can bear to be separated from the only thing in the world one gives a tinker's damn about."

"What do you mean? This house?"

"You know perfectly well I mean Philip." She gave me a quick, bright smile intended to tell me that I was the first to be let in on her secret. "By the way, would you rather have your Christmas present now or wait? You know this year, for the first time in my life, I'm actually looking forward to Aunt Lucy's Christmas tree even though there is something really revolting about the way she hauls the servants up and gives them ridiculous presents. Do you know that once she gave Ethel two decks of cards in a monogrammed leather case for Whist parties?"

Wishing to have these pointless preliminaries finished, I said, "I'd like to have my present now."

"Oh, darling! How impossible of me! I just remembered it won't be here until tomorrow. It's a phonograph and several albums of records."

I was touched by her generosity and when I thanked her, she said, "After all, it was the least I could do, wasn't it?" The remark erased the kindness from her gift, told me with its frank interrogation that it was even less than solace but was the payment of a bribe the necessity of which she had anticipated, even though she had declared a little while before that she was not aware I dined with Philip. Hearing then her condescending negotiations, I was like the child who is told that he may not go to the picnic but for his supper may have a cream-puff. In his grief he believes he is offered a choice and cries, "But I don't *want* a cream-puff!" and cannot believe that his franchise is specious, nor can he persuade the governor of the nursery that while he likes cream-puffs and any other night would welcome them for supper, this is not the night; he *wants* only the hard-boiled eggs and the cold chicken that are to be on the menu of the picnic. I did not want the phonograph although for several months I had been wishing for one, and while I could not say, like the disappointed child, that I did not, I could, like him, point out certain drawbacks in the gift. The child would say, "I don't want a cream-puff and it's silly because nurse told me we were having steamed pudding for supper and we can't have both and I think they're horrid anyway," and I said, "But I wish you hadn't bought me any records because our taste is probably not the same at all."

"Oh, Sonie, I'm sorry!" I had really distressed her and thought I even saw signs of tears in her exhausted eyes. She said, "I've tried so hard!" and thinking that she meant she had tried so hard to please me and my ingratitude was more than she could bear, I quickly said, "Oh, don't! I've really longed for a phonograph, and I've no doubt the records can be exchanged if I don't like them."

"I didn't mean that. I meant I had tried so hard in other ways. Well, it was all lost a long time ago and it's useless to try to regain it. I mean my balance was lost, my integrity, whatever it is in the name of God that keeps one together."

She poured herself another glass of sherry. "Do you want to hear an ugly yarn?" she said. "I haven't been 'studying' in New York at all, as Auntie knew and everyone must have suspected. I was going to a psycho-analyst and paying out fifteen dollars an hour for his nasty mumbo-jumbo. He had shaded lamps and old copies of the *New Yorker* and big divans in his waiting room where we all sat, so scornful of one another, pretending, every damned one of us, that we weren't there on business but had just come to pay a social call or had just dropped in to rest our feet. He had two Siamese cats that I grew to hate so violently that the doctor declared I had a cat complex, and he was beside himself with triumph when I volunteered, merely to pass the time, that Aunt Lucy had a cat that she kept locked up in her bedroom. He really said 'Eureka!' as though the whole problem were settled and it would only be a matter of minutes to find the cure. It's exactly like a dream and I can't really believe that he advised me that day to go out and buy a cat, *not*, mind you, a Siamese but a Persian tortoise shell like Mercy although I kept telling him that I had no objection to Mercy and it was his own wretched animals that I detested. He said I had come to substitute himself for my aunt! I kept going back because it quickly became a habit and at the same time I was doing just the same things I'd always done before because now I had confessed my sins they didn't seem very bad. He told me I wasn't co-operating and I got the notion that I was getting by with something because I was deceiving him the way I used to deceive the teachers at school and then Aunt Lucy and I enjoyed it all the more with him because he was powerless. I took the keenest pleasure in doing all the things I pretended I hated. His name was Dr. Ragsdale and I would tell him my dreams in which it was changed to 'Dr. Ratsbane.' He was pigeon-breasted and so evil I always knew he was homosexual and alcoholic as well as clinically insane."

"But why . . ." I began.

"Why, indeed? I kept thinking, I suppose, that I'd develop such a horror of my nature and the way he mauled it that I would at last be able to change. But I didn't. And so I have come back to Boston. *Here* maybe I can. There's probably a devil in me, one straight from hell like those in the Salem witches my ancestors used to burn."

She was sincere. A silence followed her words in which that evil she believed in and urged me to believe in was like a third person in the room; or it was like an innovation in the furnishings which was felt but not immediately perceived. I remembered, in that quiet, a series of small incidents which had puzzled me but which I had put out of my mind: once, the year before, when we were on our friendliest terms, she had brought me a present of a chartreuse evening gown which she had bought for herself and had afterwards discovered was too large. Chartreuse was a color I could not possibly wear as there were tints in my skin inimical to any variations of green or yellow, and since Hopestill and I had discussed this very misfortune sometime before when we had been shopping, I was naturally surprised at her gift. But in order to please her I put it on and went down to the sitting-room. Hopestill and her aunt were both there. "For heaven's sake!" cried Miss Pride.

"Where did you get that frightful dress, child? You're the color of bile! Run back up this minute and change to that pretty blue of yours." "Yes, do, Sonie," agreed Hopestill, "it's awful." I was glad enough to change and went out, but stopping in the hall a minute to glance over a pile of letters I had put on the table to make sure they were all stamped, I chanced to hear Hopestill say, "I can't think what got into me when I bought it for her. I was so proud of myself to remember her size, but imagine my forgetting that she couldn't wear that color," so that I knew she had not bought it for herself as she had told me. Another time, she had told me that she wanted me to meet a very distinguished cousin of hers who had married an Oxford don and was visiting for a few weeks in Milton. She said she had arranged a small dinner party and particularly wanted me to come because she thought I would find Lady So and So very amusing. And yet, when the day arrived and I warned her that I might be a few minutes late as I had to run an errand for Miss Pride in Cambridge, she said, "As a matter of fact, Sonie, Aunt Lucy asked me to tell you to stay at the Cock Horse for dinner and she'll send Mac around for you at nine. We're having a little dinner party for a cousin of mine who's a great bore and a stickler for family and that kind of thing."

Her malice was conscious, but its genesis was abrupt and unplanned, or seemed to be, though actually it must have been calculated painstakingly in the craters of her subconscious mind, so that probably she had intended to buy the dress for herself but a sudden impulse had made her select my size rather than her own and she had forgotten, in her guilt, the story she had told me and had told her aunt quite another. Now, having discovered the diathesis predisposing her to these brutalities I looked upon her with detachment, and thinking that what she wanted tonight was not to be with Philip but to spoil my evening (a desire which came from the same mischief that had prompted her to give me the dress), I resolved to keep my appointment with him.

Her mood had changed from one of restive worry to a sort of mild elation. She stretched out full length before the fire, her hair like the beams of a monstrance as it lay gleaming on the green carpet. The arc of her wide turquoise velvet skirt was broken by her small feet shod in gold dancing slippers.

About her throat she wore a tightly plaited gold chain from which depended a scarabeus fluted with lapis lazuli. We were so still we heard Miss Pride moving about her room on the floor below us.

"It's late," I said. "I'm afraid I must go down."

"Go down? But I thought you had agreed."

I stood up. "You know I didn't. But if you insist on it, take his flowers." As I unpinned them, I pricked my finger and I thought how ruinous and beautiful this jewel of blood would be if it were to drop and glisten on her blue-green skirt.

She received the camellias, but as she pinned them to her shoulder, a shudder streamed from her face to her frivolous feet. "I wonder if he . . ."

"If he what?"

"If when he bought them he touched them with his hands. Oh, God!" She covered her face with her fingers, but her eyes were visible through the interstices. She stared up at me with a plea which, being unable to fathom, I could not grant. But as I turned to go, leaving the issue constructed between us like a barrier with no purpose, the girl's seemingly diverse moods which she had addressed to me since our first words in the drawing-room at tea time now appeared as an unbroken concatenation, and I was enlightened as I saw the uniformity of her whims. I divined, through an intuition which had never been exercised in me before, either because of a physical immaturity or because of the want of circumstances, that there was a sole exigency that could drive her to this corner where, for all her insolence, she was terrified. And as I realized that not the satanic particles but the organic chemistry of her composition had led her to this replacement of myself for the evening (a replacement she was determined, I now knew, to make permanent), I was ready to withdraw any claims I might have had since her need was so much greater than my own. My delay at the door, occasioned by this certain understanding, may have communicated its derivation to her, although she said, to my surprise (for in this instant after I realized that my hand had been half a minute on the door knob, I almost expected her to confirm my suspicions, to admit frankly that she was pregnant), "Take back the flowers and go to dinner with him. I will see you all at Berthe's." I had not fully turned around

and I envisaged the flowers, their magenta petals protecting
the golden filaments of the core, and as I went back to retrieve
them (though I no longer wanted them, for by their exchange
of hands they had been bruised and their significance had been
polluted) my eyes traversed the window where, by arc light
from Louisburg Square, the cold December snow was falling,
and I remembered, as we remember comfort when the crisis of
our pain descends and hints of our recovery are given us, that
Philip had told me once that camellias bloomed in midwinter
in New Orleans.

The single peal, three flights down, preceded a moment the
six bells struck by the nautical clock on Hopestill's mantel. "It's
Philip," I said, as I bent over to take the flowers. My utterance
of his Christian name, upon the heels of my recollection of his
report that camellias bloomed this time of year in the south
(for, unable to visualize such a phenomenon, I had merely
thought the words, Philip said . . .) imparted to my flesh an
inchoate, sensual delight, similar as I perceived to that I had
experienced when, identifying my own body with Hopestill's
to make my diagnosis of her altered nature, my comprehension
had not been established by logic but by the completion of my
own ripening. Hopestill still lay before the fire in her strategic
immobility. It was strategic because she appeared transfixed
by an invisible pinion to the floor as if, like the possum or the
dung-beetle playing dead, she would come to life at once upon
my departure. Her eyes, apparently shut, took in each motion
it was necessary for me to make to unpin the flowers from her
shoulder and, glancing at the bits of shining eyeball, visible
through her long, sparse auburn lashes and seeing once in that
brief space of my perusal, the gold-flecked iris that enshrined
the eye's soul, I knew myself to be in the presence of desperation so rarefied at this climax reared up by the signal at the
outer door that it resembled lethargy. And simultaneously, I
knew that no one else would see what I had seen and that she
would go scot-free. Although at this point in her there was
ambush and a cause for it, both would be obliterated; the sins
would be exorcised not by the psycho-analyst but by concealing
custom.

When I had left her and had stepped into the corridor,
the sensation that summarized the scene in Hopestill's

sitting-room was not one of anger or indignation, had nothing in it more unfavorable to her than my old and now enfeebled antipathy to the child in the Barstow dining-room. I directed the movement of my body to partake of the grace of my dinner dress, desiring, as though Miss Pride's dim hallway were lined with spectators, my organism to proclaim through its flattering draperies that the force inspiring me was one of fleshly love, akin to the passion that had undone Hopestill and with devoted obstinacy still clung to her in her dilemma. The love I felt, which like a rapid poison circulated throughout me, had no object, and until I was on the last flight of stairs from the top of which I saw Philip's hat and gloves on the vestibule table, my desire did not focus, for until then, the elusive lover I had tried to construct was that unnamed, unacknowledged man whose impregnation of Hopestill was also an exegesis of my own changing self. Then, attaching my attention to a well-known object, for the space of ten seconds, I was determined to finish with him what I had so indecisively begun. But the moment my desire materialized, it vanished; the shame that recalled me to my usual timidity was incommensurate with its cause: at the same time that I took in the doctor's bowler and the gray suède gloves, I heard Miss Pride's voice through the closed door of her bedroom: "You may go now, Ethel. I am ready to undress." The direction, which was probably superfluous to the well-trained maid who knew by heart her mistress's habits, fell upon my ear like an injunction repeated to herself by a nun, and I could no more imagine Miss Pride in the deshabille she painstakingly kept for the eyes only of her mirrors, than I could have imagined a Mother Superior in her nightdress. I took no pleasure now in the décolletage of my new frock, and thought it would be improved by the addition of a shawl thrown about my shoulders. But the atavistic reaction was not complete as it had been formerly, when I was a child and had loathed my mother for those qualities I had now discovered in myself. For I had gone too far, by becoming myself a protagonist, to believe blindly any longer that Miss Pride's was the ideal pattern: there was, in the tone of her voice, cold and neutral, a suggestion of ingrown, conceited lewdness which, having no sexuality to modify, advertised the secret nudity of the old, arid carcass.

The doctor had been shown into the library where he stood inaudibly conversing with a large young man, shaped like an athlete, but one whose muscles had relaxed already and beneath whose chin a soft second growth had begun. They turned to greet me and Dr. McAllister introduced me to his friend, Frank Whitney. The doctor was nervous and would not sit down. He said, "I've just lost my first patient and if there's anything here besides Grandfather Pride's port, I'd like to resort to the traditional sedative. Do you keep any whiskey here?" We did. I brought out a decanter of whiskey and a tumbler. Philip poured the glass three-quarters full. "I can blame only myself, although some kind-hearted person said the x-ray reading had been at fault. It was a skull-fracture and I advised against operating." He drank half the whiskey and then, pausing, with the glass still in his hand, he said, "How stupid! I poured out three times as much as I wanted," yet his hand remained suspended, clasping the tumbler and I knew that he wanted the rest of it, indeed, probably wanted another double portion, but that his will denied it to him.

"Hopestill is here," I said. The response on his face to my announcement was a compressed version of what I had seen on the first afternoon I met her when he raised his hand and touched her hair. But his look was not one of surprise and I wondered again what she had written him.

"That's convenient," he said. "Frank decided at the last minute to come along. We can all go together. By the way, some friends of Hope's rang me up a little while ago and said they were stopping by here . . . perhaps we can offer them a drink, what do you say?"

"Hope wasn't expecting to have dinner with us," I said.

"I'm sure we can persuade her," put in Frank Whitney.

"Oh, yes, I have no doubt we can," I replied. "She's very anxious to see you, Philip."

"That's good of her."

"She's come back to stay. Did you know?"

Hopestill entered the room. The animal that had matured in Philip's disciplined person, despite the herculean efforts of his Puritan will, strained towards its meeting with that other specimen of the same genus that I had seen rioting in the cold prison of the girl recumbent before her hearth. I turned away as he went to greet her and discovered Frank Whitney's dreamy brown eyes regarding me with wonder. I had picked up Philip's half-emptied glass and downed it. "Do you often do that?" inquired the young man. "I mean, drink that much whiskey neat?"

"No," I told him. "But it's a good idea."

Philip was telling Hopestill that her friends were coming here. "The person who telephoned me was named Morgan," he said.

"Oh, yes, of course. I know him," replied Hopestill. "He's from Long Island. From a branch of the family famous for its lack of fame. Quite a barbarian he is, but I'm rather fond of him."

"Morgan?" said Mr. Whitney as if it were a name he had heard in some unsavory connection. "I don't know any Morgans." He uttered it as an accusatory epithet, as if its etymology had vested the name with respectability but its root meaning glared forth in the pronunciation; it was as if he had said, "A rum runner? I don't know any rum runners."

The door-bell rang, bringing us, in a moment, Mr. Morgan and a couple who were introduced with a great deal of laughter as the Cabots, the reason for the hilarity being that their name was really Babbitt. Mr. Babbitt who, because of an unfortunate obtrusion of his mouth, resembled an animal that rhymed with both Cabot and Babbitt (I pointed this out to Frank Whitney later and he said gravely, "That's not our kind of joke."), came up to me as if we had known one another all our lives and said, "Where's the booze, honey?"

"The drinks are coming now," I said. Ethel had brought in glasses and ice at Hope's order.

"That's dandy. Are you going to Berthe von Happel's shindig?" I replied that I was and remarked that I was sure it would be a very lavish party since the Countess had dispensed with the dinner party and had expended all her efforts on the midnight supper.

"Oh, she'll give us our money's worth tonight, bless her royal heart. I nipped in this afternoon for five minutes to see if I could lend a hand, and had a look into that gorgeous drawing-room of hers. Would you believe it, she has a Christmas tree—a *tannenbaum*, as she insists—reaching to the ceiling, an absolute smack in Louis Quinze's face. And she has poinsettias in green tubs all over the house, for all the world like a department store."

"She's really appalling," said his wife, "but it's impossible not to adore her."

This was a brazen untruth, but Hopestill, Philip, and Frank Whitney all enthusiastically seconded it. The irony of the expressions, "Isn't that absolutely the case!" "I love her parties, particularly her Christmas parties," and "She's a jewel, I'm head over heels in love with Berthe!" was so deeply embedded that had I not known that the authors of these praises actually despised the Countess, I should have thought them a cult convening to eulogize a high priestess. Thus, when they described her drawing-room to someone who had never seen it, they appeared to find it enchanting, and it was only the initiated who knew that some such statement as "She has two spurious Watteaus which are so charming one doesn't mind their being frauds," was actually inspired by the most savage spitefulness. The stranger, whose ear missed the note of contempt, at once admired the Bostonians for their defense of the Countess and felt little interest in the house itself, believing the word "charming" had been used out of simple generosity.

"Do you suppose Kalenkoff will be there?" asked Mr. Babbitt and the whole room laughed. Accustomed to their own habits of inbreeding and holding the common notion that royalty east of Austria was worthless because it was so abundant, these American aristocrats seemed to frequent the Louis Quinze salon chiefly for the purpose of snubbing its titled habitués. An obscure professor of physics from the University of Paris fared better at their hands than an arch-duke, and the dashing Baron Kalenkoff was invited nowhere while a wealthy British manufacturer of photographic equipment had a standing invitation to the best houses and clubs. They were so perversely American, so vehemently uninterested in any culture but that which their ancestors had found acceptable that they even went out of their way to offend the Countess' friends by their intentionally inaccurate pronunciations of German place names or their smug misconstruction of political philosophy or even, though this was regarded as *démodé*, by bragging of the excellence of the American sanitary system. On the one Saturday the year before when the Admiral had put in an appearance, he had said to Baron Kalenkoff, "Is it true, mate, that you Russian chaps sleep with dogs in your bunks?" The Baron flashed him a friendly smile. "It is customary," he said. "And when our guests are shown to their rooms they do not find detective novels and magazines on the night table to amuse them but they find the master's best dog in the bed. If the guest is any kind of gentleman, he will refuse this extravagant kindness and will insist that he be given the *second* best dog. You may be sure, sir, that if he does not hesitate to climb into bed with his host's prize wolfhound, he will never be asked again." The Admiral was flabbergasted by this leg-pull and moved away, remarking gruffly to Mrs. Frothingham who quite agreed with him, "Those Russians have no sense of humor."

Mr. Morgan alone did not join in the laughter and I surmised that he did not know the Countess. He had said nothing after the introductions and I quite erroneously thought that he was ill at ease. But when the laughter had subsided, he stepped forward shakily and said, "Don't you know I'm to be congratulated?" Mr. Babbitt then informed us that Mr. Morgan was celebrating his coming into a vast fortune through the death of his grandmother. To my astonishment, I heard Philip propose a toast.

"Thank you, thank you," said the heir, bowing at his stocky waist. "Somebody is missing from this conference, isn't somebody? It looks like a damned little conference, and what is this place we're holding it in? The Atheneum?"

"The missing person," said Mr. Babbitt, familiarly nudging me with his elbow, "beg pardon, the missing link is Miss Nanny Brewster whom you left in the ladies' retiring room at the Ritz bar."

"Nanny Brewster?" cried Hopestill shrilly. "What do you mean by bringing that street-walker to my house?"

Morgan patted her shoulder and said soothingly, "There, there, she isn't in the Atheneum. Didn't you hear John say she was in the W.C.?"

Frank Whitney abruptly presented his back to the company, whispering to me, "I remember him now," and began to read the titles of a section of books on Far Eastern studies. In a moment I joined him, preferring his pastime to the discussion of Miss Brewster's whereabouts, but not before Mr. Babbitt murmured to me with a moist laugh, "I don't know which one of them is getting the run-around." We were some distance from the others, Mr. Whitney and I, when he growled, "Bad blood is the rule with those Long Islanders. How can Hope stomach a buffoon like Harry Morgan?" And then, because Mr. Babbitt seemed to be approaching us again, he said, taking a book down, "Here's a funny thing, a Japanese novel translated into German. I call that too much of a good thing." Then when we saw that we were to be left alone since Mr. Babbitt was joining his friends, Frank Whitney told me about Morgan.

Mr. Harry Morgan was thirty years old. His equine face was being elongated year by year by the withdrawal of his black hair, and was being softened year by year by good living which the death of his grandmother, happily coinciding with Christmas, was evidently to make even better. We read in the newspapers that scions of famous families have gone to Hollywood to join, usually in a social capacity, the "film colony," and it is hard to tell, from the impartial journalists, whether the colonists or the immigrant are hereby benefited. Mr. Morgan was such a person, although, if his credentials had been gone into, it would have been found that he was so distantly related to any of the celebrated tycoons whose name he bore that he was no more entitled to a share in their glory than is a person named Shakespeare entitled to the homage of literary people. But it happened that this Mr. Morgan was extremely wealthy and few knew that his money came from the maternal side of his family, named Schumacher, and had been made in a variety of enterprises, including brewing, the manufacture of artificial limbs, razor blades, hooks and eyes, and the breeding of long-horn cattle. But the fact of the money, not its history, was the important thing. It was likely that had his father's name been Schumacher and he had not used Morgan at all or had used it as a middle name, he would have been as readily accepted in California. However, "the wealthy young Morgan" was a title of more tone than "Schumacher, the artificial limb heir." At the same time that he maintained an establishment in New York near a café called the Lancelot Club which he owned, he not only frequently visited Sun Valley, Idaho, and while he was about it looked in at his Beverly Hills cottage, but he was also, and had been for years, a student at Harvard College. There was a rumor, Mr. Whitney told me, never confirmed, that he had once made application for a Rhodes' scholarship.

"I won't go anywhere if that tart is going along," Hopestill was saying. "Really, Harry! And you're drunk."

"Let's not anybody quarrel," he replied amicably. "You had at least five or six drinks too many in the club car, sweetheart, you can't fool Harry. And how come you weren't on the train you told me to meet?"

"I got off at Back Bay," she said shortly.

It was as though we had come into a moving picture half-way through and because we did not know the beginning of the plot, could not adjust this scene to the foregoing action. Philip McAllister, standing witness to the intimate tiff, looked suddenly faint. "Excuse me," he murmured and backed away. For the second time, he told Frank Whitney and me about the skull-fracture case, of whose fatal termination he had learned over the telephone just after he had left our house at tea time. "Let me show you," he said, taking a pencil and envelope out of his pocket, "what it was in the x-ray reading that deceived me," and he began to draw a skull, but his hand trembled so, either from his surprise at Hopestill's almost domestic shrewishness with Morgan whom she had pretended to know only casually, or from a relapse into his earlier shock, that the outline was pinked like a valentine. Above his insistent explanation, I could hear the others talking and I was so intent on their conversation that from the doctor I learned only that the skull might be likened to an egg, which, broken on one side, might break simultaneously on the other, that his patient, struck on the temple had "sustained" an occipital fracture which he had misread as merely the widening of a suture line.

The Babbitts and Mr. Morgan had grouped themselves about the chess-table and seeing the men set up on the board, in readiness for Miss Pride's Sunday maneuvers, remarked that this was the final touch which proved that they had strayed into a club. To create the illusion that it was a commercial club, they put the board and pieces on the floor and set up in their place the bottle of whiskey to which they freely helped themselves. Hopestill, who had been standing by the fire gazing abstract-edly into the spurting logs, joined them when they threatened to put ice down her back if she didn't, and they sat, the four of them, round the little table, at play, as if they were in a night-club and had grown bored with their surroundings so that they had turned to their own private jokes and gossip for entertainment.

I interrupted the medical monologue. "Listen, Philip," I said, "this makes me nervous. What if Miss Pride should come in?"

"What if she should? Hope is her own mistress, isn't she?" he replied touchily.

"But such strange people," I said. Both young men stared coldly at me and I flushed.

"Helen Babbitt is Hope's cousin," said Mr. Whitney solemnly. "I must admit, though, that they *are* an unattractive lot."

Philip agreed with a laugh and turning to me forgivingly, he explained that Mrs. Babbitt had been a Miss Brooks and therefore related both to Hopestill and, by marriage, to the Countess, and while no one had ever liked her, for she was a fool and had not worn stockings to her wedding, people forgot this and came to believe that the interloper from New Jersey had made her into what she was. Admiral Nephews had remarked to her, "Madam, thou art mated to a clown," and ever afterwards it was the universal opinion that Mr. Babbitt had had the weight to drag her down. They came to Boston at Thanksgiving and Christmas to the great suffering of Mrs. Babbitt's family who were, ironically enough, related in several different ways to the Cabots.

"I suppose it's natural enough Hope's taken up with them," said Whitney. "She's probably lonely in New York."

"I would say the contrary," returned Philip drily. "I've concluded that Sonie is right: Miss Lucy would have epilepsy if she came in here now. I'll see what I can do." And he called across the room to the group at the chess-table, "Don't you think it's time we went on to dinner?"

"Why, doctor, what a childish idea," said Mr. Morgan, "we are just beginning our *apéritif.* It's my party and I name the hour. By the way, doesn't the Somerset Club serve meals?" He went back to his conversation, dismissing the interruption.

In spite of the objections one might make to his appearance or to his manner, whether one saw at once that he was crude or unscrupulous—for, although dissipation had obscured the sharpness of his face, a certain cunning remained in the eyes which did not look directly into other eyes—or whether he offended one's intellectual principles, there was about the young millionaire something so magnetic that exposure to the same air he breathed was similar in its effect to a love-philter. I had thought, in the first minutes of my admittedly enraptured regard of him, when my mind, operating simultaneously on two levels saw him on one as irresistible and on the other as repellent, that the sensuality manifest in his face was the forerunner of the corruption into which Dr. Galbraith had helplessly sunk. But presently I revised the prophecy that in twenty years he would be as damned a soul as the old doctor. For while he was sentimental—this was apparent from his slang, that badge by which we recognize the members of an egotistical and tenderly self-indulgent order—he was also shrewd, noncommittal, and even tonight when he was drunk, constantly on guard against involving himself with Hopestill, with Philip, in a sense, with this very room.

There are some people whom we know at first glance will never marry. How we know, I cannot say, but we know as surely as we know that other people have taken a dislike to us at the moment of our presentation to them. Harry Morgan was such a man. What appealed then so strongly to me that it was only with an effort of will that I was able to look away from him was the challenge flung down by his self-sufficiency, which could not but rouse in any woman the desire to conquer him, and I felt a revival of that light-headedness—anticipatory, perhaps, it had been—in which I had descended the top two flights of stairs.

Hopestill, handing him a pair of ice-tongs, said something we could not hear and he replied, whispering in her ear as he put an assured arm about her shoulders. She lingered beside him the briefest time and then moved away. There was a look of outrage on her face, but not that he had been familiar amongst strangers, rather that he had with such facility, such untroubled certainty of where he stood with her, communicated to all of us: "I can take you or leave you alone," for his gesture had been at once possessive and indifferent.

I doubt if Philip or Frank Whitney discerned the agitation into which Morgan sent the three women in the room, for even Mrs. Babbitt, although she was obviously accustomed to him, looked at him worshipfully. Neither of the men could have sensed the source of his charm since it required the intuitive simplicity with which a woman perceives in a man the very embodiment of temptation. This is one of the mysteries of their sex by which men are infuriated for, being unable to solve it, they believe it to be a hoax: "Why, So and So is a perfect bounder. What can you see in him?" they ask of the women who can only reply, "I can't explain it."

"Listen, Harry," said Mr. Babbitt, "I want you to sing that song Miss Nanny Brewster taught you. You'll love it, Hope. It's funny as hell the way Harry does it."

"I'm not interested and I don't want to hear it. I think it's time we went on to dinner."

But Mr. Morgan had already risen to perform. He moved unsteadily across the room and stood before the Governor Winthrop and in a moment began to sing. Above his strange head, like a moon at half eclipse, Miss Pride's father stared at the trophy case. His loosely clenched hand rested on a table at his side as if he were about to make it into a fist and pound. The wavering Long Islander sang with a tuneless, distended insolence, rolling his eyes and suddenly closing them as, stopping dead in his song, he stroked imaginary female hips of extraordinary dimensions. The Babbitts, half in tears with laughter, kept filling his glass with straight whiskey, for at the end of each line, by way of punctuation, he drained off what he had. The lewdness came chiefly from his pantomime and his catarrhal voice, for the words that issued from his boneless face were only:

> I love to go swimmin'
> With bow-legged women
> And dive between their legs.

"Isn't he a scream?" shrieked Mrs. Babbitt.
Frank Whitney was pale. "Let's get him out, McAllister.

He's drunk as a catfish." He started towards the offender, but Hopestill, who without trying to stop the song, had been gazing up at her grandfather as if supplicating him either to forgive this indignity or to put a stop to it, raised her hand in an apostolic gesture which said, "He has asylum here."

"He's perfectly all right, Frank," she said. "He's only gay. He inherited two million dollars yesterday and he has every right to sing if he wants to."

"Repeat refrain!" cried Mr. Babbitt, covering his face with his hands while his thorax hopped convulsively like a jumping bean. Mr. Morgan obliged him and the words traveled slowly through his nose.

The door to the library flung open and crashed against the paneling. Miss Pride, dressed for dinner in garnets and black silk, stood on the threshold appraising the terrain. The first to speak was Harry Morgan who, going towards her with the sober countenance that appears in certain stages of drunkenness, said, "Mrs. Mather, I presume?" Miss Pride's enameled lenses suddenly could focus only on distant objects. She looked at me and said, "The letters, Sonie, which you promised to mail," and held them out. Mr. Morgan's rejected paw faltered uncertainly to his side.

"Good evening, Helen." She addressed Mrs. Babbitt frigidly.

"Good evening, Cousin Lucy," said Mr. Babbitt, bounding toward her, "I'm glad to see you." Miss Pride did not share his pleasure but glared straight through his head as if the gimlets of her eyes could puncture the optic nerve. She came to me with the letters. "Hello, Frank. Is Mary coming on for the holidays?" and as she took his hand, she gave me the bunch of envelopes and adroitly, so that no one could see, she pinched the fleshy part of my thumb between two fingernails so hard that I nearly cried out with pain.

For half a minute she stood there while Frank Whitney gave her news of his family. She did not release my thumb until he was finished and then she said, "I must go this minute. Hopestill, bring Frank when you and Philip come to the Countess'. I know Berthe will be delighted."

"We're all coming, Auntie," said Hopestill. "This is Mr. Morgan, Aunt Lucy,"

"Good evening, sir," said Miss Pride and glanced up at the

portrait of her father. "Papa looks *en prise*. Do set his men up again, Philip." And she left the room. The only proof I had that she had been angry were the two white crescent marks on my thumb made, in her rage at something with which I had no connection, in the way one hurls a teacup to the floor because the contents of a letter have infuriated him.

"Waiter, bring me my bill," said Mr. Morgan with a foolish grin. "And cancel my membership in the Somerset. The bouncer gives me the creeps. Are you coming, baby?"

"No," said Hopestill. "Before you go, Harry, will you apologize to all of us?"

"Now I suggest," said Mrs. Babbitt in the voice of a peacemaker, "that Harry and John and I all go eat dinner by ourselves and let the ladies and gentlemen alone. Nobody's mad now but if we don't go right along everybody will be dreadfully mad except me."

"I won't be mad," pouted Mr. Babbitt. "And Olga won't be mad, will you, Olga?"

"Well, I'm damned," said Mr. Morgan, using his hands as binoculars and directing them towards me. "Is *that* Olga? Troika-ho, Olga!"

They left, Mrs. Babbitt's giggles leaving a wake behind. If I had been able to speak, I would have been profane, would have used every blasphemous and scatalogical oath I knew to tell Hopestill how I was affected by the knowledge that I had been the object of amused discussion. Olga! Her malice was so rich, so inventive that even now, exposed by the babblings of her drunken friends, she tried to hoodwink me. "I don't think Sonie looks all that Slavic, do you, Frank?"

The evening lay in ruins. My disappointments, my humiliation, and my scorn bustled through the branches of my nerves, created a tic here and a tingling there, an ache in my skull and fever in my eyeballs.

Mr. Whitney touched my arm. "Will you have dinner with me?" he asked.

Hopestill smiled. "Give the poor child a stout drink," she said. "She isn't used to the lower classes."

"Oh, I'll have a lot to drink," I said, and she and Philip laughed. They had forgotten us already before we had even reached the threshold. Hopestill was saying, "Well, darling, I've come home to stay. Aren't you glad?"

As soon as I could I left the Countess' salon and got my cape, but as I was starting down the hall towards the stairs someone laid his hand on my shoulder and I turned to find myself the captive of Mr. Pingrey. He said, "Sonia, Amy is in a tiz over your cutting her. You come straight along with me, you baggage. Mr. Hornblower is here and you have to meet him. He's just been telling the most delicious thing about Mr. Roosevelt. Did you know that the name is really Rosenfeld?" I was in no frame of mind to meet Your Esteemed Uncle Arthur Hornblower and told Mr. Pingrey that Miss Pride had asked me to run home to fetch something for her.

"Oh, stuff!" said Mr. Pingrey, flapping his hands limply in my face. "You're a perfect imp sometimes. Very well, but I will absolutely disown you if you don't meet him when you come back. Do you realize that he knows everyone of importance? Gandhi, Mussolini, Hitler, Trotsky, the Lord knows who. He's the most literate person here by far."

I felt this to be a slight exaggeration, but said I had not been aware that the Countess' parties were intended to be the meeting ground of minds.

"Well!" he gasped. "Frankly I don't know what you're talking about. Why on earth would one come otherwise?"

"Why, to drink," I said.

Mr. Pingrey did not drink or smoke, making his abstention from alcohol, tobacco, and highly seasoned food a fetish as obstinate as a vice. He put his hand to his heart as if he had been wounded there and might, after his valedictory, topple over dead at my feet. "I cannot, I simply cannot understand this transformation in you." His eyes, similar to Amy Brooks' (both of them were victims of excessive thyroid secretions, a bond which strengthened their friendship, I am sure, and played a strong part in their marriage and their subsequent production of two children with the same glandular vagary), bulged forth as he bent his ruddy face down towards mine to gaze upon the frog which, before the gods had been provoked to wrath, had been a charming maiden.

"Then go on to your . . . punch bowl!" he cried, and stepped aside to let me pass. Had I lingered a few minutes longer, he would have used such words as "wassail" and "negus" and "sack" to show that his acquaintance with alcohol was purely literary. Once, at an informal luncheon, he had inquired of his hostess if her servants made the mead themselves. "Mead? What is that?" she asked. He indicated the glasses of Chablis. "Oh," said the lady, who did not like him and was also vain of her learning, "No, my athelings have lost the receipt. This is a simple grape concoction made by the Christians in Gaul."

I was halfway down the stairs when he leaned over the bannister and implored, "*Do* meet Mr. Hornblower. He wants us all to come to tea at his house tomorrow. He's terribly anxious to meet you and says he will be ever so interested to hear your political conflicts—I told him, you see, that you were half Russian and half German."

As the next day was Sunday, I could not go. "I will be away tomorrow," I told him.

"Oh, but you must come," he protested urgently, "because Mrs. Hornblower will be there too!" as though, if it were a rare thing to meet Mr. Hornblower it was an even rarer one to meet his wife. I repeated my refusal and Mr. Pingrey withdrew his head but not before he had stuck out his tongue at me like a peckish child and flung out, "Crosspatch!"

I had gained the outer hall when the door to the dining-room opened and the chauffeur shot past me like someone on a surf-board. He was carried along over the carpet by the leashed Doberman and the boxer to whom he applied, under his breath, the word "bitches" with venomous accuracy. Through the door I could see the supper table with its dishes arranged as tastefully as if they had been bouquets of flowers and were to serve no purpose other than ornament. The Countess had been planning this for months, ordering the strangest of the foods through importers, scouring Boston and New York for the finest Liebfraumilch and Niersteiner and champagne, herself supervising the decanting of the sweet wines and the liqueurs, and living through each step of the lengthy preparation of the *daube glacé* as if upon the proper contents of the bags of herbs depended her social success.

I had hoped to find the Countess here alone so that I could make my excuses to her, and I was annoyed to see that she was not in the room at all, but that wandering back and forth before the table were Baron Kalenkoff and a Jewish brain surgeon who were making hearty meals of the *daube*, the cucumbers in sour cream, the herring and salmon and caviar, the cheeses, olives, salads. Every now and again they abandoned the table only to repair to the side-board where the wines were cooling. The two accommodators, hired for the evening, and the Alsatian waitresses stared stonily at the carnage, stood near-by the gormandizers waiting to pounce upon the empty dishes and bear them away to the dumb-waiter to be, if possible, replaced.

I entered the dining-room intending to seek the Countess in the pantry. This room alone had been left untouched by the new mistress of the house; its walls were hung with Audubon's eagle attacking the inflated white belly of a fish, his Iceland gulls and curlews, and interspersed amongst the birds were Currier and Ives Maine landscapes and paddle-wheel boats. Miss Pride said of it, "I could digest my food there as well as I did in Josie Brooks' day if only Berthe didn't let her livestock run free."

As I paused in the doorway, the Countess appeared, coming out of the pantry with the intention, probably, of having a last minute look before she allowed supper to be announced. It must have been shocking for her to come upon two guests who had gobbled up visible portions of the food and had destroyed the appearance of half the dishes by their wanton hunger and who greeted her with their mouths full, one hand holding a slice of bread piled high with a layer of pickled herring, a layer of jellied partridge, one of salt salmon, and topped by a round of marinated onion, the other hand clasping by its neck a liter of cold wine. But the Countess' hesitation was the briefest possible. Undismayed, she advanced and she said, as though she were delighted by what she saw, smiling, her large fair face aglow with hospitality, her diadem of sapphires forming for this perfect hostess an angelic halo, "Oh, you didn't find the Niersteiner. You're drinking that flat Moselle. Here, let me get you some real wine."

Then, having finished her ministrations to the vandals and

having caught sight of me, she cried, "Ah, angel! I was just going to look for you. What are you doing with your cape? Going? But you've only been here five minutes!"

I told her I was feeling a little ill, I believed I was catching cold. "Oh, no! How shocking! I won't have you taking cold." She thrust a plate of lobster *en mayonnaise* in front of the Baron and said, "Try this, Alexy, and give me your honest opinion. Will you excuse me for a moment?" And taking me by the arm, she led me into the hall and towards the yellow sofa.

"Now!" she said, adjusting the camellias at my shoulder to her liking. "Now tell me why you're playing such a trick on me."

"But it's no trick, Countess. Really, I am all chills and fever."

"Oh, adorable monster! But I'll keep your secret. Is he gifted? Is he a gentleman? Darling, don't think I'm prying, but I love you! I could not bear it if my Euphrysone weren't treated well!"

Anxious to escape and afraid that if she kept me any longer I would blurt out the whole story of my wounded dignity, I put my cape around my shoulders and laughed, "He, Countess, is only Dostoievsky whom I shall read when I've taken an aspirin for my cold."

"Seriously," she said looking, indeed, very serious, "I am only thinking how Lucy Pride would feel about it. You know her anti-Semitism. But you do as you like, my dear pet! I will let you go *only* if you promise to be amused!"

"Oh, I do promise!" I assured her and I extended my hand in farewell, wishing to end this baffling dialogue. The Countess got up, kissed me, and went to the stairs. "How stupid of me! I forgot to tell you that he's waiting in the library."

I had known, even before I opened the door, that I would find Nathan Kadish in the library. He was standing in the lamplight, his birthmark towards me.

"Well," he said, "aren't you surprised?"

"Hello, Nathan. I'm glad to see you."

"I should hope you might be, you poor girl! What you must have been through! Had I only known I would have come to solace you months ago."

"How did you get in?" I said, amused and pleased that he had not changed.

"It was a very neat coup. I saw you come in here with that St. Bernard—what a moron *he* looks like—and waited a minute and rang the bell myself. I must say I was ready to give up when I got a gander at that butler. He was tough sledding, but the lady was a pushover."

I saw that he was going over, with an admiring eye, the details of my attire, and I likewise allowed my look to travel upwards from his feet in muddied white shoes, over his immaculate gray suit and bright red bow tie to his face.

"Well, Sonie? Well, how would you like to get drunk? I very much regret that as I am currently in love with someone else, this is the only amusement I can offer you."

It was the only amusement I was capable of enjoying. Even the prospect was sedative. As we went into the hall, Nathan said, "I assume that you won't mind doing the boozing in my sort of saloon?" We met the soulless face of the butler who, opening the door for us, said to me, "Good evening, Miss Marburg. I hope you won't find it too wet underfoot."

"Want to come along?" said Nathan to him, but the man, ignoring him, said to me, "Of course you have a very short walk home."

"She's not going home, you buzzard," said Nathan, looking closely into the snobbish face. "Slave!"

Both the man and I were too shocked to speak. The white door slowly closed and I was certain that I looked for the last time upon the Countess von Happel's brass knocker.

Chapter Four

Now on the glossy Sunday after I had stayed until four o'clock in the morning with Nathan Kadish at a café in Scollay Square, I had as my traveling companions not only shame, jealousy, and despair, but in addition a headache that pounded and reverberated through each convolution of my brain and stretched to bursting each tunnel and cove of my skull, a tidal nausea, a chill as dry and plunging as a winter wind. Last night's snow was deep and glazed, played on by bright sun, and the pavement over which we drove was like a polished blade casting upward shimmering filaments of frosty light. The spruce, hibernal landscape, simplified like a conventional design in which the vitality and the heterogeneous shades of autumn had been discarded for a white and mortal rigor, gave to the condition of my body and the state of my mind an incisive accent, and I could neither see nor imagine a source of warmth (chilliest of any detail in this fixed scene was the dun tendril of smoke ascending from a white chimney), nor could I be reminded by anything presented here of the good, the gratifying, the ennobling, or the pleasing elements of life. For I could observe only contrast, and in personifying nature as one will sometimes do in illness or in melancholy or conversely in well-being or in joy, I saw myself rebuked by the immaculate, inflexible earth for having been the night before exactly the opposite, just as I had been rebuked earlier this morning by Miss Pride whose wintry eyes in her bone-clean face had extinguished my heart's heat so that I had stood like a stalagmite beside the chess-table receiving her terse lecture.

Nathan and I had revived and rescaled our friendships with mixtures of rum and soda water, the number of which a persistent, unsolicited clerk in the back of my tortured head kept trying, this morning, to count from memory. And at sometime these scorched, half-blinded eyes of mine had seen a chorus of footsore girls dancing on a platform to a rompish paraphrase of "O, Come All Ye Faithful." They had been dressed like Santa Claus, if Santa Claus had been a girl in red, fur-trimmed underdrawers and a brassière of gold stars and had worn, in place of the smile of a kind-hearted old innocent, a grin of the most

workaday lewdness. Either before or after this travesty, which
at the time I had taken for granted but which this morning
possessed the impossible quality of a comic dream, a sailor in
His Majesty's, the King of England's, employ had briefly joined
us and in exchange for my wilted camellias which he requested,
declaring that he would preserve them to the end of his days in
his mother's prayer-book, he gave me a picture post card that
we all regarded as irresistibly droll. It showed, in vivid colors, a
small, libidinous, middle-aged man staring at a bathing beauty
about to dive into the ocean while his portly wife, surveying a
group of new cottages, remarked: "Look at the seaside development, George." For some purpose, lost forever to memory,
the sailor had laboriously printed his name, Sam Casserly, on
the back with an obtuse blue pencil.

The iconoclastic antics of the dancing girls and the transaction with Sam Casserly together accounted for perhaps fifteen
or twenty minutes out of the five hours we had spent in the
crowded room where the green and red lights, veiled by smoke,
made the atmosphere crepuscular. But I remembered that we
had not been idle and that our intake of noteworthy amounts
of rum had been accompanied by unflagging talk which,
although its substance was irrevocable, seemed, on retrospect, to have issued altogether from my lips. I could fairly see
Nathan's face patiently registering courteous sympathy with
my complaints, amusement at my mirthless anecdotes, respect
for my moral and literary judgments. And yet, gradually, as if I
were reading a book which I had forgotten I had read before,
so much of my companion's current history came back that it
seemed impossible, in view of the fact that I had learned all this
in just five hours, that I could have uttered a word, but that
the solo voice had been his, interlarding the calendar of his
love-affairs and his scholastic enterprises with expositions of his
character, guesses about mine, and childhood reminiscences
common to both of us. He was now, he told me, at Harvard
and had been for two years, studying literature with the support of a fellowship. He was also tutor to Harry Morgan and
was making so much money (he lived very simply) that he had
saved almost enough to go to Paris after his graduation. Before
the flight from America, he thought he might marry a Japanese
girl whom he described as superbly beautiful, or else an elderly

French fly-by-night who had no attractions for him but who spoke both German and French and could therefore act as his interpreter. And I believed, though I could not be certain, that when I reminded him that I was also bilingual (this exaggeration had evinced no comment from him), he had accepted my application, but had made it perfectly clear that he was in love with the Japanese girl.

I could not, though I exerted a supreme effort, retrace the paths I had traveled in our conversation, but I knew, if from nothing else than from the simple observation of human nature, that I had not been silent this whole time. What troubled me, therefore, to the point of tears which bubbled out of my red-hot eyes, was that I had possibly so involved myself with Nathan Kadish that I dared not cut myself off from him at once, must see him immediately again to ascertain how much and from what irascible or sentimental viewpoint I had revealed. And yet, because I could not dissociate him from my malaise, I desired nothing so little as this second interview.

When we had traversed another mile, I remembered that we had made an engagement for that evening when, at eight o'clock, I was to call upon him at his apartment in Cambridge for the purpose of meeting the Japanese girl. Simultaneously, I recalled my astonishment at hearing him ask me, "Does Shura live by herself in Chichester now?" I had been in control of my wits sufficiently to tell him nothing but I had found, by careful questions, that he had not heard of my mother's commitment to the asylum, for he had been back to Chichester only twice in the past two years and by that time, I suppose, some new scandal was of more immediate interest.

I had no difficulty at all in calling to mind what had happened after we left the café in Scollay Square. Emboldened by my renewed friendship with this charming young man, this paragon, as I often told him as we ascended the back side of Beacon Hill, of sense and sensibility, I did not hesitate to adopt his suggestion, when we got to Pinckney Street and I found I did not have my door key, that I call out to Miss Pride while he bombarded her window with snowballs. For Nathan said that the procedure was more practical than rousing the whole house by ringing the door-bell.

"Hello, up there!" I cried. "Miss Pride! I'm locked out!"

"Hey!" shouted Nathan. "Hey, lady! Come down and let a person in! It's cold out here!" To our delight, one of the snowballs went in the window. I congratulated Nathan on his marksmanship and we shook hands, gazing at one another with deepest admiration. Presently Miss Pride's head appeared. "Hush! I'm coming." Nathan backed away and as he receded into the whirling snow, I had the impression that like the Cheshire cat, he was leaving his smile behind. He whispered, "So long, madam," and vanished as the outer door opened and Miss Pride stood shivering on the threshold in a brown wrapper. Her scanty hair was unpinned and it bristled about her collar. I was not in the least frightened. On the contrary I felt loquacious and was on the point of asking Miss Pride to join me in a drink of her whiskey as I was suddenly urged to tell her what I knew about Hopestill. But before I had opened my mouth to speak, she said sharply, "Come in at once and go upstairs, you wretched girl. If one whisper of this reaches anyone, I'll turn you out of the house." She said no more, or if she did, I did not understand her. But in the morning when I went to the library, she spoke at length.

The sight of the glass of sherry beside the chess-board made me gasp and lift my eyes to Mr. Pride, but the thought was at once in my mind that he and Dr. Eliot had one time eaten Brazil nuts with their wine. There was no corner of the room without its alcoholic associations: here Mr. Whitney and I had stood drinking whiskey, there Mr. Morgan had constantly refilled his glass, and Miss Pride, mercilessly smelling the bouquet of her wine between leisurely sips, reminded me that I had been drunk, had been drinking heavily, had had too much to drink, had reeked of alcohol, that I must learn to refuse the third glass of whatever it was, whiskey, rum, gin, brandy, wine. She had learned from the Countess that I had pled illness and had left the party (I could have wept with gratitude for the Countess' discretion), but she had also learned from Mr. Pingrey that I had said I must run an errand for her. The latter, comparing notes with his hostess, had been furious. Moreover, I had made no apologies to Mr. Whitney who had been kind enough to give up his evening for my sake, and I had refused point-blank to be introduced to Mr. Hornblower who was Miss Pride's cousin and who had had the generosity to show an interest in what he had heard about me.

In view of my egregious misdemeanor, I was to be punished by exclusion from a series of parties to some of which I might otherwise have been invited. These parties were to be in celebration of Hopestill's engagement to Philip which had been announced at the Countess' shortly after I left. The marriage was to take place in three weeks' time. On the day following this, a dressmaker was coming on from New York and Miss Pride had planned that she and I, for these pre-nuptial weeks, would dine together at an early hour, and the rest of the time, she implied, we were to make ourselves as scarce as possible except in those quarters dedicated to our work.

Just as one cannot be surprised at death when it has been prepared for by a long illness, as the liar cannot be surprised by the consequences of his lies, so I was not surprised by Miss Pride's news, for I had known from the moment Hopestill spoke Philip's name the afternoon before that it was her intention to marry him by fair means or foul. And yet, want of surprise does not cancel out grief over the death nor regret that the lies have been found out, and I did not hear Miss Pride without desolation. I mustered up what politeness I could, said I was sure she was happy over the turn of events, that it must have been something of a thunderclap since it was so sudden. Miss Pride assured me that on the contrary no one had been in the least taken unawares, but naturally everyone had been delighted.

What a revolting business appeared my sodden, sentimental interlude in the slums of Boston! While we had sat in dirty tumult, Hopestill in her turquoise dress with fresh camellias at her shoulder which Philip had bought her (probably at the same stall where earlier he had bought mine) was elegantly, forthrightly playing her game and playing it with an éclat which disguised her guile even to herself.

I was too absorbed with my diversified pains to determine, from Miss Pride's manner, whether the damage I had done myself in her eyes was irreparable. I recalled the pinch she had given me last night when she had discovered Mr. Morgan in the library. It had been a sort of gesture of fellowship, as though she had wanted me to know that she knew that I, her pupil, shared fully her revulsion. How appalling then must have been the sight of my disheveled person, the sound of my thick voice as I stumbled into the vestibule!

No apology was forthcoming from my dry, swollen lips. I swayed, dumb and contrite, before the chess-table, awaiting my dismissal. She gave it finally and with a stingy smile, but one which made my heart leap for joy, she said, "I have been told that Bromo-Seltzer brings relief to your kind of suffering," so that I knew my exile would not be permanent.

If only the short space of three weeks would cure my other ill, my stifling and manacled envy of Hopestill! It was like a fretting child that having a limited experience of the mercy of time believes that the mumps and his imprisonment will last forever and that the time at playing he has lost can never be made up but must blight his whole life. Love, commingled with envy, confounds the mind like drink or fever and the world narrows to the size of one's own soul. Archimedes, if he could have got off the earth, could have moved it. The wretched person, if he could get outside himself, could find the proper physic. But one does not learn, believes with laic obstinacy that the efficacious remedy is the homeopathic one: the common cures, impotent as a broth of newts' eyes and bats' wool, are the escape from love into love, or into writing verses about one's love or reading others' verses, or into a recital to friends of one's love and its debacle. Our obfuscated faculties cannot comprehend that the addition of fuel to the fire will make the blaze brighter and the heat more intense. Thus, I desired to replace Philip with someone who looked exactly like him, who had the same sort of voice and the same kind of mind and had even the same stiff back.

2

Eleven o'clock each Sunday, when Mac and I started out for Wolfburg, was the hour at which the descendants of believers and a few believers gathered sociably before Emmanuel and Trinity, the furred issue of the limousines offering to each other hands in gloves, white even in the winter, or a caress that served as a kiss in these days of so many colds and "catching" coughs, but was rather the light pressure of cheek against check. Along Commonwealth Avenue, others briskly walked in typical pairs: the middle-sized man with a black mustache, a bowler, a Chesterfield, and gray suède gloves, was formally but devotedly protective of his wife or sister in a short mink coat, adorned with last night's gardenia for whose longevity the ice-chest was responsible, a dress of which the gentle-colored skirt showed beneath the coat, a small hat topped with a crinoline posy. Now and again, as we drove past, I saw someone I had met at Miss Pride's or at the Countess', and if my nod were acknowledged, even though its target showed by her thought-ful scrutiny that she could not "place" me ("That's Lucy Pride's chauffeur," said the perplexed eyes, "but who can the girl be?"), I felt mildly triumphant. But mildly, because the luxury which embraced me—the camel's hair lap-robe, the shining glass between myself and my impeccable driver, the thermos bottle of consommé provided me in case I should get cold, my own expensive coat imported from the woolen mills of New Hampshire—made these outward signs merely the superfluous confirmation of my good fortune. If my greeting to one of the Sunday promenaders was not received, I felt no disappointment for, if I needed them, I could summon any number of explana-tions for the slight, none of which reflected unfavorably on me: Mrs. Frothingham was without her spectacles, Mrs. Coolidge was flustered because she thought she would be late to church. Admiral Nephews did not fail to know me. "Hello!" he cried as we stopped before the red light on Exeter Street. "Where are you going on this day most calm, most bright?" He pointed me out to his frail wife who leaned upon a cane, and she nodded amiably but tugged at his arm to remind him that this was no time to dally.

On Commonwealth Avenue on fine Sunday mornings, there was an absence of children and of poor people, as if the terri-tory were "restricted" like apartment buildings which will not let space to Jews or the owners of dogs. Down the mall towards the Public Gardens, there strolled the débutantes, airing their doe-eyed cocker spaniels, or laughing with their beaux whose cropped, uncovered heads and Cantabrigian costumes—long tweed coats with leather patches at the elbow, trousers that did not match, bow ties, cinereous summer shoes over the tops of which lazily cascaded woolen socks—were the badges of privileged youth who, having other things to do, did not go to church. A fair-haired, solitary girl in riding clothes, who was exercising a prancing black shepherd, called out a greeting to one of the older generation who kept to the sidewalk. "Good mahning, Mr. Pukins! I heah Billy's going to Chiner. I think it's mahvelous!"

Mr. Perkins, lifting his bowler, faced her across the engine of Miss Pride's car, his white teeth revealed in a smile that agreeably elevated his little mustache. "Good mahning, Susan! We're having a little dinnah pahty for him next week. You've been told to come, haven't you?"

"Indeed I have!"

They bowed and smiled again and as he replaced his hat, Mr. Perkins added jestingly, "I see you don't go to church."

The roar of traffic, commencing to move along again with the green light, drowned out her reply, but I had faith in her and knew she would not make a fool of herself with a serious counter. Probably at Billy Perkins' farewell party, when his parents made their appearance during cocktails, after which they would leave the "youngsters" to themselves, the sally would be repeated, and Susan would say something like, "I really enjoy church, you know! But Sunday is such a lovely time to exercise my dog!" making her neglect of religion rather endearing as well as temporary for, her gentle, wistful tone implied, she was prepared for the inevitable and would graciously assume her duties towards God as soon as she had settled down either as a matron or as a spinster. And Mr. Perkins, into whose glass was being poured a second cocktail while the girl extended her fingers over her glass to show that she had had enough, would say that he absolutely agreed with her and that when he was her age he probably would not have gone to church either if it had not been compulsory. "Things were so line and rule," he would say, making the staid girl's heart flutter at this testimony of her generation's liberty. "You wouldn't have had a cocktail, for instance," he would continue as she gazed proudly into her Martini in which the olive was still an inch from the surface of the liquid.

As one tenacious of sleep in the early morning, I hoarded the moments of the drive along the avenue against the time when we would turn off towards Boylston and then into the Fenway. For to me, as to those whom the Countess derided when she said, "Boston is a very small place," the city ended precisely at Massachusetts Avenue, and all the rest of it, the cold, uncrowded medical college, the spacious Brookline parkways, the large houses of new materials and derivative architecture, the wide modern drives, did not belong to Boston with its narrow houses and painted doors, and I felt that the expatriates dwelling in Jamaica Plain and Hyde Park and Milton were but wealthier versions of the bourgeois Brunsons. I admired the horseback riders along the bridle paths which bordered Jamaica Pond and the ice-skaters, but did so only because I thought they merely used the resources of these fertile outskirts but returned, at the end of their diversion, to Pinckney or Marlborough or Beacon Street. I felt altogether differently towards such towns as Concord, Lexington, Bedford, Lincoln, and these, together with certain parts of Cambridge and what I called "Boston proper" constituted in my mind "greater Boston" whereas everything in between, even though nearer to the State House, was clearly excluded. I could not revise my map even when I learned that eminent families lived, and had for generations, on Blue Hill Avenue in Milton, in Needham, in Newton.

In an hour's time, we had reached the country and drove between fog-filled woods. Fresh snow, still scathless, lay between the trees where only a few weeks before the stained leaves had lain; the natural paths, rejuvenated by the graduation of the landscape into winter, crept in their immaculate renascence back into the far blue shadows; and not too long from now they would waver forth in the marine spring. We had not gone more than two or three miles when to our left there rose up the high red walls of my mother's asylum; covered with woodbine that had caught the snow, they blended with the landscape. Presently they broke for an iron gate guarded by a fat, unpleasant man who let us in and said sardonically, "This way to the booby-hatch, folks." I had told Miss Pride of the gate-keeper's manner which no longer offended me but which I thought must horrify the relatives of other inmates, for I believed that Miss Pride, with the flourish of a pen, could have the man removed and a courteous one installed in his place.

She did investigate and found that this greeting was only for our car, as Mac and the man had been companions in grammar school, though there was never the slightest sign of recognition on Mac's misanthropic face.

My mother came into the reception room, like a nun coming from the cloister, in her gray uniform, her eyes observing something beyond me or above my head. I nearly always took her flowers and as she sat down, her head bent to study them, she appeared to be waiting for the roses and the carnations to be given the gift of tongues. Then she lifted them to her ear. "Pretty *things*," she would say to them. She would turn towards me her lovely eyes that could see me only as a little child and drawing me to her she whispered so that no one could hear, "Darling, we're going visiting today. The flowers won't wilt if we wrap them in a wet newspaper." Then we rose and walked, arm in arm, down the long, gray hall, followed at some distance by an attendant, and entered the common room where the daffy, harmless women rocked and sang, nodding and smiling, their tender eyes roving private worlds which they sometimes found so amusing they had to laugh out loud. My mother's fancy-work and mine were brought to us; together we worked for an hour and my mother praised the tailless birds she had taught me how to make. "But, dearie," she would say, "there's something wrong with it, I don't know what. See mine, see how it goes?" And she held up the identical bird, bereft of its tail feathers, embroidered in green and yellow silk.

Sometimes my mother's affection (she would suddenly drop her work to kiss me) spread like an epidemic through the room and the demented creatures who that day had no visitors shouted and cooed and goggled their eyes and beckoned me with rapidly wagging fingers. One mild and motherly woman with white hair and dimpled cheeks would hold up a pink candy box that rattled when she shook it. "I'll show you what's inside, Ellen, if you'll just come to Granny," and when I shook my head, smiling politely, she would take a man's white handkerchief out of her bosom and cry a little and blow her nose. Once an attendant let her come sit beside us to show us her treasure, fifteen gallstones of varied sizes and shapes. My mother was charmed. "That's a fine one!" she cried as she picked one up, but the old lady snatched it out of her hand.

"No you don't, my good woman," she said sharply. "Do you think they grow on trees?"

Most of the others had neither fancy-work nor gallstones to keep them occupied, and so they merely sat about, batting their eyes, grinning and purring like happy cats. The malcontents, arms crossed on their breasts, sat apart, muttering motley diatribes: "I called the police. No, couldn't make it, too busy they said. Busy, yes, no doubt of that, I said, busy taking the bread out of poor people's mouths, that's what you're busy doing. Called the newspaper. No, didn't handle such matters. Why not, I said. Do you mean to stand by and watch the people of your community suffer because dentists' brothers are politicians? Yes, ma'am, no, ma'am. Don't yes, ma'am, no, ma'am, *me*, I told them and hung up. It is a crying shame that you can't carry x-rays of your teeth in your pocketbook without gangsters, hired by dentists' brothers, following to steal them or substitute the real ones with other people's teeth or dog's teeth, for that matter. I merely walked into the restaurant and two men with revolvers were waiting. Merely stepped inside to have a cup of tea after the dentist's visit, and there they were waiting." The less articulate of the persecuted stared in silence at the attendants, their faces fixed in a monotonous sneer.

My mother no longer felt that she was victimized, for much had been deleted from her memory: if she ever spoke of a place other than the asylum garden or of the room we sat in, it was of Luibka's house or the officers' tavern, but not of Chichester. She did not forget me, although, because her sense of time had gone, she thought I was eight or nine years old, and the six days when she did not see me were like the six hours when formerly I had been at school; nor did she forget the cold, but she would rub my hands between hers in the old way and complain with sorrowful resignation that "they" put snow in the stoves instead of wood. "They" were unreal shadows, harmless, stupid, servile ghosts who required a good deal of pampering; because she did not wish to offend them, she always spoke in whispers. "A new one came this morning just after you left, darling," she would say, "and left the door wide open so the snow came in. That's why it's so cold."

She talked very little. For the most part we worked at our birds in silence. And so long as I was there, with the living proof before my eyes that she was not aware of her surroundings, I was not depressed but was even comforted by the soothing, aimless motion of my fingers as they plied the embroidery needle. I would wonder, watching her serene face, if I would ever achieve the degree of her beauty, for, if I still looked upon Miss Pride as my model for character, I was no longer deluded by that old hallucination in which I saw her as a beautiful person, and, at least on Sunday, I was as ambitious to look like my mother as on all the other days I was to be like Miss Pride. Unfortunately, I had a variable face so that my mirror showed me a different person half a dozen times a day, for I had inherited some features from both my parents and each set of genes struggled for pre-eminence: my hair was black like hers but my eyes were blue like his, and though my mouth was a facsimile of hers, its pure outlines were corrupted when I smiled and showed my father's crooked teeth.

Gliding, these hours, in brainless daydreams, fashioned from anonymous places and times, I would sometimes hear, like an echo, a voice of a familiar timbre. Like the person who, awakened by a scream, deduces from the cold sweat on his forehead and the trembling of his arms that the sound has come from his own throat, so I, recognizing the voice as my own, thought I had spoken. But in a moment, the words, which my nerves had retained though my mind had not yet comprehended them, were repeated: "Poor little blue cold hands," and I knew that it was my mother who had spoken, not I. Conversely, when I was not with her, when, for example, I was at the Countess' on Friday and everyone was chattering loudly, I was thinking of something far removed from the conversation of which I was a part and I heard my mother speaking; yet when the words returned they formed the banal, effortless answer to someone who had asked me if I had ever been to Ipswich.

The hours in the bright common room were like those a solitary traveler spends in a strange railway station, after a sleepless night, so that his weary eyes impose a glaze on colors; half-dozing, he wakes suddenly, thinking he has been asleep for an hour and sees that the old woman on the bench across from him who had taken out her handkerchief when he went to sleep has now begun to blow her nose, and that the man who sweeps up the burnt-out cigarettes on the floor has progressed at the most two feet. He sleeps again and wakes to see the old woman returning her handkerchief to her pocketbook, the cleaning man twelve inches farther along. Or they were like those moments when, succumbing to ether, the conscious mind suddenly revives, rises like the bobbing head of a drowning man, and hears the end of the sentence the anesthetist had begun as he attached the cone. The boredom of the traveler and the horror of the patient are unendurable when memory makes them so and pessimism complains that they may happen again. I never failed to dread Sundays nor to be distressed as we left the asylum, but at the time I was with my mother, I had no feelings save sensuous ones and nothing from the outer world accompanied me here. On the contrary, when shame or jealousy or despair had dogged me like a shadow all the way to Wolfburg, the moment the door to the common room was opened to us, I was beholden to no one and to nothing.

Each time, my mother was allowed to sit in the car for a little while before I left. An attendant sat in front with Mac, glancing often at us in the mirror over the wind shield. The meeting of my eyes with his trained ones, keen as a surgeon's (the medical effect was enhanced by the mirror in which he studied me, like the mirror of a nose specialist), produced in me a self-consciousness that warmed my cheeks and dried my tongue, and I blushed when I made some reply to my mother, although the glass was closed between us and my voice was inaudible to the men in front. What disturbed me—and marked the end of the hypnotic state that had enabled me to endure the visit—was that those watchful eyes included me as well as my mother in their vigilance. When my mother had been led away after a final sighing embrace from which it would have taken me hours to disentangle myself if I had been alone, and Mac had started down the drive, the embarrassment became a vague, irrational fear which was then followed, as the dénouement to Ivan's fits had been a coma, by a benumbing, anarchical depression which possessed me until finally, late that night, back in my room on Pinckney Street, I fell asleep.

3

It had never been so great a solace as it was today to sit in my accustomed place beside my mother in the unchanged common room, having no need to make explanations to anyone, not even to myself. Gradually the aspirin tablets which I had begged from a nurse (I had not liked to ask Mac to stop at a drug-store for Miss Pride's prescription for me) began to take effect and my nausea and headache were replaced by a sweet, feverish sleepiness. I had brought my mother some apples as well as the customary flowers, and their clean, wholesome smell was drawn from their satiny hide by the excessive warmth of the room. The last time, she had asked me to bring them. "Bring me some red apples, darling," she had said. "I know how smooth they are." But today when I opened the paper bag for her to see them, she had said, "What are these?" "Apples," I had replied, "You asked for them." She had put the bag on the floor and every now and again glanced at it. After a while she had said, "Sonie, tomorrow see if you can find me some apples. Bring me some little yellow apples. I've forgotten how they taste."

My mother was not well. For some Sundays past she had had a cold in the head and now today I saw that it had settled in her chest. She coughed considerably and her breath sometimes came with difficulty. An attendant had whispered to me that I must leave sooner than I usually did, for she had been in bed in the infirmary for several days, though she had been allowed to get up for a few hours each afternoon. Never talkative these days, she was more disinclined than ever to conversation, and we worked for a long time in silence. The lulling, soporific warmth, the wordless muttering of the woman persecuted by dentists' brothers, the odor of the apples, and the steady stitching of the birds so satisfied me as an opiate that I proposed to myself, with the seriousness that makes a dream of a five-inch man or a German-speaking dog or an encounter with a camel seem useful or irritating but not in the least strange, that I spend the next three weeks in this well-heated and peaceable place.

When I had finished inventing plausible lies for Miss Pride about where I should be and had imagined myself installed with a few books and my phonograph in one of the cells, something in the room, a voice or a falling object or the rattling of the gallstones, awakened me and I suddenly laughed. My mother looked up from her work and said, "You have caught my cold!" And when I assured her that I had not, she said, "But you just coughed. I heard you." She beckoned to an attendant who was sitting near-by reading the Sunday comic strips avariciously and without the slightest amusement and when he came she said, "Do you know where they keep the cough syrup? Sonie coughed and she'll be ill." I attempted to make a sign to the attendant but I was hampered by the fixed gaze of my mother as if she were waiting for the devil inside me to make me cough again so that she might pounce on him. He went back to his chair and from the table beside it, took a bottle from a box which seemed to contain first-aid equipment and returned to us, gravely offering it to me along with a spoon. My mother resumed her needlework and I said to the man, "But I didn't cough, I only laughed."

"Laughed?" he said, as if that were a kind of action unfamiliar to him. "Why did you laugh?"

"I don't know. But anyhow I don't need the cough syrup."

"Take it," he said, nodding in my mother's direction and he poured out a spoonful which he handed to me. It was strong and not unpleasant, tasting a little like Cointreau. I thanked him and he went back to his funny papers, but for the next hour he glanced at me from time to time over the top of Elmer Tuggle and Gasoline Alley (he read thoroughly and very slowly) as if he were trying to fathom my laughter.

For a long time there was no other interruption, and in this cataleptic tranquillity, my mind was blank, or, rather, was occupied by certain abstractions such as "warmth" or "absence of pain" or "motion." In demonstrating to myself the last of these, I felt myself sinking through boundless space; I was at once pressed down and pulled down, in the first place by a weightless force from above and in the second by gravity, of which the principle I experienced in a manner more entire than the simple, conscious observation of a falling object could ever induce, just as, at other times when I had been fatigued for some days together, I fancied I could sense in my tired muscles the slow vertigo of the earth. When I emerged from

this ethereal baptism, I was more than ever at ease, and I was
so freed of any anxieties, in this isolated place and in this par-
enthetical time, that my mind could roam like an innocent
child, at will, through grouped reflections and through favorite
daydreams.

I had been following a string of associated memories which
began with a clambake held about this time two years before
by the senior class of the high-school. I had seen Ruby Beeler
filing a boy's right-hand fingernails, and I proceeded from that
to Mr. Henderson who all one winter had had a blue nail on his
little finger. Abruptly the concatenation was unlinked by the
obtrusion of a single, clear-cut image which could not be worried into any sort of relationship with what had gone before.
Irrelevant, impulsively independent, there was before my eyes
a room which I had never seen, but a room in which there was
hardly an object that was unfamiliar. It was possible that I had
briefly fallen asleep and had dreamed of such a place, and yet it
did not fade upon my scrutiny of it, but, static, pictorial, it was
present to me like a projection on a screen.

It was a dark and rather shabby room in which the solid,
heavy draperies were threadbare, blotched and rotten in the
folds. One of two casement windows was open, giving onto
a court, and from it were visible frail balconies where mop-
buckets and potted geraniums stood, and all the tattered, dirty
overflow of kitchens, the rags and cans and empty cartons.
On window-sills were bottles, bowls, and sleeping cats. All
the windows were red, reflecting a sunset; the light had an
autumnal quality, discernible only through feeling since no
other circumstance hinted at the season of the year. There were
no trees in sight, yet had there been, they certainly would have
been releasing their fissile yellow leaves. Probably if the room
had been animated or if from its visible contours I had proceeded to list its likely attributes in other sensory perceptions,
it would have included a coolness, a musty smell, and through
the windows, the voices of boys loitering on the way home
from school.

The furniture of the rectangular room was ponderous and
dark and was crowded together, forming angles and recesses
and deep shadows like hiding places. In the middle of the
room, quite by itself, was a small round table covered with

a white cloth which was clean but limp, as if in the ironing it had not dried properly. A bottle of red wine, bearing no label, stood in the center. The bookshelves which lined one wall and extended nearly to the ceiling were full and contained well-worn volumes largely, it seemed, in French and German. The titles were arranged in confusion. Among them was a bound medical manuscript dating from the fifteenth century. There was a book called *Der Traum der Roten Kammer*: its binding simulated rice-paper and there was a singular discrepancy between the design (a delicate torii and a path scattered with the petals of red flowers) and the curly German script of the title. Between the two windows stood a little Victorian writing desk, open, and revealing a portfolio of cheap Italian leather, dyed green; on it rested a horribly ingenious tortoise-shell letter-opener of which the handle was fashioned into a lobster's claw, cleverly grasping a solid sphere of agate.

It was like the room of some student of wonders and curiosities who had returned the books to their shelves for the afternoon and had got himself this bottle of red wine to enjoy as he looked upon himself in leisure, asking whether his study of prodigies had affected him in any way.

I reviewed rooms in which I had been, as far back as I could remember, but I could not place it, and while, as I have said, it was by no means unfamiliar and all the objects were as real as if I had owned them for many years, I could not, nevertheless, actually identify any of them. I cannot say how long the "vision" of this red room lasted, but while it did, I experienced a happiness, a removal from the world which was not an escape so much as it was a practiced unworldliness. And it was a removal which was also a return. The happiness was not unmixed: as I gazed at the red evening sunlight winnowed through the brick chimneys of the court, I was filled with a tranquil, mortal melancholy as if I were out of touch with the sources of experience so that I could receive but could not participate: that is, I could *assume* that boys were shouting on the street, but I could not hear them. The mitigation of the light seemed to sadden me even more, for it had a potential quality of "bursting" in upon me and yet upon my windows, it was a layer of rich opacity which did not, however, prevent me from seeing quite clearly the balconies and the sleeping cats.

From another world, from the streets of the anonymous city where the room had been in readiness for my return to it, a voice ascended and as the windows were blackened and the room disappeared in a darkness as complete as that immediately after the lights have gone off in a theater, I heard my mother say, "I'm in the crazy house!" Her eyes blazed with the anger of a terrified animal as she was forsaken by the merciful anesthesia which for these months had made her live burial tolerable to both of us. Those powerful eyes now saw the barred windows behind the coy, concealing blinds, saw the inimical, impassive strength of the attendants, saw the moonstruck women grinning and gurgling like babies and they saw, completing the circuit, wider with each new revelation, that I was not a little girl just home from school but was a grown woman whose fine tailored suit and costly shoes cried aloud my treachery. Her lips twitched with panic and vivid splashes, induced as much by fever as by her fright, appeared on her cheeks.

When she had spoken, it had been softly in a breathless voice, as though she must state her discovery but must do so quietly lest she not hear another noise, and she had not immediately looked for a door through which to escape but had surveyed cautiously her dangerous surroundings. But though I thought I alone had heard her, the vigilant attendant, trained to hear and see things that did not attract other people's attention, had laid aside his comic strips and sat poised on the edge of his chair, ready to spring forward. Thinking to adjust things quickly, lead her back to her world of tailless birds and little yellow apples, I put my hand on hers and said, "Mamma, will you rub my hands?" But she flung me off and seizing the flowers from their pitcher on the table beside us, she stripped the blossoms from the stems and hurled them like rocks into my face, spattering me with drops of water as a shower of petals fell into my lap and obliterated the embroidered bird. As in the faithful dog that turns on his master, the stimulus for her assault was mysterious. She wanted to inflict pain on me, and in her rage she could not see that the soft rosebuds touched my face as tenderly as snow, and as if blood from wounds was pouring from me, she hissed, "Beast! Cheater!"

I could not remember what I had used to do with her in her exuberant furies, and with relief I saw the attendant approaching us, casually so as not to alarm the other patients, and knew that he would capably manage to quiet her. I had forgotten to be grateful that I was no longer responsible for her, but just as a woman whose children are grown recalls, on seeing a baby, the nuisance of infantile care, and as we are sometimes profoundly thankful as we witness the seething turmoil of adolescence that we are not and can never again be sixteen, so I counted my blessings as I watched the attendant draw my mother from her chair and, gently embracing her, move towards the door. Upon a signal from him, immediately after her first outcry—though it had been little louder than a whisper it had sounded like thunder in his alert ears—the other attendants had busied themselves with the patients, fussing with their clothing or asking after their wants, so that the crazy calm, the disruption of which had been threatened when my mother, pelting my face with the flowers, had become the cynosure of inquisitive simian eyes, continued as if there had been no hiatus.

I brushed the petals off my coat and finding no other place to put them, dropped them into the bag of apples which I picked up intending to take home with me. With the stubborn health of a strong animal despite what had just happened, I was hungry, for I had had neither breakfast nor lunch and the smell of the apples had so tempted me that it was all I could do to restrain myself from biting into one as I left the room. The rattle of the gallstones reached my ears as I crossed to the door and turning, I saw the white-haired old lady smiling beseechingly as she crooked her index finger at me. "Come here a minute, Ellen," she said. "Granny has a surprise for you." But one of the wise and lifeless matrons sat down beside her, saying, "Mrs. Andrews, may I see what you have in your little box?" Delighted, the old lady opened it up and said in her kindly voice, "Ellen gets them all when I die."

As I went into the white-walled corridor down which my mother and her guard were strolling, like lovers, her head upon his shoulder, his arm about her waist, a doctor, who had been writing something in a notebook as he leaned against a radiator, stepped towards me. "Are you the daughter?" he asked. I replied that I was and I remarked that my mother seemed to be approaching one of those crises with which I was so familiar.

The doctor, bluff, corpulent, with a large, limber face in which broken capillaries running in all directions made it look like crazed pink porcelain, shook his head and answered, "On the contrary. We think she is recovering."

Instinctively, as if to prove that he was wrong, I looked down the passage towards her and as I did so, she turned her head. "Sonia, Sonia!" she cried, sobbing like a child, but the attendant tenderly bent her head again into his shoulder and they disappeared into a doorway marked "Infirmary."

"Oh, no!" I said to the doctor. "She can't be getting well. Why, she's much worse today than she has ever been before!"

"No, you're wrong, my dear girl. Dr. Tudor and I have lately been much more hopeful about her. To a large extent, she has shaken off that intermittent amnesia, and a good part of the time she is at least semi-aware of where she is. We're now of the opinion that she will recover, perhaps not completely and not permanently. But it is possible and, indeed, very likely, that in another three months you can take her home."

I said nothing. My silence drew a smile of understanding to the florid face. "I've been over the case. I understand you had her brought here because you hadn't money enough to get someone to take care of her."

"Yes, I have no money."

He did not fail to scrutinize my clothes. "But you're well enough off now?"

"I am secretary to a wealthy woman," I told him, "but I have very little actual money."

"Mmm," he mused. "You're qualified to be secretary to someone else, I suppose? To someone who would pay cash for your work?"

"I can't!" My fingers tightened round the paper bag of apples as I imagined this future life he proposed for me: the rumpless birds gradually crowding us out of our house, the endless cups of tea before a fire so violent it threatened to burst from the stove, the incorrigible maudlin affection manufactured at top speed by the indestructible engine in her person, unvarying in its pattern. I could think only of my return after work in the afternoons: day after day and year after year of her pertinacious life, I would hear my name reiterated in different tones and in combination with a few simple phrases, falling from her lips like tears or like a molten substance used to solder one thing to another in obdurate unity.

"Why can't you?" inquired the doctor with interest.

"Because I am afraid," I confessed. Until I said the word, I had not been afraid. My feeling had been anger that I must give up my life in Boston as it was now for the lonesome, tedious sort the girls at the business college had been prepared for. And I was as defiant of my mother as if she had conspired against me with someone, perhaps with this optimistic doctor. But I knew, as soon as I had spoken, that I spoke the truth, that I was afraid, not of any harm that might come to my mother through my inexpert treatment nor of any physical harm that I might suffer at her hands. When the doctor asked me, I told him, "Because I think sometimes *I* might go insane."

Still, when he questioned me further, I could give him no reasons save that I could not bear to be alone in the room with the Countess because she reminded me of Mamma and each time, after she had kissed me, I ran through the Common to Boylston Street and then ran back again to Pinckney as though the whistling wind, my pounding heart, my smarting face, could efface the memory of that plastic bosom and those full, intemperate lips. Sometimes my distress was so acute that I was obliged to send down word that I could not eat dinner because of a headache, and all evening I was numb and visited from time to time by an abortive retching, a spasm of inexplicable terror. And I could tell the doctor how sometimes Miss Pride's eyes and sometimes Philip's were watchful and that the guard who sat with Mac in the car perused my face for signs of madness and that all these eyes, on certain nights, watched me from the corners of my darkened room.

The disclosure shocked me: it was as if I spoke of an absent person, sketched impersonally the strange behavior of a fictitious character. But I was not creating. These things were true but until now I had not articulated them nor even recognized them. For months, though, I had felt presences in my room which came in that hazy interlude that foretokens sleep, and I had had the feeling that I was being watched, but like my mother I confused one sensation with another and said that the hallucination had come from the sound of the fire which, dying, soughed like a forest wind.

I did not convince the doctor. Even to myself my story did not sound like history but like an impromptu fabrication. I had neither the vocabulary nor the analytical gift to state my case in full, arguing from the past as well as from these present idiosyncrasies. But he was not unsympathetic, although he smiled with what may have been contempt.

"You must control yourself. If you want your mother to be well, you've got to help, you know."

"But *well*, sir?" I said. "I mean, how far will she be cured?"

"Why, I should think you'd be as good a judge of that as I. She'll be restored, we hope, to her original state of mind. From what we've seen here, we know that she is by nature an unstable woman and for that reason could never be thrown on her own. If she had no relatives and were completely alone in the world, I expect we would keep her here, give her some little occupation like helping in the kitchen. But you wouldn't want that, would you?"

"Oh, no," I hastened to assure him. Then, against my better judgment I went on. "There was a time when I would have given up my whole life to her, but that was before I saw that nothing, no change of atmosphere, no improvement in our standard of living, could make her anything but what she has always been since I was a young child."

"And what is that?"

"A millstone," I whispered. "But I know I'm duty-bound. You needn't tell me."

"I had no such intention. I'm not a moralist."

I closed my eyes for a moment to shut out his professional smile and as I did so, I seemed to descend once more through the wide, moving air and then, purged, absolved, emptied of all that did not pertain to solitude, I saw the red room with its wedges of shadow, its prospect of eternally slumbering cats. When, with the opening of my eyes, the room disappeared, I thought of adding to my list of suspicions about myself which I had just given him, this phenomenal apparition. For whatever had been the emotions with which I had received the impression for the first time a few minutes ago in the common room, surprise was not one of them: the part of my mind, the spiritual optic apparatus, so to speak, had registered the details of the room so singularly tangible—down to the title of a book in

German—when the details were some of them extraordinary, that the exercise could not be mistaken for a daydream or a dream and I knew (but how could I expect anyone to believe this subjective testimony?) that it was not a memory. But I concluded that this morning was *not* the first time I had seen it, but that something in the external world upon which I could not lay my finger had by accident dislodged it from the populous, diffuse, chimerical mazes of my subconscious mind. I had this second time, as before, felt safe and comforted. And it was because of this that I did not tell the doctor, out of the fear that if I told him, I would lose the room forever. Then as I looked again, straight into his eyes which regarded me with curiosity, I was visited briefly by a feeling of guilt and uneasiness like the thief who, having cached his plunder, feels that he has been observed though a second survey shows him that no one is near. When I spoke—and it seemed to me that a long time had elapsed since his last words—it was with a stammer: "I can't explain . . . I . . . perhaps you don't believe me . . . that is, perhaps there's nothing to what you say. You say she has had fever. Well, often before, when she had fever, she seemed rational. It's nothing more than that, I can assure you." I cursed myself for this unsure speech, so insolent in its ambiguity, and as my eyes faltered and fell away from his astonished stare, the doctor said, "Why, you *are* at sea, aren't you? You must stop worrying. Go on back to town and see a movie and try to get a good night's sleep."

I thanked him and apologized for my hysteria. "Good-by," he told me and, as I retreated down the corridor, I could feel his eyes still on me.

As we drove back towards Boston, I ate one of the apples. My thorough enjoyment of its flavor and its frosty grain bitterly amused me: my perturbation was not of heroic enough proportions to kill my appetite; it was even likely, I thought, that I would sleep no worse than usual tonight. The satisfaction of my hunger urged me on to further practical action, and I proceeded to sound out for their utility the several impulses that came to me. My first and strongest was to go at once to Philip. It would be possible to tell him honestly why I could not live with my mother again, for he did not draw a sharp line between sanity and insanity but saw innumerable nuances between the two poles. But would a conversation with him now be as easy as in the old days, now that our incompleted gestures, their instigation unplumbed, were between us like a transgression that was not confessed because, having the appearance of accident, its premeditation on the part of either of us could not be proved? On the other hand, perhaps if I appealed to him now in my trouble and now that he had entered into a contract which precluded the maturation of that fumbling, dumb desire which had fled from the one of us as soon as it had made itself known to the other, perhaps now we could step backwards and, starting fresh, proceed as before. *As before.* But could I, in this darkness, find my way back through the détour where shaggy shapes misled the eye: the shapes of *might have been* and *still might be*? And where, at such an hour, would I find him? Even if he were at home in his three large rooms on Beacon Street, would it not be highly improper for me to call upon him there even for advice? But he would not be at home. He would be somewhere with his fiancée. They were undoubtedly already being fêted. Someone would have arranged an impromptu cocktail party for them and they would be there now, receiving congratulations. Even if I went to him, even if he had nothing else to do but listen to me, he would not be able to keep his mind on what I said.

Would it be better to warn Miss Pride at once? Should I go directly to her bedroom where she would be resting until tea time and beg her for help, telling her that she alone in all the world could give it to me? She was angry with me; she had made it clear this morning that she did not want to be troubled with me for the next three weeks. Another time she might be sympathetic, might even suggest some way to preserve the separation from my mother, but the marriage of her niece was of more importance to her now than anything else; my life, beside it, was a project like the memoirs which must be set aside for the time being. I could not risk it. I would wait until the wedding was over, and then some evening, just before she picked up the *Boston Evening Transcript*, I would say, "Miss Pride, may I ask your advice?"

Or should I now at this moment pick up the speaking tube and say, "Mac, turn around as soon as you can and drive me to New York." When I was alone in the car, Mac gave in to his temptations and drove both fast and recklessly. While sometimes I recalled with terror the talk of the old ladies who declared that he had heart disease and might suddenly die at the wheel, today his speed and his narrow escapes thrilled me as if he were already obeying my command to take me far away and swiftly to a new life. But the squat shops and movie theaters of Mattapan were already huddled on either side of us and we slowed down with the thick traffic. Nudged on one side by an endless line of cars and on the other by the trolley that lurched slowly forward with loud ejaculations, at times we barely moved and I was gradually invaded by claustrophobia so insistent that the ligaments of my arms and legs began to ache as if I were actually cramped into a small space. How patiently our moral nature bides its time, how adroitly sets its stage, parting its curtains suddenly. As unprepared as Gertrude or her king, we willy-nilly witness our own villainy played out. It had not crossed my mind until I felt myself hampered, buried alive by the creeping machinery all about me that perhaps what the doctor had said was true and that my mother fully knew she was a prisoner whose release depended on me. Was it not the meanest beastliness even to think of flight? I caught a glimpse of myself in the mirror above the wind-shield, and saw my black hair. What if I unpinned it some time as she did always in her frenzies? What if my own passions became hopelessly entangled in a desperate disorder and what then if Miss Pride cold-bloodedly, like me, disburdened herself by sending me off to an asylum and stopped her ears to my entreaties? For ours were not the kind of aberrations that Hopestill's fashionable psychiatrist could cure.

I suffered from my punishment. But I made a bargain with my sense of duty: I said that the red room would be my refuge, that when the time came I would resume the battle on the condition that I might always return to it, as a warrior pauses to pray. The milder, though not sovereign, wardens of my being, granted me permission, and a little comforted, I sank back on the cushions as we pushed on.

The house would be silent and my room would be cold. I did not want to go home. I remembered Nathan's invitation, and although it was not yet five o'clock, I directed Mac to drop me at the Copley Square subway station. My reason for going to him was no longer to find out how great a fool I had made of myself the night before. It was that I wanted company and I could think of no one more appropriate than my old friend whom I had used to watch reading on early winter nights.

4

The overwashed young man, his birthmark veiled in a shadow, was hard to establish in the surroundings of last evening and equally hard to establish in this cold, filthy, malodorous subterranean suite of two small rooms densely populated with furniture so shabby, fractured in so many places, that it seemed to be totally useless rubbish. I saw, as soon as I went in, that on his sick and sober awakening, Nathan had had no stomach for the visit he had suggested and that probably he had hoped I would not come. Not without irritation, he said, "Oh, it's you. It's only five. I thought I told you eight."

"I know," I replied. "I just had nothing else to do. I brought you some apples."

Perplexed, he took the paper bag from me; as he withdrew an apple, a shower of rose petals fell to the floor. "What the hell's going on?" he said.

I looked brightly about his place, ignoring the question, and said, "Well, you're cozy here." He was anything but cozy. The only light came from two small, high windows through which I saw a steady parade of legs marching briskly past as if they had been amputated but had retained their power of locomotion. There was no rug on the cement floor and this accounted, I supposed, for the galoshes that Nathan had neatly fastened over his trouser legs. There was a couch, covered with a foul green blanket, burned and stained; two over-stuffed chairs with ruptured seats from which batting and horsehair indecently protruded; a desk, littered with papers, orange rinds, dirty cups, soiled handkerchiefs; a bookcase; a standing lamp with a paper shade decorated with a sailboat on a blue sea as flat as a table top. In the corners there were bundles, the wash or merely rags I could not tell, and stacks of magazines and pasteboard cartons full of trash. The air was damp and weighted with a strong odor comprised, I thought, of stale cigarette smoke and scorched coffee and fried meat. And yet the occupant of this squalid cell was cleaner than I had ever seen him. I thought at once of the young man, Mr. Garvin, whom I had met at the Countess' and who had impressed me because he gleamed so brightly with soap and water. I said, looking from Nathan to the unsightly blanket on the couch, "Do you sleep here?" and he turned down the cover to show me a pair of clean sheets.

"At present personal cleanliness is my principal fetish."

"Do you know a person named Garvin?" I asked.

"Certainly. And you knew I knew him. He reported to me at once that he had seen you at that fat German's house. And, yes, you're quite right, I got the washing habit from him."

"She's not German, she's Viennese," I said. "He did tell you he had met me? Why didn't you look me up?"

He shrugged his shoulders and with his old, still breathtaking gesture, drew his long fingers over his cheek. "Our last meeting—I mean in Chichester, not last night—didn't leave me with the feeling that you would want to see me again."

"But you misunderstood me!" I cried.

"I had hopes that that was the case, but since you never tried to explain, I assumed you didn't want to explain. And there's no use in your doing it now, because I have other fish to fry."

I was irritated that he thought I had come to resume our adolescent flirtation. "And what makes you think I haven't? You're as vain as ever, I see."

He did not reply. I sat down on the couch and for a time we were silent while he ate his apple. When he had finished he wiped his lips with the back of his hand and reaching down behind the desk brought out a gallon jug. "I suppose you want some of this? I haven't any glasses but I have some teacups. It is sherry, the poor dipsomaniac's drink. Well?" I thanked him, forgetting Miss Pride's admonition. He went on. "Yes, I am glad to see you. The past, that is, the past prior to that aforesaid encounter, comes back rather pleasantly. The fog, for instance. I hadn't thought of it for months."

His eyes narrowed dreamily to show that he was thinking of it now with enjoyment. Likewise, to me, the past came back, for he had presented me with the brilliant cheek and my fingers tightened round the handle of the teacup, restraining themselves from reaching out to touch the skin.

"Oh, rest assured I didn't forget you. I merely set you aside as something completed, the way I did when I finally had to admit that your father wasn't coming back."

"You said last night you hadn't been in Chichester. Why not?"

"Why should I? Oh, I probably neglected to tell you my family moved to Lynn. But my family would never be a reason for my going back there anyhow. I did go back though, twice, just out of curiosity to know what the dump looked like. The first time it was in the summer and all I did was get a bottle of Moxie at Bennett's and get out as quick as I could. There was one of those Barstow hags in the store buying a stick of camphor ice. But the next time I went it was in the winter and it made me sort of nostalgic to walk past your house late in the afternoon. At first I thought I saw a light in the window but it was only a reflection of the sun. Does your mother live there by herself?"

"No," I said. "No, she isn't there any more."

He did not press me and while I longed to tell him where Mamma was, I checked myself and instead poured out to him the story of my meeting with Miss Pride last night and this morning, putting into my account all the feeling I had about my talk with the asylum doctor. Nathan, at first surprised that I had taken my scolding so seriously and then disturbed because he felt he was to blame, comforted me with sincere little speeches which I applied privately to my future with my mother rather than to the one with Miss Pride. He said such things as, "But it will all be over and forgotten," "No one in the world is that important," or "Things will be the same as ever in a little while."

"But you don't *know*," I said. "You don't know *her*."

"Why do you care so much? She sounds like a bitch. May I have another apple?"

"Certainly. I brought them to you."

"They're good apples."

As he ate, the fresh odor reached me through the other smells, and I said suddenly, almost without plan, "Look here, can I come to see you every Sunday?"

He looked at me over the apple in surprise. "That's a very peculiar request. How do you know you will want to come here or that I will want you to? Why Sunday? It's a very inconvenient night for me as I have an early class on Monday."

"I'm sorry," I said, blushing. "I don't know why I said it. Do forgive me."

"But what is there to forgive? You're very much odder than you used to be."

"Perhaps I am, but it's also odd of you to tell me so."

He smiled and filled our green teacups again. "I'll confess to you now—now that I don't feel the same way any longer—that I hoped you were so drunk last night you wouldn't remember that I asked you to come. I woke up thinking, Now I've done it again, got myself involved with the past again when it's all I can do to stomach the present. But I'm glad you did remember. And I'm touched by the apples. The rose petals mystify me, though."

I wanted to tell him how I happened to have the apples; I wanted each Sunday night thereafter, through the winter and the long spring, but I was kept silent by indecision, for I did not know how my words would sound to him, whether they would elicit fear or sympathy, or how they would sound to me, whether I would be ashamed or comforted. Though the hours before I came to his apartment remained my secret, so that Nathan was still a stranger to one half of my life, nevertheless to me he became connected with it just as a landscape will seem to be inextricably involved with a remembered event although, at the time, it was hardly noticed. It was as if by giving him the apples that my mother had fingered and had not understood, I had joined them in an alliance which, for all its artificiality, consoled me. It was not that I had felt any disappointment in my mother's not welcoming the apples, nor that I appreci-ated, by contrast, Nathan's enjoyment of them. It was not in my power to please my mother. It was more, also, than the comparison I naturally made in coming from a madhouse into the presence of a normal person. It was, in effect as a symbol, that I saw the execution of this kind of duty to be worthless both to the agent and to the recipient, for my mother derived no benefit from my gift and had I not brought it, she would not have been aware that I had failed to fulfill my promise. And I, being commissioned to bring the following week essentially what I had brought this week (smaller apples and yellow instead of red) was walking a treadmill. This was what I had wanted to convey to the doctor, but I had known that I would never be able to make him understand and therefore the only hope I had lay in the verdict handed down to myself by myself: whether the obligation, imposed upon us all by the Fifth Commandment, was to be taken literally or was to be interpreted. But since I knew of only one kind of action which could follow if my decision finally was that I owed my mother no more years of my life, that action being the flight I had thought of as we drove home, I could not tell anyone of my debate. For flight, no matter how it may be justified, no matter how necessary it may be to the maintenance of life, is an act of cowardice. One's alternative is protest; but to protest without fear, one must be convinced that right will win, and if it does not, must accept, at least temporarily, the triumph of wrong. The conscientious objector to war is generally regarded as a moral man, if too philosophical, and immune, through some strange means, to the infectious patriotism that sweeps his country in time of war; he may be criticized but only a few will call him a coward. But the man who kills himself, the man who hides himself away in the mountains or in the swamps to escape conscription, is abhorred by everyone. Yet it is possible that his refusal to fight is neither out of the fear of danger nor the dislike of regimentation, but that it stems from the same moral principles as those upheld by the objector.

I was not certain of this argument; yet, as I sat that afternoon with Nathan in his dirty room, I laid the foundation for the edifice that would please me, not the one that was sure to be the soundest. I was persuaded that when the time came, my decision would be impartial, that in the end I would not favor myself, but that in the meantime I was entitled to play with the idea of going away, as unconditionally as my father had done, as far, perhaps, as Nathan was going.

"What are you going to do in Paris?" I asked him. "Write?"

He laughed savagely. "I've got that nonsense knocked out of me. What a pipe-dream!"

"What are you going to do then?"

"You really want to know? It's not nice. It's a damned colossal bore."

"I do want to know."

"I'm going to study Old French and I'm not going in the fine, careless, romantic, high-spirited way I let on last night. I am going on a fellowship and it is my thrilling ambition to make a critical study of Bernard de Ventadour. On my return to America, one year later, I will present this study as a thesis for the degree Master of Arts. Then, oh, then, dear friend, I will be ready for that next step to glory, the Ph.D. And after that, if I am very well-behaved and keep my nose clean, I may get a job teaching beginning French to the boys and girls of the Chichester high-school."

But what had happened to his earlier plans, those he had made on the steps of the Barstow in the fog. "I just grew up," he said sorrowfully. "But this has its compensations. I get a certain sense of power making footnotes on my papers on various medieval subjects: '*Ysonde*,' I write learnedly, 'is a rare Scottish form of the name, usually rendered *Ysolt* or *Isolt*, or sometimes *Iseult*.' You know I wanted to go in for *Mittelhochdeutsch* and work on Walther von der Vogelweide just as an excuse to go to Germany, but that's out now, of course. I'll show you what the University of Heidelberg sent me last year." From an untidy drawer, he produced a prospectus containing photographs of the baroque *Alte Gebäude* half hidden by flowering lime trees, of the Castle in its massive decay, of the Old Bridge spanning the river, and of the Protestant cathedral with bookstalls stuffed between its buttresses.

"There are hills on either side of the river, you see," he said. "Garvin spent a summer there a couple of years ago. The first thing I would do would be buy a rucksack and take a long walk. Or maybe before I did that I'd buy a bicycle and go to Heilbronn. I know the map of South Germany by heart and just what the distances are and just where I'd stop overnight." He broke off and took the prospectus from my hand. "It makes me Goddamned sore that I've got a name like mine. Do you think I look Jewish?"

"Not very," I said, thinking as I did so that I had never seen a more Hebraic face than this one.

"Well," he said dully, "let's change the subject."

I was surprised to find that Nathan was essentially unchanged but that my whole perception of him had altered. Where before I had seen formidable brashness, now I saw only a nervous arrogance which, at times headlong, was at other times so timorous that I had only to disagree in the mildest way to make him retract, apologize, abjectly humble himself. He began pontifically to talk of books as if he had forgotten that I could read, had, indeed, been instructed by him, and when I took exception to his enthusiasm for a writer whose short stories were then much in vogue and which had, he asserted, revolutionized the art, Nathan's face expressed his amazement that I had even heard the writer's name, then distrust of himself, and finally he said, "Of course! He's a charlatan! Why didn't I see that before?"

When, in our conversation, he hit upon a poet whom I also admired, he was overjoyed; he fairly frolicked with our kinship, treating me with a connubial warmth, congratulating both of us on this marriage of minds. Our enthusiasms were, indeed, so commonplace that he would have lived in limitless polygamy if he had courted further. His transports would be over Shakespeare's sonnets or Heine or Blake or Yeats whom he would come upon suddenly with as much surprise as a traveler who has been over a road many times will feel if, on one journey, he finds that a handsome new house has been built at the side of it since he last rode by. He told me that it was precisely because of his confusion that he had gone in for medieval studies. "Your taste doesn't matter much there. You don't have to commit yourself on whether you think *The Agenbite of Inwyt* is good or bad."

I asked him if he had ever gone back to the Communists. "No," he said, "but I hate the upper classes more than ever. Harvard College for Boys teems with them. I am employed by one of them, as I told you, a party named Morgan. I have tutored him in German for two years and I bleed him of a great deal of money and learn twice as much German as he does. But this is the kind of thing he'll do: we'll be translating along—he's a moron, of course—and he'll stop suddenly and say, 'Beg pardon, baby, I've got to make a phone call.' He *always* calls me 'baby.' He will call the air line and say, 'This is Morgan. I want a ticket on the five o'clock plane and I want to be booked through to Las Vegas. Put it on my charge account, will you?' His *charge account*, mind you. We go on with the translation—and you couldn't believe his illiteracy—and the telephone will ring. It will be a dame and Morgan will say, 'Honey, I love you, I love you, but right this minute I've got to hop a plane for the Golden West. I'll be back day after tomorrow. I've got ten drunks from Metro Goldwyn Mayer at my place and I've got to go out and police the joint.' We start out again and maybe do one, maybe two paragraphs of *Immensee* and his door-bell rings. His butler (butler, I said) comes in and says there is a little lady outside. 'Well, baby, let's let the Hun go for today. I've got to lay this little lady before I hop a plane. Come around next Tuesday. Tell my man to fix you a drink.' Need I assure you that I do not tell that fat, patronizing penguin that I want a drink?"

With some effort, I brought out, "Do you ever see any of the little ladies?"

"No. And I never want to. But I see their mink coats lying in the hall when I go out. And don't think for a minute I feel the least bit sorry for them. I would rather go to a whore-house myself. But why should he be successful with women? He's stupid and he subscribes to *Esquire*. Now I am extremely intelligent and once you get used to my face, I'm not really ugly. But do I have any success with women? Can I ever be sure of them? If I am sure of them, it's because they're too uninviting to be unfaithful and then they bore me to death. That middle-aged French baggage I told you about won't stir from my door-step and she annoys me so much I could strangle her without the least remorse. But on the other hand I never have been so in love as I am with Kakosan Yoshida and I can't trust her. She lies and deceives me and when I most want her she doesn't show up. And that was the way it was with you. When I specifically wanted to do nothing else in the world but drink Budweiser draft with you at Red's, you wouldn't do it."

We had been sitting in the dark for sometime and now he turned on the lamp. He was as angry, I saw, as he had been on the way to the Brunsons' house, but I was equally angry and rose to go. As I reached for my coat, he grasped my hand. "Don't go," he pleaded.

"Oh, you make me sick," I said.

"I know it. I'm sorry. But please don't go."

"But your friend is coming. Your beautiful Japanese lotus flower."

"She won't come, and if she does, what good will it do me? I want to ask you a question, Sonie. Please sit down again and drink some more sherry or I'll make you coffee if you'd rather. The thing is this, do you think it will work, my going to France this way? I mean, if I don't marry Kakosan? I was joking when I said I might marry Andrée, she's impossible. Do you think it would work if l went by myself?"

I could not have answered his question even if I had had the time, for I did not know what it was he wanted except to live in Paris for a year and for that length of time to have a holiday from Mr. Morgan and his kind. At that moment there was a delicate triple knock on the door and Nathan rushed to unlock it and to admit his Japanese mistress, Kakosan Yoshida.

"I can't stay," she said, remaining on the threshold so that, because the hall beyond her was dark, I could not tell what she looked like. I could see only that she was diminutive; the clear, dissonant notes of her voice were like a string of brilliant, hollow balls. "I cannot come in. I am sorry. You must not be angry, please. I promised to go to the séance. It can't be done without me."

"But you promised three days ago to come tonight," said Nathan.

She hesitated a moment. "Yes, that's true, I did. And I would rather stay with you. But they said they couldn't make the séance work without me and so I have to go. Please understand."

"Let me go with you, then."

"Oh, but you said you hated things like that. You hate me to go to them. I told them this would be the last time I would come. You wouldn't like to go."

"Yes, I would like to go," said Nathan firmly. "Is it cold out? Should I wear a coat?"

The high voice was desperate. "But you would hate it. It would be all right if just the *real* people were there. But riffraff is coming tonight. It's not by invitation tonight. Please!"

"That's all the better. If there are a lot of people I can leave if I want without offending anyone. Is it cold out or not?"

"Very well," said the girl angrily, "I won't go then. I told a lie. It's not for everybody. It is very exclusive. They wouldn't let you in. No, I won't go. I will sit here with you. But first I must call and tell them I'm not coming."

"All right," said Nathan. "You can use the janitor's telephone."

"No, I must go to the drug-store anyway. I must buy something. I will be back in a little while."

Nathan sighed. "Go on to the séance if there is a séance. But come in and meet an old friend of mine, an old, and up to a point, faithful, friend."

"I am too faithful!" she cried. Then, "Oh," she said as she saw me, "Why does he want me if he has company?"

She tipped her little saffron face up to him and smiled. He could not resist her, although he knew that there was no séance, that she was going to meet another lover, and taking her small, lovely hand, he kissed the lacquered fingertips. As she stepped into the full light, she seemed unreal, less human than animal material fashioned in the image of figures of painting and sculpture and the ladies of poetry so that it was almost necessary to understand the ideal in Oriental art before one could truly appreciate how authentic her beauty was. I would say of my mother's lips that they had the color of a rose, but of Kakosan I would have to say that her mouth was like a "mallow flower" for her loveliness was something so unfamiliar that the old words and metaphors would not do, and to say her lips were like a rose would be to say that they were beautiful but not to specify them as Oriental. She wore, under her incongruous American polo-coat, a dress of purple silk brocaded with gold. In the glowing blackness of her hair was pinned a white carnation, and on either hand she wore a jade ring. She was, with this costume, with her symmetrical, unblemished face, her tiny body as limber as a grass, something so conscious, so tastefully assembled that she was like a bejeweled ornament of incalculable worth. It was hard to imagine her in the arms of an Occidental man, harder still to imagine her as promiscuous as Nathan had implied she was and as I had gathered from her unskillful lie about the séance.

She sat down on the couch beside me and handed Nathan a parcel elaborately wrapped in white tissue paper and tied with pink ribbons. "It was to take my place," she said. "I found it in the store and thought you would read it tonight while I went to the séance. Do you know the spirits?" she asked, turning to me. I replied that I did not, and she informed me that I had missed half my life by not becoming acquainted with the supernatural. She told me that she had not only heard spirit voices imparting news of the other world, but had also been witness to the unaided peregrinations of chairs and tables and vases of flowers and, on one occasion, to the levitation by will alone of one of the sitters. "A year ago, my uncle, the tea-merchant, spoke to me. He died in Kobe three years before. He told me I must not marry according to my father's choice. I am a Samurai daughter. How can I disobey my father?" She laughed. There was in her laugh something controlled and artful as if it were part of a song. "*He* should be happy at what my uncle said, shouldn't he?" and she pointed her finger at Nathan who was undoing the ridiculous pink bows on her present. "What would my father say," she whispered to me, "if he knew I had a beau like him? In a place like this? I call him *Gacho*. It means 'goose.'"

"And I call her '*hototogisu*' which means 'cuckoo,'" said Nathan bitterly. He had succeeded in removing the wrapper from the parcel and he withdrew a book. "Oh, thanks," he said, "I've wanted to read it." And he put it down on his desk.

"Now I must go," said Kakosan. "I am so obliged to meet you, Miss Marburg. Will you please go to the movies with me sometimes? Do you love the movies?" I said I had no burning passion for them, but I would be delighted to go to a matinée some day.

"Let's wait until the Garbo comes. I love the Garbo best of all. If I were not a Japanese girl, I would most like to be a Swedish girl."

As Nathan accompanied her to the outer door, I went to the desk, looking for the prospectus from Heidelberg. The book which Kakosan had brought was lying face down and I picked it up, curious to know what kind of writer she would choose to keep her lover company while she was deceiving him. The title was in German: *Der Traum der Roten Kammer*. The cream-colored binding was decorated with a black torii between whose posts lay several scarlet flowers; beyond the gate three cedar trees were visible. Although it had been in the shelves with all the others in my imaginary room, and I had only seen the back, I had known exactly how the front panel would look! When I heard Nathan's footsteps returning down the hall, I dropped the book suddenly as if I had done something shameful. But between the time I heard him and his entrance, the room appeared to me. This time, three positive things happened. I wondered if there were more rooms down the hall from mine and if the buildings forming the court had a continuous passageway. Simultaneously a German word, *Gesäusel*, came into my mind and I seemed to stand in the doorway of the room, remarking the onomatapoeia of the word which meant "murmuring." Moreover, I recognized the writing desk as Louisa May Alcott's, on display in the Alcott house in Concord which old Mrs. McAllister had taken me one day to see. Upon this desk and under glass, I thought, had been Miss Alcott's diary, opened to pages of small, unreadable writing with the coppery look of aged ink. The town, from the windows of this room, eternally dead amongst its elegant trees, had seemed grandly harmless, and the glassed-in meditations of the gentlewoman were like a last testament begun at birth, like a happy, lifelong requiescat, and I remembered feeling as if I were in a different century. My lame and wattled companion, smelling of some faint, old-fashioned scent, had said to me, "Do you like the room? It is what I call a *gentle* place." But Louisa May Alcott's was not my room and we had not gone there at sunset, but in the early afternoon. Philip and Hopestill had driven to Walden Pond after luncheon to watch the skating, and Mrs. McAllister had said to me, "We mustn't stay in on this golden day. Let me take you to the Alcott House. It is closed for the winter, but the caretaker will let me in." And we had gone out in the pure yellow light of the winter afternoon.

Nathan touched my arm. "A trance?" he asked me. "Isn't it revolting the way I let her lie to me? I should have told her never to come back again or else I should have beaten her to death. And that book! Do you see what it is? A Japanese novel translated into German. Can you tie that for a pure waste of time?"

But for me, it was not a pure waste of time. His words were but a slightly altered version of what Mr. Whitney had said as we stood last night in Miss Pride's library and he had taken down a book from the shelves. I did not remember having looked at it at all. I was weak with relief that I had seen another copy like Nathan's, and I began to laugh. It was a deep, interior, physical laughter, as beyond my control as hiccoughs, the

kind that afflicts children in grammar school who bend their
little shaking bodies forward and hide their heads in their
folded arms and want to stop but cannot even when the teacher
reprimands them.

"But it's not funny!" cried Nathan.

I could only splutter a reply, and after a time when I was
quiet, I explained to him that I had not been amused by anything, that I was only nervous, probably from all our drinking
the night before and the dressing-down I had got from Miss
Pride. He looked down at me contemptuously. "Nervous, is it?
You're more fashionable even than I thought. I suppose you
are being psycho-analyzed."

"Certainly not," I rejoined with some annoyance. "You want
to know too much."

"I assure you that I have not the slightest interest in knowing why you laughed. If you are a giggler, more's the pity. It is
particularly offensive when it comes late in life."

I wrapped my muffler about my neck, resolving not to come
back again. Although a little earlier I had wished to explain
why I had not drunk beer with him at Red's, I now wished
only to expunge him and the memory of him from my mind.
But, as often in the past, he disarmed me. He sat at his desk, his
birthmark hidden by his hand and regarded me with a piteous
entreaty. "Did you really mean it when you said you would go
to the movies with her?"

"Oh, I don't know. Probably not. It seems very unimportant."

"You could help me if you only would. If you could convince
me that she's a bitch, possibly I could eventually break off."

"I'm not interested, and now I've got to go home."

"I'll be lonely if you go. Will you come back again next
Sunday?"

"No," I told him. "You're too rude."

"You can't hate a cat for killing a bird because it's the cat's
nature, and you can't get sore at me for being rude because
that's *my* nature. Please, Sonia!"

"All right," I said. "I'll try once more. It will be a little later
next Sunday, I expect." We shook hands and said good-by with
an exaggerated warmth.

I walked quickly between the banks of snow which lighted
the streets like moonlight. A few doors from Nathan's building,

I heard someone playing a recorder and I paused for a minute to listen. It was a tender, doleful tune like some Irish lamentation. The bold blood rushed to my face and fingertips. I passed on and peered into the uncurtained ground-floor rooms of students, for no other purpose than to see that they were all clean and comfortable, all unlike Nathan's and unlike my red room.

The room had been a little random daydream which I could have again, or it was like a lengthened *déjà vue*, that evasive quasi-memory which is a sort of unlearned knowledge of the soul. I could, I knew, in time, name in its real place each object in the room, and I felt confident that even after my vivisection, the room would accomplish again its impeccable synthesis, a fused and incomprehensible entity. It was a sanctuary and its tenant was my spirit, changing my hot blood to cool ichor and my pain to ease. Under my own merciful auspices, I had made for myself a tamed-down sitting-room in a dead, a voiceless, city where no one could trespass, for I was the founder, the governor, the only citizen.

Chapter Five

THE DRESSMAKER who had been imported from New York to make Hopestill's trousseau was known by her trade name, Mamselle Thérèse, which she herself always substituted for the nominative case of the first person singular pronoun, as though she were her own interpreter. "Mamselle Thérèse does not touch the potatoes," she said on her first evening to Ethel who frankly tittered. She said to me, "Mamselle Thérèse goes to a night-club twice a week in New York," by which I understood she wanted me to supply her with the Boston equivalent of this diversion, but I did not respond as she had hoped and thereafter she made no more such overtures but amused herself (and presumably me) in designing costumes which she said would "bring out" my personality. She spoke of Chanel, Lilly Daché, Mainbocher as if they were Brahms, Bach, Mozart, or Plato, Descartes, and Hegel. "Daché composed a superb number for an archduchess last month, a really revolutionary turban. People were simply swept off their feet." Like the bald barber recommending a hair restorer, like the dentist whose teeth are false, Mamselle Thérèse dressed most frumpishly. She wore a strange assemblage of seedy garments, too large for her spare, nimble frame, out-of-date, soiled, frayed, reminding me of the hand-me-downs that two or three times a year the Brunsons' Boston relatives sent them to be given to me. And it was not only that the little modiste had clothed herself out of a rag bag, but that she had very bad taste, burdening herself like a fancy-woman with gimcracks from the five and ten cent stores: wooden brooches in the unreasonable shape of a Scotty dog or of an ice-skate or of a Dutch shoe or of a football; enameled beetles or dragonflies or cobras made of tin, with blinding rhinestone eyes; earrings in the shape of oak-leaves or candlesticks; and with any costume, upon her right arm, she wore nine thin silver bracelets which she clanked interminably. Her shabbiness could not be explained by poverty, for she had a flourishing business, and the expensive dresses of her two assistants who had been lodged in a house on Joy Street, suggested that she could afford to be generous in their salaries. She was charging Miss Pride a shocking price for this assignment, as I knew from the estimate she had handed in on the day she arrived. She spoke quite openly of this as "a good thing."

"Now for you, angel," she said, "Mamselle Thérèse would sew for next to nothing, but for them, the price is in the hundreds, sometimes in the thousands. It is an art, *ne c'est pas?* Wouldn't they pay ten thousand for a picture by Rousseau? Then why shouldn't they pay ten thousand for a dress by Chanel? Mainbocher? Mamselle Thérèse don't kid herself. She knows she isn't in that class yet, but she works slow and sure like a mole. Five years from now Mamselle Thérèse will be in the movies like Adrian."

Her ruling passion was business, and she could see nothing except in terms of its commercial value. Thus, when she learned that I had gone to a secretarial school, she said, "You must keep your eyes open and when the time comes, rush in and nab yourself a plum. Mamselle Thérèse's advice to a young girl like you that has a good head on her shoulders is: be a secretary to a big-time lawyer. There's the money! There's the prestige! I'm telling you. What good are you doing yourself fooling around up here with that *vieille furie* when you could be on Fifth Avenue, New York? Mamselle Thérèse has a girl-friend working at Number One, Wall Street, on the thirty-fourth floor and she makes fifty dollars a week. I'm telling you."

She talked ceaselessly in a hoarse whisper as if we were two business men making a slightly shady deal. Often she worked arithmetic problems with the tip of her finger on the polished table, so obsessed with the imposing figures of her last year's state and federal income taxes that she did not leave off even when I warned her that her nails would scratch the finish. It was of no matter to her that I contributed nothing to the conversation but answered only with a monosyllable or a forced smile when she put such a rhetorical question to me as "Does Mamselle Thérèse know all the answers in the business world?" Her chief ambition was to receive a commission from visiting royalty; it deeply thrilled her to imagine some queen or princess finding, after she disembarked, that she had not brought enough evening gowns: "'I must run right to Mamselle Thérèse. She will make me a *chose merveilleuse* for the White House ball.' Wouldn't Mamselle Thérèse be knocked off the

Christmas tree?" Sometimes, impassioned by the memory of a gown that Mainbocher had executed for some foreign personage or by the contemplation of vast sums of money owed her by her "élite clientele" she would pursue me to my room, having given a peremptory order to Ethel as we left the dining-room, to bring our coffee to the third floor.

Occasionally, out of self-defense, I would deliver her a little lecture, on how much I liked the town of Concord and its environs or on the splendor of the Countess' Saturdays, but Mamselle could attend nothing of what I said and the moment I paused, she burst in with a raging river of facts and figures to obliterate completely my little trickle of talk.

But she was not, as she seemed, out of touch with human affairs. She was not especially interested in them, but nothing escaped her shrewd French eye. Believing me to be Miss Pride's secretary and nothing more, she spoke unguardedly of the household. "*Mon dieu*, that bridegroom! Angel, he is a fool, I'm telling you. Mamselle Thérèse don't need to make his acquaintance to know that like she knows the palm of her own hand. She only has to contact the fiancée, *ne c'est pas*? That rich *renarde*."

"Why do you say she is a *renarde*?" I asked.

"You can tell by the eyes. They are sub-zero. You know? It is on her part a *mariage de convenance*."

"And how do you know that?"

"Because they haven't slept together. And how does Mamselle Thérèse know that?" She tapped her forehead. "*Par intuition*."

"But perhaps it is a *mariage de convenance* on his part too?" I suggested.

"Maybe. Yes, maybe. It is a cold place, this Boston. He marries her because she is rich, beautiful, what-not. Because a doctor should have a wife. She marries him because she is *enceinte, ne c'est pas*."

I should have laughed and denied the charge, but I was so astounded at the woman's wizardry that I could not gather my wits together for a moment and when I did, knowing that her conviction was not only right but that I could in no way shake her from it, I said, "You may be right, but I beg you to say nothing to anyone. It would kill Miss Pride."

Mamselle Thérèse was offended. "Why should Mamselle Thérèse gossip? She is here for the money. She don't care a damn about the *mariage*. Angel, it is a dirty business and not for me. This little up-and-coming *couturière* stays single, I'm telling you. Plenty of boyfriends and not a husband. Don't mix business with pleasure, angel. So why should she interfere with someone else's *mariage*? Mamselle Thérèse won't talk to the interested parties. She is interested only in the money from the interested parties."

We were sitting in my room at the time of this conversation and it was rather late, perhaps eleven o'clock. Both Miss Pride and Hopestill had gone out for the evening. Presently we heard light footsteps coming up the last flight of stairs and Hopestill's door was opened. Evidently she had come back to get something for in ten minutes, she went out again and back down the stairs. Mamselle Thérèse, not so much through the fear of being overheard as through boredom with the subject, dropped it instantly on hearing the footsteps and began telling me about a new costume she had designed for nuns which would be at once more sanitary and more beautiful than their present ones. She had interviewed innumerable Mother Superiors and had written to various bishops and to the secretary of the Archbishop of New York. As she had what is aptly known as "total recall," she repeated verbatim each conversation, each letter, and each reply, all of which seemed, on the part of the ecclesiastical authorities, to be stubbornly hostile to her proposition.

But the soliloquy, which lasted for half an hour after Hope left the house, did not prevent me from hearing through the wall which separated our rooms, the soft collapse of the girl's body on the *chaise longue* and a sob, stifled at once as though she had pressed her face into a pillow. The sound would probably have escaped me if I had not heard it before and had not come to expect it as the expression, in a sense, of the reason for her visit to her room during the evening. Almost every night when there were dinner guests, she came up two or three times, and usually I heard that secret, frustrated outburst like a checked curse. On such evenings, she might stay as long as a quarter of an hour and hearing her footsteps back and forth across the carpet, muted so that I could not be sure if I really heard them or only felt the vibrations of the floor, I sat at my typewriter unable to strike a key, embarrassed because she must have heard the clatter of the machine which stopped as her door-knob turned.

I could not immunize myself to her misery and pitied her for whatever punishment her conscience was meting out to her. I was impelled to go in to her in the way one may start, hearing a human cry in the night and think it is someone lost or hurt and in need of help. Beside a warm fire in a light room, an impression of the night's cold and darkness superimposes itself upon the altruistic impulse, and one rationalizes, says the cry comes from the throat of a drunk or of a cat that can sound like a woman or even that it is the lure of a thief. I would wait until I heard her going down the stairs again and then I would shrug my shoulders with a resolute indifference and say aloud, "It's her affair, not mine."

Before my brother was born, I could not bear to have my mother speak of miscarriages and of "the pains" because I was sure that pain must be much more terrible to other people than to myself. And when Miss Pride reproved the Gonzales boy for stealing her soap to carve his little Virgin, I would have been glad to exchange places with him in order not to see the shame in his downcast face and the limp arms hanging at his sides, the palms of his hands turned out in broken-hearted supplication. And now while I did not minimize the discomfiture of my own position and spent a good part of every day in sorrowing over my unjust luck and even thought that in the end, my lot was much the worse, I felt that I was somehow better equipped to endure than Hopestill. She, the frail sheep lost from the herd, could not find her way back nor could she make her way alone. She knew already, as these flights to the privacy of her room showed, that she could not carry it off, for even if the discovery of her deception were long postponed or never made at all or made only by a few people who would not blame her or, if they did, would keep silent, she had nevertheless ruined herself in the only *milieu* for which she was trained. She had ruined herself even though there might never be suspicions or rumors, for she would never be *sure* that she was not suspected: she would hear the most innocent remark as a *double entendre*, the most amiable question as put with an ulterior design. It was possible, too, I thought, that after the secret gratitude to Philip for unknowingly saving her from disgrace had expired, she would commence to hate him, as the impoverished libertine, her father, had hated his martyred wife whose rich dowry had provided him with the means for his philanderings.

Long before this, Hopestill had damaged herself, though not irremediably, by her connections with "the Bohemians." She had occasionally brought young men, who let their beards grow and who dressed most unusually, to the houses of her friends and her aunt's friends, exhibiting them like trained poodles. Unconventional and explosive, they alarmed the hostesses whose disapproval could not find its exact target and fired nervously upon all sides. The poverty of these barbarians was thought to be an intentional and Communistic affront; they were believed to be practitioners of free love, companionate marriage, and atheism; their painting or their writing was eyed with distrust as revolutionary or satirical. The Boston hostess, finding herself at the mercy of a novelist (she had not heard of him and therefore could not tell if he was a satirist or not) guarded her words against the escape of a stupid or a typical remark, yet most typically, most stupidly, said, "I hope you won't put *me* in one of your novels."

It would have been tolerable, everyone thought (according to the Countess, my faithful informant), if Hope had been content merely to bring her friends to parties for, despite their appearance, they behaved usually quite well. It was that Hope had given herself such insufferable airs, sprinkling her talk with the cryptograms of literary critics, explaining, unbidden, the meanings of abstruse poems. She had painstakingly studied out an erudite essay on "psychical distance" the year before and for several months judged thereby every book, painting, play, or movie that came up. But as someone remarked—someone who probably had never heard of the esthetic principle she used so boldly—she shot only at sitting birds, and she was openly laughed at when she was heard to say to Amy Brooks, "The trouble with your Oyster House pastel is the figure in the foreground, which is under-distanced. He is simply too much the pitiable bum. He actually brings tears to one's eyes, and that won't do."

To be sure, she was over her "intellectual" phase and no longer carried marinated herring to the obscure studios. But she had not become any more manageable. Exactly what she was doing in New York no one knew. Indeed, no one knew her address beyond the vague fact that it was "in the fifties." When someone said to her, "I wish you'd look up my friend so and so. She has a charming place on the Park and I know you'd find her amusing," Hope replied with a warm smile, "It's terribly sweet of you. Of course one *never* does anything one wants in New York, but do give me her address anyhow." Only once had anyone seen her and that only by chance. A Miss Bradley, an elderly spinster, idling away an hour between appointments in Central Park, had come on Hopestill staring raptly at the sea lions who were being fed. "Oh, aren't they beautiful?" the girl had cried. "Oh, aren't they wondrous! Oh, if only I had seen them when I was a child. You know, Miss Bradley, that Aunt Lucy never let me go to the zoo." Miss Bradley, reporting this uninhibited speech to Amy Brooks, said, "I expected her to give me a lecture on child psychology, but she spared me and we had a very pleasant little chat."

Now that she had made the full circuit and had returned to the starting point, she was generally forgiven all her past peculiarities, and there was universal rejoicing in Miss Pride's circle that the marriage, prophesied for so long, was at last to come off. In my exile, I was obliged to rely entirely on the Countess for my information, and she assured me that both Philip and Hopestill were ecstatic, that it made her quite giddy herself just to be in the same room with them. Hope, she said, had never looked so well or so handsome.

I would have been glad to believe the Countess, but I could not because of that testimony of Hopestill's misery that I heard nearly every night. As soon as her footsteps had died away, I would give in to a vicarious fear that set me trembling and, suddenly cold, would go to the fire to warm myself. I would muse into the brilliant coals and shut my eyes. The inner wall of my lids retained the clarified red of the flames like the surface of one of those freakish hot pools in certain places where minerals behave in a fanciful way. Willfully I would force myself downward through a red wind until the door to my imagined room was opened and I stood upon its threshold. Recently I had identified the lobster-claw letter opener as belonging to a very aged woman who lived in Chichester and had rendered some service to my mother when I was about five years old, so that we went to call on her one afternoon at tea time. I had been given the letter opener to play with and I was horrified by it, but I was bashful and did not want to be rude to the kind old lady, and so I had twirled the agate sphere and stroked the reptilian claws until I was nearly sick and had to refuse the hot cocoa which had been made especially for me. Still, the aged woman's room was not my room. I remembered distinctly that she received us in her bedroom because there were no fires in the rest of the house and that the spool bed had been covered with a blue and white quilt with a design of five-pointed stars and crescent moons, and that I had sat on an ottoman covered with scarlet oilcloth and that the tea things had been on an old-fashioned washstand through the half open door of which had been visible a chamber-pot with pale roses painted on the side.

My memories of rooms where I had been were delineated with the perfection of detail of truthful photographs. I saw Miss Pride's room at the Hotel as it had been one day after a windy rainstorm. A cherub pillow had been by the open window and one of the castles was dark with dampness; an elm leaf was flattened against the screen, and a letter which had been on the sill had been blown to the floor. One day I recognized the unlabeled bottle of red wine. It had been in the Countess' music room one afternoon, late, when I had gone there to listen to some records and had been alone. I had tasted the wine, but it had gone sour and I concluded that it had been removed from the cabinet to be taken downstairs but had been forgotten.

My visits to the red room were infrequent. Though I was convinced that there was no harm in it, that it was, if anything, an achievement of will that should be envied and applauded by other people who had not so sure a refuge, I was, at the same time, loath to make my seclusion there a habit. I entered it only (rather, I stood upon the threshold, for I was never actually in the room and could not visualize myself taking a book out of the shelves or sitting at the desk) when I felt that I could not withstand the onslaught of worry or of loneliness. Whenever

I realized that Sunday was approaching and I must go again to see my mother and probably to have another conversation with the doctor, whenever Miss Pride reminded me that I was in disgrace, and whenever I came to think of Hopestill, then I would turn to my ghost of a sanctuary as I might turn to a drug.

When there were no guests but Hopestill and Miss Pride had gone out and Mamselle Thérèse was in her own room working at her sketches of a renovated nun, the stillness of the house unnerved me and if by chance there was a wind lamenting in the trees of Louisburg Square, my heart was plucked quickly like a taut gut. It was not that I feared sneak-thieves or murderers or Kakosan's spirits, nor did I feel, at this particular time, the watchful eyes of people who thought I might repeat my mother's pattern. It was a fear I could describe only approximately as a fear of *myself.* It was not a new experience. Sometimes in Chichester, I had taken care of children in the evenings at a lonely house almost at the Point. An old, one-eyed Airedale kept me company, snoozing on the sofa. Abruptly he would waken and lift his head, pointing his nose toward the door, and then, assured that there was nothing outside after all, he would look at me with his one intelligent eye. This look, so companionable and preternaturally wise, frightened me more than his attention to the door, beyond which he had sensed the lurking of some unknown thing: I was afraid the dog would speak. This droll idea, of brief duration, was but the envelope for another fear: the fear of my own mind which had conceived so awful a possibility. Like the motorist through dense fog at night who has proof of only himself, his automobile, and the road, and must accept *a priori* the fact that the rest of the world has not been dematerialized, I could not demonstrate the external authorship of myself and the dog nor our independence of one another. What proof had I that the dog was not the creation of my own mind and being such might, if I willed it, speak to me; conversely, what proof was there that I was not the dog's idea, evolved in those mysterious, perhaps Olympian, brains behind the obtuse snout? What broke my ghastly reverie was the registration of sound on my mind, the footsteps of some later walker, or the rustle of a bed above me as one of the children turned in his sleep. I argued that since my mind had been altogether on the dog, it could not have produced a noise in the distance. My hearing re-established my spatial relation to the outer world's complexities and immediately thereafter my judgments were restored.

Similarly at Miss Pride's on silent nights, what unbalanced the poise of quintessential self (a play on words would come to me: the eye was the proof of I, not only of my own eye or my mind's eye, bur the Cyclopean eye of the Airedale) was the protesting, bewildered cry of Miss Pride's cat shut up in her bedroom. It would come toward the middle of the evening and was no more than one prolonged off-key yet musical howl which petered out on a descending scale.

I had seen Mercy only once or twice in all the time I had lived with Miss Pride. When I first came, I had been told that she was jumpy and unfriendly because her kittens, begot by an unauthorized tomcat during the summer when she had been entrusted to the care of the Hornblowers in Concord, had been chloroformed as soon as they were born, and the mother, her instincts baffled, hunted them with piteous persistence, crying and snooping through the closets, the bedroom, the bath, and her own apartment, a storeroom no longer in use. Until her mesalliance and its results, she had been allowed to roam at will throughout the house, but Miss Pride, attributing a high degree of intelligence to her, thought that by way of revenge, she might now defile upholstery and rugs, in her search might overturn vases and clocks, might in her despair and anger scratch visitors and claw their stockings. By this time, she had surely forgotten her kittens, but Miss Pride had decided to make this limited arena permanent, for what reason I do not know. Each morning, I saw Ethel putting Mercy's sand-box (called by Miss Pride "the kitty-cat's water-closet" but by the embarrassed servants "the cat's carton") shrouded with last night's *Transcript* on the dumb-waiter to be emptied and filled with fresh sand. This and the lonely cry at night were the only evidence I had that there was an animal in the house.

One night I thought that it would do no harm if I let the prisoner out for an hour or so, bringing her up to my room which was not a spacious place to romp in but would at least be a change of scene. I went down. Miss Pride's room was dark except for the fire that had burned down to a rich glow and at first I could not see the cat. When I was accustomed to the shadows, I perceived a pair of sulphurous eyes which, seeming to be suspended in the air four feet from the floor, regarded me with the unflinching stare of the hypnotist. I switched on the night-lamp beside the bed and in its weak light saw the animal perched on a chest of drawers beside the fire-place. For a moment she did not move but only looked at me. She had a short, square face and silver whiskers that curved downward from her tawny cheeks, marked on each side with two black stripes. She sat with her front legs straight and her luxurious tail curled about her feet. I moved toward her and she started, thrusting her head suddenly forward so that I could see the pure white fur under her chin. "Kitty, kitty," I said. She leapt from the chest with a chirrup of fear and ran to her room, a streak of fur that blended shades of red and yellow and blue, all overlaid and softened with a cloudy silver and striped with black. As she ran, her tail dragged on the floor like a train. I did not pursue her, for there had been in her face as she saw me coming toward her a look of primitive terror that could, I thought, easily become the rage of a wild beast. I ran back up the stairs two at a time to my cheerful room where all the lights were burning. Three or four nights later, again hearing the cry and again wishing to bring her upstairs, I went down to try a second time. I found the door to Miss Pride's bedroom locked.

It was easy enough to explain the locked door. I remembered that in my haste the first time to get away from the cat and to end our mutual fear, I had neglected to turn out the night-lamp, and Miss Pride, finding it and realizing that someone—probably a servant, she would think—had been in her room, henceforth took precautions against Mercy's escape. She preferred to do that, I reasoned, rather than to shut the door to the storeroom. But ever after that, when I passed through the hall on the second floor, the fact struck me as potentially sinister that I had never heard Mercy's call until these last weeks when I, too, was virtually a prisoner, heard it only at night when I was alone except for Mamselle Thérèse and the servants who were all on the floor above me. As I went on and ascended the flight of stairs to the third story, my common sense returned and told me that heretofore I had been reading aloud to Miss Pride at this hour, and that on the nights when she was at home, I used my typewriter, the racket of which shut out all but loud noises or very near ones. But there is a side in us that courts and would like to believe in the fanciful. "Of course it was no more than coincidence," we say, but we would like our audience to share our wonder and reply, "Coincidence, certainly, and yet . . ."

2

By day our house was the scene of what Miss Pride crossly called "a needless hullabaloo" for which, as a matter of fact, she was largely responsible, for while Hopestill and Philip had wanted a small wedding, she had insisted that a step of this kind be taken with public pomp. It was typical of her to speak of it as "a step of this kind," as if it were some sort of sensible negotiation which had been undertaken after several other "kinds" had been discarded. It was she who had wired Mamselle Thérèse (recommended by the Countess and deplored by Hopestill who had her own modiste) and she who had sent out invitations to three hundred guests for the wedding breakfast, and she who had persuaded a notable clergyman who had left Boston several years before to perform the ceremony. There had been some argument about this last detail. Both Miss Pride and Dr. McAllister's father were Unitarians and did their best to dissuade Hopestill from being married in the Episcopal church in which, adopting her father's rather than her mother's sect, she had been confirmed. She was adamant and requested, moreover, that the minister from whom she had received the Eucharist at her first communion be brought back for the occasion. In only one other particular had she insisted on having her own way. She refused to be given away by her uncle Arthur Hornblower or any other relative and before even consulting her aunt, conferred the honor upon Admiral Nephews.

I thought that she wanted to be married in the Episcopal church out of a nostalgic attachment to her childhood, as it had been a better and happier time. I could find no other reason, for she was altogether without religious conviction and never went to any services. I divined, too, that in denying any member of her family the right to participate actively in the ritual, she was relieving them, symbolically, of any accessory responsibility.

In the week before the wedding, my duties were many and complex. I acted as the intermediary between Miss Pride and the representatives of florists, liquor dealers, caterers, and took great pleasure in ordering such things as twelve cases of champagne and thirty pounds of filet of sole. Miss Pride would have preferred to attend to these matters herself because all tradespeople were scoundrels and I was both gullible and extravagant, but she was occupied with other things, among them with ridding the house of kinsfolk who came in droves beginning at nine o'clock in the morning, expecting to be asked to luncheon and then tea and even dinner. They infuriated her by telling her that she looked "worn-out" and that they were going to make her go to bed while they themselves took over, lock, stock, and barrel. To such a suggestion, Miss Pride would say, turning her eyes like pistols on the offender, "If I want crutches, I'll *buy* them, Sally Hornblower." They were full of plans for what she would wear to the wedding (I knew what she would wear: a new black broadcloth suit and a green beaver hat) and for the most decorative way of arranging the display of gifts. She would nod her head and say, "I dare say that would be nice. But I shall just muddle on in my old way. You can't teach an old dog new tricks." Once, after this cliché, she gave a mirthless "ha! ha!" and sounded, indeed, like the dog that could not be taught but had learned in his youth the trick of biting trespassers.

The continual stir of the house was intoxicating. On my way out of the house to run some important errand, I would glance into the upstairs sitting-room where the presents gradually were accumulating. Hopestill might, as I passed, be unwrapping something that had just come. She would hold up for me to see a blue plum-blossom jar or a silver pitcher. We could hear the bee-like flurry of the sewing machine and the animated conversation of Mamselle Thérèse and her two assistants. The door-bell and the telephone reiterated their clamorous demands until the servants were beside themselves. Leaving Hopestill surrounded by her treasure, I would go downstairs to receive a final instruction from Miss Pride. Nearly always, on one of the tables in the hall, there was a silver bowl half filled with water on whose surface floated the disintegrating but still fragrant flowers that Hopestill had worn the night

before. I was curiously moved at the sight of them, and imagined her coming in late, the dangers of another day behind her,
Philip's car already pulling away from the curb. I wondered if
she would not ponder her face in the mirror above the table as
she unpinned the orchid or the gardenias just as I pondered
mine a moment before I left the house. Which face would she
see? The one with which everyone was familiar or the one I had
seen on the day she had come home when in her distress she
had seemed old and plain?

The churchly odor of old wood and stone was sweetened with
the perfume and boutonnières of the wedding guests assembled twenty minutes early. A beam of sunshine came through
the open door and extended the length of the central aisle
until, at the sanctuary, it joined in a pool of opaline light with
another laden shaft sifted through the stained glass windows,
of which the three segments were so detailed that I could read
in them no narrative but saw only brilliant colors throwing off
the glitter of jewels. Then, through the gilded haze the altar
was visible, furnished with a massive cross, two golden urns
of white azaleas, and pale candles still unlit. The sun and the
flowers and the open door made me think of spring, though
I had only to look at the fur coats to remember that it was
not yet midwinter and that the cool of the church was withal
warmer than the outside temperature. The freshness of the
bath I had just taken and the clean, acrid odor of my new
clothes combined with this pleasure to give me a general sense
of well-being and excellent health, as if I had shaken off the
aches and miseries of one season and had entered upon the
next under favorable omens, like the day on which we realize
that our blood has expunged the last particle of disease. Two
incidents the day before, which was Sunday, had lightened my
heart. When I went to the library in the morning, I found Miss
Pride more cordial than she had been since the night of my
defection ("The night," she called it, "when you came home
in such an informal state of mind."), and by way of showing
that I was being recalled from exile, she gave me a glass of
her fine personal sherry and told me that I must not fail to be
at the wedding and the wedding breakfast the following day.
Then, at the asylum, I was told that I could see my mother for

only a few minutes as she was very ill and was confined to her bed in the infirmary. The doctor, the same one I had talked with before, admitted that he was not so confident of her cure as he had been. He was positive, he told me, of her ultimate recovery but thought she could not be moved for at least six months instead of three as he had told me before. The extension of time seemed like an act of benevolence performed by the doctor himself out of the goodness of his heart and I so ill concealed my gratitude that I drew from him a smile and a companionable pat on the shoulder as he wished me a Merry Christmas. I was, moreover, in good spirits today because the end of my suspense was at last in sight and henceforth I would not hear Hopestill weeping into her pillow nor catch in her face an occasional look of alarm.

From where I sat at the back of the chapel, I could see Miss Pride in the front pew sitting between the Reverend McAllister and his wife. She was wearing a new suit, but as it was made in the same pattern as all her others and cut from the same wool, perhaps I alone knew that it was new, for I had seen the tailor's bill. She had made one concession to her relatives, and in place of her green beaver wore a small hat planted with red posies which caused her so much consternation, because she thought it would fall off, that during the ceremony, as she told everyone later, she could think of nothing but the moment when she might take it off.

She and the clergyman, in their sober black, whose forebears had not taken passage on the same boat with the Tory Almighty who had lodged in this chapel since pre-Revolutionary times, sat rigidly, staring straight ahead with disapproval at the Popish paraphernalia of the altar which, as Miss Pride said, was "tantamount to a repudiation of the Declaration of Independence." Distrust of the high-church folderol as well as of her headgear gave her face the dour immobility of a Protestant martyr and she did not smile once or look either to the right or to the left from the moment Frank Whitney ushered her to her seat of honor until she left it. The Reverend McAllister, on the contrary, sent his eyes meddling into the nooks and crannies of the "temple," as he spoke of it, and glowered upon the kneeling attitudes of some of these first cousins to the Roman Catholics, into whose ranks he was heartily disinclined to release his son.

The Reverend was a man of extraordinary obtuseness and had he ever taken the trouble—as his wife and mother did—to observe his future daughter-in-law even to form an impression of her external appearance, he would have been freed at once of his suspicions that she was leading Philip to the Pope, would have been far more worried that she would lead him to atheism. I had heard that at the time Al Smith was running for president, Reverend McAllister had been the victim of a recurrent nightmare in which a company of dwarfs (presumably Catholic dwarfs) attempted to stuff him into a confessional box, and he remarked to several people that if Smith were elected, he would die. Very likely he would have. He had presented himself at the house this morning to pay his respects to Miss Pride and as she was then engaged, I went down to entertain him until she would be free. He was a teetotaler and refused the port I had been commissioned to offer him. For five minutes he listed some facts to me which he had gleaned from his reading the night before, among which was the sagacious custom of polar bears who, when stalking seals, covered their black noses with their paws so that there was nothing about them to show that they were anything but mounds of snow.

Philip's mother who, although she would have preferred to wear black as a sign of mourning for her son, had finally decided that it would be too much of a good thing if all four of the chief relatives were attired as for a funeral, and was dressed in pale blue, becoming to her rosy checks and her white hair and her blue eyes, which had not been reddened but made only prettily clouded by the incessant stream of tears they had released ever since the engagement was announced. She had lost her appetite, had been unable to sleep a night through, and had not appeared at any of the pre-nuptial parties. It was said by her husband that her heart was temporarily "out of kilter." She had several times written Hopestill begging her to come to Concord: "We have so much to talk about," she wrote. "I feel there are many things you must know about Philip which only I can tell you. The hastiness of your wedding has prevented us from getting really well acquainted, but perhaps we can make up for lost time if only you will agree to spend two or three days with me." Hopestill, either because she was harassed by the business which the wedding involved or because she could think of no way to refuse the invitation graciously, did not answer, a breach of manners that had already had serious consequences. The elder Mrs. McAllister had told the story everywhere and, making use of her daughter's unwittingly accurate phrase, repeated often, "The wedding is too hasty for me. Marian and I both wish they'd wait until June. It is breaking Philip's mother's heart that she can't have a garden party for them. And since the poor thing's ill now, she can't even have an indoor party for them. I do think it's inconsiderate." The heart-sufferer, through a supreme sacrifice of her health, had managed to come to the wedding, though she would not be able to come to the breakfast. Her excuses, "doctor's orders," had been made through her husband this morning, as if she could not bear even to speak to Miss Pride.

The Countess, resplendent in a gray suit and a fox scarf, was sitting with Amy Brooks some pews ahead of me but she had spied me and was mouthing something which I could not catch and so mouthed back, "I can't understand what you're saying." It came out later that she had been telling me to be sure to look at Mrs. Hornblower, who had oddly enough come in evening clothes. I had, as a matter of fact, been on the lookout for Mrs. Hornblower who had heretofore seemed mythical, for I had learned on asking someone why it was that the tea-party to which I had been invited was such a remarkable event because the host's wife was to be there, that while she was on the friendliest terms with her husband, she did not share his house or his servants but lived in her own establishment fifty yards from his, a path leading from one door to the other. I asked my interlocutor—it was, as I remember, one of the girls at the Countess' Friday—to explain this. "They're just cranks," she said, shrugging her shoulders. "Mrs. Hornblower used to come to tea with my grandmother now and again when she was in town and she was at that time wrapped up in spiritism. It made poor Grandma have bad dreams about Mrs. Hornblower's astral body, and once when she said, 'Mary, I can simply walk through that wall if you only have faith in me,' Grandma shrieked, 'Nellie!' at the top of her lungs and it made Mrs. Hornblower furious although Grandma passed it off very nicely by saying that she just wanted Nellie to bring some more muffins. After that she took up the cause of Sacco

and Vanzetti, but she didn't come to call any more for, as she
told someone who of course repeated it to us, she didn't think
my grandmother was interested in ideas." She had given up the
occult for more pressing matters, but every now and again she
would put in an appearance at a séance for old-time's sake, and
at one of them, Kakosan had met her. Mrs. Hornblower had
been a tremendous success and Kakosan, who assumed that
because I lived opposite Louisburg Square I was intimately
acquainted with everyone of consequence, had begged me to
arrange an introduction. Mrs. Hornblower was a person of fine
bearing, a large woman of whose face one immediately said,
"She must have been lovely when she was young," and now,
pitifully palsied, her white hair stained with yellow, she was
still handsome. Much larger than her chubby husband who,
although he was her senior, was better preserved and still wore
black hair in which there was not a trace of gray, she bent
toward him the loving and respectful looks of the obedient
young wife.

Sitting at the aisle in the middle of the church, casually
dressed in tweeds, Mr. Morgan slouched against the side of
the pew, his chin in his hand, his eyes closed. He had not been
invited, as I well enough knew because I had checked over
the list of guests. But I was not in the least surprised to see
him although I could not be certain of his motive, whether
he had come to tease Hopestill or if he was in love with her
and wished to torment himself, or if it was that desiring to
escape suspicion he had thought it the better policy not to
hide himself away. He had, if this last was his intention, made
a serious mistake in his costume and continued, throughout
the ceremony, to make an even graver error in his indolent
attitude and his drowsy grin, for he was most conspicuous in
that church full of people whose dress (with the exception of
Mrs. Hornblower) was all so similar it was virtually a uniform,
and thus he was set down by everyone who saw him—and he
escaped the notice of very few—as vain and impudent for in
gainsaying the decrees of custom, he was usurping custom's
power. His presence relieved me on one point and troubled
me on another. Evidently Hopestill had not been seeing him,
as I had suspected from time to time, for if she had she would
have told him not to come. I had suspected meetings between

them because I had learned from Nathan that Morgan was in town all the the time now and there was no falling off of his visits and telephone calls from young women. What disturbed me—vaguely because this morning I felt detached from the whole business—was that since he apparently thought there was nothing odd in his coming this morning and coming with so blatant an air of indifference, there was no reason to suppose that Hopestill and Philip and their friends would be deprived of his company in the future.

Nathan, after two years of anatomizing his pupil, had come to the conclusion that he was not really selfish nor cold-blooded but that he was one of those unfortunate people in whom is missing the talent for falling in love. Such people do not give up but suppose that love will come at last in the person of some now unknown woman, just as other people do not relinquish their hope that belief in God will at last batter down the impregnable battlements of the soul. He carried on two or three affairs concurrently and was equally tenacious of each of his women because it was possible that *she* was the one who would, under an abrupt and accidental change of circumstances, become his solitary objective. This being the case and if Morgan's need for the centralization of his life about one woman was as urgent as Nathan would have me believe, would not Hopestill's marriage be an obstacle of slight consequence to him? I could only conjecture what had taken place in New York, but I was sure that if Morgan offered to marry her (and I imagined that he did, for he was the kind of person who could, with the left hand, dispense a sort of sentimental honorableness at the same time that the right hand was composing a love-letter to another woman) Hopestill had refused, not because she did not love him, not even because she was unwilling to support his infidelities, but because her pride had been mortally wounded and its resuscitation could be effected only if the accessory to the crime were out of sight and, eventually, out of mind. The refusal (I continued my hypothesis) impressed her lover who had not reckoned on so easy an acquittal and after his first sweet sensation of relief, he became tantalized with the possibility that he might have fallen in love with her on the revelation of her stern character which, in spite of her yearning, had firmly dismissed him. Perhaps he had come today, then, for the simple reason that he wanted to see her, to refresh his memory of her beauty and to determine, from the expression on her face and the way she walked, whether his siege of her would be rewarding.

In the hush that forewarned the wedding march, a hush that fell upon the flesh as well as on the ears so that the guests froze briefly in their postures of kneeling or leaning towards their neighbors, a faintness passed over me, obliterating the vigor of a few minutes before. And as from its rich reservoir, the organ's voice ascended, translating the march from *Lohengrin* into its ecclesiastical language, I was apprised of the crisis of my complex feeling about this wedding, so similar to the sickness of the flesh that it was as if the very guardians of my body's fluids had told me of my disequilibrium. My dizziness had no cause more serious than excitement, was but another and more acute version of that agitation which caused the women in the church to apply handkerchiefs to their eyes. And yet, the anguish, that one moment inched like a cold worm through the tunnels of my flesh and the next kindled a fire that spread from branch to branch until I was all aflame, was so much fiercer than any emotional distress I had had before that for a time I believed I was really "coming down" with some disease. Tears boiled over my eyelids and half screened the four bridesmaids in their green tulle dresses, preceding the maid of honor whose medieval velvet gown, a deeper shade than theirs, was like the outer leaf and theirs the paler inside ones. As I was on the verge, I thought, of toppling forward over the back of the pew ahead of me, my mind, like a rapid finger flicking through a book to find a special passage, went over possible diseases and diagnosed my weakness by presenting to me Hopestill's face, shrouded in shadows, as I imagined it might look in the mirror above the table in the vestibule. Certain then that my symptoms were not physical, I sought to efface them by an effort of will. My eyesight, still somewhat deformed by the tears, cleared enough so that the maid of honor was less nebulous than her vanguard. With a smile directed towards nothing but an abstract point of the compass, she addressed to her gait as much science and regard for the rhythms of the music as if she were executing a step in a difficult dance. But although I saw her thus and

followed her slender body and the head whose black hair was
caught in a cap of gold and perceived that in her hands she carried a bouquet of yellow roses, I saw her also through the hot
vapor of my tears as a mobile stain upon the undulating curtain
that obscured the church and the wedding-guests. Similarly,
while the music advanced from chord to chord, it clung, at
the same time, in my ears, to one deep, roaring note everlastingly renewed by its infinite vibrations. Closing my eyes, I saw
repeated on the black waves of my blindness, the same green
smear which my sightless pupils pursued until it swam out of
their ken, yet entered again at once when the ball rolled back
to its central position.

With the passing of the maid of honor, I felt a temporary
return of strength. The vertigo ceased and my mind cleared.
Across the heads of the audience, who were turning to behold
the bride, I saw Philip entering from the chancel, and through
some unstudied sophistication, I saw him separate from the
person I had known but instead, as a total stranger who, in a
few minutes, could no longer lend himself in my imagination
to romantic equations of which I was the other magnitude. He
underwent a second metamorphosis and became "the physician." It was under the auspices and according to the rules of
this genus that I should henceforth govern my relationship
with him. In the service of my own interests, I was then able
to transmute the smile of a young man about to be married,
who at this moment had caught sight of his bride as she entered
the chapel, into the smile of the understanding healer who
by his attentiveness seemed to exist for me alone. And taking
this clean-boned Yankee together with his opulent and august
setting, I was, despite my frustration, glad that our flirting had
come to nothing, that he would be unchanged when throughout the years I sought his advice.

The dazzled guests watched the proud flower for whose
protection and enhancement the leaves had been created: a
chaste and perfect column draped in satin as pure as the wax
of the tapers on the altar and outdoing their flame with the
hair that blazed through a calotte of pearls. Her face, white as
her finery and her lilies, wore an expression of solemnity befit-
ting the occasion, although, as I heard someone whisper, there

should have been something of a smile in her countenance, if not upon her lips, then at least within her eyes, for joy should be in proportion equal to the other feelings of the partaker of this particular sacrament. Her look, to me, was one instinct with death, yet death less chill than that which now like a layer beneath her skin gave off a waxen luminosity and imparted to her movement a brittleness as if the soft integuments of skin and cloth concealed a metal mechanism. Her thin fingers were tightly curled on the Admiral's arm. Harry Morgan had turned, with all the others, and while I could not see her face, I knew by his, when she had passed by, that a sign had passed between them, for his mouth curved into a serene smile as if he had half won his battle.

It seemed to me, as they joined before the minister, that Hopestill shuddered as she had done when she took the camellias from my hand. If this was seen by anyone else—indeed, if it occurred at all—it was attributed to her nervousness, the understandable and appropriate reluctance of a girl about to relinquish her virginity by so public a ritual. With a tidal rustling, the audience sat down, arranged their hands in their laps and adjusted their spectacles like people anticipating a well-known and beloved piece of music. It was, to be sure, an artistic performance, for the minister, wreathed in benign smiles, posed his literary questions and offered up his prayers with the intonations of a Shakespearean actor, which grace of pitch and diction was afterwards to evoke from Reverend McAllister the remark that the service had been "nothing but rhetoric." I was astonished at the brevity of the cross-examination, and before I had accustomed myself to the idea that something of great importance was going on, the whole thing was over and the man and wife were coming back down the aisle, arm in arm, smiling to their well-wishers, their faces illuminated by the sunlight into which they were walking. Hopestill did not fail to include her husband in her dispensation of impartial smiles, but her hand that clutched the bouquet of flowers was clenched like stone.

The drawing-room, the library, the dining-room overflowed with cawing guests and the stairs were packed with two lanes, one ascending to view the wedding presents, the other coming down. As soon as I had offered my congratulations (the bride and groom were stationed before the bay-window. Both of them had protested against this lavishness and were so harried that they seemed not to recognize me at all), I pushed my way through the throngs who, because they blocked the way between myself and my room for which I longed, offended me as if they were being intentionally hard-hearted. Outside the drawing-room door, I met Miss Pride who had got rid of her hat and looked refreshed. I told her that I thought I was ill and wanted to go to my room.

"Nonsense," she said. "I've never seen you look better. There are two or three things I want you to attend to in the pantry. Come along with me and I'll show you."

I said, "I thought that if I went to bed now the cold wouldn't have a chance to develop."

"Oh, I know your kind of cold, you vixen. I'm not as easily taken in as Berthe, though, and won't let you off. What I think is that you're just concerned too much with yourself. After this is over, we must have a long talk and straighten things out."

I followed her docilely down the hall to the door of the pantry where she instructed me to post myself in order to see that the dirty dishes were immediately sent down on the dumb-waiter to be washed and sent up again so that everyone might be served. The waiters, who were perfectly capable of managing by themselves, regarded me with such wounded displeasure that for the half hour I stood on guard I did not utter a word, but leaned against the window where the sunlight was warm, drinking the remains of the champagne in the glasses that came out from the other rooms. Once I closed my eyes to feel the sun on my lids and when I opened them again saw Harry Morgan lounging up against the door giving me what I could only call "a once-over." Fearing that if Miss Pride chanced to come into the pantry and saw us there together she might surmise that I was responsible for this intrusion, and being, moreover, greatly perturbed by his prowling eyes, I exclaimed, "My God!" and he, straightening up, extended his hand as he said, "May I share your quiet inglenook, dear, just we two?" One of the accommodators, a portly middle-aged

man with a bald head and a frowning face, turned on him a
look of avuncular disapproval as he pushed past with a tray of
glasses and I said, "It's very crowded in here."

"Well, then, let's find a place that isn't crowded. I can't go
back into that crush."

"Nobody asked you to," I said, so nervous that I was obliged
to put down the glass I was holding for fear of dropping it.
"Nobody asked you to come in the first place."

"What kind of talk is that? I am guest Number One. I came
at the urgent invitation of the doctor himself. No one asked
me, indeed!" He laughed openly at my perplexity. "Well, in
that case," I said, "you ought to join the party."

I myself, feeling that my services in the pantry were dispens-
able, went out, taking up a place between the long buffet table
and the doors to the drawing-room which had been slid back
all the way there to examine the implications of the conversation I had just had. I was prevented from a long study by
the Admiral who, with old Mrs. McAllister, appeared slowly
making his way toward the refreshment table. "Ah," he cried,
spotting me, "here we have an ally. Sonie, what could you do in
the way of a hot bird and a cold bottle for two old fellows? I'm
hungry as a bear. I tell you, giving away a young lady is hard
work. It's a strain on the heart! Particularly if you wanted her
for your granddaughter-in-law." He winked at his companion.
"Well, all's well that ends well, as they say. And while I'm about
consoling myself, ma'am, let me congratulate you on getting a
pippin for the boy."

"Much obliged," said Mrs. McAllister coldly. "I think Hope
looks ill."

"Ill? Why, ma'am, though you're a woman, you don't know
women. What female creature ever looked well on her wedding
day? I always say the expression shouldn't be 'white as a ghost'
but 'white as a bride.' And the whiter they are, the prettier,
what?"

Mrs. McAllister received a plate of sole and salad and a glass
of champagne from me. Refusing from that moment forward
to discuss the wedding, the wedding breakfast, or the bride
and groom, she commenced on an analysis of Amy Brooks'
water colors in which she displayed more affection than intelligence. "The sweet thing, knowing that I don't get about,

brought a whole portfolio full of them to me yesterday and I was perfectly charmed. She has real talent." She went on to describe in particular a little scene Amy had done of the hemlocks in the Arboretum. While I nodded with interest and even volunteered a few comments ("How much I should like to see the picture. No, I have never been to the Arboretum, but I hope to go on Lilac Sunday," etc.), I was actually engrossed in staring at Harry Morgan who had belatedly followed me out of the pantry and was in conversation with the Countess who, from her smiles and laughter, appeared to find him delightful. A surge of people presently obliterated them and I turned my mind again to what Mrs. McAllister and the Admiral were saying. The Arboretum had led her to her own garden in Concord, and Concord had led her to the bitter announcement, corroborated by her son, Reverend McAllister, who edged his way up to us, that "I suppose you've heard Philip Senior has given the young couple a handsome wedding present? That house on the Bedford Road left to him by my husband."

"I declare!" cried the Admiral. "That *is* handsome of you, Phil. Why, that's a humdinger of a house. Up on a hill, ain't it?"

Mrs. McAllister sighed deeply. "The loveliest house in Middlesex County, Lincoln. One of the loveliest in New England. I have always said we ought to turn it over to a historical society."

"No, Mother, not in my lifetime. I hope the children will get some pleasure out of it. I've never cared much for the house myself. Would have sold it long ago, Lincoln, but Mother here didn't like its being in the hands of a stranger."

The old lady pursed her lips, said nothing, but obviously was thinking that the house *was* in the hands of a stranger.

Her son asked me then, "How much champagne would you say Lucy Pride ordered for this collation?" I told him exactly: twelve cases. He raised his eyebrows, appalled. "If all the money spent on drink were handed over to the missionaries, we would have a Christian world."

Mrs. McAllister, who had wanted her son to go into the navy, had often been heard to speak like a pagan. She snapped at him, "I hope that time never comes, son, for I feel that there are times when one *needs* alcohol. Now, for example. At weddings and at funerals." Her voice had risen to an impassioned shriek and her son put his finger to his solemn lips. "Hush,

Mother, they say it takes very little to go to one's head when one is advanced in years."

The Admiral snorted, "Your mother can take care of herself, old man. She hasn't had enough to drink, that's her trouble. Hand me your glass, ma'am, and let me refill it."

"Good afternoon," said Miss Pride crisply from behind us. "Ah, Sonie, I see you're taking over out here. I don't know what I would do without you. Well, and have you seen our poor lambs, Sarah? They're complaining that their arms ache from shaking hands and their faces hurt from smiling. They groaned when I told them they must stay another hour at least."

"At least," rejoined the old lady, staring hard at Miss Pride. "Why, I dare say that less than half of Boston has had a chance to congratulate them. My dear Lucy, you have outdone yourself!"

Miss Pride smiled pleasantly and turned to the Admiral. "I haven't even thanked you, Lincoln, for contributing to the occasion, but I'm angry with you for not wearing your decorations."

"Not with mufti, ma'am. Not me, thank you!" returned her friend, beaming all over his pink face in gratitude for her mention of his medals.

Old Mrs. McAllister, determined to find one barb at least to pierce Miss Pride's composure, at this said, "How did Arthur Hornblower feel about it?"

But she did not fell Miss Pride who retorted, "I expect he breathed a sigh of relief when he knew he wouldn't have to perform in that church. You know his objection is not to the Romish atmosphere but to the English. He's a great Anglophobe."

"Oh, I'm quite aware of *that*," said Mrs. McAllister with considerable asperity. "We've had several disputes. I tell him he's provincial, he tells me I'm a snob and we get nowhere."

"You would have quarreled with Papa, Sarah. I have always been glad that he died before war was declared because, since he liked neither France nor England, I have no doubt he would have made himself talked about in Boston. Oh, I don't mean to imply that he would not have supported the Allies whole-heartedly as far as the United States was concerned, but he would have turned a cold shoulder on England, I'm sure. His sister, my aunt Josephine, had what Papa called 'the hebetude' to marry a baronet and to be called henceforth 'Lady Fulke.' It was the name, even more than her large and totally inconvenient country establishment, that struck Papa so ridiculous. And I recollect that at the time I was presented at court and we were perforce staying with my aunt and my uncle Geoffrey, Papa consistently introduced her as 'Mrs. Faneuil' or 'Mrs. Fuller,' being unable to bring himself to say 'Lady' or to utter a name so peculiar as 'Fulke.' But I remember, also, that my sainted father was worsted on one such occasion by Mr. Henry James who turned to an English woman and said, 'One may forget other names, but Faneuil Hall is always on the tip of the tongue.' Papa was no backwoodsman: he blushed to the roots of his hair and never returned to England again or permitted the names of Mr. James and Sir and Lady Fulke to be spoken in his presence."

"Ha! Ha!" laughed the Admiral who was well-known himself as an Anglophile. "Lucy, you're a real raconteur!" But old Mrs. McAllister, pretending that she had not heard the story, groped for my hand which she pressed as she said, "My dear, do find Amy Brooks for me!"

As I went in search of Hope's cousin, the Countess, fragrant as a whole garden, came towards me with outspread arms, bumping everyone who stood in her way, among them the easily terrified Mr. Otis Whitney who immediately fled through the drawing-room in the direction of the door and was not seen again. She had nothing to tell me of any more consequence than that she loved me and that I was not to wear anything ever again but the same shade of green that I had on today and that if I did not come to hear the "Scarlatti I've dismembered, dismembered, my angel," at her next Friday, her heart would be broken into a thousand pieces. As she embraced me at our leavetaking—she had of course given me a welcoming hug and had let me go for only about a minute—she dropped her effusive tone and spoke as if we were contemporaries: "I'm not pleased, Sonie! I'm much distraught. I've been talking with a young man who has given me a real fright. You . . ."

But she could not finish for, to my great vexation, we were interrupted by one of the girls who came to the Fridays. Martha Dole was a large, plain bluestocking whose embonpoint was apportioned helter-skelter so that the thin, rectilinear legs did not harmonize with the bossy torso and likewise the long, willowy neck was inadequate support for the full-blown Norman face. She, like the other young ladies, had always shown me great cordiality in the Countess' presence, and had two or three times sent me tickets to the theater or to concerts with which, to be sure, she had parted because she could not use them herself but which were accompanied by a flattering note which told me I was more deserving than she to hear the music or to see the play. Only three nights before, I had gone, thanks to her generosity, to see *Hamlet*, but this had not prevented her, on the following day, from becoming suddenly so engrossed in her companions that she did not see me, even though I passed directly in front of her, when I entered the cocktail lounge of the Parker House to keep an appointment with Nathan and Kakosan. Yet, her first remark to me this afternoon was, "Who was that lovely girl, Japanese, Chinese, whatever she was, that I saw you with the other day?"

"At the Parker House, do you mean?" I asked experimentally, watching her face to see what degree of confusion would be recorded there. If there was any, it was too infinitesimal to be measured, and she said, "Was it at the Parker House? Yes, of course, that's right. She was exquisite! We were all quite enchanted and I was greatly set up to be able to say that even though I didn't know her, I did at least know her companion. She looked as though she had stepped out of a fairy tale. You would have fallen in love with her, Berthe!"

The Countess gave me an indulgent spanking. "What do you mean, you wicked creature, keeping all of this from me? No, no evasions! I want to know all about her. Oh, such a betrayal!"

I explained that Kakosan was a stenographer in some firm, the exact nature of which I had never determined, for she always referred mysteriously to "the commodity" which might have been anything from ink to corsets. I told them also that she was the daughter of a nobleman in exile, a cultivated patriarchal gentleman who preserved all the customs of his country and his class, writing *hokku*, painting water-colors of the Yanagawa from his faithful memory of it, sitting beside his pool in the American duplicate of his garden in Kyushu, in contemplation of the Zen-Buddha to whom, each day, he paid his ceremonial respects in the tea-house. As I observed the mounting interest in the Countess' face, I regretted I had made Nathan's mistress sound so interesting for I had no wish to bring her to the salon. My reason was that I could not trust her to exercise any restraint in her conversation. The several times that I had seen her (in my exile, I had welcomed her invitations to the movies), she had been naïve enough to tell me, when we had stopped at Schrafft's for raspberry frappés, about her lovers previous to Nathan whose attentions she described with a thoroughness that made me blush. I had no reason to suppose that she would be less candid with the Countess and the Boston girls.

"But she sounds charming!" cried the Countess. "Just imagine a real Samurai daughter simply at large in Boston! I've never heard anything so exotic! I command you to bring her to hear the Scarlatti on Friday, and if you do not, Euphrysone, I'll think up some really humiliating punishment for you. I'll make you spend a whole evening with Kalenkoff playing omber!"

I agreed, with misgivings, to bring Kakosan, and started to take leave of the Countess to go in search of Amy when Mrs. Hornblower approached us and halted me with an upraised and trembling hand. Gently with a dreamy, timid smile on her face—entirely out of keeping with her reputation of being a firebrand in political discussions, of being a sly one, and possibly engaged in subversive activities on the behalf of the Third Reich and Mussolini, having long since lost her interest in Sacco and Vanzetti—she said, "Lucy Pride told me where I'd find you. Someone told me you were acquainted with a young lady whose address I'm very anxious to get hold of. I mean the little Japanese girl, Miss Yoshida, or, rather, I should say, Yoshidasan without the 'Miss,' shouldn't I?"

"Ah, it's an epidemic!" cried Miss Martha Dole. "Imagine Sonie being in the key position!"

I told Mrs. Hornblower that I did not know Kakosan's address but that I should be glad to give her a message as I often saw her in Cambridge. "I'm getting up a benefit party for the Rebels in Spain, and I want her to come, partly for decoration, partly because I suspect that she's a sympathizer. Wouldn't you like to come too? Or don't you believe in Franco?" I had no strong feelings for either party in the Spanish Revolution and agreed with Miss Pride who said, "When the pot calls the kettle black, I shan't back either one."

"No, I can't say that I do think Franco's right," I said, and the Countess, a rabid Loyalist supporter, squeezed my arm and said to Miss Pride's cousin, "Sonie and I would be driving ambulances if we could, wouldn't we, darling?" This was not in the least true. The Countess supported "causes" solely in her drawing-room and the drawing-rooms of her friends, and I, for my part, was too ignorant of world affairs to be anything but apathetic towards them.

"What a pity," said Mrs. Hornblower. "I have not found many recruits here. Countess, have you stolen everyone for yourself?" And turning to me, she said, "I had thought that you . . . your name, you know, such *echt deutsch* . . . might be of our persuasion. *De gustibus non est disputandum*." She moved off murmuring half to herself, "So few people are willing to take the long view, the *Weltanschauung*. But the time will come." These words, proceeding from a face so venerable and harmless, gave me such an unaccountable fright that for a moment I stood looking after her, and what occurred to me as she was swallowed up by a crowd of people in the doorway was that perhaps my father, if he had gone back to Würzburg, had become a Nazi.

Martha Dole, espying an old friend, left us and the moment she was gone, I said to the Countess, "You were telling me about Harry Morgan."

"But he told me something extraordinary! Something too really strange! Don't misunderstand: I like him although he's rather racy in his language. I'm only wondering how everyone will take it."

"Take what, my dear Countess?" I cried with impatience.

"Oh, it's probably nothing at all. It's only that he told me that Philip has asked him to take charge of doing over the Concord house, and it only struck me odd because of the way Mrs. McAllister feels about the place. And of course, no one *knows* him. D'you understand me, Sonie?"

"Yes, yes," I said. "But what I *don't* understand is why Philip asked him. He hasn't known him for longer than a month."

"Precisely!" said the Countess with a wink and then, perceiving that her stepdaughter was at her side, added, "It is precisely as you say: a 'four-square' sonata, as tedious as a wooden block."

Having delivered to Amy the message from Mrs. McAllister, I made my way into the drawing-room where the crowd was beginning to thin. Hopestill beckoned to me. "Go up with me, will you, Sonie?" she whispered. I glanced towards her maid-of-honor and she said impatiently, "I've arranged that, don't worry." Philip's face was fixed in a smile that revealed his teeth which were so regular and white they looked almost false. The adjective "sanitary" flashed across my mind as I took in his clear, intellectual eyes, his fair hair, his meticulously cared-for person, and in that moment, I preferred his bride upon whose cheek there was a light streak of dirt and who was frankly exhausted and was making no attempts to conceal the fact. I told her that I would meet her in her room and she left when she had said something to Philip who, looking at me as if he had never seen me before, formally shook my hand, not altering his grin in the least. I laughed uneasily and said, "I've already congratulated you once, don't you remember?" and he replied, "How stingy you are! Can't you congratulate a man twice on the happiest day of his life?" But there was in his voice a note of such staggering unhappiness, so taut an irony that I could make only a feeble rejoinder, told him I must hurry up to Hopestill, that I wished him all the happiness, that I . . .

Hopestill had flung her bouquet down the stairwell, but one flower, limp and ragged at the edges, was caught in the pointed cuff of her wedding dress. She was waiting in her sitting-room for me and she could have been waiting ten years, she had changed so much. The structure of her face was loose, as if the sagging muscles had weakened the mortised bones. There was a starched pallor on her thin lips, a narrow canniness in her eyes, and the skin, in the brief time since I had seen her in the church, had lost that shimmer which had seemed to be touched by the moon rather than the sun, to have been inoculated by the spring rather than the summer, was ashen now, darkening to a bruised blue beneath her eyes. She had had a drink and when I came in, put down her glass. There was a newly opened bottle of whiskey on the table near where she stood.

"By God, he can wait for me!" she cried. "I'll go down when I'm God damned good and ready." And she sank into one of the wing-chairs and poured herself another drink.

"It was a very nice wedding," I said.

"Lock the door, Sonie. I won't have any of them coming in here! I won't! I wish I were dead!"

I locked the door as she ordered me and reluctantly returned. She directed me to sit down opposite her and she said, "I really mean it: I wish I were dead. Now if I were you, I wouldn't wish that, but strictly *sotto voce*, strictly *entre nous* I wouldn't predict what you'll be feeling if you go on living with Aunt Lucy for another two years."

"Well," I said, "it's not quite the same thing. It's not the same at all, Hope."

"Listen to me, you child, you baby, you innocent little girl: the time will come when you see through that woman and know her for the bitch she is. It's that she's got to have power. All of us do here: we are obsessed by it. Philip is. I am. As soon as Aunt Lucy saw she couldn't control me—up to a point she could because she was my guardian and doled out my money nickel by nickel—she got a cat! That's the vile perverted thing she did! And kept the cat locked up in a storeroom deodorized by pine-scent! Oh, she fed Mercy well: the best tinned salmon, the finest kidneys, the richest milk, and every now and again the 'Persian fat lady,' as she was revoltingly referred to, was allowed to come down and purr for Aunt Sarah and Uncle Arthur and Admiral Nephews. Until, mind you, she had a chance to perpetuate her species and have four hybrid kittens and then she was permanently incarcerated."

"Oh, that's not the reason," I said, determined to defend Miss Pride.

"Hush! Let me finish. But a pussy-cat wasn't enough, and now she's got *you*, and she intends to have the time of her life with you because you're helpless. You're dependent on her. No matter what *gaffe* you make, if you get drunk and use obscene words in front of Mrs. Frothingham, Aunt Lucy will find some way to keep you."

"I am not property!" I cried, angry with Hopestill and at the same time perturbed.

"Well, dear, that's beside the point. All of this is beside the point. I'll have a drink if you'll pour it for me, please, and tell you what *isn't* beside the point." I filled our two glasses. I was muzzy and out-of-sorts with this oblique diatribe. "What isn't beside the point," she continued, "is that all I've accomplished today, all I've accomplished in my whole life, is that I've transferred myself from one martinet to another."

"You didn't have to marry him."

She got to her feet and glared at me. "I'm sure I don't know why I've taken you into my confidence, and you can jolly well forget this. Now I'm going to dress."

The crowd had thinned considerably when I went down. In the vestibule, I heard a woman remark, "I wouldn't mind if my income were cut to fifteen thousand. I'd just go out to my farm for the whole year." And another voice replied, "Of course it wouldn't go hard with you, Augusta. Why, you have a fortune in your roses if you'd only do something about it." Augusta, whom I immediately knew to be the aunt Philip had visited when he drove me to Wolfburg from Chichester, laughed heartily. "That's what my nephew tells me, but he's a pipe-dreamer. I'm so glad that at least one of his pipe-dreams has come true. Hope is the sweetest girl in Boston, I've always felt."

"Wasn't it strange," said the Countess to Miss Pride, "that Mrs. Hornblower brought her present with her?"

"I didn't know she did," said Miss Pride. "It was peculiar enough of her to come in an evening dress."

"That's not all. She unwrapped it herself as well, and what do you suppose it was? A dozen perfectly horrid souvenir coffee spoons."

"My dear!"

Hopestill was coming down the stairs and in her carefully composed face there was no sign of the fright and anger that had made her burst out to me in her room. She joined Philip at the door and they went out, sped on by the uproar of the guests who had lingered.

"At any rate," Miss Pride was saying at my elbow, "I haven't lost this one," and she slipped her arm through mine. Through the sleeve of her black suit, I felt her bone on my flesh like a steel wand or, as she bent it into a hook, like a thin, inflexible staple. "And now," she went on to the Admiral, "now I'm going back to my memoirs."

The Admiral smiled radiantly. "When is this celebrated volume to be finished?"

Miss Pride returned his smile. "I dare say it will be years. At least that's what I intend, for I want something to occupy me so that I won't get foolish, and to occupy Sonie so she won't forsake me. Am I selfish?"

"No, ma'am. You're the most generous woman in Boston." He bowed deeply and then said to me, "And you, Mademoiselle, are the luckiest."

It was with a sort of sudden desperation that I saw that the drawing-room was empty and that the accommodators were taking down the extra tables in the dining-room and that through the open door to the library only Reverend McAllister was visible, holding open in his hands a large dark green book which I knew was a volume of the *Encyclopaedia Britannica*. Voices still came from the upstairs sitting-room, but presently a little group of people appeared at the head of the stairs and as they came down in a gust of talk, I could tell that even that room was empty now for Ethel, who had evidently been waiting for her chance, crossed the hall and went in with a tray to pick up the glasses that had been carelessly left there by the sight-seers. I wished to detain these last few guests but they were saying good-by. Gratuitously they told their hostess where they were going: to the matinee of *Richard II*, to the Country Club for ice-skating, to Brookline to shop at Best's. Amy Brooks and Mr. Pingrey, shy with one another because Amy had caught Hopestill's bouquet which she clutched tightly against her quivering breast, shaken with silent giggles, passed by me without a word because they could not see me or hear me though I called out to them, "Oh, don't go yet!" Their only thought was to get through the door and away, by themselves. They hastily told Miss Pride good-by and Amy screamed, "It was lovely! I caught the bouquet, Cousin Lucy! Edward and I are going to Agassiz! I am going to do the glass flowers in pastels for Mrs. McAllister!"

They were gone then, the last. Miss Pride, still holding my arm, linked her other in the Admiral's, and three abreast we went down the hall towards the library. "We'll quickly get rid of Ichabod," whispered Miss Pride, nodding in the direction of Reverend McAllister who was still absorbed in his book, "and then we three can have a nice talk."

"Right-o," said the Admiral. "Ain't it a pity my wife had to miss this! Why, Lucy, I haven't had such a good time since I went dancing at the Country Club, unless it was a month ago when Rose Park gave the cocktail party for her Community Chest people. I'm gay as a lark. Aren't you, Sonie?"

"Oh, yes, sir!" I cried. Miss Pride released us both and after she had gently closed the door behind us, switched off the ceiling light. The sun had gone behind a cloud and the library was shadowy and cold. "There now," she said. "It's cozy. It's just right to have this sort of *dämmerung* follow a wedding. It is the anti-climax to these affairs that I like most."

Chapter Six

PHILIP MCALLISTER, I was thinking, was one of those men in whom there lingers the perfectionism of childhood, who, when his stature was Lilliputian, saw the world as titanic, saw love centered in a goddess as a principle of salvation, as the meaning of that large, floating life, seeming so shapeless and so wonderful, like the shifting clouds of summer which veil and unveil the sun, that life he thought might vanish before he had sprung forth from his dwarfish body. We say of such people erroneously that they have never "grown up." We should say instead that they grew up too quickly, skipping certain years and finding themselves flowering, alone, and in the snow, months before the spring. The phantom he had been pursuing all his life, and which he believed was at last entrapped in this girl whom he had loved intermittently for many years, had escaped him and the love with which he thought to imprison her had dematerialized, leaving him without love and without an object to try to love.

I was coming from the Countess' and was on my way to the young McAllisters' house where they were having a cocktail party and I was going over, with distaste, the conversation I had just had with my earlier hostess. Having summoned me over the phone that morning to have luncheon with her, she began, the moment we had left the dining-room for the library, to state her object. It was nothing more than simply to satisfy her curiosity. For some months past, indeed, ever since Philip and Hopestill had come back from a wedding trip to Canada, everyone had been slightly or greatly (depending on the extent of his prejudices) shocked by the almost constant presence in their house of Harry Morgan. The Countess von Happel wanted to know what I thought of it. Had I any idea why such otherwise attractive people set loose upon their guests a person of such execrable manners, such unrelenting buffoonery? He was addicted to imitations and in the course of a single evening recently, the Countess declared, had "done" President Roosevelt at a cocktail party, Katharine Hepburn at a psychiatrist's, a Negro on trial for murder, a priest confronted by Mae West. There was little to distinguish one from another and no one

could understand how he could delude himself into thinking
he had the least gift for mimicry. "If he's as inexpert at architecture as he is at imitations," remarked the Countess, "the
Concord house will be a scandal." The Concord house was
already in a sense a scandal, for Hopestill and Morgan spent a
great deal of time there, often without Philip and without any
more chaperonage than that of the carpenter or the gardener.

Did I believe, as some people did, that Philip was perhaps
endeavoring to show Hopestill how detestable his predecessor
was by forcing the man upon her, much in the way some mothers allow their children to eat their way into an indifference
for candy? And was this newly announced pregnancy part of
Philip's plan to tame the wild creature who had lived amongst
wolves so long that she had come to howl like them?

I was disinclined to confide in the Countess my own opinion
for she was a notorious gossip and was not above naming the
sources of her tidbits, and so, to all her queries, I only replied,
"Oh, I suppose he amuses them," or "He's not such a bad sort
when he isn't clowning."

But I was not to be let off so easily. The Countess, who
enjoyed nothing so much as contemplating people's motives,
continued her anatomizing.

"I cannot accept the attachment between Philip and Mr.
Morgan as altogether genuine. And if he is trying to teach
Hope a lesson, isn't he a bit innocent? I mean, my dear Euphrysone, one can't help hearing things. One hears of Mr.
Morgan's reputation."

We are instantly put on our guard by the effeminate man
who, as if to dispel our suspicions, says, "You know, homosexuals interest me very much psychologically and I must confess
I have a number of good friends among them whom I would
like to have you meet," or takes an even bolder stand and says,
"I am so amused by the rumors I have heard about myself that
I have been tempted to give people really something to talk
about by having my hair curled and my fingernails painted"
(so that we know, in the first instance, that if the homosexuals
have admitted him to their minds which he is investigating in
the interest of his hobby, they have as well admitted him to
their arms, and in the second that curling his hair and painting his nails are probably what he will shortly do, but not for

the reason that he has prepared us). Just so, the confidence that Philip placed in Harry Morgan made the astute Countess suspect that he did not trust him at all, that he was jealous of those New York days and New York evenings to which the young millionaire so casually referred, calling upon Hopestill to confirm the name of a restaurant or of a mutual friend.

"Pretend you're a European, darling! I love you! Don't be shocked! Tell me, dear angel, if you don't agree with this evil-minded old woman that Philip McAllister has some reason—don't interrupt, Sonia—for being disappointed in that lovely bride of his? And . . . Come sit beside me. I don't know where that Filipino child of mine is. And that he does not really adore her so much as he appears?"

"I don't follow you, Countess," I said nervously.

My friend pouted and then laughed. "Of course you don't *follow* me, precious scamp, you're a mile ahead of me."

I was by no means averse to gossip but I did not enjoy it with the Countess who, for some reason unknown to me, was reined in by no inhibitions when she spoke to me although I was certain that she was discreet with others. She seemed to be under the impression that my moral view had the same generous, continental latitude as hers. My disquietude, as I fumblingly put down my coffee cup, was transmitted to her and a small silence came between us, as precise as a picture hanging on a wall.

The Countess went on, more gently. "Oh, I have not been nice at all! But you and I, Sonia, observe things other people don't. Don't we now? Wouldn't you agree with me that probably you and I are the only people, besides the principals, of course, who know that Mr. Morgan was Hope's friend before her marriage?"

"Friend?" I repeated. "But of course they were friends."

"I use the word in its European sense, darling, as you perfectly well know." She crossed the room to the bell-pull, and stood poised a moment, the light from the window enlivening her fair hair with brilliant undulations, her nose aloft. There was something at once so childish and so wise about her pose as well as about what she had just been saying that I smiled. She caught my smile, returned it, and said, "Don't try to pretend any longer that you're not a spy. You were spying on me just then. We will have some more coffee and something very special, a beautiful brandy."

Bit by bit, in the course of the afternoon, my hostess' conjectures came out. Some she revised, others she left intact; I proffered nothing new, but I was forced, by the sheer weight of her intuition which had synthesized random elements into a composition as clear as a case history written in a book, to agree with her. I did not, however, know any ease even with the assistance of the crystal-clear brandy, for I felt somehow that simply by listening I was letting Hopestill's cat out of the bag.

Berthe von Happel, through the same sort of almost physical insight that Mamselle Thérèse had employed, had known from the beginning why Hopestill had suddenly decided to marry Philip. In another sort of society, her guess would probably have immediately occurred to anyone who did not believe that the girl was in love. But it would never have crossed the mind of, for example, Amy Brooks. Hopestill might be disliked, might be criticized for her inability to get on with her relatives-in-law, for her sharp and often cruel treatment of servants, for her bland disregard of charitable works, but no one would have dreamed of accusing her of so great a crime as the one she actually had committed and the one the Countess took matter-of-factly. For whatever else she was, Hopestill was a member of a society which did not countenance illegitimate children, which, in a sense, did not believe in them, just as the prim Victorian who is told for the first time of sodomy says with a firm scoff, "I never heard of it before. I don't believe it. It's merely a bit of obscene nonsense." To be sure, shop-girls and servants frequently ruined their lives through such misdemeanors, but the people one lunched with and invited to dinner chose other means: dipsomania or betting on the horses. Bastardry was not acknowledged as a possible function of the upper classes. (I recalled, in a momentary flare of anger, how the first time I had met Philip McAllister, he had accused me of coming to him for an abortion.) But there had been a time, the Countess declared, when New England had not been so naïve, when sin was looked for in every stratum and duly punished.

Had I never seen in Philip McAllister's eyes the fanaticism of a Puritan? Had I never noticed how, at a dinner party, his flushed face did not turn when he spoke to someone but was kept tensely in an attitude that allowed him to keep a constant vigil on his wife, as if he were trying to read the thoughts in her deceitful head, or as if he wished to convey to her some message that would inform her he knew everything and forgave her nothing? Oh, to be sure, most people took this as a look of love. Indeed, the sole criticism of him was that he prolonged beyond the point of decency, his look of nuptial rapture and the vagueness which rendered him, in conversation, slightly stupid.

It was true, as the Countess said, that in public his eyes, across the cerulean azure of which there passed a flare of hotter blue like the quick, staggering stab of sun to the heart of a diamond, never left his wife but studied her as the rapt jeweler studies a rare stone through the little magnifying glass enfolded in his eye. And while he watched her, he praised her to everyone within earshot: no one had her genius for dress, or her hair, or her enchanting voice in a high minor key, or had that pearly shining flesh in which only the mouth, the palest pink or, in some lights, faint lilac, broke the lily-like monotony. In these first months of her pregnancy when it had not yet made itself cumbersome, she had reached the pinnacle of her loveliness, like the forced flower, blossoming under glass and out of reach of the distractions of other flowers and the alteration of its color by the sun or by the shade. No less embarrassed than her guests was Hopestill whose protests only made her husband the more extravagant, the more hysterically flattering: "And her greatest charm of all is that she doesn't know how charming she is!" he would cry.

I told the Countess that I did not quite see the logic of her argument: if Philip was aware that he had been tricked, and if, as she maintained, he was a throw-back to early Puritanism, why did he not divorce her or punish her by depriving her of all society, or, at the very least, refuse to have Morgan in his house?

"Oh, don't think he wants anyone to know. He wants them to suspect, probably. But he can't punish her openly, can't divorce her—for I have no doubt he feels strongly about divorce—can't burn a scarlet letter in her forehead. Darling, unconsciously he's imitating Dante: Don't you remember that the lovers' punishment is to embrace forever?"

I could not bear to listen to any more and got up. "I'm due at Hope's house now," I said, "though I'm sure I don't know how I'll face her."

And she replied, "Why, be that same inscrutable Euphrysone we know so well. You cannot fool me! You have known all along! I love you! Give Hope a kiss for me!" And she deposited a kiss on either cheek, one for myself and one for Hopestill which I did not propose to deliver.

The Countess' house, like her person, was overheated and over-fragrant, and it was a relief to be on the street. I idled, taking the longest way to Hopestill's house, and finding an organ-grinder on Marlborough Street, I stopped to watch his monkey. I did not really attend the sad little dressed-up animal, but I put penny after penny into his leather hand and dreamily looked at him and at his soiled old master who could easily have been his father. The trees had been out for some time and although now, in the twilight, it was cold, there was a quality of spring in the air. I wished that I were in the country or that, at least, I might stay out of doors until it was quite dark, doing no more perhaps than paying the monkey for the windy tunes.

I moved on. Undoubtedly the Countess was right. Philip's disappointment had made him hate Hopestill. And his hatred, coupled with his atavistic, vindictive morality, prompted him to torture her, to batten himself upon the love of the two sated and now unwilling people. But simultaneously, as he caused them to remain at their revolting banquet, though they were gorged, caused them, like Paolo and Francesca, to embrace forever and be embraced by hell, he, as overseer must also be in hell, must see to it that they rendered him the true accounts, and did not embezzle from eternity one instant of relief.

Only for Harry Morgan did I have no pity at all. The Countess, while she had deplored him, had seemed to accord him a measure of sympathy as the victim of Philip's persecution, although she could not deny my charge that he was in no way bound to accept invitations to Hopestill's house. There was one reason and I suspected two why he continued to come. The first was simply that he was a snob and had no intention of cutting himself off from the one house where he was welcome; he was a climber and would have given a good deal to be "in" as he was in other parts of the country. A fortune, he had discovered, was not the open sesame in Boston that it was elsewhere and he had once observed to me with a sort of bitter wonder that he could count on the fingers of one hand the débuts he had been invited to in this "city of the dead, this town where human life is at a premium." But there was, I thought, another reason why he did not refuse to come to the McAllisters' dinner parties and that was the new addition to Hopestill's gatherings (and the Countess', too, for that matter), that is, Kakosan Yoshida. Whether they saw one another anywhere save on Commonwealth Avenue, I could not tell, nor did I know if their friendship had progressed beyond the raillery they engaged in over cocktails, but I had perceived that they nearly always separated themselves from the rest of us before dinner and, by the time the highballs were served, had drifted to the sofa at the end of the drawing-room farthest from the fire-place. What they talked of, I could not dream, for I was sure that Kakosan had not told her new friend that she was acquainted with his tutor. Certainly, I had not told Nathan of any of this. He would have been maddened with jealousy if he had known that they were ever in the same room.

Kakosan had been an immediate success on the first Friday she had gone to the Countess'. Her conduct, of which I had been uncharitably dubious, was exemplary and her beauty, set off by a yellow satin dress embroidered with white flowers and a white carnation in her hair, distracted everyone so much from the music that the Countess was a little reserved in her conversation afterwards and we left rather earlier than usual. But Berthe von Happel bore no one a grudge and in a very short time she appeared at the Fridays and the Saturdays as often as I did. Likewise, she was taken up by Hopestill, and even Miss Pride, on one occasion, invited her to tea, though she confessed afterwards to me that she "found it a very pretty head but uncommonly empty."

If I had not let it be known that Kakosan was a typist, no one would have suspected that she had any other occupation than that of arranging flowers in a bowl or playing jackstones in a garden complete with torii and tea-house. For she was one of those people who have the enviable knack of keeping their addresses a dark secret without appearing to hide anything, of answering ambiguously or not at all questions about activities, backgrounds, preferences, antipathies. If someone said to her, "Where did you live before you came here?" she would reply, "My father, you see, has copied his villa on the Yanagawa. You should see it! He is a great gardener. And how sorry he is he cannot have the *tsubaki* in this country he loved so much in his beautiful homeland. Do you know what it is? It is red like fire and sometimes it blooms in the snow. But he has some of the Japanese flowers, you know, wistaria and cherry trees and iris. He has to have flowers, of course, for he is a Zen-Buddhist and must decorate his tea-house. And do you know that even though it never snows where his villa is, just as soon as winter comes, he covers the lanterns with straw mats as he used to do in Kyushu?" A persistent busybody, charmed with this information but nevertheless determined to know whether the villa was in California or Florida or Louisiana, might say, "Where did you say he has his villa?" As if she had not heard the inquiry, she would go on, "Oh, yes, and he has two red pines which he sprays twice a year, for it is the custom to remove every single dead needle." This was a side of Kakosan that I never saw when she was with Nathan or when she and I made our expeditions to the movies. With us, she talked only of her chief interests which were the "spirits," film stars, and some disreputable young men with whom she often conversed in the Common on her way home from work on a subject she called "nationals" and which we translated roughly as "politics." Or she would tell us the little adventures that took place in her office which sounded so remarkably like those I had heard from my classmates at the Back Bay Business College that I automatically envisaged Mrs. Hinkel as I listened to her.

But in the Boston houses, she was remote from anything worldly or anything Occidental, and I, along with everyone else, was captivated afresh each time my eyes came to rest on her dexterously wrought face as, when a conversation was in progress into which she could not enter, her golden mask became immovable and the eyes showed her to be humble before her intellectual superiors while the proud arch of her neck showed that the nobility of her blood forebade her too free participation in the meaningless talk of people who were "without tea." She was apparently the "real thing" and seeing her thus, I longed for Nathan to possess her forever as the reward for his generous overlooking of her faults. But the moment she dropped her "company manners" and exchanged a few words with me in private, I hoped that the affair would be swiftly over. The repugnance I sometimes felt for her (when she revealed herself as being so far from the "real thing") was the kind one feels toward anything that is not true to its origin if its origin is admirable or attractive: the book that begins well and peters out in mawkishness, the picture which at first seems profound until, on further study, we find that it has only the virtue of brilliant draftsmanship. She used only as ornaments the Samurai code, her father's gentlemanly pursuits of religion and art, and they were as removable as the flowers in her hair.

Nathan, feeling that he was required to justify his love of her to me (rather, to himself, for he was sometimes agonized by the discrepancy between his vast love and its mean, elusive object) often denied that she was unchaste and stupid, not stating his denial with a negative but offering me instead instances of her talents which opposed and triumphed over her defects. He did not say, "She is not stupid," but he said, "In some ways, she is very intelligent," and as an illustration of her insight, he told me that she had once observed something in him he believed he had perfectly concealed. "No, really," he said, "since I'm so generous with her, how could she know that I'm a miser?" I did not point out that the very energy of his generosity gave him away. Nor did he say that she was not promiscuous, but that she had been "misled." At one time, he would declare that she was not a harlot because she had been in love with each of her bedfellows. At another time, in a fit of jealousy of all those unknown possessors of her, he said, "She has never been affected by any of it. I am quite sure this is the first time she has been in love."

In the past month, she had been required to go to so many séances (some of which I knew to be imaginary, to be, actually, the Countess' Saturday. For some reason, probably a clever one, she had never told Nathan that she had been "taken up" by Boston.) and had broken so many appointments with him that he had become hollow-eyed with anxiety, unstrung with the suspicion that she had another lover. It was this, combined with their very evident enjoyment of one another, that made me think Kakosan and Morgan had at least entered upon the preliminaries of a love affair.

2

I had no more than let myself in at Hopestill's unlocked door than I was confronted with the proof of my suspicion, and it resulted from an incident which, by one of those almost supernatural timings of chance, occurred within the same hour that Nathan, two miles away and across the river in Cambridge, made the same discovery, his evidence being but slightly different from mine. The hall, through the carelessness of a servant, was not lighted yet, although it was quite dark, so that I could not distinguish the two people standing at one side of the door, possibly in an embrace, possibly helping one another with their wraps, but I heard Kakosan's high-pitched voice, suffused with childish laughter, cry, "Gacho, don't!", the name by which, it will be remembered, she called Nathan. And Harry Morgan said, "Okay, baby, but wait till I get you home." I was shocked, not only by the frank implications of these elided remarks, and the foretokening in them of Nathan's heartbreak, but also by the boldness of this love-play, a dozen feet from the drawing-room door. I concluded that they had already been to the party and had been relaxed by the cocktails. This, at any rate, was an advantage, for I should not now be obliged to talk with either of them. It would have been too much, I felt, if I had had to be omniscient witness to the antics of these two as well as of the McAllisters'. I hurried past them and as I went up the stairs, caught Kakosan's terrified murmur, "That was Sonie Marburg!"

Hopestill's drawing-room was so spacious that despite her many guests, it did not seem crowded. As Miss Pride said of the room, "It's not the temperature but the color that makes one think of an ice-chest. The fire in that pallid hearth gives no more warmth than the ones in the theater made with flashlights and red tissue paper." It was called the "blue room" in contradistinction to an even chillier chamber, "the white parlor." The floor was carpeted in silvery blue; the graceful chairs and sofas were upholstered in gray satin and heavy blue curtains hid the violet panes in the bay-window at the far end of the room. Bare of pictures ("I can't afford originals and one doesn't have prints," she had said), the white walls were striated with gray shadows, for the room was dimly lit by a single bulb under the blue-green shade of a Chinese lamp. There was, as the Countess complained, nothing to look at in the room, for Hopestill detested bric-a-brac, having had her fill of it in her life at her aunt's and, influenced perhaps by her prejudice against the maidenhair ferns and Aunt Alice's Birthday Trifle, did not even put flowers on the tables.

"Oh, it's California, very likely," Miss Pride was saying to a youngish woman I had met before. "Most of them settle in the west, you know."

When Miss Pride spoke of "the west," it was as if she said "somewhere." It was not quite a void, but it was something stretching interminably behind one's back. Yes, she replied to her friend, she had been "out" once, and had not the least desire to go again.

"I dare say their rugged life and bad climate make the people hardy. But I must confess I find the Rocky Mountains quite hideous, quite lacking in style. They're too much of a good thing, so to speak. Even if the landscape didn't offend me, though, I couldn't endure the place more than ten days at a time. There is a crackly feel in western speech that sets my teeth on edge."

Her friend had spent three months in Saint Louis and countered, "But you should go to the middle west if you want to hear really peculiar speech. Of course Saint Louis is neither fish nor fowl nor good red herring. I could not get the key to the city. Is it southern? Is it mid-western? Is it an imitation of a German industrial town? I don't know. But I do know that their accent makes it almost impossible for an easterner to understand what they say. If someone told you, 'I lived tin yars in Versales, Mazura,' would you have the least idea that he meant, 'I lived ten years in Versailles, Missouri'? By the way, isn't Versailles an amusing name?" The woman, whose home was in New Canaan, pronounced "idea" with a clear final consonant.

I was curiously soothed by this colloquy which was the first thing that came to my ears, for Miss Pride, no matter what scandals and disasters were perpetrated under her very nose, would never change. I assumed that she and her companion had been wondering where Kakosan's father lived. Miss Pride's announcement, "Most of them settle in the west, you know," made the Japanese immigrants as remote and unconnected with the world in which she lived as if they had never left their native shores, and Kakosan Yoshida herself went up in thin air. So long as Miss Pride was here, I thought, I could face anything. I was comforted to see that while she disdained the tray of canapés held before her by a maid, she exchanged her empty glass for a full one when the butler came round, so that I knew she would stay a little longer at least.

Feigning great interest in someone's proposed walking tour through Brittany, and someone else's plan to present Hopestill with a set of lawn bowls for her Concord house, and Edward Pingrey's recent attack of bronchitis, I actually only heard Philip's voice, superimposed upon all the others. He was not yet drunk, but he had reached a stage of animation which often just precedes almost hysterical excitement.

"What so amuses Hope and Harry about my father," I heard him say to Mr. Otis Whitney, a life-long friend of the Reverend McAllister, "is the titles of his books." And he went off into a spasm of pointless laughter in which Mr. Whitney joined with only a pained smile. His father was well-known as a mountain climber and had written three small volumes called *To the Jung-frau and Other Adventures*, *The Challenge of the Medicine Bow Range of the Rocky Mountains*, and *A Hymn to the Himalayas*. The titles, of course, amused everyone. But what variety of madness was making Philip's tongue wag on in so embarrassing a *gaffe*? One immediately pictured his wife and Morgan poking fun at his father while he indulgently looked on. It was no secret that Philip had no respect for him, but he had never expressed his contempt, had been friendly and even affectionate in his occasional little jokes about him. It sounded now as if his wife, through some obscure wile, had so corrupted him that neither taste nor common decency was left in this erstwhile dignified young man.

Evidently they had been discussing the renovations of the Concord house and the Reverend McAllister's name had come up in this connection, for Mr. Whitney, putting his glass on the mantel and murmuring that he must be going on, said, "I shall want to see the place when it's done."

"Oh, it will be a gem, I can tell you, Mr. Whitney!" cried Philip. "You should see the fire-place Morgan has designed. It doesn't look any more like a fire-place than you do."

I hoped that others were not, like myself, concentrating on the over-pattern of our host's voice. When Mr. Whitney had excused himself, Philip moved on to another group and repeated the reason why Hopestill and Harry Morgan were so amused by his father. Alcohol flings back, almost illimitably, the boundaries of humor so that we can find uproarious things which our poor sober friends miss altogether. It is necessary, if the joke is really good and really should be shared, to repeat it time and again until finally it penetrates those solemn skulls. Philip had for the third time cried out the names of his father's books. "I had never realized how terribly funny they were until Harry Morgan and Hopestill pointed it out!" Hopestill, detaching herself from Amy Brooks and two other earnest girls, came swiftly to her husband's side and slipping her arm through his, said, "Darling, Admiral Nephews wants to talk to you. Do rescue the poor old lamb. He's over there, you see, with Mr. James who's boring him to death." Perhaps, in one of those flashes of sobriety that intermittently punctuate the state of drunkenness, he realized that he had gone far enough and he obediently followed his wife, pausing to speak to me and to say, in an undertone, "Is there something up between Morgan and your Japanese friend? I shouldn't like that at all. I'll talk to you about it later."

I could keep my mind on nothing that was said to me and I moved with my cocktail to the fire-place where Hopestill's powerful dog, a Doberman, lay on the hearth, lifting his muzzle to me as I approached. Kurt had once belonged to *Herr* Speyer, the German who had mistaken me for his daughter as I waited in the lobby on my first musical Friday. When he left the country, he gave Kurt to the Countess who, having three dogs already, had handed him over to Hopestill. Despite his savage appearance, he was gentle and welcomed the advances of strangers who could not fail to be impressed by his gleaming black coat and his sharp, intelligent face. I never saw him without being reminded of his owner and the encounter with him that had given me so keen and so long-echoing a pleasure.

I sat down to contemplate the play of the flames on the short black hair and in the wise eyes that were now amber and now jet, and to restore the Nordic face that I had seen that day through the flittering shadows from the sconces and the voice, overlaid as by a filigree, by the music that descended to us from the room above. "Here, boy," I said, patting my knee. The dog wagged the stump from which his tail had been amputated, lifted his head to me, but did not get up. I wheedled a moment longer, then said, "Kurt! *Kommst du!*" and he bounded to me to put his forepaws on my lap, his shorn hind-end prancing. I was deeply attached to the affable animal who, though he bore only this resemblance to them, that is, that he could not talk, inspired me with the same joy—best known in memory—that certain things in nature did, and, in particular, through association with *Herr* Speyer, the August day when my father and I had seen the plover. Frequently Hopestill, who knew I was fond of Kurt, asked me to take him walking. We would hurtle down Clarendon Street to the esplanade and race along the river-bank. His strength and grace were communicated to me through the leash by which I restrained him and I was exhilarated with the swimming speed he demanded of me. Suddenly he would stop, listening. A growl would purr in his throat, but the bark it heralded did not come and instead, he would turn his head towards me, his companionable eyes informing me that he would not desert me after all for the excitement he had heard or smelled, far off, and we would resume our run.

Now Nathan and I, dreaming of Germany, had borrowed from libraries innumerable of those travel books which are written with a missionary's zeal, quick to report slighting comments on their darlings in order to refute them. Amongst these enraptured Valentines to Baden towns, we had found one that was full of photographs, from long study of which we had come to feel familiar with the walks, the bridges, the castle gardens, the cafés, the parks, the University of Heidelberg. As I walked with Kurt (born in Garmisch-Partenkirchen and intended, with his siblings, for a career on the Munich police force), I imagined that I was on the north bank of the Neckar

River, proceeding towards the suburb of Handschusheim, the
hills rising to my right, while to my left, across the river, I could
see the mansard roofs of the old University and the spire of
the Cathedral of the Holy Ghost. Just as in Chichester, I used
to fancy Miss Pride's house in the shadow of the State House
dome, so, taking the cathedral spire (the *locum tenens* being
Eliot House across the Charles) as my landmark, I placed my
red room somewhere to the left of it. Unless he was too impatient, I persuaded Kurt to stop awhile and I sat down on a stone
bench. I ran my hand along the space between his pointed ears
and like a child speaking to a doll, I told him about the room
which had now acquired a locality, which was Heidelberg, a
town plucked at random, and a temporal dimension which,
owing to the peculiar light that stained the windows, was
specified as autumn. At some change in the tone of my voice,
the dog, hoping that we would move on again, would part his
jaws in a grin, and I would say, "*Ja*, Kurt, *Ja*, Kurt!" and then
take pity on the imploring tilt of his head and the little whine
that sounded like a puppy's.

"*Doch, ist's so spät?*" I said to Kurt who was nuzzling my
hand with his busy nose. I repeated the sentence in imitation of
his former master and as I did so, tried to hear my accent which
Nathan declared was more Russian than German. Experimenting a third time, I heard my mother's voice and experienced
the now familiar sensation that it was actually she who was
speaking. Instantaneously, upon my image of her which accompanied the sound of her voice through my lips, she vanished
like the will-o'-the-wisp and what stood before me was the red
room. The apparition had never been quite like this before:
through the windows, instead of merely other windows and
sleeping cats upon the sills, I saw, framed by soiled and motionless curtains, in a flat opposite me, a real face but one which I
could not see clearly since it appeared to be obscured by a sort
of mist. It was an old woman's face whose eyes seemed to be
urged from their sockets a little, staring at me with malevolent
fixity. The mistiness evaporated: Miss Pride was there, in the
flat across the courtyard and the sunset had changed the color
of her olive hat.

When I vainly tried to see not the room but Hopestill's bare
white walls and gray chairs, when I strained to hear the voices

of her guests and could not, I knew that my game had got out of control and that Miss Pride had found me out in my retreat and was judging me a lunatic. It occurred to me with a terror that elevated me to an unimaginable height, that the only remedy for my obsession was a desperate one: that I must find the room in the real world before the real world intruded, as Miss Pride's face was doing now and confused me to the point of madness. For at this moment—and it was only a moment that I was conscious of her scrutiny—I was seized with a madness that was like an intense pain and was something outside myself, a violent force which urged my footsteps for the first time across the threshold onto the threadbare carpet with its faint green design. The knowledge that something external had precipitated my entrance was confused by a vertiginous and inarticulate emotion and for the present, I could not name the frenzy that had threatened but had not yet gained entrance. Despite the agitation into which the watchful eyes had flung me, I thought I sat serenely at the writing desk and sometimes smiled and other times rubbed my forehead with the tips of my fingers and then turned in my chair to examine the books on the nearest shelves. I noticed that the chair was exactly the right height, made so by a cushion. I was proud of my medical manuscript so beautifully preserved. The voice of my remembering self, roused from its sleep, said, "It was on Dr. Galbraith's desk the day you went to get him for Ivan." But my peace did not last. As Miss Pride's face moved closer, leaning out the window, her eyes pursued me and I whirled like a spinning top, whisking from corner to corner, fleeing them. I was strung out long like a bright wire that ended in brittle rays of copper, shining and pointed and raw. The eyes, like a surgeon's knives, were urged into my brain. The edges of the knives screamed like sirens; their sound curled in thin circles round my hot, pink brains. I crouched in a corner of the room, down behind the bookcases, safe, I thought. But I was plucked up by the burning yellow flares that went in a direct path like a sure blade. Miss Pride blinked her eyes. The room vanished. I had not moved but I felt an overwhelming tranquillity as if my brain were healed again, was sealed and rounded and impervious, was like a loaded, seamless ball, my hidden and wonderfully perfect pearl.

"Well!" said Miss Pride jocularly. "What a profound slumber you've just had."

Her niece stood beside her and both of them looked at me so curiously that I quickly said, "I was trying to remember a name." I was still trembling from my shock and I wondered if my voice had betrayed me. What shall I do? my eyes inquired of Kurt. His elongated face was up-pointed, immobile, and alert. I answered myself, "I must find the room or I will be like Mamma and then Miss Pride will find out and lock me up!"

Miss Pride said, "Hope tells me she wants you to stay here for dinner. I must be going on now."

"Oh, don't go just yet, Auntie," said Hopestill, her eyes wandering away from us as she sought her husband.

"I must," said her aunt. "I am behind in my political articles. Do you follow Mr. Roosevelt, Hopestill?"

Hopestill, who prided herself on not reading the newspapers and who, at the moment, was too distracted to comprehend what Miss Pride was saying, replied, "I haven't seen him in ages. I had dinner with him two years ago in a very muggy place in Cambridge. Surely he isn't *still* at Harvard!"

"Oh, no," answered Miss Pride, winking at me. "He's in Washington now."

"Really? As I recall, he was driving a banana-wagon that evening."

Disliking the prospect of having dinner alone with the McAllisters, I said to Miss Pride, "You said this morning, you know, that you wanted to do a little work this evening. Perhaps I should come along with you now."

"Oh, work is out of the question. Hopestill has made me quite tipsy. You stay here and enjoy yourself."

She turned away and Hopestill, leaning towards me, said in a whisper, "Why don't you want to stay, Sonie?"

"I didn't say that," I told her. "But the fact is that I wanted to make a telephone call. I . . ."

"Go into Philip's study if you like. You won't be disturbed there. I especially want you to stay. That is, I'm afraid if you don't, I'll have to eat alone because Philip will obviously pass out before dinner."

I relished no better the thought of being alone with Hopestill.

The Countess' conversation, my knowledge of Kakosan and Morgan, and the visitation of the red room had combined to put me into an unsettled state which I knew only a normal evening with Miss Pride on Pinckney Street could cure. And, still, recollecting how her eyes had tracked me down, I was not sure of myself, felt I might suddenly cry out as she opened the *Boston Evening Transcript* or, more dreadful yet, the room might take me unawares again as it had done this afternoon and I would be obliged to explain my trance to her. Abruptly, I was stormed by a claustrophobia so violent that every element of the scene before me assumed the proportions of destroying force: there was no reason for this gathering, no reason for this elaborate amity amongst people whose civilization had pruned down their impulses to a set of manners which imperfectly concealed a dead indifference, no reason why I should be sitting here in this wealthy drawing-room when I, so far from being embourgeoised, could find pleasure only in the society of the dog, Kurt. I was alarmed by Philip who, damaged, loud, unrecognizable, was repeating anecdotes he had heard from Morgan and, to the even greater horror of his guests, was telling professional secrets about his own colleagues. Under what influence, wifely, personal, friendly, it was not known, he had, for some time past, seemed discontented with his profession. But he had not discussed it; people had only had a "feeling" that he was going through some crisis which would undoubtedly be happily resolved. Equally alarmed was I by Hopestill in whose eyes, strikingly like her aunt's today, there was an insistent plea that I remain. She had selected me, I reasoned, because she was perhaps actually afraid to be alone with Philip and because I, of all the guests at the cocktail party, could be trusted not to carry my observations to the fastnesses of the Vincent and the Chilton Clubs.

If anyone was in need, I thought, it was myself. It had been true, as I told Hopestill, that I wanted to make a telephone call. It was, though I did not specify this, to Nathan, or rather, to the janitor of his building who would occasionally understand (he was quite deaf) what I wanted and call my friend to the telephone. For I felt that I must see him at once, must make him understand fully where the apples came from, must impress upon him the necessity of my finding the red room. Moreover, I wanted to see, simply by looking at him, that he did not know who his rival was.

And I did not want to telephone from Philip's study. I had thought of a booth in a drug-store on a certain corner from which, and only from which, I had always put through my calls to Nathan, so that I had come to associate with his distant, often blurred voice, the wooden counter visible to me through the glass door of my little cell, where a pharmacist of Hellenic beauty stood as if guarding his rows of amber glass jars full of pills, his curly golden hair occupying the place of greatest light under the neon legend: "Prescriptions." It was nearly always necessary, since several minutes elapsed from the time I got the janitor until I heard Nathan's dazed "Hello"—these calls were even now a surprise to him—for me to deposit a second or third nickel in the slot. The young god, pushing aside a ciborium of nuxvomica, called, as I hurtled out of the box, "Here, I'll change it for you," having two nickels in exchange for my dime already waiting in his outspread hand. I had not time to thank him, for I was afraid my connection would be cut off, but when I had hung up and was leaving, expressed my gratitude and made a vague promise that it would not happen again. His large, heavily-lidded hazel eyes twinkled, either because he felt he was in on a secret (perhaps he thought that my parents would not allow me to see the person I was telephoning and that I was arranging a secret rendezvous) or else because he was amused by my absent-mindedness or by the loquacity which made all my calls cost double. He said: "I always have change back here any time you need it," as if he had no wish to be deprived of the spectacle of my flurry. Once I had got Nathan immediately, for he was passing by the janitor's door as the telephone rang, and the original coin I had deposited sufficed, my message being short. The pharmacist, who had been slowly doing up a package, glanced at me through the glass door from time to time and when I came out, rapidly produced two nickels from a box at the end of the counter. I thanked him but said I had finished and he exclaimed, "You didn't get your party, then!" in a tone something like disappointment.

It was in that place where, creature of habit that I was, I wanted to make my engagement with Nathan. Superstitiously,

I felt that if I telephoned from this house, its owners would be drawn into my maelstrom whereas the pharmacist could not since he knew nothing of me and I knew of him only his youth, his beauty, and his deep voice containing the vestiges of a Nova Scotian accent. I was afraid, moreover, that if I did not make the call and see Nathan tonight, my determination would wane and by morning would have perished altogether so that the day to which I opened my eyes would be identical to all other days save that the danger was nearer, but not near enough, in the bright sunlight streaming through my familiar windows, to make me remember clearly enough how terrified I had been by Miss Pride's eyes.

When Hopestill motioned toward my untouched glass and asked me if I did not like the cocktails, I realized with a start that I had been here only a few minutes. I drank quickly and guiltily, gave Kurt a parting caress and, at Hopestill's injunction, set out to find the Admiral.

Throughout the half hour that I exchanged quotations with Admiral Nephews and soberly discussed, with Frank Whitney, the horrors of Communism, listened attentively to a drunken middle-aged man whom I had never seen before who was writing a book on a subject which he did not divulge, one part of my mind was busily casting about for an excuse to leave before dinner. Why did I not now slip upstairs, get my coat, and leave without saying good-by, then go to the drug-store or directly to Cambridge? In reflecting on one's own or in considering another's frustrations, one sees them as unnecessary, forgetting that the amenities of society, arbitrary and often absurd, beset us at every turn and it is only in larger things that one's will is really free. Thus we cannot, unless we have expert tact, or unless we are resigned to being called rude or erratic, turn from our door an unexpected visitor who arrives in the midst of a quarrel or an intimate conversation which we are loath to break off, or when we are at work. Yet, by suffering the intrusion, we accomplish nothing but ill, for our visitor senses that he is unwanted and does not understand why and we, on the other hand, are so displeased with him for not understanding that we fill our stilted, sporadic talk with little barbs, deeply offensive, so that when he leaves he may be resolving never to see us again. For there is, in the patois peculiar to the guest-host relationship, an ambiguity that penetrates to the very roots. Thus, the hostess who for the past hour has been grimacing with swallowed yawns, has, almost unconsciously, been emptying the ash-trays and collecting the glasses, begs us, when we get up to leave, not to go yet, that it is still early, that she wants another drink and cannot have it unless we stay. If we do remain, there eventually comes back to us, percolated through our mutual acquaintances, the remark she has made over the telephone the next morning, "So and So is very nice but someone should explain to him that there is a time beyond which one does not prolong a visit," or, "Like all great talkers, he's quite unaware of time. I was simply nodding in my chair and he didn't notice at all for he was only conscious of the sound of his own voice."

Philip was studiously avoiding me, and while the last thing I wanted was to talk with him, I was disturbed by the way in which, whenever our eyes met, he seemed not to see me at all and, if he found himself by accident standing near me, he immediately moved away, sometimes in the midst of a conversation. Hopestill, on the contrary, was almost constantly at my side. Her voice became progressively louder, as if she were trying to drown out Philip.

Guests were beginning to leave and there were only a dozen or so left in the drawing-room, loitering over a last cocktail. There came a general lull which was broken by Philip's clear voice saying to a young woman, the wife of a colleague of his, "I can't persuade Hope to go to Dr. Masters. She goes to a New York doctor just as she goes to a New York modiste. Fortunately our good friend Harry Morgan is decent enough to drive her down for her appointments."

As everyone knew, Hopestill was under the care of an obstetrician who served all the matrons of her circle, whose office was a few blocks from her house on Dartmouth Street. This very afternoon, she had been comparing notes with someone who had recently had a child and who declared that the process, under the supervision of Dr. Masters, was actually a pleasure. Hopestill had agreed warmly that she was devoted to him. Moreover, it was known that she had been only once to New York since her marriage and that time in the company of the Countess and Amy Brooks for the purpose of shopping and going to a Picasso exhibit. Yet, if she denied what her husband said, it would appear to the guests that she was in the habit of making trips either to New York or to some trysting place with Harry Morgan (Concord! thought the guests. Would she have the *nerve?*), using to her husband the excuse that she was visiting a doctor. Consequently, although the young woman with whom she had discussed Dr. Masters was still in the room, she said, laughing, "Oh, I only go to Dr. Ragsdale for good measure. I am quite loyal to Dr. Masters." Dr. Ragsdale, evidently the first name that came to her, had been her psychiatrist.

Philip smiled innocently across the room at her and said, "Why didn't you tell me you were seeing Dr. Masters, darling? I would have been greatly relieved to know that the product was not to be labeled 'made in New York.'"

The guests stared in hopeless embarrassment, full of pity for this naïve cuckold and regretful that he was so trusting of his wife that he had all but published her shocking subterfuges, and full of indignation that he had reached such a state of mind that his social sensitivity had been completely dulled. Specific pregnancies were not and never had been openly discussed in so loud a voice.

I waited for no more but left the room and went directly upstairs. As I picked up my coat from Hopestill's bed, I heard women talking in the dressing room adjoining. "Isn't there something in the Hippocratic oath he's disobeying?" said one. "He has the taste, thank fortune, to mention no names, but, for example, there's only one person he could have meant when he was ridiculing plastic surgery. It's frightening to see how high and mighty he is." "I've never particularly cared for him," said another, "but I find him quite impossible now. And of course Hope has such strange notions. I dare say she picked them up in New York." "New York won't hurt a flea if it's a good flea," returned the first. "Mother says it's a question of blood. 'By their fruits shall ye know them,' says Mother." "Everyone was devoted to Mrs. Mather, you know, although I've heard she was a neurasthenic. And of course her father! No wonder Hope is what she is."

I was surprised by this comment on Miss Pride's dead sister for it was like the statement of the anti-Semitic, "To be sure I have known Jews whom I've liked. I was very fond of So and

So, for instance, though even in him, you must admit, the objectionable characteristics of his race were not completely obliterated." Summary pronouncements upon personalities are common to people in society who, looking upon families as units almost as disjunct as nations, acquire a prejudice against or an affection for one member, make a declaration of war against or an alliance with the whole but make certain reservations in either case, in order to appear fair. In a moment, I overheard the first voice remark, "Miss Pride has always been rather underhanded, Mother says. It's perfectly absurd, at her age, to continue to regard Admiral Nephews as her beau especially when poor Mrs. Nephews is confined to her bed most of the time."

My departure, observed by no one, gave me a feeling of security, and painful as it might be to try to explain my dilemma to Nathan, I looked forward with pleasure to this evening which I would spend in his grubby rooms. On the way out, I bought a bottle of Liebfraumilch which came, green and dripping, out of an ice-chest, and, to take home later to Miss Pride, a bunch of mountain laurel which came, I was told by the vendor, from West Virginia. The jade-green leaves and the pink flowers like little bonbon cups made me think of Kakosan and her father's garden and the garden that Nathan had promised, in the delirium of his rapture, to build for her in some distant time and space, a castle in Spain, a vine-covered cottage, that shrine which varies according to the experience of the lovers, but is an essential of love's culture.

He had been trying for the last hour to telephone me and as I came through the murky basement, ducking under the obese pipes of the furnace that stretched out like the arms of an octopus, I found him emerging from the janitor's flat where he had been making one last attempt to reach me. I knew that he was in severe distress for it had been agreed at the beginning that he was never to call me at Miss Pride's. He told me tonelessly as his baffled eyes roved my face as if he half hoped to find there what he had lost, that two hours before, he had gone, by appointment, to Morgan's apartment to give him a lesson and had found that he was not there. But there was a note for him which the butler went to fetch. As he waited in the hall, he saw lying on the table a copy of the book, *Der Traum der Roten Kammer*, identical to the one Kakosan had given him. He could not decide whether to go away at once, leaving it untouched, maddened with uncertainty, or to probe its pages for evidence of her guilt, for marks, inscriptions, a chance slip of paper. He concluded that he must know, once and for all. First he opened it and smelled the pages which gave off, just as his did, a fragrance of her favorite scent (he had given her a flagon of it only a short time before), for it was her romantic habit to spray her letters and gifts. And then, upon the flyleaf, written with the curlicues of penmanship she effected only in notes to intimate friends, was the same girlish, warm-hearted endorsement that appeared in his—and both in red ink—"For dearest Gacho from his Hototogisu." He had then torn a page from his notebook and written to Morgan that the pressure of examinations would prevent him from giving any more lessons.

Somewhere the block-flute which we often heard gave out a waggish excerpt from *The Well-Tempered Clavichord*. The surface of our cool, golden wine was marred by floating bits of cork. Nathan's face was three-quarters turned towards me and his birthmark looked like a shadow. I was conscious of these things in terms of a painting. They were a flat surface with only a representation of dimensions and I projected them into Paris, pretending that we were there and presently would go out for a *pernod* at the café Nathan had always said he would visit first, the Closerie des Lilas. Or I imagined us wandering through the crooked streets and over the bridges of Würzburg where, at any moment, we might pass my father or jostle the elbow of my cousin Peter. Or I was in Heidelberg and the block-flute became the song of a foreign bird entering through the windows of my ruby room.

If Nathan had been listening to me as I told him what I had come for, if he had heard me taking off, layer by layer, the wrappings of my jewel, I might have lost it forever. To my own ears, my revelation sounded banal, my terror was flaccid, unimportant, trumped-up. And I was surprised that I could not make him see what I so clearly saw myself: this churchly, peaceable hallucination. I had reached the end of my account and said, "I want to find the room, you see." But I was not really conscious of this need which, until now, had seemed so urgent, and when Nathan said, "I'm sorry. I haven't been listening. What did you say?" I was comforted that I had not, after all, admitted a trespasser. I returned to his immediate and frenzied world, feeling wise, mature, and safe.

3

In the spring, the young McAllisters opened their Concord house where they spent week-ends. Frequently they entertained and their country parties were more successful than those they had had in town, not only because there were more things to do—Hopestill, although she could not participate herself, organized horseback parties by moonlight, fitted up a badminton court with lights, arranged half a dozen other diversions that appealed to her guests, and gained for her the reputation of being a highly resourceful hostess—but also because Harry Morgan was no longer in evidence and Philip had for all practical purposes become once more the person everyone had liked and admired.

Guests, approaching the house at night, were deceived by its size. Under the influence of the darkness, out of which the ell loomed suddenly, incandescent between the blooming apple trees, it seemed of manorial proportions. The impression, actually false, was strengthened by the landscape. On two sides, there was a wide sweep of lawn bounded by low stone walls in the shadows of which grew violets and lilies-of-the-valley. At the back was a grove of pines, the entrance to which had been cleared into a precise avenue where I sometimes took a walk in the early morning, relishing the blackened trunks of the pruned trees and the rich brown of the resilient needles out of which, here and there, a shell-pink mushroom thrust its tender cap.

It was not the house itself that had been renovated in Harry Morgan's startling manner, but a smaller building which had formerly been Philip's grandfather's study. No one, not even the older McAllisters, could complain that there was anything amiss in the main house. The room into which one entered was ancient, stiff, yet withal charming. The wide, thickly knotted boards of the original floors were darkened to a rich red-brown. The dresses of some of the ladies and the hides of some of the hounds in the narrative wallpaper had faded from red to the color of a wine stain and from yellow to a sandy pallor. At one end of the room was a long fireplace whose white mantel was laden with pewter plates and tankards and, at either end, ivy cascading from amber bottles. It was not a room for casual lounging. The hostility to comfort seemed to have been intentional and every article of furniture had been designed to punish the flesh: the high-backed, cane-bottomed chairs, the cruel, three-cornered "roundabouts," the cherry settle, as harsh as a pew. But the eye was pleased by the pure white doors and by two corner cupboards facing one another at the far end of the room which showed, through leaded panes, old red china, silver goblets and a flurry of bibelots.

It had been a shock, on the night of the housewarming, to go from this eighteenth century parlor to the "studio." It was like the transition from one extreme of temperature to its opposite. The studio was a box in two stories, the lower one being given over to one large room, at the end of which was a completely outfitted bar, curved and equipped with a chromium foot-rail and high maple stools upholstered in red leather. On either side, French doors opened out, on one side to a path leading to the open slype between the main part of the house and the ell, on the other, to the pine grove. The new, waxed floor was bare. Here and there, scattered about its long expanse, were massive leather chairs of an obtuse structure, but one which afforded great bodily comfort. For tables, slabs of flawed plate glass with a greenish tinge lay on iron frames. Sofas, chairs, tables, bookshelves were low as if the people meant to use them had shrunk from a normal stature but had, at the same time, become uncommonly wide. The tall, thin guests, engulfed in the cavernous chairs, had seemed fragile and undernourished, no match for the thick, pint-sized and blood-red glasses out of which they drank.

A pair of pyramidal green vases stood on the mantelpiece and, with their insistent geometry, influenced the tulips springing from them to resemble also a "new idea" so that they did not belong to the world of nature but to that of mathematical design. There was a card table in whose four legs were inserted wedge-shaped shelves to hold the drinks of the players; a pair of crystal andirons for the remodeled fire-place which, as Philip had once said, looked no more like a fire-place than did Mr.

Otis Whitney, and which he referred to as "the antrum." It was a low, square hole overhung by a vast rectangular marble shelf. A fire there could be tended, Miss Pride said, only by a dwarf and even he would be in danger of dashing his brains out. On the hearth stood a sandstone carving which represented three plump women in a happy embrace and was entitled "Breadline."

The Reverend McAllister, leading his mother about the room, had been less distressed by the bar than he had been by three pen and ink drawings which hung over a bookshelf and which produced an optical illusion: from one point of view they seemed to be illustrations of the myths of Venus and Adonis, Orpheus and Eurydice, and Narcissus, but by a slight change of focus, one saw that their subject was phallic, an assemblage of genitalia in coy half-ambush behind fronds, lotus flowers, and broad leaves of palmettos. The pictures had been a present from one of Hopestill's former friends on Joy Street, and although she was quite aware of their intention, if someone gasped and whispered in an appalled hiss that she evidently did not know what they were, she replied, "You're not the first person to tell me that, and I'm beginning to think there really *is* something ambiguous about them, though for the life of me I can't see it." It was quite true: she had seen the symbols in her first glance but had thereafter refused to let her eyes see anything but Orpheus holding his lute and Adonis lying in Venus' arms. As the latter, they were wholly without distinction, so that people thought either Hopestill's taste had gone terribly downhill or else that she was lying. As the clergyman stood before them, a dark blush stole upward from his stiff collar and he exclaimed to his mother, "I seem to be seeing things!" The old lady fetched her lorgnette from her handbag and moved up close to the pictures, although her son made an abortive attempt to stop her. She turned away, ferreting Hopestill out to kill her with a look, made particularly baleful by its filtration through her haughty instrument. Afterwards she was heard to say, "I shall never go into poor Edward's renovated library again. It gives me the same feeling of distress that I would have if the Old Manse were turned into a Howard Johnson." Miss Pride, refusing to acknowledge Harry Morgan's authorship of the changes, said of it, "Berthe von Happel, for all her eccentric notions about decorating an interior in Massachusetts, could not have produced that monstrosity. I do believe that children are born with a mental disease these days." And the Countess, looking with frank horror upon a kidney-shaped writing desk with a bakelite top and two chromium legs, one obese, the other as thin as a rail, murmured to me, "I dream! There has not yet been devised a machine to make anything so out of the question as this."

It struck me that the studio was a rarefied extension of that state of mind which had sent Hopestill to Dr. Ragsdale's consulting room. It was the demonstration, in meaningless shapes, in dislocated structure, of the rebellion to which she had become addicted without volition. Rather, the volition had existed in the beginning as a defense against her aunt, but it had now evaporated. What had taken place between her and Philip after their cocktail party, I never guessed, but none of us saw Harry Morgan again, and from that time forward, Hopestill was altered. It was difficult to say exactly what was changed in her except her appearance. She seemed to have gone beyond fear and beyond rebellion, beyond, indeed, all feeling and to exist automatically. Perhaps she had surrendered completely to Philip's hatred and had allowed her physical being to share in her moral disintegration. The demolition of her beauty was, everyone thought, merely temporary. After her child was born, her skin would regain its luster and her eyes their animation; she would be as brilliantly organized as she had been before. I wondered, though, if she would ever again be beautiful, and I thought that perhaps what we had seen as beauty had not been beauty at all but another quality, an emotional or intellectual force so powerful that it actually appeared in her person.

It will be remembered that when I was a little girl, I thought Miss Pride was beautiful. Later on, I did not call her that, but neither did I call her ugly. It was that my feeling had changed: from admiration of her carriage and her clothes, I had progressed to love of her. If by saying "she is beautiful," we mean something more (as I must have meant even as a child), we mean this as a commentary on our relationship with her, we have actually said, "my gaze is freighted with feeling and my love has urged this face to resemble my sweet memory of it." And that "feeling," like the catalyst which remains stable, must remedy, through its unchanging agency, the imperfections of what we see. Conversely, when we hate, our hearts can deceive our senses so that we find hideous what has beauty inseparably in it. In this way I, at the time I had said Miss Pride was beautiful, had simultaneously said that my mother was ugly or else that her beauty was something gone bad.

Now it was not only Hopestill's illness that made me think she had always been ugly. There was a force at play in my altered perceptions that was subtler and stronger than that which had come from my expanding knowledge of beauty, or that gradual repudiation of childhood criteria, or that vision, enriched by maturity, which allows one to speak of "types of beauty." Rather, it was that I had slowly come of age in knowledge of her and of her *milieu* into which I had willed myself. What marked the advent of my adulthood was a moment when I, standing in the doorway of the studio, saw her lying bare-footed on the couch. She was alone and Kurt lay on the floor beside her. Her small, bony feet were busily prehensile, spryly fiddling with the cushions, the toes opening and shutting like a cat's claws, the arch bowed tightly. I thought of her green slippers and how I had longed to be Hopestill or a girl just like her. Now, receiving her greeting, hearing her barren voice, I thought, "Why, it is her life that is ugly and has been from the beginning."

"What shall I do, Miss Pride?" I asked.

She deliberated the chess-board, not my question, and replied, "And how do you feel about it? Do you think she will be cured?"

I told her my opinion and then I waited, my heart palpitating at the sight of her as in her green beaver hat and black suit, whose nocturnal sobriety was relieved only by the white collar of her mannish shirt, she moved the men across the board. I knew that today after church, she was to have luncheon at the house of a Coolidge and that the guest of honor was to be a Mrs. Roosevelt, née Cabot. "Thunder!" she said suddenly. "I've made a mistake. You've rattled me and it's all spoiled. Well, Sonia, I would regret parting company with you, my dear girl, for I find your services useful and your manners steadily improve. I suppose there are other establishments besides the one your mother is in now? Of a different character where one would pay her keep. At any rate, I shall investigate."

She had set the men up to begin again and was referring to her manual, holding it at arm's length in the far-sightedness of age which she would admit to no one but me. I believed I was dismissed and turned to go, but she said, without taking her eyes from the diagram she was following, "Sonia, let us say for the sake of argument that I *do* agree to set your mother up in a private sanitarium: What returns will you make to me?"

Thinking that she wanted to know how I would repay the money, I replied, "I don't know what I *can* do for many years, Miss Pride. But perhaps I could set her up myself. I don't spend what you give me, you know."

She squinted in my direction. "My dear child, the pin money I give you wouldn't go very far in one of those places. Mind you, I know all about them. They're run by bloodsuckers and don't be told anything different. Mrs. Eppington's oldest daughter, who is named something remarkable like Margarine, though of course it isn't that, married a Russian who went quite mad and was sent off to one of those fashionable bedlams at a ruinous cost that led her eventually to opening a little tea-room in Newport, where all you could get for love or money, was some horrid red soup and salads made of Bartlett pears. Not that the marriage wouldn't have been absurd anyway. They had an apartment facing Washington Square, furnished as we don't furnish apartments in Boston, with couches that became beds and a bar in a closet, and I believe he had an icon, though he wasn't that sort of Russian. But I wander. No, Sonie, returns of that sort are not what I have in mind."

I started to speak, to assure her that I would not leave her. But she held up her hand for silence.

"If I undertake to support your mother as well as yourself, I shall be doing it with no thought of being paid back. I must repeat—although I am sure you return my devotion—that this is, I know, not much of a life for a girl your age. You have your moods, as we all do in our youth, our sentimental dreams of adventure, our fancied love affairs. Here, I've moved the rook too far." She changed the man's position. "You're unusually steady to be sure. I have only had inklings of a certain restiveness at times. I had it, for example, one evening not long ago, when you brought me that charming mountain laurel." She paused and glanced up at me. "Sonia, my father, a blunt man, but one who husbanded his words, brought me up in the belief that silence was the ideal policy, that honesty was next best, and that falsehood should be reserved for state occasions. For example, the only lie I ever heard him tell was to Mr. Charles Francis Adams' secretary who, under the impression that Papa was Mr. *Stanley* Pride, Consul General of Madrid, asked him to renew his acquaintance with the Secretary of the Navy at a dinner party at the Yacht Club. Papa said, 'I shall be delighted to renew my acquaintance with Mr. Adams.' He claimed that this was an equivocation rather than a direct lie, for he did not say Mr. *Charles Francis* Adams, and he could have meant Mr. Richard Chilton Adams or Mr. Archibald Revere Adams, two perfectly bona fide Adamses with whom he lunched every day at the Harvard Club. But silence, silence was what Papa chiefly counseled, and while I have so far as possible followed his precept, I must confess that there are times when you are a little *too* silent. Sometimes I cannot compass you. You become a cipher. I am afraid you will disappear altogether, vanish utterly. On that evening, for example, that you brought me the mountain laurel, I had the feeling while we talked that you were paying no attention to what you said. I did not ask you where you had been, though I had heard from Hopestill that you had not stayed for dinner, and I do not ask you now. But, my dear child, I cannot live with an image of you! If you are troubled by something, I implore you to let me know."

"That night," I said, "I had had too many cocktails at Hopestill's."

"I'm not entirely satisfied with that, but we shall let it go. You will keep me company, help me with my little book in the twilight of my life? You will not go away from Boston?"

"But I have no intention of going away from Boston!" I cried.

She drew her game to a close and glancing up at the clock which indicated twenty minutes before eleven, she waved her hand toward the cabinet where I went to pour out her sherry. I noticed that her hand shook; she seemed to shrink as I watched and her hand, curled into a trembling, beseeching cup, was like a beggar's, asking for alms. It was not the sherry that she reached out to seize, but it was myself. Putting the glass down beside the chess-board, she extended her old claw to me.

"Agree!" she cried. "Agree never to leave me until I die!" She smiled, but the terror of death was in her yellow eyes and in her voice, and although I took the proffered hand and smiled back at her, my whole soul retreated from her in the appalled vision of her awful dependence, her hideous cowardice. "Agree!" she was crying.

"I agree," I said, but my voice was unnatural and I could feel perspiration collecting on my upper lip.

"I thought you wouldn't fail me. Poor Hope failed me but I dare say it was partly my fault. Lord, I must get to church! I wish you could hear our new Reverend Jackson, from New Jersey, oddly enough, but he preaches admirably. Good-by." And she went from the room, her martial tread echoing with a decreasing resonance down the corridor until the diminuendo ceased with the opening and closing of the outer door. Ethel peered into the library to announce that Mac was ready.

On the way to Wolfburg, I was fretful, then scolded myself for my directionless discontent. My problem had been solved, and I could ask for nothing more. It was perhaps only the spring air that made me suddenly *wanderlustig*. Perhaps it was Nathan's preparations to leave for Paris that inspired me with thoughts of leaving Boston. He had often told me that he had money enough to pay my passage. I envied him his mobility; my double servitude, that to my mother and to Miss Pride, lay heavy on me, and now, since our conversation in the library this morning, the die was cast. I could not, morally, disappear. Just before we reached the asylum, I regained control of myself, said I loved my mother and I loved Miss Pride and Boston and that nothing could ever shake me from my resolve to live the rest of my life exactly as I was living it now.

My mother had been over her illness for some time, and as I waited in the corridor, I determined to outdo myself in tenderness and to tell her, if she was in despair, that she was to be moved soon to a house that she would like. One by one the visitors were summoned to the doctors' cells and I saw them then going off to the reception room, their hands full of flowers or fruit or magazines. And presently I was quite alone save for the tireless, ethereal voice warbling for Dr. Finkelstein and Dr. Short. A doctor crossed the hall and seeing me, said, "You aren't Miss Marburg, are you? Well, then, will you just step this way a moment?" We went into "my" doctor's office and my escort put his arm about my shoulder in a paternal affability. Another doctor besides mine was sitting on the window-ledge.

"Miss Marburg," said Dr. Tudor, "Dr. Burns, who spoke to you last winter about your mother, has presented his findings to us and we have been going over the case." He cleared his throat and said something in an undertone to his colleague at the window who then went to a filing case and brought back a bulging manila folder. "As you know, psychiatry is not a definitive science any more than medicine is. And diseased minds are as liable to relapse as are diseased bodies. And, if anything, they are more difficult to diagnose accurately. Now let us say we have concluded that a man with pulmonary trouble has fibrosis. His symptoms, blood-tests, x-rays corroborate our opinion. He is kept in bed sufficiently long to remedy the trouble and we let him get up. But his fever rises, he begins to cough blood. We put him through another examination and find that he has tuberculosis of the lungs. We were probably not wrong in the first place. He *did* have fibrosis, but the tubercula bacilli, present in everyone, were working under our very noses, so slyly that none of our tests registered their progress. And now we must change our offensive, go back to a point near the starting line and begin again. Sometimes this happens in diseases of the mind. Originally we called your mother a 'manic depressive' and we had hopes of her complete recovery by simple treatment. But recently, particularly since her last attack of bronchitis, she has at times revealed symptoms of another disease, that is, katatonia."

The doctors all were watching me, and I had the feeling that they were taking note of everything, that they saw, and afterwards would discuss, the slight tic that began at the corner of my right eye.

Dr. Tudor continued, "I must tell you frankly that what we have concluded is not hopeful. No treatment we know of can certainly arrest the course of katatonia. Two days ago, your mother, who is now in a room by herself, was seized with a violent attack of vomiting, after which a muscular rigidity set in which has continued with rare intervals of relaxation. Sleep is possible only if we give her opiates. Her hallucinations have increased and have become so diverse that they appear entirely unrelated to anything we know of in her history. It is bad news, Miss Marburg, but like all bad news, it is better to know it at once."

"Do you mean, sir," I said, "that my mother will never be well again?"

"We can't talk in positive terms like that, as I have said. Patients have recovered. Many have made partial recoveries. Your mother may be one of those fortunate people who do regain their health. But it will take a long time and we can promise you nothing."

"Does she know? I mean, is she . . ."

"You mean, is she unhappy. Subjectively, that is. Let me assure you that she is in a world of her own. She is frightened, yes, but nothing we can do, nothing anyone can do, can remove the cause of her fright."

"Perhaps I could! Perhaps if I took her away, back to Chichester, she would be better."

The doctor rose and came around his desk, standing over me with a benevolent smile that was yet somehow hasty as if he wished to draw our interview to a close. "Believe me, there is nothing you can do. For the time being, your visits will be of no use. She is very sick."

"Poor Mamma," I murmured.

"You go on home now. When we have anything to report, we'll drop you a line. Some day you can see her again."

"Some day? But when?"

"That, I can't say."

"Will you give her my flowers?" I asked him, holding out the waxy Easter lilies I had bought that morning at Mr. Quince's. Dr. Tudor laid them on his desk and, finished with my case, led me to the door. The corridor was silent, for all the other visitors had gone to their melancholy meetings. My footsteps on the hard, rubbery floor sounded wet and loud, and the sunshine which stopped halfway from the door seemed remote, a golden bay. The indefatigable voice pursued me to the door, calling after me, "Doctor *Fink*-ull-stein! Doctor Shor-ort! Doctor Baaxter!" I was conscious of the terrible permanence of the asylum: forever, in the same inflections, the voice would chant and bleat the names of the same doctors, would echo through the glistening halls where every surface and every shadow was rounded, where even the doctors, at their most precise, smoothed down the sharp edges of what they said. Only the shafts of sunlight were sharp, but they were laden with round motes.

Poor Mamma! The red room, now that I needed it, would not come. Instead, there came to me the kitchen in Chichester and the hot night I had lain on the floor at my mother's feet. Suddenly, with the same kind of uneasiness I had felt when I thought Father Mulcahy said "God's warning," rather than "Good morning," I believed that her change had come about through my own treachery. For several days my conscience did not allow my thoughts to stray from my crime, and it tormented me, saying, "You must not believe them when they tell you she isn't conscious of her misery." But at last I conquered the moral voice, and when I told Miss Pride that henceforth I should be free on Sundays to accompany her to church, and she did not ask me for any explanation, the recrudescence of the pain and remorse was momentary. For the time being, I had walled up my mother into the farthest recess of my mind, knowing that the time would come when I must let her out again.

4

I had only just learned to smoke. Like most tyros, mistaking the habit for an exciting vice, I had elaborate equipment: holders, lighters, cases, and expensive, unusual cigarettes with which I sometimes vapored through a whole evening without requiring any other entertainment than that of watching the smoke I expelled ascending in lively indirection, the thin columns expanding or splitting, and of feeling an occasional pain in my diaphragm when I inhaled deeply as if a weight had plummeted downward through my esophagus and simultaneously had delivered to my skull a faintly dizzying blow. My imagination, consigning insidious properties to the cigarettes as if tobacco were cousin to opium, through its perhaps intentional error, rendered to my thoughts a dreamy quality, the reality of their objects being interrupted just as my vision of the walls, the windows, the furniture was interrupted by the smoke. I experienced, as in illness, an imperviousness to time, feeling that I was an inviolable bystander before whose serene eyes the raging world catapulted through arbitrary, mechanized hours.

I was sitting one afternoon in the Concord cemetery, leaning against a mossy tree. Below me was a green, stagnant pool into which now and again fell a twig or pebble but it made no sound for the surface of the water was velvety with mold. From behind me came the sound of the gardener's lawn-mower and the occasional click of a trowel on stone. The faintest wind soughed in the branches and brought me the smell of pine-needles and lilies-of-the-valley which grew in profusion there amongst the graves. As I had come up the slope called "Authors' Ridge," I had seen tourists gazing respectfully at Emerson's clumsy pink quartz gravestone and at the slabs marked "Alcott." I had known by their pronunciation that they were outlanders, for they accented Thoreau on the last syllable and pronounced Alcott with a short "a." Miss Pride detested sight-seers who visited the cemeteries. One day she had seen a man set up a tripod and produce a great lot of photographer's contraptions to make a snapshot of Longfellow's sarcophagus in the Mount Vernon graveyard. Taking the law into her own hands, she accosted him and said, "Look here, sir, this is not permitted." A rude man, he asked for her authority, and she replied, "I just stepped out of my house, Elmwood. My name is Mamie Lowell." No longer interested in Longfellow, he turned his camera on her and before she could collect her wits, he had taken her picture, saying, "This is even better. I'd rather bring 'em back alive than dead."

I knew that I should go on to Hopestill's house where I was to meet Miss Pride, but I was too languorous to move and repeatedly said to myself as I fitted a new cigarette into my carved holder, a present from Kakosan, that this would be the last. Between puffs, I held the holder horizontal and mused on its giver. It had been a token of her gratitude for my introduction of her to the Countess and had been sent, fantastically enough, by messenger who, in the employ of the telegraph company, had appeared vexed to be the porter of a parcel wrapped in pale blue tissue paper through whose silver ribbons three dark violets had been passed. "It ain't a telegram," he said, not by way of information since there could be no doubt on that point, but to show me that the absurd kickshaw he handed to me was in no way comparable to the important yellow envelopes which it was his proper function to deliver and several of which now conspicuously protruded from his breast pocket.

Kakosan, along with the present, had sent a note in her characteristically inconsistent style: upon a calling card giving her name in Japanese characters which ran like red bacteria down one side, she had written in a neat commercial school hand, "For a swell pal."

She, like Morgan, had disappeared from the blue drawing-room after the cocktail party, although, as I knew from Hope-still, she still received invitations. I concluded that she did not want to see me, remembering her frightened whisper, "That's Sonie Marburg," as I went up the stairs. She had made several futile attempts to see Nathan who steadfastly refused to consider a reconciliation. I had seen her only once, by accident. We met at dusk one day as I was going home along Commonwealth Avenue and we stopped beside a false magnolia shrub that had just come into flower. The white petals were smudged with pink and a lilac color; the thick, broad leaves were stiff and glossy as if they had been varnished. We talked only of the flowers and of Ginger Rogers. But on the following day, she sent me a set of brushes in an ivory box which she asked me to give to Nathan in memory of her. She had promised, long before, to teach him to write Japanese.

Nathan was torn between the desire to keep the brushes and the desire to wound Kakosan by returning them. I persuaded him to keep them since they would be a souvenir of that aspect of her he had loved. It was some time before he ever used them, but when he did, practicing the few brush strokes he had learned from her, there came to the good side of his face a look of tenderness and longing, not for the person he no longer loved nor could love, but for the girl he had known in the beginning, had pursued like a bloodhound down the streets of Boston, hiding behind the subway kiosks as she, this still unknown beauty, stopped to buy fresh posies for her hair. Finally, after months of this delightful chase, he had accosted her at a street corner as they waited for the traffic to pass and had asked her if she knew of anyone who could give him lessons in Japanese. He would put down the brushes, pass his fingers over his marked cheek, and then would pour each of us a teacup of his violent sherry and tell me, for the thousandth time, that he would never love anyone but an Oriental woman again with the same kind of wonder that he had loved Yoshidasan in the first of those days.

I looked at my watch: at this very moment, Nathan's train for New York was leaving from the South Station. At midnight tomorrow, he would sail for France. I felt no particular sense of loss. This morning when I had told him good-by in his basement room, stripped of his personal gear, his books and trash and the photographs of Dostoievsky and Heine which had hung over his desk, I had, on an impulse, taken between my hands his mutilated face and kissed him on the lips, and my kiss was not only a farewell to him but a resolute farewell to the temptations he had put in my path which had attempted to make my staid feet nomadic.

I flung my cigarette into the slimy pond and got up. If there were time, before we went back to Boston, I would take Kurt for a run through the woods behind Hopestill's house. I hoped that I would be offered one of the rum cocktails which had been invented by Harry Morgan, the household's former *arbiter bibendi*. Miss Pride had been making a tour of the Concord gardens in the company of several people whom she did not like, including the Mesdames McAllister, and I was confident that she would find herself in need of a restorative and would suggest to her niece that she "concoct a little something for us."

The old lady, all alone, was sitting on the lawn in a cane-bottomed chair. She was reading and did not hear my footsteps on the driveway. I was struck by the singular composition of the picture before my eyes: the spare black figure central in the expanse of shining grass and behind her the white house with its pedimented windows flanked by green shutters and its paneled door which was slightly ajar; burnishing the whole scene, giving to it that final fillip which distinguishes art from nature, was the clear light of early summer as skillfully executed as Vermeer's sunshine. She looked up with a smile as I approached.

"I hope you have enjoyed Hawthorne's grave better than I have done the gardens. I have no horticultural principles, yet had the great misfortune of being taken in tow by Mrs. Bigelow who feels very strongly about *tulipes noire*. I could not comfort her at Charity Brewster's, where she was confronted by several specimens."

I laughed and asked if Hopestill had accompanied her and she replied, "No. I don't know where she is. There isn't a sign of life about the place. Not even her animal is here."

Turning her eyes once again to her book, she indicated that she had spent enough time on me and I left her, making my way round the house to the studio. I helped myself generously to whiskey from the bar and put a Brahms piano concerto on the automatic phonograph. There was a sweet flamboyance to the music; it was like a plump and tender hug into which I burrowed luxuriously. Whiskey and music, I reflected, especially when taken together, made time fly incredibly fast. When the long concerto was finished, it was growing dark. A little wind had come up, threatening a storm. The air itself, more than the dark clouds, presaged the arrival of the thunder and the rain. I went back to the house to see if Hopestill had returned. Miss Pride had gone inside and the lawn was bare again save for the deepening shadows of the apple trees along the drive. There was a note for me thrust into the knocker which read: "Undone by the gardens I have gone upstairs to rest. When our tardy hostess arrives, tell her that since we have been given no tea, we shall expect dinner. Lucy Pride."

An hour later, just after the storm broke, Hopestill, wild-eyed, tousled, burst into the studio. She did not take off her wet raincoat but sprawled in a vermilion chair and the legs she stretched out before her were clad in jodhpurs, a fact that did not strike me as odd probably because her whiskey had rendered me impervious to surprise. Nor was I taken aback when she asked for the decanter of whiskey and took three large drinks neat and with a masculine rapidity.

"Do you believe in supernatural things?" she said quickly in a shrill voice and leaned forward with an eager look in her harried face.

"Some, I suppose." I regretted that I had drunk so much. I felt that there was something amiss and could not capture it.

"I mean, do you think hate can kill? There is a story about a woman who makes a doll in the image of another woman and burns it and the woman comes to some dire end, I think.

It's been so long ago that I can't remember, but lately it's been haunting me."

"I don't believe in *that*," I said.

"Where's Aunt Lucy?" she asked, sitting up. "I want to ask her something. I want her to give me Mercy."

"What about Kurt? He'd kill her."

"Kurt? Oh . . ." Although she had poured herself a fourth glass of whiskey, she put it down before it had reached her lips and her face became instantly as pale as moonlight. "Kurt is dead," she said.

"Dead?"

"He was killed this afternoon . . . run over on the Bedford road."

"Was he off his leash? Weren't you with him?"

"No. He had been with me. I was riding. I had been running my horse and he was keeping up with me. Something frightened Chiquita—you know that little Palomino mare?—and she stopped suddenly and reared. Kurt went tearing back, here I thought, but just now, as I was coming up the road, I found him."

"I wish you hadn't let him go with you," I cried. "Why didn't you follow him? Why were you a whole afternoon going after him, Hopestill? Didn't you care?"

"I had had a little accident and couldn't get back. Chiquita threw me."

Now I saw the riding trousers for the first time, wondered even in my alarm when she had got them to fit her now misshapen body, and my voice issued as a scream. "You are ill, then!"

"Yes, I suppose that I shall be very ill."

"I must call Philip." I stumbled to the door.

"Don't! He'll think I did it intentionally." She slipped off her short boots and her damp socks. "And of course I did. I made Chiquita do it. Once, I remembered, she threw me because I was wearing some Indian bracelets which rattled and the sound made her wild. I wore them today." And she pulled up the sleeve of her raincoat to show me three thin silver bands.

"You hadn't any right!" I said furiously and ran out and round to the house where, without disturbing Miss Pride, I telephoned Philip in Boston. As I waited for the sound of his voice, I could think of nothing but Hopestill's nimble feet as they had looked just now on the bare floor. They were somehow aged, for the skin was stretched and blanched and over the sharply knuckled bones, the tracery of veins stood out, blue and vermicular. When I had got Philip and he promised to come at once, I went outside and stood in the drenching rain under an apple tree and over and over again hummed the phrase from *The Well-Tempered Clavichord*, the favorite of the anonymous block-flute player. And I did not leave my dripping sanctuary until, three-quarters of an hour later, the lights of Philip's car came bobbing through the trees.

When I went back to the cemetery in October, half a year after her death, I could not remember at once where Hopestill was buried. At the time of her funeral, I had not heeded any landmarks, and all I could see, in my mind's eye, was her grave as it was yawning for her casket and, a few minutes afterward, as it became a fresh mound and pile of flowers. Built on a hill, this graveyard of a small New Hampshire town was cut by a spiraling road into four or five sloping tiers, all similar in appearance. Identical paths ran parallel to each other and every tree, spruce, or cedar, or elm, was mimicked by a twin. Hopestill was at the very top, beside her father. They were farther up even than the graveyard's only mausoleum which, in a splendor of marble and genuflecting angels, housed the bones of a distinguished bishop, native of the town, who had returned from the wide world to settle in the dust of his last vestments under his boyhood's earth. Miss Pride, the connoisseur of graves, had remarked as we drove away, "I'd *walk* if I were buried there. From what you can tell of his Grace's taste from that outrageous excrescence, he must have been a trying party when he was alive. I dare say he went in for parlor statuary."

It had begun to snow long before the bus that brought me had bumbled into the little town, and by the time I had found her stone, it was covered over by a deep layer of white which was replaced by another as soon as I had brushed it off. Indeed, there was no need for me to see it, for I clearly remembered the bare factual legend engraved on the plain granite oblong: that she had been born some time and given the name Hopestill Pride Mather, and, being married, had taken McAllister, and that she had died a little more than twenty-one years after her birth. Nor was I, uncovering it and shielding it from the snow-fall by my hunched-up body, urged by this physical symbol into recalling her better. I could not, as I crouched there, gazing, feel any harmony with her soul as it existed now or with her soul as it was arrested when her breathing stopped. I had not the faith as had her loving old friend the Admiral that her "spirit" still lived, though what he meant, approximately, was, "I have faith that Hopestill's soul continues its existence. What I *know* exists is my faith." But I granted the possibility that a soul might continue to operate in some imponderable place. There was, though, no affective coloring to the hypothesis: the grave could not become to me more than a little elevation of the soil and a flat stone and the skeleton which I visual-ized could not be hers but merely "skeleton," merely "heap of bones," and it was almost an accident that these bones had been the framework of someone I had known. I wondered when, in her grave, her hair had stopped growing and when its gloss was gone and if its dust were gray or red. I could see it yet, blandished by every change of light, the only remnant of her loveliness left when she lay in the fern-fingered casket. I shivered with the cold and with the memory of my mother's obsession over Ivan's hair which she thought had grown long in the water and was tangled with seaweed.

I had come this long way in the cold to finish her history, in a sense. I thought that if I saw her simple, conventional grave, like all the others, I would be able to efface from my memory the unhappiness of her last days. Although passion was with-held from me as I knelt and I was conscious of the cold which, chilling the dramatic core of my errand, made it folly, tears fell from my eyes, as tame as the windless snow. But they were tears almost of ennui because the death for which she had made so wild a preparation, no longer shocked me but seemed a languid petering out, like the expiring fire from which there comes a final flare and hiss of resin and then is ash. My weeping did not last and when I stood up, I saw that for a moment the snow had stopped and the air was clear enough for me to see the village's green roofs and white church spires.

The snow returned, colder than before, and obliterated the hill opposite the one on which the graveyard was built. A wind came down from the north, swift and soundless. As clearly as though it were borne by the rushing air, I heard the block-flute piping *The Well-Tempered Clavichord*, and trembled, recollecting how, all during her illness I had sat in my room on Pinckney Street humming it over and over again so that I would not hear the telephone which at any moment might bring us word that she had died. That revenant, whose single tune had joined my very blood so that its floating through the canals of my body depended for the tranquillity of its progress upon the cadences of that passage of music, purling in my ungifted throat, brought back, as the sight of her grave had been powerless to do, the person of Hopestill, not as the shrunken creature in the casket nor as the handsome girl of Boston, but of the little girl with the long red hair in the dining-room at the Hotel Barstow. All the time she had lain in the hospital dying, I had been able to think only of her bare feet and of the green slippers which I had defaced and slashed and of her recollection, that night in the studio, of the effigy-burning in *The Return of the Native*. Reason told me I was laughable and self-important in feeling myself an element in her death, but superstition rebuked me, made me deafen myself to the telephone with Bach.

She had been unrecognizable in her casket: her hair had been curled when half its beauty had been its straightness. A little rouge had been put on her lips which had never before been so treated. She was dressed in her wedding gown; she looked pinked and cooked like a frivolous cake. Mrs. Frothingham whispered in someone's ear, "Such a pretty girl to make such a plain corpse!"

I sat behind the straight, black backs of Philip and Miss Pride. Once Philip's shoulders lifted with a sigh. The Countess and Amy Brooks, the Hornblowers, the Admiral, all the cousins, and the friends wept. The McAllisters were rigid like Miss Pride and Philip. The organ music seared me as it had done the day Hopestill married, and the bright, hot sunlight on the wooden floor of the little church stole into my very brain, burning it like liquid gold.

The minister said: "One thing have I desired of the Lord, which I will require; even that I may dwell in the house of the Lord all the days of my life, to behold the fair beauty of the Lord and to visit his temple. For in the time of trouble he shall hide me in his tabernacle; yea, in the secret place of his dwelling shall he hide me, and set me up upon a rock of stone." The even voice and the words were cooling and when we knelt to pray, I mouthed the word "tabernacle" against the smooth wood of the pew ahead of me.

Outside, in the merciless sunlight, the guests, with their faces streaming, were grouped about on the lawn. The white spire of the church pointed up to a sky where shiny cumulus clouds were approached by gray rain clouds. It was impossible to tell which went behind; the rain was coming, we all knew, and we waited impatiently for the signal to move on to the cemetery. It had been quite a nuisance for some people to drive all the way up on such an uncomfortable day. Of course, it was understandable that Hopestill should want to be buried by her father. Even so . . . Little conversations, far removed from the dead girl, had started up everywhere, and I heard a woman say to her companion, "He is very interesting, I suppose, but he is so alien to anything I have ever known. He has the word 'success' written all over him like the measles and his children have come down with it, too. The boy is very fat and was unmercifully teased at St. Marks, but somehow or other he has got in with Alexander Hornblower's son and they're as thick as thieves. So he gets on, you see."

The Countess, more moved, I felt, than anyone except perhaps myself and Philip, pressed a point-lace handkerchief to her eyes and said to Miss Pride, "Ah! Let us pretend we are children again and are being escorted by our mammas for the first time through the Tuileries. Wasn't it wonderful! Wasn't it bliss to be ignorant then and not . . ."

But now the casket was borne out and she did not finish. As we got into the automobiles, the merging of the clouds was completed; no blue sky was visible. A heavy rain fell, but in five minutes, by the time we had reached the gate of the cemetery, the storm was over.

Soon after the funeral, Miss Pride and I left Boston to spend the summer in Mattapoisett. She had not liked, she said, to leave me alone in Cambridge again and although it might seem strange, at her age, to begin going to a new place, she had been rejuvenated, she said, by our work on the memoirs. We had not spoken of Hopestill at any time.

I started down the graveyard hill. When I reached the road, my depression lifted and I was reassured that what I had just left *was* a tabernacle. I felt strangely energetic and as if I had completed a difficult task. It had not snowed here, but there was the bluish fog of autumn between the trees; there was the smell, acrid and like the moist hull of a walnut, of maple leaves that had begun to fall. From a second rise, the last little hill between the graveyard and the town, I saw that the mist was vanishing as I watched, and the sun was coming out. Snug and rubicund, splattered with scarlet and golden leaves, the earth lay at its meridian.

It was late afternoon when I got off the bus on Tremont Street and I hurried. Miss Pride was giving a little dinner party, in honor of the engagement of Amy Brooks to Edward Pingrey. She had invited the Countess and the Admiral, Baron Kalenkoff, Mr. James, the Arthur Hornblowers, and the Norwegian water-color painter. We were to start with cocktails made with the second best gin, but during dinner were to have the best champagne. "Champagne, you know, shouldn't be kept too long," she had said. "I have had this two years and I really must have it drunk up."

As I crossed the Common, where the leaves were curly underfoot and the squirrels were lively in their heyday, I glanced up at the State House dome still shining brightly in the last rays of the descending sun. I used it now as a sort of register for the light. My glance told me that if I made haste, that same glow burnishing the golden sphere would still be on my windows. I hurried on across Beacon Street, down Mount Vernon, then turned into Louisburg Square. For a few minutes I stood at the farthest corner, looking at Miss Pride's house through the high black iron palings with their tops shaped alternately like sword points and sword hilts. Every seventeenth bloomed with a flower on a stalk like Grecian drapery. Frost had made the beds of myrtle droop, but the stunted evergreens were bright. Small Aristides and Christopher Columbus regarded one another across the expanse of dead grass.

The sun had left the lower windows of our house, but mine and Hopestill's on the third floor, and the servants' above were red. I knew that within, the Cape Cod lighter on my hearth would cast forth blinding spears of light. For a moment, the scene seemed remembered, not perceived; it was as if some intelligence in my eyes themselves believed that they would take in the house with its green shutters, its brass letter-slot on the pure white door for the last time now and therefore saw all details overlaid by a film, by an impalpable smoke like the twilight which presently would absorb the sun. Perhaps the time had passed and I could not, save in imagination, traverse the short cobblestoned space between my vantage point and the door to which I owned a key. But then, immediately upon the full development of my feeling that Boston was a part of the past for me just as it was so completely for Hopestill, I was brought back to the present time and knew again that these realities had not diminished in size and in distinctness. Years hence they would perhaps, after Miss Pride was dead, and they would be like the trees of an avenue which perspective reduces and shrouds.

Through the doorway of the building on which an inscription read: *Per Angusta ad Augusta*, a man and woman emerged. The man put on his bowler, then drew on his gray suède gloves. Their voices carried across the quiet square.

"Is it too late to look in at Lucy Pride's?" asked the woman.

Her companion took his watch out of his pocket. "It's six. Wouldn't that rush us? I dare say it wouldn't, but even so I'd rather not at this hour. Lincoln Nephews is usually the only one left by this time, the old loiterer."

The woman laughed. "You're only angry because he gave you your comeuppance in charades."

"*Ulalume!*" cried the man with bitter scorn. "Who but the most egotistical pedant would act out such a thing as that!"

They moved on down Pinckney Street and I ran across to Miss Pride's house. As I fitted my key to the lock, I noticed that the last of the rosy light had gone and that over the steep street lay a topaz patina. Far below, the fragment of the Charles was pure, cold, blue, and across it, a single sail, like a perfect iceberg, moved slowly. From within the house came the Admiral's voice, so close to me I knew he was about to open the door and I withdrew my key to wait for him. "Good-by, Lucy. I'll be back in an hour. Back to Lucy's cot where she dwells in untrodden ways. Ma'am, that was a bang-up tea you gave me. I'm so stimulated I could go waltzing and not peter out till morning."

"Nonsense," came Miss Pride's voice. "My rum cakes have gone to your head, Lincoln. Run along now, do." The Admiral laughed and with him laughed his friend. "Ha! Ha!" her rare bark burst upon me and when the old man opened the door, he found me on the step laughing too, for what reason I was not sure. She was there, behind him. Under the lamplight, she appeared vigorous and even youthful, as if her age which she had passed on to her niece were buried along with Hopestill in New Hampshire. She looked again as she had done when I was five years old in Chichester; her flat, omniscient eyes seized mine, grappled with my brain, extracted what was there, and her meager lips said, "Sonie, my dear, come out of the cold. You'll never get to be an old lady if you don't take care of yourself."

THE MOUNTAIN LION

A friend loveth at all times, and a brother is born for adversity.

PROVERBS XVII, 17.

Chapter One

RALPH WAS ten and Molly was eight when they had scarlet fever. It left them with some sort of glandular disorder which was not malignant, but which kept them half poisoned most of the time and caused them, frequently, to have such bad nosebleeds that they had to be sent home from school. It nearly always happened that their nosebleeds came at the same time. Ralph, bleeding profusely, would stumble into the corridor to find Molly coming out of the third-grade room, a handkerchief held in a sodden bunch at her nose. Their mother could not bear the sight of blood and her distress, on seeing them straggle up the driveway, never lessened even when these midday homecomings had become a habit. Each time, she implored them to telephone her so that she could send Miguel, the foreman, in the car. But they never did, for they liked the walk home, feeling all the way a pleasant superiority to their sisters, Leah and Rachel, who were still cooped up in school with nothing at all to do but chew paraffin on the sly.

In the September following their illness and on the day Grandpa Kenyon, their mother's stepfather, was to arrive for his annual visit, they met with gushing noses outside the art supply room and seeing Miss Holihan through the open door at the paper cutter with a sheaf of manila paper, they walked on tiptoe, giggling silently until they reached the stairs and then they ran. Once outside in the empty school-yard, they congratulated each other; Molly would not have to draw an apple on Miss Holihan's paper and Ralph would miss both Palmer Method and singing. Actually, they would gain nothing by getting home some hours before the school bus since Grandpa's train did not get into Los Angeles until the middle of the afternoon and then it was another hour before Miguel brought him up the driveway in the Willys Knight. So they dawdled more slowly than usual, not certain that they would find anything to absorb them at home, but certain, on the other hand, that their mother, fussing and chattering as she always did when they had company, would be as cross as sixty when she saw them.

It was a narrow, winding country road they walked along. On either side ran clear small ditches, making a mouth-like sound. Now and again they stopped and dipped their handkerchiefs and wiped the blood off their hands and arms. On their right was an orange grove from which, at all seasons of the year, came a heavy fragrance and where they sometimes saw flocks of such bright, unusual birds that they thought they must have flown up from the South Seas or westward from Japan. Some of the little pyramidal trees were always in bloom and some were always bearing fruit. There was a man on a ladder in the grove today and he turned when he heard them coming. He took off his hat and wiped his forehead on the sleeve of his black shirt and called, "Hello, you kiddoes," but as he was a Mexican, they did not reply and scuttered on, terrified, until they no longer heard his derisive laugh.

Next they passed Mr. Vogelman's huge clean dairy. Mr. Vogelman was a fat German who wore a white coverall and who had once been stoned by a group of second-graders when they learned what the Huns had done to the Belgians. Their mothers, fearing that he might take his revenge by treating the milk with tuberculosis germs, had written him an apology. But as the demonstration had taken place on Hallowe'en, Mr. Vogelman had misconstrued it and did not understand the letter at all. He had Guernseys whose hides gleamed in the sun like a metal, not so yellow as a banana and not so blue as milk, but something in between. Today there was a new calf near the fence, its fawn-like face wearing a look of melancholy surprise when it saw the human children staring. Its outraged mother bellowed at them, her great black nostrils hugely dilated, and they ran away for, although they would never have admitted it, they were afraid of cows. They knew a joke about a cow which they had read in *The American Boy*, and when they were safely beyond the pasture, they recited it as a dialogue:

Ralph: What are shoes made of?
Molly: Hide.
Ralph: Hide? Why should I hide?
Molly: Hide! Hide! The cow's outside!
Ralph: Oh, let the old cow come in. I'm not afraid.

They laughed so hard that they had to sit down in the road holding their stomachs and the laughter made their noses bleed twice as fast so that, convulsed and aching, they dabbed desperately with their handkerchiefs, screaming with pain, "Oh! Oh!" Finally, when they were sobered, Ralph said, "I guess I'll tell that joke to Grandpa," and Molly said, "Me too." Of late, Ralph had had moments of irritation with her: often, when he had finished telling a joke or a fact, she would repeat exactly what he had said immediately afterward so that there was no time for people either to laugh or to marvel. And not only that, but she had countless times told his dreams, pretending that they were her own. He did not want the joke about the cow to fall flat and so, after a reluctant pause, he agreed to let her tell it with him as they had recited it just now. It was not as long as one of the darky pieces Leah and Rachel spoke together, but it was so much funnier that they were sure Grandpa could not fail to laugh in that big, roaring way of his, slapping his knee and saying, "By George, that's a good one."

They proceeded, thinking of Grandpa, joyfully scuffing the white dust of the road until their oxfords were all powdery, even the shoelaces. Next to the dairy was a deep, dry arroyo called "the Wash." It had been hollowed out by a flood that had come in the spring of the year Leah was three, but they had so often heard the details of its devastation that they were certain their impressions came from memory and not from their mother's and her friends' talk when there was nothing new to discuss and they had to return to the thrills of the past. Mr. Fawcett had gone across a raging creek on a horse named Babe, long since dead, to rescue an aged woman whose house was later washed away. He brought her home flung over his saddle like a gunny sack of feed and gave her artificial respiration on the kitchen floor. Thousands and thousands of finches came out of the pouring rain to perch on the front porch; there were so many Father said it looked like a regular bird sanctuary; Fuschia was baking a cherry pie and Father asked her if she wanted four and twenty finches to put in it. A grapefruit tree came floating right down the driveway, roots and all, and Father planted it beside the solar tank. Every year it bore one grapefruit, which was smaller than a golf ball and almost as hard.

On the floor of the Wash, Ralph and Molly could find bright-colored stones, pink and green and yellow and blue. After a heavy rain, there was sometimes fool's gold in the puddles. Strange harsh shallow-rooted flowers grew all over the steep slopes and clumps of mallow that yielded bitter milk. There was one place where the mud dried and cracked into wedges like pieces of pie and when Molly was very small, she thought that this was where the sandwiches lived. All mystery and evil came from the Wash. Those smooth colored stones they gathered were really stolen jewels and the thief was a coal-black Skalawag who slept in the daytime in Mr. Vogelman's cornbin but kept watch at night. They did not venture down into the Wash when they had nosebleeds because the Skalawag could smell blood, no matter how far away he was, and he would get up and come legging it after them. So they passed it quickly with sidelong glances. Last autumn, when they had taken Grandpa Kenyon to see the Wash, he had said, "Well, now, that's something like it. There's too damn much green in this here California. But that dried-up little old crick bed down there makes me think of a place that *is* a place." He swept his black eyes round the scene and breathed shallowly as if the sweetness of the orange blossoms offended him and he said, "To think there ain't any winter here! Why, I'd as lief go to hell in a handbasket as not to see the first snow fly." The children were a little angry and shy and sensing this he explained to them—though they did not understand what he meant—that Nature here offered a man no real challenge. "You take that place of mine in the Panhandle. Nature ain't any ornrier anywhere in the world than she is right there, but she's a blooming belle of a fighter." When he had bought the land, there had not been a drop of water on the whole forty-five thousand acres of it, not a stream, not a pond. Everyone said he was a boob to buy it. But he turned in and bought it anyhow and then he took a little forked switch of holly and he chose a place on a rise just to the west of where he meant to build his house. He stood there with his holly wand, holding a fork of it in either hand. By and by, the rod bent down: where she showed him, there was a deep clear spring that had never yet gone dry.

The Wash, after that, had a new meaning for Ralph and Molly and they came to believe that the Skalawag was so watchful because he feared someone might come with a divining rod and once water was found, all his gems would be washed away. And now, too, whenever they went past, they thought of Grandpa's ranch in the Panhandle and Ralph, sighing, would say, "Golly *Moses*, I'd like to go out West." For they believed Grandpa Kenyon when he told them that California was not the West but was a separate thing like Florida and Washington, D. C.

For example, out West you would not find such falderal as Miss Runyon went in for. Miss Runyon lived next to the Wash in a little white house with green shutters and begonia in all the windows and Molly had loved it before Grandpa called it "a devil of a note." The flower garden came straight down to the road and standing among the beds of phlox and bachelor's buttons and oxalis were all sorts of curious creatures: a huge green frog, three brownies, a duck and four ducklings, two bluebirds as big as cats, a little Dutch girl in a sunbonnet, and a totem pole. There was a sign over the front door of the house which said "Dew Drop Inn." Next to the house was a doghouse built exactly like Dew Drop Inn and over its door was a sign that said "Dun Rovin" because Miss Runyon's sheep dog was named Rover. Under the eaves on the front porch was a bird house built like the other two but its name was not so ingenious: it was simply called "Jennie Wren, Her House."

Miss Runyon was the postmistress and was known as a character. She drove an automobile herself which she called "Mac"—short for "Machine" which she humorously pronounced "MacHeinie." She ate neither meat nor spices, for she was a follower of Dr. Kellogg. She occasionally invited the Fawcetts to a picnic supper on her lawn and served them hamburgers which were really made of Grape Nuts agglutinated with imitation calves'-foot jelly. She always came on Sunday afternoon to read their paper and made no secret of the fact that she liked the funnies as well as any child, reading them with the same unamused absorption that Ralph and Molly and Leah and Rachel did. Once she said that she was tired to death of Elmer Tuggle and his everlasting baseball mitt; Happy Hooligan was her favorite. In spite of her aggressive good nature, she was very timid and could not sleep alone in a house, so she had living with her a little Japanese woman named Mrs.

Haisan. If ever Mrs. Haisan had to be away, Leah and Rachel went there to sleep, although they never wanted to, for the first time they stayed with her, she suddenly looked up from *McCall's* in the middle of the evening and said tensely, "Hark! I heard a human swallow!" Ralph and Molly thought it was likely that it had been the Skalawag swallowing and the possibilities of *what* he had been swallowing were so numerous and terrifying that they could not hear the word without trembling.

It was thought, jestingly, by Mrs. Follansbee, the pastor's wife, that Miss Runyon had set her cap for Mr. Kenyon, part of this supposition being based on the rhyming of the two names; and it was true that several times during his visits she had invited them all to come and take "pot luck" with her but they never went, for as Mrs. Fawcett said in the bosom of her family, "I am sure I don't know what a hearty eater like Mr. Kenyon would do if he had to have an evening meal of cereal, I don't care how she disguised it."

Ralph thought perhaps he could tell Grandpa a funny story about Miss Runyon, not a true one but one in which he just used her name, and he stood leaning upon the picket fence, pondering and allowing his nose to drip on the palings so that two of them looked like spears that had struck home. Or maybe he could tell one about Mrs. Haisan. Mrs. Haisan had two children about his and Molly's age who lived with their aunt, a tiny little thing who was Mrs. Fawcett's washerwoman. Their names were Maisol and Maisako and one of them had been born on the Fourth of July and the other on April Fool's Day. One terrible day they had come with Hana and had made Ralph and Molly go down to the watermelon patch with them and not only had they cut up an unripe watermelon with a putty knife but they had said things and hinted at others so awful that Ralph and Molly had to fight them. They won very easily, of course, because the Jap kids were much smaller.

Ralph could not think of a single joke except the one about the cow. He thumbed his nose at Miss Runyon's house and chanted, "Runyon todunyon tianigo sunyon, tee-legged, tie-legged, bowlegged Runyon!" And then, seizing his sister by the hand, he ran like the wind because simultaneously Mrs. Haisan had appeared at the door of Dew Drop Inn and Rover at his door, and while Rover was as harmless as a ladybug and

Mrs. Haisan more than likely had only wanted to give them a candied kumquat, it was pleasanter to think that they were rushing out in anger like the Skalawag, and as soon as the house was no longer in sight, Ralph knelt down and put his ear to the road and jumping up cried, "Hey! They're a-gainin' on us!" and they did not stop running until they had turned down their own road.

When they had gone a hundred steps, they could see the palm trees that marked the boundary of their land. On this last stretch, Molly always thought for some reason of Redondo Beach where they went for a few weeks at the end of the summer. Looking up into the blank blue sky, she could feel that she was barefoot in the hot sand, hunting starfish and sand dollars, hearing the cries of the frightened ladies to their wading children who petulantly cried back that the waves were not high. The thought of the beach made her restlessly nostalgic and sometimes made her whimper, because she always remembered a feeling of queer and somehow pleasant horror when once a gull had winked at her and she had seen that his lower eyelid moved and not the upper one. But today she did not cry: Ralph was too gay, she knew, to comfort her and that was the only pleasure in crying, to be embraced by him and breathe in his acrid smell of leather braces and serge and to feel, shuddering, the touch of his warty hands on her face. It was always possible for her to will herself not to think sadly of the beach but to think instead of her dead father, of whom she had no memories but only the knowledge that he was up in the sky with Jesus and would miraculously recognize her when she came to heaven even though she had not been born when he died. This was the most thrilling thought she ever had and it had made her almost delirious ever since the day she and Ralph agreed not to die until he was ninety-nine and she was ninety-seven so that when they got up there they would look much older than their father who had died at the age of thirty-six.

As soon as they turned in the drive, Ralph began the game of Dead Horse. He said, "I saw a dead horse lying in the road." Molly answered, "I one it," and they went on: "I two it." "I three it." Just as they got to the side of the front porch, Ralph cried out, "I eight it," and Molly screamed hysterically, "Mother! Ralph ate a dead horse *again*!" But their mother was not sitting on the front porch as she usually was, and they looked at each other in numb embarrassment.

They should have known that she would be in the kitchen, preparing for Grandpa. Now they could hear her bustling across the front hall in her French-heeled slippers, anticipating what she would see and crying, "Oh, I declare I just don't know!" And then she stood in the screen door, arms akimbo at her small waist in her pearl-gray skirt, unable to decide whether to be angry or worried, too upset for a moment to utter a word. The children waited on the bottom step like well-mannered dogs and their mother, seeing their humility, chose to be anxious and flew down the steps, embracing them but carefully so that she would not stain her white smocked shirtwaist. She smelled of orris root and gingerbread and the children, sniffing, sensed the arrival of company even more than they had when they saw Miguel drive out this morning to meet the train. He had gone early to shop for delicacies in the Los Angeles markets; among other things, they were going to have black cherries and Turkish Delight.

"Oh, the poor chicks!" she cried, her blue eyes quickly full of tears. "Oh, dearies, *why* didn't you telephone? *Why* must you aggravate your mother?"

Molly said, "If we had telephoned it would have been silly because Miguel isn't here and neither is the car and even if the car was here it would still be silly because nobody but Miguel can drive it."

Molly's logic always made Mrs. Fawcett angry and now she drove them into the house and upstairs to the bathroom, ejaculating unfinished sentences: "I simply never . . . !" "No matter how hard I try . . . !" "Today of all days in the year . . . !"

The nosebleeds almost always stopped as soon as they got home, a phenomenon that obscurely vexed Mrs. Fawcett, and once she had spoken of it in their presence to Mr. Follansbee, who had replied, with a catarrhal chuckle, "Well, you know, Rose, that puts me in mind of my sainted mother who was stone deaf *except* when she wanted to hear something." Neither Ralph nor Molly had any idea what he meant but they caught an undertone of ridicule in his voice, and fearing and hating him, they went up to Ralph's room where each of them printed

"Rev. Follansbee" seven times on sheets of drawing paper and then burned the papers in the gilt Buddha incense burner.

Washed and dressed in their company clothes, they went outdoors and sat under the umbrella tree playing mumbly-peg, hurriedly concealing the knife when their mother came to the door to call some warning about their clean clothes or getting too much sunlight. Mumbly-peg was forbidden as everything was that was attended by the least possibility of danger, for Grandfather Bonney, their real grandfather, had died of blood poisoning. José, the gardener, was trimming the palm trees, and as he deftly wielded his banana knife he sang songs which they knew were bad although they could not understand a word of them since he sang in Spanish. They knew, because he was a bad man. Once Rachel had dreamed that he pursued her on a bicycle without holding his hands on the handlebars, that same banana knife between his teeth, one hand brandishing a monkey wrench and the other the Civil War saber that had belonged to Great-uncle Harry Fawcett, about whom not another fact was known. And once José had called Ralph a son-of-a-gun and threatened to burn his eyes out with a red-hot poker if he took any more berries off the bittersweet for his pea shooter.

Budge, the kindly cat, lay sleeping on the rim of the frog pond, and the only kitten that had been spared her out of her last litter gazed fixedly down into the slimy green water. Mrs. Fawcett, who did not like animals even in their own place, believed that Budge had brought the scarlet fever germs to Ralph and Molly, for goodness only knew what sort of houses she visited in her search for food and tomcats, and she would have had her destroyed if Ralph had not heard her talking with Miguel under his windows one morning when he was thought to be asleep. Weak with fever, he tottered to the window and called down the stern promise that if Budge were not still on the place when he got well, he would leave at once for the Panhandle and would never come back in a thousand million years. There were times when Mrs. Fawcett feared for the reason of her two younger children: they had natures of such cold determination that she trembled to think what they might do if they were crossed in a matter very close to their hearts. She could never imagine where they had got this streak, certainly not from her side of the family, and although Mr. Fawcett had by no means been a mollycoddle, he had been very mild-mannered and had always been able to see the other fellow's side of an argument. Budge remained. And then the astonishing Molly had literally read her mother's mind one evening. Mrs. Fawcett was looking at Budge asleep on the hearth and Molly said, "If anything ever happens to Budge, like poison or something, I'm going to set the pumphouse on fire."

From the cool-looking house—the dark green blinds were drawn to keep out the sun, though the turquoise berry was so dense it admitted little light—came the dulled sounds of Mrs. Fawcett and Fuschia as they made the dinner. They had been cooking for two days. They had made pineapple upside-down cake, boiled dressing, potato salad, beet pickles, baked beans, brown bread, sugar cookies, lady fingers, Sally Lunn, and temperance punch. Fuschia had brought in the new Schmierkäse that had been swinging for three days in its muslin bag in the icehouse and she had got six bottles of grape juice from the preserve closet to put in the refrigerator. Ralph and Molly, the afternoon before, had cracked a bowl full of last year's walnuts from their own grove and today Fuschia had glazed the whole meats and put the broken ones into penuche. The duck was in the oven, baking in a bath of orange juice. Before school, Leah and Rachel had polished the Bonney silver and had laid out the morning-glory tablecloth.

The afternoon seemed to have no end to it and yet the children were not really impatient to have it pass, for looking forward to Grandpa was in some ways as pleasant as having him there in the house. The sun appeared to remain in exactly the same position and the shadow of the umbrella tree to be unalterable. The bees, restless in the blossoms of the lippia lawn, and the humming birds, lancing the turquoise berries, worked at top speed as though eternity were not time enough to accomplish all they had to do. Mrs. Fawcett and Fuschia were forever softly banging things and chirping in muted screams, and José was forever at his palm trees. It was very quiet. The Mexicans harvesting the walnuts in the grove were silent. Once a dog began to bark and stopped so suddenly it was as if someone had seized his jaws and held them together. "That's Schöneshund," said Ralph. Schöneshund was a mean and hideous mastiff owned by the German family next door and Mrs. Fawcett was never willing to allow that the name had been chosen ironically; she preferred to think that the Freudenburgs simply did not know any better, for they were not "our sort." "If I could not have a carpet in my parlor," she said, "I would have some sort of inexpensive grass rug, or I would leave the floors bare. I certainly would not have linoleum." Ralph, identifying Schöneshund's bark today, wondered suddenly if Grandpa had any dogs on any of his ranches and he regretted that in the years past he had asked the old man so few questions that he knew very little about him. The two weeks he was here were always so short. Too many new impressions were crowded into the dazzling days, the smells of school that he had forgotten during the summer, the frightening complexities of the new arithmetic book, the surprise of finding in his lunchbox a hard-boiled egg colored magenta with beet-pickle juice, and over it all, the wonder of the rich old man who was different from anyone else in the world. Always before he had been too unbearably excited to plan a way to catch one of these bright hours, but he promised himself that this year he would gather facts to think about in the winter: the kinds and the names of Grandpa's dogs for one thing, whether he had ever been to a prize fight, if he had always had a beard, the name of the town in England where he had been born, and how many silver dollars he could carry in his money belt at one time.

The sun, in time, brutalized even José, and he stopped singing and worked more slowly. The children's game was languid and they had given it up long before the school bus came and Leah and Rachel trudged down the driveway, swinging their schoolbags in one hand and their lunchboxes in the other. They were cross at Ralph and Molly for coming home early and did not speak but went directly into the house and appeared half an hour later, bathed and dressed in the new Scotch plaid tissue gingham dresses that Aunt Kathleen had sent them from Marshall Field's. They came out to pick dahlias for the parlor and for the table. They walked past without looking at their sister and brother. Rachel said, "I *was* going to give Molly my extra Cashmere Bouquet just out of the kindness of my heart, but I'm not going to now." And Leah said, "I know. I was going to give Ralph my Colgate's shaving soap, but now I wouldn't give either of them anything but a swift kick." Ralph and Molly ignored them, but when they had gone on, Ralph, looking after them with scorn, said, "If I didn't have anything better to do than send for free samples, I'd go jump in the lake." And Molly, agreeing (she and Ralph sent for gun catalogues and booklets on things like "How to Care for Your Glenwood Parlor Burner"), said in a whisper, "Do you think they're going to be sassy to Grandpa?"

"I guess they'd better not," said Ralph. "If they do you and I will make them a pie-bed that'll be so tight they'll both break both their legs."

Leah and Rachel, almost young ladies, had, along with many other people and many habits, outgrown the soiled and rumpled old gentleman and looked with the same disfavor their mother did upon his table manners, his rough and ungrammatical speech, his clothes, and his profession, even though it had netted him three million dollars. He had four cattle ranches: one in Missouri, where he lived, one in Oklahoma, one in Texas, and one in the mountains of Colorado which his son, Claude, Mrs. Fawcett's half-brother, ran for him. How Leah and Rachel could imagine their mother's distress when her mother married this second husband! What a contrast he was to Grandfather Bonney, that noble person in the portrait over the fireplace in the parlor! And how different the life must have been for her and her sisters on his ranch in the northern part of the state when they had been used to the hustle and gaiety of St. Louis! Last September, when Grandpa left, Leah, watching the car go down the drive, put her arm around her mother's waist and said, "I could simply *cry* for you, Mother, when I think how you must have missed St. Louis." Mrs. Fawcett, who was wonderfully plucky, smiled fondly down upon her perceptive child and answered, "Well, dear, you know we can't have everything in this life." From that time onward, the two older children heaped upon the absent Mr. Kenyon an articulate and savage ridicule, commingled with resentment which was at once aimless and precocious: shortly after he had left the Colorado ranch last October, he had gone to Europe, as he frequently did in the winter, and while heretofore these casual trips all over the world had been something to admire and to refer to in conversations with other children who had no such traveled relatives, the girls this year were angry, realizing fully for the first time that their mother had never been abroad. And their anger was inflamed when Mrs. Fawcett from time to time remarked that often in the years she had lived in his house, taking charge of his child, he had taken these long journeys, not giving a thought to her. And you can imagine what those lonesome winters in the country were like for a girl who had been brought up in the city!

But Ralph and Molly, in a smaller world, would rather go to reform school than live in St. Louis. The one time they had been there they had been in tears half the time at all the poor old men selling shoelaces and lengths of elastic and at all the homeless dogs with sore eyes and limping legs; the smell of smoke and the horrid noises and the terrifying pace of the trolleys had almost made them sick. Their mother, introducing them to Mrs. Waite, their hostess, had said, "And these are my two little country bumpkins. They already want to go home. Can you feature it?" They had not really wanted to go home; they had wanted to go visit Grandpa Kenyon, but their mother wouldn't let them, falsely declaring that they would be bored to death for there would be nothing there to do. There was certainly nothing to do in St. Louis and all summer long Mrs. Fawcett and Mrs. Waite had had whispered conversations about Fatty Arbuckle so that Ralph and Molly were in a temper the whole time because, when they asked, the ladies only said, "Little pitchers have big ears."

At Grandpa's place they could have done what they pleased. Their mother didn't know anything. She said that she knew from experience that there was nothing to do. Had she not spent her boarding school holidays there with Aunt Rowena and Aunt Kathleen? All those long, still summers when there was nothing to distract their thoughts from the heat! The immense lawn, going down to the river, was bare of trees so that one had an unobstructed view of the Mississippi: one of the Bonney girls' few amusements was to watch the barges and the steamers going down toward Hannibal. Sometimes the sound of a banjo was carried to them on the motionless air, making Rowena, the least controlled of the three, so restless that she would cry, "Oh, why doesn't something *happen*!" Behind the house was an apple orchard, kept as formally as a garden, and in the center of it was a clearing with a little summer-house where they sometimes sat through the airless afternoons, fanning themselves with palm leaves, homesick for St. Louis. It was ten miles to the nearest town, and once you got there there was nothing to look at or to buy and no one at all congenial to call on. Aunt Rowena and Aunt Kathleen amused themselves by riding horseback and driving the buckboard, but their sister Rose would not join them. She would not because Grandfather Bonney's blood poisoning had been the result of a scratch from a nail in the railing of a paddock when he was watching her take her first jump, and ever afterward, feeling that she had been the cause of his far too early death, she vowed she would have nothing to do with horses.

If the Bonney girls had not all been great readers, they would have been half out of their minds with boredom. Fortunately, Mrs. Bonney had brought a good part of the library along from St. Louis and they almost put their eyes out reading Mrs. Gaskell, Dickens, and E. P. Roe. In some ways, the very worst thing of all was the conversation at mealtime. If the girls had been given half a chance, they might have elevated the tone of it by discussing the books they were reading, but there was never any opportunity. They *could* not take an interest in the talk of cattle and hogs after the cultured life they had led with their own father! And that was all Mr. Kenyon talked about; their mother talked right along with him, seeming to be really keen on hearing how many steers were being shipped to Chicago and how many bulls were being sold off the Texas ranch and how much feed would have to be bought for the Colorado place over and above the timothy that would be put up in the harvest. Table talk in St. Louis had been quite a different matter. Grandfather Bonney, who had owned a button factory, never brought his business home; he would say that he wanted to "forget the cares that infest the day" and besides that he had great respect for conversation as an art and once a year, on New Year's Day, he read selections from Boswell's *Journal of a Tour to the Hebrides*. He directed the talk at his table as adroitly and interestingly as a professional forum leader. He would start the ball rolling by saying something like this: "Today I was just wondering how much you girls know about Apollo. Do you realize how often he figures in poems, pictures, and statues?"

And that would lead to a very enlightening discussion from which the girls derived far more facts than they ever would have done in a cut-and-dried schoolroom class. They talked of everything under the sun, often examining such concepts as "justice," "charity," and "truth." Some of Mrs. Fawcett's most cherished values had been developed at that table.

In the late spring of Rose Bonney's last year in boarding school, two years after her father's death and a year after her mother's unseemly second marriage, her mother bore Mr. Kenyon a son. She was then past forty—she had been much younger than her first husband—and to her daughters there seemed something shameful in this middle-aged child-bed. Shameful and obscurely disloyal to their dead father. Five months later, she died a lingering death. Mr. Kenyon, so unimaginative in his innocence, thought that he was honoring Rose in asking her, her mother's eldest survivor, to keep house for him and rear the baby, Claude. It was not, of course, that he was the least bit stingy and did not want to hire a nurse and a housekeeper, for of course he did that anyway. Poor soul, he really thought Rose would like to do it. Can you imagine anyone understanding girls so little? But how could she refuse? Well, she just couldn't. Thus for ten years she buried herself alive, ten years of stupefaction enlivened only by the weddings of her two sisters on which Mr. Kenyon had spent nearly a fortune. (Grandfather Bonney would have done it for half as much and with twice as much dash.) In all that time, she felt so little intimacy with him that she never called him anything but "Mr. Kenyon" and she never called the child by any name at all, just "you" and "he."

And then at last, when she was twenty-nine and nearly hopeless, she had been released from her prison by Mr. Bruce Fawcett, who had taken her to California to a house very much like the one she had known in St. Louis and all the niceties were restored to her that her father had taught her constituted reality. Mr. Fawcett, the children gathered, had been similar to Grandfather Bonney, although he had been a fainter and imperfect copy, lacking the vitality of the original. (For example, his jokes were never quoted and the children doubted if he had ever made any.) She had brought all the treasures that had been in the storage house these many years and those she had kept in Mr. Kenyon's house: the portrait of her father, his books, and the man himself, a heap of dust in a graceful urn whose handles were shaped like flat-headed snakes and whose top ended in a little knob shaped like a water lily.

Both Mr. Kenyon and his stepdaughter dreaded his annual visit, but they looked upon it as a duty which they would not have dreamed of shirking. He set forth from home on the first day of August, visiting first his Oklahoma place, then his Longhorn ranch in the Panhandle, and after a short trip to Mexico to buy presents for the children, he came on to Covina. Once the courteous preliminaries were over, Grandpa seemed to enjoy his stay, for he was fond of the children, especially of Ralph and Molly whose coloring was that of their grandmother and their half-uncle and, curiously enough, of himself. But Mrs. Fawcett enjoyed none of it, and for the whole two weeks was so flustered that when he left she always went to bed for three or four days with a prolonged sick headache.

To the children, this visit was a season as special and separate as Christmas or Easter, and days before he came they conjectured what surprises he would bring them this time in his big shabby grip, crammed with stiff socks and dirty shirts and scraps of useless paper with the writing worn off. All other visitors wrapped up their presents in tissue paper and tied them with ribbon, but Grandpa just handed them out the way he had got them, sometimes loosely wrapped in a crumpled piece of cheese paper. These gifts were not the sort of souvenirs the children saw in the boardwalk shops at Redondo Beach nor were they like the presents their aunts brought: toys for Ralph and Molly, hair ribbons and round combs for Leah and Rachel. Grandpa brought them heavy, hand-made objects, rings and knives and boxes, and Ralph, ever since he could remember, had loved to hold something small but solid in the palm of his hand. Once Grandpa had given him a miniature contour-globe made of Mexican silver. It was his favorite belonging.

Mrs. Fawcett, while she did not conceal her regret that he was coming, made as extensive preparations for him as if he were someone like Aunt Rowena or Aunt Kathleen whom she really welcomed, and for a week beforehand she threw the house into a turmoil of cleaning and arranging and putting away and getting out, not failing to remind the household from time to time that it was singularly obtuse in Mr. Kenyon to come at the very busiest time of year when there was canning to do and when the nuts were being gathered. But there was no help for it: one of the precepts she had learned at her father's table was: "Never be near with your hospitality." Conventions, as a result, had grown up around these visits, so that just as they associated turkey with Thanksgiving and ham with Easter, the Fawcetts thought of duck and wild rice, of Sally Lunn and fig preserves as the only possible fare on the night of Mr. Kenyon's arrival. And on the last Sunday of the visit, Mr. and Mrs. Follansbee came to a buffet supper served on the front porch at which they had chicken pie and hot biscuits with salmon-berry jam. This supper was invariably a fiasco, but Mrs. Fawcett, an incorrigible ritualist, repeated it year after year. Mr. Follansbee was a voluble man, given to telling anecdotes which usually involved a passage from Scripture or from Shakespeare, and he embarrassed Mr. Kenyon, reducing him to a glassy-eyed stupor which Mrs. Fawcett earnestly strove to end by asking him questions about people in Missouri of whom she had no desire to hear nor he to speak. More often than not, he had a seizure of yawning, almost like a spell of some kind, and he yawned exactly like a dog, making a noise at the end that sounded like a thwarted howl.

Except for this one evening, Mr. Kenyon's visit was not interrupted by any social occasions, and he was only that one time required to dress in what he called his "store clothes." Mr. Follansbee, who had known her father, was the only man Mrs. Fawcett met, so to say, in the drawing room, and it would have been quite unthinkable for all concerned to invite any of the ladies of her various circles to be introduced to her stepfather. There existed between the two a cool formality as if they actually had been estranged in some way and did not simply dislike one another; Ralph knew instinctively that it had always been like that and this was one of the reasons his mother perplexed him. She was quite smiling and flirtatious with Mr. Follansbee, almost as silly as Leah and Rachel, but with Mr. Kenyon in whose very own house she had lived for years and years she acted like an impatient schoolteacher. And Mr. Kenyon, for his part, seemed shy and gawky. But there was no such aloofness between him and the younger children. He was amiably talkative with them and treated them as if they were men of about his age. They spent the hours with him after school, rambling till suppertime through the orderly avenues between the lines of English walnut trees. He had been everywhere in the world and had hunted every animal indigenous to the North American continent: deer, antelope, moose, caribou, big-horn, and every game bird you could name. He had caught wild horses in Nevada and had tamed them "into the gentlest little benches a man ever saw." He had killed rattlers as long as a man is tall; he had eaten alligator and said it tasted like chicken. Two things he never had been partial to were possum and beaver tails, though some people counted them great delicacies. The old colored cook at Claude's place would as lief eat beaver tails three times a day.

It was natural, Ralph supposed, for girls not to be so interested in hunting as he was, but that did not give Leah and Rachel any right to say, as they had been doing all this year, that Grandpa made his stories up. They were obviously all true and Molly, who was very smart, believed them. He thought he had never really liked his older sisters, that he had always suspected they were not what Mrs. Fawcett called "true blue," and that this turning against Grandpa proved that he had been right.

Now, in the garden behind him and Molly, they were talking in low voices. They had many secrets and were in love with two brothers named George and Kenneth Taliafero whom Ralph and Molly detested because they put bay rum on their hair and they called Ralph "hot water Fawcett" and Molly "cold water Fawcett." Now and again the girls' golden hair appeared over the tops of the tall flowers, as bright as the petals. They wore plaid hair ribbons to match their dresses. Leah's was blue and Rachel's was red. Their hair was as soft as down, and when it was washed and Mrs. Fawcett was brushing it, it crackled with electricity. She was ever so proud of it and said crossly, "*Oh, this pesky stuff!*" They were very pretty girls. Their mother carefully protected their fair skin from sunburn and freckles and it was uniformly the color of milk. There was a blue vein in Leah's high forehead which made her look delicate. Their faces were oval and narrow and somehow old-fashioned like the tintypes and sepia photographs of their mother and aunts when they were young ladies. Their bones were small and in time they would be prettily padded as Mrs. Fawcett's were. In addition to their winning faces, they had what the members of the Sorosis called "the poise of ladies of thirty," so completely at ease were they when they passed the cakes at tea or played duets, never having to be coaxed. Mr. and Mrs. Follansbee, who were childless, were devoted to them in a way Mrs. Fawcett found quite touching and sad. After church, when he shook hands with her, the minister often said, "Rose, if you ever get tired of these two little ladies of quality, you know where you can bring them." Leah and Rachel kept this love alive by calling on them frequently and drinking cambric tea and by making presents for them at Christmas and Easter, sending them Valentines and making them May baskets. In return, the Follansbees gave them tokens of piety, small New Testaments, packets of Bible scenes, and books of a moral flavor. Ralph and Molly, for their part, wouldn't have been seen at a dog fight with either of the Follansbees.

It was hard to believe that the two girls had had the same father and mother as Ralph and Molly, who were shy and sometimes impudent out of embarrassment. Since their illness, moreover, they had been thin, pallid, and runny-nosed. From some obscure ancestor they had inherited bad, uneven teeth and nearsighted eyes so that they had to wear braces and spectacles. Their skin and hair and eyes were dark and the truth of it was they always looked a little dirty. They were small for their age but they had large bones, and it was predicted with pity that they would shoot up suddenly in that dreadful ungainly way so many children do, going then through several years of coltishness, painful to behold. They were so self-conscious that they could not sit on a chair without looking as if they perched on a precarious cliff, and if they were suddenly addressed by a strange elder, they swallowed in the middle of their words and tears came to their eyes, steaming their glasses. They were always getting cut and bruised and bumped, and this seemed so inconsiderate (of course it wasn't at all, the poor youngsters couldn't help it, but it *was* peculiar) when Mrs. Fawcett felt the way she did about injuries which could so easily turn into lockjaw. Last year Molly had run a sewing-machine needle straight through her index finger and

Mrs. Fawcett had fainted clean away. This had seemed to all Mrs. Fawcett's friends not only a deliberate accident but one brought on by the most reprehensible circumstances, for Molly was making a quilt on the machine, not to be outdone by Leah and Rachel who were sewing their pieces together by hand in the regular way.

At home Ralph and Molly were hot-tempered and rebellious, but elsewhere were so easily intimidated that the enemies among their contemporaries called them cowards. And while Leah and Rachel had dozens of fast friends and were invited to innumerable slumber parties and donkey parties every year, Ralph and Molly had none but one another and at Valentine's they had to stuff the boxes in each other's room at school or they would not have got any at all. In some ways the most disturbing thing about them was their precocity. Mrs. Follansbee, who was discomforted by intellect in anyone, said that their reading excesses were very likely the result (not the cause) of their having to put on eyeglasses at such an early age: first they *looked* studious and then they *were* studious. Their tastes, in point of fact, were not in advance of their years, and they really preferred Howard Pyle to Dickens though they did make rather a show of themselves by memorizing the scene in which David Copperfield gets drunk and entangles himself in Steerforth's curtains. Their reputation really derived from their ability to say off the alphabetical syllables on the backs of the *Encyclopaedia Britannica*, no volume of which they had ever opened except "Ref to Sai" where Ralph, with great disappointment, had read the article on Reproduction.

There was only one thing about Molly he did not like, Ralph decided, and that was the way she copied him. It was natural for her to want to be a boy (who *wouldn't*!) but he knew for a fact she couldn't be. Last week, he had had to speak sharply to her about wearing one of his outgrown Boy Scout shirts: he was glad enough for her to have it, but she had not taken the "Be Prepared" thing off the pocket and he had to come out and say brutally, "Having that on a girl is like dragging the American flag in the dirt." He wished she would not tag along with him and Grandpa. How splendid it would be, he thought, if only the two of them went walking together! How fine if he could tell the cow joke by himself! He lay back on the lawn, crushing the little lippia blossoms, feeling her eyes follow every movement he made. And then, as he had known she would do, she lay back too.

The day seemed strange to him, the very air unusual. It did not possess quite the quality of a dream, but it lay beyond him as the days had done when he had scarlet fever and all the noises on the first floor had been thin and ephemeral. He remembered that late one night he had seen the sky glow suddenly with heat lightning and he called to Molly through the door that connected their rooms, "Heat lightning for the sky is the same thing as scarlet fever for us." Sick as she was, she clapped her hands and cried back, "Oh, Ralph, you always think of things!" He would have asked her now if she, too, felt funny, but he was afraid that if he shared it with her the feeling would leave him and so he lay in his selfish speechlessness pursuing the red globules that sped downward behind his closed eyes.

"Hey," said Molly and abruptly sat up again.

"Straw's cheaper," said Ralph automatically. He wished she wouldn't talk.

"No, listen. I've made another poem."

He opened his eyes in astonishment and looked at her. She was twisting her head around with excitement and he realized that she had not been thinking the same thoughts he had at all and that perhaps she had not even been looking at him when he lay back. Once Grandpa had said that Molly was "a deep one" and Ralph almost thought this was true. He had said it because she insisted that she had learned Braille in kindergarten, and though people would explain to her that what she was thinking of was the beads on a frame which you moved about to learn to count, she replied, "I said I learned Braille and I mean it."

"Will you listen to my poem?" she said pleadingly.

"How long is it?" Ralph did not care for poetry.

"It's real little." And then, without waiting for him to say "All right" she went on. "It's called 'Gravel,'" she said, "and this is it:

> Gravel, gravel on the ground
> Lying there so safe and sound,
> Why is it you look so dead?
> Is it because you have no head?"

"Say it again," said Ralph, puzzled now. And when she had repeated it, he said, "It doesn't make any sense. Gravel doesn't have a head."

"That's what I said. 'Is it because you have no *head*?'"

"Well, I don't know what you're talking about."

"You're merely jealous because you can't write poems yourself," said Molly, close to tears. She took her handkerchief out of the pocket of her middy and snuffled into it and beginning to cry, she said, "Now you've gone and made me have another nosebleed."

He did not even open his eyes. He knew that she didn't have a nosebleed and he was so tired of her poems that he was just not going to make any effort to understand this one or to praise it. But neither did he want her to have a mad on him because that would spoil Grandpa's arrival and so he said, "Why don't you go write it down on a piece of paper and then maybe I can get the drift of it?" It was true that he never could hear things as well as he could see them and until just this year he had always thought that the song was "O Beautiful for Spacious Guys."

"I will! I will!" cried Molly and she ran to the house, chanting her poem.

Now, with her gone, he was completely at peace. The unusual feeling came over him again and he held on to it. It was almost as if he were clutching his broad mold-colored geography book to his chest. Later, Ralph felt he had had, on that long afternoon, some prescience of what would happen when Grandpa Kenyon finally came, but probably he had not and it was only desire that made him remember those hours as peculiar and significant, though they were without event.

Chapter Two

A T FIVE, the children were sitting in a straight row on the railing of the porch like cats on a fence. There was a temporary truce between the two older and the two younger, but they were not friendly enough to talk. Although Leah and Rachel for a week had groaned to think of the arrival of "that old hobo," they were as greedy as ever for the presents which he would take out of the rank gray bundles in his grip. When finally they heard the car slow down at the opening of the driveway, all four of them began to giggle aimlessly and to pound their heels against the uprights of the railing. They did not move until he was actually on the porch, watching his descent from the car spellbound.

He was a big old man, stoop-shouldered and bowlegged. He looked like a massive, slow-footed bear as he heaved himself out of the car which seemed dwarfed just as Miguel, that long, lithe man, seemed small and somehow womanly. Grandpa stood for a moment with his legs wide apart, looking around the yard, glancing at the house and the garden as if to make sure that he had come to the right place, and then he took his grip from Miguel and came stomping up the path, peering at the children over his spectacles. As he passed a clump of turquoise berry, he tapped a sprig lightly with his shillelagh and Ralph, tense with excitement, wondered why and then wondered why he had wondered: why had he suddenly begun to notice all these pointless little things? Then, when Grandpa was actually on the porch and was setting down his bag, the boy observed nothing more and abandoned himself to the joy of shaking the strong, toughened hand—it was inconceivable that Mr. Kenyon had ever kissed anyone. Ralph was always the last to greet him and Grandpa always said, "Well, sir, I'm here again." It was true that if one of the girls had been the last to shake his hand, he still would have said "sir," but Ralph, in establishing this rite, felt personally, privately addressed, man to man.

He pushed his black hat back on his forehead and they could see the sweat running down to his whiskery eyebrows. He sat down in a wicker basket chair and took off his boots and then opened his grip and got out the soft-soled moccasins which had been made for him by a Cherokee named Daniel Standing-Deer. He would wear these all the rest of his visit, even on the night the Follansbees came. As he tugged at his boots, he said genially, "By the Lord Harry, it's as hot as Tophet."

Ralph was always surprised at Grandpa's clothes even though they did not vary from year to year. It was that no other man he had ever known dressed with such unconcern, with such a deliberate second-hand look. His store clothes were a suit of scratchy gray material, cut without relationship to his measurements. The trousers were too short and the cuffs were three inches wide, and beneath them stuck out his tremendous black boots with rawhide laces and his cattle brand, a bar and a K, burned into the leg of the left one. The coat was long and the pockets were so misshapen from the things he carried that they looked like panniers on a donkey. He carried a watch which he called a "turnip," and a jackknife with four blades, a collapsible tin cup, two pipes, a fly-book, a compass, a good-luck scarab, a collection of bolts and nuts and screws and the coins of foreign countries, and a plump brown leather notebook in which he kept his accounts and in which Ralph had one time seen an old entry, headed "Dodge City," which read:

> Mo. steers sold $6,000
> Purchase 1 pr. shoes $1.75
> Purchase 1 rum for Borchard $.10
> Purchase 1 rum for self $.10

Grandpa's vests were his only fancy in the matter of clothes. He had a great many of them and while they were all cut alike, coming almost to his beard, they were a variety of colors and patterns. His finest was made of black velveteen with silver buttons, in the center of each of which was a small turquoise. This vanity had taken root in him many years before when Jesse James and his boys rode into his yard in Missouri one night and asked for quarters. "I can't go any farther," said Jesse. "If you haven't got a bed, you can hang me on a nail." Jesse James had worn a waistcoat of dark green velveteen with large mother-of-pearl buttons which matched the handles of his side arms. Today Grandpa wore a vest of gray doeskin faced with printed challis, as delicate and feminine as the most stylish dress goods.

He tugged and mumbled, preoccupied and at last got one boot off and then the other, then deeply sighed as though the job had been a hard one. He winked at Ralph and said, "Those are damned fine boots, son, but on a hot day like this they try a man's feet." Leah went into the house to call their mother and to take Grandpa's boots to his room and Rachel sat down on the top step, humming "A Capital Ship for an Ocean Trip," hoping that she would be asked to sing out loud for she had a gifted voice. But Grandpa ignored her and turning to Ralph and Molly, scrutinized them fixedly, seeing for the first time the change in them since last autumn. "By Jupiter, you two are poor," he said. "What in the world has laid aholt of you?"

Rachel explained as if the younger children were mutes. "Oh, they had scarlet fever last March. Leah and I didn't though because Mother sent us to Aunt Kathleen's. Don't you love Aunt Kathleen's house, Grandpa? The way it's right on Lake Michigan?"

Grandpa looked at her politely: "I never was to that house that I recall," he said and then turning to Ralph and Molly, "Well, I declare that's a hell of a note. I reckon I'll have to take you back to Claude's place with me and let that coon of his fatten you up. You ain't any use this way."

"We don't *hurt* anywhere," said Ralph anxiously and Mr. Kenyon laughed, showing the glossy coral gums of his false teeth.

Mrs. Fawcett came out, chattering like a bird. "It's so good to see you, Mr. Kenyon! My, you must be hot and tired after that pesky train! Won't you rest here on the porch where it's cool before you go up, and I'll bring you a glass of nice cold punch. Molly, dear, do you think you can run in and ask Fuschia to get the punch out of the icebox? And tell her to put in a nice big piece of ice? And tell her to be *sure* to wash it first? And then bring out some glasses and we'll all have a good cool drink."

Molly started to the door but Grandpa stopped her. "Just bring your grandpa a small tumbler. I have in my valise here a quart bottle of Bourbon drinking whisky which I had the good fortune to purchase in El Paso at a king's ransom. I think that'll do more for what ails me than your punch, Rose, no offense intended."

Ralph trembled all over with delight and dread. Once he had seen a bottle of dark red wine on a shelf in Miguel's house, but he had never seen whisky nor had he ever seen anyone drink. Mrs. Fawcett bit her lip and flushed. Grandfather Bonney had never used spirits but took a glass of claret or port now and again on special occasions and if he had lived to see the Volstead Act passed, he would have forgone even that.

"Just as you like, Mr. Kenyon," she said, her cheeks still bright and her eyes blinking with indignation. "I only thought you would like something *cool*. In that case perhaps we'd better go inside."

"Why?" demanded Ralph.

"Because I say so," she replied tightly.

Leah giggled. "Goody-goody Mother! She means Miss Runyon might go past and see Grandpa's bottle of you-know-what and tell the policeman on him. But if she did see it, Mother, we could say Grandpa sprained his ankle and was putting Sloan's liniment on it." She and Rachel laughed and lovingly ran their fingers through their fine hair.

"Dammit, Rose," said Grandpa, "I'm tired, and if it don't make a world of difference to you, I'll take the liberty of drinking my whisky right here."

Mrs. Fawcett took her defeat in silence, but it was clear that she thought this beginning indicated an even more trying visit than usual. She rolled down the bamboo screen on the south side of the house so that the Freudenburgs (who went right on making beer in spite of the new law) would not see Mr. Kenyon's bottle and wrongly think she had given her approval or, even worse, that she was sharing it with him. She said brightly, "Now tell me all your news, Mr. Kenyon. I'm on pins and needles to hear about everyone back home. I was just saying to Fuschia that good as her duck smelled what I was really hungry for was news."

Grandpa reported that a Dr. Taylor had been operated on for kidney stones and was not expected to live; indeed, since he had been away for five weeks and had had little word from Missouri, it was possible that the old gentleman was already dead. Mrs. Fawcett said, "You remember Dr. Taylor, don't you, girls? He and Mrs. Taylor gave us those nice little salt spoons you like so much. Isn't it too bad he's not well?" Leah and Rachel were moved and Rachel said, "Poor Mrs. Taylor. When you write her, Mother, will you give her my love and tell her I keep my best hankies in the darling case she sent me?"

Ralph, sitting on the arm of Grandpa Kenyon's chair, hesitated a moment and then plunged, "Ain't Dr. Taylor the one you told me was crooked as a dog's hind leg?"

"Ralph!" cried Leah. "You awful little Hun! And you said 'ain't' too!"

An unhappy, beating silence fell, ended finally by Molly's return, and the conversation set forth again, a plodding drudge. Grandpa, never interested in these chronicles of deaths and marriages and illnesses which he dutifully recited for his stepdaughter, seemed even more bored than usual, more inaccurate with names and more uncertain of his facts. He said that someone called Geneva Whatyoumaycallit had had erysipelas and it had disfigured her almost beyond recognition, but as he could neither remember her last name nor where she lived, the news was not thrilling but only tantalizing. He said that on second thoughts she might as easily have been named Mildred and he was not at all sure she didn't live in Oklahoma. One Maude Pease had asked him to tell Rose how much she had appreciated the metal casserole of candy she had sent as an anniversary present. (Leah said: "Mother, is that the one that had the alfresco wedding?" She brought this up whenever she could and it always made Ralph and Molly furious because they never could remember what "alfresco" meant.) The family on the place next to his had had a run of bad luck with their wheat—had rust—and had had to sell their automobile. He said then, "I can't make out what you want to keep that bus of yours for, Rose. Why don't you get a new one? By George, a man of any size feels like a galoot in that tom-fool outfit of yours."

Mrs. Fawcett winced; she could not bear the word "bus" and did not any better like "flivver." She herself always spoke with dignity of "the machine." The Willys Knight had been extremely expensive and, although rumors had come to her that it was out of style, she had great affection for it. She replied exuberantly to Mr. Kenyon that she did not know what she would do without his advice, that it was one of the things she had wanted to talk over with him, and that she also hoped he would take a look at the shaft in the pumphouse in the morning for she felt that it needed to be replaced, even though Miguel said it was sound.

Ralph stared listlessly at a small tear in the knee of Grandpa's trousers and wanted to ask him what countries he had gone to last winter. But it was a convention that he never spoke of his travels in Mrs. Fawcett's presence. He had been to Siam, to Borneo, India, Spain, Sweden, and even to such out-of-the-way places as Lithuania and the Shetland Islands. A trip to Sydney or to southern Mexico was no more to him than a trip to Riverside to the Fawcetts. Once he had written a picture postal card to Ralph from Melbourne saying that he was bringing him a monkey, but Mrs. Fawcett had replied for her son, requiring him not to. The boy never forgave her and sulked whenever he recalled it. Mrs. Fawcett had remarked acidly that it was typical of Mr. Kenyon to select the one sort of pet that could not be housebroken. He had gone by steamer to Alaska and there had seen the northern lights and had gone out in a sealing vessel in the Bering Strait: before they even spotted the seals there had been a thundering great storm and the whole crew had nearly lost their lives; the waves were as high as the Fawcetts' pumphouse and the downside of them was as steep as Mt. Baldy. The noise of the gale had had the tongue of Hades in it.

Now and again Mr. Kenyon looked at Ralph and smiled and patted his knee with a thick, out-of-shape hand. He looked rather like an Indian with his strong cheekbones, his lank black hair and his sun-stained skin and his humped nose, but of course no Indian ever had a beard like Grandpa's: it was as thick as the top of the umbrella tree. He finished his second tumbler of whisky and put the glass on the table. Spreading his hands out on his knees, he looked at his stepdaughter and said, "Rose, you had ought to be ashamed of the looks of these two. You hadn't ought to hold out on them the way you do: you had ought to send them to Claude of a summer."

"But, Mr. Kenyon! What do you mean! Why, they're much too delicate to be away from me and Dr. Haskell!"

This was a controversy that was repeated annually. Mr. Kenyon, whose scorn for Mrs. Fawcett's picayune walnut grove was boundless, saw no reason at all why the children should not summer in the Colorado mountains and each year he offered to pay their train fare; he felt it particularly unjust that she did not at least send the boy who ought to be learning the ways of a man.

"This Dr. Haskell," said Mr. Kenyon contemptuously, "is he the only sawbones in the world?"

"Oh, I didn't mean it that way, Mr. Kenyon, I surely didn't. I daresay Claude has a very fine physician up there in the mountains. I only meant that they're such babies . . . they need a mother's care. I just don't know . . . with all those horses and cows there, just danger everywhere."

Ralph, knowing beforehand that nothing would come of this argument, wondered if he might not now tell the joke about the cow since his mother had mentioned cows, but she hastened on. "You know how I have always felt about horses, Mr. Kenyon."

He replied, "Rose, there's not a damned thing on God's green earth I know any better than that. But it don't make sense that you should want to turn in and spook this boy as well."

Mrs. Fawcett blushed and vigorously fanned herself with a palm leaf, though the breeze was cool. "I want only one thing, Mr. Kenyon: I want him to be a gentleman."

The flame died in Grandpa and he said wearily, "I don't aim to judge in the matter of gentlemen but my son Claude is a fine man."

Mrs. Fawcett put her fan down suddenly and sat up straight. "Mr. Kenyon, I think perhaps we had better discuss this some other time. You were going to tell me about Roberta Wagner's fire. How did it start?"

"Oh, a kerosene lamp or some damned thing or other in the barn."

Reluctantly he allowed himself to be steered back into tame channels, but presently there came a long pause. He could think of no more facts and Mrs. Fawcett was out of questions. They were all so bored! The children waited impatiently for their mother to go in to speak to Fuschia, for this was the signal for Grandpa to give them their presents. But because she revered custom, she would not move until it was really

necessary; she did not want the dirty, tippling old roughneck
to think he was not welcome, not even when she was so angry
with him that she could cry.

Grandpa filled his glass for the third time. Ralph got off the
arm of his chair and moved to the railing of the porch where
he sat with his hands under him. "Grandpa," he said, "have
you got any dogs?" The old man put his glass down on the
round wicker table while he corked the bottle. Then, without
warning, his head fell forward on his chest, his hat slid off and
lay, crown upward, on the floor, and the bottle rolled unbroken
to the railing, directly under Ralph's feet. His hands relaxed
and lay over the arms of the chair; his breath came unevenly
and deeply like wind through his loosely opened lips, and his
eyes appeared quite blind though they were open. There was
a moment of quiet so long and so pure that it seemed like an
hour of dreamless sleep, and Ralph was again reminded of the
scarlet fever days when the neat, still hours had been in a row
like boxes. He stared intently at the long unkempt hairs in
Grandpa's eyebrows and at the coppery gloss of his beard. The
old feet, swollen, lay turned on the ankles and the boy saw
that the moccasins were not completely on and that the heels,
in white cotton socks, stuck out. In one there was a careful
darn. He realized that he did not know the name of Grandpa's
housekeeper, though he did know that Uncle Claude's was
named Mrs. Brotherman.

Then Mrs. Fawcett cried, "José! Fuschia! Quick!" José, still
holding his banana knife, came silently across the lippia lawn,
the grin now gone from his face. Ralph was sent to telephone
for Dr. Haskell and Molly went with him into their father's
den. Leah and Rachel had run sobbing in terror to the garden.

Ralph and Molly stayed in the study until they heard José
and Fuschia help Grandpa up the steps. There were gasps and
moans and curses and the sound of those old helpless feet pad-
padding up in the soft slippers. Then they heard the door to
the guest room close, and still, for some time, they did not stir.

Unable to understand this unmanly collapse, this strange
dissolving of a rock, Ralph fled the thought of it and viewed
his father's study, wishing he were alive. This room was kept
as he had always kept it, but there was no clue to what sort of
man he had been. Its simple and business-like furnishings had

no idiosyncrasies and there was little to distinguish it from Dr. Haskell's waiting room. There were no pictures on the walls and the only books in the shelves were government tracts on the growing of walnuts and a set of dusty, yellow-leaved volumes called "Letters and Messages of the Presidents." On the desk there was a surveyor's telescope in a black box and an arrowhead in an abalone shell. The only article that had, so far as he knew, any history at all was the serape on the black leather lounge: his mother had smuggled it in from Tia Juana on her bustle. This had been the only act of daring in her life and Ralph admired her for it, but today he realized that he was tired of the story and he wondered what his father had been doing all the time she was having her perilous adventure with the customs inspector. The man had faded away like smoke. Even Leah, who had been six when he died, recalled almost nothing of him, and the few impressions she did have grew paler and paler until she could no longer give definite answers to any of the other children's questions but would say vaguely, "I *think* he used to say 'jiminy crickets' but I'm not sure." What was truly amazing was that the old woman he had saved in the flood was still alive!

"Oh, I'm lonesome," Ralph said to himself, and then, against his will, he saw Grandpa again, slumping in the wicker chair, and again he wondered why he had tapped the turquoise berry with his stick. And now, clear-headed, he turned on Molly in a cold, exhilarated anger and said, "Why do you always have to follow me?" He went out to the porch and sat motionless in the swing, hearing his sister sobbing and heaving about on the lounge. José had left his cruel curved knife on the round table beside Grandpa's little glass of whisky which he had not got to drink.

It was the last time they saw Grandpa Kenyon until, five days later, he was brought down to the parlor, dead, where he waited two more days until Uncle Claude came to bury him.

The children did not go to school for the three days between Grandpa's death and the funeral. Mrs. Fawcett felt that this was a necessary gesture of respect to the dead man, but it was an unhappy time for the children. Leah and Rachel sorted and arranged their free samples and quarreled with one another

saying, "Move *over*, what do you think I am anyway?" and
Ralph and Molly roamed silently from room to room trying to
think of something to do. "Why don't you settle down with
a book?" said their mother. They talked, dispiritedly, in Pig
Latin about Molly's poem which Ralph still could not understand. The house was quiet and dark and the Mexicans in the
grove were afraid to raise their voices above a whisper. All that
time, Fuschia was canning and making piccalilli and the whole
house smelled deliciously of mace and dill, and yet it could not
obscure the fragrance of all the flowers that lay in the parlor
with Grandpa. Ralph was acutely conscious of all the smells,
and he was able at last to name what it was that had been so
distinct in the odor that clung to the old man: he had smelled
like a raisin.

Mr. Follansbee came twice in the evening to call. The
second time he left a leather-bound book of solemn aphorisms
called "some Starbeams of Solace," which Mrs. Fawcett read
frequently with moist eyes. In his sermon at the funeral, the
pastor spoke of Grandpa as a man whose "many interests and
travels destined him for an active rather than a contemplative
life," but since it took all kinds to make the world, there was
no reason to suppose that the Lord would look on him with
disfavor. "Among men, too," he said, "there are the Marthas as
well as the Marys." By way of gratitude, Mrs. Fawcett, enriched
by her stepfather's will, subscribed a thousand dollars toward
a central heating unit for the church. She would have liked to
have a stained-glass window put in in his memory, but she was
by no means certain that Mr. Kenyon had believed in God.

The night after Grandpa died, Miss Runyon brought some
roses, and because Fuschia was busy with the dishes and Leah
and Rachel wanted to listen to the ladies talk and Molly was
in bed with hiccups after getting too much sun, Ralph was
sent to the parlor with them. Only one lamp was burning, the
smallest one of all. It stood on a round marble-topped table at
the foot of the coffin and it scarcely illuminated Grandpa's face
at all. Although there seemed to be no opening in the room,
the flame was unsteady and shifted behind the thin china shade
with its design of tulips against a pale green ground. There
were flowers everywhere, brought by all the neighbors, not
in tribute to Mr. Kenyon since none of them had known him,

but in sympathy with Mrs. Fawcett in whose house this had unreasonably happened. It had been one of his orders, repeated throughout his lifetime, that he be buried wherever he died, for he had no use for pomp and thought that the transportation of a corpse from one part of the world to another was wasteful of money and of time. Mrs. Fawcett would gladly have accompanied the casket back to Missouri or even to England, and in her first telegram to Claude had said so, but he wired back: "Must bury him like he said."

Ralph tried not to look at the body which, even though it had shrunk in death, made everything else look small as if the importance of its metamorphosis had taken on a physical dimension. He put the vase of roses down on the library table where the Bible lay open and as he did so, a petal fell off onto the finely printed page. Simultaneously the tip of a spray of fern in a tall vase of carnations brushed against his cheek, startling him with its subtle touch. He turned quickly as if he had been spoken to and looked full into the dead man's face. He now could see the big hooked nose jutting up and casting a shadow of itself on the satin pillow, and could see the dead white wrinkled eyelids under the ragged brows. Someone had brushed his beard and his square, corrugated fingernails had been cleaned. Ralph put the palm of his hand on Grandpa's cold cheek, feeling the formation of the bones. He was neither afraid nor disgusted: the skin under his fingers was as smooth and meaningless as the fallen rose petal. But then, when he had taken away his hand and had stepped back, he was frightened exactly as he had been frightened last summer when he went onto a submarine in San Diego with Uncle Ernest and he had looked through a periscope; it was so far, what you looked at, and so watery and so strange.

In the days just past, when Grandpa had been dying, the mystery had been withheld from all the children. Rather, it had been obscured by the bustling, the quiet coming and going of Dr. Haskell and of well-wishing neighbors with napkin-covered offerings of custards and broths (the Freudenburgs had sent, of all things, some spiced dumplings!) and the ringing of the telephone, and Miguel's innumerable trips to town to fetch medicine and to send telegrams. The guest room was at the back, in an ell, a part of the house Ralph rarely went into since besides this room there were only his mother's sewing room, the linen closet and a storage cubby; yet in these past days he had been drawn to it, bewitched by the silence, and sometimes for an hour had stood in the sewing room, tossing a bobbin of blue silk thread up in the air and catching it again, trying to hear something through the wall, hearing nothing but the nightlike silence, the silence that muted the hurried commotion of the errands and the calls.

Now that everything had ceased, it was possible to look back and to realize that the soft sounds and the agitation had been only trifles superimposed upon a great, unviolent force. Grandpa was like a big river, he thought, but one that had dried up and was gone forever into the ocean. He could take in the finality of this, but he could not understand how the drying up had happened: it had been too quick. He had just been sitting there corking the whisky bottle; Ralph had just asked him if he had any dogs.

Ralph understood that Grandfather Bonney had been dying for some time, in excruciating pain, and he knew that he should be glad—as his mother had said a dozen times—that Grandpa had not suffered at all. No matter how hard he tried, though, and no matter how often he heard the story of Grandfather Bonney's tragic ending, he could not feel really sad as Leah and Rachel did, nor did he wish as they did that he had known the gentleman whose portrait he now looked at in the fluttering light. Beneath the gold-framed picture, on the mantel which was black marble and had been taken from the house in St. Louis, stood Grandfather Bonney's christening cup and the Florentine urn which held his ashes. Between his Alpha and Omega stood a multitude of small mementoes of the intervening years: a silver snuff box embossed with a salamander; a miniature Venus de Milo made of brass which he had used as a paper weight; a gold stamp box with his name engraved on it in German script; a red leather jewel case which held the studs and the cuff links, the tie pins and the Masonic ring which Ralph, who was named for him, would get when he was grown.

Everything in the face and bearing of Grandfather Bonney showed that he was truly the character in his daughter's legend, that is, that he had been a scholar and a gentleman. He was plump and bald, but fat had not obscured the vigor of his face.

His gray eyes intelligently searched those of his beholder and in them resided a great self-possession which appeared also in his luxuriously full lips shining as though he had licked them, which were closed and unsmiling above the faintly grizzled and elegantly kempt Imperial. He wore a pink carnation in the lapel of his morning coat; a silk hat and a gold-headed stick, a black Chesterfield and a pair of white gloves lay on the hassock beside his chair. He was so spruced up that the children could never get over the idea that he had not just come from a funeral at which he had been a pallbearer, but Mrs. Fawcett assured them that this was the way he had dressed on the most ordinary occasions. He sat at a large round table laden with gold-clasped books, the same books which were now on the same table in the bay window, opposite the fireplace. The one that was open under his hand—a finger pointed to the middle of the right page—was Tennyson's *Collected Works*. The chances were strong, said Mrs. Fawcett, that the poem he pointed to was "Break, Break, Break" which he had liked especially. Still, it was hard to believe that he had been reading and had suddenly been moved so much by a passage that he had stopped to meditate upon it, for there was no softening of reflection about the lines of his mouth and eyes: they were tense as if he had just come to a decision and intended to abide by it sternly. The picture had been painted when he was in his prime, in his middle fifties. It was very soon after that that he had died.

Leah and Rachel and Ralph and Molly could not remember a time when they had not known that Grandfather Bonney had personally met Grover Cleveland at the Democratic Convention in 1888. He had himself been a Republican and had always voted a straight ticket, but all the same, he never had anything harsh to say of Mr. Cleveland although he was naturally glad that Mr. Harrison had won the election. This connection of her grandfather with the history of the United States had led the eldest child, Leah, to several confusions which she had passed on to each of the others in turn. Chief of these was that President Cleveland, wrong-headed as he might have been, was second in importance only to George Washington. They believed that during his administration the capital had been Cleveland, Ohio. They could not place Abraham Lincoln in time but they could easily do so in space, for Uncle Ernest, their Aunt Kathleen's husband, had gone to the University of Nebraska where, but for a fluke, he would have graduated *summa cum laude.*

Furthermore, because in the delirium of his last illness, Grandfather Bonney had several times spoken of his meeting with Cleveland, they associated the President with blood poisoning and with profuse perspiration and Molly could never hear his name without immediately seeing in her mind's eye a brown custard cup in which her mother had burned sugar to dispel the fetor of the sickroom. Similarly they linked Tennyson with their grandfather, for his last articulate words, spoken to Aunt Kathleen as she was arranging his pillows, were, "It's no use, Kate. I am at the crossing of the bar." Each of the children envisaged this trinity, the poet, the President, and the grandfather, in a different way: Ralph saw them fat, hatless, wearing morning coats, walking abreast along an endless beach, eternally nearing a sand bar. Leah saw them sitting at a round table drinking coffee out of mustache cups while in the distance a band played "When You and I Were Young, Maggie." Through Rachel's mind, they marched in single file down the central aisle of the First Presbyterian Church with such calm and ceremony that they made Mr. Follansbee seem remarkably rustic. Molly, who was often ill, saw them lying all three in one enormous bed with a moon like a jack-o'-lantern shining in on their big rosy faces through a dormer window.

Ralph, glancing from Grandpa Kenyon's dead face to Grandfather Bonney's living one, felt lonely and beset, knowing with unwilling shame that he should mourn them equally because, in a sense, he really knew Grandfather Bonney better than he had ever known his successor. For example, he knew all about his grandfather's fox terrier who had been named Liliolukilani and had been as sharp as a tack: she could pray and she could jump through a hoop and she knew commands both in English and in German. Ralph could see the man as clearly as he could call up the image of Mr. Follansbee. What a sport he had been! How full of jokes and pranks! He had always been the merriest one of all at skating parties (to tease the girls he once wore a fascinator to a skating party!) and at wiener roasts, at formal halls and informal Sunday evening chafing-dish suppers. He had had gallant manners with ladies, preserving such customs as kissing their hands and paying them compliments which always contained a word or two of French. What young lady did not delight in having him say to her, "Mademoiselle's frock is truly *distingue*"? Besides being chivalrous, he could play tricks that were a scream and afterward he would say, "Forgive me, ladies and gentlemen, but I felt an uncontrollable desire to tickle my risibles." Once he had put burnt cork all over his face and had pretended to be a darky and his imitation was so good that everyone had been taken in for at least five minutes. Another time, he had sneaked up under an open window one dark summer night and when there was a pause in the conversation, he suddenly said, in a spooky voice, "Boo!" and Mrs. Bonney and the girls had nearly jumped out of their skins. At breakfast he would ask a visitor if she wanted onions in her cocoa and he would say it with such a straight face, she wouldn't know what to answer. Once, though, he had been beaten at this game, for a perky friend of Rowena's had answered back quick as a wink, "Not on your tintype, Mr. Smarty," and Grandfather had laughed until the tears came to his eyes. He had always been up to some frolic like that. Now it would be a joke on one of the colored servants (he loved to tease the old colored cook who was *just* as superstitious), now a lark down the river on a steamer to Memphis, now an outlandish slide mixed up with the scenes of Venice in the stereopticon: suddenly you would see a pair of flannel underdrawers flying from the middle dome of St. Marks! He used to say that "one is only as old as one feels" and he never felt old, not even at the last of his life.

The boy felt neither fear nor sorrow for either man. He felt only this unkind solitude that waited for him like a surly dog. In a brief foreknowledge of maturity, he thought how curious it was that it had been possible for them all to eat three times a day the same as ever: they had actually eaten the duck and Sally Lunn the night Grandpa was, as they said, "taken," and Leah had not bothered to take away his place so that it was still there, opposite Mother, the emptiest space Ralph had ever seen. Even now, after dark, alone in a room with a dead person, he was not afraid, and he was able to notice little, useless things like the dust rag Fuschia had left behind on the bookcase beside the vase of cattails. He remembered that his mother had said that just before Grandfather Bonney died she had been in her

Chapter Three

JUST AS five days before when they had waited for Grandpa Kenyon, Ralph and Molly lay on the lippia lawn, waiting for their uncle. An airplane flew across the sky. Its pilot was stunting and as they watched, breathlessly, he took a nose dive. "The big fool!" cried Ralph. "He's going to hit the pumphouse!" And then he smiled as he saw the plane cleverly climb up again. It occurred to him with pain that Grandpa Kenyon, who loved all unusual experience, had died before he had ever gone up in an airplane. Nor had he ever got to see the racing fellow, Barney Oldfield, of whom he had often spoken with admiration.

What would next September be like without him? Associated as he had been with the renewal of crowded days after the tranquil ennui of the summer, he had seemed to the children, after he had gone, half legendary like a figure known only in his identification with a particular place or a particular day of the year. He was a sort of god of September, surrounded by the gold, autumnal light. What Ralph missed most already was the early-morning ceremony in which he alone participated with Grandpa. The old man kept his usual hours when he visited in Covina and always got up before daylight to make his own breakfast. The fragrance of the coffee he made was so manly and stimulating that Ralph could reproduce the sensation of it at will throughout the day and could therefore daydream under the most adverse schoolroom conditions. Ralph, creeping downstairs in his stocking feet lest he awaken his mother and sisters, would find Grandpa Kenyon sitting by the stove in the half-light, his black hat pushed back from his forehead and his glasses midway down his nose. He would be waiting for the griddle to heat up for his flapjacks, but the coffee would be made already and the kitchen would be full of its strong, rather rancid smell. They did not speak to one another until the meal was over and Grandpa had lighted his pipe; at this point, he always took off his hat, Ralph could never guess why. At these times he told no stories but instead talked with homesickness of the chores that were now proceeding on his ranches: just about now in Texas the whole outfit would be fixing to go up to the range and cut out the beeves to be shipped to Panama; in Colorado, where they kept lazier hours, the old colored woman, Magdalene, would be calling the men to breakfast. As he stated these facts, he kept his eye on his watch. When the second hand had completed its circuit, he would say, "She's settin' the coffee pot down by Claude." Ralph discerned contempt in Grandpa's glance through the window at the tidy grove with its toy-like trees where the Mexicans would not come for two hours yet, and when he heard the milkman come, he sometimes grew angry, thumping his fist on the table and shouting at the boy, "Lord God Almighty, she could keep *one* cow anyway. She had ought to be ashamed." She was not ashamed but Ralph was, and once he declared that he would not touch milk again until she got a cow. Her reply was a familiar and irrefutable one: "Our sort of people don't have cows."

Ralph wondered if, after all, Grandpa would have liked the joke about the cow. He wondered, too, if he dared tell it to Uncle Claude or if this would seem unbecoming on the day of the funeral. Uncle Claude. Uncle Claude. Uncle Claude. He said the name over and over to himself but it brought no picture to his mind. He could not imagine what Grandpa's son would be like and because he could not, the thought of meeting him made him shy.

At the same time that he became aware that Molly was crying and had been for some time, he saw the car coming round the bend in the lane where the blue cedars grew and with no plan at all in his mind he jumped to his feet and ran at top speed across the lawn and past the solar tank. As he ran, he thought: Now I pass the garden and Leah and Rachel haven't seen me. Now I am passing the solar tank. Now I am passing the den and in the den I am passing the deer-head and the deer-head hasn't seen me. Now the pantry and Mother isn't there and Fuschia isn't there. And now I am safe. He ran to the pumphouse and climbed the ladder as quickly as a mouse. Once on top, he squatted on his heels on the round roof. His heart pounded as deeply as the pump pulsed below him. He had no idea why he had not wanted to see his uncle. It was as if he had got to control himself by a complete physical escape, by exposing himself to the perfectly empty sky and by enclosing himself in this perfectly round small area where shapes and colors were of the simplest: the sanctuary was round, its floor was black, the sky was blue, and he was alone.

He would not look down but he could hear voices. His mother said, "Dear Claude. It is a sorrowful time for all of us."

If the air had not been so still, Ralph would not have heard the man's reply for his voice was so soft. It was so soft and sad that Ralph thought he must be sitting on the steps with his head between his hands in anguish. He said, "Can I see Mr. Kenyon, ma'am?"

The boy saw his uncle all by himself, casting his shadow on a white desert, on the terribly unearthly stretch of land he had seen from the train the summer they had gone to St. Louis. There had been miles and miles of nothing but sand until finally the train passed a giant pear cactus and Mrs. Fawcett, in an explanatory voice, had said, "You know, that little bit of shade would mean a great deal to someone who got stranded here."

Mr. Follansbee and his wife came to luncheon after the funeral. Mr. Follansbee sat at Mrs. Fawcett's right and told jokes which the children and Uncle Claude did not understand, although Leah and Rachel pretended to. He was an unpleasant-looking man with a small upturned chin and a large, down-turned nose and his whole face was thin and malign. Mrs. Fawcett said he had a "typical Yankee face," but Ralph could never reconcile this with the song "Yankee Doodle" which was, he thought, about a man something like Santa Claus. Molly had decided, though, that if Uncle Sam were clean-shaven, he would probably look a good deal like the minister. He wore a morning coat; Mrs. Follansbee, like Mrs. Fawcett, was dressed in black. Each child wore a sign of mourning: Ralph wore black knickerbockers and black stockings and the three little girls wore black Windsor ties at the necks of their middy blouses. In this decent gathering, Uncle Claude was a gaudy incongruity. His suit was chocolate brown, his shirt was a rich deep blue, and his tie was scarlet; there was no black about him save for his black hair and his black eyes. His whole color scheme was like that of a rooster. He was a younger and slighter version of Grandpa.

His jawbones were broad and his cheekbones high, but his chin was rather small and Ralph realized with a shock that probably Grandpa's had been too and that was why he wore a beard. Uncle Claude's shoulders were massive, bullish, and his arms hung forward from them in an animal heaviness, terminating in the biggest hands the boy had ever seen. These hands, whose fingers had been enlarged and discolored as his father's had been, were long but were so wide that on the damask tablecloth and handling the coin-silver spoons, they looked scarcely like hands at all but slabs of meat with the rind still on. Leah and Rachel, scornful of his cheap ugly suit (it looked like the one the Watkins man wore), had said that he looked simple-minded and they hoped they would not have to sit next to him at the funeral. It was that his face was so innocent; he did not seem to know what had happened to him, and this house, these little girls, the appointments of this table were not in his line. You could tell he wished he had not come; but he was not simple-minded.

He had hardly spoken at all since his arrival. After he had seen his father, he had gone to the guest room and had remained there until it was time to leave for the service. Molly, hugging the trunk of the umbrella tree, had seen him standing at the oriel in the upstairs hall, looking down when the men came to fetch away the coffin to take it to the church. His silence had infected the others, and even Mrs. Fawcett's tongue had been stilled on the drive to the cemetery and home again. But now that all was over, she believed a lighter tone should prevail to efface, if possible, the sorrowful reason for their gathering together. The talk, therefore, at the luncheon table was jovial and irrelevant. Mr. Follansbee started it by telling a story about an earnest young lady, the daughter of a remote cousin of Mrs. Follansbee's, who had been sent to them with a letter of introduction for a short visit before she entered a boarding school in Pasadena.

"Oh, Rose, you will like this, I know," he said. "I can just imagine your good father in a similar position." To Uncle Claude, he explained, "I, an immigrant to California like everyone else—these four little Fawcetts are the only California natives of my acquaintance, ha, ha—and in the dim dark past I had the honor of hearing Mrs. Fawcett's father hold forth on cultural subjects far into many a night. I must confess that sometimes, for me, the midnight oil gave off soporific fumes but—ha, ha—as that most learned gentleman would have said himself, *aliquando bonus dormitat Homerus*, that is, 'even good Homer sometimes nods.'" Claude Kenyon, flanked by Ralph and Molly, looked bashfully at his plate of jellied soup and did not even pretend to smile. The preacher, with a hint of exasperation in his face, but none in his deep oratorical voice, continued, "This good lass came with loads of luggage, all of it as heavy as lead. Full of books, do you see. As pretty as a picture she was, and no earthly reason for her to be smart as well—look there at Leah and Rachel pricking up their ears! Yet she *was* smart, but the pity of it was that she wasn't really bright. You call that a paradox? Well, I have a funny sort of little old mind and I maintain a person can be intellectual and not be intelligent. But don't let me make a sermon right here! On to the story! Well, sir, the first night the pretty little slip of a thing was with us, we were taking our coffee in the library, a custom I have not been able to outgrow even after many years in this new-fangled nation of California, and lo and behold and *mirabile dictu*, milady says to me, very seriously, very soberly, 'Mr. Follansbee, have you ever read Shakespeare?'"

Mrs. Fawcett, who had been ready from the beginning of the anecdote, now laughed until she had to wipe her eyes. Mrs. Follansbee, who had been present and could not be expected to react quite as she had done at the time, was milder. Leah and Rachel covered their mouths with their napkins, through which came peals of laughter. But the minister had expected this applause and did not so much as glance at any of them but fixed his eyes on Uncle Claude with a look of malicious amusement. When Uncle Claude blushed, his skin took on an apoplectic blue and Ralph, who had not been able even to grin, shuddered when he looked at him.

When there had been enough laughter, Mr. Follansbee, still looking at Claude, said, "Sir, I envy you your snowy winters. I miss them here in California. Back in Missouri, on snowy nights, I used to go through the historical plays. Read them and reread them to my great edification. I imagine you do much the same thing. I expect when you're snowbound the time may hang heavy on your hands. Literature is a great medicine: it takes us out of ourselves."

Claude put his spoon down clumsily and it made a loud clatter on the plate under his soup cup. His ashamed eyes lifted waveringly to the minister's as he sighed. And then he said, "I couldn't rightly say I find the time hanging heavy. I have a sight of cows to feed."

"All the same," cried Mrs. Fawcett, frantically embarrassed, "I expect you manage to find the time to read! Mr. Follansbee, Claude was the most precocious youngster you ever saw, and who should be a better judge of that than I? Why, he was reading *Lorna Doone* when he was just a little bit of a thing!" This profession fell flat, but she barely paused. "Don't you remember the many many times we used to go out to the summer-house and read Tennyson aloud? How you loved *The Idylls of the King*!"

For several minutes she talked rapidly and distractedly about Tennyson, Claude's early love for him, her own love for him, her father's love for him. She did not relinquish the conversation until it was at a safe distance from the question of how Uncle Claude passed the time on a winter evening. Later on she confided in her children that she had been on tenterhooks for fear Claude would tell them what he did read. For she assumed that his tastes would be like those of his father who had never been seen reading a book and who had never mentioned any but the novels of Gaboriau which certainly could not be called "classics." As far as the ancient languages went, these might have been the Dark Ages for all Mr. Kenyon had known of them, and Mrs. Fawcett suspected that his son had not known what *mirabile dictu* meant.

Mr. Follansbee experimented with another gambit. His hobby was taxidermy and his house, which smelled of mud, was full of stuffed skunks, raccoons, woodpeckers, bluebirds and cottontails, the corpses being brought to him by his obedient flock, some of whom felt that for a minister the pastime was unduly skittish. He asked Uncle Claude if he had any interest in the subject and when Uncle Claude replied that he had never thought about it one way or the other, Mr. Follansbee said, "I'm just like a boy about it, as my long-suffering better half will testify. Why, yesterday I got a new batch of supplies and I stopped work right in the middle of my sermon to open the parcel. They had made a rather comical mistake. I had written for eyes of a vulture and they sent instead the eyes of the extinct auk."

Molly spoke for the first time. She closed her eyes and chanted, "A is for auk who lives in the wet, B is for blackbird with wings of jet." And Uncle Claude turned to her and smiled.

But Mrs. Fawcett, to whom actually the minister's handling of dead animals was extremely repugnant, told her not to interrupt and she asked what on earth he had done since obviously one could not substitute an auk's eyes for a vulture's eyes. He answered that he had sent them back and would, until the "genuine article" arrived, work on a gopher which Kenneth Taliafero had brought him. At this mention of her lover's name, Rachel giggled. Mr. Follansbee reached across the table and delicately pulled her hair. *Oh, stop it!* thought Ralph.

The meal progressed as if the silent outlander were not there. Leah and Rachel, interrogated by the minister, showed their wares boldly. Yes, indeed, they surely *were* glad they were going to boarding school next year in New Haven where they would have an opportunity to study French and music, but most of all to study elocution under someone of more gumption than the rather ungifted and certainly homely Mrs. Sawhill to whom they went on Saturday afternoon after their dancing lesson with the equally uninspired but less plain Miss Lanier. Both the minister and his wife laughed happily when Rachel, speaking of Mrs. Sawhill, said, "And I never can keep my mind on the piece I'm speaking because she mouths the words and I'm afraid her false teeth are going to fall right out because they do wobble so." Leah, not to be outdone, said of Miss Lanier, "Yes, but that's not half as bad as in ballet when she takes off her slipper and rubs her *bunion*." It was said that Mrs. Fawcett was brave to let her little girls go all the way across the country even though Aunt Rowena would be near them to keep an eye on them. It was observed by the girls that they were already homesick.

Molly bubbled her water and said, "A child in my grade has the itch."

"Molly," said her mother, vigorously shaking her head. "Shame on you." Everyone ignored the impossible child.

A hideous accident attended the serving of the dessert. Uncle Claude had failed to remove his finger bowl from his plate and when Fuschia brought around the raspberry ice, he put his portion into the water, splashing it on the table. Leah and Rachel could not contain themselves any longer and burst into laughter. To double his humiliation the others chose pointedly to pay no attention to the calamity and Mrs. Fawcett, in a flash of venomous discourtesy, said, "I declare I do not understand why these girls can suddenly laugh their heads off at nothing at all."

Ralph felt physically sick and was afraid that if the meal did not end quickly he might disgrace himself right there at the table. Never had he so passionately despised Mr. Follansbee's cruel, smug face, his pince-nez on a black ribbon, the effeminate white piping of his vest. Grandpa Kenyon had, next to merchants, disliked clergymen more than any other people, and Ralph agreed with, him, for he was sure they were all like Mr. Follansbee. Grandpa's shillelagh had been sent to him from Cork by his brother who was a clergyman and who "had undertaken to preach the Gospel English style to those poor backward natives." By the way he said it, the children knew that he did not think the Irish were poor and backward at all and that he was really making fun of his brother. He had another brother who was also a clergyman, a missionary in China, and his sister Nan was an Anglican nun. Mrs. Fawcett always told him, before the Follansbees came to the buffet supper, that it would perhaps be just as well for him not to mention his brothers and sisters as Mr. Follansbee had very decided opinions on anything the least bit Romish. She was afraid he was secretly displeased that her land adjoined that of the Freudenburgs who were Romans and went in for all kinds of superstitions like fish on Friday and statues of the virgin on top of the piano. Ralph wondered if Schöneshund had to eat fish on Friday too. Probably they gave him potatoes instead.

The horrible pastor looked at Ralph and for some reason winked his light green, reptilian eye. The boy trembled and looked away and this time glanced with ardent loathing at Mrs. Follansbee's round puffy face whose vulgar snub nose complemented her husband's downward curving one. He particularly hated her nose because she had chronic catarrh and tried, because of it, to identify herself with him and Molly who were similarly afflicted. While she was therefore ostensibly becoming their contemporary, she spoke of their kinship in baby talk and in the loud voice ladies used in addressing servants and foreigners. The only thing that could be said in her favor was that she did not talk as much as her husband. Otherwise, she was just as bad, and Ralph wished both of them would get bubonic plague.

"Who has the itch?" he suddenly asked Molly.

"Ralph!" cried Mrs. Fawcett. "This is not to be discussed at the table."

But Molly said, "Beulah. The one that stole my nickel."

"That will be enough, Molly," said Mrs. Fawcett. She dipped her fingers into the crystal bowl of water and dried them on her napkin and everyone did the same except Uncle Claude who could not wash in his dessert. Ralph's nausea and resentment ebbed. In a moment it would be over. There would only be two more meals and the Follansbees wouldn't be at those. While he wanted Uncle Claude to like him, he was glad that he was leaving the next day so that Leah and Rachel would stop giggling at his wrong clothes and his table manners and his language. He was determined not to let him go, though, without explaining to him that he and Molly were different from the rest of the family. And there was another thing: there were the presents Grandpa had not given them, so now they would really be Uncle Claude's presents. But how could he ask for them? Again he wondered if he could tell the joke about the cow, but it did not seem quite right; Uncle Claude seemed too serious even though he had smiled at Molly when she recited the alphabet thing.

After lunch it was suggested that Uncle Claude would like to take a nap for he had really had no rest at all since he left home. The fact that he had unaccountably come all the way from Denver by day coach was not alluded to before the Follansbees. The minister, who was the host in any house he entered, thought a game of Twenty Questions would be as decorous an amusement as any; Mrs. Fawcett, agreeing, said that afterward Leah and Rachel could recite their new Scottish dialogue. They sauntered slowly to the parlor, Molly and Ralph and Uncle Claude at the rear. As Uncle Claude turned toward the stairs he said, "If that Beulah stole your nickel, it serves her right to have the itch."

Most of the flowers had been taken out of the parlor and laid on Grandpa's grave, but the air was still heavy with fragrance. The room was altered. Although nothing had been moved or added, it was not the same place it had been before, and Ralph could not imagine the ladies of the Sorosis sitting here eating ice cream in tiny bites off the tip end of their spoons and talking, giving prices, of the January white sales in Los Angeles. But no one else appeared aware of the transformation. They all picked their chairs and settled down and looked around as if nothing at all had happened, as if the long old dead man had not been here just a few hours before. For a little while no one spoke: it was as if they were all consciously digesting their lunch. They heard Uncle Claude move down the ell, quietly like a dog. It was warm so Mrs. Fawcett took off her black broadcloth jacket. She wore a pink crepe-de-Chine guimpe through which showed the deep lace yoke of her camisole, and at her throat she wore a cameo brooch which Grandpa Kenyon had given her as an engagement present. She did not especially like it, finding it too large to be really refined, but she had often worn it during his visits.

"Well," said Mr. Follansbee at last. Ralph, closing his eyes, could believe that they were in church and that Mr. Follansbee was standing before the pulpit while the deacons, Mr. Brewster and Mr. Prater, sat behind him, monumental, bald, inexorably dull, looking very much like Grandfather Bonney. The sermon presently would begin; his voice always trailed dramatically down at the end of every sentence during the last twenty minutes so that you were deceived a hundred times, thinking he was nearly through. He was not quite ready for his flock to play Twenty Questions. Instead, looking up at the portrait, he made an astonishing statement. He said, "Well, Ralph, my boy, it wouldn't be hard to imagine *him* as the President of the United States, would it?"

Ralph was too dumfounded to reply and Leah said, "It certainly wouldn't, Mr. Follansbee. Why do you suppose he never was?"

Mrs. Fawcett touched her point-lace handkerchief to her eyes. There promised to be a scene of sadness and memory but Rachel, who had been seized all day with the giggles, prevented it by giggling, burying her head in Leah's shoulder, and saying in a stage whisper, "Imagine Grandpa Kenyon as the President, though!" Leah said, laughing, "Now you just stop it, you horrid girl." But Rachel could not stop and she went on conjecturing how the Senate would like it when Mr. Kenyon said, "By the Lord Harry," and how funny he would look in a top hat like Mr. Harding's. The grown-ups pretended not to hear, but they were smiling all the same at the wicked, witty little girl. Ralph and Molly, side by side on a hassock, kept a glum silence until at last Ralph said bitterly, "Nobody but a boob would want to be the President."

It was the first time in his life that he had ever shown temper in the presence of anyone but his immediate family, and it gave him a feeling of lunatic power. Rachel looked slapped. His mother, most likely deep in a dream of boating parties on the Potomac and picnics on the White House lawn, looked at him reproachfully. The minister, unaccustomed to having his speculations rejected, arranged his cunning, vulpine face to give him his comeuppance, but Ralph got ahead of him. He said: "Did you know that Grandpa Kenyon killed a man once, Mr. Follansbee?"

Mrs. Fawcett said, "You poor silly it! You should never take any of Mr. Kenyon's stories seriously. He was only telling you a western yarn, Ralphie boy."

Mr. Follansbee could scarcely conceal his curiosity, but he said, "They are the salt of the earth, those tale-tellers. The farther they get from the truth, the better the tale."

"Oh, no, this wasn't a made-up one," insisted Ralph. "Grandpa really did kill a man. Probably more than one, I guess, but I only know just about this one."

The man folded his hands and slightly teetered on his chair and said indulgently, "Let's hear this true confession, laddie."

"Oh! Do you think it's right?" asked Mrs. Follansbee and her pop eyes strayed to the place where the coffin had so recently been. "Don't you think it seems a little disrespectful?" But her husband, quoting in his brief homily from "Some Starbeams of

Solace," assured them all that the deceased would have enjoyed this himself.

Ralph began with self-assurance, but it waned as he went on. He could not tell the tale as Grandpa told it: he himself was shocked and disbelieving and could not recapture the feeling of wonder he had known that day the year before when he and Molly and Grandpa had sat together under a tree in the grove. He had been telling them that when he had been in Texas the week before he had had to take measures about some sheep that had got into his pastures and that he had not a bit liked to blow those little lambs to glory, one in particular that he would have liked to bring to Molly. Ralph immediately saw the lamb that Jesus carried in the Bible picture, one awkward leg hanging over His arm. Molly said, "Then why *did* you blow the lamb to glory, Grandpa?" And the old man answered, "Well, I'll tell you, Molly. I'd rather kill the sheep than kill the shepherd."

He stopped to light his pipe. They were far from the nut gatherers now, at the north end of the grove where the trees had been stripped and the ground gleaned. There was an acrid smell everywhere of the splitting hulls and the bleaching acids.

Ralph said, "Did you ever kill a shepherd?"

"Yes, sir," said Grandpa. "I own I did."

As he told his story, Ralph could see him, a young man, riding like the wind through the dark Texas night, his money belt full of silver and gold, his twin revolvers ready to be drawn. Months before he and his outfit had driven a shipment of steers to Dodge City and he was coming back home again. He had left the train at Amarillo and had come horseback the remaining fourteen miles. "My horse was called Pearl," he said, "and she was a dandy piece of jewelry." He had been in sight of his place and had seen a light in the bunkhouse, down in the hollow, some way off yet, when a couple of men had charged him suddenly, riding at a lope out from the shadows of a thicket of screw-bean. There was no moon but the night was clear and he was able to tell who they were by the starlight. They were brothers by the name of MacNeill, not good Scotch, as the name sounded, but half-breed Creeks, murderous and thieving. There had been ill will between them and Kenyon for a long time, for they had used his land to pasture their flocks and if he or any of his men caught a MacNeill sheep there, they disposed of it after giving the boys good warning. In retaliation, the skalawags rustled his cattle. The pattern was an endless circle. As they came on him tonight—they must have heard somehow that he would be riding in alone and with tolerable money on his person—they fired into the air to frighten Pearl, for they were that underhanded: they wanted to unseat him and have him on the ground at their mercy. Grandpa did not wait to find out what their business was and he stuck to his saddle as if he were nailed to it, though his mare leaped in terror. He shot the taller of the two cleanly through the heart and the other turned yellow and rode off the way he had come, not even dismounting to pay his respects to his dead brother. Ralph remembered that, when he had finished, Molly had asked if in the morning the two ravens of the ballad Grandpa sometimes sang had come to pluck out the man's bonny blue eyes.

The way Grandpa had told it, it had taken a long while, fifteen minutes or more, but Ralph, half crying, took only two or three, and at the end he realized that he did not believe a word of it. Leah pursed her lips. "I don't think it's nice to make up stories about killing people. I think it's awful."

Ralph turned on her and with the maniac laugh he and Molly had invented, shouted, "You mean because Mother killed Grandfather Bonney?"

But suddenly a mocking bird, in this broad daylight, began to sing. Mrs. Fawcett clasped her hands together and said "Oh!" as if the sound hurt her. Her large diamond ring, in the gesture, came into a ray of sunlight and two green needles shot out from the stone. Then Mr. Follansbee was across the room in one stride, shaking Ralph's shoulder. "You little cad," he said between his teeth, "you get down on your knees and beg your mother's pardon. On your *knees.*"

For a moment he defied the minister by remaining motionless, but the long bony hand on his shoulder propelled him off the hassock and at last he knelt, not feeling sorry, feeling nothing but rage, as painful as a deep cut. He could not utter a word, though this delay was agonizing, and they were all watching him and they were all waiting. He could hear Mr. Follansbee breathing heavily. Then Molly, half under her breath, said "I wish you were a fairy, Mr. Follansbee." Rachel giggled, but

Mr. Follansbee did not think this was funny and he snarled, "What's this? Why do you wish I were a fairy, young lady?" And Molly whispered with deadly hatred, "So you'd vanish."

And now he could speak. Now, with this ally beside him, kneeling and clutching his hand, he could tell the lie: "I'm sorry, Mother. Please forgive me, Mother." Molly said it after him in that queer, hoarse whisper in which she had insulted Mr. Follansbee.

Mrs. Fawcett patted his head, but she said firmly, "You may leave the room, Ralph." Molly did not get off so lightly. Mrs. Fawcett slapped her face, not hard, but so that it made a sound. "Mr. Follansbee will never want to come to our house again after this terrible thing you have said. You may go ask Fuschia to lock you in the closet."

Ralph did not go to his room which was directly over the parlor but to Molly's. On the little white desk under the window she had laid out the presents from Grandpa Kenyon in the order in which he had given them to her: a doll made of straw with a sombero that could be taken off; a suède bookmark with a burned-in design of yucca; a pair of bearskin slippers which were now too small; a totem pole, three inches high which listed like the leaning tower of Pisa; a jewel box made of fragrant lemon wood and carved all over with squash blossoms; a beaded belt. Ralph touched them, one by one, and thought of his sister standing in the dark in the coat closet which smelled of naphtha and of buttons. His anger had given way to fear, to the fear of the sermon Mr. Follansbee would preach next Sunday, two days away. They always sat in the very front so that there was no escaping his darting eyes and you had to pay attention every minute, even when you had a hangnail or something like that to play with.

There was a copy of "Gravel" on Molly's desk and he read it again and *still* it didn't make any sense to him. There was also a letter which she had written to their cousin Mildred whom she did not like at all but to whom she wrote once a week because Mildred had sent her some stationery for her birthday. Ralph read it even though he knew it was against the law to read other people's mail.

Dear Mildred.

How are you? I am fine and hope you are the same. How are you getting along in school? Do you think long devision is hard? I do.

The Snake and the File

A snake one day crept into a blake-smiths shop and chaunced to knock against a steel file. This hurt the snake slightly, and, flying into a rage, he at once bit the file as hard as he could. The hard steel file cut the snake mouth, but when he saw the blood he though it was the file that bled, and so he bit it again and again until he had damage his own mouth very badly.

When we try to hurt other people we are much more likely to get hurt ourself.

Isn't that a funny story?

I guess that is all I can say so I will close your cousin.

Molly F.

He put the letter down, baffled. Molly was going crazy, he decided, and the thought made him nervous. If it were true, that was all the more reason he should get to be Uncle Claude's best friend, because if they had to take her to an asylum, he certainly wouldn't stay around here with those women; he would have to go to Colorado. He wanted to go into Uncle Claude's room, but he might be asleep and if Ralph woke him up, he might be angry; on the other hand if he were just sitting there, thinking of Grandpa, perhaps he would be glad to have company. He debated, looking at Molly's presents. Soon he heard them all go out to the front porch and almost immediately Leah and Rachel began their recitation. Now and again the grown-ups laughed and then, when they had quieted down, the girls went on. It was about a girl and a boy named Jock and Jean and at the end of it, they would sing "Comin' Through the Rye." He felt suddenly that he could not bear to hear the song which always reminded him of the time Miss Runyon had come over to play Snap with them and at the end of the evening sang that song in a trembly voice and to make it all the more terrible, there was a piece of fudge on her front tooth. Hearing more laughter from the porch, he got up and went down the corridor to the ell.

Ralph was surprised to see that the door of the guest room was open and Uncle Claude was lying in the middle of the double bed flat on his back with his arms straight at his sides. He had taken off his bright orange oxfords and his coat so that Ralph could see the black and green horsehair belt; it had a design like a snake's back. The shades were drawn. Grandpa's grip was still on the luggage stand and Uncle Claude's small Boston bag, unopened, stood in the middle of the floor. A cigarette was burning in the pin tray on the dresser.

As he stepped across the threshold, Ralph was uneasy and he would have gone back to Molly's room if his uncle had not heard him and jerked up on his elbow.

"Your door was open," he said.

"You can close it now," said Uncle Claude.

Ralph hesitated, his hand wetly grasping the doorknob. "With me outside or in?" he asked.

"Suit yourself."

He went into the room and closed the door. Something inside him twitched like a cat's tail and he was afraid he might have a nosebleed. Fuschia and Miguel were having their lunch in the kitchen directly below the guest room and he heard a soft and urgent conversation. It was possible here only to hear the voices on the front porch as an uneven murmur; he was sure Uncle Claude had not heard what had happened in the parlor. Desperately he looked around the room: "Oh! Can I bring you your cigarette, Uncle Claude?"

His uncle got up and went over to the bureau and brushed his hair with two military brushes that had belonged to Ralph's father. He wore his hair parted in the middle and slicked down on either side. He ground out the cigarette and lighted a fresh one and then he sat down in the white rocking chair by the window and said, "Is this the room where he died?"

"Oh, yes," said Ralph. "Don't you see his grip still here?"

"I know," said Uncle Claude. "I thought maybe your mother just put it here to make me feel at home."

He was scrutinizing Ralph now and Ralph knew what he saw: a thin, sallow creature with his knickers hanging down to the middle of his spindling legs, hideous braces on hideous teeth, glasses that made him look ninety-nine years old. He felt that he must quickly speak before his uncle passed judgment on him and denied him permanently, but he could think of nothing to say. It would be unkind to tell him what it had

been like when Grandpa had had his attack; it would be useless
to apologize for his sisters and his mother and Mr. and Mrs.
Follansbee; what was there to say? Finally, in a thin, singsong
voice he told Uncle Claude the joke about the cow, realizing
with each word that it was not a bit funny, just as he had known
a little while ago that Grandpa's story about the MacNeills was
not true. He did not even finish telling it, and when his voice
trailed off, Uncle Claude did not even pay any attention so that
Ralph knew he had not been listening.

After a long while, Uncle Claude said, "My father thought a
lot of you. He was always saying he wished you'd come to visit
me on my place." Then, with a smile which disarmed Ralph so
that he nearly cried, he added, "But I guess you wasn't of the
same mind."

"My mother . . ." Ralph began.

"Oh, well, hell," said Uncle Claude. He had a funny way of
smoking. He drew so deeply that the ember took great bites
in the paper. Ralph remembered evenings when Grandpa had
sat on the porch smoking and the glow in the bowl of his pipe
went on and off like a firefly. Uncle Claude said, "She never got
over that about horses, did she? She would of kept me off 'em
if she'd of had her way. But Mr. Kenyon was stronger minded
than her."

"Well, I guess she worried, you know, about riding a horse
and Grandfather getting the infection while he was watching
her." He made his voice tentative. He did not really wish to be
disloyal and so he said, "I don't really think she killed him,
though, do you?"

"Jesus," said Uncle Claude. He sounded tired. In a minute
he said, "What do you do around here to keep busy?"

There was very little they did that would interest Uncle
Claude. They were not allowed to climb trees because splinters had been known to get into the bloodstream and travel
to the heart. They did not have bicycles and they were not
allowed to build things (the very thought of a nail brought
tears to their mother's splendid blue eyes) nor to have roller
skates or wagons. The girls played jacks and had all sorts of silly
different kinds of games called "Dropsies" and "Allsies" and
"Cart before the horse." He did not think that Uncle Claude
would be interested in knowing that the most exciting thing

he and Molly did was to watch Miguel harness the team; if Star and Swanee offered any resistance and tossed their heads, the Mexican slapped them on the nose with his gloves or gave them a wallop on the rump. He was not in the least afraid, even when they neighed at him angrily and their velvety lips rolled up, showing green teeth and a line of grass-stained foam on the underjaw.

And Ralph was sure that Uncle Claude did not want to hear about their indoor pastimes. They had sets of water colors and boxes of plasticine and Mrs. Fawcett guided their fingers so expertly and so patiently that the results made everyone believe the children were unusually gifted. In the evenings and on rainy afternoons she played games with them. They played "Lotto" and "Authors" and "Parchesi" and "I Spy," all of which Grandfather Bonney had enjoyed. Sometimes she read aloud to them from *The Little Shepherd of Kingdom Come*, *Sevenoaks*, and *The Old Curiosity Shop*. When it was cool enough for a fire in the fireplace, they popped corn over the flames while the Edison played records of Grandfather Bonney's favorite songs: "The Green Hills of Home," "All Through the Night," "Old Black Joe," and "I Dreamt That I Dwelt in Marble Halls." All of them, by the time they were six, could recite "The Brook" and "The Chambered Nautilus," and often they said them in unison, standing in a row in front of the bay window, their mother smiling proudly at them when she looked up from her crocheting. Leah and Rachel embroidered dresser scarves and tops for pincushions and talked in a grown-up way with their mother about clothes, to his and Molly's embarrassment. Once Mrs. Fawcett had said, "I am making some curtains for Molly's sitting room," and held up a pair of bloomers, right in front of Ralph.

Ralph could not possibly tell Uncle Claude what a sissy life he had to lead. But he had to say something and so, doubtfully, he began, "Well, Molly and I got sick last year—that's why we're so funny looking but Dr. Haskell says we'll outgrow it. I didn't used to look like this. . . ."

Uncle Claude said nothing, and there was no possible way to tell what he was thinking for he did not smile or frown or have any kind of look on his face at all.

"Anyway, we are too skinny or something to do anything much. We play mumbly-peg a lot . . . we do a lot of things. I'm in the Yosemite Patrol. I'm going to tie knots at the Jamboree next spring."

Why had Uncle Claude asked if he wasn't going to listen? He went back to the bed and lay down in the same position Ralph had found him in.

"Don't you feel well, Uncle Claude?"

"I don't know."

"Did you ever hunt savage animals, Uncle Claude?"

"You mean like tigers?" he said. "Or do you mean like deer?"

"Either kind," said Ralph.

Uncle Claude narrowed his eyes reflectively. "I get me a deer now and again, but a man couldn't call a deer a savage animal. I never seen a bear or a mountain lion. The chances are they might put up a fight if you didn't hunt them just according to Hoyle."

"Is a mountain lion really savage?" said Ralph.

"Why, son, if you was a setting hen, he'd tear you limb from limb," said Uncle Claude and laughed.

A fat autumn fly thumped and fretted against the screen.

"Uncle Claude?" He put his hand out and touched the handle of Grandpa's grip. "Uncle Claude, I think that maybe there's something that belongs to me in here."

Uncle Claude did not open his eyes but he smiled and said, "Sure, help yourself."

The catches sprung back easily and the mouth of the grip gaped wide, showing the familiar gray wads of clothing, a suit of winter underwear, nearly black around the neck, a few blue work shirts, a pair of denim overalls. Ralph took out everything and shook it and looked in the pockets and in the toes of the socks, but there were no presents. He came finally to the bottom where Grandpa's big blue-black revolver lay, and though he again shook each garment as he put it back in, he found nothing but Grandpa's own belongings. So what had happened? Had he felt bad in Texas, too bad to go to Mexico? You would think that in that case he would at least have brought some rattles off a rattlesnake. It was incredible and it gave him a creepy feeling, knowing that this autumn they had been far from Grandpa's thoughts. And now he could not make Uncle Claude include him in *his* thoughts: he wondered suddenly if anyone in the world were thinking about him, Ralph Fawcett, at this moment. If anyone was, it was Molly sitting on top of the galoshes in the closet. For some reason he thought of the crazy pilot banking his plane like a hawk and he said to himself, "Pilot, whoever you are, I am thinking about you."

"Do you want to hear something funny, Uncle Claude?"

Uncle Claude shrugged his shoulders. "I'd just as soon."

"Well, the other day, I went to get some brown sugar and I put a whole lot of it in my mouth and it wasn't brown sugar at all. I'll give you three guesses what it was."

"Corn meal," said Uncle Claude.

"No, no. I mean it looked like brown sugar all right."

Uncle Claude next guessed dried milk and oatmeal even though Ralph had explained that it had *looked* like brown sugar.

"It was nitrate fertilizer that Miguel had got to put on the four-o'clocks!"

Uncle Claude chuckled. At last Ralph had won. Pleased as he was, he was a little disquieted because this had happened to Molly, not to himself, so he quickly said, "But don't tell anybody because it would make Mother mad."

"I won't breathe it to a living soul," said Uncle Claude. "You know it's a funny thing. At lunch I was just thinking about the time Mr. Kenyon got this here impetigo and then your sister said Beulah had the itch."

Why, he was wonderful! He didn't talk like the usual kind of grown-up at all. Ralph thought he was probably sincerely glad that Beulah got what she deserved for stealing Molly's nickel. He said, "I like you, Uncle Claude."

Uncle Claude stretched out his hand, beckoning to him. "I like you, too, Ralph." Then he lay down beside his uncle, careful not to touch him. They lay there for a long time, dozing and waking. In all that time, Uncle Claude did not say a word, but twice he put his hand on the boy's thin shoulder. For the first time in days Ralph was free of the smell of flowers. Uncle Claude had a smell something like Grandpa's but it was younger and had less raisin in it, perhaps because he smoked cigarettes and his father had smoked a pipe.

Soon after they heard Mr. Follansbee cranking his car and driving off, Uncle Claude sat up and yawned and said, "You come on out next summer to my place and bring What'shername along."

"Well, I don't know if Molly can come. I think maybe something is going to happen to her."

"Like what? Is she going to have her adenoids out?"

"No. They're already out. I mean . . . well, Uncle Claude, strictly speaking, I think Molly's going crazy." Then he recited "Gravel" which he had read so many times that he knew it by heart.

Uncle Claude laughed but he was puzzled too and he said, "I wouldn't worry if I was you. I always did think that the folks that wrote poems were bughouse but harmless. No, you bring her along."

Ralph sucked at a wart on the heel of his hand, at first refusing the daydream, but he could not hold out against it and he allowed it to overtake him and to crowd from his mind all else: Grandpa's neverness, the sermon next Sunday, the darkness of the coat closet, the embarrassment of the meal they soon would eat.

When his mother called to him from the foot of the stairs, he left his shoes where he had put them, right beside the orange oxfords. But once again, when he had closed the door, the smell of flowers greeted him like an ocean wave. He moved toward his mother, toward Leah and Rachel, toward the portrait in the parlor. She called again sharply, "Ralph! How many times must I ask you to come downstairs."

"Hush," he whispered, leaning over the banister. "Don't you know Grandpa's dead?"

Chapter Four

THE BIG dining room was dim because a hop vine grew over the windows. The foreman, the six hands, Mrs. Brotherman and her daughter, Winifred, Uncle Claude, and the Fawcett children all sat at one long narrow table which was covered with mottled red linoleum. In one corner of the room stood a gun cabinet which looked like an upended coffin and showed, in this half-light, the blue glint of a dozen barrels. On the long wall behind Uncle Claude, casting an enormous shadow of itself, was the head of a bighorn. The horns, like white half-moons, curled rakishly away from the stupid and dignified face; it did not look dead but only despondent, unlike the head of the doe in Mr. Fawcett's den which Mr. Follansbee had once said looked more embalmed than stuffed. Ralph realized that this was the first dining room he had ever seen in which there was not a still life of fruits or fish or a rare roast of beef. From this eccentric omission, he proceeded to observe other peculiarities: the knives and forks did not match and the dishes did not all have the same design; the spoons were in a tumbler in the middle of the table.

The men ate quickly and efficiently, bending their heads low over their plates and not straightening up even when they spoke. The girl, Winifred, who sat nearest the kitchen door, kept a close vigil on the dishes and took them away the moment she saw they were empty and brought them back refilled. The food was strange and Ralph and Molly ate with mistrust. There was strong, tough meat which Uncle Claude told them was "buckskin." Too tongue-tied to ask what he meant by that, they listened for a clue and finally got it when Mrs. Brotherman made the chance remark that this was the last of the deer. There were string beans cooked until they were almost brown and there was fried mush with gravy. At either end of the table stood a quart can of strawberry jam and the men took out tablespoonfuls of it and ate it with their forks. Globules of cream floated on the top of Ralph's glass of milk and he could not drink it. Before each plate was a smaller plate with the dessert, a fried pie which was shaped like a rubber heel.

No one took any heed of the newcomers; perhaps they were as shy of the children as the children were of them, and Ralph and Molly endeavored to be as silent and small as possible and did not look around save when the talk was general and the speakers were off their guard. Ralph's first impression was that all these men were the same size and shape and color, that they were all large, spare, and red-brown, and this, in general, was true, but as the meal progressed, he saw that one of them was very blond, that another was handsome and had auburn hair, that a third had a flattened nose like a prize fighter's. Similarly, their voices had at first seemed indistinguishable from one another but in time he heard variations in the timbre and even, slightly, in the accents.

The talk was endless but it seemed to be made up almost altogether of non sequiturs. The men did not interrupt one another, but they did not listen. Questions were answered, but were usually reshaped to fit a statement that was uppermost in the speaker's mind. At the very beginning of the meal, Uncle Claude asked Homer Armitage, the foreman, if he thought it might not be a good idea to put in a strip of electric fence along the pasture where he kept one of his prize bulls, and Homer replied, "I never was a man for electric fence. If the current goes off, where are you? Old man Terry put some in once but I don't know if it was ever worth the money or not. Don't remember ever hearing anything more about it, only just that he put it in. I seen old man Terry today and he said he seen elk sign half a mile this side Wolf Forks. He said it was as clean as a whistle, and I aim to go up there this coming Sunday if the weather's good."

Uncle Claude and Homer retired into silence, the one to think of electric fence, the other of his hunting trip. Then one of the hands, who was named Dump, said, in the direction of Homer who was now bowed over his plate, "Bernard Tobey's got his still up there to Wolf Forks."

The man next to him said, "I knew Bernard Tobey in Glenwood. He was a barber there. I guess he got tired of drinking bay rum."

"Some people like Tobey and some don't," said Dump. "One that don't is Agnew Prescott. Those two hate each other like poison and have for a dog's age."

"Kenyon," said another man, "did you hear that Prescott took his bulls out to Denver last night?"

"No, I never heard that," said Uncle Claude. "I ain't taking any of mine till fall. I'm studying on whether I ought to sell Advance Anxiety."

Homer exclaimed with surprise and alarm, "Why, you must be touched! Why, my God, he's the best bull you ever had on this place."

Uncle Claude said, "You may be right. I reckon I won't sell him. I wonder if it wouldn't be kind of a good idea to put up a strip of electric fence around that pasture where I got him."

They had all been to a horse sale that afternoon, but each man made a different report. None of them had seen the same people or the same horses and none had heard the same bids, so that it sounded as if there had been eight different auctions in eight different places. And yet each knew what the others were talking about. Homer, who had not known that the blue-eyed stallion had been sold to a dude for seven thousand dollars— though, from Uncle Claude's account, this must have been the high note of the afternoon—said, "You mean that ugly old paint that Bill Prescott sold to Roger Campbell here awhile back? You mean that colt that was that little wild mare's, that one B. F. Ward got in Idaho?" They all knew the names and the lineage of all the horses in the country and they spoke of them as if they were people in the way, Ralph thought, fishermen would speak of boats. They talked of Ruth, the cow pony whose master had once hitched her up with a team horse when his other team horse had lost a shoe; of Poncho, a dandy little chestnut who had thrown Prescott once when he was three sheets to the wind; of Meadowlark who was herself an ugly piece of business but had foaled two good colts.

The children were tired from the long, halting journey over the mountains from Denver where they had parted from their tearful mother. The train had not been like any they had ever been on before. Instead of little rooms with white towels on the backs of the seats and a little shelf by the window where the porter put the glasses of lemonade, there were just rows of bronze-green seats which were straight up and down and so hard you felt after a while your bones were going to come right through. The windows were dirty and the car was full of smoke. All the towns they passed through, pausing for a long time while freight was unloaded, were exactly the same. The buildings along the wooden walks had high square façades and on them, in faded letters, were printed "Livery," "Odd Fellows' Hall," "Assayor's Office." Undernourished dogs meandered about the streets looking for food in the ruts they already knew by heart. There seemed to be no trees in any of the towns, though the great shaggy mountains beyond were densely forested. The train had labored up and up, going right through the mountains, through tunnels too many to count. They spoke very little but each was conscious of the other's misgivings, and they did not eat any of the Martha Washington candy their mother had bought for them. Once Molly almost cried when they had stopped at a town called Blackriver and a man with a bandanna around his neck looked right in the window at them and then turned and spit tobacco juice at a cat. She felt the same surprise and anxiety as she had one morning when she woke up and saw a grasshopper on her pillow, looking at her.

They were bedazzled by the mountains and the ranch. They had not bargained for anything on so large a scale; it seemed beyond their compassing and they had already begun to withdraw. Ralph looked at the guns in the cabinet, so much bigger than he had imagined them to be from the catalogues, and now, while the whole point of coming had been to learn how to ride horseback, he was afraid. For months he and Molly had planned how they would defy their mother's injunctions ("If there is a Shetland pony there, you may ride that if someone is with you," she had said. A Shetland pony, indeed!) and how they would disobey Mrs. Brotherman who, through frequent letters, had promised that she would exercise the most stringent discipline to keep the children away from guns and horses. The moment they had met the sad, mild-mannered housekeeper, they had known that she could easily be shaken from her resolution and this, in itself, was enough to cloud their passion. Yet, though they no longer felt daring but on the contrary were afraid, there was no waning of their determination. They knew, both of them, that they would try to escape, would invent headaches, would have nosebleeds, would hide behind books, but they would not, in the end, successfully evade Uncle Claude; they were bound to learn.

It was the presence of the genteel Mrs. Brotherman that had finally persuaded Mrs. Fawcett to allow Ralph and Molly to come to the ranch. They had given her no peace after Claude had left and had had tantrums whenever she suggested the alternatives of Puget Sound or Lake Tahoe, and then, when Dr. Haskell said he thought the mountain air might be good for their catarrh, she finally wrote to her half-brother, inquiring whether he had any trustworthy womenfolk in his house who could watch out for the children's baths and clean underwear and health. She put faith in Mrs. Brotherman because she was from Salem, Massachusetts, and Grandfather Bonney had been born in Boston. Besides this, Mrs. Brotherman was herself a mother and a widow and could be expected, therefore, to be more responsible than a spinster or a woman with a husband.

Ralph and Molly had been prepared to dislike and mutiny against the housekeeper. They saw her as a stout, ill-natured and red-faced woman with all the power and habits of a school principal, so that this afternoon they had been astonished and almost disappointed to find her a fragile, dispirited gentle-woman who appeared to find everything in the world immea-surably sad and who spoke mostly in the past tense. She did not say, "I think you will want to wash before supper," but "I thought you would want to wash." She was the widow of a Swedenborgian minister who had come West to die in the sun of tuberculosis. After his death, she had not gone East again because her daughter was said to have a "tendency." Winifred was fourteen, a tall and lovely girl who did not look in the least delicate. She was very brown and clear-eyed; she had thick dark hair which she wore short and which lay in tight little curls all over her head. She had her own horse, a sorrel gelding named Noel since he had been Grandpa Kenyon's Christmas present to her the year she was twelve. Grandpa Kenyon had given her silver mountings for the bridle and a crop made of snakeskin.

Winifred was the first of the household they had met. They had stood, begrimed with train smoke, miserable, already homesick, in the shadow of a cottonwood tree while Uncle Claude got their suitcases out of the back of the car. The ride

from the station to the Bar K had been difficult; Uncle Claude
had three times inquired after the health of their mother
and sisters, twice had said he was glad to see them, and this,
together with the children's monosyllabic replies, had constituted their conversation. Now, in the shade of the summery
tree, they felt doomed to failure. Unable to take in the huge,
snaggle-toothed mountain ranges that completely encircled the
valley where the ranch lay, alarmed by the rapid rushing sound
of the river which they could not see, frightened by the steady
commotion of animal noises—cows bellowing, horses neighing, dogs barking, birds screaming—they had been glad to fix
their attention on one single thing, the girl who came riding
her horse across the bridge which spanned a slough to the west
of the house. She dismounted quickly and looped the reins
around the hitching post across the lane from where they stood
and when she started forward Uncle Claude told them about
Noel, as if this would establish a bond between her and Ralph
and Molly. But the gleaming horse, stamping his delicate foot
and flicking his handsome tail, made the presents Grandpa
had given them seem paltry and perfunctory. However, Ralph
remembered that Grandpa had wanted to bring him a monkey
from Australia. So, in a moment, he shook hands with Winifred, noticing as he did so, with a shock of pleasure, that her
blue jeans were stained with dung, and he thought with contempt of Leah and Rachel who had never got their clothes dirty
in their lives.

"I'm mighty pleased to meet you," she said and smiled showing small, even teeth. Ralph and Molly were taken aback by her
words and her slow, uninflected speech. They had been taught
that the expression she had used was vulgar. You were supposed
to say "How do you do."

Molly said loudly, "Who are you?"

The girl looked startled but she smiled again and said, "I'm
Winifred Brotherman. I know who you are."

"I don't suppose you write poetry, do you?" said Molly.
Ralph wished she would stop that kind of talk. She had recited
"Gravel" to the conductor just as the train pulled out of Los
Angeles and although he had smiled and said the poem was
fine and dandy, it had been perfectly clear that he had not
thought much of it.

"Why, no," said Winifred. "I reckon I don't. I've got to go now and get the cows."

She mounted and rode off, over the river this time. Ralph hoped that Molly and Winifred would be friends so that he could spend all his time with Uncle Claude, and when he had finished his unpacking he went into her room and said, "I think Winifred's peachy, don't you?" Molly replied, "She has Nell Brinkley hair," and said no more.

Now, watching Winifred as she moved from the kitchen to the dining room on silent moccasins, Ralph admired her and glancing sidelong, he saw that Molly, too, followed her with fascinated eyes. Suddenly a wave of pity for his sister came over him and he impulsively touched her hand which rested in her lap. His pity was focused on her clothes: she wore a flowered batiste dress with a full skirt, smocked at the waist and at the neck and the prettiness of it made even more ridiculous her thin, freckled arms, her ugly little face framed by black hair with which, Mrs. Fawcett often remarked, nothing could be done. Molly, at the touch of his hand, turned and looked him full in the face and smiled wistfully. Ralph met her eyes only for a moment and then looked away, looked at Uncle Claude and saw that he was watching them inquisitively; he read the look as a question of his worth or of his manliness, and abruptly, despite all these lean, red-faced strangers who, now that the meal was over were thoroughly picking their teeth, he said, "Uncle Claude, when are you going to teach me how to ride horseback?"

Mrs. Brotherman, putting her napkin in a bamboo napkin ring, gazed vaguely at the hop vines. His uncle smiled. It was again that winning, bone-enfeebling smile whose memory he had kept since last September; he was as friendly as a child and he said, "Is first thing tomorrow morning soon enough?" Then he got up and led the way into the living room, patting Ralph's shoulder as he went by. The others followed him in single file, all with a slouching gait as if they would otherwise be unsteady on their high-heeled boots. Ralph longed to join them but Mrs. Brotherman, in her unhappy way, said she was sure he and Molly were tired and should go to bed at once and Ralph realized that he was, indeed, so tired that he could hardly bear to think of going up the stairs and getting undressed.

Before he went to bed, he had a conference with Molly who came into his room and sat on a bench, hugging her knees. She had taken off her glasses and she looked like a black-eyed rabbit.

"Whoever heard of calling an animal Advance Anxiety?" she said.

"I thought of that, too," said Ralph. "But what would you do if you were a man and your name was Dump?"

"I would dump it."

"No, you would have to lump it."

They laughed, delighted with one another. Ralph had decided that Molly was not going crazy after all, although there had been a period of a month during the winter when she thought she was going to be kidnapped and had worn a Hallowe'en mask in the school bus every day. She was just different from other people, he supposed. He liked her when they were alone, but she embarrassed him in public because she said such peculiar things. For instance, she said to Mrs. Brotherman this afternoon, "Do you have any opinion on the false Armistice?" and when Mrs. Brotherman said no, she really had not, Molly had said, "Oh, of course you don't live in California so you wouldn't have seen the Los Angeles *Gazette*." What she was talking about was the old newspaper they had with the one word PEACE printed in letters four inches high on the front page, but how was Mrs. Brotherman to know?

"Do you like it here?" said Ralph.

"I don't know. I'll tell you later. I don't like the food, I must say. String beans are the bane of my existence."

"I liked the buckskin."

Molly frowned and said nothing for a moment and then she said, "You know, I don't think I'll learn to ride horseback tomorrow. I think I'll wait for a few days as I have an idea for a short story about an amateur kidnapper."

How he regretted his headlong contract with Uncle Claude! He heard a horse snorting in the pasture right under his windows and his hands turned as cold as ice.

"Darn you," he said angrily to Molly, "darn you to heck. You *always* make up an excuse." He knew he was quite unreasonable; Molly had said nothing about learning to ride, but it seemed so unfair that she could always get out of anything by saying she wanted to write something. "All right for you," he said, "if you don't come tomorrow, you can't ever come anywhere with me again."

"My literature is more important to me than you are, Ralph Fawcett," she said coldly and left the room, pausing in the doorway to make donkeys' ears and say "Hee haw."

For the first weeks of this first visit to Uncle Claude, Ralph and Molly were not happy and most of the time they were afraid. The landscape itself was frightening. Above timberline the snow was thick in the deep gashes; to the north were two long glaciers which sometimes shone pink through the haze; this pinkness came from bacteria which inhabited the glacier snow, and when he learned this Ralph was curiously disgusted, he did not know why. Below timberline and above the dry sagebrush of the foothills, the forests of conifers were dense, their dark blue-green here and there interrupted by a small grove of golden aspens or a bright upland meadow where Winifred often went to gather columbines. The mountains were at once remote—their summits were often enshrouded by clouds—and oppressively confining. The children had been used to summers at the seashore and the sea, even in a storm, was something that could be taken in at one glance; its evils, however, were quite hidden, so that sharks and sting-rays, hurricanes and calms seemed only legendary and needed not be reckoned in their impressions; and even when they went out in a glass-bottomed boat and saw the fish all golden and green and huge, looking up at the passengers, they did not feel any of this was real but was only like a movie.

But the mountains wore peril conspicuously on their horny faces. Through Uncle Claude's field glasses they could look directly at the ledge from which a packhorse had slipped and fallen to her dreadful, screaming death. They knew the place where a bold dude had frozen in midsummer, having lost his way in a cloud when he was scaling an arête. The foothills were alive with rattlesnakes. At dawn the coyotes wakened them and through their windows they could see the small, shadowy sneak-thieves on the rim of the hill to the south of the house; the howling had a cold and beggarly sound, sometimes intolerably like an outraged human voice.

The house, spacious and rambling, made of white brick, faced north upon the fast stream called the Caribou River which cut the pasture land in half. On its banks grew cottonwoods and weeping willow trees, and dense amongst them, chokecherry and sarvis berry bushes. Here beavers made their clever dams and here hoot owls warned at night: there was no place that was not alive with something. A bridge led to the pasture on the other side of the river where the milk cows grazed and where there were cattails five feet high and where often the children saw blue herons. To the west was a broad, treeless field of timothy, bound on one side by the slough that ran along the red road; its west fence was parallel to the railroad track where the slow mixed train went past in the early evening, ringing its lonesome bell. The foothills leading to the summer range were to the south and the view of them was cut off through the lower windows of the house by a line of eight Lombardy poplars. Between the house and the road was the pasture, and the barn and the many sheds lay to the east.

Everything and all the people, with the exception of Mrs. Brotherman, made Ralph think of Grandpa, and he had the feeling that the old man's other ranches (which now Uncle Claude would visit once a year in September) were similar, save that this was the only one in the mountains. The men were skillful, good-humored, hard, living within the present time and on a large scale. When they got drunk on a Saturday night, they did so with abandon, behaving exactly as drunk people in the movies did. Their lawlessness seemed natural. It seemed altogether reasonable that they hunted at all times except during the open season when, as Uncle Claude said, "there was too much danger of getting shot at by them dudes from Denver." The revenue officers and the game wardens intimidated no one; strangers to the country, they could not police all the hundreds of hiding places for stills in the mountains, nor could they catch the poachers who wanted wild meat and proposed to have it.

Ralph thought of the house in Covina with all its flurry of little objects, little vases and boxes on little gilt tables and whatnots hanging in the corners; and then thought of the big, bare rooms of the ranch where the furniture was heavy and solid as if it were nailed to the floor and the only small things were catalogues from L.L. Bean and Montgomery Ward, boxes of buckshot, fly-books, odd bits of leather and metal which had no use but which remained undisturbed, week after week, on the mantelpiece and the tables. He thought of the delicate food they had at home and then of the sage hen and puffballs and head cheese they had here, and Ralph felt that when Grandpa left them he must always have gone away hungry.

But the most amazing contrast of all was between Fuschia and Magdalene. Fuschia was young and pretty and good-natured but full of respect so that she called them "Miss Molly" and "Mr. Ralph." But Magdalene! She was the first Negro besides Pullman porters they had ever seen up close. Molly was so frightened when the old woman took her hand in her skinny black one with its pink palm like a monkey's that she wanted to go home at once. Magdalene seemed hundreds of years old, so old that if she lived another century or two, she would not look any different. Her skin was not yellowish to show that she had white blood; it was rather as if it had faded to a bluish gray. Her lips were purple and they had so many lines that they looked like narrow grosgrain ribbons; her brown eyes were as mean and watchful as a chipmunk's, and the scraggly fuzz on her little head looked like dirty snow. She was not in the least kind; she was always smoldering with an inward rage or a vile amusement over something sexual or something unfortunate, and she spoke chiefly in obscene or blasphemous expletives. But she was wonderfully wise. She knew when it was going to rain and when someone was going to get sick and when a cow was going to get through a fence. Her wisdom was something antediluvian and cosmic and the almanac she went by dated back a million years before the fall of man. She was, Molly thought, the wife of the Skalawag at the Wash. She had her own little cabin between the barn and the bunkhouse and she raised white rabbits in a hutch beside it. No one ever saw the interior of it, but the children imagined that it must smell frightful, for not only were the rabbits so near, but she cooked strange things on her stove, things like beaver tails and the lungs and testicles of freshly butchered calves.

Up on a hillside, a mile behind the barn, Magdalene kept some goats of her own, milking them every morning before sunrise and again in the evening while the others were finishing their supper. One afternoon Ralph met her coming around the corner of the corral, carrying a dead and bleeding goat slung over her shoulder. In her free hand, she carried a small hatchet, bright with thick neck blood. Ralph asked her why she had killed her goat and she replied, "I was hongry, that's why, you lil ole June bug, so I went out and botched 'im on the haid." Uncle Claude could not remember where Grandpa Kenyon had found her, and she would never tell the children where she had lived before. When once they asked her where she had been raised, she said, "I wa'n't *raised*. A cow-bird laid me in the sagebrush and the sun hatched me out." They did know that she had two sons, named Salem and Jordan and a daughter named Psalmetta. Once Jordan sent her a bottle of Ben Hur perfume and while she laughed like a lunatic with contempt, she poured it all over herself and the kitchen reeked. It smelled like the cheap chocolates with pink fillings they got in Covina, four for a penny.

Magdalene's territory was the kitchen and she never went into the other part of the house, for besides bringing the food to the table, Winifred made the beds and did the cleaning. Magdalene did not like to have anyone fussing in her kitchen. She did not mind the men hanging up their chaps there or even having a cup of coffee in the middle of the morning if they were working around near the house; and she suffered Ralph and Molly to poke into the cupboards and watch her make pies so long as they did not ask for anything to eat, although occasionally she would give them bits of raw potato, always with the remark, "Knew a horse died of 'em." But she would not stand for Mrs. Brotherman, whom she called "Miz Bo-Bo" or "Miz Budmanny," or Winifred to hover over her, and if, in the morning, she discovered that after she had gone to her cabin for the night someone had made fudge with her sugar in her pan on her stove, she swore a blue streak half the day through.

Molly got the idea that she looked like Magdalene and for some time thought that she was probably her daughter. She had never been at all certain about the circumstances of her infancy for Leah had told her that for the first years of her life she had been only the size of a talcum powder can and they had kept her on the mantel beside Grandfather Bonney's ashes.

This was, of course, a big fat lie, but all the same there were some peculiar things about those early years. For example, she clearly remembered riding an elephant and the more she looked at her, the more certain she became that Magdalene had been the driver. But she did not ask her about it because Negroes were essentially the same as Mexicans and if you did not keep your distance from them there would be the dickens to pay. But she watched her and listened to her and in her diary she referred to her as "Mrs. Skalawag."

The one part of the ranch that was anything like home was Mrs. Brotherman's sitting room directly above the parlor. Mrs. Brotherman and her room always smelled of apples, giving the children a feeling of perennial Hallowe'en. Everywhere there were small baskets and bowls on the tables and hanging shelves, full of McIntoshes and winesaps and of Golden Grimes. As vivid as the smell, almost, was the sense of oldness in the room, coming from the furniture and the oddments and coming, as well, from Mrs. Brotherman's Boston accent and her strange syntax. Close as they lived to the Brothermans—the Fawcetts' rooms were across the hall—they were invited so seldom into the sitting room that it always held an air of foreignness for them, and because they never got so used to it that they could take it for granted, the fruity fragrance always surprised them. So also did the coolness and the furniture which sat upon a dim cabbage-rose carpet, between walls on whose yellow paper were tidy rows of dark green laurel wreathes which cast oblique and questionable shadows. In the center of the room there was a large round table with a single stout leg. It was covered with a blue velours and the four corners hung straight to the floor, weighted and decorated with wiry gold tassels. On the table was an armadillo sewing basket which Ralph found so revolting that if Mrs. Brotherman asked him to fetch her scissors from it, he shuddered. There was a music box on the table which played first "O Mistress Mine" and then "Why Does Azure Deck the Sky?" There was a bust of Socrates on a shelf and a picture of George Washington over the fireplace. There were two wing chairs covered in chintz with tatted antimacassars on the arms and the backs, and there was a terrarium with a peaked roof in which grew brake fern, partridge berry, and wintergreen. She had a silver candle snuffer and a glazed bowl holding aromatic pine cones, a Van Briggle vase of everlastings, and a souvenir sofa pillow from the Garden of the Gods. There was nothing chipped or marred or stained or dusty; only time had altered the looks of things by draining away the colors as it had drained them away from Mrs. Brotherman's cheeks and hair and eyes. She was as secretive almost as Magdalene about her past life, but once, in a thin burst of expansiveness, she told them that before Winifred was born, she and Mr. Brotherman had gone to Manitou Springs for two weeks, and she showed them a photograph of herself and her husband, sitting on a rock, holding up two folding cups of mineral water. In the background was a cement pop bottle ten feet high. They both looked bleakly into the eyes of the camera. The children could tell by the looks of the narrow-faced and wasted man that he had been as sad as his wife; they concluded that she had been born that way and it was not her widowhood alone that had cast her into eternal twilight. They often spent hours with her helping her weed in her flower garden which was famous for its roses; she dried the petals for potpourri and gave them to the ladies who sometimes came to call in the hot afternoons to visit with her in her sitting room and drink iced tea and eat gingersnaps.

They liked Winifred more and more, although at the very beginning they had been in doubt about her because she had taken them swimming in the pool behind the barn and had said she was going in without her suit. But she didn't, of course, and after a while they realized she had only been teasing. They started a detective agency and found clues all through the foot-hills; they believed that Dump was running a gambling den in a gulch and they collected a great deal of evidence against him, but he outsmarted them all summer long.

Ralph could not make up his mind about Uncle Claude. One thing was certain, he was not as nice as Grandpa. He laughed unkindly at their blunders and told about them at the table. Once poor Molly asked who milked all the cows up on the range and he laughed so hard he made her cry. Mrs. Brotherman explained to her that this was a breeding ranch, not a dairy farm, but she was unconsoled and hated Uncle Claude for three days.

And still, he would occasionally give Ralph a friendly push or invite him to ride along with him in the pick-up to town, and when he did this he smiled with the same sort of generosity in his mobile face as Grandpa used to. The trips to town, though, were never a success. The sun was always so glaring on the asphalt that Uncle Claude was too preoccupied with his driving to talk, so Ralph stared at the fields where the whitefaced Herefords grazed and at the dreary, unpainted farmhouses that stood here and there along the road, unprotected by any tree, bleak and dusty in a grassless field. Then, on the way back, Uncle Claude was wrapped up in remembering what news he had heard in town and the purchases he had made, and while he was talkative enough then, Ralph was really not interested in learning that Bernard Tobey's horse had the sweeny or that Shorty Peterson had hired a Mormon kid who had been baptized a hundred and twenty-five times or that Roger Campbell, always as independent as a hog on ice, had refused to give back Claude's hackamore, maintaining that possession was nine-tenths of the law.

There were times when it seemed to Ralph that Uncle Claude was somehow trying to get even with his mother. Every time he took them riding, he would say, laughing as he got into his saddle, "I reckon your mother would have a set of dishes if she could see you now." It both thrilled and frightened them to think what she really would do, probably send them to the penitentiary. He and Molly rode only the oldest and safest horses, but something always went wrong. Uncle Claude told them that a horse had a sixth sense which could judge whether his rider was afraid and would, out of pure orneriness and show-off, play tricks on him if he were. So that the old white horse Eye-Opener whom Molly rode would pretend that he was half blind and would deliberately stumble into gopher holes so that she pitched forward, clinging desperately to the pommel with a flushed face and wide, staring eyes. And Studebaker, the black Ralph rode, refused to wade the streams. "Give him your spurs!" Uncle Claude would cry and Ralph would tentatively push his heels into the horse's flanks. "Harder! Give him something to think about!" So that Ralph would dig harder, driven by shame, mortally afraid of being thrown into the water. Then Studebaker, snorting, would fling back his head and rear so that Ralph had to rivet himself to the saddle to keep from falling; but he did not, like Molly, grasp the horn, for Winifred had told him that this was something only dudes did.

Although, more and more often, he enjoyed the rides through the ripe meadows and along the red roads, beside the river where the sarvis berry brushed its cinnamon-smelling flowers against his face, into the cow pasture as the sun was setting, Ralph did not outgrow his uneasiness at being so high off the ground and being dependent on so capricious an intelligence as that which lay in the long black head. And when he began to saddle his horse himself, it was hard to keep back the tears when he put the bit in Studebaker's enormous mouth with its enormous square teeth and yellow-green tongue. Uncle Claude occasionally praised him and his confidence grew, but he was so mean to Molly ("You set on that bench like a sack of potatoes," he would say to her) that she seldom went with them but stayed at home to help in the garden or to write. She was now writing an article for *Good Housekeeping* called "My Summer at the Bar K."

In the latter days of June a series of tragic accidents took place, following one another as if by a spiteful plan. A horse, frightened by the backfiring of a car, stumbled and fell on the rain-slick highway, breaking his leg and crushing the foot of his rider, Homer Armitage. Nauseated with pain, Armitage roused himself enough to shoot the horse and then lay half an hour in the road until a passing motorist found him. The men at the Bar K carried the dead horse in a truck up to the place where the coyotes gathered most often after they had robbed the henhouse, and they poisoned the meat with cyanide. Later, a magpie brought a chunk of the meat down into the yard where Uncle Claude's favorite dog, a beagle, found it, ate it, and died in convulsions. Ralph never forgot his uncle's rage when Magdalene brought him the news at dinner. He got up and went at once to the gun cabinet and then strode through the kitchen. Dump said, "I reckon he'll pick off a magpie. A man cain't blame him." Everyone was silent, waiting for the shot.

There was only one report from the .22, but Uncle Claude did not come back to his dinner, and someone said he had probably gone to bury the dog. When the meal was over, Ralph went out into the yard and there, beside the milk house, he saw nine magpies standing in a circle round a tenth which was dead. They were scolding in unison, their harsh, hawk-like voices clawing at the noontime quiet. Their impeccable feathers, coal-black and snow-white, gave them the look of professional mourners, formally attired. Ralph approached, but they did not fly away; instead, two turned and faced him, shrieking abuse and hopping with anger. Their racket continued until one of the men came out of the house and tramped through their circle to pick up the dead bird and fling it with disgust into the slough, crying back to the others, "Shut up, ya goddam buzzards." They left the ground then, but for a long while afterward sat in a neat row on the fence, remembering from time to time to mourn raucously.

Uncle Claude was mending fence today, Ralph knew, and after a decent time had elapsed, he got on Studebaker and set out for the farthest pasture, up behind the barn. He had hesitated as he mounted, partly because he had never ridden so far alone before, partly because he was not sure that he should intrude upon his uncle's sorrow, just as he had not been sure after Grandpa's funeral. But he thought that since the circumstances were so similar, they might again reach the same kind of amiable understanding they had done the other time.

It was hot in the sun and he had forgotten to bring his hat; the glare on the meadows was as blinding as if it shone on tin. There was a violet heat haze hiding the tops of the mountains toward which he rode. He was stupefied by the silence and by his solitude and by the even trotting of his horse who, today, behaved himself and even forded the river at the shallows with hardly any persuasion though Ralph, for an unseen audience, gave him his spurs and felt the rowels spin lightly against the tough flesh. Only once was he afraid, for it occurred to him that Uncle Claude might have finished the fence this morning and was mending somewhere else; the possibility of not fulfilling his mission made him uneasily self-conscious; he would feel like a sap when people asked him at supper where he'd been and he would have to say, "Oh, I just went for a ride," for no one here did anything without an end in view.

He ascended a ridge and then, across a wide field of alfalfa, he saw Falcon, his uncle's horse, cropping peaceably near the fence. Falcon, a young palomino and the handsomest horse on the place, was sought after by all the other horses, but he had singled out Studebaker as his particular friend and in the early evening, as soon as they were unsaddled, they trotted up the lane together and then went running up the road to disappear in the foothills. When they were pastured with other horses, they were stand-offish and if one of them came too near, Studebaker would rear up and kick the air with his hind legs.

Studebaker, catching sight of Falcon, neighed, his whole body shuddering with vibrations and then, though Ralph tightened the lines, he broke into a lope and then into a run. Ralph was claimed by the wildest terror he had ever known. The hot wind stung his cheeks and ears and his feet, flexing in the stirrups, his knees, hugging the horse, ached so intolerably he could have screamed with pain. Blinded by the speed and by the sun he could not see his uncle but he did see Falcon, huge, blond, his creamy mane waving, come running toward them, whinnying passionately. In his quick agony Ralph scanned the field in vain and screamed his uncle's name. Instantly from some place he could not determine, his uncle shouted "Falcon!" and the palomino slowed down with a final, disappointed whinny. But Studebaker paid no heed and raced on. Then Uncle Claude, appearing suddenly from nowhere, came running bare-headed across the field, hollering words Ralph could not understand, and when he was fifty feet from them, Studebaker changed his gait to a gallop, but swerved suddenly to avoid the man and in doing so, reared, not high but so abruptly and surprisingly that Ralph's feet flew out of the stirrups, his sweaty hands turned loose the lines and he went crashing down into the sweet, gentle clover, his glasses falling off to lie unharmed beside his nose. He closed his eyes and listened to the hooves retreating and the lunatic neighs saluting and responding, listened to his uncle approaching him on running feet: "You damned little numskull, are you hurt?"

He did not know whether he was hurt and he did not care now that he was safe on the ground, but the annoyance in Uncle Claude's voice wounded him. Uncle Claude knelt down beside him and Ralph opened his eyes. The sunburned, sharp-boned face was, when Ralph first looked at it, so stern that he thought, "Now he will send me back to Covina." But then the look gave way to that rare smile and Uncle Claude said, "You better see if you're hurt. You can't trust that fool bench when he's around my horse."

Ralph sat up cautiously and pulled up his Levis. His legs were not hurt except for a big bruise on his left knee. His elbow was skinned and there was a bump on his left temple, but these were his only injuries. He was giddy, though, and the meadow swam like fishes under the high sun; then he realized that his glasses had fallen off and he groped for them with both hands as if he could not see at all.

Uncle Claude found them for him and handing them over, said, "What's the matter with your eyes that you have to wear those things?"

"I don't know. I've always worn them ever since I had scarlet fever. The nosebleeds come from that, too."

"Will you always have to wear them?" There was a curious eagerness in his voice. This was the first really personal question he had ever asked Ralph.

He replied, "I don't know. Dr. Haskell never said."

Both he and Molly had grown so used to their glasses that they did not even mind particularly being called "Four Eyes" by other children; indeed, there were times when they took pleasure in their weakness which distinguished them from others and which served, as well, as an excuse for not playing baseball or pom-pom-pull-away at which, before scarlet fever, they had been so poor that they were the last to be chosen on a team.

"Well, you look a whole hell of a lot better without them," said Uncle Claude.

"Thank you," said Ralph, although he realized it had been what his mother would have called "a left-handed compliment."

"What did you come up here for anyway?"

"I came to see if I could help you bury Juanita," he said.

"Well, that was nice," said Uncle Claude and Ralph, once more unsure of himself—despite the smile—thought he used the word "nice" contemptuously. "It wasn't much of a job. She was a little dog."

"Ken Burkhardt threw the magpie you shot into the slough."

"Did he now?" said Uncle Claude, but he was preoccupied; Ralph could not get through. He remembered a time when he and Grandpa were in the grove one Sunday morning; for some reason he had not had to go to Sunday school and he was exuberant with a holiday feeling, but he could not make Grandpa talk to him. He asked for a story but the old man refused, not crossly but distractedly. Ralph had felt compelled to force him to talk and so he began to ask questions: Was it true that if you swallowed a lemon seed a lemon tree would grow in your stomach? Did he like Post Toasties? Had he ever seen a buffalo, not in a zoo? Did he not think that monkeys looked a lot like people? Did he have very many dreams? At first Grandpa had answered briefly, but not unkindly, but then suddenly he jabbed the ferrule of his shillelagh into the ground and said sharply, "Dammit, lad, can't you see I've got something on my mind?"

Today he felt that same compulsion, even when he remembered how hot and faint he had been after Grandpa's rebuke, and seeing his uncle light a cigarette and lie down full length in the alfalfa, covering his eyes with his handkerchief, he said, "Where did you bury her?"

"Yonder," said Uncle Claude vaguely motioning toward the river. "By the shallows."

"Oh! I must have passed the place."

There was a silence. Studebaker and Falcon had calmed down now and were cropping side by side in the middle of the meadow. It was not really silent; there was a steady undercurrent of the noises of the land, but they were so closely woven together that only a sudden sound, like the short singing of a meadowlark, made you realize that everywhere there was a humming and a rustling. And then, the separate sound, the song or a splashing in the river, was like a bright daub on a dun fabric.

Ralph said, "Are you going to get a new dog?"

"Sure, I'll get me a new dog. I'll miss that little old hound but I'm not a fellow that goes to the mope-house over a dog."

"What is a mope-house, Uncle Claude?"

"It's a place where the niggers go and mope when somebody dies."

Uncle Claude grew rather talkative after that. He told Ralph that there were towns in Oklahoma where only Negroes lived and at the outskirts there were signs saying "White man, get out of this town before sundown." He said Ralph could come along with him this fall when he went to look at Grandpa's ranches; he'd be glad to have company.

"I haven't finished school yet," said Ralph. "I don't think I'll go on past the seventh grade. How far did you go?"

"Eighth. I wouldn't of gone that far if it hadn't been for your mother. Mr. Kenyon used to tell her and tell her that you couldn't make a silk purse out of a sow's ear but she didn't believe him. I reckon she believes him now, all right, after the way that preacher showed me up that day."

"I'll tell you something funny, Uncle Claude, about that day." And he told what Molly had said to Mr. Follansbee. Uncle Claude laughed so that his belt buckle hopped up and down on his stomach like a jumping bean. "That Molly!" he cried. "She's a caution."

"Do you like her?" said Ralph.

"Sure I like her. Sometimes she's too many for me but she's as funny as a crutch. Sometimes I don't think she is on purpose." He sat up, laughed again, and said, "Come on and help me mend this outfit. Just as quick as I get one stretch mended then she busts out in a new place. Beats me."

All afternoon Ralph worked like a grown man, holding the posts steady while Uncle Claude nailed on the barbed wire. He was happy at first but gradually he got cross from the heat; the smell of alfalfa became cloying; a dozen times he asked his uncle what time it was. He was depressed at the thought of having to mount that crazy Studebaker again. Uncle Claude had said, when they were working on the first post, "A fall like that one don't amount to anything, but the first time it happens to you, you feel kind of worried." Ralph had replied, "Oh, I wasn't scared!" He wanted the time to pass quickly so that he would be safe at home again, but when he thought of the moment of getting into the saddle, he trembled all over and wished the sun would never set.

But when the time came, he was not afraid. Claude had something of a time catching Falcon who took it into his head to run around in circles like a trick horse, but he was outwitted at last and Uncle Claude led him to where Studebaker stood, for once oblivious of his friend. They were almost like people who were temporarily not on speaking terms. Ralph mounted and realized intuitively that he was in complete control of his horse. He spurred him at the river and Studebaker leaped forward at the pricking and then, when he had crossed the water, resumed a steady gait. Uncle Claude pointed out the place where he had buried Juanita and said, "I don't know why I wasted a bullet on a magpie. A dead magpie ain't going to bring back my dog." He said he would bring Ralph up here at dusk one day and see if they could catch the beaver that was damming up the west slough that ran off from the river at a right angle. He went on then to talk of hunting trips he had made and hunting trips he would like to make. This year he would miss his expedition to the Bear's Ears because he would have to make the rounds of the ranches. At the Bear's Ears, he hunted elk and deer and it was there that he had got the bighorn whose head hung in the dining room.

Two things he had never seen were bears and mountain lions. To be sure, they weren't anything a man would want to eat, but he'd like to see them anyhow. About fifteen years ago, before Uncle Claude came here, there had been a raft of mountain lions in this country, but they seemed to be all gone now. At least no one he knew had ever seen one.

"What do they look like?" said Ralph.

"How should I know? I just got through saying I never seen one."

"Well, I'd like to see one." He wished he would be hiking by himself in the mountains one day and suddenly come on a lion's den. He would shoot the mother and the cubs and then take Uncle Claude up to see. He could just hear Uncle Claude suck in his breath and say, "Well, I'll be a son-of-a-gun."

Chapter Five

ON A winter Sunday afternoon when Ralph was fourteen, the Follansbees had come to call and he and Molly were sitting in their Sunday clothes and Sunday solemnity on the hassock in the bay window. Looking at the portrait of his Grandfather Bonney, Ralph read into his face vacuity and self-pride; he saw the plump hands as indolent and useless and believed that in a handclasp they would be flaccid. He understood now why Grandpa Kenyon, when he had used the word "merchant," had uttered it like a curse. He decided that the world was made up of two groups of people. The first he called "Kenyon men" and this included those who, like Uncle Claude, knew the habits of animals and subjected themselves to the government of the seasons and who, with age, became neither fat and bald like Grandfather Bonney nor bony and ragged like Mr. Follansbee. The other group he called "Bonney merchants" and this included everyone he had ever known with the exception of the people at the Bar K, Grandpa, and Molly. The fundamental distinction between the two groups was, he thought, their attitude toward horses and, vice versa, the attitude of horses toward them.

For four years now Ralph and Molly had divided their year between the men and the merchants. Their lives were like those of the children of divorced parents who spend a season of each year with their father and the bulk of it with their mother and who feel themselves thus split in half and sometimes find their memories confused, so that they cannot be sure what books have been read, which ideas acquired, which sounds and shapes perceived in the two separate households. Their own relationship was likewise a double one. At the ranch, they all but ignored one another, but in Covina, alone with their mother now that Leah and Rachel were away at boarding school, they were still close friends.

Their estrangement at the ranch had begun on a day late in August in the very first summer they went to Uncle Claude's, a day on which Ralph's whole life had been changed. Uncle Claude had taken him and Molly and Winifred up to the nearest of the glaciers. They went horseback as far as they could, a little below timberline, then hobbled the horses at an abandoned mine and climbed the rest of the way. Uncle Claude's clowning Newfoundland, Walter, charged into every pool they came to and slunk out, shuddering and coughing. Claude and Winifred were skilled and tireless mountaineers and the two of them went straight up without stopping, leaving Ralph and Molly far behind. When the children finally got to the top, weary, cold, hungry, and exasperated, they almost cried to see that the others had not waited for them there but had gone on and had climbed a cluster of rocks near by. They were sitting on the topmost one, side by side, and they laughed down and waved, turning then to one another to say something the children could not hear. Ralph was too depressed and too tired to take any interest in the vast slide of ice to which he had been looking forward for weeks, nor in the strawberry snow at the head of the glacier. Warm with resentment of Uncle Claude's desertion, he glanced around him casually and then joined Molly who had begun to pluck the waxy yellow orchids growing profusely there, for they had promised to take a bouquet to Mrs. Brotherman. Actually he was less angry than perplexed, for he did not understand why Uncle Claude should prefer the company of a girl to his nor, on the other hand, why Winifred should desert a child for a grown-up. Suddenly it occurred to him, stunning him, that Winifred was really not a child but was as old as Leah. This realization made him feel colder and tireder than ever and he would have lain down amongst the flowers if this would not have appeared an act of weakness to the sitters on the rock. He looked at his weedy sister with dislike as she crouched on her heels, plucking the lilies all around her, and when she looked up at him, her large humble eyes fondling his face with lonely love, he wanted to cry out with despair because hers was really the only love he had and he found it nothing but a burden and a tribulation. She kept a diary in which she recorded everything he said and everything he did and she insisted on reading each entry to him before they went to bed. At first he had been flattered but now he was only embarrassed. She was especially rhetorical on the subject of his shooting at which, if the truth were known, he was quite inferior. Molly would not learn to shoot, and she did not like to touch a gun even when it was unloaded, for their mother had frequently warned them that it was the unloaded ones that always went off. But she went on about Ralph's handling of his .22, under the tutelage of Winifred, as if he were a champion. His first game was only a portly pack rat which had got into the potato cellar on the side of the hill, but later on he shot two jackrabbits and a sage hen. Molly wrote in her diary that he had shot three Rocky Mountain laughing hyenas.

For the most part she did not pester him much but hung around Winifred on whom she had a crush. But he was always conscious of her, always nagged by the suspicion that she felt left out. Half the time, though, it was he who was left out like right now when Winifred had stolen Uncle Claude.

Later, after they had eaten their lunches of salmon sandwiches and Baby Ruths, Uncle Claude offered to let Ralph look through his binoculars to see if he could spot any automobiles on Cuthbert Pass, and when he took off his glasses, Uncle Claude said, "Why don't you leave them things off all the time?"

And Ralph obeyed. He began by not wearing his glasses for an hour at a time and then for two hours and then for whole days except when he went out to shoot. It caused him at first to have hammering headaches and they, in turn, made him eventually vomit and then writhe miserably on the settle in Mrs. Brotherman's sitting room with a damp washcloth over his forehead. But he persisted, and within a few weeks his headaches came infrequently and he was able to see almost as well as he had done with his glasses. Molly tried it too, but in vain: her eyes were much worse than his and without her glasses she was as blind as a mole. After that, everything happened. For example, Uncle Claude took him one day to a deep wet-weather branch where a cow was calving and at the moment he saw the horrible little hoof appear, he felt a painful exultation and he tried to remember what Maisol and Maisako had said that day in the watermelon patch. He was not in the least embarrassed, only filled with wonder at the bewildered wet calf that was finally born and immediately stood up although it was so small and weak it swayed piteously under its mother's big rosy tongue. But when he told Molly about it, she stuck her fingers in her ears and screamed at him, "You're a liar! You're a dirty liar!" and her nose began to bleed.

And Uncle Claude always let him help with the butchering when he was doing it himself. He would shoot the steer through the skull and then would fling his pistol to the ground and run to slit the creature's throat. He stood back after that while the blood gushed out and waited until the reflexes stopped and the dainty legs ceased kicking. Most of the process was sickening, but there was one part he liked and this was the skinning of the carcass after it was strung up. The tight hide came off like an eggshell under his sharp knife and he was always surprised that there was no blood at all and that when the hide was off, nothing showed but another skin of white fat. It looked like someone in winter underwear. He turned his head aside when Uncle Claude commenced to draw it, for the blue guts were hot and steamy and as they slithered out, they stank like a backhouse. Sometimes, by accident, the knife went into the stomach and then green grass came bulging out, fetid and slimy like the stuff around the stems of zinnias that had been too long in water. Ralph carried the tongue and the liver in a pail to the kitchen and the bloodthirsty old Negro woman looked on them as greedily as a scavenger bird.

For four summers now Ralph had been his uncle's constant companion. Occasionally they went into town in the early evening to visit one of Uncle Claude's friends. They would sit around the kitchen table drinking iced tea or sometimes home brew; Ralph had Coca Cola or Orange Crush which Uncle Claude would buy at the drugstore on the way. They talked of murders, of hunting, of horses, of dudes. Some nights, though, Uncle Claude went in alone, not telling anyone what he was going to do, and deeply and secretly Ralph suspected that he was going to a particular street whose nature he would not allow himself to imagine. It was a street one block long and on either side of it were small white one-room houses; at the end of the block there was a larger house made of red brick where lived a woman named Dago Mary who one day had called out to Ralph as he was hurrying by at dusk to meet Uncle Claude at the post office and had asked him to run down to the drug store to get her a package of Luckies and an ammonia coke. He had not even refused; he had run on, his heart pounding. Often, on those nights when Uncle Claude had set forth mysteriously, Ralph thought of how, before he had seen the birth of the calf, he had been like Molly, savagely refusing the knowledge of such things, but now, bad as he knew it all to be, it sometimes gave him a warm feeling like cocoa on a cold night.

Winifred did not like him and he did not know why. In the very first year he had tried to win her by praise, by telling her jokes, by teaching her Boy Scout knots, but she was always aloof with him. And then one day, they had a real falling-out. They had gone hunting and he had shot a prairie dog but she had not hit anything. They sat down to rest on a knoll near the river and Ralph, on an impulse, asked her if she had ever heard about the time Grandpa Kenyon had killed a man. He had assumed, in his possessiveness of Grandpa, that she would not possibly know and his question was rhetorical, holding the expectation of her astonishment and eagerness to hear the story. He even forgot for a moment that Molly knew and that Leah and Rachel and the Follansbees did; he felt that he was offering Winifred a new and precious gift, so that he was completely taken aback when she said she had known it before Ralph was "dry behind the ears." She spoke with such ferocity that he blushed deeply. Molly turned on Winifred, enraged. "He was not your grandfather! He was *ours*!" Winifred jumped up, her eyes blazing, and she said, "He was as much mine as he was yours. He wasn't any *kin* to you, you dirty little snobs!"

Recalling this now as he looked at the portrait, he wondered if there were not some kind of operation you could have to drain off the Bonney blood in you. You could then have a transfusion from Uncle Claude. The terrible danger was that he might get fat like his mother; it was awful that she had named him for Grandfather Bonney and that she kept saying all the time that she wanted him to be exactly like him when he grew up. Sometimes he really hated her just as he had moments of intense hatred for Mr. Follansbee when, listening to the sermon, he knew that he did not believe in God. Especially he hated his mother when he hurt her feelings and she cried. The tears did not move him, nor was he taken in when she blubbered that he was all she had left in the world, but he could not bear the display: her pretty face became dropsical and red and she made piping noises like a fretful kitten. She was a Bonney merchant, through and through.

Ralph handled the symbols of his life delicately like superstitions. Round Grandfather Bonney's portrait and urn he walked with care lest he arouse his ghost, and when, on the anniversary of Grandpa Kenyon's death, he went with his sister and his mother to lay flowers on the gravestone, fixed his attention on the impersonal junipers that hugged the slopes of the low mound and refused himself the memory either of the living man or of the corpse in the parlor. For he believed that if he did not allow even his most hidden mind to prefer one dead man above the other, Grandfather Bonney would not creep forth to haunt and discolor his days at Uncle Claude's where his whole existence betrayed his mother. She knew, to be sure, that he rode and shot and was around dangerous machinery and she cried a good deal over this and there was always a wretched scene in Denver when she saw them off on the train to the Bar K. But she was secretly glad to be rid of her volatile two in the summer and to bask in the sunny dispositions and pretty faces of her two older children.

Today, in the damp twilight, Ralph seemed unable to escape the man in the portrait and he was filled with a terrible physical disgust. Momentarily he closed his eyes and allowed the voices to seep into his mind. His mother was speaking of him and she was saying, "You know, Mr. Follansbee, the single disappointment in my father's life was that he had not studied law at Harvard. It is my dearest wish that Ralph will."

Mr. Follansbee, who had a "digestive condition," belched slightly and perfunctorily sought pardon. He said, "An excellent plan, Rose. And how about it, sonny, how do you feel?" He did not expect an answer; he was a rhetorician and cared little for give and take. He made a speech as if he were in the pulpit, scattering Latin phrases where they fell and bringing in such subsidiary matters as a friend named Dr. Lucius Kennedy who lived in Somerville, a felicitous conversation he had held with a Mr. James Brooks on a bench in the Boston Common, and a Pasadena lawyer of high reputation who had been discovered recently to be the owner of a still in the neighborhood of Carson City. He concluded, addressing Ralph directly, that it would be an ungrateful son who did not grant his mother's dearest wish. He pointed to the portrait and said, "Emulate *him*, my boy. For he was a man among men, a man whose motto was the single word 'Honesty.'" Ever since the scene in this room on the day of Grandpa's funeral, Mr. Follansbee had been spitefully on the look-out for ways to nettle him and Molly. He would refer obliquely to "tall tales," to Paul Bunyan and Baron von Munchausen and pinching Molly's sallow cheek would say, "Hello, hello, my pretty little fairy. Take care you don't fly away."

Now he spoke of the fine blood that ran in Ralph's veins (it was as if he had read his mind!) and went on to speak of the love that bound a son to his mother. Ralph's embarrassment—the preacher ruthlessly kept his eye upon him—was so febrile and agitated that he could not keep his feet and hands still and they danced foolishly. He tried in vain to envisage Uncle Claude, but could see, in his mind's eye, nothing but his mother, bending over him anxiously as he lay sick of scarlet fever, the neck of her gray silk blouse open so that her breasts showed. And then, once, her image was replaced by that of Grandfather Bonney, Tennyson, and President Cleveland plodding arm in arm toward the sand bar.

When Mr. Follansbee had paused, Mrs. Fawcett said, "I know many things may happen in these years before he is ready to go to college, but I do not feel that anyone has ever suffered by taking the longer view of things. Besides it is not much more than two years. When the time comes, I will sell this place and we will go East to live."

"Not me," said Molly.

Mrs. Fawcett smiled. "Molly doesn't want to do anything anyone else does."

"The rugged individualist," said Mr. Follansbee with a chuckle. "Well, Molly, what do you want to do?"

It was, Ralph knew, all she could do to keep from sticking out her tongue. "I want to stay here with Grandpa," she said.

They all were shocked. The depths of this child were unfathomable and Mrs. Fawcett at times was really afraid of her. Somehow time did not soften her, did not make her have thoughts and feelings like other children. Now Ralph, although he was still unusually sensitive and in some ways eccentric, had normal interests—much as she wished the object of his admiration had been someone of more culture and refinement than Claude Kenyon, Mrs. Fawcett was bound to admit that it was right for him to enjoy the company of a grown man—and, moreover, he was beginning to look . . . well, to put it bluntly, to look like a human being. But poor Molly, although she had shot up and was taller than any of her schoolmates, looked just the same as she had done when she was eight. And the things she said!

Mrs. Fawcett faltered, "Molly, dear, you mustn't say things that make us sad." Molly stared at her and curled her lip. Mrs. Follansbee rescued them, asking in her domestic voice, what sort of house Mrs. Fawcett would buy in the East. She said she would settle somewhere in Connecticut, near Aunt Rowena, and that in the winter she would rent a house in Cambridge so that Ralph would not have to lead the irregular life of the dormitories. It was planned, parenthetically, that Molly would go to a boarding school in the vicinity of Boston and would then go either to Radcliffe or to Wellesley. Mrs. Fawcett said, "I should like *one* of my daughters to be a college woman, and the other two give me no hope—they write of nothing but beaux."

It was time for tea and Mrs. Fawcett rose to wheel in the table from the dining room. As she passed her son, she stooped and kissed the top of his head and with a small, sweet-smelling hand, patted his cheek. And then, as a sop to her conscience, she ran her fingers through Molly's hair. The preacher and his wife smiled benignly on the scene, exchanged the sorrowful glances of the childless, and the man belched, the woman sighed. In the few minutes that Mrs. Fawcett was gone from the room, the Follansbees changed their pious, general tone and inquired of Molly and Ralph lightly and condescendingly—Mrs. Follansbee speaking in a very loud voice—whether they did not keenly look forward to going to college.

Molly said, "We're not going to college, neither one of us, and we decided that before you were born."

Mr. Follansbee humorously clucked his tongue. "And what do you Methuselahs intend to do?"

She said, "We will get married and stay right here with Grandpa." And then she turned to her brother and said, "Won't we?" She would never believe him when he told her that marriage was not what she thought it was. The first summer at the ranch she had wanted to marry Studebaker and a long time ago she had told everyone at school that she was engaged to Schöneshund. The Follansbees looked at her with horror and

Ralph whispered in her ear, "Don't say anything more. I'll tell you why later."

There was always a long, uncomfortable pause when the water was coming to a boil over the spirit lamp, and no one seemed to be able to think of anything to say. Today, as always, there was an expectant hush and Mr. Follansbee's stomach made a noise like a querulous voice. Disgust overwhelmed Ralph. Would they never take their awful Bonney bodies away?

He took a drink of his tea and said, "The milk is sour, Mother."

"Nonsense," she replied. "I poured it into the pitcher myself. Mr. Vogelman brought it this morning."

He drank again and repeated, "It's sour, I say."

Sour spit flowed from behind his jaws into his mouth and he swallowed desperately. He tried to think of something else but he could think only of milk and of its smell. Shaking like an old man, he returned his cup to the tea wagon and said, "May I be excused? I am going to be sick."

"The milk is fresh," insisted his mother. "Sit down, son. It is very rude to behave this way."

"My brother will be sick," said Molly dully, stating a fact. He put both hands over his mouth and ran to the door. His illness lay in small pools of froth on the carpet and all the way up the stairs to the bathroom. When he had finished being sick, he went to his room and lay down on the bed with his eyes open, watching the green sky darken and the rosy clouds divide, assume new shapes, then disappear from sight. He did not know what had happened to benumb him in this way, and he knew that the milk had not been sour. But he felt as disabled as he had done when his tonsils were removed and the ether mask had been fitted over his nose. He had never forgotten the blue, spicy smell; now, six years later, he could remember it accurately and he gagged again.

He could take no pleasure in thinking of the Bar K. Next summer would bring him closer to the end of these summers, nearer to New England, a cloudy abstraction no more imaginable than the world of sleep. He knew that his mother would not let him go back, once she settled in Connecticut. He could not bear the thought of not seeing Uncle Claude again and the ranch itself and the mountains which both he and Molly loved as if they owned them. Sometimes he went swimming naked in the cold, amber pool of the Caribou behind the barn. (How long ago it seemed that he and Molly had been horrified when Winifred had said she was going in without her suit!) Alone in this rustling, humming wilderness, he pretended that he was an Indian. Later, coming back to the house, he paused on the ridge to the west of the barn and surveying the buildings and the pastures, he imagined himself as Uncle Claude's partner, saw himself riding in a caboose to Mexico with carloads of stock in front of him, saw their consultations in the office on what to buy and what to sell. In time, growing taller and filling out, people would take him for Kenyon's brother, Grandpa's younger son. Often he went climbing with Molly and Winifred. They hunted for beaver dams, filling their pockets, for no reason at all, with the chips of wood that littered the ground around the fallen trees. They found sweet piñon seeds which covered their hands with pitch that smelled like medicine. Winifred had taught them how to climb without getting winded and to go up the chimneys of the pinnacled red rocks, their hands on either wall, their rubber-soled shoes squealing at their pressure against the narrow footholds. Each time they went into the mountains, something unusual happened: they would come upon a ranger's saddled horse, cropping in a field of columbine, an old man panning for gold in a stream. Once they found an empty whisky bottle covered over with pine needles in a place so far from everything that they could not imagine what sort of person had put it there. From a favorite cliff they looked down into the valley and could see the pretentious dude camp west of Uncle Claude's, set in a barren waste of scrub oak and sage. A cattle train, puffing out a clean-lined cloud of white smoke, burrowed through the red banks like a mole, disappeared, and sent back a faint, protesting valedictory. There was always the possibility that they might see a mountain lion; they never did, but often they saw eagles.

The very life would be crushed out of him if he were deprived of all this! Of late, he had been wild with all sorts of angers and with an anxiety which he could not name but which pestered him continually so that he could not keep his mind on reading and sometimes he could not even pay attention to the movies. Sometimes he loathed his physical being for the alterations that were taking place in it: when his voice cracked, he wanted to die of shame, and when Molly laughed at him, he was abjectly humiliated. He was filling out now; he had lost his pallor and his eyes, quite strong, were clear. He would have taken pleasure in his appearance if it were not for Molly with her ugly face and her lankiness and the slouching, round-shouldered gait which she had developed and which caused her enemies to call her "the crab." There was something wrong with her and while he still loved her, he wished oftener and oftener that she did not exist.

The sky darkened suddenly and in a few minutes it began to rain. The calm sound of it in the turquoise berries outside his window soothed him. He lay as still as a stone. He thought: there was something preying on Grandpa Kenyon's mind that day—perhaps he knew he was going to die—and that was why he had absent-mindedly tapped the turquoise berry with his shillelagh. That was the sort of meaningless thing you did when you had a great worry.

As soon as Ralph left the room, Molly returned her cup to the tea wagon and said, "If you will pardon me, this is the pause in the day's occupation which is known as the children's hour."

Mrs. Fawcett shook her head and sighed, "She's simply not happy unless she can be with Ralph. If he's asleep, don't wake him."

Mr. and Mrs. Follansbee said, "Good-bye, Molly," and Molly said, "So long," so that she had to come back and curtsy and say it properly. She stepped around Ralph's sickness which the grown-ups had chosen to ignore. It was just spit and it was already sinking into the carpet.

She had no intention of going to Ralph's room. It had been perfectly clear that he was not going to marry her and she suspected that he was going to marry Uncle Claude. She went down the hall to the kitchen. It wore its Sunday-afternoon look of lifeless cleanliness. Fuschia did not prepare their supper on Sunday night but left a pot of soup to bubble slowly on the back of the stove. This was all they had except toast and peanut butter and a chocolate drop a piece. The funny papers were on top of the refrigerator and she read "Out Our Way." It was very funny today. The two kids and their father were out cleaning the backyard and getting terribly dirty. They had to pass the living room door to get upstairs to the bathroom to wash and the mother was having company. So they took a sheet off the line and the father said they would all get under it and it would just look like a white flash going past the door, but it didn't work because they got mixed up and went *in* the door instead of *past* it. She laughed for a moment and then, looking in the mirror over the sink, she said, scarcely moving her lips, "Ha. Ha. Tee. Hee."

Molly let herself out the back door without a sound. Budge, who was old now and insensate, lay on the top step, unmindful of the rain, but she did no more than look at her and murmur, "Hi, purr-cat."

She went to the shed where the bleaching vats stood ready for the next year's harvest. There was a chemical smell here and this, together with the murkiness and the drizzle against the window panes, made her think of *Dr. Jekyll and Mr. Hyde* and she proceeded as if she were walking in her sleep. She went directly to the beakers of acid on their racks which Miguel had warned her and Ralph against since they were tiny children, pulling out their stoppers to show the sour blue vapor emerging from the hidden heat. One drop of it, he said, on the bare skin would hurt like a red-hot poker and he put an eye dropper of it on an old piece of canvas to show them how quickly it would eat through any substance. Miguel had taken a correspondence course in chemistry and the shed looked almost like a laboratory with test tubes everywhere stained purple and green and bile color; there was a Bunsen burner and a collection of beakers of bizarre and attractive shapes. He experimented with all kinds of things; once he had let Molly and Ralph watch when he combined his spit with something and it turned bright green. Ralph asked him if the acid would burn off warts, but Miguel said no.

There was a test tube marked H_2SO_4 which Molly knew was the most dangerous of them all. That was what was used to make the walnuts pale. She took the small flat cork out and smelled the nasty smell. Then she held her left hand over a basin and poured the contents on it. At first it did not hurt at all; it stung a little like the liquid soap in the basement at school, but that same blue smoke came up from her hand and

almost at once big puffy blisters came out, as white and opaque
as mushrooms, and there was a new and terrible smell. The
smell, not the blisters, alarmed her and sent her plunging to the
sink where there was a cold water tap. But the more water she
allowed to flow over her hand, the bigger the blisters got and
when she took her hand away and sniffed at it, the smell was
worse than ever. Then she began to cry, not with pain but with
terror at this odor of her destruction and she stood in despair
in the shadowy room, full of the sound of rain.

She ran out of the shed as if she were being chased and back
through the kitchen sobbing, "Mother Mother! I have hurt
myself!"

Ralph was in the kitchen cutting himself a piece of raisin
bread so she knew he had not been very sick, and when he
heard her, he stumbled out, dropping the knife on the floor.

"Look," she moaned, "look what happened to me."

The pain was not severe; it was the knowledge that the acid
was *eating* her, the way the Follansbees were eating cake, the
way Ralph had been about to eat the raisin bread, and in this
revulsion she paid no attention to her brother who was saying,
"What *is* it, Molly? What did you *do*?"

She sat down at the table and put her head on her right arm
and stretched out her left arm in front of her so that Ralph
could look at the burn and she wept with pity. Ralph stared
and impatiently repeated, "What *is* it?" until finally she was
able to say, "Miguel's acid," and then he went crying along the
corridor to the parlor as she lifted up her head and screamed,
"Help! Help!"

Molly lay on the lounge in her father's den and refused to
answer any of their questions. Through her half-open eyes she
saw them standing in a row beside her: her mother was wearing
a pink dress with an accordion-pleated skirt and her cheeks
were as pink as the cloth with passion as she insisted, "Tell
Mother, my baby. Mother is not cross with her little girl," but
Molly knew that this was a lie for she heard the anger in her
voice as clearly as she saw it in Mr. Follansbee's eyes which were
green like the cases of fish in the aquarium. He stood at the
foot of the lounge, looking from time to time at his watch. He
had promised Mrs. Fawcett that he would stay until the doctor
came, but he was nervous for fear he would not have proper

time for his supper before Epworth League. Mrs. Follansbee, who had declared herself to be "chilled to the marrow," sniffed into her handkerchief and often repeated that the best thing in the world for burns was butter. Molly thought slyly: then the acid would eat the butter; the acid would have a buttered hand sandwich. Ralph stood at the head of the lounge and she could not see him but every so often he stroked her forehead and said, "It won't hurt in a little while."

At last they heard Dr. Haskell's car in the drive and Molly said, "I don't want you to stay in here."

"Young lady," began Mr. Follansbee, but Mrs. Fawcett checked him with a wave of the hand and said, "Yes, sweetheart, if you are sure you won't be afraid."

"Ralph can stay," she said and Mrs. Fawcett looked at Mr. Follansbee and said, "You see?" and then they left the room.

Both Molly and Ralph had always been fond of Dr. Haskell who did not take their mother seriously and who had a nice angular face and curly red hair. When they had scarlet fever, he brought Molly a brown candy reindeer and Ralph a bear. He drew up a chair and glancing at Molly's hand said, "Molly, you give me a pain in the neck. I was just sitting down to my supper and I was going to have waffles."

"I can't stand waffles," said Molly, and Dr. Haskell laughed.

"Now tell me what you did this time," he said, picking up her hand and touching the blisters lightly with his finger.

She could have told the truth without embarrassment, that she had done it on purpose to punish Ralph, but while she liked Dr. Haskell, she did not entirely trust him. Once he had told Mrs. Fawcett that she and Ralph were "nervous" and their mother was stricter than ever after that, saying, "I think you need a little rest. We don't want to get tired out and then be nervous, do we?" The word "nervous" came to be as disgusting to her as "body." So now, if she told the truth, she had no assurance that Dr. Haskell would not tattle—for that matter she was no longer even sure of Ralph, and she said, "I went out to the shed to see if I could find my art gum."

Ralph said quickly and suspiciously, "Why would it be in the shed?"

"I thought maybe Miguel had borrowed it." Now she was disquieted and her heart beat strongly. "I was looking around there but it was dark as a pocket and all of a sudden I knocked over a little bottle of stuff and it went all over my hand."

Dr. Haskell went to the door and called across the hall, asking for a basin of hot water. Coming back, he said quite matter-of-factly, "And the cork was out of the bottle?"

"Yes," said Molly. "Yes, it was."

The doctor clucked his tongue. "That is very careless of Miguel. We must speak to your mother about it."

"Oh, no!" she cried. "Oh, please don't! Miguel would knock my block off. It wasn't his fault."

The doctor's smiling glance went straight through her and he said, "This time, then, I won't. But if it should happen again, Molly . . ." And his smile went off like a street light.

"What did you do then?" asked Ralph.

Molly, remembering the basin where some of the acid would still be lying, remembering the cork which had just been sitting there beside the rack of test tubes, was afraid now and her hand began to hurt dreadfully. She whimpered, "I put my hand under the water faucet, but it didn't do any good."

"I guess not," said Dr. Haskell.

Mrs. Fawcett, returning with the basin which steamed into her face, asked, "It isn't serious, is it, Doctor? I cannot tell you how often and often I have warned them about the acids."

Dr. Haskell said, "It isn't too serious. There is danger of infection, though, if we are not careful."

"Infection!" cried Mrs. Fawcett, stumbling from the room, her hand pressed to her bosom, and Molly's heart said, "Goody! Goody!"

For some weeks it seemed possible that Molly might lose her hand. She wore upon it a cast of paraffin, for Dr. Haskell was afraid that if air got to the wound and a scab formed, the acid would continue to eat its insidious way through the flesh. In time it began to have so unpleasant a smell that she lay in bed with her arm stretched out, her head turned to the wall and a sachet of lavender pinned to her pillow. The pain was never great, but she was obsessed with the horror of being consumed alive.

She did not go to school for a few days and as this was a time of cold rain, she stayed indoors reading *Bleak House*. It was not like being sick, for she did not have to stay in bed but could go wherever she liked in the house. Sometimes she sat in the parlor and sometimes in the guest room, but usually she sat in her father's den. People rarely came in there except to use the telephone so she would not be bothered in the middle of a paragraph by someone saying, "How do you feel, Molly girl?" or "Would you like some Ovaltine?" People were always looking at her and she knew none of them believed it was an accident. Ralph hadn't, from the beginning, and the night it happened Ralph came into her room and whispered, "If you have to do dumb things, I don't see why you have to be so dumb about it. I went and got the cork."

"I did it to punish you," she said.

"What did I do to you?"

"You said we were not going to get married and stay here."

"Molly!" he said irritably and then, more kindly, "I never said that."

But though she asked him every day if they were going to get married, he always somehow changed the subject. She had almost come to the conclusion that she would marry Dr. Haskell.

One day Mrs. Fawcett came into the den to sew. She had never done this before, but Molly could tell by the way she frowned as she bent over the buttons that she meant to tell her something of importance. Molly glanced at her from time to time over her book.

"Molly," she said at last, "what do you do at Uncle Claude's all the time? Do you play with other children your age?"

"Of course not," said Molly. "What do you think he lives in? A *town*?"

"But what do you *do*?"

"I swim. I hike. I ride Eye-Opener. I talk to Magdalene."

"Magdalene? Oh, the cook. I wouldn't talk too much to a darky if I were you, Molly."

You would, thought Molly, if you were probably a darky yourself and Magdalene's own child.

Molly said, "What do *you* do while we're gone?"

"Why, just what we always do," said Mrs. Fawcett with surprise. "Do you know, Molly, I sometimes think you and Ralph are happier with your uncle than you are at home."

"I do not believe in happiness," said Molly.

Mrs. Fawcett bit her lip. "That is a very foolish thing to say. You are a very foolish girl, Molly." She had something up her sleeve. She said two mysterious things. She said, "Well, I used to think it was wrong to let you go, but now I think it's a very good place for you at your age. There must be lots of cunning little calves and lambs and colts and so forth." Molly did not know what her age had to do with it; the colts and lambs and calves were a lot younger than she was. And the other thing was, "I hope you don't try to tag along with Ralph too much." Molly replied with falsehood, "I am with him every minute every day every week every month."

They did not talk for a while and Molly went on reading about the man who went up in spontaneous combustion from drinking too much gin. Shortly before the school bus came, Mrs. Fawcett let the cat out of the bag. She said, "Molly, I wonder if you and Ralph wouldn't like to spend a whole year with Uncle Claude?"

"Why?" said Molly. She was not at all sure she would like to spend a whole year at the ranch. The public library was too far away, for one thing.

"I just wondered because, well, Molly, I may as well tell you. Now I don't want you to be disappointed because your turn will come. I am going to take Leah and Rachel around the world."

"When?" said Molly tensely, closing her book.

"As soon as Rachel has finished school. This spring." Leah had finished the year before but she was staying with Aunt Rowena so that she could enjoy the cultural opportunities of New York.

Molly, thinking of the pictures in her geography book of the Taj Mahal and the pyramids and the Rock of Gibraltar which her sappy sisters would get to see, threw *Bleak House* on the floor and stamped both her feet. "See if I care!" she howled. "You just wait till I tell Ralph!"

"There, there," said her mother. "Don't fuss, Molly. Didn't I say your time would come?"

"I'll be too old by then."

"Would you like to go to boarding school instead of to Uncle Claude's?"

"No. I want to stay here if I can't go around the world."

"But you can't, Molly dear," said Mrs. Fawcett nervously, "because the house will be sold."

She had done all this behind their backs. She wasn't content to make the far future look horrible, she had to make it start right away. Molly stared at her bandaged hand in which now and again there was a slow pain. Dr. Haskell said she was out of danger now and she was glad that she was not going to lose her hand but she was also glad that the burn would leave a bad scar. Her mother was going on talking about how necessary it was for her to take the girls around the world because she did not belong to a society to which she could present them; this was a substitute, to be sure, but she felt a very satisfactory one. As for Ralph and Molly, she thought the year in the mountains would be very character-building and she was pleased with Molly's wisdom in not wanting to go to boarding school. In public school one learned a great deal about responsibility and democracy. Fortunately Leah and Rachel had sterling characters and had not become snobs; all the same she realized now that sending them to so fashionable a school had been a dangerous experiment.

"But, Molly dear, before we go, I want to have a long talk with you about a few things."

"About what? Go ahead. Shoot."

"Not now, not yet. Goodness, Ralph is late. The roads must be bad." She put her sewing away and got up. As she left the room, she said, "We're having your favorite dessert for dinner tonight, lemon pie."

When April came and Molly looked at the spring in Covina for the last time, she was homesick as if she were only remembering the sweet orange blossoms in the Freudenburgs' grove, the palm trees, the bee-filled lippia lawn, the workmen with their doe-like eyes. She visited both the graves of her father and of Grandpa Kenyon and she sat for hours in the shade of a blooming tulip tree in the cemetery. She was restless when she thought of strange children lying under her umbrella tree and strange women cracking the walnuts.

Now and again her care-worn melancholy made her suddenly self-contemptuous and she brushed it off like a spider.

Once to prove to herself that she was not a crybaby, she took a still live wood mouse from a trap and drowned it in a milk bottle half full of water, rejoicing brutishly in the swimming and the squealing which became slower and fainter and at last ceased while the small speckled body swelled and the sharp teeth showed themselves in an angry grin.

Ralph was as sad and jealous as she. They often quarreled. She wondered sometimes if she liked him as well as she used to. Once they were walking home from school together when a girl on a bicycle came riding by. Her name was Ardis Wester-lund and she enjoyed the distinction of having fainted several times in school. She was frail and pretty and had long yellow hair which was held in place with a round comb; her mother dressed her to look like Alice. This year she had given Ralph a Valentine and once Molly had seen them earnestly talking together by the parallel bars at recess, and when the bell rang she saw Ralph touch his fingers to his lips and blow Ardis a kiss. Today, as she went whizzing by, she cried, "I name Molly for the prettiest girl in school!"

Both Molly and Ralph halted and Molly snarled, "Why don't you stop breathing?" but Ardis Westerlund was far away, streaking past the Wash.

Ralph made a convulsive gesture to take Molly's hand, but she brushed him off and said in a cold, level voice, "I know I'm ugly. I know everybody hates me. I wish I were dead." Unappealing, unloving, she continued to stand motionless in the bright sunshine. She knew the light made even yellower her yellow skin with its hundreds of shining bronze freckles. She could see herself as clearly as if she looked in a mirror. A blue Indian-head jumper hung on her slackly; her ruffled organdy blouse was mussed and soiled from the long day at school; one knobby knee was covered with a scab from a wound of two weeks before; one of the ear pieces of her glasses was bound with adhesive tape. Molly was not only ugly, she had a homemade look, a look of having been put together by an inexperienced hand.

She closed her eyes and teetered. Ralph shook her, "Come along, Molly, we've got to get home."

"I haven't got a home," she said and she let go her schoolbag so that its books and pencils and loose-leaf notepaper scattered in the dust at her feet.

"Listen, Molly . . ."

"Go away. I wish they had had to cut my hand off."

"All right!" he cried and his voice rose to a shout. "All right! Why don't *you* stop breathing?"

Molly smiled a particular smile that always made him crazy-mad. He spat at her feet and yelled, "I hate you. Damn you, I hate you! Stay here all night for all I care!" When he had gone, running down the road, she picked up her books and her papers and wiped the dusty pencils off on her skirt.

Chapter Six

M RS. FAWCETT and her elder daughters, on their way West from Rachel's commencement, met Ralph and Molly late in June in Denver. As in former years when only their mother had been with the children, they stayed at the Brown Palace hotel. While Leah and Rachel and Mrs. Fawcett were shopping and Molly was at the Museum of Natural History, Ralph sat in the lobby where one looked up past gallery after gallery to a fretted dome, and he imagined the days of the gold and silver harvest when towns sprang up in the mountains to exist for a few opulent years and then to be abandoned. The train that took them to the Bar K passed through several of these ghost towns: the sagging, rotten, tall Victorian houses, windowless and with the porches maimed, still wore traces of their original elegance, and there was something deeply mournful in the sight of a cupola whose gingerbread remained intact but which listed like a hat on a drunk man's head. Patches of gilt still clung to the pillars of the boarded-up opera houses; the saloons and gambling dens, as haggard as death itself, still wore their flush names: The Golden Horn, The Gold Nugget, The Silver Dollar, The Silver Moon. The mouths of old mines yawned blackly beside the pyramids of ore. Grass grew in the streets, all the houses were tenantless, and even the trees looked dead.

The Brown Palace had been part of those days, and while it was as flamboyant as ever with its profusion of marble, of tall rubber plants, of gilt-framed mirrors and of frescoes, it failed to recall the life of the Eldorado as clearly as did the derelict opera houses. It seemed like any hotel in Los Angeles, and the businessmen who sat in the modern leather lounge chairs, smoking good cigars, were pale-faced and stout, not Western- ers. Only occasionally did ranchers, unmistakable by their gait and their hewn faces under tall buff hats, amble through the lobby like restless dogs; uneasy in their city clothes they picked the chairs behind the rubber plants so that they would not be seen. The others, the buyers and the sugar merchants, were often in the company of women who were too young to be their wives and Ralph, against his will, was pleased by this just as he was pleased that his mother and Leah and Rachel were the objects of admiring, libidinous stares when they came into the dining room.

On the eve of their departure, the family gathered in Mrs. Fawcett's bedroom for a farewell visit. Mrs. Fawcett talked of her grief at leaving her two babies behind, but brightly promised that they would have their trip around the world in that most far-off future "some day." She was grateful for her own bravery in being thus able to face a year without them, but said she knew that it was for their own good. "It will be very good for you to be on your own. Grandfather Bonney used to say, 'Solitude is the greatest tonic in the world. Loneliness is the poison put into solitude by weaklings and cads.' And I know you aren't either of *those*. Molly, you must ask Winifred to use the fine-comb on your hair after you wash it. And when we come back—you'll see how quickly the time passes—we will all be together in a lovely new home in Connecticut."

Molly, who had been captious for days, said, "How many times must I explain to you that it is incorrect to use the word 'home' in that way? You mean 'house.'"

Mrs. Fawcett smiled patiently. "Very well, my dear, *house* since you know so much more than your mother. May I continue what I was saying when you interrupted me?"

"Molly, you are becoming an intellectual snob," said Rachel, taking out a gold and white Coty's compact she had got for graduation.

"*Becoming?*" said Molly. "I have been one ever since I was nothing going on one."

Ralph, while he was in entire agreement with Molly on the distinction between "house" and "home" and had, in fact, suggested it to her in the first place, hated the smirk on her thin ill-natured mouth and hated the unblinking vigil of her nearsighted eyes. This disconcerting stare often caused people to falter nervously in their speech or to flush, and frequently, in front of company, her mother scolded her, "Molly dear, you must *not* stare. It is very much like pointing." And in school these eyes, missing nothing, intimidated her teachers, already intimidated by her intelligence and her talent for writing themes of a savagely satiric nature. Everyone said that she had the brains of the family, but as Mrs. Fawcett was not interested in brains, she thought this a handicap rather than otherwise and often told Molly that there were other things in life besides books. But, thought Ralph, what else could there be for that scrawny, round-shouldered tall thing, misanthropic at the age of twelve? It was curious that she bore so close a resemblance to him. She had the same coarse, straight, black hair, the same heavy eyebrows, and the same prominent nose that looked as solid and unbreakable as a stone. But in a girl such ruggedness was not handsome as it was in him and Uncle Claude, and nothing could be done to improve the features nor, probably, would she have permitted any alterations even if they had been possible, for she took a vindictive pleasure in her plainness. She would stand before the mirror in the hall and when someone passed by would point to her reflection and say, "Admit I'm prettier than Mary Pickford."

Looking at his older sisters with their fine, tender faces, their shining hair, their dresses of flowered pongee, catching their clean, delicious smell of soap and talcum powder, he wished Molly had never been born. He was still contemptuous of the others, but he was so conscious of their beauty that sometimes he desired, to his horror, to put his lips on their smooth white necks or on the long green veins in their arms. They had been completely oblivious of Ralph and Molly and had talked about esoteric things like "the Winter Carnival" and "the Yale-Harvard game," "the sixth-form dance at St. George's" and "Olivia's coming-out."

Mrs. Fawcett's voice went chattering on, joined sometimes by Leah's or Rachel's (once Rachel said, "But, Mummy, I think it will be too *poky* not to stay in Paris for at *least* two months." Ralph and Molly exchanged glances and each formed the word "Mummy" soundlessly). It was hot. Ralph's pants stuck to the varnished chair and he drank water slowly out of a sweating hotel pitcher. He gazed greedily at his sisters and the desire to kiss them became almost irresistible so that he had to blind himself from time to time by staring into the blazing ceiling light. Then, suddenly, he thought of Winifred Brotherman and in an instant, he was floundering in his first real love. For a few minutes he sat motionless; then, from somewhere in the hotel, a jazz band began to play "The Sweetheart of Sigma Chi." The woodwinds, grieving their hearts out, the dancers he imagined with their eyes closed, the dimmed lights he saw, the smell of the girls' perfumed hair and of the boys' breath sweet with gin, made him tremble like a tree. He thought of her as he had seen her once last summer, lying on the lawn, a bottle of Coca Cola, half drunk, forgotten in her hand. The sun seemed to darken her skin as he watched and her curls looked molded out of metal. He had been pleased to look at her, and now he understood why he had stood so long at his window looking down at her, keeping Uncle Claude waiting for the knife to skin a beaver.

On the pretext of a headache from the movie they had gone to in the afternoon, he went to his own room across the hall and lay in the darkness with his hands crossed on his chest. The music here was louder than it had been in his mother's room. Each time the tempo changed, the scene in his mind changed. With the fox trots he imagined them dancing, although he did not know how to dance; with the waltzes he saw them sitting in Uncle Claude's car in the darkness, outside the dance hall or driving up Cuthbert Pass until they came to an unfrequented road where they would park the car to kiss for hours. This was nothing like what he had felt for Ardis. That had been a sweet and nebulous romance and its only incidents were that once she had given him a Valentine and had blushed and said that someone else must have signed her name and once he had blown her a kiss. They had loved in their silences and in their sidelong glances exchanged in study hall. It gave him a sense of almost conjugal comfort to know that Winifred was three years older than himself. It did not occur to him that she might already be spoken for; he felt that this was not a sudden miracle but that it had been prepared for since he was a little boy and it must, therefore, have been simultaneously prepared for in her. How curious it was that in all these years he had barely been aware of her! How curious that she had seemed to dislike him!

Toward eleven o'clock there was an intermission, and when the music ceased, his mind wandered perversely to Leah's high, cool forehead, and as if he were already married and already unfaithful to his wife, he exultantly felt her enclosed in his arms while he first put his lips and then the tip of his tongue upon the small blue vein which marked it like an artist's signature. Then, when the music began again and he returned to Winifred, he fashioned out of his sister and out of memories of girls in movies and girls in books the rival to whom he would allude in his first days with her. He wished to miss nothing and when he remembered, at first with pain, that she would be away at college, he rejoiced that there would be love letters and that she would come home for the Christmas holidays and then in the spring. He whirled round and round in his rapid love; it pricked him on the breastbone like a needle. He wanted to be shut up in a small space to think about it. He wanted to grab it and eat it like an apple so that nobody else could have it.

At the train, Mrs. Fawcett and Leah and Rachel all cried, for departures and railroad stations required sorrow and they honored ceremony. They had brought farewell presents. Mrs. Fawcett's and Rachel's were boxes of candy, but Leah gave them nothing except an envelope which she pressed into Molly's hand, telling her not to open it until the train left. Kissing them all good-bye, Ralph felt a twinge of envy of the boat they would sail on but he did not fail, as Molly stubbornly did, to wish them a bon voyage when his mother said, "Now aren't you going to wish us a bon voyage?" He and Molly waved from the observation platform until they could no longer see three separate figures but only a single clump, and then they went back to the rusty green seat where their presents were. They opened the envelope first. On a sheet of thin Japanese writing paper with a heading of two ladies drinking tea, Leah had written:

Dearest Molly girl and Ralphie boy,
    Mother made me *promise* not to tell but she can't do anything now since by the time you read this I will be on my way to China!!!!!! On the third finger of my left hand, I am now the proud wearer of a diamond ring! Mother is quite silly (don't we all know it!!!!) and says I cannot announce my engagement for a whole year and that's why I have to go around the darned old world. Of course she's the limit, but I must say I am looking forward to the Taj Mahal not to mention the Holy Land. Garden of Eden, here I come, right back where I started from. (Apologies to California.) If you are good and don't breathe this to a soul, I'll bring you back a whole trunkful of

presents and will write you every day about what we have seen and the adventures we have had.

I will hang my close on this line,

Loads of love,
Leah

P.S. The Donor of the Famous Engagement Ring is named Robert Appleton and he is a senior at Dartmouth. I'd give anything to see your faces when you read this.

Molly went over the letter, sentence by sentence, devastatingly, and when she came to the parody of "California, here I come," she put her hand over her mouth and said, "Hasten, Jason, bring the basin, ulp! Too late, bring the mop." Recently she had been very much attached to the word "bourgeois," and she used it as if it were the most venomous in the language. She had once said to her mother that she thought the Sorosis was "as bourgeois as all outdoors," and of Ardis Westerland, once she had recovered from the shock of her insult, she said, "Why should I bother about that lousy bourgeois stick-in-the-mud?" So now Leah's letter, Leah herself, and the trip around the world were, she said, the most bourgeois things she had ever heard of in her life. "Bonney Bourgeois," she said with finality.

Ralph was deeply disturbed by the effect of the letter on himself, feeling somehow cheated and, furthermore, he was ashamed that Leah, engaged to be married, was the very figure he had meant to use to rouse Winifred's romantic jealousy. He felt, as well, a terrified guilt as though he had despoiled his own sister, and now, to make everything even more sinful, her letter, a clear confession of a relationship with a boy, tempted him again to think of her high forehead and again to imagine his lips upon it. The wickedness fluttered round him like a moth-miller which he could not catch.

As a safeguard against betraying himself, he changed the subject quickly and said, "Will I be glad to see old Studebaker!"

And Molly said, "Will I be glad to see Eye-Opener!"

Now they were really glad to be going to the ranch and they talked with amiable venom of their mother and sisters and said that, among other blessings, they would not have to hear Mr. Follansbee again as long as they lived. They planned and remembered, and then Ralph, looking in a pause at Molly's hand which was still puffy and blue, pointed to it and said, "Why did you do that?" But Molly said, "I'm through talking now," and opened *Les Misérables* so that Ralph had to contemplate once more his evil thoughts.

At the end of ten miles he was already tired and Molly was deep in her book, leaving it only now and again to goggle at the open box of candy on the seat beside her and, with maddening regularity, to select a gum drop. The journey always made Ralph homesick, not for people or for a place, but for cleanliness and comfort and orderly houses. For always on the train were the most pathetic travelers in the world. Not the ranchers, returning from Denver or Omaha, rumpled but still well dressed; and not the rodeo riders on their way from Pendleton to Frontier Days in Cheyenne; nor the dudes in their mottled silk shirts and ten gallon Stetsons, but the others who belonged in no classification. Each year there was always a group consisting of a gaunt young woman and three or four small children who ate graham crackers out of an oiled paper parcel and whined nasally. Years of hard work and bad food had given the women a canine look in the mouth and eyes; their skin was brown and old; if their teeth had been replaced, the false ones were gold, but generally there were only spaces where they had rotted and fallen out. The groups varied little, but they could not always have been the same one, for the children were the same size. The mother's hair was always reddish brown and hung about her sunken face like dirty strings, but her children were tow-headed and their eyebrows were too light to see. Sometimes they had skin diseases or birthmarks or Hutchinson's teeth. If another passenger struck up a conversation with the mother, the car usually learned that they had been to Denver to a doctor and the complaint was always something dangerous like mastoid or rheumatic fever. They would get off some hours before Ralph and Molly did at a bleak, treeless town where a mustard-colored depot and a mustard-colored water tower glared in the sun, and where small cottages and outhouses with drooping doors straggled up the dry sides of the foothills. The halts were so long that it was often possible to watch the whole progress of the woman and her children up the dirt road onto the porch of the house itself. They moved so slowly they did not seem to be glad to be at home at all. The scene gave Ralph great thirst, and when the train moved on again, he would go to the back of the car and drink cup after cup of tepid water.

This time the woman wore a tall, tan hat which sat on her head like a pail; it was spotted with mildew. Her dress was a sleeveless evening frock of azure georgette and its scalloped skirt was longer in the back than in the front. A flower made of orange crinoline with spiny, life-like pistils was pinned to her shoulder, and she wore a choker of pink beads. As the train mounted to the high country and it grew chilly, she put on a black satin coat with a neckpiece that looked like toasted cotton. She smoked cigarettes in a carved bone holder and ground them out on the floor of the car with the heel of her tennis shoe.

There were only two children this time, a little girl of about three and a boy a little older. They stared vacantly with pale blue eyes at their fellow-passengers and ate Cracker-Jack with their mouths open, forgetting what they were doing and allowing the boxes to fall from their laps, spilling their contents everywhere. They were silent for the most part, but now and again, for no visible reason, they wailed loudly as if they were in pain and then stopped as abruptly as they had begun. They absent-mindedly plucked at the tussocks of their mother's collar and she told them, without any feeling, to "lay offn' me."

He tried to read *The Girl of the Limberlost* and could not. He worked at the crossword puzzle in the Denver *Post* but gave up when he came to "the soubriquet of Ferdinand II." He endeavored and in vain to feel the rapture of last night and he even hummed to himself some of the songs they had played: "Glow Worm," "Sleepy-Time Gal," "I'm Looking Over a Four Leaf Clover." He fled from Leah's face but it gained upon him and was before his mind's eye, doll-like and china-white. The train, the slowest on earth, seemed to rocket up the peaks and hurtle down the valleys and through the long tunnels, taking him, at this mad rate, miles away from Leah, miles on the way to Winifred whom now he was bound in conscience to love in order to purge from his heart the unholy image of his sister.

At noon they went into the forward car where there was a small buffet at one end. An amiable Negro sold dry ham

sandwiches and coffee of a strange buttery flavor. Opposite
Ralph and Molly, sitting with a table between them, were four
ranchers, drinking whisky out of Lily cups. Farther up the car
was a sandy-haired little man with a small, spiteful mouth and
blue pop eyes. He wore a cerise silk neckerchief and a black
and yellow braided belt; his Levis were stiff and new and he
had turned up the cuffs to show his black boots with curlicues
burned into the tops of them. He had a bottle too, but he
did not fool with a Lily cup; instead he put the bottle to his
mouth and gurgled loudly. Molly continued to read as she ate,
having made the statement when they came in that Napoleon
was a man she wished she had known platonically. Ralph gazed
out the window at the deep gorge of the Wolf River, full and
foaming from the big thaws. The train slowed down so much
for a steep grade that he saw a fat woodchuck calmly eating
something on a rock at the edge of the track-bed. They came
then into a brilliant valley, checkered with neat fields, and here
the river was deeper and was the color of dark, dim gold.

A large Germanic man who smoked a pipe said, when they
stopped at Peacetown and he had scrutinized the landscape,
"Don't Luke Fisher live up there? Yonder, I'm talking about,
past them cottonwoods? Seems to me like he does."

His companions first agreed, then doubted, then denied, and
it was established finally that Fisher lived twenty-seven miles to
the east. But this did not dissuade the speaker, as it would not
have done a man at Uncle Claude's table, from talking further
of Luke Fisher. "He done mighty well with them kids after his
wife died, that's one thing you can say for him. All of them
but the oldest boy and that one, Milton, turned out ornery
as a bobcat. You ever hear about the time he was working for
Roger Campbell and turned loose a stallion with the saddle
horses? You know the stallion I mean? He was an ugly bastard
of a paint with one blue eye. Campbell bought him off Prescott
and sold him to some blooded dude here a while back for seven
thousand dollars. Well, this here Milton—Milt, they called
him—was wrangling Campbell's horses up there one summer.
Campbell used to have a whole hell of a lot more dudes than
he's got now, don't ask me why because I don't know. Anyway,
I guess this Milt got aholt of a bottle of rotgut whisky and

drank it one Saturday night because the next Sunday morning when the dudes went out to get on their horses, there wasn't anything in the world in the corral but that ball-face stallion kicking the bejesus out of every goddam bench on the place. Campbell had some good horses too. Bought a colt off him myself once, pretty near the finest horse I ever had. Ken Burkhardt's got her now down to Kenyon's place."

It was not unusual for Ralph to hear his uncle's name in these conversations. Indeed, he could not remember a time when Uncle Claude had not come up in connection with something or other and it gave him a sense of security and pride. His name was as well known here, as much taken for granted, as that of President Hoover. Sometimes he and Molly talked loudly to establish their identity so that the men would speak to them, but they never did, although usually they knew who the children were, and when they got off at White Woman, someone would look out the window and say, "Well, there's Kenyon's pick-up, so the kids won't have to walk home."

Between swallows, the solitary man cut his nails with a jackknife and whistled tunelessly between his teeth. He finished his whisky as they sat there, and when he had tucked the bottle away under the seat, he smiled at the men across the aisle. His smile was only a physical adjustment of his lips; it was like the grin of a panting dog. He spoke with a Texas accent, and he said, "I don't like to horn in on you boys if you're discussing something private, but I was studying on maybe one of you all having an extra bottle of corn whisky that I could buy off you. I aimed to stock up better than I done, but I'm a stranger to Denver and only got just this one pint. Hadn't stocked up on the password was my trouble." There was a pause during which he did not close his mouth. The four men shrewdly sized him up, and although it was clear that they did not approve of him, one of them nevertheless fetched down his valise from the luggage rack and got out an unlabeled pint bottle. The Texan handed him three silver dollars and the man pocketed them wordlessly.

The stranger drank and then, to the men who had not taken their eyes off him, he said, "Well, no offense intended, but that ain't worth three dollars and it ain't worth two. If a man felt right free, he might give six bits for it. By Jesus, they got us coming and going between the goddam government and the goddam bootleggers."

His listeners' faces were expressionless. Presently, the tall Germanic man said, "Where you from?"

"Well, Mister, as of seventy-five hours forty-five minutes ago, I'm from San Fernando Hospital, San Anton'. I laid on a bed for six holy months. Broke my leg bulldogging a steer on Christmas day."

He had recovered now and was on his way to Laramie to put on an exhibition for a millionaire and his pals who had hinted of Madison Square Garden. "Can you feature a rodeo indoors?" he said. "I can't, but, Momma dear! I *can* feature the cash in them New York dudes' jeans." He had never been through this country before, he said, but in Reno once last November he had met a man from here. He had met him at a gambling table and he would swear on a stack of Bibles that he had never seen a man with such luck. "I can't call his name, though I'd remember if I heard it. But anyway, that man had the most gorgeous luck I ever saw in my born days. He won him one hundred twenty-five dollars before he said quit, and if I'd of been in his place, I would of gone on. But then, I always was a sucker."

It was agreed, finally, that the lucky gambler was Homer Armitage and the details of his fortunate career were reported, how, at Spit-in-the-Ocean, he had bluffed his way into a twenty-dollar pot, had never been known to lose a cent at Stud, and was the one man in ten thousand that could make a slot machine pay off. The stranger said, "He cheats, don't he?" and grinned.

The four men sat up straight and the one who had given him the whisky said, "You had ought to watch the way you talk, Mister. Homer Armitage don't cheat and you're among his friends."

Molly looked up from her book and laughing noiselessly, said, "Ride 'em, cowboy." Ralph, who until then had seen nothing amusing in the native's defense of a fellow-citizen against an outlander, scowled, annoyed that, as usual, she was twice as quick-witted as he even though she had appeared to be absorbed in her book.

After that the Texan drank in silence, sucking his bottle like a baby, and the others did not speak to him again, but went on talking of Homer. When his luck at cards had been exhausted, one of them said, "Hear Armitage bought a quarter interest in Kenyon's place. If the man's got money to do that, I don't see why he don't get his own place. It ain't any good working for somebody else."

"Kenyon ain't bad to work for," said another. "He pays his men good."

A yellow-haired and cross-eyed man said, "Hear Kenyon's going to get married."

"You don't say? Who to?"

"I haven't got the foggiest. Just something my wife picked up and told me. She didn't know either. I asked her."

"Well, it's time. It ain't that girl of Kennedy's, is it? The one that has the school up to the Forks?"

"Christ, no. She's Harmon Tucker's girl."

"Well, I'll be damned. I wonder who it is."

Molly closed her book and leaning across the empty plates and cups, whispered, "Did you hear that? Do you know what I think? I think Uncle Claude is going to marry Magdalene."

He did not bother to be irritated with her. The thought was immediately in his mind that Uncle Claude was going to marry Winifred, and now the blustering passion of last night returned. Imperfectly, as if he looked through waves of heat, he saw his sister's forehead furrow with surprise and then smooth out again as her lips curled in a smile whose intention he could not grasp. He thought: what has given me away? But Molly said nothing and prepared to go back to the other car. For one interminable moment he sat still. The train was picking up speed, for they were coming down off Booth Pass. Between this and Cuthbert there was a ride of three more hours during which they would pass through fourteen tunnels, one of which, the longest, they were rushing toward now. This was the part of the journey he and Molly had always looked forward to. Sometimes they saw a man standing in a niche at the side, the pale light from the lamp on his cap giving his grimy face a corpse-like luminosity. Once a bat had flown against the very window at Molly's elbow.

As Ralph lurched through the buffet car, he heard the train

hoot, protracting its note of warning so long that he knew they were almost at the mouth of the tunnel. By the time he had passed through the vestibule, the lamps in the car were turned on. They were not powerful and the blackness of the tunnel, even at its entrance, was so complete that the light was crepuscular. Coal smoke, forced back from the locomotive, seeped through the door of the observation platform. His mouth already tasted foully of sulphur. He made his way toward Molly. The woman with the children leaned out into the aisle as he passed by and she said in a flat voice, "You got a match?" He flushed in the dimness as he shook his head, ashamed that he did not smoke. He saw that she wore no wedding ring.

He sat down beside Molly, although the seat in front was pushed back so that they could be opposite one another. Partly he did not wish her to read any further in his face and partly he wanted to feel her near by. He thought of her as if she were the last foothold beneath which the world fell away in a chasm: it would be so easy to lose his footing, relax his fingerholds, and plunge downward to wedge his bones in a socket of rocks. Vile fogs baffled him and vileness was below him. Molly, alone, he thought, did not urge him to corruption.

For the moment he was protected by her elbow and her knee which touched his, and by the sexless odor of her new white shirt which she wore with a pair of black sateen gym bloomers. He saw the tunnel as an apotheosis of his own black, sinful mind which had incestuously coveted Leah (he trembled to think of Mr. Robert Appleton) and the girl who might well be his aunt-by-marriage, the mind that had observed with delight that the mother of the seedy children had no wedding ring. He urged the train to make haste. Once out in the bright green meadows of the valley he thought he would be safe from the thoughts that swarmed about him like a dream of reptiles. As long as Molly was here beside him, though, he could hang on.

And then he knew he had been wrong, that he was not safe; he was weakening and ready to fall, and now he actually slumped down in the seat so that his shoulders were on a level with Molly's and he said, in the lowest voice, "Molly, tell me all the dirty words you know."

He heard himself almost with relief. Before there was time for Molly to move away or to utter a cry, they had emerged into the light which streamed like glory through the dirty window panes. The sun was high and the fields shimmered. Round them, for miles, as far as the eye could see, were the violet mountains, clean-lined, clear of haze. The eye could not detect a single impurity in all the scene.

Ralph's childhood and his sister's expired at that moment of the train's entrance into the surcharged valley. It was a paradox, for now they should be going into a tunnel with no end, now that they had heard the devil speak.

Chapter Seven

WHEN THEY came into the long living room late in the afternoon, Mrs. Brotherman was waiting for them as she had always done in former years. She sat, thinner, sadder, more pearly than ever, beside a table where she had put a bowl of apples and a pitcher of cider. These days of early June were still cool in the mountains when the sun was setting, so there was a fire in the hearth and the housekeeper, whose aging blood was pale, leaned toward it with a wan, inadmissible hunger. Ralph recalled the gritty heat in Denver: it had been as recently as last night that, sweating in the hotel bedroom, he had listened gluttonously to the music of the jazz band which was itself suffused with summer heat and moistness. The room had been cleaned that day and it shone dustlessly in the light from the fire and the light from the setting sun that burned through the windows. All the catalogues and the magazines of western stories were stacked up neatly and there was a feminine order in the arrangement of sacks of Bull Durham, boxes of cartridges, and tins of pipe tobacco on the big varnished table, an order Uncle Claude, seeming almost driven by necessity, at once demolished by seeking cigarette papers with a planless hand.

Familiar smells came to Ralph faintly after he had been greeted by Mrs. Brotherman and had sat down for a ceremonious moment of silence. There were the smell of fat meat cooking in beans, the smell of the apples and of the pitch in the spitting pine logs; over them all was the nameless smell of the house itself whose elements comprised leather, saddle soap, oily ramrods, dogs and drying hides. With the well-known smells came the sounds of a cow bellowing for the calf that had been butchered that morning; the team horses, turned loose, neighing as they ran foolishly in circles round their pasture; the barking of dogs on distant farms; the clatter of milk buckets down at the barn; the obstreperous arrival of the tractor across the bridge over the big slough.

He could taste the apples in the cider and he wondered if wine really tasted of grapes. Often in the past summers Uncle Claude had given him a glass of Dago red, but it had only tasted thick and faintly sour. He had liked, though, to sit in

618

this room with him and the other men on special evenings—
Saturdays or when it was storming—and watch them pass the
gallon jug back and forth as they filled their teacups, bragging
that they were getting as tight as ticks, although Ralph could
see no difference in them.

Uncle Claude now stood with one leg flung over the end of
the table, rolling a cigarette. His hat was pushed back and a lock
of black hair lay on his forehead like a leech. He had not shaved
and the small blue spines made his jaw look sunken. Although
he was otherwise unaltered, this detail made Ralph quickly
alert to him, not as his uncle nor as the man's man, drinking
bootleg wine, but as an almost anonymous man, old enough
both to have a heavy beard and to marry a girl. Indeed, he
had never known how very old Uncle Claude was until today,
on the way from the station, Molly had asked him and he had
told her that he was thirty-six. "You're the same age as my
father," she had said. Further, Ralph observed that if he himself
had been looking for the cigarette papers, he would not have
messed up the other things and he wondered if there would
ever be a time in his life when he could be untidy without being
self-conscious about it. At this moment of resentment, as if he
had spoken his futile envy aloud, Uncle Claude said, "Where's
Winifred?" Ralph was sure he heard a note of possessiveness
in his uncle's voice and that when Mrs. Brotherman's reply
came, he saw a flush under the stubble. "She went to see *The
Scarlet Pimpernel* with one of her beaux." Molly gave Ralph a
rapid, spiteful glance and then looked at her feet, smiling with
dreadful secrets. It seemed to him that something was going to
happen and there came to his mind, quite inexplicably, the idea
that an arrow was going to be shot from an unseen bow the
length of the room to imbed itself in the neck of the antelope
on the south wall. But the charged moment ended when Mrs.
Brotherman, refilling Molly's cider glass, said humbly, "How
nice for your sisters and your mother to go all the way around
the world. I expect they will have wonderful tales to tell when
they get home."

"I suppose so," said Molly, "if you happen to like that sort of
hogwash and soul-butter. I happen not to be the type."

Uncle Claude laughed. "Hogwash and soul-butter, that's a
new one. Where'd you get that one?"

Molly said, "In a book I read when I was a child. A book by Samuel Clemens."

"Listen to Grandma," said Uncle Claude.

Ralph was quite unable, even though he concentrated so hard that his head began to ache, to feel any emotion at all over Mrs. Brotherman's announcement that Winifred was at the movies with a beau. And not just "her *beau*" but "one of her *beaux*." The word had a fusty, old-fashioned sound and made him think of his mother who would say, "When I went to a taffy-pull with a beau," or "a beau of mine gave me the souvenir spoon from the Alamo." All that really took his fancy was the fact that Winifred was seeing *The Scarlet Pimpernel* which had, to his regret, been scheduled in Covina for the week after they left. He wished somehow to convey his indifference to Molly, but she sat, incommunicable, enclosed within herself, staring at the flames as she munched her apple, an enemy to both the fire and the fruit. It was barely possible that he had misread her smile in the buffet car, and in this case, silence was the only possible policy.

Uncle Claude and Mrs. Brotherman asked them questions about who had bought the walnut grove, the name of the ship on which the travelers were sailing, whether Mrs. Fawcett had spoken to the caretaker about Grandpa's grave. Molly replied in pig-like monosyllables, watching Ralph as he politely filled in and then, in his turn, inquired after Homer Armitage who, for some inscrutable reason, was taking a correspondence course in shorthand and who had not, as the man on the train declared, bought an interest in the Bar K; and after Magdalene who had made more than a hundred dollars last winter by trapping skunks; and after the men to whom, it appeared, nothing at all had happened.

"When's the wedding?" said Molly at length, biting an apple seed between her front teeth.

"What wedding?" said Uncle Claude.

"Yours and Magdalene's."

"Molly!" cried Mrs. Brotherman, horrified.

Uncle Claude looked at her as if they were exactly the same age. "If you don't watch out, they're going to put you in the booby hatch. I never seen anybody in my life with such damn crazy ideas."

"Well, if you're not going to marry Magdalene, who are you going to marry? Me?"

"Shut up, Molly," said Ralph, beside himself with embarrassment, and then, to Uncle Claude, he explained what they had heard on the train.

"Well, I'll be," said Uncle Claude, pleased. "It don't happen to be true but I'm obliged to those boys for thinking I'm a ladies' man, which I am as far from being as Molly is from having good sense."

"Then you *aren't* going to get married?" said Ralph with an eagerness he could not suppress.

"You bet I'm not," said Uncle Claude.

Molly said crossly, "Why isn't there any salt for the apples?" and glared balefully at Ralph.

It was only a question of minutes, he thought, before the grown-ups would begin to suspect that some issue had been raised between him and Molly, even though neither was quick to observe such things, Uncle Claude because he wore his own feelings clearly on his face and expected everyone else to do likewise, and Mrs. Brotherman because she had imposed on all the world a smooth, unruffled sadness in which all events were exactly the same. She returned with a melancholy warmth to the world cruise and asked Molly if she were not proud of the travelers.

"Why?" said Molly. "Why in the world would I be proud of them? I could have gone too if I had wanted to, and now I'm sorry I didn't."

"Why, Molly," said Mrs. Brotherman. "Why, Molly, what a thing to say. Your uncle will think you aren't happy here."

"I'm not," said Molly.

Uncle Claude colored and Molly, fearless and level-headed, looked from him to Ralph and back again, disliking them both. It was true, of course, that she had never been close to Uncle Claude and had held a grudge against him for ending her companionship with Ralph; but if a word of criticism were spoken against him in Covina, she was savagely defensive, principally because he was Grandpa Kenyon's son and Grandpa Kenyon continued in her rapt memory as the only hero of her life. Today, in her fault-finding gaze, there was something besides this old resentment, but Ralph could not put his finger on it.

Mrs. Brotherman was distressed and said, "Oh, dearie, you are worn out from the journey. Have another apple, do." Molly took the apple, her third, and slumped down in her chair to eat it in small bites like a squirrel, mumbling once, "I prefer bananas, of course," and then subsiding into a vigilant silence. Everyone but this forthright monster was embarrassed; black-haired, studiously misshapen, noisily nibbling, she tyrannized them into a gawky silence and then suddenly she kicked Ralph sharply on the shin. It made him gulp with pain but he said nothing although he could feel the very skin draw tight over his cheeks.

Uncle Claude looked curiously at them both and said, "Did you two have a scrap somewhere along the line?"

"No," said Molly shortly and returned to her apple. Anyone else would have been fighting back tears, but Molly's tantrum was controlled and dry-eyed.

"Then what's eating on you?" Often Uncle Claude did not, as Mrs. Fawcett would have said, "know when to let well enough alone."

"None of your beeswax, Mr. Kenyon," she said, "and that's that."

Uncle Claude was furious. For a moment Ralph thought he was going to pull her hair or twist her arms behind her back, and he did take a step toward her, but checked himself and pretended he had only moved nearer the fireplace to throw his cigarette away and then, ignoring her entirely, he said to Ralph, "Come on up to the gallery. I want to show you something."

The gallery ran the length of the short wall of the room. Most of the space was taken up by the poker table and the chairs, but at one end there was a sort of alcove, called "the office," with a rolltop desk where Uncle Claude kept the registration papers of his pedigreed bulls and all sorts of other documents of an important historical nature, such things as land grants, dark yellow with age, signed by Buchanan and Lincoln, a trap-shooting certificate belonging to Homer Armitage and Uncle Claude's birth certificate in which his middle name was written down as "None." Over this desk, obscured by the shadows of a lodgepole pine which grew close to the house and thrust its needles against the window screen, was a picture of Ralph's grandmother. It was a journeyman portrait with a background of a blue lake in the distance and nearer at hand an ailanthus tree in flower. She wore a lace cap over her brown hair which hung in ringlets to her shoulders, and in her hand she held a white silk fan. Mrs. Bonney-Kenyon had a firm Scotch face with narrow lips and a small thin nose which ever so slightly tilted up. None of her children or her grandchildren bore any resemblance to her at all, but this, really, was no wonder, since both her husbands had been such powerful characters. Ralph could not tell whether she looked humorless or beaten or whether the unhappy look in her hazel eyes, set close together, came from embarrassment at the anachronistic curls which beset her plain face. As he came up the stairs behind Uncle Claude, he glanced in at her and he was struck with terror, thinking of how she had died giving birth to the man ahead of him.

They went to the window opposite the poker table and Uncle Claude pointed out to a bull in a small pasture by himself. He had a hairball in his jaw the size of a grapefruit. The vet had not been able to come to operate yet and the beast suffered noisily. As they watched, he faunched up the grassy ground around him and then, bellowing with pain and fury, rubbed the great tumor against the trunk of a poplar tree. He seemed to stare directly into their eyes with hatred as if they were responsible for his torment. There was something horrible in the spectacle and Ralph was absorbed by it. His uncle, likewise, seemed half hypnotized, and in this brief time of their brutal preoccupation, their companionship was so complete that it almost frightened Ralph; it was as though he had set forth on an adventure whose terms were so inexorable that he could not possibly change his mind and go back, as if they were on a boat in the middle of a landless sea. He looked at the heavy, small-chinned face in which, as the dark clear eyes studied the sick bull, there was a certain ponderous stupidity, a sort of virile opacity, an undeviating dedication to the sickness and health and the breeding of animals. The bull, by acquiring this infirmity, had temporarily become a nothing since he could not perform his function as a sire. It was almost as if he had made a fool of himself, for surely the smile that came and went in Uncle Claude's face was a mocking one. While this discovery appalled him, he was determined never to be degraded in the man's eyes as the bull had degraded himself, as Molly had done, simply by being the kind of person she was, bookish and unhealthy. Even so, he was mixed in his feeling about Uncle Claude and his resolution was the result not of a refreshed admiration but of the desire to go unnoticed by having no shortcomings. Because his own masculinity was, in its articulation, so ugly, and he could therefore take no pleasure in himself, neither could he respect it in anyone else, and he was sorry now that he had heard Uncle Claude use dirty words to Magdalene. Was it possible that even Grandpa had been like that? He quickly thrust away the dishonorable thought.

Mrs. Brotherman, in her sighing monotone, was telling Molly about the bad luck she had had last winter with her house plants. Several times Molly said something in reply, but Ralph could not catch her words which she uttered as softly as a secret. Poor Molly, so unflower-like, should have been interested in something like minerals, but she loved flowers, and at times, when her writing was not going well, thought that she would be a nursery man. Mrs. Fawcett always sent Leah and Rachel for the delphiniums and the roses, but Molly picked the marigold and the calendula. They would come across the lippia lawn, Leah and Rachel in front, carrying dozens of full-faced roses whose gentle petals touched their perfect little chins, and Molly following behind with her sidelong lope, clutching the hairy stems of the harsh, scentless orange flowers. But Mrs. Brotherman, leaving the winter's woe to talk instead of her summer hopes, included Molly in her gardening plans and once Ralph heard his sister say, without a bit of cynicism, "Do you think we can *ever* have a rambler, Mrs. Brotherman?"

Suddenly Uncle Claude put his hand on Ralph's shoulder and said, "I'm mighty glad you've come to stay a while this time," and Ralph, while he did not move, felt himself grow cold with withdrawal and with something like distrust for the enthusiasm in his uncle's voice, so boy-like that it actually cracked. For right now he did not want any attention paid to him at all. But when Uncle Claude went on, he realized to his relief that it was not he that had so inspired the man, but the tale he now commenced to tell him.

"Don't you know how I've always said I wanted to get me a mountain lion?" he said. "Don't you know that? Well, I'm on the trail of one now."

He paused and smiled, waiting to be questioned and Ralph cried, "Where?"

Uncle Claude had seen the lion in the foothills before you got to Garland Peak. He had seen her only once early in April and had gone back time after time to have another glimpse of her or of her mate. He had been so bent on having her hide that he had wasted a lot of hunting time just fooling around looking for her and he hadn't got a piece of game this year, though there had been plenty to be had and the boys had stocked up well. She was about as big as a good-sized dog, he said, and she looked for all the world like an overgrown house cat. He thought about her so much that he had given her a name; he called her Goldilocks because, running the way she had in the sunlight, she had been as blonde as a movie star. He had told the boys, including Homer, that he would fire any one of them that drew a bead on her because if anyone got her, it was going to be him. Old Magdalene had ragged him a God's plenty, saying that *she* was going to catch the lion with fresh kid meat. No one had quite understood why he was so all-fired crazy to get her and he could not quite make it out himself. "But you know, every now and again a man will get a bug like this and there's no more rest for him." Sometimes he would go up and spend the whole day, packing his lunch along with him, and by sundown he would be cursing her, talking to her image as if she were a person.

He had decided that he was going to let Ralph hunt her too. They were never to hunt alone and were, when they separated, to keep within hailing distance of one another. This singular honor made Ralph feel as if he were actually rising in the air and he warmly thanked Uncle Claude while, deceitfully and unsportingly, he resolved that it would be *he*, not the man, who got the lion. For a few minutes his joy was immediate and unspoiled, and then it was smashed and he remembered again what he had said to Molly in the tunnel, for through the quiet—all other noises were suspended for this new sound— came the roaring of a car, tearing along the road with the cut-out open, and he could see it, a scarlet Model A roadster with the top down as it appeared and disappeared in the lacy sarvis berry that grew along the bank. He knew at once that this was Winifred and her beau, and when the car came fully into view and turned in at the lane with a brash squeal and he saw the girl (*his* girl!) sitting beside a boy in a porkpie hat, he was overcome by the most painful sensation he had ever known and thought he was going to become too limp to stand up straight. And yet, in spite of his consuming daze, he had the presence of mind to look quickly at his uncle and to see, with another emotion that he could not name, that nothing had registered in his face at all, that he did not even glance at the car but turned to look at the sick bull again, saying, "Laid up thisaway, that bastard is losing me money right and left."

The car now passed out of sight, drawing up to the front of the house. Its engine was suddenly raced and then it idled like a loud whisper. Molly and Mrs. Brotherman continued their secret conversation about the roses and Uncle Claude muttered to himself about the bull. Only Ralph was conscious of the laughter of the boy and girl which, high, prolonged, gasping, was immodest and exciting and he felt himself to be in extreme danger. At last there was an antiphonal good-bye which, lacking the greed of the laughter, rang out mournfully over the yellow valley and the sudden car went back up the lane like a clowning dog.

He heard her come through the screen door and he turned jerkily, leaning against the railing of the gallery. Uncle Claude did not stir. Winifred raised her hand in salutation to him, smiled widely, and said, "Hi, chum," and then went to Molly and kissed her after the manner of cousins and grown-up women friends. She was plump now and so mature and feminine that Ralph could not recognize in her the shooting companion of earlier summers, that rather negative and taciturn person who, without playing a role, had seemed like another boy. Now she was a positive creature, self-assured, beautiful and glowing with an interior smile. She threw her polo coat over the back of a chair and sat down on the milking stool before the hearth. She was wearing a white dress, sleeveless and low in the back and low at the neck, and her flesh looked as brown as Fuschia's against it. He could not remember ever having seen her in anything but blue jeans and a faded work shirt; she was shorter than he remembered. There was, somehow, a settled look about her; she had a tender, untroubled, and vacuous gaze, and it would have been impossible for anyone to tell what she was smiling at.

He was uncertain. As soon as he no longer heard the red car, he was no longer jealous. And when he saw her sitting there, as native to the stool as a cat, he felt nothing at all, but the void was not painful; rather it was like a great soothing boredom. He turned to Uncle Claude and said, "What'll we hunt her with? A thirty-thirty?"

But Molly drowned out his uncle's reply with a sudden laugh. Her voice was deep for a girl and her laugh was slow and muffled but, though now she laughed her same laugh, it seemed to Ralph it had in it some of the same immodesty Winifred's had when she lingered with the boy, and in panic he thought, "She has *told*!" He knew this to be untrue, but the pleasure of the hour—scattered as it had been and filled in the interstices with embarrassment and guilt—was gone. Darkness was beginning and he felt friendless, separate, unclean. Again he tasted the sulphur at the back of his jaws and again he saw the woman in the train and her claw-like, ringless hand.

After supper Molly refused to play Continental Rummy because there was too much danger of having to speak to Ralph, and she went directly upstairs to take a bath. She drew the bolt and turned the key in the lock as well and she pulled down the window shade even though there was nothing outside but night. She was very dirty from the train. Dirt had seeped through her basketball shoes and her feet were a sight. Her arms were uniformly gray, beginning at her wrists and going up to her elbows which felt like dried-up biscuits. She had washed her hands before supper so that she appeared to be wearing a pair of pinkish gloves. Molly enjoyed being this dirty; when you were not black or at least gray, bathing seemed wasteful and self-indulgent just as did making your bed if you had not mussed up the covers much. But if you were properly dirty and could take a long, large bath, it was fun.

She had brought to the bathroom with her a Boston bag which she kept locked and hidden away on the topmost shelf of her closet. It contained green bathsalts and violet bathsalts of so inferior a quality that no matter how hot the water was, they did not melt but lay, as sharp and shining as quartz on the bottom of the tub so that it was necessary to sweep a place clean with her hand before she got in. Even so, they gave off a sweet fragrance and she could imagine that she was in a garden. Besides the bathsalts, there were a cake of soap in the form of a yellow rose, a can of Armand's talcum powder, a bottle of Hind's Honey and Almond, a jar of Daggett and Ramsdell vanishing cream, a bottle of Glostora shampoo, a jar of Dr. Scholl's foot balm, a jar of freckle remover, some scissors, a nail file, a toothbrush, some dental floss, a comb, a brush, a buffer, a chamois skin, and a pearl-handled corn parer. Covering them all was a maroon bathing suit.

She hung a towel over the back of the chair and moved the chair in front of the keyhole to thwart any Peeping Tom. Then she stood on the chair and took off her blouse and her gym pants and threw her wrapper around her shoulders while she took off her undervest and bloomers and got into the bathing suit. She sat on the chair waiting for the tub to fill, thinking of nothing, for there would be plenty of time once she was in the bath. It was unlikely that any of them would come up and try the knob because they were all sitting around the table in the gallery, all but Mrs. Brotherman who spent her evenings, and always had, crocheting a bedspread for Winifred for when she got married. They would be sitting there, those illiterate men, scratching themselves and getting the ends of their cigarettes wet and saying things like "he don't" and "you was" and "those kind" and if the subject came up, pronouncing "apricot" with a short "a." As likely as not, if Winifred had decided not to play, they would drink whisky and wine which, as everyone knew, was nine-tenths fusel oil and the chances of going blind on it were ninety-nine out of a hundred. However, they were quite unimportant to her. Under the roar of the hot water, she said, "*I* should ishkibibble if they all commit suicide."

She turned off the water and got into the tub, but she had run in too much cold and had to get out again and run in some more hot, for Molly never sat in the bathtub while the water was running: a slender snake might come right through the faucet. At the thought of snakes, she shivered all over and remembered every single encounter she had had with them, beginning with the very earliest when she was four and was too little to go to school. She was waiting one day under the umbrella tree for the bus to bring home her sisters and her brother. When she heard it coming, she walked across the lippia lawn to the patch of clover and there she stepped on a coiled-up snake which uncoiled under her bare foot and slithered off. She had stood there, unable to move but screaming at the top of her voice until Miguel came running and picked her up. She had never known whether it was the feeling of the snake under her foot or the smell of Miguel's sweaty shirt that made her throw up over his shoulder as he carried her to the house. "Aren't you ashamed," said her mother. "Why, it was nothing but a harmless garter snake." Ralph found it and killed it with a rock and took Molly out to see, but the sight of it, even dead, only made her scream again until he had to carry her piggy-back to the porch so that she would not have to step on the ground. There was another time when she and Ralph, acting out "The Little Swiss Twins," had taken a lunch of cheese and crackers to the Wash and all of a sudden Molly discovered that she was sitting right beside a bright green grass snake. This time Ralph was not kind to her. When she screamed, he slapped her face and said, "Oh, you make me sick, you big fat baby." The worst of all had happened right here, the first summer, although a real snake was not involved. She had been reading *The World Almanac* one day in the leather chair in Uncle Claude's office and had taken a horse hair out of a tear in the arm to play with in her mouth because she had forgotten to bring a match and quite unexpectedly she had swallowed it. She went down to the kitchen to ask Magdalene what to do and Magdalene said she must quickly drink a glass of water or it would turn into a bull snake in her stomach and eat up everything she ate so that she would die of starvation; Magdalene had known at least eleven people that this had happened to. She rushed to the sink and Magdalene said, "That's hard water. That ain't no good for what ails you." So she ran upstairs to Mrs. Brotherman to say that she had better get right back to Covina so that Dr. Haskell could operate on her and Mrs. Brotherman told her that Magdalene had made the whole thing up. She returned to the kitchen and said, "You're a nigger," and Magdalene replied, "You're pore white trash."

Mrs. Fawcett said she would outgrow this fear as soon as she was able to distinguish between the harmless snakes and the poisonous ones, but Molly knew this was not true because she did not even like to look at the pictures of them in the illustrated part at the back of the Unabridged. It enraged her to be told that they were useful because they ate destructive insects, and when Leah and Rachel said that if she had any sense of beauty at all, she would see that their colors and patterns were wonderful, she replied, "Who cares about a sense of beauty? I'd a whole lot rather have a sense of *proportion*, you conceited Elsie Dinsmores."

Molly lay soaking in her bathing suit so long that her skin became white and ridged. Every now and again, she got out and stood dripping on the rag rug while she ran more hot water in. She washed her hair in the bath water and let it drip down her back, the drops crawling like flies. Lying full length sometimes she let her feet and hands float to the surface and saw that they looked like something drowned; she thought of the flood when her father had brought the old woman into the kitchen. The only other thing Molly knew about the old woman was that it was said that when she was a child she had lived in a goiter belt, so now she had to drink iodine in her water.

She looked at her long feet which she allowed slowly to sink again. But for the most part, she was not conscious of her body (she was never conscious of it as a *body* and had never spoken this word aloud and almost died when one of her sisters would jokingly say, "Don't touch my body"; Molly thought of herself as a long wooden box with a mind inside) but of what had happened that afternoon in the train and she went over the whole scene time after time, each time redeeming the brilliant hatred that had spread over her exactly like bath water. Often she had hated Ralph but she had always got over it. She hated him for a month once because, when she showed him a picture in tempera of a New England kitchen, he had laughed so hard that he spit and made the red and white checked seat on the rocking chair run. Once he had brought her a little horseshoe magnet and told her that the teachers had voted to give it to her as a reward for being so diligent in collateral reading, and when she went to thank Miss Bandy, Miss Bandy said, "Why,

Molly, I think this is just something out of a Cracker-Jack box."

But while she would never forget these injuries, they no longer made her feel as if she were going to have a nosebleed. This new outrage, though, was a horse of quite a different color, and she vowed several times, raising her right arm out of the water, that she would hate Ralph Fawcett for the rest of her life. She was not certain yet how she would show him that she was his permanent enemy, but she was in no hurry to decide. For the time being she could simply lie here in the tub, safe behind a locked door, and contemplate the thing he had done, so terrible, so blackly wicked that it was thrilling. It was sharply pleasant, too, to think that she could now add Ralph's name to her list of unforgivable people, a list that included almost everyone. There were some doubtful cases (she was not completely sure about Winifred and Uncle Claude), but there were only two people who were purely forgivable and these were her father and Grandpa Kenyon. She did not forgive her father simply because she had never known him, or Grandpa just because he was dead; after all, Grandfather Bonney was a foremost unforgivable and even Grandmother Bonney was a doubtful. She often wondered, proudly, why she hated people. Sometimes she could figure back to the moment the feeling began. For example, she had hated Pinky Freudenburg beginning one day when she had stayed in at recess to work on her long division and he had stayed in too; she had gone to the pencil sharpener and he had sneaked up behind her and kissed her on the cheek and at that exact same moment, a front tooth fell out onto her tongue. She had liked Pinky until then because he made up dances to illustrate her poems besides others which he made up on his own. There was a "Pineapple Dance" and a "Ten-Cent-Store Dance" and a "Mashed Potato Dance." They were all rather alike but very exciting to watch, and Molly was sorry that she had to put her handkerchief over her eyes every time he did one of them in the playground. She had known, too, the moment Grandfather Bonney had become unforgivable. It was the day Ralph threw up in the living room and she poured the acid on her hand. She had looked at the portrait just before Ralph said the milk was sour and had thought "I

h. that man," and had known that this would be true forever and ever. But she could not remember when she had begun to hate her mother and Leah and Rachel. As for the Follansbees, of course, she had hated them before she was born.

It occurred to her as her fingers grew more swollen and furrowed that she hated them all for the same reason, but she could not decide what the reason was. You could say, Because they were all fat. But this was not true of Mr. Follansbee and it was not true of Ralph and strictly speaking it was not true of Leah and Rachel although they talked in whispers of corselets. But fatness did have something to do with it. There was something fat about the way Mr. Follansbee belched and the question Ralph had asked her had been fat. She remembered, closing her eyes to see precisely the horrible image, the day early in April when the Follansbees had gone with them one Sunday to Redondo Beach, and Mrs. Follansbee had come out of the bathhouse in a bright red swimming suit. Her thin, knock-kneed legs were traced with thickened varicose veins; her stomach was soft and pendulous and made Molly think of a cake that had run over the side of the pan. But Mr. Follansbee was every bit as bad in his emaciated half-nakedness; his spindling legs, covered all over with black hair, came out of long, loose trunks with a white band around the edge and his arms were hairy too, but his neck was as white as a fish. She would not go in swimming with them but sat on the beach, writing her name and grade in school in the sand with a piece of driftwood. Her mother came once, dripping and glistening, to sit beside her and plead with her to "be a good sport," and she looked at the dimples in her mother's pink knees and hoped she would get bitten by a crab. Ralph had been embarrassed that day, too, and when they had their picture taken against a fake background of the ocean with sea gulls painted on the canvas, both children had refused to be in it and Ralph had muttered, "I wouldn't be in a picture with those ginks if you gave me the Statue of Liberty." But it was clear that no one could be trusted, Ralph least of all. He had always hated the right ones before and now he had become one of them. It did seem a shame, really, that he had turned out so badly. He had told her in so many words that the day he got sick over the tea it had happened because he had seen through Grandfather Bonney, and they had been best friends for a month or so after that, marveling that it had come to them at the same time.

After a long while she pulled up the stopper and let the water run out, slipping down her sides, tickling a little, and deep in her throat she imitated the sound it made as it gurgled down the drain. If she ever got fat, she thought, or ever said anything fat, she would lock herself in a bathroom and stay there until she died. Often she thought how comfortably you could live in a bathroom. You could put a piece of beaver board on top of the tub and use it as a bed. In the daytime you could have a cretonne spread on it so that it would look like a divan. You could use the you-know-what as a chair and the lavatory as a table. You wouldn't have to have anything else but some canned corn and marshmallows, and if you got tired of those, you could let a basket out of the window with a slip of paper saying, "Send up some hot tamales" or some hard-boiled eggs or whatever you particularly wanted at the time.

But she doubted if she would ever get fat enough to have to live in a bathroom. She looked at her thin upper arm and gave it a monkey-bite. There were too many simple ways to avoid it as well as the drastic one of getting a tapeworm. She did profoundly hope, though, that Ralph would get fatter than Tweedledum and Tweedledee put together, and she put both her fists in her eyes, thinking with rapture of how tightly his pants would fit over his seat and his shirt would just barely button over his awful stomach. His cheeks would get so fat they would nearly cover up his eyes. All this time she, Molly Fawcett, would be getting thinner and thinner until she was practically famous for it, and when the time came, she was going to drop the fat name of Molly and be called Clara after Aunt Clara, Father's sister, of whom there was a full-length portrait in the album. Aunt Clara had been as straight up and down as a yardstick and she had enormous stick-out teeth. In the picture she wore a straight black skirt and a straight black jacket, black gloves, black shoes, and a black hat with a wide brim so that all you could see of her was her crooked nose and her great big teeth resting on her lower lip. Molly often stood before the mirror holding her teeth out and saying "Clara?

Clara?" as if she were calling to her in the grave, calling to tell her that she would try to look just like her. Otherwise, Aunt Clara had not been very admirable as she had died having a tumor removed, and Mrs. Fawcett, in telling this, would say, "Why, girls, it was such a big tumor that everyone thought she was in a certain condition." She would lift her eyes questioningly and Rachel and Leah would wisely nod. Molly would not have dreamed of asking what the condition was, but she supposed it had something to do with all that tommyrot with which people were constantly trying to ruin her life.

Finally the last of the water was gone and she stood up, putting one foot on the rim of the tub and drying it and then standing on the rug while she dried the other. She gently moved the chair and tried the knob in case anyone had picked the lock while the water was making so much racket and then, taking off the bathing suit, she dried herself and bound her stomach with a piece of outing flannel. She wrapped it so hard and pinned it so tight that it gave her a pain and she had to lie down on the floor to get her slippers because she could not bend over. Then she put on her long-sleeved, high-necked pajamas, and the nightcap she had made over her drenched hair. It was her desire to have tuberculosis, and at the ranch, where she was not supervised, she often went to bed with her hair soaking. She had tried for years to find out where Winifred kept her toothbrush.

She packed up the Boston bag again, having used out of it only the soap and the bathsalts, and let herself out. The voices of the card players came twanging up the stairwell and there were no lights showing under any of the doors save Mrs. Brotherman's and she got to her room without being seen. If she had been seen by anyone, she didn't care who, in her wrapper on this particular night, she would simply have dissolved like a slug with salt poured on it. When she got to her room, she pushed the washstand against the door and she didn't care who heard her. If they did, they did not bother; they bothered about very little around this place and this was one of the few good things about it.

When she had hung her bathing suit up in the window, she got into bed and took up her diary which she kept under her mattress. She wrote:

Ralph has gone beyond the pale. I am his permanent enemy and do not know whether I will ever speak to him again as he has literally beat a rivet of hatred into my heart by a remark he passed on the train today. I am not sure about Winifred this year. She is too fat but she told me a good joke and for the first time in a month of Sundays it was funny enough for me to laugh at.

WINIFRED'S JOKE

You call someone up on the telephone and say, "Are you the lady who washes?" and the other person says, "No," so you say, "Why, you dirty thing," and hang up.

I am not sure about Winifred, as beforesaid, because she told me that she had been to the show with her steady and when I asked what she meant by a steady she said the boy you were dippy about and was dippy about you.

But getting back to the subject of my former brother, what he did is so devilish I could like Leah by comparison in spite of the letter she wrote that made her sound non compus mentis. I will not mention the subject of this letter nor will I write down what Ralph said to me in the train, but I can assure you, Molly, that they were plenty bad. I intend to read all of Sir Walter Scott, Dickens, Stevenson, and James Fenimore Cooper while I am here so that I won't have to have anything to do with R.F. He and Uncle Claude were talking about hunting a mountain lion. I can think of nothing more boresome personally. Uncle Claude looks very old. Naturally. He is thirty-six. I am not sure that I tolerate him. He didn't know what I meant when I said "hogwash and soul-butter" and I am perfectly certain he didn't know that Mark Twain's real name was Samuel Clemens. There are only two I am sure about, Mrs. Brotherman and Magdalene. Mrs. Brotherman will let me do the roses with her, but I do not know whether they will be any good because I read on the train in the Denver *Post* that the aphids are going to be very bad this year. I have not as yet conversed with Magdalene, but she said she had a rabbit foot for me which is said to bring good luck.

Resolution: think all the time about Ralph getting fat. Tomorrow I must look at the pictures of the stout men's underwear in the catalogue and decide which one I want him to be.

Chapter Eight

I N FORMER years, ever since he had seen the calf being born, Ralph had been excited to a point of ecstasy by the robust and perpetual birth of the farm creatures. He had trembled all over at the sight of a mare being carried away in a truck to the stud farm and he had been on hand at every calving. He regretted always that the lambing came in the spring before he got there. Molly, of course, had steadfastly held her ground, and once, two years before, when he had tried to explain to her the difference between a stallion and a gelding, they had had a serious quarrel. She would not be shaken from the belief that they were simply two different breeds of horses. He had not, in any conscious way, really connected his knowledge with people, as now he did, to his shame and sorrow, wondering, with especial revulsion, about the Follansbees. He found himself compelled to study the faces of the men at the dinner table and to look with stunned amazement at Mrs. Brotherman.

Now, this summer, he took no pleasure in the colts and in the sucking calves, and he was glad that his horse and his uncle's had a pure masculine friendship and that they ran away from Winifred's mare whenever she came near them. Winifred herself made him shy and uneasy but he was not in love with her; yet he thought, in a cloudy way, that if he had not committed the crime in the tunnel, he would have been.

For a time there was little, indeed, that he took pleasure in. When, now and again, he lost himself in some small enjoyment, his guilt started and the world was spoiled. He was obsessed with the phrase "the bowels of the earth" and imagined blackened intestines spilling forth from the carcass of a gigantic steer strung up on a pulley as high as a mountain, butchered out by a knife as long as a train. Wakeful at night, he lay with his head under the pillow to shut out the brilliant starlight; he was alert to every sound, hearing Molly, who despised him, turning and grumbling in her sleep; the owls cautioning in the cottonwoods; the men coming home late from White Woman. On these cool nights, full of the clean, unripe smells of June, he could not summon any daydream. For now he aspired to be nothing but what he had been before the evening at the Brown Palace, and he could not even pretend to be that person again because Molly knew his secret, nasty nature. Not even his favorite and foolproof image would come, that of himself as Uncle Claude's partner. If he did not become Uncle Claude's partner, what would happen to him? He had no variety of ambitions as had Molly who, in the course of a week, would plan to be a salesman for the *Book of Knowledge*, a grocer, a government walnut inspector, a trolley conductor in Tia Juana; of course her real vocation was writing and these were to be only sidelines.

Ralph was troubled by the loss of his desire to enter Uncle Claude's world completely. He had continued, against his will, to remember how he had looked at the sick bull and he thought, "If anything happened to a *person*, he'd be the same way." How was this possible, though, when Grandpa Kenyon's death had broken him up in pieces like a plate? Perhaps it was not death that annoyed and disgusted him but only the circumstances leading to death, and Ralph remembered that he had not asked a single question about Grandpa's attack or his three-day illness.

He would brood for a while about Uncle Claude and then brood about Molly. In time he invented a reason, abstruse and clever, for his defection in the tunnel. He said that something, some dark creature like the Skalawag, had cast a spell over him and he had been powerless to break from it. The fact that Molly had been the victim was pure chance; he could as easily have abused the anonymous woman in her dispirited party dress. At times he could almost believe that he had said, "*It* told me to ask you to say all the dirty words you know." But this was little consolation, for he could never explain it to Molly; he could never refer to what had happened in the slightest way, even though she herself mercilessly used the words "tunnel" and "dirty" so often and with such contriving that he felt sure someone would one day remark it. She never spoke to him except to say something unkind. Once she clapped her hand over her mouth and through her fingers gasped, "Oh, my gosh, for a minute you looked just like Grandfather Bonney." And another time she said to Winifred, "You know it runs in our family to be fat. It's bad enough for a woman to be fat but don't you think fat men are terrible?" And she had looked at him as if she wanted him to get fat.

There was no escaping his anxieties, and plagued as he was by them, he sought solitude, but Uncle Claude, who could not bear to be alone, frustrated him, insisting that he go mending fence, hiring the hay crew, fishing before daylight. Ralph found himself hiding when he heard his uncle call. He would hide in the barn in a grain bin or behind the skins in the slaughter shed, his heart trying to burst out of his shirt and his mouth as dry as paper. Often, on butchering days, he went off to town right after breakfast, hitching a ride on the highway to spend the whole day lounging with the high school loungers in the doorway of the old livery stable or in the booths of the drug store. Sometimes a tangle of hysterical girls would come sweeping down the main street, shrieking, into the booths with porcelain-topped tables. It was a prolonged giggle there in the drug store, a battle of wits with the boys who sat in separate booths and courted them by tossing over wet straws and wadded-up paper napkins. Occasionally Winifred and John Fulbright, the boy with the scarlet car, sat in the very last booth, silent and bedazzled.

Uncle Claude was puzzled by this desertion and he said, "I can't make out what's got into you. Why, I thought you was going to turn into an A Number One butcher," and Ralph could only reply, lightly, "I don't rightly know why I'm off it myself." He began even to resent the fact that he was obliged to speak like Uncle Claude in order not to sound impolite.

They were leaning one afternoon against the railing of the corral, their hats over their eyes to keep out the sun. Ken Burkhardt and Dump were hog-tying the sick bull, and the vet, a fat, dapper little man in green gabardine trousers and a pink silk shirt, was sorting his instruments beside the gate. Ralph had not wanted to come, but Uncle Claude had insisted. "It's part of your education," he had said. The bull was thrashing and bellowing and Ralph, certain that he was too much for just two men, did not put his foot up on the railing but stood alert, ready to run.

When the operation began and the knife went in, he had to keep his jaws closed tight and he shut his eyes, swaying sickly.

There was a smell which hit them in a hot wave, and the bull made a wailing screaming sound that went splintering though his skull. He dared not look but kept his eyes fixed on the green ball and the two red arabesques that floated behind his eyelids. While all this was going on, while the poor beast was being cut up like a piece of food, Uncle Claude said, "We'll go fishing tomorrow up to the Hell Hole."

He felt no anger, but he was determined not to go, and he said, "I am sorry, Uncle Claude, I can't."

But Uncle Claude only said, "You be up by four. It ain't any good if you wait longer than that."

"I can't go," said Ralph. "I'm going to do something else tomorrow."

"My eye," said his uncle.

"I am. I'm going to play pool."

"At four in the morning? Where you going to play it? In the swimming pool?" He poked Ralph in the ribs, laughing at his joke. Ralph moved away irritably. The bull roared and the vet said good-naturedly, "Take it easy, old man, we're comin' right along here."

"I can't go fishing tomorrow, Uncle Claude," said Ralph stubbornly.

His uncle said, "Well, I ain't going fishing to the Hell Hole alone and I ain't going to take your sister, so it looks like I'm taking you."

"Looky here," cried Ralph, "looky here, not you and not anybody else is going to tell *me* what to do, goddamit to hell." He left the corral, walking in enormous strides back to the house, immediately remorseful, his pride receding. He knew— and even when he had had his tantrum he had known—that Uncle Claude did not want to impose his will upon him, he just wanted company, and when you came right down to it, a man couldn't deny another man that. So he would go as he had known all along he would go and as Uncle Claude had known.

Never had there been such weather. It was clear and hot in the day and cool at night. Curds of bruised clouds hung motionless in the sky. If rain came, it came as a spectacular storm, beginning with brilliant lightning and thunder which sometimes stuttered far away in the distant ranges and sometimes was so close at hand that it sounded like blasting at the very base of Garland Peak. The rain followed with a push like the heavy wings of an eagle, obscuring the mountains, the timothy fields, and the outbuildings. During the storm, everyone sat moody and damp in the parlor, stubbornly listening to the radio over which came nothing but an outraged cackling and, at great intervals, a thin wisp of song. Uncle Claude paced the floor restlessly. He hated rain just as he hated illness or anything else that kept him indoors.

Very late on one of these days of storm, a man stopped by, riding at the head of a string of twenty blooded horses. He asked for quarters for the night. Uncle Claude, who never turned anyone away nor asked a stranger what his business was, said he could sleep in the bunkhouse and his horses could shift for themselves in the cow pasture. It was nearly as dark as night when Ralph and Uncle Claude rode out with him to lead the horses, but now and again the sky was split with lightning; the frightened neighing of the horses and behind that sound the thunder seemed unreal, like something in a western movie. Ralph experimented; he spurred Studebaker to a run and standing up in his stirrups he screamed but he could not hear his own voice, he could only feel it in his throat.

The stranger, by his very coming, elevated everyone's spirits. Uncle Claude built up the fire and he said to Ralph, "Go tell that coon to pack up a jug of Dago out of the cellar." But Ralph went himself although Magdalene argued, saying that she didn't want him "amessin' around in my spuds and my engerns and my conserves." He was so excited by the storm and the stranger and the twenty horses that he could not remember, once he was down there, what he had come for. He turned the flashlight over the shelves and a pack rat ran with a glittering eye behind a crock. When the light fell on the jugs of wine, he remembered, and instead of taking just one, he took two.

Warmed by the fire, freed by the wine, the man talked volubly, and all the other men and Ralph and Winifred sat around him listening and laughing as if they were outcasts to whom at last a visitor from the world had come. He told them that he was riding to Vernal, Utah, to take his horses to a gambler (he pronounced it "gambular") to whom he had lost them on a bet. Uncle Claude said, "That's a long ride, Mister. Would you do better to put them in some boxcars?" The man had a long, lopsided chin and rheumy eyes. He laughed and replied, "He took my fare as well as my riding horses."

The lights went off and they had to eat supper by kerosene lamps. They did not come on again that night, but the fire was bright all evening and they crouched around it, some of them sitting on the floor like Indians. Molly was learning to play the ukulele and she sat in the darkness on the gallery, plucking the unresonant strings and singing softly over and over again, "My dog has fleas." The stranger would not tell them what the bet had been for which there had been such high stakes, and all of them passionate with curiosity and with the wine and the howling storm that did not abate for more than a minute all evening, questioned him time and again, sometimes impatiently, sometimes uneasily. Now and again he looked quickly over his shoulder, but this was only meant to tantalize them for afterward he laughed in their faces.

Ralph drank several glasses of the wine and the effect of it was as odd and elusive as the atmosphere which the stranger had imparted to the evening. He was by turns drowsy and keenly awake. Winifred sat crosslegged in front of the fire on a deerskin, saying nothing at all, but looking up with an abstracted smile at the stranger sometimes and at Uncle Claude who was the company's principal spokesman. It was one of the few nights since Ralph and Molly had come that she had stayed at home, and the men had teased her about it at supper, saying they guessed her boy friend was no great shakes if he let a little thing like rain keep him away. Her mother gently remonstrated, "Winifred has better sense than to make herself sick by going out in the rain," and the man who had started the raillery mumbled an apology, recalling her "tendency."

For the space of this long evening, secure in the darkness from questioning eyes, safe from Molly whose meaningless plinking was as steady as the rain, Ralph allowed himself to think of Winifred and a guiltless desire ruffled warmly over him. It was hardly possible, he thought, that she and John Fulbright did not kiss. Often he heard them coming down the lane at midnight, coasting quietly, and then there was an interval

of a quarter of an hour or more before the car went away and
he heard Winifred coming up the stairs so softly she must have
walked in her stocking feet. She was not like the other girls
who were boisterous and brash, liking to walk loudly in their
high heels across the drug store's tiled floor and, in the booths,
suddenly begin to sing. They were loud-mouthed and postur-
ing and could perpetrate their tomfoolery for hours together.
But Winifred was demure, soft-spoken and almost pensive, and
always upon her lips was that enchanting, mysterious smile.
Ralph had heard in the town that she was a very good dancer
and he marveled that she had this skill as well as the masculine
ones of riding and shooting. When he first heard this, he said to
her, "I have a t.l. for you." She said, inadequately, "Homer says
you are the best help irrigating he ever had." When he told her
what he had heard, she said nothing and was not at all embarrassed, as if this were her simple due. Molly who, according to
her custom, had been lurking unseen in the room, sidled forward, *The Pathfinder* folded over her thumb, and said, "What
I heard is of far more import than that. I heard you could read
Latin at sight." Winifred frowned and cast down her eyes as if
her character had somehow been impugned.

Winifred stirred, and looking around at Ralph, she said,
"Where are they now?" so that with surprise he realized that
she, too, had not been listening to the men.

"Where are who?" he said.

"Your mother and Leah and Rachel."

Everyone listened as he said, "I don't know. The last letter
was from Hong Kong."

The stranger peered at him closely. "Well, I'll be. So your
folks are in Hong Kong. I was there once and I seen one of
them mongooses kill a cobra snake."

The ukulele immediately stopped and Molly, out of the darkness, said, "I doubt that. The mongoose is native to India."
Her voice was firm and clear and its effect upon the stranger
was so prompt that sweat came out on his forehead, glittering
in the firelight, and his hand trembled so that some of the
wine spilled on his khaki Army and Navy store pants. He did
not dispute that voice, like the voice of conscience there in
the pitch blackness, but he replied quickly and nervously, "By

golly, that's right. I must of been thinking of Bagdad." Molly laughed derisively and began to play again.

The men wanted to hear of the stranger's world travels, but he would not tell. The most they could get out of him was an account of an opium den he had been taken to in the San Francisco Chinatown.

Ralph thought, half enviously, of his mother and sisters. All summer plump letters and picture postal cards came to him and Molly from Yokohama, Tokyo, Shanghai, Canton. They gave the cards and envelopes to Magdalene who kept them on a shelf in the kitchen in a Roi-Tan cigar box which until then had only held an announcement of Grandpa Kenyon's funeral and the business card of a Watkins man named Edward P. Otto-lengui. Leah and Rachel, in their letters, alternated between a formal essay style ("You will next want to know about the peculiar vehicle they have here which is called a 'rickshaw' and is the equivalent of the American taxicab") and a gushing coquetry ("our nice new suitcases have been just ruined by all the awful stickers the hotels put on them"), but Mrs. Fawcett always wrote in the same way; her tone was a combination of the sisters' two styles, half educational, half jocular. She wrote, "Luncheon has become a 'movable feast' for us since we never can tell what adventure is going to o'ertake us in the forenoon to keep us from our victuals. And, my dears, the victuals when we finally do get to them are just as strange. I'm afraid my persnickety Molly would have to change her habits if she came here. We have become very partial to bean sprouts! (How is Uncle Claude's garden, by the way? I hope you are both helping Mrs. B. in it, for that is a very nice way to show your gratitude to C.K.) What would the Orient do without bean sprouts and rice, I often wonder, but I dare say there is no danger of at least the rice giving out, as from every train window you see nothing but fields upon fields of it, dotted all over with coolies in their picturesque hats like those on the postal Leah sent you yesterday."

It was not the nonsense of the letters that disturbed him. Indeed, he was rather relieved to find that traveling had no effect upon his mother's silliness. What made him dread the daily mail was that each letter contained a passage on that happy future when the family would be reunited in Connecticut. There was an implication of ponderous finality in this reunion. Between the lines, he read that she would bury Uncle Claude as completely as she had buried Grandpa, and while this year he was often discontented and often wished to be elsewhere, whenever he thought of his mother and of Connecticut, he clung with passionate devotion to his uncle and to Colorado. He was, at these times, like someone who has been told that his lover will die soon and who, unable to conceive the metamorphosis of his habits and thoughts after her death, becomes the closer bound to the necessity of this love so that when the hour comes and she is gone, he feels that he has not been prepared at all. Such, he brooded, was the shape of the earth that the farther away the world-travelers went, the closer they came to the Atlantic seaboard and to their inexorable plans. In a short few months from now, his father's gravestone and Grandpa Kenyon's would be separated from him by the whole width of the continent, but Grandfather Bonney, portable, ubiquitous, reposing for the summer in a safety deposit vault, would always be at hand. And so, always at hand, would be Molly who could ruin him, blow up his world if she chose. He knew, but for no reason he could name, that she would do nothing so long as they were here, but in that bare wasteland where they were to live under the shadow of the trinity of fat men, he must guard himself against her weapon.

In the middle of the evening, Uncle Claude complained restlessly that the rain was getting on his nerves and that the wine was not doing him any good. Suddenly in the room there was a sense of fear and Ralph saw Dump look furtively at the stranger. The man, mean-mouthed and nasty-eyed, sat with his chair tilted against the fireplace. He had got over the nervousness Molly had caused him and had for some time been asking about the hunting in these parts. At first the men talked enthusiastically, blandly and casually interrupting one another, but bit by bit they withdrew and one by one fell silent. Uncle Claude for a while did not sense their dim suspicions, and having the floor to himself, told story after story. Then he said that he had not done much hunting this spring himself as he had in years past, but he told how many pounds of elk and deer the other boys had brought in, most of it hanging up out there in the icehouse this very minute. He recounted their adventures as if they had been his own.

"But you say you ain't got none of this meat yourself?" said the stranger. "How come?"

This was a question he had wanted to be asked and he smiled. "I'll tell you. Along here in April I was scouting around in the foothills having a look for a good fat beaver and one day I seen . . ." He paused. Now his men's distrust had made itself known to him. It was almost as if they were shaking their heads at him and even Winifred sat up straight, tense and waiting. He finished, "I seen something that took my fancy."

"And what in the world was that?" said the man. He let his chair down slowly and leaned forward, holding his wine glass in both hands.

"Well, that's a question I don't feel called to answer," said Uncle Claude.

Ralph was perplexed. He knew that what had stilled the men's tongues was that they had begun to wonder if the stranger were the Law in disguise and had come to collect evidence against them to settle their score with the game authorities. But why had they not wanted him to know that there was a mountain lion on Garland Peak? There was no bounty on them. Perhaps it was no more than a cumulative resentment of the man who had drawn their secrets out of them but refused to tell what the bet was that he had lost.

Hearing the thunder once again burst in the mountains, the thought of the lion enraptured him and he wondered where she was and if she were asleep now in her den. They had looked for her day after day but had never seen her, though twice they were sure they found the prints of her paws in the squelchy ground near the beaver dam. Then he knew that the reason Uncle Claude had not named Goldilocks by name was that she was his own property, his and Ralph's. The other men could know because they could be trusted not to hunt her. But you could not trust this ugly man who now, laughing out of his uneven mouth, said, "I wouldn't think you'd have to go to the mountains to hunt that kind of game. What's the matter with the little lady settin' here? Settin' right here with all us big grown men?"

Uncle Claude slowly turned his eyes to Winifred who had

not even seemed to hear and he said reproachfully, "That's no way to talk." He sounded hurt like a misunderstood child. "I was talking about something else."

Soon after this, they all went to bed. Ralph lay for a long time listening to the rain and to the frequent thunder. Often the lightning shot like a flare through the curtains and illuminated the posts of his bed which ended in carved pineapples. There was too much noise outside for him to hear Molly in the next room, and for the first time in weeks he did not think of her, but only of Uncle Claude whom now he thought he understood. He had never grown up and his hunt for Goldilocks was a childhood game; his men indulged and protected him like an innocent. They wanted him to be happy and so they wanted him to have the mountain lion.

The day dawned in a dry brightness. But the stranger was gone before sun-up, leaving no trace but the marks of his horses' hooves in the mud of the lane. The sheriff came at noon with a posse and gave Uncle Claude a proper dressing down. "So, though he don't account for himself and he's drivin' twenty thoroughbreds, you don't catch on. By God, Kenyon, you must of got dropped on the head when you was a baby. And so must of your whole outfit here." He tapped his forehead with his finger and said, "To let." But all of them, including the sheriff and the mock-angry men who rode with him, were delighted that the stranger had been a thief. The Bar K outfit, at dinner that day, said they had known it all along. "I knew it from the start," said Dump. "I never let on but just played into his hand to watch the show. I knew from the start he wasn't no Law, he was an *out*law."

From that time forward, the summer was a rush of pleasure. In late July there was a forest fire in the mountains to the north and the unhealthy sun, remote behind the smoke, was as small and lusterless as a withered orange. People twenty miles away from the burning trees coughed and their eyes watered. All the men from the Bar K went to help fight it. They rapidly dug trenches in the soft ground, slippery with pine needles. Ralph's hands were blistered by the handle of his quick ax and his face was swollen with the heat. After twelve hours, when the fire was under control and there was nothing now but smoldering in the underbrush, Ralph and Homer Armitage and Uncle Claude went to the ranger's look-out where Ralph had his first drink of whisky. He did not enjoy the experience; he was hot already and the liquor set him ablaze. It was just dawn and he had had nothing to eat since the evening before. At first the light-headedness was pleasant; his ears rang as though he were holding shells to them and he heard the men talking as if from a far and golden distance. But in the next stage he was heavy-limbed and heavy-eyed and it was thus that he began the long walk home. He had to calculate each step before he took it lest he fall down. The other men had gone on ahead, and by the time they got home there was no one in the house but the womenfolk who were sitting at the table in the dining room drinking coffee and waiting to hear about the fire.

Ralph did not want to eat; he wanted only to lie full length on his bed and sleep, but he forced himself to lift his coffee cup with a sore hand to his parched lips and he ate part of a fried egg though it sickened him. He was aware that Molly was watching him, but he was too weary to care, and when finally, unable to sit up any longer, he excused himself and she said, half under her breath, "So you drink, too, Ralph Fawcett," he was not in the least afraid of her. He said crossly, "So's your old man," and joggled the back of her chair.

At haying, a whole new gallery of people came, Mormons and people from Oklahoma with outlandish ways. A family named Prevost came to live in the house. The man was clumsy and once, out of simple awkwardness, fell off his rick. The woman, in unbroken silence, helped Magdalene with the cooking. They had brought with them a tow-headed girl of nine named Darling and a boy of three named Gasper. They had come on foot, carrying a shuck mattress and a couple of laundry bags which bulged with everything they owned in the world. They were from Muskogee and had accents so grotesque that not even Molly, an able mimic, could copy them. Although Uncle Claude offered them two rooms on the third floor, they preferred a small back bedroom downstairs off the kitchen, and they all slept in the same big brass bed. When their eldest daughter, Opal, lost her job in a café in town (a circumstance enshrouded in mystery) and came to stay with her parents, they still remained in one room. And then, in the last week of the harvest, three of Mr. Prevost's cousins, two women and a man, drove by to spend the night, and all of them slept in the same small room, eight of them together, six of them grown.

The cousins had come in a tall green Reo, as rusty and sorry as something left to perish on a dump. They left the next day at sundown, not even waiting for supper, taking the Prevosts with them. The Reo made loud gusty sounds and the driver, a dreary man they had called Cheesie, played the fool with the clutch so that the car shook back and forth in a paroxysm and with a racking cough until it died in the lane while the curious horses watched, hanging their long heads over the fence. Cheesie and Mr. Prevost got out and lifted up the hood and tinkered for a long while until Ralph, who was watching from the porch, went to tell his uncle that they needed help. They worked uselessly until dark. The mute women, once the light was gone, got out of the car and built a fire in the middle of the road. Gasper and Darling went to the slough with a pan and they brought it back full of water and Mrs. Prevost made coffee, crouching over the small blaze like an unhappy gypsy woman. Uncle Claude gave the Reo a push with the pick-up over the bridge, but Cheesie had not understood his instructions and instead of turning down the road, he kept on straight ahead so that the Reo plowed up into the sage and stopped there, hugging the hillside for dear life.

They did not debate at all what they should do. The uncomplaining women and children stamped out the fire and joined the men and in the darkness they set out on foot, carrying their laundry bags, disappearing in the luminous sarvis berry. The Reo remained there, but the Prevosts, seen once in a strong light, were never seen again. The car disintegrated almost as one watched. The doors swung open and the hinges loosened until they all but fell. The tires collapsed; the running boards sagged and the top, on which the magpies impertinently sat, acquired blisters and dents. Whenever he looked at the car, Ralph remembered Opal, a yellow-haired girl with acne all over her face, who had spoken to him only once and had said, "Did you know my daddy used to raise goats?" Her dead voice was full of damaged pride; she had not asked a question but had stated a vanished fact. The Prevosts, like the downcast women of the train, existed lifelessly like the senile Reo in which the former animation, now quite gone, was unwilled.

When the quiet autumn came, inching redly over the valley, and Winifred had gone to college and Uncle Claude had left for Missouri, Ralph roamed through the days like a sleeper, barely conscious of anything but the irrational feeling that if he could only figure out the way, he could make the world break open at his feet, even in spite of Molly.

Chapter Nine

IN THE winter, Molly would go on Saturday morning up to the summit of Garland Peak where by chance one day, turning over a stone, she had found it red with hibernating ladybugs. No one at the ranch or at school had ever heard of this phenomenon and the president of the Nature Lore society, a boy of fifteen, told her it was something that ought to interest the people at the agricultural college. Accordingly, she sent the entymology department thousands of them, packing them into matchboxes and wrapping them carefully in heavy brown paper. She got no acknowledgment at all except for one typed postal card without a signature which notified her that her parcel—it was the eighth—had arrived. She was not at all disheartened and continued weekly to gather the sleeping bugs, sure that an investigation was under way and that in time her name would be mentioned in a monograph in a scientific journal. She went even on the coldest days when the snowdrifts were deep and the pine needles in the glades were ossified with ice. The shapes of the high blue trees were obscured by the snow that encumbered their branches and they looked like formless ghosts. Sometimes the wind came fiercely down the trackless slopes, blowing sharp pellets into her face. On the upland meadows the sun was blinding, and walking there was difficult because the crust was thin and the soft piles of snow beneath were deep.

Garland Peak had always been her favorite to climb. It was one of the lowest in the first range, lying to the north and west of the ranch. In the summer she went up the face of it, but since this involved scaling three chimneys, she had to change her route when the storms came and was obliged to approach it indirectly, first climbing half way up a higher peak and then cutting across a mesa, down a gulch, and up the opposite bank to the northern base. The ascent was not an easy one at any time of year, but it was worth all the fatigue. From the summit she commanded a view of the entire valley, of the range as far as the eye could see, and of Cuthbert Pass beyond which, disappearing finally in a gauzy blue, were the highest mountains of all, the Arrowheads, which seemed as far away as the end of the world. In the summer the mesa below was like a sheet of rusted metal with densely growing Indian paintbrush, and there was a part of it where columbines grew at the edge of a stream in which, down near the gulch where it broadened out just before it joined another stream, there was the largest beaver dam in all the hills around. In earlier summers, when Winifred or Ralph had gone with her, they had often seen deer grazing among the blue flowers, but she had never seen anything, not so much as a rabbit when she was alone.

She had been here in the fall when the aspens shone like money among the conifers on all the foothills and the high fields were dark green with the first shoots of winter wheat. The hay had been up for weeks by then and the stubble in the meadow was short and even and had an itchy, barbered look. The highway, a narrow glitter, went between red banks until it vanished midway up Cuthbert at a pyramidal stone called the King's Tower. At that time, through Uncle Claude's field glasses which she took surreptitiously from his desk (Grandmother Bonney's eyes, each time she did this, seemed to follow her), she had been able to see the cattle moving down from the summer range, their white faces bobbing up and down like buoys as they ran; it was hard to see the bodies behind them for the soil up there was almost as red as their hides. She could clearly see Uncle Claude's place. One day she heard a shot ring out and she could see Homer running across the yard to a flapping turkey. She knew it was Homer by his black shirt. Another time she saw Mrs. Brotherman moving about in the kitchen garden and Molly, spying on her, said aloud, "Miz Budmanny's at the muskmelons."

Until she had found the ladybugs, Molly had gone to the mountain to be undisturbed at her writing. She carried her materials with her in a small knapsack on her back: three notebooks with glossy blue covers on the inside of which was printed the multiplication table and information about weights and measures; a pocket dictionary; pencils and a pocket knife to sharpen them with; a safety-match box full of paper clips and one of rubber bands; and, though she had no use for it, several sheets of carbon paper. She had found an ideal glade for her study. It was very small and surrounded so densely by trees and chokecherry that they were almost like walls, and right in the middle, as if planned for her, was a big flat rock.

The first thing she had written there was a long humorous ballad called "The Fierce Mexican" which she was able to admire for several weeks, rereading it nightly when she was in bed, but she turned upon it finally with such loathing that she tore it up into tiny little pieces and tried to forget it, but she could not. The imperfection of the rhyme of "Mexican" and "Mohican" stuck to her mind like paste. She had quit writing poetry after that and had simultaneously begun a detective novel called "The Mystery of the Portland Vase" and a short story about a leper colony. The novel was not successful because it was too short. Furthermore, the reading public would have immediately found her out because the article in the Sunday supplement of the Denver *Post* from which she had got the idea had said that the vase had just been found and had been put under lock and key in the British Museum, about which she knew nothing. But she was well pleased with the short story and thought of submitting it to the *Scholastic Magazine*. The hero was a man named Lord Garnsborough who had so wasted away that all that was left of him was one tooth; he and his close friend, Launfal Hottentot, who was all gone but the lobe of his right ear, traveled about together in a glass cage, visiting people in worse conditions than they. An especially pitiful case was that of Malachi Strattonbottle who had nothing left but a small spitcurl of oleaginous hair.

Now in the winter she wrote in her bedroom in the evenings and on Sundays and she kept a meticulously detailed account in a separate notebook of what she had seen on her ladybug trips. The ladybug place was very near her studio and she always looked in; completely covered in snow, it was as if it lay under dust sheets waiting her return in the spring. In some ways the view from Cuthbert was more exciting at this season than at any other. On a clear day it was possible to see the men on the ricks in the pastures, pitching down feed to the herd which appeared to be hundreds of small red blocks on the glaring snow, as small as her ladybugs. The Caribou was frozen solid and all the trees on either side of it were bare. Molly loved the snow. When she had seen her first snowfall, she pretended to have a sore throat and did not go to school that day but stayed in bed, watching the snow flurry in imperfect circles over the poplar trees.

Both Ralph and Uncle Claude thought Molly's enterprise was absurd and they said they imagined her boxes of ladybugs had given rise to all sorts of jokes in the laboratory. Uncle Claude said she called to mind a cranky friend of Grandpa's who had shot magpies for three weeks and had tried to sell the feathers to a veterans' hospital to use for burning out the sickroom smells. She did not care a red cent for the opinion of either one of them on this or on any other subject. She rarely talked to them, but now and again if she particularly did not want to talk to Mrs. Brotherman about plants—she was rather outgrowing her interest in them as a result of Mrs. Brotherman's preoccupation this winter with snakeroot which Molly found singularly unattractive—and if she had finished a book and did not want to start another, she would play Double Canfield with one of them or Casino with both. They were so stupid and slow-witted that there was no sport in playing with them, but it was fairly fun to watch them make mistakes.

It seemed to Molly when she was alone in the mountains that she had been by herself for years now, really ever since Grandpa had died. It was as if Ralph and her mother and sisters were no blood kin to her at all, as if nobody ever had been except her father and Grandpa Kenyon who was really only what you called "a connection." She was entirely solitary at school which she disliked this year. She disliked the harsh mountain voices of the children and the teachers and the smell of winter clothes, and she hated riding Eye-Opener over the river and then two miles into town every morning when the sun was just barely up and then back in the late afternoon when it was already going down and the light on the snow-covered meadows was blue. The children in her grade were so backward that she had to be given extra work to occupy her and she made notebooks of advertisements clipped from magazines showing different types of "Houses," "Landscapes," and "Occupations." The motto for the Occupations notebook was "Give us, Oh, give us the man who sings at his work." When she was not unhappy, she was bored. The only things that really gave her pleasure were the ladybugs, her writing, and her plans for a horrible life for

Ralph. She became so obsessed with the idea that he would turn into Grandfather Bonney that she almost believed that he looked like him already and on the flyleaf of her diary she drew a farcical facsimile of the portrait under which she wrote "Ralph Bonney, Jr."

Every Saturday she took her Brownie along. She did not have much luck with photography and in her pictures the sky took up more space than anything else and trees and buildings tended to be diagonal. But she hoped that she would one day see Goldilocks and could take her picture. Uncle Claude and Ralph, timid of the snowy slopes ("Typical! Typical!" exulted her scornful heart), had left off their hunt and said they would find her in the spring. But just as always before, she never saw a living thing when she was alone.

And then, the very day they came with her, they caught sight of the mountain lion. On the Saturday before Christmas Uncle Claude decided that they must have a Christmas tree. They said they would go to Garland with Molly and on the way down would cut a big fir, and they took a sled along, leaving it at the foot.

There had been a big snowfall on Thursday and there had been no thaw. The sun was warm on the slopes and mesas and brilliant in the branches of the evergreens, but the air was cold and the wind was raw in the unprotected clearings. Uncle Claude said it might drop to twenty below that night. They had got the ladybugs—Uncle Claude scraped them up with his hunting knife to Molly's exasperation for she used a spatula which seemed more humane and also more scientific—and had started down. Uncle Claude was the first to get to the opposite bank of the gulch and just as Ralph and Molly began the ascent, he turned around and motioned them to come quietly. It was an easy climb and the path was deep in snow so that they made no sound. Once Molly broke off an ice-covered twig on a chokecherry bush but the noise was slight. Their uncle stood absolutely still, watching something. He had moved into the cover of a small deformed scrub oak laden with snow and he beckoned them to join him. They stepped carefully in his boot-prints, not seeing yet what he did. Then, when they were beside him, he pointed to the east side of the mesa and there they saw the mountain lion standing still with her head up, facing them, her long tail twitching. She was honey-colored all over save for her face which was darker, a sort of yellow-brown. They had a perfect view of her, for the mesa there was bare of anything and the sun illuminated her so clearly that it was as if they saw her close up. She allowed them to look at her for only a few seconds and then she bounded across the place where the columbines grew in summer and disappeared among the trees. Her flight was lovely: her wasteless grace and her speed did not make Molly think immediately of her fear but of her power. When you saw a running deer, you were conscious only of its instinct to flee danger. The lion had sensed peril and yet they, the watchers, sensed peril in her, under her tawny hide, in the way her tail had moved against the glint of the snow, in the way she streaked across the flat land. Molly shivered to think she might now have climbed a tree like a tame cat and might be sitting there observing them with large green eyes.

"Goddamn," said Uncle Claude. "This would be the day we'd see her when we never brought our guns." His face, in the snow glare, did not show so much disappointment as anger, as if he really hated the mountain lion and wanted to kill her for that reason and not for the sport of it. Ralph did not say a word but continued to look at the place where she had been, smiling a secret smile. She was afraid and thought she could never come here again. The lion grew to huge proportions in her reflection. She imagined its claws, its teeth, the way it would hiss. She remembered a lioness in the zoo at Balboa Park who had stopped in her prowling now and then to lift her lips and grumble deeply; she had not reminded Molly at all of a cat with those heavy dewlaps and puppy-like paws, and it seemed incredible to her that their pansy-faced Budge belonged to the same species, though Leah and Rachel and Aunt Kathleen kept insisting that she see the close resemblance. Afterward, Molly often had a dream that she was being chased mile after mile through the streets of San Diego by the lioness who almost overtook her at every mailbox.

When they started down, she twice looked back over her shoulder and she kept close to Ralph. When they got home, she did not wait to help take the tree off the sled but went straight into the house, feeling unsafe until then. Mrs. Brotherman was in the living room putting up the holly wreaths and when

Molly came in to warm her hands at the fire, she said, "A friend just sent me a box of Delicious apples and I do think they're quite the best I ever tasted. Let me finish this one wreath and then we'll go upstairs and have one." Molly looked at the scar on her hand and then she thought again of the golden cat and her fear left; in its place there came a soft, inexplicable sadness. On the way down, her arm had once brushed against her brother's and remembering this, she felt weak.

The warmth of Mrs. Brotherman's sitting room and the smell of the apples, the sight of the widow watering a pot of begonia with a small sprinkling can, the bright winter sunlight through the dimity curtains made Molly even sadder. She was full of wishes. She wished that she had yellow hair like Leah's and Rachel's and the lion's. She wished she could go to London and become a famous writer. She wished she did not have to wear glasses; she wished she were only four feet five.

Mrs. Brotherman, blowing up the fire with a pair of small red bellows, said, "I am always sad at Chistmas here, although your uncle does everything he can to make it a happy season." The statement must have come at the end of a long string of thoughts, but in that even, toneless voice there was no clue to their nature, whether Christmas made her conscious of her widowhood or whether she longed to be a child or longed to be in Salem. Molly was embarrassed and quickly said, "Oh, I forgot to tell you. We saw Goldilocks."

Mrs. Brotherman sat on a bench before the fire, clutching her hands together in her lap, and even though Molly could only see her profile, she saw fear arrive in the twilit face and remain there. Then, turning, she said, "There is nothing here but danger and there never has been, but this is the worst yet. I had hoped Mr. Kenyon had been mistaken."

"Oh, a mountain lion isn't dangerous," said Molly, courageous in the presence of this adult cowardice. "They're just as afraid of people as deer are."

"Perhaps. But I will feel safer when it is dead. I hope you will not go back there. If the men must go, they must, but it's not right for a girl to be alone in the mountains with a lion loose."

Molly threw her apple core into the fire and heard it hiss briefly. She, too, would not feel safe until the beautiful animal was dead. She would never be unafraid at Garland again because in the back of her mind she would always know that the big cat might be watching her from the crotch of a tree or from behind a rock.

She left the sitting room and went to her bedroom where she wrapped up the last of the ladybugs she would ever send. She could not keep her mind on anything; it kept darting around like a darning needle and she did not know what was the matter with her. If only she had yellow hair, she thought, she would be an entirely different kind of person; she would not be cross all the time. At the very thought of her crossness, she began to grow very angry and it became clear to her that Ralph and Uncle Claude had gone with her today, knowing they would see Goldilocks, just in order to spoil her ladybug project. They had *known* that she never saw any wild animals when she was alone and they had come today deliberately so that everything would be ruined. There had been absolutely no reason for them not just to stay at the foot and cut down their idiotic Christmas tree. She personally would have nothing to do with the tree as she thought the whole idea of it was too sentimental for words. In fact, she thought Christmas itself was bourgeois and she had never got anything she wanted but just things like a patent-leather hatbox or yarn flowers that you were supposed to pin on your coat, as if you ever *would*. There was going to be a piece of mistletoe hung in the door between the dining room and the living room and the thought of it gave her gooseflesh because she remembered once in Covina Mr. Follansbee had kissed Miss Runyon and Miss Runyon had squealed and said, "Of all things! Aren't you the foxy grandpa!" And besides that, Uncle Claude had bought a lot of grain alcohol and rotgut (*rotgut!* People ought to be put in jail for using words like that) and kept saying that they would all "get stinko and then I'm gonna trim every jack man of you at Red Dog." It was not hard to imagine. They would all pile up to the gallery and clank their silver dollars together, acting as if they were in a movie.

And Winifred was coming home. She was coming on the evening train tonight, in fact, and there was no doubt at all that she had acquired insufferable airs. Molly knew because she had got a letter from her in which she sounded exactly like Leah and Rachel. "My sorority sisters are griped because I am the only pledge who has already got dated up for the Junior Prom."

Molly had replied, "Personally, I have never heard of a Junior Prom. Possibly you are thinking of Promenade. I thought you went to college to study Cicero's essays and I must say, Winifred, that you do not sound as if you are making much effort to be an outstanding *bas bleu*." It had been a severe measure, but one thing no one could ever say about Molly Fawcett was that she was wishy-washy. Decisively she got out her diary and added Winifred's name to the list of unforgivables and then, because he had wrecked the ladybug business, she also put down "Claude (Club-Foot) Kenyon." Recently she had learned that Claude meant "lame," and she had decided to put a new character in the story about the leper colony called Claude Binks who only had one toenail left.

She lit the incense in the gilt incense Buddha burner which she had brought from Covina and very briefly prayed that the mountain lion would either clear out of the hills or would step into a skunk trap; she hoped neither Ralph nor Uncle Claude would get her. Molly had not decided yet whether she would be a Catholic or a Buddhist but she had narrowed the choice down to these two as she certainly had no intention of being either a Presbyterian or a Christian Scientist. Magdalene had told her about the Holy Rollers, but Molly did not think they were her style. Her final decision depended on what would make Mr. Follansbee the maddest, and now she sat down at the table and wrote him a letter, frankly asking him. She also wrote a letter to President Hoover and one to Henry Ford. They were identical and read:

Dear Gentleman:

I have been apprized of your outstanding munificence with regard to helping people along the highway of life and so I wonder if you have any typewriters that you don't need. I am very needful of one myself and if you could see your way clear to sending me one, I will be very grateful.

I think what you have done for other people is wonderful and hope it will come to pass that I will have first-hand knowledge anent this.

Respectfully yours,

Molly Fawcett

P.S. There is no Railway Express here so you will have to send it by freight.

These were quite useless, she knew. She had already asked ten other people of lesser importance—including Dr. Haskell—and had got only one reply (except for a comic postal from the doctor on which he wrote "If at first you don't succeed, try, try again," and so she had) and that was from Spencer Penrose's secretary saying that Mr. Penrose was out of town, was, in fact, in India, but would attend to her letter when he got back. Of course the blatherskite never did, and he had been in Colorado Springs for two months now and she had not heard a word from him. Furthermore, she had read in the Denver *Post* that he had bought an elephant to bring back to the Broadmoor (what for? thought Molly) which seemed really unfair considering how badly she needed a typewriter and how much cheaper they were than elephants.

She sealed her letters and then stood in front of the mirror with her teeth sticking out. "Clara? Clara?" she said. Then, without leaving the bureau but leaning on one elbow, she reached for her diary and her pencil and to the list of unforgivables she added her own name. She burst into tears and cried until she was hungry, and all the time she cried she watched herself in the mirror, getting uglier and uglier until she looked like an Airedale.

Easter came late that year. The pasque flowers were already paling on the mesas and the cactus was in bloom, smelling like melons. This time of year was full of wonders. Even the howling of the coyotes had a queer charm for Ralph, and after they had ceased, the meadowlarks sang freshly for an hour or so. The light lying on the meadows just at dawn and then again just before dark was a singular ominous yellow, giving to trees and to animals a submarine remoteness and ambiguity of outline. But then in the broadlight and then when the night came the shapes were separated. There was always a haze on the far mountains and sometimes it bedimmed Garland Peak. The evenings were cool and light; through the open windows came the smell of the first new leaves of the hop vines and the upturned dirt of the flower garden. There were clear, nocturnal sounds from the direction of the Caribou where the Negroes from the mines fished in the dusk and then when night came built fires on the river bank to fry their trout and to drink whisky and sing spirituals amongst the weeping willow trees.

Ralph dreamed of the mountain lion and thought, "Oh, if I don't get her, I will *die*!" He saw himself standing where they had stood before Christmas, taking perfect aim, shooting her through her proud head with its wary eyes, and then running across the mesa to stroke her soft saffron flanks and paws. Ralph had always loved cats and when Budge had died this spring of old age, he had been wretched for days, mourning the lost purr and the quiet feet. He would not skin the mountain lion, he decided, if he got her, but would have her stuffed and keep her in his room all his life. If he had to go to college, he would take her along with him. He wished that Uncle Claude were not so keen as he, for he felt, somehow, that he had more right to Goldilocks: he wanted her because he loved her, but Uncle Claude wanted her only because she was something rare. Besides, Uncle Claude would be here forever and could get another, but this was Ralph's last chance. Sometimes, indeed, he forgot that he was not her only hunter, and at such times he seemed to sink into a golden bath of joy.

They saw the mountain lion on Easter Sunday. This time she was beside the stream, nearer the gulch than the place where she had vanished before, close to the beaver dam. They had only a momentary glimpse of her and then she leaped away and was out of sight before they could even raise their rifles. They ran to the place where she had been and found that she had left her food, too startled by their voices to carry it off. A half-eaten woodchuck lay beside a tree stump, its entrails chewed but its silly head intact and twisted to a sheepish angle. It had been mauled and slobbered on and its grizzled hair was clotted. There was blood on some of the chips of wood left by the beavers when they had gnawed down the tree.

Uncle Claude, frustrated, angry, moved around the stump, examining everything as if he expected to find a clue which would lead him to her den. Sighing, he said, "Blast the yellow bitch."

And Ralph, feeling himself on the verge of tears, said desolately, "What'll we do now?"

"Go home, I reckon," said Uncle Claude, "but by damn, I'm going to get me my cat yet."

Ralph kept the edge out of his voice but his heart was rapid. He said, "You mean, I'm going to get *me my* cat."

Uncle Claude glanced sidelong at him but said nothing and they started down the creek bank. The creek was swollen from the thaws and there were places where the water sprayed like a geyser in the hollows between the rocks. Between two boulders at a widening, Ralph saw the points of a set of antlers sticking up out of the water and he waded in, not bothering to take off his shoes. But what he found was not just one set of antlers: he found the skulls of two deer with horns so tightly interlocked that he could not get them apart. They were wedged in between the rocks and he had trouble getting them loose. The water was cold and insistently flicked up his pants legs and once he lost his footing and slipped on a rock. When he came out with his trophy, he found Uncle Claude sitting on a patch of grass smoking, watching Ralph without the least interest.

"What'll you do with them now you got them?" he said.

Ralph did not immediately answer, but tried again to get the horns apart. His heart constricted when he conjured up what must have taken place: the two bucks charging one another and then, by lunatic accident, being joined as one, toppling into the water to drown, still struggling to get free. But it was not so much the violence of this wilderness death that made him quiver; it was his uncle's indifference, the same indifference he had seen when he had looked at the sick bull. His passion for Goldilocks went over him like an ocean wave, for he was determined that she, at least, would be killed not out of this cold calm of Uncle Claude's but out of his own love for her golden hide.

Uncle Claude repeated, "What'll you do with them?"

"Why, I'll take them to Magdalene as a present," he said. "Or, no, I'll take them to Molly."

Uncle Claude laughed shortly. "You'd better take Molly a box of candy to sweeten her disposition. What's the matter with that kid anyway?"

Ralph took in his breath sharply. "Search me," he said.

Later, when he took the antlers up to Molly's room, he found her lying on her bed with the counterpane over her head. She pulled it down and stared at his present with terrible woe but without scorn. They exchanged, at last, after these months, a look of understanding and Molly said, "Thanks, Ralph. I'll shoot them with my Brownie."

Finally school was over. On the night of commencement, he sat in the hot auditorium where the June bugs bumbled foolishly against the window screens and the teachers sat among the baskets of gladioli and the potted rubber plants on the stage, listening to a boy in glasses deliver the valedictory. His voice broke twice, rising to a plaintive scream once on the word "emperor" and once on "romance." He used phrases like "elegiac cadences" and "poetic counterpoint" and he said that Vergil had been born to "the purple of classical literature." When he came to the end, he begged permission to finish with the lines of a "devotee of Roman literature more mellifluous than myself, *id est,* Alfred Lord Tennyson," and he recited *Frater Ave Atque Vale.* Ralph immediately saw the portrait of Grandfather Bonney and he was clutched by terror at the shortness of the time. He felt that his mother and sisters, who were now in Venice, were speeding, were about to overtake him, and there was no time to lose for he *must* have Goldilocks before they came. He looked for Molly who was to receive an eighth-grade diploma. She was sitting three rows away from him and when the boy had finished, she turned round and looked directly at her brother, puffing out her cheeks to look like a fat person.

The day after that they took the car, Ralph, Winifred, and Molly. Winifred drove and they went as far up Garland as the red road went. She and Molly climbed the face but Ralph could not manage the chimneys with his gun and went around the other way. Uncle Claude had taken a mare to stud and he had told them that when he got through, he would come looking for them in the hills and he would pack some food along so that they could cook out.

Ralph met them at the stream. Red dust had come off on their hands when they climbed the chimneys and they washed it off in the cold water, letting the fool's gold run through their fingers. All three of them lay down, crushing harebells, and looked straight upward. A chicken hawk lazily banked and coasted across the sky; behind them, in the forest, the chipmunks and the bluejays sent up their absent-minded racket against the wind which was always present in the pine trees like a voice. Hearing it, Ralph wished he were at the foot of a tree in the strange and smoky shade and were lying on the pinkish-brown pine needles; but the high, hot sun was too excellent to leave. Winifred held her arm over her eyes and Ralph noticed the tiny golden hairs on her wrists and on the backs of her hands. She was not going back to college next year; she was going to marry John Fulbright on the first of July and they were going to the eastern part of the state to start a truck farm. Mrs. Brotherman, too, was leaving the Bar K, now that her daughter was grown; she was going back to Salem. Ralph was sure that the odor of apples would cling to her rooms. He thought how lonely his uncle would be next winter and was sorry for him. The winter was an idle time for him and in this year Ralph had seen that idleness aged him. He did little of the feeding himself because, some years before, he had ridden into town without chaps, had been delayed, and coming back after the sun had gone down and when the thermometer registered twenty-five below, he had frozen both his legs and he was afraid thereafter of freezing them again. He hunted a little, emptied his traps, and took care of his beaver and ermine hides, gave a hand with the milking and gathered the eggs for Magdalene. The rest of the time he spent at his desk, studying the histories of his bulls and writing letters on lined paper with an indelible pencil to his foremen on the other ranches; playing a kind of Solitaire called "Once in a Blue Moon"; and reading books like *The Count of Monte Cristo*, *Graustark*, and *Beau Ideal*. Ralph pitied him so much at this moment that he almost wished Uncle Claude would get Goldilocks, but his generosity was brief-lived. Where was she now? How wonderful she must be in this hot sun!

The smoke from Winifred's cigarette went straight up and then opened out into a horn like a blue lily. Ralph thought somnolently: the lilies of the field are numbered. He saw in his mind's eye that wide, bare plateau at the glacier where the yellow orchids grew. Now, years after their expedition there, he thought how curious it was that he and Molly had not been tempted to eat the strawberry snow, for it had looked as delicious as sherbet. That was the day his friendship with Uncle

Claude had begun and the day on which he had abandoned Molly. It had begun in a look of recognition.

He fell into a lazy meditation. He wondered if Montreux where the travelers were going next was similar to this and if the Alps were as tall as the Rocky Mountains; he wondered if their hotel would be like the Brown Palace. He pretended that he lay on the thick carpet in the center of the lobby looking up at the dome as if it were a motion-picture screen. He saw ladies in taffeta dresses and small velvet toques, mitts and pointed satin slippers, saw the gambling tables where the croupiers used heavy shovels because the money was all in gold bricks. In those days, the ladies had bathed in champagne in gold-plated tubs. Everything that presented itself to him was gold: the bark on the palm trees in Covina, the whisky in the glass that Grandpa had left when he went upstairs to die, Leah's hair above the tall chrysanthemums, the clasps on Grandfather Bonney's books. He did not will any of these images but they came in a stately promenade. There was a small gold brooch of two clasped hands in his mother's button box and in the same box was a tarnished heart-shaped locket on a fine chain. He remembered Jesus' halo on the cards given out at Sunday school, the gilt star of Bethlehem on the Christmas tree, his Tenderfoot pin.

Once they heard a freight train going out and once, from somewhere miles away, a blast of dynamite. Contented as he was with this present time, he was idly trying to think what it reminded him of and when at last, opening his eyes, he saw the chicken hawk again, he remembered the airplane those long years ago when he and Molly had lain on the lippia lawn, waiting for Uncle Claude to come and bury Grandpa.

He said, "Molly, do you remember the airplane that day of Grandpa Kenyon's funeral?" His voice sounded submerged and hesitant to him and he found he was trembling for her answer. She paused a long time and then, leaning across Winifred, she looked straight at him and said, "All I remember in the whole wide world is that I hate you and I hope you will get fat."

Winifred laughed. "You've got the worst temper in the county."

"I beg to differ," said Molly. "It is the worst in the state, in the United States, in North America, in the Western Hemisphere, in the world, in the universe." She said this rapidly, letting her voice rise powerfully.

"All right, be a bad sport," said Ralph wearily and closed his eyes again.

"You'd be a bad sport, too," she said to Winifred, "if you knew what he said to me."

"Molly!" he cried and sat up straight.

"What did he say?" asked Winifred, amused.

"Molly, if you tell, I'll . . ."

"You'll what?" She looked at him coldly. Then she stretched out her long thin arm and pointed in the direction of Cuthbert Pass and said, "If we had the field glasses, we could see the tunnel from here."

"What did Ralph say to you, Molly?" insisted Winifred.

"Oh, I don't intend to tell *you*, Winifred Brotherman. By the by, don't you think Ralph is getting fat?"

He jumped to his feet and picked up his gun. "I'm going now," he said tightly.

"What for?" Molly smiled at him teasingly, twirling a harebell between her fingers.

"Cat fur to make kitten breeches," he snapped and then was annoyed with himself for using the childhood joke.

"That is a very good pun, I'm sorry to say," said Molly. "I surely don't think you knew you were making it as I have never known anyone more unfurnished in the upper story."

He did not know what she was talking about; he did not understand the pun he had made. Striding through the harebells, he enjoyed the feeling of crushing the blue flowers under his feet. Winifred called after him, "Good luck," but he did not turn back. He could not have any luck, for even if he saw Goldilocks, he couldn't shoot until Uncle Claude came. He went downstream toward the beaver dam, making too much noise at first in his irritation with Molly and then treading lightly on the mossy, resilient ground. He passed the place where he had found the antlers and thought how wrong he had been the day he had given them to Molly and had thought they had understood one another again. He felt suddenly that he was going along this stream for the last time.

Molly had spoiled everything and he could not even care about Goldilocks. Damn her, he said, damn her. It was only

Goldilocks that had made him able to forget the tunnel. Now she had wrecked it all. It was possible that even now she was telling Winifred, but on second thoughts, this seemed unlikely: she was too smart; she would save up and use it when the right time came. She was always saving up something and always had; she saved her candy at Christmas until everyone else had finished and then, a day or so later, she brought all hers out and ate it in front of them and wouldn't give them a crumb of it. And she saved up all the jokes she heard and the things people had said and other people's dreams so that she had the reputation of being interesting, although no one could stand her because she was so sarcastic. She would, for instance, take the pun he had made and pretend it was her own.

He sat down finally on a lichen-covered rock beside the beaver dam. One day late in October he had come here by himself, not to hunt for Goldilocks but to escape Uncle Claude who had wanted him to go to look at the winter wheat. The day had been cold with a wind and a chill that crept along the skin, not quite penetrating. The sky was heavy and the leaves were all fallen and were all brown. The skinny trees were already gray with winter and the ferns underfoot crumbled, making a faint sound. He had seen a weasel and had thought how in just a little while its coat would turn white and it would be an ermine.

At the very moment he remembered the weasel, a salamander, black and orange, streaked through the fern brake beside his rock, making him think of Grandfather Bonney's snuff box. Was there anything in the world, he wondered, that did not make you think of something else? From the snuff box he went on to the night Miss Runyon had brought the flowers and he and Molly had sobbed silently for Grandpa on the floor beside his coffin. Nothing had ever been really right since then, but why? He perfectly saw the old man and perfectly heard him sing:

> Oh, we'll sit on his white hause bane,
>   And I'll pyke out his bonney blue e'en,
>   Wi' a lock o' his gowden hair,
>   We'll theek our nest when it blaws bare.

"I'll never be happy again," he said softly and aloud. Neither would Molly, but Molly did not want to be happy and she wanted him to be as wretched as she. If she told his mother, if his mother gave him a moral lecture often using the expression "not quite nice," he would leave home. He would not just threaten, he really would join the Navy.

The decision made him feel better and he got up. He moved around the beaver dam, looking alertly through the trees. Just beyond this black silent pool there was a little glade he knew of with a flat rock in the center of it like a table. He thought he heard someone across the dam and stopped to listen, but he concluded that it had only been a bird rustling. It had occurred to him that it might be Uncle Claude, but he realized that he could not have got back from the stud farm so soon. Quiet as it was, there was, as always in the forest, a feeling of life near by and when, softly moving aside a branch of chokecherry, he saw Goldilocks in the glade beside the flat rock feeding on a jackrabbit, he was not surprised. He had been certain, this last moment, that he would find her there. She delicately moved the rabbit with her paw and then savagely ripped it with her teeth. He stood, holding his breath, utterly motionless for a minute, debating, but he could not hold out against the temptation: Uncle Claude would have to forgive him; if he didn't, Ralph would go away.

As he raised his rifle, he heard another sound but this time from the direction of the face of the mountain. Goldilocks heard it too and lifted her heavy head; before she could find him with her topaz eyes, he shot and immediately he was stone blind. His blindness lasted for an exploded moment and when he was able to see again, to see the tumbled yellow body on the bright grass, he realized that he had not been blind but deaf, for there had been another gun, another shot a split second after his.

Uncle Claude came charging through the brush, hollering like an Indian. "By God, we done it! By Jesus Christ, we both done it." And he ran to the lion, throwing his gun on the ground. She had fallen toward Ralph on her wounded side and no blood was visible. Uncle Claude turned her over to look for the wounds and Ralph stepped forward.

"She's so little," said Ralph softly, as if Goldilocks were not dead but only asleep. "Why, she isn't any bigger than a dog. She isn't as *big*."

But what mattered was whose bullet had killed her. They looked together eagerly, pushing back the hair with their hands. Ralph was surprised to find how short and harsh it was. There was only one bullet hole, and it was not in the place where Ralph had aimed. He was sick with failure, sick and furious with his uncle for coming so quietly and winning so easily.

Uncle Claude said, "No man alive can judge which one of us got her. I reckon we'll have to call it a corporation."

There was a sound in the chokecherry bushes beyond them, opposite where Ralph had stood to shoot. It was a sound that could come only from a human throat. It was a bubbling of blood. Uncle Claude and Ralph stood up and looked at one another in an agony of terror and for a moment they could not move but stood, hatless, the sun blazing down upon them and upon the lion at their feet.

"Somebody . . ."

Uncle Claude, bending almost in two at the waist, ran across the clearing and Ralph followed, his body a flame of pain. Molly lay beside a rotten log, a wound like a burst fruit in her forehead. Her glasses lay in fragments on her cheeks and the frame, torn from one ear, stuck up at a raffish angle. The elastic had come out of one leg of her gym bloomers and it hung down to her shin. The sound in her throat stopped. Uncle Claude knelt down beside her, but Ralph stood some paces away. He could as clearly see the life leave her as you could see fire leave burnt-out wood. It receded like a tide, lifted like a fog.

When Uncle Claude stood up, Ralph began to scream. He threw back his head and with his mouth as wide as it would open he let the sound flow out of him, burning up the mountains. Then he was too hoarse to scream any longer and he threw himself down on the ground and pounded the pine needles with his fists and with his feet, moaning, "I didn't see her! I didn't hear her! I didn't kill her!"

Uncle Claude came to him and seized him by the shoulder roughly and made him stand up. "Cut it out," he said sharply. "Get the hell out of here and go get somebody."

He stood with his arms hanging at his sides and said, "I didn't know she was there."

"Goddamit, I know *that*. Shove, now. Go on. *Get* somebody."

In a minute, he thought, just let me have a minute. He knelt down beside his sister and touched the blood on her forehead, stroked her cheeks, felt of her sodden hair. "Molly," he said. "Molly girl." He kissed her blood-salty lips as if like a dog he could lick her wound and heal it. Uncle Claude kicked him in the ribs and said, "When I say shove, I mean shove."

He had to go then. He stumbled across the clearing trying not to look at Goldilocks. At the head of the beaver dam he saw Winifred running toward him and knew that she had heard his screams. He stopped and waited for her, sitting again on the rock where he had seen the salamander. He pulled from its sheath a stalk of upland bearded barley and bit its succulent stem and chewed. There was neither a past nor a future to his life in this single, yellow minute.

When she came panting up, he said, "Go on through the clearing. They're on the other side," and though her face questioned him, she ran on without a word.

For a long time, he sat there muttering like a crazy man: Molly, Molly, Molly, Molly. He said it until they came back, Winifred carrying the guns and Uncle Claude carrying his dead sister with her ruined head. They had tied a handkerchief around her forehead so that you could not see the hole but the blood had soaked through; relaxed like that in Uncle Claude's arms, she looked like a tall, slim monkey.

By the time they got her down to the car, the sun was setting. Directly, Ralph thought, there would be that evil yellow light. Uncle Claude and Winifred sat in front and Ralph sat in the back beside Molly, whom they had propped up like a person. He looked straight ahead, watching the road being devoured by the car like an endless red noodle.

Magdalene was in the front yard picking mint and Uncle Claude called to her to come and help. She came to the car and looked in at Molly. There was no emotion at all on her pleated black face, but as soon as she spoke, Ralph was able to collapse. She said, "Lord Jesus. The pore little old piece of white trash."

THE CATHERINE WHEEL

To My Father and in Memory of My Mother

Contents

Man's life is a cheat and a disappointment;
All things are unreal,
Unreal or disappointing:
The Catherine wheel, the pantomime cat,
The prizes given at the children's party,
The prize awarded for the English Essay,
The scholar's degree, the statesman's decoration.
All things become less real, man passes
From unreality to unreality.

T. S. ELIOT, *Murder in the Cathedral*

CHAPTER I

On the First Day of Summer

B ETWEEN THE marriage elms at the foot of the broad lawn, there hung a scarlet canvas hammock where Andrew Shipley squandered the changeless afternoons of early June. Books lay in heaps beneath him on the grass, but he seldom read; he had lost the craft of losing himself and threads of adventure snarled in his mind; the simplest words looked strange. His kite was stuck in the top of a tree and black ants moved militantly over his pole and tackle box. He was waiting.

He waited, in the larger chambers of his being, for the world to right itself and to become as it had been in all the other summers here, at Congreve House in Hawthorne, far north, when he had gathered the full, free days like honey and had kept his hoard against the famine of the formal city winter when he was trammeled and smothered by school and a pedagogical governess and parents whom he barely knew and certainly did not understand.

From his Cousin Katharine Congreve's house at the top of the lawn where the long windows of the drawing room were open to admit the radiant northern air and light, there sometimes came to him the voices of his twin sisters, Honor and Harriet, who, while they embroidered, sang. Idly, he imagined Cousin Katharine crossing the room to seat herself at the easel on which her needlepoint was stretched, to resume weaving a carpet of *mille-fleurs* for the delicate feet of a unicorn and of the girl who embraced his arching neck. Now and again all three of them laughed and Andrew, lonely, tried to avert the stream of their intransigent happiness, stopped up his ears, spoke vicious words aloud; he rocked the hammock violently. But the laughter bubbled down like golden balls and then the song began again.

A gust of wind brought him the sound of the sewing-machine as the seamstress, Beulah Smithwick, making his sisters' summer wardrobes, briskly paddled the treadle. Then the neighborly telephone rang its four short, three long, one short, summoning some member of the household to receive an invitation or a carefree piece of news. Elsewhere, he knew, in Congreve House and in the orchards and gardens that blandished it, the others of the ménage were engrossed in their own styles of complacency. In the mid-afternoon, he saw Mary and Maureen, the doll-like maids, teetering a bit on their high heels, go down the graveled drive on their way to the village to shop and flirt, their limpid Irish voices dipping and ascending as if every word in the language were an endearment, their prim voile dresses not beginning to conceal the graces of their plump bosoms and their pretty legs.

He knew that Mrs. Shea, the pious cook, was telling her beads on the kitchen stoop, turning her rheumatic shoulders to the sun, her glass-green eyes half closed as, decade by decade, she further lost herself in the hope of heaven and the companionship of God. Maddox, the gardener, who was in love with flowers, would be crooning to the rosebuds and calling them by his mistress's nicknames, "Kate," "Kitty," "Kathy," as he ministered to them devotedly, hunting for snout-beetles amongst their crinkly leaves. Two self-conceited peacocks patrolled their pen on the eastern lawn and the Olympian white swans, Helen and Pollux, with their brood of cygnets, rode the oval pond among the lily pads. In the stable, the quiet horses laid their cheeks against each other and Beth, the coon-cat, rubbed her flanks along their legs and purred. Adam, Miss Congreve's coachman, who was lazy, would be stretched out on an army cot opposite the stalls, dozing dreamlessly or straining his eyes in the crepuscular light to read "Scattergood Baines."

And Andrew knew that across the lake behind his cousin's house, Victor Smithwick, the seamstress's son, his friend of former summers, his confidant and guide, his teacher and his audience, was equally absorbed as he sat, wide-eyed with idolatry, beside his ailing brother's bed. This brother, Charles, a sailor, whom Andrew had never seen but who was said to be six feet three and to have a cannon and a cairn of balls tattooed on his chest, was home on sick-leave, convalescent after some unusual disease, acquired romantically in Singapore. And Victor, who had always bragged of him and quoted his scenic postal cards as if they were tidings from on high (though half the time Charles only stated that Hawaii had no snakes or that the Yangtze was a filthy river), never left his side unless it was to sprint to the village on an errand whose purpose was to comfort or divert him. Sometimes, as he raced past Congreve House on his way to fetch paregoric or *The Saturday Evening Post*, he flung a noncommittal salutation at the figure in the hammock, but he did not pause or even slacken his zealous pace and if Andrew called out, "When are you going to look at my new flies? Don't you want to see my crazy crawlers?" Victor replied, "Can't hear you," and vanished behind the lilac thicket.

It had been a joyous friendship, for it had sprung, full-grown, from leisure, and had not been predicated, as winter friendships were, on the extraneous considerations of school or dancing class or a mutual dentist. Andrew was poor at team sports, being small and, by reason of his smallness, timid, and he was therefore shy of half his school-fellows whose seasons changed with the change in the size and shape of balls and who vociferously despised non-athletes; and while he was bookish, he was also dreamy and was often at the very bottom of his class, so that he was nearly as tongue-tied and queasy with the boys who sanctimoniously honored Algebra as those whose god was the Discobolus. But Victor Smithwick, a child of nature, flung down no challenge, and because their worlds were so divergent there was between them no exhausting and carking competition, the spirit of which was upheld by the masters at Sewell as a cardinal virtue, indispensable to American, Episcopalian men. Not racing with him, Andrew had never lost to Victor and the cocoon of shyness that bound him all winter released him as soon as he arrived in Hawthorne.

Ever since they had been very little boys, their companionship had been daily and all day long, uninterrupted by homework and unhampered by parental disapproval, for Andrew's parents, far away in Europe every summer, knew nothing at all of Victor. Andrew's mother would have been appalled that the boy had smoked cigarettes since he was nine and that he had been so long acquainted with the processes and the rites of sex that only the most extraordinary variation on the theme could interest him; and Andrew's father, who was a snob, would have said, "the chap's a bumpkin," and implied that there could be no possible reward in such a friendship except a sentimental sense that one was being democratic. From time to time, Cousin Katharine had urged him to widen his circle of acquaintances; but the other native boys his age were uneasy and even hostile in his presence since usually the shoes and shirts they wore had been provided by his rich and philanthropic relative, and those who were visiting great-aunts or grandmothers in the other summer houses were no different from the boys at Sewell: they beat him at tennis and crowed and some of them bragged shamelessly about their marks and seemed to have no aim in life except to study hard at Harvard. Cousin Katharine, who believed in the pleasure principle, and who was fond of Victor, had given up the effort to socialize Andrew and he was never seen on a tennis court again.

It had been an incessant pleasure and a summer-long protection against the fits and starts of melancholy that always plagued the winter and had especially beset the one just past when, throughout his parents' house, there had hovered a vague and massive mood that had slowed down everyone, even the servants, even the bromidic, optimistic governess, Miss Bowman, who had theretofore been indefatigable. There had been some wilting, asphyxiating emanation that had made itself known negatively, through silences, omissions, forgetfulness, sometimes on his mother's part, sometimes on his father's. They had seemed forever to be standing abstractedly at windows, staring out into the snow or rain, never hearing what was said to them. Often his mother had had a tray sent up to her room after his father, in dinner clothes, went out to join a client, and when her children begged her to join them at their early meal, she complained of a splitting headache and pointed to the bottle of Empirin compound beside her bed as if this were the explanation and the cure of everything.

Cousin Katharine, in whom the children had individually sought consolation, had explained that John Shipley was badly overworked—an architect of his abilities was much in demand—and that Maeve, sensitive and loyal wife that she was, reflected the strain; that these black humours would be dispelled by their annual trip to Europe and that the twins and Andrew would forget all about it once Congreve House was opened. It was a reasonable diagnosis, for their father did look drawn and their mother's eyes were listless, but they had nonetheless been careworn and one time late in April, Honor had come into Andrew's room without knocking, had lain down on his bed and cried heartbrokenly. "What *is* it? What's the matter with everybody?" she had demanded through the muffling pillow. Never in his life had Andrew been so sad.

But he did not pity anyone except himself; he almost hated his mother for perpetually looking woebegone and he did hate his father for his irascibility when he snapped at the servants for no reason and greeted the slightest mishap with a towering rage, blaming Andrew if he could not find his briefcase; he was forever blaming someone and forever exonerating himself of charges that had not been laid against him: "It's not *my* fault you have a cold. You wouldn't have if you watched your health as I do mine," he said to Andrew who had not complained, had only sneezed and said, "Excuse me." He dressed them down before the servants, and Andrew intended never to forgive him for a public utterance (in front of a clerk in Brooks Brothers): "If you could learn to kick a ball around the field, you'd get some meat on your bones and then your clothes would fit. But I suppose that's too much to ask."

This spring, Andrew's need for Congreve House and Victor had been more urgent than ever, and he had counted not only the days but the very hours until he would alight from the slow local train at the Hawthorne station. As in every year, as the end of hibernation neared, he had begun to keep a notebook full of things to tell his friend and questions to ask him: What was the coldest it had been when Victor had fished for smelt through the ice? Had anyone escaped from the pen? How many days had school been closed on account of the snow? How often had Jasper, the retired, towheaded barber who chose to have his epileptic fits in public, been carried home in the Black Maria from the corner of Baldwin and Main? In exchange, he had to offer an account of a fierce and bloody fight between two drunks he had seen in the Park Street subway station; a description of a Norwegian sailing vessel that had tied up at T Wharf, having come across the open sea all the way from Oslo; there had been a trip to a bull-mastiff kennel that he knew would interest Victor and another one (made in secrecy, needless to say) to the morgue.

And as always, as the train toiled finally into the station and he heard the summer bee-buzz of an outboard motor on the lake and saw the gray carcass of a schooner that had lain atilt at the headtide of the river since anyone in Hawthorne could remember, he had gone to the door of the coach and over the engine's clangour and hiss had jubilantly cried, "Smithwick, I'm back!" though Victor lived miles from the depot. Still, this announcement of himself, unnoticed as it was—except by the affable stationmaster who nodded and said, "At your service, Shipley"—formally opened the holiday for him. In his exuberance he felt as if he had run all the way from Boston and still had enough energy in his legs to go straight on to Montreal. His tongue was abruptly loosed from the cat's hold and in his cousin's old-fashioned carriage on the way to her house, he chattered wildly, with himself as the center of all he said, until his sisters begged him to be still.

This year, he had run all the way only to find that there was no prize at the goal and, his place usurped, he was embarrassed as if he had spoken to someone he later realized he did not know; his shyness sealed him up again into an envelope he could not tear open. He and Victor had never written letters to each other (they exchanged comic valentines but that was the extent of their communication in the winter) and he had therefore not been prepared at all for Charles Smithwick's return. He was newly shocked each time he thought of the casual way Cousin Katharine had said, "Charles Smithwick has come on, to the unbounded delight of his mother."

It had been at lunch on the day of their arrival and as she delivered the information, she serenely fingered the pale green grapes on her plate and, as if nothing had happened, went on to extol to his sisters the charm and intelligence of the St. Denis boy, Raoul—the more remarkable, she thought, because his mother lacked both, though she was sweet, and his father had deteriorated through the years into nothing more than a businessman. She could not have distressed Andrew more if she had said, "Victor Smithwick has gone away," for he knew, because he knew Victor well, that so long as Charles was there to talk of submarines and Eastern ports, of storms at sea and of himself—a paragon of wit and strength and sex appeal—there would be no comradely clamming on the mudflats of the river, no studious explorations of the town dump, no endless rush and cataract of conversation, no badgering of Jasper ("Will you take a fit, Jasper, please? Pretty please with sugar on it?" mocked the dauntless Victor and often was obliged), no hunts for snakes or Indian artifacts.

And, indeed, Cousin Katharine, returning to the invalid in her chronicle of happenings and situations which she had been accumulating since her own arrival three weeks earlier, confirmed his fears by saying, "I was afraid that the return of the native might take Beulah Smithwick away from us but when I asked her if she could leave her Charles to come and sew for us—I have some lovely gold linen that came last week from Dublin—she said, 'That Victor is as good as Florence Nightingale with his big brother. He's not got eyes or ears for anything but Charley, Charley, Charley.' Whether that means he'll fetch the gruel on time, I don't know, but in any case, Beulah will be here tomorrow."

Honor and Harriet, entranced with freedom and the thought of dresses and of the charming Raoul St. Denis, had already cast the winter from them and Harriet sang, "Gold linen from Dublin's fair city! How perfectly celestial!"

And Honor said blandly, "How glad for us, how sad for Andrew that Victor is the lady with the lamp."

His fingers lay nerveless among the grapes and as he watched his sisters bud and blossom in the sprightly season, the winter's gray rue washed dully over him; the light itself, streaming through the long, gossamer curtains, had seemed as spiritless as city light. Cousin Katharine had appeared not to notice his despair and this astonished him because she had always before sensed his troubles and had done what she could to ease them. She should have said, "That won't make any difference. Charles will soon be well and until he is, I daresay Victor will be glad to have Andrew keep him company while he plays nurse." But she said nothing of the kind. She was as unaware of him and as scatterbrained as the twins as she talked on of short-sleeved boleros made of pink piqué, of the droll, sky-blue modern house the St. Denis family had taken for the summer on an island off Bingham Bay, and of the birds she had seen on the walks she had taken; it was more important to her that she had found a phoebe's nest than that Andrew had lost his last friend. And after lunch, when he asked her frankly if she thought that Victor would have any time for him, she was absent-minded and offhand; she said, "I expect the three of you will play checkers a good deal." The three of them play *checkers*! That was the sort of irresponsible thing his mother might say, but in Cousin Katharine it was alarming. He watched her deftly arranging a vase of sweet peas to make them look Japanese; he had the feeling that she wished he would leave the room, and nervously he realized that she had not looked at him once since she had kissed him at the train. "Why don't you go down to the alewife run?" she said. "They tell me we're having a bumper crop this year." Still she did not look at him but frowned at the flowers and Honor said brutally, "He's afraid to go to the run without Victor." Cousin Katharine reproved her, but Andrew was not convinced; he felt disliked by everyone.

But he had not given up immediately. That afternoon he had rowed across the lake and had gone to the gate of the widowed Mrs. Smithwick's house, a crooked little cottage with an undulating roof and dented walls, painted the color of raspberry ice except for the shutters which were green. He had whistled his and Victor's fraternal whistle, a bobolink call with an added note, but in answer he heard only the fussy flight of a heron he had startled and which arose, a clumsy wedge of feathers, to fly to the opposite bank. Victor's pet vixen in a chicken-wire cage at the side of the house yapped peevishly at him; he heard a distant dog and a distant clump of voices, but no sound came from the house that crouched like a pink gnome at the end of a tousled vegetable garden. He could almost feel the sickness in the quiet air, and his imagination persuaded him that he smelled medicine. He whistled twice again and finally Victor appeared, closing the screen door softly behind him; he blinked against the sun and yawned and said "Hi," simultaneously. He must have been asleep in a room with the blinds drawn; the thought of his possibly having been lying companionably beside his brother on the same bed filled Andrew with unbearable envy. For a minute he could not say a word and simply stood there at the shabby picket fence, staring at his friend.

Victor was the most peculiar-looking boy Andrew had ever seen, so freakish that it took him several days at the beginning of every summer to get used to him; after that the ugliness fascinated him. He was a parody of a boy in whom all the components had originally belonged to another species; he was as various, said Cousin Katharine, as a duck-billed platypus; Honor and Harriet called him the boy from Mars. His head consisted of a woodchuck's upper lip from which obtruded two large oblong teeth, a porcine nose that pointed skyward, a pair of amber cat-eyes, round and feral. He wore his tall ears high upon his head and they were red; his pigeon-toed feet were huge and his hands were pebbled all over with big pied warts and they were scarred with the marks of a jackknife with which he tried to dig out the unsightly nubbins. His long black hair lay on his conical head like rags and usually there was something in it, a crumb or a burr or a small twig. Once Andrew had seen a green worm in it and when he reached up to brush it off, Victor said, "Leave um be. I put um there. He's measuring me a hat." Victor, whose mother was a fortune-teller as well as a dressmaker, believed in signs—another thing in Victor that Andrew's father would have taken exception to.

That afternoon, he stood in the slanting doorway under a lucky horseshoe, looking doubtfully at Andrew as if he could not remember at first who he was and then, grinning, he whispered loudly, "Did you hear? My brother's home." When Andrew diffidently asked if they might go for clams one day soon when the tide was right, Victor, still whispering, said, "Who, me? I told you: my big brother's home."

The rebuff was genial and his manner was even generous as if Victor expected everyone to be as happy as he was. "I'd like to meet him," said Andrew.

"He's sleeping."

"I mean some other time. Maybe tomorrow? I could row over here right after breakfast."

"Well, I don't know . . ." Victor looked down at his feet and meditatively twisted a string of his hair around his index finger. "He has to sleep a lot. Charles sometimes sleeps all day. And when he wakes up, well, he sort of just likes to have me around." He smiled proudly to himself, still looking at his splayed basketball shoes. "He doesn't even care a whole hell of a lot about Billy Bartholomew comin' ridin' up here."

"My father bought me a slick new rod," offered Andrew. "And a landing net. Could you go up on the lake tomorrow? We'd take a picnic?"

But Victor shook his head. "I've got my work cut out for me," he said. "I guess you wouldn't fool around with fishing and stuff when your own brother was sick."

Andrew was mortified, and he did not give Victor the Hitler Jugend knife his father had brought him last year from Berlin, a knife exactly answering the description of the one Victor last summer had said he longed to own. It had been selfless love that had made him keep the knife, unused, for Victor and that had made him use up three weeks' allowance in having the initials, "V.S.," in Gothic type, burned into the handle where the *Hakenkreuz* had been; in the box from the shop in Germany, there was a card that said: "To his best friend from Andrew Shipley." The long box stuck out of the pocket of his sailing coat, but Victor had undergone so great a change that he did not even ask what it was, though he was by nature a prying boy. After a minute or two of awkward silence, he went into the house, nibbling between his rabbity teeth a tiny lettuce leaf that he stooped down to pick and over his shoulder he said pleasantly, "See you downstreet some time."

Andrew rowed back across the sun-struck lake, helplessly angry and certain that the whole of the summer would be as empty as this shell of an afternoon. It was so much worse, this negligent, smiling dismissal than an out-and-out quarrel; Victor, for all practical purposes, was not on speaking terms with him, but because the snub had derived from brotherly love and family ties were said to be sacrosanct, Andrew had no grounds for revenge. He could not himself imagine ever being in the least interested in any member of his own family, except Cousin Katharine, but he knew that his apathy was shameful and knew that Victor was behaving as everyone should. But though he was unjustified, he hated the intruder, Charles, and ambiguously he hated Victor too. He rowed slowly over the cold blue lake with islands in it where, in all summers past, they had fished for pickerel and frequently had caught eels instead and pink, whiskered horn pouts, hideous past description. On that small island yonder they had found a fossil of a beetle and farther up, where the lake widened, they had rescued a tourist who had had a heart attack and had fallen out of his rented boat. Was nothing like that ever to happen again?

Late on that same day, he drove with Cousin Katharine to Bingham Bay to buy lobsters at the pound and he gave Victor's knife to a total stranger, a man he had never seen before in his life. It was just at sundown when they reached the harbor and as his cousin made her transaction, Andrew went to stand on the dock to watch the fishermen baiting the trawl for the next day's hake catch. One of them, scraping the berries of blood off his hand with his pocket knife, hummed up and down the scales; untrue but firm and loud, the sound proceeded from his Roman nose which was pitted all over like a strawberry. Presently he looked up and shading his eyes against the evening sun, he smiled at Andrew and then he smiled at Cousin Katharine's gleaming and anachronistic black brougham, drawn by Pegasus, the bay, and Derek, the roan; Adam wore a tall hat and his summer-weight livery was bottle green and his gloves were hand-sewn yellow kid. Cousin Katharine maintained this striking equipage less for eccentric than esthetic reasons and even her friend, old Mr. Barker, who had a passion for motorcars, was forced to concede that it was far more pleasing to the eye than anything he owned, including a beloved Pierce Arrow which he had painted off-white.

The fisherman immediately recognized the brougham, for it was famous throughout the region, and he said to Andrew, "How do. My name is Congreve Smithwick." Both names were common in Hawthorne and its environs but the coupling of them seemed, on this day, deeply significant and when the man had finished tracing the complicated lineage that related him by blood to Katharine Congreve, Andrew, on an impulse, brought the knife out of his pocket and handed it to him; it was still in the cutler's box and the gift card was still beside it. Cousin Katharine called to him just then from the door of the pound to help Adam with the pails and before Congreve Smithwick had had time to see what he was to thank the boy for, Andrew was gone. It was as if he had paid Victor back by depriving him of what he awfully wanted but all the same, in some way that he could not quite define, had left behind a life-line by giving it to someone who bore his surname.

On their return to Hawthorne, through the fragrant, tree-darkened lanes, under the brilliant early stars he was exhilarated by the rush of summer in the country, imagined that he had misinterpreted Victor's behaviour and that on the next day he would be waiting beside the gate at Congreve House, alternately yodeling and whistling the private whistle, summoning Andrew. They would go then to swim in the warm salt river where seals played and sometimes teased the unwary by rising suddenly to the surface of the water and looking them straight in the eye; a pup once had nosed Andrew's stomach and had barked in his face, so close to him that he could have counted the bristles on the foolish little snout, and he and Victor had laughed so hard that they had nearly drowned. Here, at low tide, they would dig for clams in the velvety mudflats and Andrew would give his harvest to Victor who would sell them all at the general store. As often as not it was Andrew's own clams, bought by Cousin Katharine from Mr. Breyfogle, that went into the Friday chowder at Congreve House.

In this solacing delusion, generated by the look and the smell and the sound of evening, he put his head on Cousin Katharine's shoulder, withdrew it, interlaced his fingers with her gloved ones, saluted a black and white dog that barked at the horses, behaved, in general, with such abandon that Cousin Katharine, her affectionate self again, smiled down at him and said, "How you flatter me to like the summer in Hawthorne so much!"

He leaned into the orbit of her flowery perfume and thought delightedly of the first ceremonious dinner at Congreve House when they would have lobster and minute green peas, cloverleaf rolls and brandied peaches. Afterward they would darken the drawing room and make the magic lantern cast on the wall its watery, wavery pictures of John Drew as Hamlet and Maude Adams as Peter Pan and its scenes of Windsor Castle and the Bridge of Sighs. After all that and a game of Hearts and a late meal of sandwiches (there were no sandwiches in the world like those that came out of Mrs. Shea's kitchen; they were made of anchovy and olives and watercress and were cut in the shape of hearts and diamonds, clubs and spades), there would be the first night in his remarkable sleigh-bed in the room with the window seat and the Franklin stove and two stuffed pheasant cocks on the bookcase. He would barely be able to sleep for excitement and for the bleak admonitions of the owls by the lake and the flicker of fireflies in his room and the anticipation of the morning, a drench of sun, of dew, of grass and lights and shadows.

He laughed to himself and to his cousin said, "Do you know where my clam digger is? I'll need it in the morning."

2

But Victor had not been at the gate on the next day or on the one that followed, and the habit of waiting for him grew on Andrew like gluttony. He promised himself that if ten cars passed westward on the road before the church bells rang for three, Victor would telephone. If his guess was correct and they had ham for dinner, Victor would be at the gate next day.

Often the waiting was an end in itself so that for brief periods he forgot what he was waiting for. He seemed, at these times, to wait for nothing but the passing of the listless time, told by the bell that Paul Revere had made to hang in the belfry of St. James's church. Each hour there came to his inner eye the image of the verger, a fat, lame idiot who, being enamoured of the bell—for the ringing of it was the only art he had ever mastered and his aged mother had to lace his shoes—wore a small replica of it on a string around his neck so that his shuffling, sidling approach was heralded by a dulcet jingle. If one greeted him, he bashfully shook the little bell in answer and from his freckled, lunar face, there came a babyish gurgle, ineffably kind. In other summers, Andrew and Victor had teased Poor Hollis, as he was known, by climbing up into the steeple and throwing down acorns on his head. But this summer, he was too inert even to gather the nuts and the memory of the smell of bat dung sickened him a little.

For hours his lazing body floated away from him, as light and shapeless as the luminous clouds swimming through the aqueous sky. He read fantastic apotheoses into the clouds and the intricate patterns of the elm leaves: pink, hairless tapirs; vast polliwogs; Rip Van Winkle still asleep. Or he mused on the vireo's nest that hung, purse-like and pendulous, from a branch in one of the trees and pondered the clever and courageous instinct that in autumn would take its tenant south, to Louisiana perhaps—he liked the name—where Cousin Katharine had one time trod upon a water moccasin and another time had fainted when a night-blooming cereus had finally opened out in an explosion of perfume. The vireo might build its nest in a chinaberry tree. *Chinaberry tree*: he envisaged twigs dripping breakable lozenges like the filmy pink beads Aunt Dora had given the twins for Christmas or like the yellow pearls his cousin plaited in her hair when she wore it in a coronet. If the bird came whirring to its nest, he lay quite still and listened to his heart. Deep in the pine-woods to the west of Congreve House the blue jays bickered. "'Tis!" "'Tain't!" they nagged.

But all of a sudden, his lethargy would end in a pang and he was alive with bitterness; his stomach ached as if he were starving. And then he could not help his thoughts from straying backward to the irretrievable days when Charles Smithwick had been no more than a mythical hero, as insubstantial and therefore as tolerable as someone in a book. He thought of how, in the old days, when he and Victor were clamming, Victor would pause, holding his digger up-ended and pointing down the river that vanished in the summer haze, he would say, "The high sea is there," and his tone was so rapt and his desire to follow in his brother's footsteps was so keen that it was as if he had stripped the intervening seven miles of their forests and farms and hills and dingles and were looking directly at the North Atlantic; as if, in his revery, he could stride titanically to the very pier of his imagination and board the very battleship his mind's eye saw moored there. With a sigh, he returned to his tame digging and did not speak again. But later, when they started back to the village to sell the clams, he would indicate that he had thought of nothing but the sea and ships by saying, "Do you know where he is now?" And because "he" always meant Charles, Andrew clothed a faceless stick figure, six feet three, in a middy blouse and bell-bottomed trousers and situated him, in the posture of a trapeze artist, atop a mast. "He's in Panama, the lucky stiff," Victor told him. Or Charles was in Yokohama or in Manila and from these exotic harbors, he sent back snapshots of himself, embracing native girls ("One of the local products, not for export"), striking a comical attitude with a knife between his teeth ("Yours truly as Captain Kidd"), standing stiffly at a quayside with a waste of sea behind him and looking, in such solemn portraits as these, as if he had just got his comeuppance from a superior. Charles was so strong, said Victor, that he could have been a wrestler if he had wanted to or a circus strong man, "one of them that lifts the weights," and, indeed, he had considered both professions but in the end he had elected the navy because he liked to be "on the move in a big way." He liked to ride on things, said Victor, on trains and trolley cars and motorcycles, on horses, in rickshaws, on every kind of water-going craft. One time when the high-school track team had gone to Portland for a meet, he had got so interested in riding on the streetcars that he had altogether forgotten to go to the stadium and Hawthorne High had lost because he had not been there; his specialties had been the broad jump and the shot-put and people who were in a position to know said that he could have been top man at the Olympics. Last summer, Andrew's father had gone to the games in Berlin and after hearing him describe the Finns, Andrew doubted that anyone—and particularly Charles Smithwick—could have beaten them.

And while this Galahad and Douglas Fairbanks and Admiral Byrd rolled into one was not handsome—this was evident from the pictures and Victor himself who lived in a glass house and should not have thrown stones admitted that he was "no looker"—he had not one but several girls in every port. When he had left Hawthorne, he had left a string of broken hearts behind him and Victor was by no means sure, he said and smirked, that he had not left some children.

For proof of his popularity, Victor once showed Andrew Charles's high-school autograph book, inscribed in purple ink and brown and green, with rococo capitals and luxurious serifs; the "i's" were dotted with hoops and the "t's" were crossed with unfurling banners. The signatures belonged to Dorothy, Edie, Trudy, Flossie, Janet, Josie who all enjoined him never to forget some rendezvous or secret. "Remember the night you and I didn't go to the Junior dance accidentally on purpose?" "By any chance did you ever watch the sun rise from Coot Isle?" "Is it fun to get stuck on the top of a ferris wheel—or isn't it?" Andrew and Victor had gone through the book carefully and matter-of-factly, as if it were a table of statistics, sitting side by side in two rocking chairs in Mrs. Smithwick's parlor-sitting room and all the while the old, moulting parrot that could not talk but could only laugh, chuckled pruriently as he paraded up and down in front of them on the floral-patterned Congoleum. It gave Victor an obscure but assertive pleasure to point out one of Charles's former girls in the village, settled already into the fat or the gaunt lean of bucolic motherhood, hauling along a child by the hand or carrying a baby in her arms. And though the girl had been the one robbed of her youth, it was the husband Victor defended by saying, looking coldly at her, "Charles was smart. She would have done that to him if he'd of given her half a chance. You take these girls, you give 'em an inch and they'll take an ell."

In Mr. Breyfogle's store, spare, reddened men collected amongst the bins of dusty navy beans and the racks of guttapercha overshoes and while they waited for their groceries, they cleaned their square fingernails with Bowie knives. "How's the admiral?" they asked Victor. "What's weather like on the bounding main?" and Victor, haggling with the grocer over the price he was to get for his clams although it was fixed and had been from the beginning of their contract, smiled, sunning in his brother's glory and repeated the text of Charles's last letter or postal card. Charles was generally regarded as the most interesting of Hawthorne's younger citizens and though he had not been home once, until this summer, since he had gone away, everyone kept so well informed of his activities through his mother and brother that if he had stepped off the train unexpectedly one day, no one would have been at a loss for words but could at once have asked him specific questions about his ship, his officers and his friends.

What chance had an untraveled twelve-year-old to compete with a celebrity like that? He could do nothing but wait for Charles Smithwick's departure, either through death and burial or recovery and the return to his ship. And whether the news from the tip-tilted house was good or bad, his spirits rose in the same degree. If Beulah reported, "Charley's perky as a squirrel today," or mourned, "He's bad again, Miss Congreve, my fellow's low," Andrew's satisfaction was the same. The *status quo*, however, depressed him and he could feel his mouth drooping when at lunch Cousin Katharine, imitating Beulah, said, "Charley's holding his own, thank you. Not well enough to leave us lonesome but not poor enough to make us blue."

Though he did not have in them the blind faith that Victor had, Andrew furthered his interests through incantations; on wishbones, first stars and on loads of hay, he wished that Charles would die; at night, genuflecting quickly (he did not think it necessary in the summer to kneel since Bowman, a phrenetic High Church convert, was miles away out West) he prayed Christianly for the immediate restoration of the sailor's health, calling on heaven to make him "better than new" so that he would be able in the future to resist all disease and never come back to Hawthorne again. He did not care at all which fate awaited Charles; he wanted only his removal and the end to this heavy stupefaction that had gone on like a bad sleep for months. His resilient sisters, busy with the business of girls, their enormous correspondence with their school friends (they were extremely popular), their needlework, their lessons in ladyhood at Cousin Katharine's feet, their dates with boys who drove from miles away to see them, had entirely forgotten the miasma of the winter. But Andrew, though he could not distinctly remember the details of it, felt it still drugging him and dragging him, pushing him mysteriously down and down and to his alien, absent friend he called "Help! Help!" But Victor would not listen and the quagmire sucked.

Day after day from his hammock, he watched the traffic on the road: Victor rushing up or down the hill, fleet-footed for his brother's sake; Billy Bartholomew, the loafing old blacksmith, sprawled bareback on his white horse on his way to visit Charles; Mrs. Smithwick scuttering past, her sewing finished for the day, with a pot-shaped basket full of food for him; Dr. Taylor, a child-sized man from Bangor, honking nervously at every tree as he drove past in a rattletrap coupé to minister to the famous invalid. Far from the center of the world, Andrew lay torpid and individual on the periphery of it. Lethargically he shuffled through his favorite daydreams, of being on a buffeted boat in the Baltic Sea with Victor, of catching one of the river seals and training it to balance a ball on its nose, of having an eye on the end of his finger. But nothing seemed worth while and he continued to mark time, waiting for Charles to die.

3

He would lie in the hammock until the spurs of light began to recede from the ground and a general shadow to invade the lawns and meadows. The sound of early evening came on the timid wind in the high tree-tops, of cows ringing their bells in the small pastures that lay all around, of children calling good night to their friends as they went home for supper, of the final stutter of an outboard motor as it came to shore. His sister, Harriet, came out the front door and called to him, "Tea, Andrew, tea!" and, almost absent-mindedly, she assumed the five positions of ballet, framed between two of the classic pillars that stood before the house. After a moment, Honor appeared, to look for tail-feathers that the peacocks might have dropped and as she sought, she sang, "On the first day of Christmas, my true love brought to me a partridge in a pear tree . . ."

He was absorbed then into a mauve and female hour and with his sisters and his cousin, all three of them as soft and beautiful as flowers, beside the swan pond, he ate *pâté* and cake, listened to Cousin Katharine read aloud his parents' letters and those that came each week from the hortatory governess, played "I Went to Boston" and was, in spite of himself, consoled.

"Don't you get bored doing nothing all day long?" Honor would cry; she was a restless girl who never finished anything. "I would *die*. Mrs. Shea says you look 'laid out.'"

And Harriet said, "It's exactly what Mr. Baxter told Daddy. He is 'markedly anti-social.'" She elongated her face to mimic the elegiac headmaster at Sewell and they laughed because she did it well.

But Cousin Katharine, full of tact and affection, said, "I *like* to see you cogitating in my hammock. I like to know that the man of the house is within hailing distance."

And though he knew that this was nothing more than flattery and that she was facetious when she said "the man of the house" he was warmed with a fugitive glow and when she offered it, he took her long smooth hand and touched her round ring paved with rubies. He almost wished to be a small child then, a baby even, and be held in her arms and rocked and crooned to.

There was a short space of every day in which he was taken out of himself and caught glimpses of a larger world as he had used to do when he voraciously read history and the lives of Napoleon's generals. Just after they had finished their light, delicious meal, Cousin Katharine, who was pensive at this hour, told them a story that some trifle in the course of the day had brought to mind. They sat some time after Maureen had cleared away the tea things, hearing her account of an odd meeting in Rome, a curious twist of fate in Vienna, a dream that had come true. This artful, graceful, fanciful woman, their mother's age (yet seeming, because of her white hair, to be a generation older and seeming, at the same time, because of her light heart, to be the Shipley children's contemporary) did not accommodate her manner or her facts to the youth of her audience, just as she did not alter her mode of living because the times had changed.

"There is only one time," she said, "and that is the past time. There is no fashion in *now* or in *tomorrow* because the goods has not been cut." And so her anecdotes were as archaic and yet as timeless as her carriage and as the ostrich-feather fan which she carried with her when she went out to dine with Hawthorne's summer gentry. It was not that she "relived" her stories but that she seemed to exist in two tenses simultaneously. The children moved with her from memory to memory as if from case to case in a historical museum and they were excited, as sight-seers would be, to find in one display a shard identical to one they had seen in another gallery: if a Bavarian named Max Pirsch whom they had originally heard of in a tale of a ball at a baronial house in Munich reappeared on the passenger list of a steamer that had taken Cousin Katharine to Budapest, they were as satisfied as people who recognize in a novel a place where they have actually been.

In her rarefied world, she countenanced no change, and she had faith that the Dublin and the Rome where the elder Shipleys went each year were in every particular the cities she had known as a girl and had not revisited for eighteen years. Once she had commissioned Maeve Shipley to buy her some gloves at a shop in Venice—no substitute would do and she was firm on this point—and when Maeve wrote to say that the shop was no longer there nor anywhere, Cousin Katharine was shocked and disbelieving and she said, "Maeve went to the wrong street or she's playing a trick on me." She did not choose to recognize political alterations in the countries she was fond of; Mussolini and Hitler she looked on as demented eccentrics whose day would soon be over, and she would not be persuaded that their power, moral and philosophical, was more than superficial. In her reflections, she was like someone looking at a Chinese painting, allowing his eye to begin at the bottom and to travel slowly upward to the top of the mountain and the houses beside the waterfalls, as large as the ones in the valley; there was no progression in time because there was no perspective and therefore no shrouding of the past; the present was exactly the same size as the past and of exactly the same importance and except in the most minor and mechanical of ways, the future did not seem to exist. Andrew had always clung to her in her unchangingness, as he had clung to Victor. After his first fears on the first day, when he had believed that every single part of the world was spoiled, and even Cousin Katharine was different, he had been reassured: she was the same as ever. She never spoke to him of Victor, but he reasoned that this was not out of a lack of sympathy or understanding, but simply that she did not want him to see that she knew he was humiliated.

Often these stories of hers had no point that Andrew and his sisters could see and were no more than the descriptions of a scene, but so warmly did her gray, lovely eyes and her articulate long hands support the role of her fluid, gently monotonous voice, that they were carried with her and they looked as closely, heard as vividly, smelled as keenly as she did. The parks and the palaces of foreign cities were brightly projected for them, and the rivers of Germany and the bare, gray islands of the Outer Hebrides.

One day, she put on the tea table a fragile, spiraling seashell and she said, "I found this in the pocket of a jacket I haven't worn since the day I acquired it. The day seems like yesterday but actually it was eighteen years ago."

"The year you went abroad with Ma and Pa!" cried Honor, for Cousin Katharine, their mother's first cousin and best and lifelong friend, had gone to Europe with the Shipleys on their honeymoon, a fact that Honor and Harriet found so debonair, so airy and jocose that they brought the subject up whenever they could. They had gone on John Shipley's fabulous yacht, the *Empress Katharine*, which had long since been sold to a Cuban parvenu who had changed her color from midnight blue to apple green (in moments of ill humour, John Shipley fumed, "How dared that Dago take such liberties?") and Honor and Harriet, now that they had grown sophisticated and outspoken, took extraordinary pleasure in the knowledge that they had been conceived in the middle of the ocean.

"The *annus mirabilis*!" exclaimed Harriet.

"Yes, that was the time," said Cousin Katharine, picking up the shell again as if the touch of it would transport her to the far time and place. "We had gone for a picnic to a beach near Naples, taking the funicular and then carriages and though, when we started out, we congratulated ourselves on selecting a perfect day, we had no sooner got to the seashore than thunderheads began to gather and the air was so heavy that we could feel it pressing down on us like mattresses. I remember it all, down to the clothes we wore and the word 'Bulgaria' printed on the shells of our eggs. We had forgotten to bring salt and the wine was undrinkable. Maeve hated the blue lizards that went slithering through the ruins and what disappointing ruins they were! They were nothing but hunks and heaps of rubbish from which we couldn't get a sense of history at all. A band of children materialized out of nowhere to beg from us. One little girl was blind and she sang us an uncommonly sad song. Another child juggled two of our own oranges and a big boy, about fourteen, did a very wild dance—I think he was supposed to represent a whirling dervish. Your papa paid them handsomely to go away."

"Our papa disapproves of fun," said Honor.

"Not fun," said Harriet. "He disapproves of children."

Ignoring them, Cousin Katharine continued, "It was Ronnie Pryce who gave me the shell. He picked it up and said, 'Put this in a pocket to remember this day.' And so, you see, I have done as he asked. Just after that, a storm came up and as we scrambled for the shelter of the carriages, we could see the lightning far out at sea and suddenly, quite magically, the ruins that we had been so contemptuous of became weird and splendid in this new light and we all grew thoughtful in spite of the wet."

Ronnie Pryce, as they all knew, had been one of Cousin Katharine's many admirers. Long ago they had seen a picture of him standing in a formal garden beside his father's Georgian house in Gloucestershire; fair, silkenly mustached, he had looked so aristocratic and so English, so reticent and dignified that it was hard to believe that he had been a practical joker, fond of exploding cigars and spurting boutonnieres and, as Cousin Katharine described him, "a man in whom garrulity was a malignant disease." In another photograph he wore his Lancers uniform and when Honor had seen it first, at the age of eight, she had asked, "Is that the king?" It was only years later that the children understood their cousin's answer, "If that were the king, don't you suppose that I would be the queen?"

Harriet picked up the shell. "It's pretty," she said, "but it's awfully small. You couldn't use it for anything. You couldn't even hear the ocean waves in it."

"Why did Mr. Pryce ask you to remember that day?" asked Honor. "Did he propose to you?"

"Did he?" Harriet was enchanted. The twins literally could spend hours speculating on why Cousin Katharine had never married. This was the darkest of all tribal mysteries and Andrew was sure that not even his mother knew the answer. "What did you say to him?" insisted Harriet.

"If he did, and I don't recall that he did—he was certainly much too line and rule, in spite of all his buffoonery, to propose marriage in a cable car or in front of a troop of mendicant urchins—I must have told him 'no.'" She laughed, finding the memory of the man ludicrous but sweet. "Perhaps the day was memorable to him because he was to leave Italy that evening to go back to England and from there to Australia where almost at once he made a fortune raising sheep. He *looked* rather like a sheep. And baa'ed continually."

"He went to Australia because you broke his heart," exulted Harriet. "How many people's hearts have you broken, Cousin Katharine? Tell us! We promise not to tell."

"Ah, where shall I begin in that long list?" teased Cousin Katharine. "I can't. It's far too long and I must concentrate on the conquest of Mr. Barker who's to be my dinner partner tonight."

"Mr. Barker's eighty!" screamed Honor delightedly.

"But he has at least eighty million dollars," said Harriet. "And his cars are perfectly stunning."

"I know for a certain fact that you broke Raoul's father's heart," said Honor. "Because Raoul told me. Do you know what I said when Raoul asked me why you never got married? I said, 'The answer should be very obvious. No one in the whole wide world was good enough for her.'"

"When did you see Raoul alone?" said Harriet sharply.

"Oh, once upon a time." Honor went to the edge of the pool and dabbled her fingers in the water. "What difference does it make? He thinks that you are me and I am you. He got so rattled once he called me 'Honoret.' He'll call you 'Harrior.'"

Poor Hollis rang the bell for six and Cousin Katharine got up to go and dress for dinner, taking her shell with her and patting Andrew on the head as she left, saying, "You are my favorite child because you mind your own business."

"Andrew is the strong, silent type," said Honor. "You may *think* he minds his own business. But he doesn't. He listens at keyholes."

With Cousin Katharine's leavetaking, he was suddenly lethargic again, too sad and bored even to defend himself against his sister. Besides, her charge was true. He loved to eavesdrop and read other people's mail; locked diaries tantalized him.

Cousin Katharine said, "You must not forget, you three, that tonight is the night for letters to the voyagers," and she moved across the lawn, forgetting them all, humming an Irish air to herself.

"It was awfully snide of you to say that to Raoul," said Harriet, still angry. "It implies that his father wasn't good enough for her."

"Well, he wasn't. That fat, terrible thing? The only person I can possibly imagine being worthy of Cousin Katharine is the Prince of Wales. Or was."

"He isn't tall enough for her," said Harriet.

Disputing, the twins went off to the picking garden to cut flowers in the cool of the dusk and Andrew, left alone again, returned to his grief which was all he had to keep him company. Victor would not come this night or any other night to invite him to go and watch the fish in the alewife run by moonlight or to play grave-robbers in the creepy churchyard. Last summer, Andrew would not have depended so heavily on the tea hour and his sisters' silly prattling; he would, half the time, not appear at all but would still be prowling with his friend who, wise, ragged, raffish, prodigiously *au courant* with scandals and crimes knew, through his clairvoyant mother, what murders were to be committed, what houses robbed, what bastards born and what escutcheons blotted. He knew by a sixth sense where to go on the lake on one particular day at one particular hour to catch bass, knew by the stars or the moon or the color of the sunset where a salmon would await him the next day; he knew the habits of birds and the deer that came to drink at the lake's edge and the stoats and the skunks and the porcupines. Days in advance, he knew when a caravan of gypsies would come to camp on the ridge above the lake; he knew by their first names the itinerant tinkers and revivalist preachers and traveling salesmen.

At this hour, in other days, they would be scuffing slowly up the hill from the village to Congreve House and Victor would be yodeling. The grotesque, good-natured warbling had always grown louder as they approached the summit and at the gate, it reached its peak, Victor's signal of good-by. He would go on and not look back, taking the winding lane to his mother's incarnadine and rhomboid house to feed his vixen and laugh at the parrot who laughed at him. His voice came rippling thickly back; in one little hollow, it caught an echo and after that, Andrew could hear it no longer. With that, the day was done. He plaited his way between the shadows of the maple trees that bordered the drive, walking carefully as if a sudden jolt might knock out of his head all the sensations and impressions and witticisms he had garnered through the day. But when he had opened the front door, he raced across the entrance hall and took the stairs two at a time, sped to his room and wrote down everything before he could forget. Afterward, a family child, he washed and went downstairs to apologize for missing tea. He sunned in the memory of the day that had passed and in the thought of the one to come.

Now he lay on his back on the grass and waited for the first star to appear. Patient, contemplative tears that never overflowed ebbed and surged in his eyes as he considered how everyone he knew was supported and comforted by some intimate conjunction: Victor had Charles and the twins had each other, his father had his mother, Maddox had the roses that might as well be people the way he carried on, and Mrs. Shea had God. Cousin Katharine, universally adored, had everyone. She was the world round which all lesser worlds revolved; her houses were the Shipley children's second homes; she was their sponsor, playmate, teacher, second mother, their father's second wife, their mother's second self. In the winter in Boston, she came two or three afternoons a week to the Shipleys' house a little before tea to talk to Andrew's mother in her bedroom as they sewed or addressed invitations to the cocktail and waltzing parties they gave jointly. They were as forthright and sometimes as quarrelsome as sisters.

Andrew, listening at the door (his sneaky habit was so obdurate that his father had spoken of "taking steps"), heard his cousin call his father a wastrel and his mother reply, "How *can* you be so presumptuous, Kate, when you're not married to him?" Sometimes, though, the shoe was on the other foot and he heard Cousin Katharine defending John against Maeve's charge that he was irresolute. "What do you expect," retorted Cousin Katharine, "in an age when the will has ceased to exist?" He had never heard anything more revealing than this sort of thing; the one thing he was sure of was that neither his mother nor his cousin particularly liked his father, and it was no wonder: a man as cross as that could not expect to have friends. And yet, when the three of them were together, they seemed to have a wonderful time.

Cousin Katharine and his mother had effected an armistice by the time they went down to the library to wait for his father who walked home from his office in Franklin Street (he was a great one for exercise and health foods, a faddishness for which the two ladies often teased him), arriving punctually every day at half past five. He always paused in the doorway a moment, surveying his domain, and then he advanced across the rosy Aubusson to kiss his wife as she sat behind the urns and pots and to present to her the wine-red carnation that he brought her every day; and she received it with a quotidian smile of love (although, with his own ears, Andrew had just heard her say that he was, in some ways, weak and, being weak, was cruel), put it in the silver vase that yesterday had held its predecessor and asked him whether he would have rum in his tea or cream. Then he bowed to kiss the other lady's hand, murmuring his pleasure in seeing her as if he had not seen her two days earlier in this same place and had not had with her this very morning his daily conversation on the telephone, lasting for three minutes, shortly after ten.

Though this short section of the day was jocularly known as "the children's hour," since at no other time except at Sunday lunch were the family together, it was nothing of the kind but belonged to the three adults who, in their solidarity, excluded everyone from their twilight eucharist. Their jokes were so old and complex and personal that even they could not have dug down through all the laminations to the source of them. Their gossip was esoteric and to an outsider it sounded, often, as if the people they excoriated and anatomized were creatures of their own invention and not, as they really were, men and women they had lunched with or had seen at the theater or were going to dine with that evening. They seldom used proper names but spoke allegorically of "our charity" and by the laughter in their voices indicated that they did not feel charitable toward him at all, of "our court jester," and "our Karamazov." There was "the *arriviste*," "John's club Macaulay," there were "Maeve's poor ladies" (at the instigation of Cousin Katharine's mother, Aunt Alma, who was public-spirited, Mrs. Shipley headed armies of women who knitted furiously for the destitute of half the world) and there were Cousin Katharine's "young men," a retinue of dazzled youths who came in droves from Cambridge on her "day" to be inspired to sonnet-writing by her beauty and her charm. In speaking of these people, in terms as incomprehensible as a foreign tongue, such was their community that they gave the impression of being three aspects of the same person and not three separate persons. This indivisible trinity, established long before Maeve and John were married, was looked on as the most winning friendship in Boston. Cousin Katharine, who believed in the stars, counted it beneficent that they had been born under signs congenial to one another, Cancer, Pisces and Virgo. In anger or frustration, the children called their parents by their zodiacal symbols, their father "Fish," their mother "Crab"—though, actually, it was the other way around—and, until they were reprimanded by Miss Bowman, they had, in moments of familiarity, called Cousin Katharine, "Cousin Virgin."

On these snug afternoons of winter when the thick velvet curtains were drawn in the bay against the sneak-thief wind in the bony trees of Mount Vernon Street and the orange fire flicked and lapped the shining andirons, Honor and Harriet, protected by each other and by their inborn pride, sat apart and read while they drank their tea. But the lost boy, diffident in the farthest corner of the room, was as random and unfixed as a floating island and sometimes he blushed darkly though no one saw. He pretended to be reading the inscriptions on his father's yachting trophies, but really, out of the corner of his eye, he was enviously studying first one group and then the other, the three friends and then the twins. The miracle of his sisters' identity baffled and enraged him as if, in His production of the Shipley family, God had played favorites. The unity of their outward pattern and color gave to them an inner oneness, like a culture or a nationality, so that their responses to everything, unrehearsed, were exactly the same, neither of them taking a cue from the other but both simultaneously exclaiming in delight, dismay or scorn. He thought it unlikely that twins could ever know the slightest twinge of loneliness; nor would he ever if a magic spell could invest with dimensions the image of himself in a looking glass. He was at times as frantic as his cousin's cat who, believing herself to be two cats, boxed her reflection in a mirror and hunted for herself behind it.

These people were as cool as that smug cat or as the horses, Pegasus and Derek. Peggy received offerings of sugar lumps and apples as his just due and gave in return no more than a perfunctory nudge of thanks and retreated at once into his lofty ruminations. Like Beth and the horses, the peacocks and the swans, his friends and relatives were all engaged in something of their own so that they were perpetually self-sufficient. Often, even so, they beckoned to him, they called, they sometimes went so far as to wheedle and then, when he came abreast of them, they had retired into their private and inscrutable worlds, as concealed and convolved as the flesh within their hiding clothes. He had never forgotten and never failed to smart when he thought of it, an incident in the first summer in Hawthorne. They had gone to the seashore, to Pemaquid, and had found a plot of sand although the coast was rocky there. Harriet and Honor wore faded blue jackets and pleated white skirts and their black hair was braided into pigtails that reached to their waists. Harriet cried out that she had found a ladybug on a whelk shell but when he ran to see, the fine sand squelching between his toes, she would not show him; she held the shell in her eclipsing hands and though he stood at her elbow, complaining, impatient, perplexed, she would not look up but kept her cool, large eyes fixed tenderly on her phenomenon. What had made her court him if she only meant to send him away? She had let Honor see and as if he were going to steal or defile her shell or her bug, she had said to her twin, "Don't let Andrew see!" Yet she had called *him*, by name, had cried over the windy roar of the waves, "Andrew, come and look at what I've found! A ladybug on a seashell!" He had to pretend that he did not care; he had appeared to be interested in nothing in the world except a parade of snails inching toward the withdrawing waves, between the tracks of sandpipers, but he had listened, yearning, to his sisters' merry speculation on how on earth the ladybug, idling in a place so out-of-the-way, would ever get home in time to save her children.

Just so did Cousin Katharine sometimes evade the consequences of her invitations. She would say, "Be a pet, Merryandrew, and bring me my knitting," but by the time he had found the tapestry valise she kept it in, she was out of the mood, was telephoning the pastor's wife to beg from her a start of lovage or was telling her own fortune with a deck of Tarot cards; or, worst of all, had decided to write a letter to his mother and father beginning (oh, he had seen it written there in her old-fashioned, grand calligraphy) "My darlings."

Victor Smithwick was the only one who had ever *really* paid attention. Victor had *really* belonged to him for five solid summers. The evening wind up off the river said, "Heavy, heavy hangs over thy head, what will you do to redeem it?"

"I will wish on the star," he moved his mouth to form his answer to the wind and scanned the sky and wished on

Venus and then stared northward until another star appeared, a minuscule point of blue, perhaps not big enough to make the charm work. His superstitions had become so labyrinthine that he did not trust his way among them. But the small star would have to do for he could see no other and he wished that Charles would die. Then he turned to considering what would happen after the wish had been granted and Charles was in his coffin. Would they bury him in his sailor's middy? How many days must pass after the funeral before Victor would come and call for him with his digger and his pail? A week at the most, he thought. Seven days of marking time? A hundred and sixty-eight more hours like this? He could not wait! He pleaded with Victor to shorten the time of grieving. The daydream made his heart race and he hugged himself until, like ice-cold water in his face, crudely down his back, reality awakened him and he whispered, "Oh, hell fire. Charles Smithwick is immortal. He is an immortal snot."

His mind, fumbling and prehensile like a baby's hand, groped, then wearied, but even when he fell heavily into his familiar lassitude and seemed actually to sink into the springy sod, his loneliness stayed like a bone in his heart.

He heard Maureen exclaim, "It's the prettiest summer in all my life," as she stood in the back door, breathing in the pastoral smells and heard Honor, her hands full of pansies, agree as she and Harriet came up from the garden, "It is! It's the divinest summer that ever was!" He hurled a pebble at the swans to ruffle and deflate them but they did not turn their haughty heads nor were even the cocky cygnets disturbed.

"It's the worst summer in all *my* life," he paraphrased Maureen, who was in love with someone though no one knew with whom. And because the summer was the only part of the year that counted, he went on, "It's the worst *year*, in case you'd like to know."

His sorrow winged assertively down on him like snow until the sun was altogether gone and the peepers began to chirp and the daft loons cried in the cat-tails and another meal was nearly ready in the cool, vast dining room. His sisters, learned and frivolous by turns, would either discuss capital punishment or describe the dresses they prayed their mother would bring them from Paris. Andrew, without an appetite, would try to gather into his spoon all the bits of chive on the surface of his vichyssoise.

The girls gave their flowers to Maureen who buried her smiling face in them and then all three of them went into the house. His solitude was a cage or a suffocating glass bell and he felt that everyone in the house was looking at him, making fun of him because he was unpopular. For a moment he felt close to Ronnie Pryce who had been rejected even after he had given Cousin Katharine the seashell and he had a wild wish to write to him in Australia and ask if he might come to visit. Now that Hawthorne had lost its meaning, it was a waste of time to stay on. Abruptly he got up from the grass and went into the house and to the telephone in the library and asked the operator for Victor's number. He was going to say, "Listen, Victor, you come over here tonight or my cousin will fire your mother." But the line was busy. In a panic of claustrophobia and in an agony of disappointment, he swung the cage of cut-throat finches and made them squawk and twitter with alarm and then he stood still, his hands limp at his sides, and let his slow tears fall.

CHAPTER II

My True Love Took from Me

AVING ARRANGED the lilacs, the last and the most beautiful of the season, in twin tall alabaster vases on the mantel in the dining room and having reminded her cook that today was Tuesday and, since she was therefore at home, an undetermined number might be present at tea, Katharine Congreve went up to her sitting room for her customary mid-afternoon hour of privacy, pausing in the door of the drawing room to enjoin her cousins to wear something pretty for Raoul St. Denis who was driving over with his parents from Bingham Bay.

The supple, slender, black-haired girls, sedulous copies of their mother as she had been at their age, looked up from the handkerchiefs they were hemstitching for Christmas presents and Honor, smiling, beginning with a happy laugh that candidly anticipated the meeting with the boy who had set them both off into dreams of love and of engagement rings, said, "We've talked of nothing else for hours. We've decided on the lavender shirred batistes. Do Southerners like lavender?" And then with a dramatic moan, suppliantly holding out her hand that still wore its silver thimble and addressing her sister, she cried, "But what good will it do us? He's already in love with our old, old second cousin. Every man in the world is in love with Katharine C." And returning for a moment to childhood, plunging with her whole heart into a new mood, she lay at length on the sofa, hung her head over the side of it and seriously asked, "Cousin Kate, when you were my age, did you *long* to walk on the ceiling?" Her twin said, "Honor is mad," and neatly bit a thread.

Miss Congreve assured them that the lavender batiste dresses would be appropriate, admonished Honor not to let the blood rush to her head and Harriet to use her scissors and not her teeth to cut the thread and then proceeded up the curving stair, pleasurably observing a hummingbird as it gyred in the bittersweet that grew beside the window of the landing. Fair, not rare, this day in June was like all the days of all the summers and as she rose, step by step, up the spiraling stem of her beautiful house, serenity ripened in her face and she parted her lips in a fond smile, cherishing everything she surveyed and smelled and heard, the dimming medallions of the wallpaper and the Audubon prints that ascended the wall; the commingled fragrances of sunning foliage and old, oiled furniture and flowers everywhere, within the house and out, all bound together by the fresh salt breeze, a constant wraith in the curtains, a perpetual touch, feather-light and tentative, on the pages of open books and the tassels of velvet table covers; the multitudinous bird-song, the far-off bells of buoys.

She was not really contented anywhere except in Congreve House and she reflected on a wasted summer when she had gone to Puget Sound, unwillingly accompanying her mother who, as Progressive as Katharine was Conservative, had gone to attend a convention of formidable women and then had lingered on when she had found a whole colony of vigorous sympathizers in the innumerable causes to which she had dedicated herself: she was a Baconian, an anti-vivisectionist, an advocate of buttermilk and rat control. Except for that year and two others when she had cruised with John and Maeve on the *Empress Katharine*, she had come to Hawthorne from May until October since her infancy. But Congreve House, after thirty-eight years, still took her breath away and she never came up the avenue of maples without rejoicing in her immaculately proportioned and pedimented front door and the seven classic pillars of the façade. Large and white and regal, ensphered by orchards and gardens and acres of lawn, Congreve House had been built at the top of a monarchical hill and because its construction had been supervised by Katharine's great-grandmother, a Huguenot from Charlottesville who had made few concessions to the North (there still existed in this otherwise homogeneous region a small settlement of Negroes, descended from her servants and bearing still her maiden name of Delessert), it had a Southern amplitude, a height and a depth and a spaciousness of rooms and prospects that recalled the airy generosity of the houses of Virginia. This long dead ancestress, whose hauteur was centralized in a stony hooked nose, looked forth from a journeyman portrait that hung in the library, appearing to be staring out of countenance the shelves of books confronting her that dealt with the War between the States.

The long, embrasured windows of the house commanded, at the back, a view of the wide blue lake ringed with thin pines that cast their Oriental images blackly over the waving water. From the drawing room and the dining room, one looked out on the green swirl of the tidal river, spangled with the silver wings of gulls and the white pouches of spinnakers. From the east windows and those on the west, Katharine looked toward meadows, magisterial and vast, two oval yellow seas bounded by black country lanes. Beyond the western meadow there was a dense blue forest where the sun could never penetrate and where there always hung a gun-blue haze between the trees, where, in certain places, there were dells as green as Ireland and the mossy earth was bejeweled with monkshood and bluebells.

Her friends and relatives granted that her house was splendid, was perfect of its kind, but the life in Hawthorne! They flung up their hands and cried, "You're beyond me! It may be an ideal place for a waif of ten or an invalid of fourscore years and ten, but for an active woman in the prime of life! You owe it to yourself, Kate, to try Newport or the North Shore." Her critics' dismay was understandable enough in terms of themselves, for they were gregarious and uncontemplative and when, once in a blue moon, one of them made the long, uncomfortable journey to visit her, there usually arrived, soon afterward, an urgent telegram summoning him back; the pretext of business or of ailing uncles would not have deceived a child and, in a flutter of relief, the visitor scampered back as fast as he could to midday cocktails upon the humid sands of Bailey's Beach.

Hawthorne had nothing at all to offer any generation except the oldest and the newest, no club, no proper swimming beach, no summer theater, no sailboat races. Katharine's fellow summer colonists, as old as the hills, occupied (and had since they were children) vast, sprawling cottages that hovered on the outskirts of the demesne of Congreve House and which, with their gingerbread and their trailing porches and their purposeless stained-glass windows (a murky, morgue-like light entered Mrs. Wainright-Lowe's dining room through the leaded bodies of Paul and Virginia) appeared unkempt like tasteless but kindly frumps in the entourage of a famous belle. The cottagers entertained in varnished drawing rooms, darkly paneled in chestnut, wherein were situated copses of wicker furniture upholstered in cretonne and round tables on which stood stereopticons and albums, quadrupedal jardinieres planted with oxalis, chipped alabaster figurines and all the other outmoded bits and pieces that were unpresentable in town but "good enough for the country." In every house, since Katharine could remember, there had been a commingled smell of vanilla and of lemon oil which, like willow-ware tureens and cracked Waterford bud-vases, she would always associate with midsummer and septuagenarians.

Katharine had endeared herself to the halt and stooping citizenry because not only did she continue to return loyally each year but also intrepidly to withstand the inroads of what Mr. Barker, in spite of his worship of fast automobiles, petulantly called "these ultra-modern times." The customs in Congreve House remained the same that they had been in her father's day. She had conceded to electricity, to modern plumbing and the telephone but to no ungainly fads like radios or vacuum cleaners, canned soups or boisterous evenings of The Game. Her dinner parties were long and she dispensed with no formality (Hawthorne heard, more sorrowfully than angrily, that in Bingham Bay, the ladies did not withdraw and Miss Margaret Duff predicted, "Next thing you hear there'll be mixed swimming parties *au naturel*"); at her occasional balls, usually outdoors on a platform festooned with crepe-paper lanterns, there was only waltzing and the music was slow to oblige stiff knees. The servant staff was smaller, the tennis courts had given way to an herb garden, new objects had been introduced into the rooms, but nothing else had changed upon this lordly hill since her father, whom she had idolized, had died.

In great peace, she mounted the stairs, slowly as she did every day, slowly and then even more slowly until, three steps from the top, she was nearly immobilized as if her feet themselves were reluctant to leave the deep grassy carpet and her hand to quit the wide white banister.

Confronted by the portrait of her father that hung at the head of the stairs, she did at last stop still, her daily habit, and renewed her memory of his black eyes whose vital brightness the paint had not obscured and his full, versatile mouth, one corner upturned and the other set implacably, and his strong bones, having in them a Hebraic aggressiveness or a Hellenic one, a validity and an inherent pride so that they flattered rather than were flattered by the moon-white skin that rose to perish in tight, coarse curls of blue-black hair. Her own face, deriving from his, had been softened to a female role, the colors modified (her eyes were gray and a cloudy pink suffused her cheeks), and the aspect transformed from that of a humanist, steadfastly ironic, to that of a leisured, tranquil woman. These fine long faces were civilized. They were the faces of people so endowed with control and tact and insight and second sight that the feelings that might in secret ravage the spirit could never take the battlements of the flesh; no undue passion would ever show in those prudent eyes or on those discreet and handsome lips. For there was no doubt here, no self-contempt, but only the imposing courage of sterling good looks and the protecting lucidity of charm. So compelling was the integrity and the impregnable, intelligent self-respect that as Katharine looked at the masterful painted face, her source and counterpart, euphoria at her good luck extended her height and the length of her narrow hands and narrow feet and she felt as heroically proportioned as the statue of Minerva that stood in a summerhouse at the end of the pergola which her father had had made as a present to her on her fifteenth birthday, astonishing everyone who had imagined that, like other girls, she would have preferred necklaces or frocks.

"The poor Humanist is dead," she said and she said it in the same unaccented way she had done the first time she had said it when, finding that her father's heart had stopped in his sleep, she had gone into Maeve Maxwell's room and tugged her awake in the green light of early morning.

"Why did you go first to Maeve and not to me? *I* should have been the first to know, *I* was his wife." Even now, years later when wifeliness had lost all its meaning for her, Katharine's mother, a woman who insisted upon rights, upbraided her for this extraordinary defection and she could only repeat her apology and her explanation that she had been too bewildered to think clearly.

Who could ever understand or fail to condemn her that it had been essential to her own tears of grief that Maeve's fall first? If there had been no Maeve, no uncertain poor relation, no orphaned cousin, there might have been no tears at all. "And that would have puzzled you far more, Mother," she sometimes said in her imagination. For Katharine, who had never learned to demonstrate, could only imitate. She would never know, because of the timidity and the apologetic vagueness that obscured all of Maeve's human relationships, whether she had taken in that calm, comic use of the epithet, "the Humanist," spoken through a mouth that wore the same double expression this painted one did and she would never know, therefore, whether Maeve's immediate and authentic tears had come from shock at the news of the tragedy or shame at the way it was announced. "Don't cry," Katharine had said and the articulation of the word had permitted her then to burst into bitter, hopeless tears and to arouse the household with the sobbed outcry as she flung open her mother's bedroom door, "Father's dead! Oh, my God, my father's dead!"

When, later that morning, John Shipley had come to Congreve House for second breakfast, he had found his fiancée consoling Katharine, murmuring to her like a nurse or a mother, and he was touched at first only perfunctorily by the calamity but, on the other hand, was moved so deeply by Maeve's goodness that he had said, "You are an angel," before he had so much as offered a commiserating handclasp to Katharine; before he had composed himself to the atmosphere of sorrow, he had smiled, head over heels in love. Katharine's bereavement had been double that day but she knew that neither John nor Maeve had seen in her careful face anything but the loss of her father. "My skeleton would not have pained me so if John Shipley, mine by rights of discovery, had called *me* an angel and given *me* those ingenuous, amorous looks." She could not recall ever having cried again except occasionally in her sleep; then she would awaken from some irretrievable dream to find her pillow wet and her eyes streaming from a buried wretchedness.

She moved at last, turned all the way around to look down the stairwell and into the heart of a pale pink water lily in a milk-glass cuspidor on a table in the entrance hall. It must be replaced today, she thought, her affectionate husbandry overtaking her, and then a fresher memory flicked across her mind, of the quite unwarranted *succès fou* she had scored the week before when, telling Edmund St. Denis that this was, indeed, as he had suspected, a cuspidor, she had added, "But you see, I dignify the profane vessel with a pristine *nymphaea*." This kind of lapidary speech, while once it had been a conscious affectation, was natural to her now, as natural as her daily carriage drive or as her Japanese fans for hot evenings and her Spanish shawls for cool ones. These eccentricities, having so long been her second nature, were no longer eccentricities and she was surprised when Edmund, whom she had not seen for fourteen years, had laughed, exclaimed, repeated the word "vessel" as if it were obsolete or superlatively witty, had, in the course of his applause, used the phrases "a sense of humour" and "from the sublime to the ridiculous." He had seemed, in his torrential mirth, to be about to slap her on the back. He did slap his own soft thigh resoundingly. The tribute disappointed her; she had looked forward to the company of Edmund and his wife (a cipher, badly dressed, but oddly appealing) but she could not be at ease in the face of such voluble appreciation. Indeed, she was more than disappointed, she was affronted that a man she had nearly married could understand her so little: she had not meant to make a joke.

The boy, Raoul, had been embarrassed at his father's exhibition just as Edmund himself, when he was young, had been embarrassed by his own father when Katharine, just after her father died and a year before Edmund married Madeleine, had visited him in Louisiana. General St. Denis, a professional gallant, shamelessly lecherous, had grossly flirted with her and so monopolized her, fascinated by what he called her "black abolitionist tricks and dodgements" (he referred to nothing more regional than a few New England expressions and an indifference to hominy grits) that his enraged and jealous son had been reduced to plotting ways to steal her away for himself. The older man had not seemed to belong to his perfect and patrician house just as Edmund must seem out of place there now.

It had been a strange, exotic land. Through the vast, rank grounds at Thibodaux, thirty peacocks had strutted, and there was a cage where a summerhouse should have been in which there spat and grimaced and bawled an old, indecent chimpanzee. She remembered, feeling faint, the heavy-headed flowers and the great ubiquitous insects and the hypnotic air that sucked like a parasite until the mind was benumbed. The large family dined sumptuously and excessively beneath a fan that whirled and whirred like a colossal crazed bug. They spoke in the French of the region, these violet-eyed and small-boned women going plump, and the loving, hedonistic men, red in the face from all their luxuries of food and drink and infidelities. They had seemed, all of them except Edmund, continually to flirt—with each other, with the household dogs and cats, with the servants—until all experience became with them no more than an elaborate structure of artifice. When it was not an interchange of *double entendres*, conversation had been occupied with the perverse nature that smothered the land, with the purple water hyacinths that choked the bayous, the plagues of river rats and termites, the fevers and the nameless affections of the Cajuns and the Negroes, the snakeskins cast on the verandas, the tree-toads in the magnolias, the crocodiles seen from pirogues in the hidden waterways. Ceaselessly, the warm rains fell, rotting and mildewing; she remembered how the backs of books had been swollen and soggy.

Katharine, bred to a thriftier landscape, had liked no part of it except the peacocks and, of course, young Edmund with whom she had almost persuaded herself, in this tropical air where the senses overpowered the logic and the will, to fall in love. Then she had believed that his mind had been like the scenery, rich and dark and teeming. Just back from a studious year of *Sturm und Drang* in a solemn Paris atelier, his mind, though it was not unusual, was passionate. But now, the exercises in copying Rembrandt's drawings forgotten, the etching tools discarded, one would not know his mind from any other. Concerned so long with cotton gins and oil and the millions that fluffed and gushed from them to make for himself, his wife and his son what he was bound to call "the good life," he seemed to have forgotten everything he had ever known. He could never, except in the flesh, revisit Paris. When she had spoken of it to him the other day, he had not the faintest recollection of the ape, did not remember that his name was Julius and that when he was in a friendly mood, he let his keeper put a baby-bonnet on his head. At the time, the two of them together had spent their mornings morbidly watching him. He had congratulated her on the excellence of her memory—as if that satiric beast could ever be forgotten!—and said, "I bet we did some fine philosophizing!" Invisibly she bridled at his ridicule of himself.

It was alarming and disarming and sad to see how like that Edmund the young St. Denis was, limber and tall and fair, his oval, olive face full of poetic and boyish solemnity that would go—oh, how rapidly it would go!—when he had reached the man's estate of real-estate and fortune-building and surrender to the second best; when the skin-deep college education or the *Wanderjahr* had paled like the tan of a winter holiday and the mind was left to rust and blunt like a knife left out in the rain and instinct and reflex replaced imagination.

"Stop this. Stop this infantile tirade," she counseled herself and set her hand against her heart, pounding with anger, and entered her sitting room, turning in its lock the ponderous brass key, vehemently as if she were shutting out a heated argument that had come to an impasse. Inexorably, like clockwork, this rage assaulted her each day, having its origin in something different every time but scaling swiftly to the same pinnacle of passionate and unforgivable disappointment. Sometimes it sprang from the recollection of an endearing mannerism that the boy Andrew had unconsciously acquired from his father who had acquired it from *her* father, sometimes from the timbre of the twins' voices, indistinguishable from Maeve's: and then, as the patroness of these three innocents whom she deeply loved, she travailed as she considered what they would become, tarnished with compromise, becalmed by convention.

At first she did not recall what had set the detonation off today and then she did: five minutes ago or ten, she had happened to look across the lawn at Andrew, limp in the hammock, looking, in attitude and countenance, so like John Shipley that she had desired all the clocks in all the world to stop just then at that point when John Shipley returned to her in the person of a boy of twelve. Progress, change, stereotype, dilution: "Their minds! What will become of their minds? Andrew's, Raoul's,

Honor's, Harriet's?" On second thoughts, though, the girls would last as Maeve had lasted; like hers, their naïveté was imperishable.

The fever passed and to her reflection in the pier glass opposite, she said wryly, "It might be well to consider what is happening to your own mind, dear." And gathering her selves together she went to her desk where with a blue quill pen she began, facing the problem, to write in her journal, a massive album of tooled Italian leather which contained the history of twenty-three years of her life, on India paper, in an ample hand. She wrote:

June 16

Last night the whippoorwills were tireless and I read late. It was a struggle to keep their flagellant cries from influencing the rhythm of Thomas Browne. The melancholy birds and the melancholy prose kept me awake when I longed to be oblivious of both. I think I shuddered and wailed aloud when I read that dour forecast of Judgement Day "when many that feared to die shall groan that they can die but once" and "when men shall wish the coverings of mountains, not of monuments." Finally, well past two o'clock, the heathen whippoorwills got the upper hand and I could not take in another word. So until I could sleep, I played a new kind of patience that Celia Heminway has taught me, long and intricate and perfectly suited to her invalidism and to my insomnia. I did not give up until I had once defeated Sol. Maddox's lamp went on for a moment as I turned off mine and I watched him, wakeful with love, come out of the stable and go down to the garden with a lantern. The winter must be a sleepless grief to him when the snow and the ice implacably mask the rosary, exiling him. Mrs. Shea complains that he is sour and dumb. Poor, lonely, obsessed Maddox.

Poor, lonely, obsessed Katharine. For I am snatched by moments of hallucination when reality disgorges me like a cannon firing off a cannon ball and I am sent off into an upper air where there is no sound and my senses are destroyed by the awful, white, paining light. I know that it is only a matter of seconds but because there (wherever *there* may be) time does not exist, it is also eternity, unchanging, looking forward to no equinox, no winter, no spring, no night, no day. Upon a matter so indefinite, having no attendant symptoms, no preamble, no pattern of any kind, I can consult no one. What or whom do I serve? Solomon himself could not tell me. If there were vertigo along with it or a headache or a twitching of my nerves, I might go to a neurologist or even, though I should loathe so craven a capitulation to the vogue of half my friends, to a psychiatrist. Or if there were premonitions beforehand or visions during or afterward, if it resembled at all the *déjà vu* or a bad dream, I could speak to Beulah Smithwick and let her sixth sense explicate and extricate me. If fear or regret attended it or any other vaporing from a tangible cause, I could find the proper physic for myself. But there is no fear except the fear within the experience itself which is, to be sure, a fear of the utmost intensity: it is ideal and has no object that I can name. At the same time that I rise, ejected from the planet into the empyrean, I plummet through the core of the world.

I took this dangerous journey for the fifth time last night, embarking under the prosiest of circumstances, at Peg Duff's when, after dinner, she was showing us her newest cactus, a huge globe with a gray hide and yellow spikes that curled like talons; at the top of it there was a sort of fontanel covered with a downy growth and I was seized with a frightful desire to stab into it with the paper knife that lay beside its tray. Above the table where she exhibits all these abominable armed bladders and bulbs, together with her Western gear, her tomahawk and arrowheads and a lariat that she declares once belonged to an illustrious cattle-rustler, she has with her infallibly bad taste hung two della Robbia reproductions, more simpering than most and, because the workmanship is so bad, more lifelike. The association between those plaster baby skulls and the organic, living cactus made my impulse monstrously immoral; but as I stepped back, unable to find a suitable comment to make, Mr. Barker, from all outward appearances a good and gentle man, explored the soft fungous top with the fingers of one hand while in his other, he balanced the sharp Scots dress dagger with which Peg slits open her morning mail. And he said, "Wonder what's inside?" and Peg replied, "Know what you mean. Looks like baby hair." In varying degrees, in different ways, I knew that all the others had been possessed as I had been, but this coincidence of our crime did not absolve me, and I was swept upward, outward and pressed down by . . . by what? Shall I call these moments "trances"? When it was finished and I had, so to say, come back into the room, something peculiar and irrelevant took place: I seemed to smell something hot and acrid and the smell seemed to proceed from the array of plants. I spoke of it, not sure a fire had not broken out somewhere. But no one else, though they all sniffed vigorously, caught the odour and Peg said, "Smelling the wide open spaces. Sun on the desert sands. Dunes, you know, like the Cape." My suggestibility was remarked and then the subject was changed. I lasted the evening, played bridge and even concentrated well enough to win five dollars. But when I walked home alone through the fog, my legs were weak as if I had been through an exhausting physical ordeal; I felt that the straps of a tight harness had bruised my back. The first light had come before I fell asleep.

She closed the journal, returned her pen to its bowl of shot and went to her front windows from which, through the interstices of the Dutchman's Pipe, she looked down at the languid figure of the boy in the hammock, his bare, shadow-dappled legs ivory against the crimson, his intelligent large head turned upward to the house. The look of John in him was embryonic for he was still a child, but nonetheless, it was there, beginning, a breathtaking, reminding vulnerability, a pure and open wound of youth. In the healing, he would change. Katharine who had never healed, had never changed, and but for her white hair, she was the same as she had been at nineteen when her lover married someone else, at seventeen when she had sworn to marry him.

At seventeen when, recognizing her first real love, she had gone to the summerhouse one night and prostrated herself before the figure of Minerva, the protectress assigned to her by her learning-loving father, and had vowed by a majestic galaxy of Roman gods and Christian saints (Teresa of Avila, John of the Cross, Aquinas and Augustine, heaven's intellectuals) to marry John Shipley to whom, translating as she went, she read *The Georgics* at his request in payment for the bouquets he brought her; she had taken those naive offerings as symptoms of the absent-mindedness of his infatuation, for no garden in Hawthorne yielded anything like the flowers of Congreve House.

Unlike Edmund St. Denis, she did not make fun of that prefiguration of herself nor even of the melodrama of a passage in her journal that she remembered having written in the beginning of her rapture, "I thanked him for the flowers and could not help from putting him on tenterhooks by telling him he should take care what he puts in his nosegays for girls who have studied the language of flowers. And then I told him that when Maeve comes on Monday week, he will bring her nothing but red roses. He said, 'I shall bring nothing but stinging nettles and deadly nightshade to anyone but you.' This speech, though it was pretty, seemed to me headlong and I was relieved to have Papa come in just then to ask us to play croquet. But for all my precautions, I am devastated by the fellow. Papa believes that he will be another Bulfinch. I pray for that. I do not need to pray for his proposal because of that I'm certain, but I do beseech all the powers that be to make him an eminent architect." (Another Bulfinch! Oh, Papa, for God's sake, let us sit upon the ground and tell sad stories of the deaths of kings.)

It had not been more than a week later that Maeve Maxwell arrived, having spent the earlier part of the summer with Aunt Dora Congreve. Maeve, Katharine's father's ward since her infancy, had been brought up almost as Katharine's sister; together they had gone to Miss Winsor's and then had spent three years at a convent school in France. They bore a strong family resemblance (Hibernian but of the Protestant complexion) and it had been a natural error, in those days, to speak of them as "the Misses Congreve." The Misses Congreve, rather than the "Misses Maxwell" since the latter name was not borne by such luminaries as the former and therefore did not spring so quickly to the tongue; Maeve, erroneously congratulated once on having so brilliant a father as George Congreve had flushed and answered, "I'm only his niece. Katharine's the cream, I'm the skimmed milk."

There was a sisterly, rather than a friendly bond between the girls, and the very fact that they were not sisters but were cousins made their intimacy circumspect and incomplete; Maeve could not forget that she was a burden thrust upon an uncle who had never liked his sister, and she was continually remorseful that the money that had been left her was insufficient to cover her needs of schooling and clothes. Her humility exasperated George Congreve and filled Katharine with such unbearable guilt that, fleeing from it into resentment, she was often coldly cruel. And like everything else, Maeve accepted the cruelty without a murmur.

But when she had come on that summer, Katharine was so much in love that she overflowed with love and welcomed Maeve with abounding grace and affection. She had not confided in her (it was a miracle that she had been able to hold her tongue since she could put her mind to nothing but John Shipley) but had described to her in full detail the Norman

Gardiners' young house-guest whom Maeve was bound, she said, to adore. He had gone sailing with his host, Dick Gardiner, and Maeve did not meet him until the evening of her birthday when a supper and dancing party was held in her honor.

There had been fireworks and dancing on a platform on the lawn; the whole natural world had seemed a background constructed for this one particular night in Katharine's history to accent and deepen her triumphant blossoming. She had been so enthralled by the splendor of her father's gardens, the perfection of the moon in the sky and the clownish paper moon in the tulip tree, the green flares of the fireflies and the sparkle of the violins, the jasmine petals floating in the Moselle *Bowle* in the cool, columned temple to Minerva, the bonhomie of all the young guests lustrous in the promise of their lives to come and, above all, by the joy of a moment when she met her father's eyes and knew by the look in them, wholly altruistic, that he knew and approved and hoped for her that her young man would propose marriage to her on this spellbound night—she had been so secure in the clouds, so busy at her Spanish castles, so self-assured that, in the beginning, she had heard no dissonance in the hour's unfolding melody.

There had been no doubt of it, Maeve, that night, had never been lovelier nor had her simplicity ever been more winning. Ignorant of the cause of it, she had turned toward Katharine's ripe warmth like a leaf turning to the sun. In their bountiful mood, they had gaily worn identical frocks of rose-red *mousseline de soie* and had adorned their Psyche knots of black hair with garnet rosebuds; their beautiful slippers had been ivory satin overlaid with an Arabian design in silver threads, presents from Uncle Daniel Thornton who had enjoined the young ladies to save them until their coming out. But they had agreed they could not wait. Both pairs of slippers now stood in the bibelot cabinet in Katharine's sitting room; they had been worn only that one time and the reason Katharine and Maeve gave each other was that, exquisite as they were, they did not fit. Nor did they ever wear those diaphanous dresses again; they hung still at the back of Katharine's closet, smelling of ancient sachet.

Late on the evening of the ball, just before supper, the fireworks were announced and even then, Katharine had been too much interested in watching Adam and Maddox moving down into the meadow, supplely cleaving through the silvery grass, their arms laden with rockets and pinwheels, to see that Maeve and John, who had danced the last dance together, were standing beside her, hand in hand. A crimson girandole mounted with a hiss into the sky and fell, a fountain of blinding orange fire; the fine, showering colors were unreal and chemical, plangent pinks and purples, sharp blues and violent greens, and the rapidity with which the rockets vanished, leaving for only an instant afterward the image of their course and the echo of their explosion, so excited her that she had been lightheaded and tears had started to her eyes. As the last Catherine wheel revolved insanely on its separate planes of scarlet and green, sizzling and thundering as the wild spokes fired each other, Katharine, in an ecstasy, turned to face John Shipley. No longer than it took the Catherine wheel to spin itself to nothing and leave the summer sky to the stars did it take her to see that he could not, could never see her. So cold that her joints themselves were locked and frozen, so icy that her smile could not relax, she stared at them who, in their oblivion, stared at each other.

It had been a long, long, silent struggle in which, from the start, Katharine had had no chance, for her adversaries, blind and deaf to everything except each other's eyes and voices, had not known that a struggle existed. Throughout that tortured summer and the next one after that, two mortal summers, delaying the formal announcement of their engagement because of some parental restriction imposed on John, they had bruised her; undetected, unsuspected, the cancer spread until its progress and its malevolent pain became the armature of her whole thought and conduct.

As if it had been yesterday, she remembered her demeaning anguish when, on idle afternoons, they begged her to read aloud to them *The Georgics*. (It was always *The Georgics* they asked for, though what did they care for the pruning of vines and the keeping of bees?) They sat the while demurely far apart, stealing glances and mouthing pet names. In the intoxication of their romance, furthered—even created—by this house, these grounds, this lake, this river that Katharine's father and grandfather and great-grandfather provided them with, in this lavish, extravagant Roman holiday, they had had energy and lunacy to spare and had showered her with it. They had imagined that she had deliberately brought them together and to her, their ambassadress, had proposed that the three of them be a triumvirate for life. They had even gone one evening, after a moonlight horseback ride, into Mr. Congreve's writing room off the library where he was reading Tibullus, and had asked him to draw up a document in Latin to testify to this intention. Katharine's father had half turned from his desk and, angry at the interruption, said, "Are you drunk, Shipley? What sort of rambunctious romp is this?"

That night, when John had gone back to the Gardiners' and Maeve had gone upstairs to bed, Katharine had returned to her father at his lucubrations and that time and only that time, they had spoken of Maeve's intrusion. "Was it the real thing, Kathy?" he asked, and when she nodded, he stroked her hand and said, "Poor dear. I had hoped for you there'd be no compromise." The oil in one of the canisters of his student lamp was low and the light expired behind the fluted green glass shade as they watched. At the coming of that half-darkness, Katharine gave up, sighed deeply, brought in another lamp from the library and, Spartan to commend herself to him, she said, "First things first, Papa," and returned to his hand the pen he had set aside. It struck her, as she watched him poise the nib again over the margin of the page of poetry, that like her father, note-maker, student for study's sake, she would never participate, that she would read astutely and never write, observe wholeheartedly and never paint, not teach, not marry God. Untalented and uncompromising, she would not commit herself: her life had seemed to her to stretch upward in a dark curve and as she ascended the stairs, she seemed to tread heavily through all the days of her future years.

Maeve's wedding, in Hawthorne's St. James's church, had followed on the heels of George Congreve's funeral at the same altar, and where his coffin had stood in the drawing room, there stood the bride and bridegroom, embowered in the finest of Maddox's roses. The brevity of the interval, called indecent in the town, had been insisted upon by Katharine herself who had wanted all the business of Congreve House finished, for without her father as her champion she could not have endured much longer to look upon the lighthearted lovers. Maeve, having no relatives closer than the Congreves, could not be married anywhere else, and Uncle Daniel Thornton had come up from Newport, rather grumpily because he hated to be disturbed, to give her away. There had not, at least, been the indignity for Katharine of seeing her own father in this role. Her extremely busy mother who had had little in common with her husband (she had ordered her weeds with the same efficiency and good sense that she employed in replacing worn linens and in the same way put on her face the look of widowhood) and nothing at all in common with her daughter, had gone back to town as soon as she had buried her husband behind Minerva's temple ("I want my bones to be alone," he had said. "I'll not be buried with a multitude. You must plant me under my own fig tree in my own backyard") and dispatched her niece in a flurry of rice. She, Alma Congreve, had been too much concerned at the time with raising a private fund for an ex-sexton of Christ Church in Cambridge who had suffered a nervous breakdown, to think it odd or even interesting that the newlyweds, moved by Katharine's great generosity in the midst of her bereavement, had determined that they would postpone their honeymoon until she could go with them almost a year later. Their insistence on preserving the fiction of the triumvirate had made her think, at first, that they suspected her disappointment; later on, when they were in Europe, she realized that to them it was not a fiction, for they continued to believe that she had made the match between them and with the greatest good humour continually and publicly thanked her.

Ten years later, Mrs. Congreve was once to remark in passing as she sat in her daughter's Boston drawing room, knitting cardigans on the double quick to send to a Dublin temperance house, "It strikes me as unorthodox, to say the least, that you went abroad with Maeve and her husband so soon after their marriage. Wasn't it actually their honeymoon?" But Katharine's affirmative answer was lost on her mother whose questions were usually rhetorical and who went on with a rushing and detailed account of a charity bridge tournament she had attended the day before when, to her certain knowledge, a doctor of good repute had reneged twice and had not been caught out. She was too busy and too obtuse to realize that Katharine had been "keeping up appearances" for, like the honeymooners, she had never dreamed that her daughter was in love with John, whom she referred to, even now, as "Maeve's husband" or as "Dick Gardiner's friend."

After they all had gone, leaving Katharine alone in Congreve House, through some miraculous, compensating providence, she had been stricken desperately with typhoid fever and it was then that her hair had turned to white. The faithful Maddox and the faithful Beulah Smithwick had attended her and when she was well enough to have a mirror brought to her, she had amazed them both with her delight in this transformation. Her calendar had not changed since that time; she remained, in looks and in interior complexion, the girl John Shipley had listened to as she read Vergil's recommendations to agrarians on how to pass the winter.

2

A sigh like a sob shook her as she thought how, in the end, the patience of her charm and her rigid rejection of the second best had finally won her a Pyrrhic victory. For John Shipley, grappling in his forties for his twenties, had been fooled by his needless need and, as greedy as Ponce de Leon, imagining a source of rejuvenation, a new start, rebirth, a second chance with no strings attached, had returned to her. Except that he did not look upon it as a return; he believed he was seeing her for the first time and the bitterest pill of all the galling pills she had had to swallow was the knowledge that he had scarcely been aware of her those years ago but had only been impressed, snobbishly, by her situation as the only daughter of a remarkable man in a showplace of a house.

Now, though, he *must* divorce his wife, *must* marry Katharine, *must*—this is how he stated it—"save himself." *Must*, *ought*, words dear to the Puritan tongue telling lies between its veiling teeth and coating the vile mendacities with an ethical vocabulary. "I must save myself *no matter what!*" It was not, as she had once imagined it would be, honey-sweet; it was sand in the mouth and under the nails to see his notion of his salvation thus debased; to see him yanked like a trussed and hobbled victim toward the destiny she herself had set for him when she was seventeen on a pallid summer night, when she had loved and desperately required him, and had pressed her hands against Minerva's giant, marble sandaled feet; to see him cowed to incest and Maeve abandoned sordidly for "the other woman."

Maeve had not guessed who the other woman was; conventional and more old-fashioned, in spite of everything, than Katharine, she pictured to herself a dancing girl who kept her husband away often at the sacred hour of tea, caused him to pick humbling quarrels, mantled the house with deceit and gloom. Pacing her bedroom floor she said to Katharine, her confidante, "I want to know and I cannot bear to know. I want her to be the very soul of vulgarity with bad perfume and ankle bracelets and at the same time it revolts me to think of my successor as a tart." Katharine, warming her cold hands at Maeve's hearth, consoled her cousin with a truism, "If she's a tart, it won't last," but could find nothing to console herself for her hypocrisy, could not escape the memory of his insistent declaration that he must save himself, *no matter what*, and that only if she helped him could he succeed.

Their complicated history had begun most honestly and naturally with a conversation one afternoon when John had come to Katharine's house for tea since Maeve was gone for the day on some errand of good will. He had brought with him a portfolio of sketches he had made the summer before of the houses in Gardner's Crescent in Edinburgh; he had drawn the pleasing Augustan conceit well and she expressed her genuine delight in his deft eye. He was as pleased as a schoolboy, and eagerly and with impressive scholarship he talked to her of architecture as if he had only just begun his career and as if nothing could impede the fulfillment of his talent. On that innocent autumn afternoon, he had seemed to her as serious and as frank and charming as he had been in the very beginning and though she had felt a dim stirring of her old emotion, she had essentially been a generous friend, glad to see the renascence of his enthusiasm which, conversationally, at least, had seemed long ago to have died. For, early in his marriage, he had lived too much for his marriage and for his second love, his yacht, the *Empress Katharine*. Self-indulgent while he had the boat, incurably restless after the sale of her, he had never really worked at anything.

The sale of the *Empress*, seven years before, had been urged by his father, a commanding parent in a severe goatee who, being his son's employer in a venerable family firm, had objected to the cruises that had begun in July and ended in September and had been conducted, so he said, "as if Ash Wednesday never followed Mardi Gras." Ever since that time, John had gone each summer to Europe and these tours, even longer than the cruises, were called, a little fictitiously, "business trips," but if the business involved in them led to no contracts, led, indeed, to nothing but the depletion of an expense account, their purpose was ostensibly so elevated that the elder Shipley, who had his soft spots, was satisfied; though he described himself as "a practical man, a mason, merely," and was content to remodel department stores, he revered the artistic persuasion and he liked to think that his son was greatly gifted. "I think John's got something," he said. "I think he's by way of being a pioneer."

For many years John had been endeavouring to evolve what he called "an absolute design" for municipal buildings, but "pioneer" was a misnomer, for he was a revivalist and it was his ambition, before he died, to see a Palladian circus in every principal city of the United States. For an enterprise so daring and so elegant, it was natural that he require an annual refreshment of his memory in the classic cities of the continent. Therefore, for these seven years, he had gone abroad to look at Bath and Paris, Dublin and Edinburgh and Cheltenham, and while he was no closer than he had been before to the renovation, along the ingratiating lines of the eighteenth century, of the police courts, land offices, city halls and vehicle bureaus of Detroit, St. Louis and Bangor, he had an imposing collection of notes and sketches and his father, defending him against wags who claimed he spent his time golfing in Ballybunion and gambling in Monte Carlo, said, "These things take time."

Maeve, in every particular a constant wife, faithfully accompanied him, though Katharine remembered that once on the eve of departure, as she sat surrounded by luggage tessellated with the stickers of hotels too numerous to count, she said, "I wish I could once go to the North Shore with my children. It's sinful of me, I'm well aware, but there are times when perfection tires me." For Katharine, the arrangement could not have been more felicitous; Congreve House was too big for her by herself, she loved the children and they loved her.

It had not occurred to her until their tea *à deux* on Brimmer Street when, in his stimulation, the color rose to his cheeks and his eyes grew lustrous, that he ever had done anything in Europe but play. And even then, she mistrusted the evidence; the sketches might be nothing more than the result of training and facility. Certainly she had never taken seriously his plan to revolutionize the business centers of America and behind his back, with friends and relatives, had laughed at him. No one scolded him for deluding himself; he could afford to; he was rich; and insulated by fatherly and wifely trust, he could go to his grave believing that he had worked hard toward a worth-while aim.

And he might have done so if, on the coppery October afternoon when Maeve had gone to Concord to serve tea at a charity bazaar, he had bought a drink for a tart in an ankle bracelet in the bar of the Touraine Hotel instead of coming to Katharine's house and letting her see the drawings which he was taking home to file with all the others and then to forget. And so also might he have done if he had not, in the course of their subsequent impersonal talks, gradually begun to include himself in his talk, to speak of what he meant to do, then what he could do, then what he *might have done*, and then what he had not done. Suddenly the wasted years of his procrastination gaped open at his feet and in terror of the fading, academic blueprint of his life, he turned desperately to Katharine, persuading himself that she was the catalyst that would turn his whole world gold. But his terror had not burst just yet, it had unfolded slowly and had masqueraded as something else entirely; it had shown itself, through unresolved gestures, the warmer than cousinly greeting kisses, the pretexts for telephone calls and those for presents of flowers and books, it had shown itself to be the mild aberration of a man who knew he could rely upon his lady not to take him seriously. And she was reliable; she did not lose her head.

And finally, then, the terror worked itself out of the maze of his confusions and he had come running to her, begging her to tell him that it was not too late. (Too late for what? At the time she had not questioned but now she did. Too late to persuade the town fathers of Bridgeport to build a railroad station after the manner of Robert Adam?)

So they must save him, together, *no matter what.* But there was a matter: there was the matter of his children. She loved them warmly, especially the lonely boy who, last winter, had sometimes overcome his reticence and come to her for protection against the incubus that shambled through his parents' house. Doctoring him with lies ("Your father's badly overworked this year" and "Your mother's heart is delicate, but they'll both be as right as rain when they've come back from Europe"), she had felt, nevertheless, that in some intuitive, though still amorphous way, he knew and sensed in her drawing room that his father was a frequent visitor to it. It had been one afternoon when Andrew had come to call on her that she had suffered the first of the series of these seizures.

The day before, John had stood with his back to her, leaning his forehead on the mantel and running his fingers through his hair and had said, "I'm at the end of my rope, Kate. I can't pretend any longer or I'll be ready for an asylum. I'll admit I didn't bargain for this, I didn't want it, I don't want it now. But unless you help me, this is the end of me." She had told him to be still, had told him to pour himself a drink and then go home and when he would do nothing but stand there, woebegone, she finally crossed the room to him and in the spendthrift luxury of their embrace, promised everything he asked of her. She promised that if, at the end of the summer, after a fair trial (there is so much self-justifying in adulterers, so much good sportsmanship among ladies and gentlemen in doing dirty) he could not reconcile himself to the continuation of his life with Maeve, she would cast her lot with his, sell Congreve House, leave Boston and go with him to "begin again" in some outpost of the earth.

Childishly and criminally, they had picked out on the globe the island of Mangareva at the bottom of the world. Now somberly contracted to revenge for her ancient wound (she was an honest woman with herself and did not beat around the bush: she was and had always been "in love" with John Shipley and she did not love him and she knew that at the moment of conjugal commitment, the state of being in love would be annulled and she would never be accessible to him again through any ruse) she could not sleep that night and at last she took a soporific, left over from an illness of some months before. As the medicine began to solace her and she began to descend circuitously and slowly like a leaf falling to earth in a demure breeze, she wished, not thinking of John or Maeve or of the children but only of herself, never to awaken. For the first time in her life, she thought of life's alternative as delectable; with her whole heart she wished to die.

On the following afternoon, having observed that Andrew left his large schoolboy's tea untouched (Maureen imagined that all growing lads were gluttonous and on the days he came, set forth a trencherman's meal) she invited him to help her put together a jigsaw puzzle of the Taj Mahal. He was absorbed, head bent, his tongue between his teeth, his being concentrated on the restitution of a minaret. But when all the pieces were interlocked and the garish picture was smooth, Andrew did not smile in his characteristic shy, self-congratulatory way, did not seem to take any pleasure in his accomplishment. He turned away from the table and idly spun the globe and when it had stopped, he closed his eyes, pointing his finger at a spot in the azure matrix of the earth and opening his eyes again he read, "Mangareva. Who lives there?"

She recalled having heard from a psychiatrist at a dinner party that coincidence sometimes dogged the errant course of lunatics, and he had told her of a patient who, having escaped from his sanitarium, had gone to a distant city where he had never been before. Such was his sense of unreality that, requiring tangible proof that he existed, he had looked up his name, an ordinary one, in the telephone book in a public booth. And there it was, lightly underlined in pencil! Just as the man, terrified by a chimerical pursuer, tore out the page in the directory and went howling through the railway station, murderous with fear, until policemen came, so Katharine that afternoon, galvanized with guilt, had savagely spun the globe

and screamed at the baffled child, "No one lives there! There's
no such place!" and had shaken his shoulders. When the hurricane ended, she had acted quickly, had won him back by
saying, "That wretched, wicked Fanny Lyndon did Mangareva
as a charade and everyone got it except me. You're trying to
humiliate me." He had seemed to accept the explanation and
had laughed and amiably teased her a little further. But she
could not be sure, and she had not been sure of him since he
had come to Congreve House; she had felt his large, speculative
eyes on her and often, as if he had mesmerized her, she let fall
allusions to his father that, if he did know, he must surely be
storing up. Just now when she had looked out the window, she
had thought he was watching her even though she was hidden
by the broad-leaved vine.

Trying to hush her heart and her hammering pulses, she
stared at a portrait of herself as a bibliophile, painted in the
library, her hand upon a massive, gold-clasped book, her sidelong glance upon a cage of finches. It had been painted in that
memorable and awful summer of Maeve's birthday party, and
until he died two years later, it had hung on the wall beside her
father's desk. She recalled that when it had been unveiled, the
servants had gathered at the outskirts of the group of guests
and Maddox had exclaimed, "That isn't her!" Nor was it, for
there was no strength in the face, only a retreating prettiness
as shallow as a shell. She found herself irrelevantly curious to
know how many days before the party the portrait had been
finished and she opened her journal once again, leafing quickly
through the early pages on which the ink had faded into brown.
Two days, she learned, two days before the Catherine wheels
lighted up the night and whirled, two days before she had been
fixed upon her own Catherine wheel.

The figure was unwise: shutting her eyes against the insipid
presentation of herself, she spun upon a wrenching rack and
there came again that blinding, dumbing annihilation of reality. She did not know, as she had not known on the other
occasions, how long the agony lasted nor did she know whether
Honor's voice, singing, restored her to her senses (she noted
the accuracy of the phrase) or whether, like the pyrotechnic
Catherine wheel, it had ceased of its own accord. As virginal
and hyaline as the June day, the voice winged upward:

> "Who is Kath'rine, what is she,
> That all our swains commend her?"

The wristwatch at her waist said four o'clock and crossing again to the window just as the church bell began to ring, she pulled aside the vine and called to Andrew, asking him to row her out to get a water lily. She must find out, she thought, and in so doing, she must watch her tongue.

Now that her hour of solitude was finished, her mind grew practical. It dwelt upon the number of nasturtium sandwiches she would advise Mrs. Shea to make, on the warning that she must repeat to Beulah Smithwick against scrimping on the sleeves of a blue linen blouse.

> "Who is Andrew, what is he,
> That all my acts imperil him?"

she softly sang. He is a child, she replied, who, like his father, will become a weak man. She sat down at her dressing table where stood a grove of silver-capped and gold-stoppered vessels filled with homemade creams and lotions for her china skin. My life is seeping out of me, she thought, the nightmare vitiates my charm. For a long moment she could not lift her hands that lay, palm down, upon the cool and silvery marble. But finally the life came back to them and she clasped them over her breakable heart and she said, "Lackamercy on us, this is none of I."

CHAPTER III

The Sea's Souvenirs

HALF IN the hammock and half out of it, Andrew tortured a beetle in the grass and fretfully murmured obscenities. A squirrel sassed him from the crotch of the tulip tree and Beth, three feet away, insolently sat with her back to him. Nothing could make him feel worse, when he was feeling bad to start with, than the insult of a cat. He hated them all, and most of all he hated this black bug whose legs he slowly amputated. Between the dirty words, he talked as he worked to an imaginary twin who sat on the grass at the base of the tree. This interested and adventitious homunculus, although it was his twin, was, nevertheless, much younger than he and surpassingly ignorant.

"When I have finished killing Charles, I'll take you downtown," he said to it. "How would you like to eat an alewife at the smoke-house? What is an alewife? Why, it's a sort of herring. Okay, just hold your horses till I get this done. This will be about the only chance I'll have because day after tomorrow, I'll be too busy to bother with you."

"You mean because day after tomorrow you're going eeling with Victor?" asked the twin.

"Eeling!" he exclaimed. "My God, you don't know anything, do you? Do you think I'd catch an eel on purpose?"

The poor kid quickly changed the subject. "When will the funeral be?" he asked.

"Ten in the morning probably," replied Andrew. "Depending on the tide."

"Why depending on the tide?"

"Because we have to go clamming right afterward."

It was mid-morning but the dew was not yet dry in the shade of the elms; drops of it depended like beads from a spider web that was strung from tree to tree. Andrew had been awake since daybreak, stirred out of sleep by two wrens that had held a shrill colloquy in the vine over Cousin Katharine's window. Looking out at them, with the strong, fresh breeze on his face, he had seen his cousin's lamp go off. For a moment he was so thrilled to think of the two of them awake in the sleeping house at five in the morning that he had thought of knocking on her door and asking her to go for a swim. But he knew that the lake would be cold and anyhow, there was something too intimate and isolated about this hour of the day; alone with her in the aboriginal morning with nothing else to distract her, she might read his criminal mind. She had not come down to the dining room while he and the twins were eating their breakfast and her tray, which usually went up at half past seven, had not gone up by the time he left the house at nearly nine. There was a funny feeling in the house; the maids and the twins were quiet, and no one seemed able to settle down to anything. It was always that way whenever Cousin Katharine's routine was disrupted in the slightest.

"Cousin Katharine stayed up all night," he told his twin. "All night long she was reading my mind."

"Maybe she just turned on the light for a minute," suggested the twin.

"Listen," he said to this impudent Doubting Thomas, "listen to me. I'm boss around here. I said Cousin Katharine stayed up all night and that's what she did, no ifs, buts or maybes." The twin blubbered at the scolding and more kindly Andrew said, "Come on, half-pint. Charles Smith*wicked* is deader than a doornail."

He had decided to go down to the village because of something Harriet had said the night before when they were playing three-handed bridge. She had said he should be ashamed of himself for behaving like a baby; he couldn't fool her, she said, he wasn't reading in the hammock, he wasn't doing anything but pretending it was a cradle; she thought that anyone should have more pride than to advertise to the whole wide world that he had no friends and no resources. He had flung down his cards and told her to go to hell. But she was right and he *was* ashamed and all night long he had pitched and tossed and pummeled his pillow and deranged the bedding.

It took great courage to leave the hammock and to expose himself to the town; his mouth was as dry and his heart was as erratic as it always was when he had to be in any kind of play or exhibition. It was like a dream of going to school in his underwear. But he steeled himself; he got up, full of determination. To Honor who called out from the drawing room to ask him where he was going, he replied, "I've got some errands to run downstreet." She saved his life then, for in fact he had no errands at all but she asked him to take the morning letters to the post office. There were five altogether, the three they had written to their parents (Andrew, having nothing to say, had only made a few brief comments on the health of the animals, all of whom were well) and two in Cousin Katharine's hand, one to the Shipleys and the other to Aunt Alma. When he was out of sight of the house, he held these last two up to the light but the letter paper was thick and he could not make out a word; he would have given much to know what she had written about him.

He idled down the road and through the town, keeping up appearances by smiling to himself and, from time to time, if he passed anyone, faking a chuckle. He paused to look at an unfamiliar skiff tied up at the small pier and to speculate on its owner and its purpose and to deduce that it had sailed in from Bingham Bay on the early wind. It occurred to him to board it and get a lift to the docks to hunt for Congreve Smithwick and reclaim his knife with which to cut out Charles's heart; but for all he knew the man was out on a tuna boat, so he abandoned the idea. Lined with white houses, each with a picket fence, a square of lawn or a spring garden, a pair of lilac bushes, this road was as familiar to him as his own face and so pleasing were his sensations as he walked along it that for the time being he took heart and was happy and independent. To the ignorant little wraith beside him, he made much of the stock rural-joke Christian names on the letter boxes, Silas, Reuben, Hiram (he found them marvelous, not in the least comic, exactly as he would have found it marvelous and reassuring to know a colored man named Rastus, a dog named Fido, a cat named Tom), stopped dead still to gather and remember smells, smells of skunks, of tar, of some late riser's percolating coffee, of peonies, weigela, salt air, wood smoke. He and Victor had always felt it their right to look through open doors and windows and he did so now, frankly stood and stared at women combing their hair or punishing their children or disemboweling chickens or shelling peas; at an old man, infirm and useless, rocking himself to sleep in a Boston rocker as gently as if he were a mother and a baby in the same person and then jerking suddenly awake at a sound or the intrusion of the sun. He examined the packages on top of the letter boxes, read the addresses of the senders, applauded or deplored the knots in the string. Now and again he opened a letter box itself and diligently and with no interest at all read the postal cards and quickly leafed through the sale catalogues from Montgomery Ward, bridling with indignation at the pictures of corsets.

Eventually he came to the fish run, a complicated conduit a few hundred yards below the crescent headtide where every spring the alewives left the river to spawn in the fresh water of the lake above. He stood on a plank over the canal for a while and watched the obdurate fish that progressed by fractions upstream through the fast-moving water, or simply held their place for seeming hours, with their fins immobile and their unseeing eyes glued upon eternity. From the smoke-house came a strong and putrid reek which, on windy days, penetrated to the outskirts of the town; Cousin Katharine, at such times, closed all the doors and windows and went from room to room carrying a long burning joss stick high over her head. The smoked alewives which were bony and tasteless—until age imparted to them an unintentional pungency—and had a skin like yellow isinglass, were shipped to Haiti where, it was said, they were considered a delicacy, a fact that had led the cynical manager of the run to observe that he would not "care to sample their home-grown carrion." Once Charles Smithwick's ship had called at Port-au-Prince and on the back of a view of the Citadel, he had written that he had bought a Hawthorne alewife and that eating it had made him "(home)sick." Oh, that Charles was a wit all right, all right.

"He's a wit in a pig's valise," snarled Andrew's loyal twin.

Not because he liked them, but because it had always been a part of his and Victor's ritualistic day, Andrew begged a fish from one of the men and in the fuming shed he ate the woody, salty flesh in flakes; they were as dry as pine shavings. The genial, stinking man, pausing to wipe his sweaty face, smiled down at Andrew and said, "I suppose you and your side-kick have been too busy listening to Charley Smithwick's tall tales to come and see your old friends."

Andrew was amazed; he had thought the whole town knew that he and Victor were not speaking. He said "Yes," but he dared not elaborate lest the lie be discovered and he become really the laughingstock, and as soon as he decently could, he sped from the smoke-house and went to the general store where, with urgent thirst, he drank a bottle of tepid raspberry tonic. There in the cool of the vast room, partitioned into aisles with cases of notions and shoes and graniteware kitchen pots, he heard the news that had accumulated since this time yesterday. There had been a fire in a henhouse and you should have smelled the feathers! And a breaking-and-entering, a motorcycle accident on Route One; a boat had capsized in the harbor at Bingham Bay; a ventriloquist named Theophilus Sabatini had come to town and would be heard nightly after the first showing of the movie. Charles Smithwick had gained five pounds in the last week; Mr. Breyfogle was out of green split peas but he had plenty of the yellow.

The martial Miss Duff, barking out orders to Mr. Breyfogle for dried apricots as if she were requisitioning ammunition, turned and pointed her finger at Andrew like the man in the Moxie ad, "Is your cousin sick?" she demanded. He choked on a swallow of tonic and shook his head. "Her light was on all night," she accused. "I know because a damned rat kept me awake myself."

"You ought to try this here new 'Rightaway Rataway,'" said Mr. Breyfogle. He had a long pointed nose and beady black eyes and he looked exactly like a rat himself.

"Ought to try a shotgun," said Miss Duff, "and would if the damned outlaws weren't so wily."

"Did you say Kate was sick?" asked Mrs. Wainright-Lowe bustling up from the back of the store where she had been pawing a bin of new potatoes like a rag-picker. Mrs. Wainright-Lowe was a grass widow and she was fond of trouble. Mr. Wainright-Lowe had, for all practical purposes, vanished off the face of the globe though there was a rumor that he was living in Tibet and another that he had settled down in peaceful bigamy in Omaha. She lived with her elderly bachelor son who called her Mumma. Putting upon her round, small-eyed face a look of sympathy transparently malicious, she said, "You don't suppose she ate something at your house last night that poisoned her, do you, Peg?"

"If she did, she brought it herself."

"Oh, I wouldn't be so sure of that," returned Mrs. Wainright-Lowe. "One man's meat is another man's poison, as they say. As a matter of fact, Brantley and I both remarked that we felt a little under the weather this morning. I wasn't going to mention it to you but since Katharine is sick . . ."

"Rats," said Miss Duff and turned back to Mr. Breyfogle who, evidently under the impression that she was speaking of her own rats, held out for her inspection a can of Rightaway Rataway.

The whole town seemed to know that Katharine Congreve's light had been on till morning and everyone was wholeheartedly interested. The occupants of the summer houses of Hawthorne, whose chimneys smoked from just after thaw until the first frost, greeted Andrew one by one with solicitous inquiries as they sauntered or bustled, according to their humour, into the store and later when he sat on the porch, petting Miss Duff's beagles. It gave him a vicarious importance and he was careful not to deny or affirm any of the hypotheses that the ladies and gentlemen proposed; he tried to give the impression that he knew all about it but was not at liberty to tell. Between interviews, he dropped his role and studied the matter analytically, but he came to no conclusions; he could not imagine what on earth she had been doing and he did not believe she had been sick; Cousin Katharine was above sickness except for flu occasionally when there was an epidemic.

"Perhaps she had a guest," suggested Mrs. Tyler.

Miss Duff exploded with outrage, "The light was *upstairs*."

They were standing just inside the door and evidently Mrs. Tyler caught sight of Andrew for she hastily amended, "I meant a guest of the animal kingdom. My rats and squirrels often give me insomnia."

"Don't talk to me about rats!" roared Miss Duff. "They're driving me stark staring mad."

They moved out of earshot of Katharine Congreve's relative but he could see that they, together with Mrs. Wainright-Lowe, were continuing the conversation avidly.

Now he watched the deliberate approach of old Mr. Barker who laughed continuously (some said because he was happy and others, because he had nothing else to do) as he took his two-hour constitutional, covering the whole of the little town, his choleric Negro valet following a few steps behind, armed with an umbrella if it should rain and a palm-leaf fan if Mr. Barker should have one of his attacks of vertigo. He waved his stick at Andrew and called out, "I hear your daddy's yacht came into Bingham Bay last night, and I also hear that our own Empress Katharine is indisposed. Convey to her my distressful solicitude and beg her to call on me, her humble servant, if there is anything her heart desires." He laughed, taking none of his speech seriously. "It's my personal opinion," he shouted, cupping his hand to his mouth in a stage gesture, "that she was up all night reading *Gone with the Wind* though she would never own up to it."

Miss Celia Heminway, speeding to the post office in her wheel-chair, on hearing this aspersion, stopped dead still and, glowering, said, "Speak for yourself, Rodney. The trash *you* read!"

He continued to sit on the porch, his back against a tall milk can, knowing that he was the cynosure that morning of every eye. Aloof and smiling enigmatically, he watched as much as he was watched; he watched the parade of summer people whom Victor, even though he had known them all his life, looked on as *sui generis*, "the people from away," and watched the town's indigenous freaks and skeletons whom Victor did not find odd at all but who comprised a gallery so unusual, small as it was, that on the two or three occasions Andrew had described its members to boys at Sewell, no one had believed him. Every single person indicated in one way or another that his rich and beautiful maiden cousin had not gone to bed till morning. The French Canadian game warden of great age and rumored lunacy (he sometimes thought he was General Pershing and tried to drill the trusties when they were working on the highway) and whose hobby was reputed to be raising snakes, came riding his skinny brown mare down from the headtide for his weekly purchase of provisions; he had a reckless greed for macaroni, thereby earning for himself the nickname Yankee Doodle. As long-legged and as lean as his horse, he loped up the steps and Andrew could have sworn as he passed by, that he caught the fishy smell of snakes. He looked at Andrew with his crazy, batting eyes and he said, "Tell her to try a spoonful of honey in a glass of gin." Behind him, Miss Duff made a sound as if she were throwing up.

There was a vile old beggar woman known as Em Bugtown who sometimes wandered away from the county farm at the edge of town and went from door to door asking for food or snuff or silver spoons; it was said that she had been beautiful, been rich, been—despite all this—jilted by her fiancé and then, defying everyone who loved her, had turned to dipping snuff and so had gone from bad to worse. She had come drifting like a hobo up from New York and finally had settled here, an eyesore when she was abroad, a burden to the taxpayers when she stayed put. She smelled of onions and she wore a yellow rag, limp with Musterole, on the back of her neck to alleviate the headache she had had ever since her lover disappeared. Early this summer she had come to Congreve House and had hammered loudly at the spotless door and when Mrs. Shea came to shoo her off, she planted herself solidly on the front lawn, bony arms akimbo, and shouted, "Hark, Lady Congreve! You'll pay for your black sins." Cousin Katharine laughed but she turned a little pale and said that it did not seem fair to be so threatened simply because she would not part with her coin silver teaspoons that had been in the family time out of mind. But Cousin Katharine, who had never borne anyone a grudge, did not fail, when she made her weekly visit to the poorhouse with baskets of fruit and bunches of flowers, to take the old wretch some tins of snuff and packages of cigarettes nor to talk to her for a quarter of an hour. "Miss Bugtown and I," said Cousin Katharine, "according to Miss Bugtown, are in the same boat. She asked me whether I got 'the go-by' by letter or by mouth and when I told her 'both' I thought for a minute she was going to hug me." This morning Em Bugtown came ranging down the hill in a huge pair of sneakers, busily munching her toothless gums.

"Pick up your feet, Em Bugtown!" cried Andrew, for it was

this injunction that Victor used to make her swear. She halted, peering this way and that to find the source of the voice, her mouth still browsing greedily over itself. Seeing Andrew finally, she took a stance in the middle of the road, her feet far apart and she shook both fists at him; from her ribby lips there came a stream of words so venomous and nasty that his arms and legs and the back of his neck erupted into goose-flesh. When she had finished with her imprecations, she became malevolently unctuous and actually rubbing her twiggy hands together she said with a smirk, "You don't go scot-free for robbing the poor and defrauding the helpless, do you, dear? Didn't go to bed at all last night? But I, for one, am truly sorry for her." Humming villainously, she moved on in the direction of Mr. Barker's house undoubtedly to ask for spoons.

He saw the man with one diminutive ear (it was no bigger than a clove of tangerine and Andrew would have given both his normal ones for it) and the man without a nose but only a great bandage where it should have been; and Jasper, the epileptic; and the fabulously corpulent Bluebell James who had had a bastard baby every year since she was twelve. Every one of them spoke to him and tried to seem casual when they asked after Miss Congreve.

Not the least interesting of these autochthons was Beulah Smithwick, that sly and frowsy necromancer who could foresee the future and disclose the past in a pack of filthy playing cards or a pattern of wet tea-leaves. She came to town at a trot every morning, carrying a covered basket in which she put her small supplies of two eggs, four potatoes, half a pound of pork liver, a loaf of bread, which she left then in the cold-room of the house where she was sewing that day until it was time for her to trot home. She loitered a little in the streets—yet seemed to skip when she stood still—to gossip in a voice as high and unrelenting as a whistle with a single note. It was Andrew's sisters' fancy that Beulah and Yankee Doodle Lafontaine were married but very secretly and that they practiced black magic with the snakes and the tea-leaves. One year, when a band of gypsies came in the heart of summer and through the bird-watching binoculars, Honor and Harriet and Andrew had spied on the fat little women sidling in and out of Beulah's cottage on what errands they did not dare imagine, Honor had sworn that one of them had given her the evil eye through the glasses because the very next day she broke out in hives and she would not be persuaded that they had come from eating wild strawberries in the woods; she spoke of "the time Beulah's house-guest hexed me." Beulah wore a ruffled mobcap and winter and summer, rain and shine, around her neck, there slackly hung a many-tailed fur tippet the color of a mouse. "How come your mother wears fur in the summer?" Andrew once had asked Victor and Victor, shrugging his shoulders, countered, "How come your lady cousin rides around in that old-time whatsis?"

Remembering that, Andrew turned his face away from the street and gazed into a stand of pine trees on the far bank of the river, carried again into the past in spite of the potentialities of this morning's mystery. For one of the most puzzling aspects of Victor's snub was that next to his brother, he had admired Cousin Katharine more than anyone else in the world and Andrew had never deceived himself that it was partly because of his kinship to her that Victor had so favored him. But unless they were meeting secretly (anything was possible in this unpropitious year) he had ignored her as completely as he had ignored Andrew. It was true that he had seldom come nearer to Congreve House than the kitchen garden except during a party, but all the same, he knew the interior of it as intimately as Andrew did for, making no bones about it, he toured it in the winter when it was shut up except for the kitchen and the two bedrooms where Maddox and Mrs. Shea slept. Similarly he entered all the boarded-up, dust-sheeted summer houses, inspecting them methodically and uncritically. He said that if one kept "a sharp look out" it was possible to learn everything there was to know about a person just through his belongings. In speaking of Mr. Barker's house, he once had said, "I think it's funny for a man to keep a box of cowbells under his bed." His eye had wandered as he contemplated this vagary and then, "I bet he's afraid of the dark and has them handy to roust out his man," a hypothesis that was very likely true since Mr. Barker, who was many times a millionaire, had long ago been threatened by black-hand letters, presumably from a band of kidnappers. He had immediately retired for protection to a private sanitarium for nervous complaints, where through a gross misjudgement or a snarl of red tape, he had been put into the violent ward. He admitted freely that ever since, he had had horrifying nightmares in which the kidnappers and the psychiatrists pursued him in gyroscopes.

And speaking once of Cousin Katharine's house, Victor said, "I figure she keeps those spriggy shoes in the china closet to remember something by. I figure she wore them on some red-letter day or other, but I haven't figured out yet why there are two sets." The "china closet" was a bibelot cabinet in the upstairs sitting room and the "spriggy shoes" had been worn by Cousin Katharine and Andrew's mother at a ball he had often heard about. When he told Victor this, Victor winked and said, "It's funny to keep a keepsake for getting two-timed." But when Andrew demanded an explanation of this cryptic statement, Victor said only that he had been joking. Another time, he said, "You know last winter when I was in your house? I found out something. I found out why she never got married." And then, when Andrew asked why, Victor stood on his head and upside down, in a strangled voice, brushed him off. "April Fool," he gurgled. "I found a mice nest in a hat of hers, that's what I found."

Beulah Smithwick was a woman to whom gossip came unsolicited and copiously like particles of iron to a magnet and who, though she was trustworthy with confidences, enjoyed holding character up to a strong light. Like all inveterate gossips, she claimed she did not gossip at all but that she had only a friendly curiosity to know "what made people tick." And it could be assumed that in the winter, when she was snowbound and half the time the erratic telephone was out of order, she used her son as her sounding board and interlocutor so that it was natural that his mind had been sophisticated early and natural that he should know as much and even more about Cousin Katharine than Andrew did. For she had known Miss Congreve from childhood since she had been a maid in the house, twelve years old, when the infant Katharine had been brought up for her first summer in Hawthorne. Through the crude country boy, Andrew had learned that his cousin's gilded cradle had been made in the shape of a shell and had been lined with pale pink China silk; her frocks and bonnets and peignoirs had come from Paris and so had her saucy nanny who taught her to say "*ma bonne*" before she said Mama or Papa. Beulah had watched her gorgeously unfold, emerge magnificently from her adorable chrysalis. And Beulah had, moreover, watched Maeve Maxwell grow from a thin and tearful little orphan into a woman nearly as confident and nearly as beautiful as Katharine.

When Victor, borrowing his mother's recollections, spoke of Andrew's mother, Andrew was at once excited and discomforted: it was like a double vision or like a dream within a dream. As if he spoke of someone he had read about or someone he knew and Andrew did not, he would say, "She and the other one . . ." (and by "the other one," he meant Andrew's own mother). "She and the other one took off one night in the middle of the night and rode horseback to Bingham and stowed away on a tuna boat. They found them before they got past the lighthouse but—" and now he quoted his mother verbatim and his voice even partook of her screeching timbre—"it was a scandal that rocked our town." Then, speaking for himself again he added, bored, "Nothing happened, though." At such times, Andrew felt like an immigrant to a country where he spoke the language brokenly but had excellent connections.

He thought of how flattered he had been by Victor's envy of Andrew's relation to her, how he had questioned him on the interior of her house in Boston and had been delighted to know that she had a chemical laboratory in the basement where she had once successfully made gunpowder. His cat-eyes widened and his mouth hung open in fascination when her name was mentioned or when he saw her, tall, white-haired, dressed in her lovely clothes, her flowing cloaks and her Spanish shawls, her broad hats and her veils. He liked to see her going past in her carriage for her afternoon drive, bowing and smiling like a public personage on her way to pay visits of half an hour or to leave her card together with one of the small mementoes she always carried with her in a rattan basket, sprigs of lavender, spills of colored paper, dried morels. She greeted everyone she met by name and by her friendly questions, to do with a sick child or the progress of a new wing on a house or the loss of a dinghy or the preparations for a wedding, she indicated that the concerns of all her neighbors were her concerns.

When Victor called her "ma'am" he sounded as if he were addressing a queen and sometimes, forgetting his manners, he

stared at her, dumb and spellbound. He was rigid at the lawn
parties, the midday picnics, the strawberry teas and the evening
fetes with dancing round a maypole garlanded with roses. And
while she organized the other children into games of blind-
man's buff and snipsnapsnorum, he stood apart, unwilling to
be distracted from his contemplation of her. And while she
fed the others to repletion with profiteroles and lemonade, he
could not eat. Once, though, he had agreed to join in a game
of post office which Cousin Katharine herself had organized
and he had got a special delivery letter from his hostess and
had been required to go with her to the writing room off the
library, the "privy chamber," as she called it, a term that made
the country children blush and squirm with giggles. And here,
behind the damask portieres, he had received a kiss from her.
His look of surprise when he came out had imparted to his
hodgepodge face an unbelievable dignity which had stilled the
tongues of the others who had been on the point of teasing
him. He had stalked directly to the finches' cage over the terrarium and Andrew had seen him put his lips to the grating as
if he hoped the birds would permanently tattoo the kiss on his
lips with their sharp beaks. Ever since that time, however, he
had shunned even post office and he stood speechless on the
sidelines, unable to participate in anything although, because
the etiquette his mother had schooled him in demanded it, he
would stand on his head, he would even yodel briefly if Miss
Congreve asked him to.

Cousin Katharine had not had a single party this summer,
not for children and not for ancients. Andrew had not thought
of that before but now that he did, he could only come to the
conclusion that there was something wrong with her. "Something is rotten in the state of Denmark," he said to one of the
beagles and at that moment Beulah Smithwick fluttered up the
steps and shrilled at him, "What's this about my darling lady
being sick? Say it isn't so."

"It isn't," he said and on an inspiration he added, "She was
up all night cutting out paper dolls."

"Cutting out paper dolls?" Mrs. Wainright-Lowe inquired
with great interest through the screen door. "I think you're
mistaken, Andrew. I think Miss Duff's hot crabmeat hors
d'oeuvre gave her an upset."

Beulah flicked through the tails of her tippet and underlining every word she said defensively, "Shellfish does not disagree with Katharine Congreve and I am in a position to know, having known her from the bassinet."

"I wasn't impugning Miss Congreve," said Mrs. Wainright-Lowe. "If I was impugning anyone . . ." But just then Miss Duff, who was about to be impugned, marched out the door, ordered her dogs to "Heel, damnit," and charged off. Beulah went into the store, haughtily refusing to look at Mrs. Wainright-Lowe again.

Now that the dogs were gone and now that practically everyone in town had spoken to him, there was again nothing to do and no attitude to strike. Turning a little to the left, he said to his twin, "This is the most boresome summer A.D." It was indeed a summer not in any way superior to those of his school friends whom he had formerly pitied since they were either shunted off to camp to learn the doubtful art of making fire with sticks or to grandparents, set in their ways and in the belief that a child's sole commission in life was to be seen and not heard.

He and the twins had had one awful, unforgettable summer, to be sure, when Cousin Katharine had gone out West and they had been sent to the Stygian Newport villa of their Uncle Daniel Thornton, a queer fish who kept his own appendix pickled in a jar under a glass bell in the library. All that summer he had sought to improve his wards' minds by a nightly reading from *The Decline and Fall of the Roman Empire* and every morning after breakfast, no matter what the weather was, they had had to sit in the library, in full view of that pale inner worm of his and write an essay—or rather a *pensée*, as he more stylishly put it—for Uncle Daniel was in love with the written word and called himself "a member of the scribblers' fraternity," though he had been published only once, with an epithalamium in dimeter, in *The Harvard Advocate*. The rest of the time in Newport had been divided between orderly excursions to Bailey's Beach with an acidulous Fräulein hired for the season (their governess, Miss Bowman, who was from Santa Fe, had been refused house-room by Uncle Daniel who did not favor the West which he called "the ultramontane colonies where nothing flourishes except the solecism") and equally well-ordered afternoon picnics with suitable children as bored as they. The whole summer had had the languid, empty air of convalescence.

But so had this present one. They had not gone once to Bingham Bay to hire a boat to sail among the islands of the wild Atlantic; nor roasted corn on the rocks at Pemaquid; always before, Cousin Katharine sitting sidesaddle and wearing a perky derby and a regal habit of dark blue poplin, had taken them for moonlight horseback rides. They had not even played croquet or *boccie*.

Conceivably the world was coming to an end.

2

Billy Bartholomew, the blasphemous and long-winded blacksmith, was sitting in the doorway of his shop directly opposite the store, alternately reading a newspaper and observing the doings of his fellows with a misanthropic eye. Billy disliked almost everyone and he especially disliked Katharine Congreve who took her horses to Bingham Bay to be shod. Through innuendoes, through a maze of hints about "someone, naming no names, not a thousand miles away," through a crabbed castigation of the rich and of summer people and "certain parties that get themselves up like Lady Astor's plush horse," the shaggy, baggy, cantankerous old man had, in the past, lambasted her to Andrew when the notion took him to, when Andrew and Victor were calling on him and when he was reminded of her existence by the sight of her maids going into the drugstore or by the spectacle of Miss Congreve herself in her splendid carriage, her coachman dressed to the nines, Pegasus and Derek trotting along in their infuriating shoes. He had the caution never to make a direct attack but circuitously, speaking of "*some* people who are ruining the country by refusing to buy in the domestic market," of "people who come down here in the summer and think they can lord it over us," of "hoity-toity spinster women who think they know it all," he arrived, eventually, at his old wound which he loved and cherished and kept open, bleeding for all the town to see.

Although Billy was garrulous and tiresome and usually angry, Andrew needing company made his way across to the cool, cavernous barn, piled to its rafters with wheels and broken springs, the skeletons of sleighs, old lanterns, splayed creels, rat-chewed landing nets. On top of the cold anvil there was a battery radio which Billy kept tuned to a Canadian station; over it there came a watery wail from Toronto and, at certain times, the exultant voice of a young woman who advertised "live honey" which could be ordered through arrangement with one's local grocer; in the background, the static sometimes gave the impression of bees producing on the spot.

"Glad to have this unexpected honor," he said as Andrew sat down on the floor beside him. For some time then he read aloud the obituaries of people he did not know and the fillers in the Bangor *Courier*. In a rich, ministerial voice, he intoned, " 'There are more rats than people in New Orleans, Louisiana.' What do you think of that? *More rats than people*." Then, in two different voices, as if he were reading a dialogue, he presented a question and answer:

"Question: Why is neatsfoot oil so called?

Answer: Neat is an old Anglo-Saxon word meaning ox or oxen. Neatsfoot oil, used principally for dressing leather, is a fatty oil obtained from the feet of cattle."

He fell silent and leafed through a magazine called *The Northern Farmer*. From time to time he looked up and sneered at someone in the street. "How Albert can call that thing a car is beyond me," he said. And some time later he observed, "There's Jasper walking like a fiddler crab, sign he means to take a fit today."

Billy's pleasure, apart from mustering odd data, was to inveigh against the government and against women for both of whom he had an unremitting hatred. He led his lean (he himself was stout and red and hairy) embittered wife a wretched life, and their exchange of vituperation in public places was as much a part of the local scene as the springtime arrival of the alewives or the daily passage of Miss Congreve through the streets. Anything that was low or uncomfortable or dishonest or ugly was, in Billy's mind, either womanly or governmental and he liked to confound the two abominable species by speaking of "all those women in the White House and in Congress" and calling Mayor Curley "a damned flapper." Of his horse, an irascible white gelding with one blue eye, he said, "When he gets my dander up, I call him Carrie Nation, but generally I call him something sweeter." His sweeter name was Dave. And all the murders he recounted—he did this well; he had a histrionic flair and a sincere appreciation of bloodshed—had been committed by women whose victims, always men, had died through fiendish, housewifely tricks; they had drunk arsenic with their morning coffee, had eaten ground glass in their rice pudding and died a dog's death, had been decapitated with hatchets as they read the Sunday papers. A relative of his who had gone West and rashly had married a native had been eaten to death by a pack of dogs belonging, significantly enough, to his mother-in-law. Billy's nickname for Mrs. Bartholomew was Lizzie Borden.

"The blue, or sulphur-bottomed whale is the largest living animal, attaining a length of more than 100 feet and a weight of 150 tons," he read, picking up the newspaper again. He exhaled a breath of beer though it was not yet noon; he made the beer himself and drank it green and bottles of it, in the dark recesses of the smithy, sometimes exploded like a clap of thunder. "Here's something else," he said. " 'Dried skinks are still used medicinally in certain parts of the United States.' Doesn't say what parts or what for. That's typical of these women on the papers; they leave out half of what a man wants to know. Also I am fully of the opinion that a good part of the time these facts are not true. For example, do you believe as it says right here that 'the jaw is the strongest part of the body'?"

Andrew, to please him, said he doubted it and Billy yawned and put *The Courier* aside. "It's as plain as a pikestaff that the horse-drawn carriage as a means of transportation is done for," he said gloomily. "Now you take Charley Smithwick, when he was a little shaver he wanted to be a blacksmith and he spent more time with me than he did away from me learning my trade. He would have been a good man, but I never blamed him for throwing me over for Uncle Sam when it became the self-evident fact of the matter that the horse-drawn carriage was a gone goose. Charley, I am happy to report, has begun to rally. It is my conviction that he is one of the two or three people I have ever known who was worth his salt."

"When is he going away do you think?" asked Andrew.

"He oughtn't to go back too soon. He ought to lay around his mother's house for a good long time. Else how can he get the strength to become—as it is my full opinion that he will— the kingpin of the whole U. S. navy shebang? I am persuaded that within my lifetime I will see that young fellow bring his ship right up to headtide." The fact that Charles had neither received nor been ambitious for promotion was ignored by everyone, and he was called "the captain," "the skipper," and "the admiral" and it was believed by many in the town that his finger was on the pulse of the world. "You can't tell me," said Billy now, "that being right there on the spot in Tokyo and Shanghai and all that he doesn't know all there is to be known about this so-called Far East. But he's tight-lipped even with me, his tried and true old friend. He knows a lot he can't put out."

The eulogy went on and when he began, "I'll take my share of credit in the molding of that young man . . ." Andrew surreptitiously leaned toward the radio and concentrated on the phrenetic pops and ululations from Canada. When he ended, "You mark my words," Andrew sat up straight again.

"So the former *Empress Katharine* has come to the Bay," he said, "and her Ladyship has got the pip. My, my, there's a lot going on in the world. A lot more than meets the eye, and a lot of it that don't bear too close examination, if you get my meaning."

"I don't get your meaning," said Andrew nervously. "I don't get your meaning at all."

"Well, you know, like I said, there was a lot that Charley knows about those Chinamen and Japs that he's not telling every Tom, Dick and Harry. Well, everybody's got something like that, haven't they? Not so important but something to keep in the dark all the same. I bet if you were of a mind to do it, you could tell me a good deal I'm mildly—*mildly*, I repeat—curious to know. Why lights are burning in the middle of the night or whatever."

"I could tell you a thing or two about Charles Smithwick if I wanted to," said Andrew.

"What about Charles Smithwick?" demanded the black-smith, clenching one enormous fist as if he were looking for a fight. "Be careful how you talk about Charles Smithwick."

"Oh, just about what's going to happen to him one of these days," said Andrew and ducked out the door and ran up the hill toward Congreve House. He had turned in at the gate before he realized that he had not mailed the letters.

He debated whether to go back now or to wait until after lunch. Seeing Cousin Katharine feeding the swans and not looking in the least unwell, he decided to wait and to spend the time now trying to find out why she had behaved so eccentrically. He hailed her, and she greeted him warmly. If he had had any idea of broaching a serious subject to her, he had to put it aside. She would talk of nothing but the downy woodpecker fledglings that this morning had at last flown out of the nest down near the summerhouse.

There was one thing though that, detective-like, he noticed: there was a long slim glass of pernod on the iron tea table and when she had finished with Helen and Pollux, she began to drink it, not in sips but in big swallows. He had never seen her drink in the middle of the day before. He wondered if, all of a sudden, she was going to become fast and cut her hair and even dye it. He half wished she would. But there was not even a suggestion of a crack in her façade and when she saw him looking at her apéritif, she said, "I was longing for Paris today. Nothing brings it back to me more clearly than this delicious drink."

"No," Andrew said to his importunate twin who had been asking too many stupid questions; "I will not take you there again because there is absolutely no point in eating alewives. You can go by yourself if you want to."

The twin business had begun to bore him, and there was no end to this day in sight. At lunch, each time he had opened his mouth to say that everyone in town knew that Cousin Katharine had stayed up all night and that the *Empress Katharine*— called now, horror of horrors, *La Paloma*—was in the harbor seven miles away, someone had interrupted him. Finally he had moodily asked to be excused before dessert and ever since had been lying in the hammock drafting in his mind a series of black-hand letters to be sent to Charles Smithwick, Billy, and Honor who, at lunch, had called him a gasbag though the fact was that he had not got a word in edgewise. He had not gone to the post office but had put the letters in his bureau drawer and had told himself that he would mail them when he got good and ready.

He watched Brantley Wainright-Lowe pegging along the road in shorts and a tennis visor and he saw Miss Duff, dressed in a mechanic's coverall and a baseball cap, riding past on her motor-bike to hunt for bargains in summer squash and hand-hooked rugs. "Rockabye, is it, day after day?" she hollered and was gone with a threatening pull at her police siren. She disliked boys and declared that they did nothing but crack their knuckles and ask each other riddles. "Pop! Pop!" she would say to him on meeting him in the road and give him a hard look. "When is a door not a door? Really!" He was too busy with other things today to resent her implication that he was a lazy and overgrown baby, though he filed it away to consider later, for he had found that slights and insults often served to distract him from his deeper grievance; for one whole day he had been sustained by Honor's charge that he handled his knife and fork like Mutt.

He turned over in his tree-hung cradle, his back to the road, and gazed upward at the lightning rods and the broad arched doors of the barn; the iron whale was veering east. As he watched, he saw Cousin Katharine come round the side of the house, her arms full of lilacs. She appeared and disappeared behind the sweep of columns as she approached the door and then for a moment she stood framed by the two central ones, looking into the rosary opposite where she had perhaps heard a bird, so motionless and tall, placed so symmetrically that she looked to be a part of the house itself, like the cool, impassive statue of Minerva. Today she wore a full skirt of yellow linen, a tucked white blouse with wide sleeves that were inflated with the breeze, and a ribbon crossed at her neck and pinned with a cameo; her white hair rose from her forehead in a high pompadour. She listened for a moment and then she turned and though she looked directly at him, she did not call or wave or smile, seemed not even to recognize or see him. He was non-plused by this preoccupation—or was it displeasure? He was accustomed to preoccupation in his parents and lately this had been their usual role, but not in her, *never* in her for her great-est virtue was that she immediately welcomed and attended anyone who came within her orbit. For an awful moment, there flashed preposterously across his mind the thought that she really *had* read his wicked thoughts and knew he wanted Charles to die (at night before he went to sleep, he could not help it, he kept seeing Charles's bloody, decimated body strewn all over the highway and he was sometimes paralyzed with fear that he would talk in his sleep) and she had stayed up all night long writing to his parents to tell them that they should lock him up somewhere before it was too late. He knew a boy, Teddy Throckmorton, who was only one year older than he who had gone berserk, out of a clear sky, and had threatened a cook or a maid or someone with a straight razor and had been taken away to an insane asylum. At Sewell it was rumored that he was in a padded cell and that he ate out of a bowl on the floor like a dog.

Possibly he was going crazy; it was possible that he would kill Charles without even intending to. He'd better read a book, he thought, or his mind might do something dreadful, and he picked up *Life on the Mississippi*. Over the top of it, though, he watched his cousin. She went in in a minute, closing the front door softly so that the knocker would not sound, but the image of her there persisted, poised perfectly in the exact center of the stage. Or like a judge at the middle of his long, legal pen, sentencing the prisoner to death.

> "I sent thee late a lilac wreath,
>   Not so much honoring thee,
>   As giving it a hope, that there
>   It could not withered be,"

sang Honor; her voice was reedy and clean, as pellucid as a shallow, amber pool. She sang and stopped, unable, perhaps, to continue with her paraphrase or asked, perhaps, to put the lilacs into water. The house was silent. At the back of his mind,

Andrew heard Poor Hollis ring the bell for three and heard the insatiable gulls caw hoarsely over the refuse from the smoke-house. He continued to stare at the expressionless face of Congreve House and at the after-image of Cousin Katharine. *Did* she know? Did she know that as he lay here hour after hour under his great-grandfather's elm trees he wished and prayed for the death of someone who had never done him any harm? Together with the fear and the guilt and the dismay at his atrocious inner nature, there was a kind of obscene pleasure in it and he thought how he might most dramatically blackmail himself by writing an anonymous letter to her, telling on himself. "Madam, you harbor a serpent of the male sex," he would write and sign it with a skull and crossbones.

The more he thought about it, the more convinced he became that all last night she *had* been writing to his father about him. The letter had been very thick. He was not sure that he would ever mail it.

He turned from Charles to Cousin Katharine and back again, living through the afternoon. Alternately he stared at the house and stared at the road. An hour passed. He saw Beth, pregnant, wearing her kittens like saddlebags, adroitly mount the Dutchman's-pipe to her mistress's windows and just after the bell at St. James's rang for four, its last note loitering and dissipating then in a spray of fading echoes, the owner of this belvedere appeared, assisted the cat and called down to Andrew, "Will you take me out to get a water lily for my spittoon?" and vanished, letting the vine fall back into place like a curtain.

She must want to get him alone to give him the third degree. His heart was as loud and jazzy as a dance band, but he got up and called back as naturally as he could, "Sure! Now?" and she reappeared in a blue silk wrapper. "I'm changing for a swim. I'll meet you there. Just you and I, no little girls allowed."

The twins, hearing this interchange, came to the downstairs windows and Harriet cried, "As if we cared!" and Honor happily caroled, "As if we'd get our hair all wet when Raoul is coming!"

"Beth will go with us," said Cousin Katharine, coming again to the window. She had always taught her cats to swim. When he came to think of it, Cousin Katharine was awfully peculiar;

he had always before taken her for granted but suddenly he no longer did. Why, for example, was she so attached to such old-fashioned pastimes? The game of patience while she drank her tea if she had no visitors; the simple needlepoint; the making of potpourri with sun-dried rose petals; the outmoded customs of reading poetry aloud, and mounting butterflies on pins. She even smelled old-fashioned, of some fastidious, countrified scent (Maddox made it for her from an arcane receipt) no more conspicuous and no more nameable than the general sweetness of a rural garden just come into bloom. She moved in a nebula of this and of dove-gray chiffon or lilac lawn, regarding the works of Robert Browning and the Roman poets through a shell lorgnette or watching the birds which she described in a black ledger with a thin gold pencil, rejoicing in them all except for the puffin which she found absurd and the cowbird which she deplored on moral grounds. The cat was always doomed from kittenhood to wear a bell of piercing tone.

If insanity ran in the family, who was she to have him put away?

For a moment, he was inexplicably exhilarated and he set off at a run, taking the longest way through the meadow, a field of timothy full of daisies and nests of voles and stands of wild iris. A bright snake flicked past him and he ran after it and though he could not catch it, he shrieked in the direction of the kitchen, "There's a snake here, Mrs. Shea!" Instantly, like a jack-in-the-box, the woman rose from the steps and vanished into the house, slamming the screen door behind her to finish her Hail Marys trembling as she stood upon a chair. Maddox, who was clipping the box beside the stable, paused and laughed unkindly and at once resumed his look of sullen disapproval. "If you throw any more rocks at my Seckel pears, I'll snake *you*," he said sourly.

Honor came to the dining room window to scold, "You're mean! You're a beastly boy and you'll never go to heaven. You tell Mrs. Shea there wasn't a snake."

But he cried back, "I was only telling the truth. There *was* a snake. There are millions and trillions of snakes in the grass." He stood still, his eyelids burning in the sun, and chanted, "Grass snake, water snake, bull snake, viper, red snake, green snake, cobra, adder." But the joke, like all jokes these days, palled and he sighed and his smile faded. No prank seemed worth the effort when there was neither confederate nor claque. Morose again, he plodded on.

When he had changed into his swimming suit in the damp bath-house (he hated it here; it was tiled like a public lavatory and daddy longlegs ran on stilts up and down the slippery walls) he sat in the tippy rowboat waiting for Cousin Katharine, carelessly startling two young turtles that were sunning on the rock at the lake's edge; their place was taken by an enormous butterfly that shuttered its pansy-yellow wings three times before it flew away. He plucked the beggar's lice off his socks and swaying the boat lightly as if he were still in the hammock, he crooned, "Charles Smithwick, die, oh, Charles, get well, oh, big fat nitwit, Charley Smithy, go to hell for leather."

A stream of images like a motion picture passed before his eyes. Charles was swimming off the dangerous rocks at Pemaquid and a squall was coming up; under the darkening sky, the phosphorescent spindrift shone; it was a sinister sight. Charles was too far out! He could not get back! For the third time he went down! Months later, flaccid and fishbelly white, the body was washed to shore sixty miles south at Kennebunkport. Then: someone was ringing the bell in the firehouse to summon the volunteer brigade and the cry went up through the streets of Hawthorne, "It's the Smithwick house! It's going up in flames!" Beulah was in the sewing room at Congreve House, sewing a fine seam, and Victor was at the store, but Charles was in his bed in the burning house and he died before the marshal came. Charles Smithwick ate a poisonous mushroom. His lifelong enemy stabbed him through the heart. His mother, mistaking the bottles, gave him iodine instead of Castoria and he writhed to death before the doctor had even finished cranking up his car. As they were leaving the graveyard, Victor said to Andrew, "Let's go smoke."

He was frightened again and when Cousin Katharine came down the path, he bent his head, pretending to be tying his sneakers. She was wearing a long red linen cape over her bathing suit and a straw picture hat that tied under her chin, making her look not much older than Honor and Harriet. Her cat came trotting after her, mewing conversationally, her high tail waving like a plume. She leaped neatly into the boat to sit squarely in the middle, winking her shrewd eyes.

For a long while Cousin Katharine said nothing significant. Under the white sun of summer as he slowly rowed her from this archipelago of lily pads to that, he listened to her casual stream of talk, but at the same time he followed the paths of the blue devils' darning needles that skated through the reeds and watched the holiday fishermen try for bass; once someone in a red motorboat got a strike and Andrew rested his oars to watch the catch. The struggling fish arched angrily as it twisted through the air and when it was landed, Cousin Katharine clapped her hands and cried, "What a sight! Oh, what a day!"

But on a day like this, he and Victor should be fighting with the valiant bass (his new flies, ordered for his birthday from Abercrombie and Fitch, had never been taken out of their cellophane wrappings) and automatically he looked across the water in the direction of the Smithwick house, but all he could see of it above the trees was its single solid chimney from which arose a line of smoke as narrow as a pin. And then, a minute later, from far off, he heard Victor's lighthearted approach and Cousin Katharine said, "It's a pity your friend hasn't a quieter talent. Couldn't we teach him to juggle? It would be just as droll as yodeling and it would disturb the peace far less."

Hating Victor, Andrew cut the water deeply, wounding it, and said, "He'd juggle if Charles told him to," and under his breath he went on, "He'd suck eggs if Charles said suck eggs."

"Yes, he is devoted to his big brother, isn't he?" said Cousin Katharine. "I don't think he's been to our house once this summer."

"He'll never come to our house again. Not as long as I'm there anyway."

"What a ridiculous, unworthy notion. Someone has to look after Charles."

"They could hire a nurse."

"And what would they pay her with? You shouldn't say such selfish things, dear, they make a bad impression. And you should remember that Charles can't stay forever."

"Charles *can* stay forever," said Andrew grimly, gouging the water. "And he will."

They were near the end of the lake where the water petered out in a marsh beside the road and when he glanced up, Andrew saw Victor just rising over the top of the hill on his way home; from his wide-open mouth the yodeling poured copiously like something from a pitcher. Cousin Katharine waved and called, "Hello! I hope your brother's well today," and softly to Andrew she said, "Do you suppose it's related to gargling? I must try it some time."

"Hello!" cried Victor exuberantly. "Charles is okay. He went out in the yard."

"Splendid! Give him our fond regards."

Enraged, Andrew set his jaw.

"You got the cat with you?" bellowed Victor and when Cousin Katharine assured him that Beth was there and if he looked closely he could see her flattened out now in the middle seat, taking the sun, he slapped his behind with the magazine he was carrying and shouted, "Oh, boy! I hope she don't get seasick."

"If she does, we'll give her Mothersills in her cream."

Tee hee! Ha ha! Shut up, said Andrew to himself, shut up and that goes for your damned old brother too. Not very long ago, he had heard about a man who had got a cactus spine in his finger that worked itself into his blood stream and finally got to his heart and killed him like a poisoned arrow. It wouldn't be hard at all to send some cactus spines in a black-hand letter.

"Won't you come for a row with us?" asked Cousin Katharine. Victor shook his head and flippantly replied, "No, thank you kindly, ma'am. I got to get this Albert Payson Terhune installment to my brother p.d.q." And beginning to yodel again, he marched on quickly, swinging his arms as if he were doing calisthenics.

Andrew turned the boat and doggedly rowed on. "The Smithwicks are a touching family," said Cousin Katharine. "I hope the chap recovers. If anything should happen, if Charles should die, I think poor Beulah would die herself. She very nearly did when her husband was lost at sea." She was speaking of the terrible shipwreck, before Victor was born, that had cost the towns of Hawthorne and Bingham Bay eighteen lives. He did not look at her for fear she was looking at him.

"Perhaps we should take him strengthening things, calves'

foot jelly and beef tea and all those other things in books. Do you think a bottle of my father's best burgundy would restore him? We must go and call on Charles one afternoon, you and I. It isn't Christian not to cheer the sick."

Andrew, feeling very sick himself, smiled politely. "I hope Charles gets well soon," he said.

For a short space of silence, he kept his eyes averted from his cousin's regard which, nevertheless, he could feel upon him like the silent, examining scrutiny of Dr. Townsend to whom, last winter, he had lied about the pain he had; and exactly as the doctor had finally touched the flaming spot in his right side and said, "Here, boy, you do your part and I'll do mine and between us we'll rout this bellyache," so Cousin Katharine said to him at last, with utmost gravity and sympathy, "Wouldn't it help to tell me what it is that's troubling you so terribly this summer? You can trust me."

Involuntarily, he relaxed as he had done when the doctor had seemed to enter with him into his pain and keep him company and even to feel himself the short, blazing dagger-thrusts of the diseased appendix. He remembered how then he had willingly answered all the questions. But a real thorn in the side was one thing and a figurative one another and his moment of ease was followed by deep distrust of her intrusion on his privacy. Grasping out of the air a plausible reason for his brooding, he told her that last year he had especially hated school.

"But surely I remember that your mother told me you liked it much better than before," she said earnestly. "Didn't contract bridge take the lower school by storm? And didn't Maeve tell me—I know she did—that you played every afternoon at Johnny and Allen Webster's house?"

He shook his head. It was true that half the boys at Sewell could think of nothing else but bridge last year and he had gone, twice, to the Websters' house but he could never fix his mind on the game, never was sure what was meant by "trumps" and after some *gaffe* that caused the other players to scream at him in rage, though he had not the slightest idea what he had done, he was expelled from the foursome. If his mother had said that to Cousin Katharine and had believed it, it showed how little she knew of the way he spent his time. When he did not go to the Public Library to read the New English

Dictionary, he prowled through Scollay Square, counting the sailors as his cousin counted birds, and in the doorways of abandoned buildings, smoking cubebs stolen from his mother's cook, waiting for the summer.

At first he said that it was Latin that had made him miserable (this was an outright lie for Latin was the only thing he had ever liked in school) and then he said, in quick succession, that it had been Chapel, History and Algebra. It had been Miss Bowman's interminable quotations from Poor Richard and *The Autocrat of the Breakfast Table* (the Lord knew Bowman was enough to set one's teeth on edge. He and the twins had long outgrown the need of a governess but she was kept on, combining the roles of housekeeper and secretary to Maeve although she did not relax her vigilance over the children; energetic and stoutly self-improving, she read hard books on economics and psychology and as she did so gnashed her teeth as if she lay on Procrustes' bed) and her insistence that he recite the Gettysburg Address immediately after brushing his teeth, night and morning, as an exercise in memory.

In a way everything he said—except his attack on Latin— was true and it all made far more sense than if he had said he was ready to commit suicide or murder just because some dumb country hick had never stopped to see his brand-new fishing tackle nor even whistled as he passed by. Victor had left no notes beside the lantern on the gate, he had not one single solitary time called Andrew on the telephone: he might *at least* have done that and still kept his eye on the invalid; they had sometimes talked for half an hour until other people on the party line impatiently snapped at them; Miss Duff once had roared, "Deputy sheriff going to hear about this. What if you're trying to get a doctor for an emergency and can't get through because boys are saying riddle me this, riddle me that until the cows come home?" They had retaliated by putting a ticktack on her living-room window when she was there alone on maid's night out and scaring her half to death.

"But there's no Algebra to stump you now," said Cousin Katharine, "and poor old Bowman is far away. Isn't it more that other thing you sometimes came to me about? That feeling at home you couldn't put your finger on?"

Of course! How could he have forgotten? But strangely

enough, as he began to speak of it, she interrupted him to praise the way he was so capably managing the boat with its dangerous keel and to direct him toward a far patch of floating flowers. And as if they had been engaged in nothing but small talk, she began to plan a picnic on Stork Island to which they would invite the Smithwick boys.

Rhetorically she inquired whether they should have whole lobsters or put the meat into sandwiches; should they color the hard-boiled eggs with beet juice in the old-fashioned way? And should they roast corn or should the meal be cold? Perhaps it would be a greater treat for the Smithwicks to go to Pemaquid; but she did not like the waters there, for there was no hope at all for a swimmer if anything went wrong. (His mouth was dry.) She wandered and lightly talked about the picnics of the past, beginning in a fairy-story way with, "Once upon a time, the world was a picnic and Maeve and I were allowed to drink champagne when we went to the Bois at holidays, taking innumerable hampers and silver spoons and tablecloths and chinaware. So cumbersome and so very elegant! The inconveniences, as they are called these days, didn't disturb us in the least. We were as gay as larks in spite of the fact that we had no paper plates and ate off the breakfast Quimper."

Her bewildered boatman rowed on, the recipient of her bright-eyed reminiscences and speculations, her prophecies and her stray, unprefaced facts that she interpolated without rhyme or reason; as they skirted round the smallest and the nearest of the islands, she asked him if he was aware that on a certain island in the British Virgins, the natives formally disputed whether God could laugh. Fastidiously and with close attention to its good points and its flaws, she rejected lily after lily like a woman shopping for a hat, and as they zigzagged back and forth, she talked continually, her even, undemanding voice lulling, taking him willy-nilly away from the sharpness of his discontent and his suspiciousness and even leading him part of the way into her remembered adult world. She told him about a cruise she had taken once with his parents to the Caribbean and she described to him the extraordinary fish they had seen and the sea birds and the strange plants with stranger names, the shake-shake tree and the fiddlewood and the monkey-can't-climb.

"I meant to tell you," he interrupted, "the *Empress Katharine* came into Bingham Bay last night."

"Oh, that makes me very sad. Don't tell your father when you write him. She meant so much to him."

"I know she did," he said and to prove to Cousin Katharine that he did know, he told her about one afternoon last winter when, after the tea tray had gone, he had established himself in a corner of the library to read his father's second-class mail. Though he was really absorbed in it, thinking how extremely useful a home elevator would be for someone like Miss Heminway in her wheel-chair, he could not help hearing a passage between his parents who did not seem to know that he was there. His father was standing before the case of yachting trophies looking down at his mother who was sitting on the fire bench with her head between her hands. His father said, "For God's sake, Maeve, *this* testifies that I have done something with my life," and he gestured toward the loving cups. And his mother answered so softly that Andrew barely caught the words, "Oh, yes, you were an emperor in your fashion."

Cousin Katharine frowned. "Has no one ever told you that eavesdropping is a vicious habit?"

"They weren't telling secrets. That's all they said. After that they had a drink and talked about whether they should go to Europe on a big boat or a little one." Actually, his father had said something else but he did not repeat it to Cousin Katharine because it had been so rude and it had been about her. He had said, "You've grown so like Katharine that half the time I don't know whether I'm talking to you or her. You are mad to imitate a manner that you perfectly know sticks in my gizzard. The infuriating *reasonableness* of it!"

Cousin Katharine smiled. "No, I suppose you aren't repeating anything you shouldn't, so let's forget it. Poor John! That yacht *was* a beauty." Now she saw the flower she wanted at the far back of the lake and as Andrew turned the boat toward it, stirring up a school of pickerel, she trailed her fingers in the water and began to talk again. "There is no water in the world as clear and clean as this. This is what Madeleine St. Denis envies us the most and I don't wonder because it seemed to me, when I visited there, I saw nothing but stagnant water. Louisiana was like something drawn by Doré, every inch of it covered with tendrils and naked roots and vines and that hairy moss hanging from the oak trees."

From their new position, Andrew could see clearly into the Smithwicks' yard and there, indeed, was a lengthy figure stretched out in a canvas deck-chair, the face obscured by a straw hat with a ruptured crown. Victor was standing on his head in the garden path. He looked as if he had been in that position for hours.

His cousin's self-supporting monologue went on. ". . . Like the stagnant water of a moat I remember in Chantilly. We drove out from Paris for Sunday lunch. I have never eaten such melon since. It tasted of the sun . . ."

Victor turned a back somersault and through the straw hat that capped the inert rope of flesh there came a booming voice, "Good enough, you landlubber you," and Victor patted his open mouth, favoring this time a war whoop instead of a yodel. With half himself Andrew watched the brotherly horseplay and the other half was drawn into the embrace of Cousin Katharine's voice.

"After the meal, in all ways perfect for a perfect summer day, our host and the other men practiced tight-rope walking in the park while the ladies of the party sat in a tree-house admiring one another's jewels. One of them had a golden cowrie shell in which she kept her heroin."

"*Honestly?*" he gasped and when she nodded he felt a quiver of delight run straight through him.

"While all this was going on, John took Maeve and me for a row around the moat. I can remember to this day the disgusting smells that came to us and how the oars dredged up the mud and brought to light the odious things that grow in stagnant water, a horrid, reptilian green. In some places we had to lie down flat in the boat when we went under trees that bent from bank to bank. Once John lost his balance and through some stupid accident, splattered your mother with his oar and totally ruined her velvet dress. It was no loss, really; we had agreed that it was a shade of violet that never suited her. But she was terribly nervy all that summer and when this happened, she burst into tears. She cried all the way back to Paris."

Now they had come to the lily of her choice and as she tugged at its snaky stem, the fascinated cat sat up to watch, thrust out a paw as if to help and then was quiet, her tail curled around her feet. There was to Andrew a new and exquisite quality in the air, a smell, perhaps, or the stillness of his cousin's sweet past life, or the foretaste of enjoyment, the source of which was undefined. In the end, the world might change and the cornucopia be filled again. The name "Paris" took his fancy, acquiring for him a dimension it had never had before and the words "park" and "moat" and the image of Frenchmen walking tight-ropes and of women sitting in a tree captivated him. He leaned forward in the boat and said, "What happened afterward? Did you show your jewels too? Did Mother cry in front of all the others?"

"Maeve went into the house to set herself to rights," said Cousin Katharine, dreamily, intent upon the elusive stem of the water lily, "and the rest of us had a *cassis* under a false sycamore that was bound round and round by a thick vine that corkscrewed up the trunk like the serpent going up Eve's apple tree. The *cassis* was made on the premises. It is odd the way one will carry off an isolated and prosaic fact like that from the scene of disaster. Why should I remember that Peter's *cassis* was made by his servants out of his own currants? There, I've got it!" Her eyes shone and she cradled the lily in her hands, showing it to the cat. "A prize, isn't it, Beth?"

"What was the disaster? Did the tree-house fall down?"

"I shouldn't have said 'disaster,'" she said, "because the ruin of a dress hasn't quite got that stature, particularly for the bride of a very rich young man."

"Oh, was that all?" He was disappointed.

"Yes, but actually there was more to it than that, for she found out the next day that she was going to have a baby—or babies, as it turned out—and that was what had put her so on edge. I shall always remember the taste of *cassis* when I think of the day that the Shipley children were first announced. John and I toasted her in vermouth *cassis*, for our host had given us a bottle of it to bring back."

His interest flagged and he turned again to the boys in their desultory garden. They were so near the bank now that when Charles took off his hat, Andrew could see him clearly. He was quite as unusual-looking as Victor but in a different way; he had a flattened nose and his eyebrows were black although his

hair was the color of sand. His forehead was a gleaming bulb
from which that strange stiff hair rose straight up like a tall
lawn. He did not much resemble his pictures because his illness
had whittled him down to the bone. Beulah said his legs were
rubber and his blood was water and he hadn't the strength of
a newborn babe. If he stayed out too late in the dewy evening,
he might catch a chill and die of double pneumonia.

Charles began to read his magazine; the parrot wandered
out the door and stood, laughing privately, beside the canvas
chair; Victor turned a clumsy handspring and seized his wrist
and howled with pain.

"Who told you the *Empress Katharine* was in?" his cousin
asked suddenly.

"I can't remember," Andrew said. "Everybody knows everything in this town. Maybe it was Mr. Barker and maybe it was
Bluebell James. They all knew your light was on all night."

Cousin Katharine shivered. "Go back," she said. "I'm nervous about this boat."

He knew enough not to ask her a direct question and
docilely he attended to his own business, turning the boat
once more and cutting off the pantomime of the Smithwicks'
contentment. He felt again the clutching void of summer with
nothing to look forward to except more of these long, long
days fading gradually into the gloomy winter. He wondered,
without caring a pin, whether his parents, in Dublin now, were
any gayer than they had been when he had seen them last,
sitting far apart in the back of the car, as it took them to the
station for New York, looking, as Honor had said, as if they
were going to a funeral.

"They make me furious," she said. "*We* can't not answer
when we're spoken to so why can they?" and Harriet said, "I'm
glad they're gone."

As soon as the car was out of sight, the house had seemed
to shake itself from a deep sleep; from the maids' sitting room
had faintly come the sound of a victrola playing "On the Sunny
Side of the Street" and Hal, the choreman, covering the furniture with muslin shrouds, began to sing "Santa Lucia." The
children waited in the ghostly drawing room for Alfred to
bring the car back from the South Station and take them to
the North and all at once all three of them, for no other reason

than that it was summertime, began to laugh. He thought of the silent house, shut up against the sun, holding the hush in its halls and niches and he wondered how he could ever be happy there again. Or anywhere until he was old, at least as old as Cousin Katharine. Much farther away than Ireland, more indistinct than dreams, his bemused parents seemed irrevocably gone. He said, "Supposing our house burned down or supposing they decided never to come back again, would Honor and Harriet and I live with you?"

"Andrew!" She was shocked. "The house *can't* burn down, they *will* come back. You must be careful what you think or it may happen! You must be careful what you wish for when you are young for you may not want it when you are old. What if we heard when we got home that your house *had* burned down? Wouldn't you feel as dreadful as if you'd set it on fire yourself?" He did not reply.

Now they had reached the little pier and Cousin Katharine, gently laying the flower in a mossy cave at the base of a tree, waded into the water for her swim. Knee deep, she turned again, "This must be a secret between you and me, but I'll tell you what I was doing all last night. I was planning the most wonderful party we have ever had. We shall have dancing and champagne, but the chief thing will be fireworks. Not the noise-for-noise-sake ones, for those I hate. But fountains and wheels and roman candles. Skyrockets and beautiful blood-red Catherine wheels."

As if she were descending to a bed, she entered the water; in her mild wake came Beth.

"What is a Catherine wheel?" asked Andrew.

"A spinning rack," she called. "A stupendous round of sparks. Some of them look like rose windows. They're gone before you know it."

"Was that really what you were doing, Cousin Katharine?"

But he did not believe her when she said it really had been. For a while they swam in silence and then, still silent, they climbed up the path to Minerva's temple where Mrs. Shea had left glasses and a bottle of cold birch beer. They sat on the marble benches that encircled the gigantic, helmeted goddess, sipping the herbal brown drink with the summer day lying all about them; there came, to their heedless ears, through the topaz atmosphere, the sound of the rowboat dipping in the meek south wind. The careful cat dried herself and washed her violet-veined ears.

This afternoon had been a series of multitudinous beginnings that had come to nothing; now the sun had illuminated everything, now all was dimmed as a shadow intercepted the halo of June. Was this talk of Catherine wheels and lobster sandwiches nothing but a blind under the cover of which she was seeking his central, pertinacious sin? She had said *you must be careful what you think about or it may happen, you must be careful what you wish for.* Drawn to his obsession, he could think of nothing else and in this quiet and in this nearness to her, omniscient, judging, he could not help it; he said, "Do you think you can make somebody die by wishing for it? I mean, like a dog that had bitten you? I mean like using those dolls the way they did in *The Return of the Native*?"

"You must *not* say these things. You must *not* think these thoughts! Believe me, no one in the world is so detestable that you should wish him dead."

"I was thinking about a snake I saw in the meadow," he said.

"I know you were! I know it!" Her voice was flooded with relief and to his terrible embarrassment, he saw tears standing in her eyes. Perhaps it *was* true that she was sick and hurting somewhere. But while for her sake he wanted to be purged of his vileness, his interior voice went on and on relentlessly, "Charles Smithwick, die, die, die."

They went single file back to the house, Andrew in the lead. Cousin Katharine came fragrantly behind him, her cat on her shoulder, her water lily like an offering in her hand. She was so tall behind him! Her female shadow enveloped his; she was looking right through the back of his head and reading everything that was written there. When they reached the front door, the cat leaped, purling, from her shoulder and Cousin Katharine leaned against the lintel for a moment, bending her head forward as if to kiss his cheek. She did not, but the mass of her hair swept over his eyelids softer than snow.

"Oh, Cousin Kate, shame, shame!" came Honor's taunting voice. "You're showing preference!" She stood at the foot of the stairs holding a pair of ballet slippers by their ribbons.

"If Bowman ever hears that you baby the boy, she'll send you straight to Coventry."

"Be quiet!" Cousin Katharine put her fingers to her lips and bade the children listen; in the pear tree at the entrance of the picking garden, a thrush was singing; when the intricate and formal song was finished, Cousin Katharine clapped her hands. "Bravo!" she cried. The children were infected by her cry and shouted in unison, "Encore! Encore!" until they were hoarse. Andrew snatched one of the ballet slippers from Honor's hand and running halfway down the lawn he whirled it like a boomerang and let it fly off to land in the dead center of the hammock. They raced for it through the sunlight, but even the whistling in his ears did not drown out the voice and even as he put the length of the long lawn between them, he knew that Cousin Katharine knew everything. Her eyes were inescapable. He was inundated by a wave of scalding anger and reaching the hammock first, he grabbed the ballet slipper and threw it into Honor's face. She was so surprised that she only looked at him.

"I think you're going crazy," she said. There was hardly any outrage in her voice. She seemed to be stating a fact. He did not trust himself with her and turning, without apologizing or refuting her declaration, he ran like the wind down to the orchard and when he was at the farthest part of it, he stopped and screamed.

CHAPTER IV

The Late Wedding Ring

A LETTER from John Shipley was waiting for Katharine when she and Andrew came back from the lake. In its thin, square European envelope, it lay on the table in the entrance hall, and though she changed the water in the cuspidor and took her time, painstakingly posing the lily so that it lay oblique to the burnished valentine of its pad, and though in this procedure, her hands were steady, she was invisibly assaulted. Her hands, moving with such deliberation that this might have been the creation of a masterpiece upon whose laurels she was to rest for the remainder of her life, in her imagination mauled the letter, and more vividly than she saw the chaste flower, she saw St. Stephen's Green and him upon a bench, writing to her, using a book as a desk, the opal mist of Ireland and the sweetness of being in love hanging between his faculties and the red-haired children playing among the beds of public flowers.

Importunate at her elbow, Harriet said, "Aren't you going to open Daddy's letter? Please open it and see if he promises to bring us the plaid raincoats."

Katharine shook her head, said she was busy as Harriet could plainly see and the girl, respectful but still impatient, fingered the foreign postage stamp and asked, "Then may I open it and read it to you?" With the unkind prerogative of the person in charge, Katharine severely changed the subject and more sharply than she meant to, she said, "Go up at once to dress. Honor is ready, why aren't you?" Wounded, Harriet ran upstairs without a word, but at the top she leaned over the banister and said, "I'm sorry I was nosy, Cousin Kate."

There were several further domestic interruptions before she could go to her room. Maureen had come in an excessive flood of tears to confess that she had broken a sugar bowl, not valuable, not pretty, and Katharine, aware that the girl for some time had been "carrying on" with a profligate and married lobsterman, feared that this undue display over nothing at all meant, perhaps, that she was pregnant and that in the midst of upheaval and revolution, a husband would have to be found for her. But for the time being, she refused to think about it and comforted the girl by saying that she would deduct a dollar from her week's wage. Mrs. Shea, wringing her hands and almost weeping, had reported that "the boy" had frightened her with a tale of a snake in the meadow and she could not, would not, therefore, cook fish for dinner, the bellies of mackerel being what they were, Miss Congreve knowing how she felt. She revised the menu, endeavouring to keep a rasp of exasperation from her voice. Then Maddox had appeared at the windows of the dining room to announce, sepulchrally, that his prize Dr. Van Fleet rose bush, a new and costly importation from Long Island, had been mortally felled by the blacksmith's dog whom he begged leave to shoot. Aggrieved by her refusal, he added reproachfully that a band of village children who had come to gape at the peacocks had littered the lawn with empty Walnetto boxes and gum wrappers. And Harriet's feelings were hurt and Andrew . . . Once more greeting her father's eyes, when at last her household let her go, she recalled his solacing precept, "When you are unsettled, consider yourself *sub specie aeternitatis.*"

But the strength she gained from his advice failed to serve her when she read the letter from Dublin in which John's consideration of the two of them under the aspect of eternity lacked, she could not help but feel, responsibility and compassion, was rash, was honest (bull-headedly) and unethical.

The only anachronism in you [he wrote] that I find fault with is your caution. You once called it your "indeciduous Puritanism" (how like you to use a botanical term) but I beg you to name for me any people more incautious than the passionate men of Salem. While I deplore their violence, I honor their conscience and conviction, and while I deplore the cruel act you and I must commit, I love what makes it necessary. In obedience to you, I have taken this trip, prolonging my agony and Maeve's, and nothing has changed. My decision is incontrovertible and this dissembling is torment. There are times when I am close to anger with you. Yesterday we motored down to Tara and because the day was clear (the only one we've had so far; the rain has not improved my state of mind) we could see the whole of Ireland from the summit—or tell ourselves we could—like the assembled kings and poets and when Maeve innocently said, "If only Katharine were here! This is the sort of panorama that she loves," I leaped down her throat. I snapped, "Is it some special virtue in Katharine? Wouldn't anybody in his right mind love this view?" She cried when she defended you. I tell you this to show you how wretched I am, so cantankerous in this deceit that I am driven to attack what I love above all else in life. Will you not summon me back?

But in a sober postscript he wrote:

Do not imagine that I do not have doubts. There are days when I am suicidal, thinking of the children for whom I've done nothing, to whom I shall now do much worse than nothing. And I say to myself, "This is their last happy summer." I hope they are the happiest they have ever been.

Stripped of the integument of middle age, John Shipley stood before her, twenty years old, and for one callow, callous moment, she leaned on him, abiding by his decision, a yielding woman trusting a man's strength. But then, miserably, she thought of Andrew and of the lures she had thrown to him. He had seemed to rise to every one of them, though she could not be sure. She could be sure of nothing, only that he bitterly hated someone but whether it was his father or herself, she did not know.

Within a child there lies an unforgiving heart, she thought. So then for a child, must one repudiate one's victory and love and life and go on existing in a state of need? John Shipley, in his anarchy, would say no, and the world would say yes, but in the end it was not John's place to answer the question, it was only hers. And she could not answer it now for she must change for tea and put upon herself an air of insouciance with which to confront her friends who had said that she was ill. She was ill but not as they imagined. In the boat with Andrew she had heard herself saying things she never meant to say (no one should ever know except herself the envy that had grated on her when she had learned that Maeve was pregnant); she could not bear to think that any fiber of her will could relax and she was afraid it had already begun to happen and that the ganglion of her being was beginning, slowly, to atrophy. It would take strength to live through tea.

Before the first caller came—Mr. Barker in his debonair Mercedes—she wrote a note to Boston to order the fireworks for her ball, a mixed assortment, she instructed, with a pre-ponderance of Catherine wheels. As she looked through her address file for the name of the novelty shop she knew would send them to her, she came across the name of the stonecutter who had made Minerva and later had designed her father's tombstone. Under his fig tree in his own backyard and under the aspect of eternity: what peace awaits us all!

2

Old Mr. Barker, who wore a monocle, handed up his cup to be refilled and to the St. Denis family he said, "You fellows needn't tell me that in Dixie you've got any gardens that will put these in the shade. Even in a drought—and we had one last year to make you think of the Gobi—the gardens of Congreve House are a veritable paradise."

"Hear! Hear!" cried Edmund.

"Isn't it wicked?" cried Mrs. Wainright-Lowe and in elaborate mock indignation, she shook her dimpled fist at the roses climbing up the stable wall.

"Wicked is the word," echoed the old man, still addressing the Southerners who, as if they had been relegated there by reason of their being newcomers, sat a little apart from the regular Tuesday callers on the rim of the pond. "You take my word for it, this seemingly good Christian woman says incantations when the moon is full and does her plantin' when the Widow Smithwick's crystal ball gives her the go-ahead sign."

Edmund guffawed and nudged his son who rebuffed the gambit and became absorbed in lighting a Turkish cigarette. The decadent aroma drifted on two thin blue membranes of smoke, a European smell, a smell of snug cafés, bringing to Katharine a burst of fragmentary memories of morning conversations in Rome and Venice and Madrid in the middle of sight-seeing (how rapacious for churches and galleries and historic houses she and Maeve had been!) and bringing, as well, a bittersweet nostalgia for those cities and the hopes they had held, round every turning, from every yonder elevation, before the intimations of one's immortality had ceased. Those ascending days of loving girlhood, long, long before Maeve's ball which, a few minutes before, she had told her company, to their exclamatory delight, she meant to duplicate in August. She was committed, having allowed the twins to run back to the house to write down the event, permanently in ink, on the Phillips Brooks calendar that listed, otherwise, only the probable date of Beth's *accouchement* in July.

On either side of her, Maeve's copies in their lavender dresses watched Raoul, lips parted, innocently preying. She wondered which of them would engage him in an adolescent holiday flirtation—Honor, audacious and piquant, or Harriet, serene and soft. Their resemblance to their mother today was so remarkable that even old Miss Heminway who could barely see had spoken of it, saying, "You can't miss your alter ego when you've got her double strength, right here." Katharine tried to catch Raoul's eye to see whether either of them had succeeded, but Mr. Barker, following in Edmund's raffish lead, winked at him through his owlish eyeglass and Raoul deliberately looked away and up at the weathervane on the barn.

She was touched as she had been earlier when she thought of Raoul by the youthful intermixture of his nonchalance and his uncertainty, this arrogance with which he refused to join his elders in their buffoonery that was united to the humility with which he examined his surroundings, praising the house and the swans with his large, heavily lidded eyes and remaining silent except when he was asked a question. Rebellion, intellectual or filial, had caused him to obliterate his Southern accent but a soft, slow trace of it remained. His father's diphthongs, on the other hand, and his inflections were as pronounced as Mr. Barker's Mississippi valet's, to such an extent, indeed, that after they had met him for the first time the twins, imitating him between convulsions of glee, had said, "You *didn't* think you'd marry him! You couldn't have!" But in the days when she had thought of marrying him, he had no accent either and she remembered a time when, angry with his father for something else, he had burst out, "*Will* you, for God's sake, sound your final consonants?" The whole family had rocked with laughter and an aunt had cried, "Does he mean something like Gabriel tootin' on his final horn?"

Miss Duff, Hawthorne's unofficial and undisputed dragoman, was presenting to the St. Denises a lengthy dossier on the Widow Smithwick, on whose advice Katharine presumably did her gardening, and on the Smithwick boys. She dwelt at length upon a theory that she herself had arrived at, that Charles had sprue. ("Rampant in the Orient, I'm told, sprue. Funny name.") Katharine, having ascertained that her other guests were occupied—Miss Heminway with talking in an undertone to Harriet who had now to leave off casting sheep's eyes at Raoul, Mrs. Tyler deep in conversation with Brantley Wainright-Lowe on the subject of cesspools while his mother and Mr. Barker affirmed or emended Miss Duff's statements—busied herself in a needless shifting of pots and caddies on the tea table and retired into the state of mind in which she had stumbled and floundered since the evening before, finding in it, on reflection and now that the crisis was past (one crisis anyhow), a certain excitement and even an attractiveness like something romantically forbidden, like certain kinds of pain which one should not enjoy but did—opium-eating perhaps, that imperiled the spirit but quelled the pain. Though it had disturbed her deeply, John's letter was, in the end, no more than a letter and *sub specie aeternitatis* it was even less than that, only a sheet of paper hastily inscribed.

Protected by that thought and by her guests and by her duties to them, the last flickerings of her agitation had gone. There lingered only a vague dread of the possible return of her dislocation which resembled, she now decided, her conception of death. She was sure that no one saw or sensed any change in her and in this she took a healthy and mischievous pleasure and even bent her head to smile as she thought, "If only Mr. Barker could see my nightmare!" Such must be the needs and the dangers of addicts of alcohol and thievery and setting fires, cleverly hiding their macabre manias to relish them alone. She glanced from guest to guest and thought, "Not one of them guesses that I have had glimpses of a morbid world hidden beneath my reason and my senses."

But a gust of wind rippled over her white skirt and chilled her although it came from the south and was warmed with the sun: her eyes had fallen for the first time on Andrew who sat distant from the terrace, cross-legged on the lawn, his back to the party, presenting to her the long nape of his neck. His still, rejecting attitude alarmed her, and she realized now that earlier, when she had been talking about the party, he had not joined the discussion although, since he had been the first to hear of it, she would have expected him to aid and interrupt her. Had he really repudiated her? What else could explain the indifference of a boy of twelve to fireworks? As she stared at the small, heavy-headed boy, the wheel began, in the dark vault of her heart, slowly to revolve.

Terrorized and longing for the climax of her terror and knowing that her longing was obscene, she disciplined herself, she could stop the wheel; she took a deep breath and she held a whispered conference with Maureen, deflecting the nameless experience by concentrating on the tepidity of the water in the Guernsey pitcher, and telling the anxious girl for the fifth time that the sugar bowl she had broken was not of the slightest consequence. Surreptitiously looking at the watch pinned to the bosom of her dress, she saw that she must endure for the better part of an hour and as invisibly as she had departed from them, she returned to her guests. Miss Duff's discourse on sprue was long.

Dressed in umber from her trowel-shaped hat to her imported German walking shoes, Peg Duff graphically itemized the symptoms and the sequelae of the disease which she had read that morning in a medical encyclopedia. There was no possible reason for her to imagine that this was Charles Smithwick's complaint, but there was a general predilection in Hawthorne for the out-of-the-way or the archaic or the unlikely. Since no one specifically knew what he was suffering from (the doctor would not say through over-scrupulosity and Beulah did not say perhaps because she knew how much her patronesses enjoyed guessing) and the most obscure diseases had been proposed: yaws, fluke worms, psittacosis, dengue. Actually, they were all quite sure that it was only malaria but this they would not admit; they would have looked on that as too banal to discuss. And the ordinary was not Hawthorne's line.

They enjoyed discussing termite mounds in Africa, witchcraft, medieval *fin amour*; they could exchange receipts for sillibub and mead and directions for domesticating crows. And although they were staunchly Low Church and daily read *The Book of Common Prayer*, they also studied their horoscopes, took seriously Beulah Smithwick's Delphic screams, believed in ghosts and spirit rappings. Mr. Barker's house was haunted by the shades of seven aborigines who left their burying ground in the forest several nights a week to take turns sitting in a creaky Boston rocker in his upstairs hall. The Wainright-Lowes, who were not imaginative, often heard the clank of chains. It was not entirely unbelievable that Peg Duff was sometimes troubled out of sleep by the cry of a moose cow that she had shot out of season, a felony for which Yankee Doodle Lafontaine had been obliged to hale her into court, to the delectation of the whole country, three quarters of whose population had come to the trial.

It was Katharine's father who had started this vogue, peopling his house with an august body of ghosts to whom he had given names from the novels of Thomas Hardy which he much admired; and Katharine, continuing the mythology as an essential part of Congreve House, had early taught the Shipley children and her servants to distinguish them one from the other by the sounds they made as they shuffled and padded through the attics and promenaded up and down the stairs, troubling the country quiet with their sighs and their soliloquies. Michael Henchard came to pity himself, running his stick along the balustrade and to make a sound like the cracking of nuts. And the room where Maeve had used to sleep was occupied by Eustachia Vye who knew no rest at all and wept and beat her breast until the cocks began to crow. At lunch today Honor had said, "I heard Tess rummaging through the sea-chest where you keep the croquet set," and her twin, not to be outdone, said, "Jude had a frightful night."

Fondly Katharine watched her ancient playmates nibbling sandwiches. Their appetites were nearly as huge and simple as those of the village children who came in their Sunday best of linsey-woolsey knickerbockers and huckabuck shirts and of ruffled, rumpled organdy and tin barettes, to spill ice cream upon themselves and cry, not for the damage to their clothes, but for the loss of a single drop of food. And she thought how extremely pleasant her life of compromise among them all was and how extremely careless it would be to give it up and go to live in Mangareva; she knew herself sufficiently to know that she would never find in breadfruit trees a substitute for elms and she did not think that John could reproduce Merrion

Square in palm thatch. She could not (it had been lunacy ever to imagine it) leave for naked Polynesians these vivacious creatures, brimming with gossip and personal style, loving to quote from Dr. Johnson's dictionary, perpetually happy because their work was finished and all the demands upon them had been withdrawn and they were married to their houses and their habits and their infirmities.

Miss Celia Heminway, for instance, a dry wisp lost in her wheel-chair, talking with such animation to Harriet, seemed, at this moment, to be absolutely indispensable to her. And because she knew that she was indispensable to Miss Heminway, she almost leaned forward to squeeze her crippled hand. Miss Heminway, who had read widely and was especially conversant in the novels of the nineteenth century and the memoirs of the court of Louis XV, depended upon Katharine's eyes, since her own had faded, to read passages of Saint-Simon, at which she would laugh so hard that she had to extract a handkerchief from her little beaded pocketbook to dry the pink corners of her eyes. "Trust Katharine to find that *mot* again for me!" she would cry. And Mrs. Wainright-Lowe trusted her to be an unfailing source of information on birds, and Mr. Barker relied on her to be, in his own words, "a bijou *par excellence.*"

She could not leave any of them, certainly not this heavenly and preposterous Miss Duff who, having disposed of sprue, was now delivering Hawthorne's pronouncement on the St. Denis choice of summer resort. Bingham Bay was the sort of place that catered to tourists with tearooms upon whose walls hung studies in water color of the Bristol lighthouse and with antique shops that sold, as well as china broody hens, the bone and raffia produce of Japan. It was a false, expensive, loud-mouthed mecca for *arrivistes* and Miss Duff said, "Bingham Bay is unspeakable. Can't think why people in their right minds go there. Bar Harbor even worse, on a grander scale. Will fight day and night to keep hoi polloi out of Hawthorne. Can't have people mousing around in emeralds and not enough clothes." The two beagles that always attended her looked up lornly and she gave them each a piece of cake. "Went over to the Bay on my whizzer this afternoon to get booze—don't use any of their shops except for martini mixings—and saw John Shipley's boat. Two big, half-naked blonde tarts for every one of those slinking Cuban men. It made me good and sore."

It would be out of the question to move out of the neighborhood where Peg Duff lived or where lived this beaming, baby-round and baby-bald old Mr. Barker who, having rejoiced in Peg's performance (no one had ever been able to determine whether or not she was a conscious comedienne) now returned to his earlier tribute to the gardens of Congreve House and asked her to let her friends in on the secret of her "horticultural sock-dolagers."

"The secret isn't mine," she said. "It belongs to Maddox and he'll guard it with his life. My father used to claim that he was the son of a sorcerer and a sorceress and quite possibly he *is* and quite possibly he does say abracadabra by the light of the moon." She paused and wishing still to draw Andrew into the circle, she said, "Andrew, do you know what Maddox does on moonlight nights?"

He heard her and he shook his head but he would not turn around and Edmund St. Denis chuckled, "Man at work. Do not disturb."

"He bays the moon," said Honor, cheeky for the benefit of Raoul who looked at her and smiled faintly. "What does it mean, *to bay the moon?*"

"Merely to bark," said the literal Miss Duff. "Doubtless comes from the same root, only a transitive verb in this case."

"Well, then he doesn't bay the moon," said Honor. "He stews newts' eyes in brine."

Miss Heminway drolly shook her finger at Honor and to Katharine she said, "It shows the goodness of your heart, Katharine, that you let that cynical minx live with you. Do you know that last week, in this self-same spot, she told me—in a most defiant tone, I must say—that she doesn't believe in stars or ghosts. She says there's no such thing as levitation. To hear her talk, you'd think she thought her elders were insane."

"I do too believe in ghosts, Miss Heminway!" the girl protested. "Why do you think the croquet set is up? Because Tess made me think of it, rattling the balls in the sea-chest half the night last night so that I couldn't sleep. Do you play croquet, Raoul?"

Poor Harriet, minding her manners, continued to smile and nod at Miss Heminway who, after her badinage with Honor, resumed telling an amusing but interminable story about some prank in her distant girlhood. But Katharine could see that Harriet was glancing nervously and angrily out of the corner of her eye at her sister engaged in this unfair campaign.

Raoul shook his head and his father gave his shoulder a push. "Then go and learn. No time like the present." And he smiled a conniving, match-making smile at Katharine who, taking pity on Harriet, ordered all the young to go and play a round of croquet. The blond, long-limbed boy got up and ceremoniously bowed to everyone while Andrew, his back still to the company, went on ahead down the arching pergola. Everyone turned to stare at the children as if youth were a curiosity not to be seen every day and Miss Heminway sighed, "Like something by Renoir. Those little girls, those lovely, lovely little girls." Their black hair lay free and long across their shoulders and as Edmund St. Denis followed their light and laughing retreat, there came to his rubicund face, in which the slovenly flesh sagged away from the bones, a look of hunger and regret, as if at last he had begun to remember the world of possibilities whose welcoming portals he had been too timorous to enter.

"What wouldn't I give to be that fellow's age!" cried Brantley Wainright-Lowe. "Smoking Egyptian Prettiests to impress the girls, what? I say that's the life."

"He's too young to smoke at all," said Raoul's mother. "But the young are not as young as we used to be."

"It's not really smoking when those fancy brands are involved," said Wainright-Lowe. "It's just living up to the ad, 'Be nonchalant: light a Murad.' And I repeat, I'd give my worldly goods and all my expectations to be a kid again."

"I wouldn't give a farthing," snorted Mr. Barker. "I like being old. Would you want to be sixteen again, Katharine? Sweet sixteen and never been kissed?"

She shook her head and gasped, as he expected her to do, and said, "Lord, no! What an appalling thought!"

Peg Duff said, "I was a tomboy then and I'm a tomboy now. Never wanted to be kissed, never have been kissed. Like things just the way they are."

"Oh, so do I!" agreed Katharine and she meant it; she would like to have this peaceful hour go on and on, with the sound of the twins' carefree laughter and the cracking of the wooden balls coming to her, like a testimonial of security, across the sunny lawn and with these true friends around her offering her and each other their respect and their uninvolving love.

"This is the most beautiful house I have ever seen," said Madeleine St. Denis and she gazed upward reverently.

"It is also charmed," said Mrs. Wainright-Lowe. "Congreve House has always had a charmed life. The Congreves never have water trouble, to name but one of their divine rights. When the rest of us are buying Vichy water and bathing in the lake, these favored people are lolling in their tubs like Roman senators."

"Found a mouse swimming in my well this morning," said Miss Duff and patting the dog on her left, added, "Spotty killed the bad old mouse after I ladled it out, didn't the spotted doggie?"

"As the mistress is, so is the house," said Mr. Barker who was a little deaf and had not heard Miss Duff's unseemly revelation. He looked at Katharine, infatuated. "Could a queen live anywhere but in a palace?"

"She's got no servant problems," said Mrs. Tyler, a stout old widow famous for her inability to keep a cook longer than a month and equally famous for trying, always unsuccessfully, to steal the cooks of her friends. "Are you aware, Mrs. St. Denis, that this genius gardener of hers simply materialized one day twenty full years ago and has been here ever since? I'm lucky if I can get a high-school boy to come and cut my lawn."

It was true that Maddox had, as Mrs. Tyler said, simply materialized one day in the rose garden when Katharine's father was spraying his prize bushes. In the full tide of noon the strange boy had stood stock-still and breathing in the perfume of the profuse flowers he said, "I'll work here." No one ever knew where he came from nor what his antecedents were; he had a faintly Nova Scotian accent and his coloring was Scotch. Celibate and unsociable, he was interested in nothing but flowers and shrubs and trees whose Latin names fell unaffectedly from his lips although he could not read or write. She wondered again what he did so late at night in his room in the stable and she knew that unless she snooped and spied, she would never find out, for he was a private man, as private as a child.

"To say nothing of Mrs. Shea," said Brantley Wainright-Lowe, "and Maureen and that other little Irish smasher," and it was impossible to tell whether his leer, a constitutional property of his jerry-built face, was meant for Katharine or her blue-eyed maids.

"It's no virtue in me that Maddox and Mrs. Shea stand by. He is wedded to the gardens and she is wedded to the house. Where would they go if they left me?"

"I'd take them in a minute," said Mrs. Tyler who lived in one of the ugliest houses in the town, a sepia shingled warren beset by rank spirea and shaggy bangs of wisteria that blinded every window. "If you ever give up Congreve House, will you give them to me? Hear, everybody, bear witness, I'm first bidder."

"Give up Congreve House?" The indignant cry sprang simultaneously to the lips of the five other Hawthorne citizens and by their glares they set the greedy infidel beyond the pale.

"*Give up Congreve House!*" Miss Heminway's was a cry of pain. "What *can* you be proposing? If Katharine Congreve gave up the house, I'd have a warrant out for her arrest before you could say 'knife.'"

Shamed, Mrs. Tyler snickered unhappily and Katharine soothed them all. "Perhaps I can find another Mrs. Shea for you. But I shan't give up Congreve House. I shall be buried here 'under my own fig tree in my own backyard.'"

"That's the sort of thing we mean about Congreve House and Maddox and all the rest of it," said Mrs. Wainright-Lowe to the St. Denises, personally envious but publicly proud. "There really is a fig tree beside George Congreve's grave. It is put to bed in the winter in a contraption comfortable enough for a person to be buried in."

"Ceremony twice a year," said Peg Duff. "Bedding down of the Congreve fig tree in the fall, ascension of the fig tree in the spring. A movable feast, to be sure, depending on the frost."

Small silences fell as the western sky began to redden. The tea was tepid and the cake was gone and there was no reason for them all to stay except the reason for which they had partly come; not one of them had broached the subject of her lamp that had burned all night. And finally, as if she were rewarding good children, she said, "I could not sleep last night."

They clucked their tongues as if she had given them a piece of news. "I was planning my party," she said. "I was making lists."

"Oh, lists!" exclaimed Miss Heminway, to whom the making of lists was tantamount to a vocation; now, because her hands were stiffened with arthritis, it was a labor but it was still a labor of love. "I, too, would far rather make lists than sleep. But I so seldom have a legitimate one to make." Her voice was plaintive; she seemed to look back on halcyon times of inventories.

Now that the matter was out in the open, they all gave themselves away. Mr. Barker said he had thought she was reading *Gone with the Wind* and Mrs. Wainright-Lowe said she had accused Peg's crabmeat Mornay and humbly asked pardon and Peg herself said that she had concluded Kate imagined that she smelled fire, the notion having lodged in her mind earlier in the evening when they were all looking at the cactuses.

"Glad it was nothing worse than lists," said Mr. Barker and winking at Mrs. St. Denis he said, "I'm the lowbrow here. *I* read *Gone with the Wind*. In fact I ate it up." He signaled to his chauffeur at the foot of the drive, and now the prolonged adieux began and the exchange of invitations, the apologies for drinking so much tea and eating so much cake, the reiteration that this day was beautiful and that the rest of the world did not know what it was missing by not living in Hawthorne, the admonition to Katharine that she must not stay up again all night. Miss Duff was the first to go, striding down the drive like a soldier, loudly ordering her dogs to "March!" Presently only Edmund and Madeleine were left. Madeleine, disliking the thought of a boat trip to their island off the coast at Bingham Bay after dark, went around the house to take her son away from the croquet game and when she was gone, Edmund said, "You are a wonder, Kate. You haven't changed at all."

"Oh, no, I haven't changed," she answered. His wistful scrutiny broke her heart. His jowled face was mottled with the sort of colors, mauve and washed red and yellow, that appeared on picture postal cards from Venice. "*Not* changing is my only occupation."

"I think your fuddy-duddy old friends are grand. I think *you're* grand." He crossed the terrace to sit beside her and he said, "You ought to have married, Katharine."

"But if I had married, then I might have changed and changed in a way you wouldn't have liked."

"Maybe so. Still, I think . . . I'm going to speak freely, Kate, we're old enough friends for that, it seems to me. I'm going to say what's on my mind and tell you that you ought to have married me."

The impropriety was so unexpected that she could not reply but could only stare at his soft pink mouth, much smaller than she had remembered it to be. But he did not expect a reply and he went on in the same downhearted voice, "A man doesn't really know what he wants until he's forty, but why should the poor devil be penalized just because he was brought up wrong, too damned ignorant to know that nine times out of ten the woman he marries is never the woman he needs?" It was a gross and platitudinous burlesque of John Shipley's protestations, and the man was neither better nor worse than John in his effort to struggle out of his boredom and his disappointment in himself by pleading with her to build him a castle in Spain and take him on a magic carpet to the end of the rainbow.

"A man needs a woman to inspire him," he said. "A woman can make or break a man. I am not implying that Madeleine has 'broken' me. Madeleine wouldn't hurt a fly—maybe that's just the trouble, maybe if she had put up a fight on some issue or other, I wouldn't feel now that the starch was out of me."

The piteous, self-conceited jeremiad went on; he bent his head, staring at his hands that he kneaded steadily. "I think I could have been a painter. I might even be able to paint now." (John could have been a Bulfinch, could be one now.) He did not look at her as John had not looked at her when he declared that he was in love with her. "I'm a married man, I've got a son, and I swear I've fought against this feeling, but I can't win. I knew the minute I saw you again after all these years that I shouldn't have rested until I got you to say 'yes' to me. We could have had a wonderful life together, you and I."

A loon cried in the reeds of the marsh and a single whip-poorwill prematurely began nearby in the meadow. She heard the children's voices as they came back through the pergola and then Madeleine's as she urged Raoul to hurry, "Please, son, I'm leery of the water after dark."

"You think about what I've said, hear?" Edmund lifted his head and looked at her and wanly smiled.

"The first thing I'll do is forget what you've said."

"Don't be like that, Katharine. Don't sound so angry. I surely didn't take you by surprise. You surely must have seen that I'm crazy mad about you."

Fatigue after the long night and the long day had been gathering for the last hour in her muscles and in her brain and she had to think of each part of the process of standing up and of saying to him, "Won't you have a whiskey before you go back?" The improbable exchange between them was as remote and indistinct as, suddenly, Edmund's face was; it seemed to fade to a wavering ectoplasm. She said, "I'm terribly tired. I didn't sleep last night."

"It sometimes happens like that," he said, his normal voice practical and self-assured. "You go through the day and then it hits you all of a heap."

Andrew came running across the lawn. The game, which he and Harriet had won, had lightened his spirits and he devoured the remaining sandwiches, having refused to eat anything before. "Harriet said there was a letter from Daddy. Are they going to Germany because if they are . . . Cousin Katharine? Cousin Katharine? Are you sick?"

Green clouds rose, layer after layer, for the sun-like Catherine wheel, the absolute, unburying itself and edging up behind the dogs' backs of tremendous waves. The inseparable mind sang in its bone-cell and she was wheeled outward swiftly and the purblind mind nosed like a mole through splendid mansions of ice-white bone and luminous blood, singing with the music of the spheres.

CHAPTER V

A Dream of a Dove

NO ONE in Hawthorne could remember a midsummer more comely than this. The genial rains fell in the night, spoiling no one's picnic plans or boating parties and keeping the wells and cisterns full. The elegant blue hydrangeas and the splendid lawns, sweeping downward to the river or to the lake, ripened coolly under the faithful sun. Everyone looked satisfied. People passing on the road in front of Congreve House whistled and sometimes sang and saluted Maddox in the rosary and Mrs. Shea pottering about the kitchen garden. The birds had never been more various nor voluble, fluting and trilling in the shrubs and thickets; on the lake, coots clucked deeply and two dapper cardinals came to live in the grape arbor. Cousin Katharine had to send away for another bird ledger because she used up the last page of the old one before July was half over. The bells, ringing for services and ringing for the hours, partook of this tranquil jubilation and their sound was woven into the fabric of the golden days. Even Mrs. Shea, a saturnine woman, was inoculated with the summer and in her singular good humour, she attended Beth in her childbed although heretofore she had never approved of cats, finding them wanton in their promiscuity with their own sons and grandsons; she accompanied the parturient purrs with "Lord Randal" and ordered Maureen to warm a bowl of milk for the brave mother who bore a litter of six.

For Andrew, though, the days lumbered on as slowly as they had done in June almost without incident. There had been one resplendent afternoon with Victor, but only one, so that afterward his loneliness was twice as great as it had been before. Cousin Katharine had got tickets to a circus for them and because Victor looked on an invitation from her as a command and also because Charles was on the mend and needed less attention now, he accepted enthusiastically; his spirits were obviously dampened when he discovered that Cousin Katharine was not going with them but he was mollified when she told Adam to drive them to the fairground in her carriage. All the way through town, Victor bowed and waved an imaginary hat and Billy Bartholomew looked up from his whittling and called, "You the personal representative of Lord Nelson?"

The circus was small and undistinguished but they saw a man eat a live rat and they had an instructive conversation with a hermaphrodite (Victor, though, was skeptical and quoting the everlasting Mr. Knowitall, Charles, said such people were fourflushers). They had seen a girl lion-tamer who was very skillful but who cared so little for her personal appearance that her dirty yellow hair was tied up with a shoe-lace and her bodice was held together at the back with a horse-blanket pin. They had ridden the Ferris wheel and had bought chameleons and Victor had won a swagger stick in the shooting gallery which he gave to Andrew to take to Cousin Katharine.

It had been exactly like old times, for after the circus they had gone to the smoke-house and, grimacing, had eaten their handouts until Victor remembered the rat the circus man had eaten and they had thrown what they had left into a can of gurry. They had gone to the store for tonic and had drunk it on the porch, watching and ridiculing the people who passed by, as much at home with each other as if nothing at all had happened and this afternoon had been preceded by others like it. Andrew tried to appear as casual as his friend but his laughter sometimes sounded hysterical, his praise was fulsome and he could not stop issuing further invitations to Victor who either refused or pretended that he did not hear. When Jasper Freeman had a fit beside the horse trough and the Black Maria came to take him home, Andrew laughed too loud though, in fact, he had never found the spectacle in the least funny and Victor told him frigidly to grow up. But Victor had been the one who had started it, long ago. Em Bugtown was on the loose, whining for Copenhagen from every passer-by, but Victor barely noticed her.

They went to call on Billy who, before he even said hello, read, "In Dumbarton, England, brides over twenty are married in sackcloth." An ugly stream of laughter jetted from his mouth and then he welcomed his visitors, pointed to a lard can full of cherries that they might eat and opening *The Northern*

Farmer, read them a joke. It was a dialogue dealing with the taciturnity of New England farmers and Billy read it with lugubrious solemnity:

"Morning, Si.
"Morning, Josh.
"What'd you feed your horse for bots?
"Turpentine.
"Morning, Si.
"Morning, Josh."

Two days later:

"Morning, Si.
"Morning, Josh.
"What'd you say you fed your horse for bots?
"Turpentine.
"Killed mine.
"Mine too.
"Morning, Si.
"Morning, Josh."

Andrew had thought it an excellent joke but no one at Congreve House had even grinned when he repeated it. He seemed, even in such small matters as the telling of jokes, to be doomed this summer to failure.

They had been together, as formerly, till supper time. They had gone home by way of the lake, plunging through Billy's unkempt field, littered with scraps of machinery and the foundations of outbuildings that would never be finished; in his shiftless garden, the lettuce, gone to seed, was as tall as cosmos and the cabbages were striated with the black tunnels of worms. The whole place, in the fading light, had the look of ruin and the sight of it made Andrew heavy-hearted. At the lake, they bathed their faces and took off their shoes and socks and then, with their feet in the water, they lay down, their heads pillowed on mounds of moss. From far away they heard the chug and whistle of the evening train going its leisurely way to Portland and presently the first star came out; automatically, Andrew wished on it, but he had the feeling, uncomfortable and deep, that even if Charles Smithwick vanished, things still would not be the same between him and Victor. He tried to question Victor about his brother's adventures as if he were interested but Victor said, "Oh, you know, storms and stuff . . . I dunno. You'd have to get him to tell you himself."

"Would he, do you think? Could I come and see him?"

"I'd like to ask you, but Charles is funny that way. I mean he says when he's telling a story two's company and three's a crowd."

There was no doubt about it, the son of a bitch had poisoned Victor against him. Three might be a crowd to some people but Andrew would bet dollars to doughnuts that Charles Smithwick liked big audiences for his boasting and his lies. He would bet anything that he invited every man and boy in Hawthorne except Andrew to lend him his ear.

Victor had nothing to say to him and all the way across the lake when Andrew was rowing him home, he yodeled. When he got out of the boat all he said was "See you in the funny papers."

Nothing had been recovered. The chameleon died soon and Mrs. Shea hardly reacted at all when he put its corpse on her missal; it was leglessness in creatures she objected to. Cousin Katharine had her picnic on Stork Island but Charles was sick again and he and Victor did not come, and so, instead of them, Raoul St. Denis came, bringing his house-guest, a brash seventeen-year-old dandy from Mobile named James Partridge, who had a mandolin and, inhaling, smoked Lucky Strikes, and who so swept Honor and Harriet off their feet that for days afterward they mooned and could not eat and when they were not writing in their diaries, stood looking at themselves in mirrors, stunned with foolishness. They wanted to fly a Confederate flag from the barn.

But while there had been no change in Andrew's life and the events of it had been little more than a way to pass the time, there was a profound and unnameable change in Congreve House that affected everyone and had begun, he thought, to take place on that remarkable day when Cousin Katharine, renowned for her stalwart health, had fainted on the lawn. Andrew knew why she had fainted; she had been overwhelmed by what her intuition had discovered to her about him; she had looked him in the eye and seen that he was a murderer. It was enough to make anyone pass out. There had been nothing he could do about it, for the die was cast and he could not silence the voice inside him that perpetually sentenced Charles to death.

From Cousin Katharine down to Adam, they all appeared, like Andrew, to be anticipating something; there was that sense of an impending storm which is a kind of taut quiescence or a sort of premonition of disclosure as if, at any moment, the firmament will be slashed open by the lances of lightning to reveal, if one's eyes are quick enough, the angels and the thrones of heaven. This mood was nothing like the stale blight of the winter past but had an invigorating element in it, so that while they waited, the members of the household were ceaselessly busy and even Adam, whose love of lounging was the principle of his life, stirred himself to build a doll house for a favored niece and to learn how to add and subtract on a Chinese abacus he had found in the barn. The twins were frequently fetched by Raoul and James in the latter's jazzy yellow roadster to go to rustic square-dancing parties or evening sails on the tourist steamers at Bingham Bay. And when she did not dine out, leaving the house in full and magnificent regalia at eight o'clock, Cousin Katharine entertained and though her guests were the same old ones and the evening's routine was the same—after dinner she played the virginals for a few minutes and then the company moved to the card tables except for Mr. Barker and Miss Duff who played a cutthroat game of chess—the air was gayer than it had ever been. One might have thought that Cousin Katharine, like Maureen and like the twins, was in love. But Andrew knew better. He knew that all this contagious gaiety was made up and what it was was really her fear of him. Often he woke in the middle of the night to hear her moving around in her room which was on the front of the house next to his and he knew that she was standing guard to see that he did not slip out of the house and down to the lake to row across and murder Charles in his sleep. Poor Cousin Katharine! It was a terrible secret for her to have to keep.

She talked continuously of the fireworks ball in August and the twins, who really did think she was in love (they always imposed their own state of mind on everyone around them), amused themselves by imagining that on that night a lover would appear and she would announce her engagement to him—that Ronnie Pryce, perhaps, back from Australia and less talkative now, or Max Pirsch who had had a dueling scar. However, she repeated whenever they asked, that the only thing special about this party was that it was to be unusually big and unusually elaborate but that it was to commemorate nothing more than another of Hawthorne's heavenly summers. She meant to establish it as a regular tradition, "an estival Thanksgiving," she said, "when we'll give our prayerful thanks for roses instead of pumpkins and phoebes instead of turkeys." The whole town talked of the party too and they assured one another that the fireworks show she would put on would be twice as sensational as any municipal display on the Fourth of July; Billy Bartholomew predicted that she would burn up the woods with her folderol but no one listened to him. There was an altogether groundless rumor that there was to be a set-piece of *Old Ironsides*.

Andrew, for his part, was not sure what she was planning unless she meant to send for the plainclothesmen to take him away that night. It was very clever if that was what she intended to do, for in all the confusion, no one would notice even if they handcuffed him.

The town talked also, rather less openly, of something else that had already happened at Congreve House, something that altogether baffled Andrew. For his unfathomable cousin had done the queerest thing of her whole life: she was having her tombstone made by a stonecutter in Thomas and once a week she drove over to see it as if she were going for a fitting for a dress. People of a sanguine cast of mind accepted her tossed-off explanation that there was nothing more morbid in ordering a tombstone than in making a will. Mr. Barker, in fact, thought it so excellent an idea that he considered having his own made and drafted several designs, but in the end he decided to be cremated and sent for illustrated brochures of urns which Cousin Katharine studied with him. "No one will make monkeys out of us when we are dead, eh, Kate?" the old man laughed. "We'll see to it that our houses are made in the style we are accustomed to."

But Mrs. Tyler, who was a pessimist, and Miss Duff, who was going straight through her medical encyclopedia this summer and whose thought, therefore, was largely dominated by disease (last year it had been the evolution of the automobile and Brantley Wainright-Lowe had said that if she used the word "carburetor" one more time, he would scream), connected Katharine's act with her fainting spell and a frequent absence of her mind. One day, Andrew, bearing a message from his cousin to her neighbor, had stopped under Miss Duff's open windows, drawn irresistibly to listen to the ladies' low-pitched voices, and he heard Miss Duff say, "Carcinoma of the breast or I'm a dead man, so it may be just as well she's getting ready. Must say I hate to think of Katharine pushing up the daisies, as they say, but when you're called, you're called and that's that and no two ways about it." Mrs. Tyler, who knew a thing or two herself, was inclined to suspect angina pectoris but, being shouted down by her friend, asked for evidence and was told, "Haven't got any, but have a distinct feeling. Usually right about these things. Knew about Dan Thornton's cirrhosis before the doctors did. Long before."

Honor and Harriet thought the tombstone a joke but it embarrassed them a little because they were growing more and more conventional. The maids and Mrs. Shea said she was tempting fate and Beulah Smithwick ghoulishly said, "If you ask me to run up your winding sheet, I'll refuse point blank."

Andrew did not know what to make of it and he was inclined to accept it as he had accepted all her other caprices (her manufacture of gunpowder, for example, and her passion, one year, for collecting swords), although, from time to time, he wondered if perhaps she did have some knowledge of her death, told her in a dream. (Miss Duff's theory was too ridiculous to consider for a minute.) Whatever her motive was, she had succeeded in doubling Andrew's interest in death, and he often went to stand beside his great-uncle's cedar-shaded grave, trying to imagine what the skeleton looked like and whether the shroud had rotted away; he roamed the churchyard at St. James's and he scrutinized the dead bodies of birds, slain by cats, of rabbits run over in the road and mice pinched to death in traps in the pantry.

He began to have dreams of Charles Smithwick from which he awoke in a guilty sweat and some of which propelled him into sleepwalking. He loved to think about these nightmares afterward although they terrified him at the time and one night when he woke to find himself downstairs in the library, he screamed, partly from shock and partly from astonishment at the phenomenal power of the dream that had physically carried him, sound asleep, all the way from his bed to this pitch-dark room. Cousin Katharine had heard him and she came downstairs to lead him back to bed. When she had asked him to tell her the dream, he could only babble incoherently but long after she had left his room, he reviewed its ominous details.

He had dreamed that he was in the picking garden hunting for Cousin Katharine's shears which she had dropped. The sun had set and the night was coming on; Congreve House was no longer white but was brown stone, domed like a museum. As he neared a great grille-work door, he saw Charles Smithwick, wearing a long beard, lying on the cement entry and when he tried to open the door to see if he were really dead, a black dog ran out from a shed and standing on his hind legs, bit at Andrew's neck. Then Charles, clean-shaven, loomed up over a little rise, carrying a gun and two dead birds. He called off the dog and came close to Andrew and he said, "We must not kill birds. I never kill birds," but he was carrying two and the gouts of their blood shone on his trousers. Andrew knew at once that Charles was both dead and mad, and in his wanderings through the house and grounds, he found the evidences of it everywhere, for it was the dead lunatic's whim to strew enigmas as he restlessly roamed, scattering them on the lawns, pinning them to trees, to walls or to the backs of chairs. In Minerva's temple, Andrew found one on the floor, its edges held down with stones, and it said, "I must have golden gold at once," and in the library he had pasted a banner over the front of the bird cage and this one read, "My coat of dove, my glove of deer." When Cousin Katharine had turned the light on, she had found him standing right there, beside the finches.

2

Not long before the fireworks party, Cousin Katharine and the twins went off one morning to the state prison where Cousin Katharine annually bought the handicraft of the convicts to give away as Christmas presents to maids and godchildren.

Andrew, alone in the house, was glum and when the summer's record for fair days was broken by a black rain that began to fall at noon and he knew his cousin and sisters would not be home in time for lunch, he settled into a monotonous dark mood. He could not put his mind to anything and his dissatisfaction made every act an effort of the will. At his lonely lunch, he had to think each time he carried his fork to his mouth and if he had not been careful, his water glass would have slipped from his insentient hand. He ate the peas on his plate one by one, maddening Maureen.

Afterward, he tried to read and could not; he put together a few pieces of a jigsaw puzzle but it was much too easy. He stared at each object that entered his range of vision as if he had never seen it before, but there was no excitement in his discovery, only a kind of dull confusion. That is, there was no excitement until it occurred to him to become a detective for the course of the next hour or so and, like Victor in the shut-up houses, examine his cousin's history through her belongings. He pretended that he did not know her and that he had been sent as a spy to her house; sniffing and prying and listening, he wandered in and out of the crowded rooms, lingering occasionally in the long windows to gaze out at the roiled waters of the lake. Once, for no longer than a minute, the sun came out, but the rain went on. "The devil is beating his wife," he said and his voice seemed not to come from him at all. He moved toilsomely, pausing to wonder what vagary had caused Cousin Katharine to buy or to be given a cabbage rose carved of bone and having no other purpose than to lie alone on an austere marble mantelpiece in a back bedroom; he debated which of the objects in the house were gifts and which were purchases. The milk-glass cuspidor, he knew, had been used for its intended purpose until Cousin Katharine had wrested it from a quiet old gentleman in Bath by staking ten dollars against it in a local election. From a Japanese friend of her father's had come the Samurai sword she used to prune the Dutchman's-pipe that grew over her windows; lopping and brandishing, she sometimes sang "The Volga Boatmen" in a stylish contralto to the delight of Miss Duff who generally came right over and stood below, watching. When Cousin

Katharine had finished, she called up, "I declare, Kate, you're more fun than a basket of chips."

He examined, in cabinets and miniature desks and lacquered boxes and in jewel cases, on hanging what-nots and in sewing drums the accumulation of four generations. There were banjo clocks and music boxes that played minuets; embroidered nightcap holders and stuffed owls; in nooks and turnings there were Chinese vases filled with petrified cat-tails and furry grasses as old as Mr. Barker. There were porcelain umbrella stands and trivets in the shape of ducks; there was a leather fire bucket and an artificial cedar tree of jade. In drawers, there were Japanese fans whose silk had rotted from the ivory stays, Spanish lace and Spanish combs, magnifying glasses mounted on bamboo. There were snuff boxes, camel bells, and scores of ornamental wooden boxes that contained the testimonials of moods and enthusiasms and friendships, ribbons and seashells and colored stones gathered for the sake of the gathering on beaches and along the banks of rivers; fragments of wedding cake in cheesecloth bags; scraps of Mechlin, of tribute silk, of tartan ribbon and tatted edging; sashes made of velvet, solitary chamois gloves, bald buckram waistbands. There were strawberry emeries and covered corks for bone bodkins and decorated darning eggs and cases for tapestry needles. There were marbles, jackstones, fish hooks, chessmen, golf tees, corks with silver tops in the likeness of Henry VIII and Theodore Roosevelt, water bowls from Chinese bird cages, a campaign button that pledged its wearer to vote for Grover Cleveland.

In the library, on a big round table, covered with gold-tasseled gray velvet, there were, behind the porringers and christening cups, a multitude of photographs of relatives and friends. Andrew and his sisters were there, immortalized in drooping bathing suits; each held a lobster by the tail and grimaced dreadfully although it was clear that the brutes were dead. His parents were present many times: on their wedding day they stood before the front windows of the drawing room in Congreve House and stiffly held up glasses of champagne; they posed on a beach before a dwindling Roman ruin with a company of men in collegiate-looking boaters and women in bucket-shaped hats. Several of the pictures showed them with

Cousin Katharine, ankle-deep in shamrocks beside the River Boyne, drinking tea on a steamer crossing Loch Katrine, strolling through the Arboretum on Lilac Sunday. In one of them, the two girls sat on the lawn at Congreve House, plucking the petals from black-eyed Susans to learn if they were loved or not and John Shipley, a book closed over his thumb, lay in the hammock, looking fondly down at them. "Get out of my hammock, you drip," said Andrew and turned the picture face down on the table.

Here in this room an investigator saw that the lady of the house did needlepoint but not for long at any time because beside her easel there was a table piled with books and magazines: she was reading, at this time, *Henry Esmond*, Bulfinch's *Mythology*, an old cook book, *The Illustrated London News*. Even if he had not known her, he would have seen that she did not keep her mind on anything for long, for on the other side of the easel there was a second table on which she had half finished a game of Canfield.

He edged slowly up the stairs, and considered going into his room to work on a model of the State House that he was assembling but then he remembered that he had run out of mucilage. Besides, the box of parts was in the top drawer of his bureau and he felt like a criminal each time he opened it because he had never mailed the letters to his parents that Honor had given him weeks ago. He had not read them after all, for he had not dared know what Cousin Katharine had said about him, but he flinched each time he saw the neat, stamped pile.

The loud, toneless rain shut out all the sounds from downstairs and he felt as if this were the middle of the night and everyone was asleep except himself. All the bedroom doors were closed and the long corridor was full of shadows and the smell of dank. He thought of exploring the attic, he thought of going down to the kitchen to tell Mrs. Shea some perfectly awful lie such as that his father was a Hindu convert and slept on a bed of nails, but Mrs. Shea was in a bossy mood today and doubtless wouldn't listen. And for a moment he thought of paying a call on Maddox but he gave up the idea when he remembered how short-tempered Maddox was on days when he had to stay indoors. Adam was gone with the carriage and the maids made him shy.

Aimlessly he went into Harriet's room and examined her collection of ceramic pigs. What on earth she had them for he could not guess; incongruous garlands of dainty flowers girdled their necks and their round flanks were branded with arabesques and hearts and some of them had gilded ears. She had an equally worthless assortment of souvenir spoons, some with heart-shaped bowls, others with bowls like shovels and like arrowheads; one had a mosaic handle and all of them bore some legend that could not possibly have meant less to her: St. Louis World's Fair, From Colvin to Emma, Niagara Falls. He looked at her closet full of dresses and her bureau drawers full of lace-edged underpants and all the scarves she never wore. A lanky French doll lay on a frilly baby-pillow on the bed. He picked up her Line-a-Day from her desk and finding that it was locked, he rummaged like a burglar through the jewel box and through the drawers again but he could not find the key. He did discover, to his mild titillation, a box of dark blue eyeshadow secreted in a handkerchief case. Finally he gave up and went into Honor's room, but her diary was also locked and the key was nowhere to be found. He wrinkled his nose with distaste when he found a piece of paper on top of her bookcase on which she had been canceling out the letters in her name and the name of the Alabama boy, James Partridge, to determine whether their relationship was to be one of friendship, courtship, love or marriage:

> James Partridge (courtship)
> Honor Shipley (marriage)

With her small fountain pen he wrote beneath the names, "Honor Shipley is a moron."

Kneeling at his sister's window, he singsonged, "Rain, rain, go to Spain, never come back here again. Rain, rain, go away, come back on another day." He repeated the jingles until the words lost their meaning and became no more than syllables. Then, tired of that, he read a little in a book called *The Language of Flowers* which bore the name Katharine Congreve in a childish hand on the flyleaf. He learned that mistletoe signified "I surmount difficulties" and that whortleberry, whatever that might be, meant "Treason."

Back in the spooky corridor, he mechanically opened every door on the west side—the huge linen closet smelling of pine soap; the bathroom with cold marble surfaces and the longest tub in the world and a mirror opposite so that while one bathed one could make faces at oneself, a far cry from Cousin Katharine's days in convent school when all the mirrors had been taken down from the walls on bath day and the girls had worn muslin shifts when they got into the water. How did the nuns themselves take baths, he wondered, thinking of his mother's cook's sisters whose habits looked to be a permanent integument like fur or feathers. Next to the bathroom was a storeroom filled with boxes neatly labeled "Kitchen Curtains," "Lamp Chimneys," "Coat Hangers & Shoe Trees." After that there was the sewing room where two ample-bosomed, wasp-waisted dummies, armless and legless and with a curved hook for a head, stood, sentry-like, on either side of the Singer; around the middle of one of them, he tied a girdle of bias tape; he filled a bobbin with green silk thread, wrote "Beware" with a piece of chalk on an old billiard table piled with bolts of cloth, and bifurcated the room with a tidy row of buttons, alternating black and white.

The last of the rooms on this side of the house was Eustachia Vye's. It was never used except once in a blue moon when an overnight visitor slept there. A long time ago, when he and the twins had still been very small and had needed the governess, it had been Miss Bowman's room and he remembered how, somewhat to Cousin Katharine's annoyance, she had converted it into a schoolish place, hanging up maps in place of Godey's ladies and substituting for the graceful little escritoire a sturdy golden oak office desk which she had had sent up from Boston, causing everyone trouble. There were no signs of Bowman here now. Indeed, there were no signs of anyone, for this was unlike any other room in the full house; it was swept and dead; its narrow, stripped-down bed had an air of final vacancy as if its occupant had been carried away to a coffin, as if it really were inhabited by a ghost beyond the need of any creature comforts.

And yet, by contrast, the open desk showed letter paper and a full inkwell, ready for a guest, and a vase of roses so fresh that they must have been cut that very day, stood on the top of a chest of drawers. Light books for summer reading were lined up between two square Chinese vases on the bedside table, Lear's *Nonsense Rhymes, The Memoirs of a Midget, The Green Hat.* Still in its wrapping, a cake of Pears lay in the soap dish on the commode and the towels on the rack were fresh. But the naked mattress and the frame of the bed, disrobed of its tester, were inhospitable; it was like a carcass picked by birds. He looked into the closet and found nothing there but an enormous empty hatbox from a shop in Paris. The drawers of the desk and the dressing table were empty; there was nothing in the sewing drum except a length of gray grosgrain ribbon, and on the shelves of a three-tiered what-not there was only a yellow pear made of wax with a hinged section in it, like a drop seat, which, when it was opened, revealed a minute crèche half lost in cotton.

And then his eye fell on a little box beside the vase of roses, a box that Cousin Katharine always carried with her, extracting from it lemon drops that she gave to children she encountered. She must have left it here, he reasoned, when she brought in the flowers, and though he found it peculiar that there should be flowers in this forsaken room, he found it even more peculiar that she had left the box behind. He had not imagined it had any existence except when she was making up to a child, just as umbrellas seemed to dematerialize between rainstorms. He opened the box to take a candy out and noticed, as he had not done before, that there was a photograph slipped into the inside of the lid.

It was a picture of his mother and Cousin Katharine as girls, examining the wares of a lace vendor before the doors of Chartres, and on the back of it was written, "Maeve and I buying scandalous lace gloves. M. in a black mood because of her eczema which is so severe that Sister Chrysostom thinks her skin may be permanently pitted." Eczema, how awful! Those horrid, pinky hummocks that often appeared on his own chin? He looked closely at the photograph again but he could see no mutilation of his mother's wide-eyed, lovely face. So tall that they dwarfed the lace vendor even in her high medieval headdress, the girls, hatless and wearing their dark hair in buns at their necks, gazed tranquilly into the camera, their arms entwined.

An arresting hypothesis came into his mind: if this Sister

Chrysostom had been right, he doubted that his father would have married his mother, because he could not bear disfigurement of any kind (he could hardly endure the sight of Honor whenever she had hives and when the three of them had had chicken-pox, he talked with them through the closed doors of their rooms and never once came in). In that event, he probably would have married Cousin Katharine who, then, would have been Andrew's mother. But would Andrew have been the same person? Would he have been born to Katharine on the same day and at the same hour of the day that he had been born to Maeve? And would he be standing here now in this little room, and would the rain be coming down so madly at this very hour if his father had married the girl on the left instead of the one on the right?

A distant, uncompleted trumpeting of thunder startled him and he looked out the window. The stable was directly opposite this room and in the gardener's room, he saw a light-globe burning. Immediately, as if at a signal, Maddox's face appeared; he flattened his nose against the pane like a child and scowled. The rain was heavier than ever, lunging against the windows and lashing the tops of the maple trees and making a swift muddy river down the drive. The gardens would be a mess and Maddox would not be fit to live with for a week. For a moment Andrew watched Maddox, who did nothing but glower at the ruinous downpour but Andrew felt as if those angry eyes had caught him red-handed in some wickedness and he moved backward from the window, hearing the grandfather clock strike two in the endless afternoon.

Taking the lemon-drop box, he went across the hall to put it in his cousin's sitting room, partly out of thoughtfulness and partly as an excuse to lie on the chaise longue, an article of furniture he liked next best to a hammock. Beth and her family of six blind, naked kittens lay in a basket lined with flower-printed cotton flannel; the mother cat stretched her neck to be petted and purred loudly, narrowing her perspicacious eyes.

If Cousin Katharine were his mother . . . Taking up this speculation again as he lay on the chaise longue and stared up at the ceiling, he presented himself with questions and problems as if he were taking an examination. Would Cousin

Maeve, in that case, be at the state prison today or would she be in Dublin, about to leave for France? Would it be Katharine who followed Paris styles and Maeve who wore what she wanted to regardless of fashion? He proposed a series of substitutions, imagined his mother in Cousin Katharine's little drawing room on Brimmer Street, serving tea to the boys from Harvard and, on other days, walking up to Mount Vernon Street to the Shipleys' house.

It was all unthinkable, really, because his mother would never *dare* to do the things his cousin did. It would never occur to her, for example, to take up Botany as Cousin Katharine had done for one semester at Radcliffe. When she bought a microscope and announced her intention of watching the sex cells of slime-mold conjugate, Mrs. Shipley had put her hands over her ears and cried, "Slime mold? For pity's sake, don't tell me what it is!" To use one of Bowman's favourite expressions, his mother had no "intellectual curiosity."

He changed his tack, pretending now that Cousin Katharine, as his mother, was the person she had always been and that his mother, as Cousin Maeve, was that rather vague, somehow always slightly worried, rather humble, faintly discouraging woman to whom he returned on winter afternoons. How much nicer it would be to go *from* her house to Cousin Katharine's instead of the other way around! He remembered a typical day last February when it had seemed to him that all the care-worn futility of being alive in the winter was crystallized in the person of his mother who, even while she accepted confidences and soothed tears and laughed at jokes, never gave herself up wholly but kept preoccupied with the mechanics of existence: her mind was always elsewhere—it was on the message that had come up from the kitchen that the alligator pear was bad, it was on the failure of the window-washers to appear, or the error in the address that Shreve, Crump and Low had printed on invitations to a party. If he came to her, bearing like a gift the intelligence that the word "hippocampine" meant "of or pertaining to seahorses," she did not ignore him and, in fact, she showed a considerable interest, but it was polite and after much too short an interval in which her questions were much too perfunctory, she was as likely as not to cry, "Oh, *dear*! I forgot to call the men about oiling the books," and to take up a pencil and write a note to herself; Cousin Katharine, on the other hand, would have written down *hippocampine*.

On that particular afternoon that came back to him today, he had gone to call on Cousin Katharine and had been wholly frustrated for she had to break her promise to show him a slide of tap water because, in the first place, an uninvited guest was announced, a doctor by the name of Codman who spent the time disrespectfully fingering the beard of a bust of Shakespeare and importunately telling Cousin Katharine that she ought to learn to drive a car.

And then, just after he left and they had adjusted the microscope, Andrew's father came. Failing to see his son at first, he said, "Well, thank the Lord, I find you alone," and then, "Oh, blast and damn—forgive me, Katharine—I left my briefcase in the hall. Would you get it for me, Andy, like a good chap?" He had drawn up a design for a guest house for Cousin Katharine, he said, and he wanted to go over it with her. When Andrew came back, his father commenced to shuffle through papers and to drum his fingers on the tea table and then he abruptly looked up and said irritably, "Do you mind if you cut your botanizing short today and go along home? I have only a few minutes to get through this business with your cousin." Cousin Katharine herself had let him out and winking at him just before she stooped to press her cool cheek against his, she said, "What a fusser he is! But since he's doing it for me free, I can't look a gift-horse in the mouth." He had been about to ask her where the guest house was to be and who were to be the guests who would sleep in it, but her manner hurried him and as he walked home through the cold, mean dusk, he felt cheated and scolded and he hated his father.

There was a dinner dress on his mother's bed and his mother was at her dressing table brushing her hair. "You're early. I thought you were having tea with Cousin Katharine and boning up on tobacco diseases. Wasn't it very gay there?"

"No, not very," he said. "Dr. Codman was there at first. And Daddy afterward. Just as we were starting to look at tap water."

"Tap water? What's botanical about that?"

"Bacteria," he said. "You probably wouldn't drink it if you knew what was in it. It's alive."

"Really? I never heard of that before. I wondered where Daddy was. Darling, you terribly need a haircut." She began to brush her hair again. "It doesn't matter that he didn't come home because there was no tea today anyhow. We're going out for dinner."

The purling of a pigeon on the roof came strangled down the chimney. The sound made him lonely the way the sound of a night train could do or the look of a dog staring through a window.

"I don't see why he can't let her come to his office at a regular time. Why does he have to spoil the slide she made?"

"But if it's only tap water, sweetheart, she can make dozens, can't she?"

"You wouldn't understand," he said but so softly that she did not hear.

He watched her in the soft and facile light that came from under the small pink silk shades that sat like parasols upon the crooks of two dead-white Dresden shepherd boys. From across the room he could smell her perfume; she smelled delicious, but she smelled like all her friends who bought their perfume on the Champs Elysées at the same shop and discussed the price of it, dispelling, thereby, half its magic. Cousin Katharine's, on the other hand, was brewed secretly by Maddox.

"Did she seem to like Dr. Codman?" asked his mother.

"I don't know. *I* didn't like him. He had a dead front tooth."

"I expect he could have that taken care of. Dentists are growing awfully clever. Did he do something offensive?"

He told his mother how the doctor, as he was leaving, ostentatiously reminded Cousin Katharine of the present of red roses he had brought to her and said, "An aspirin will help keep them. And be sure to cut the stems each day," to which Cousin Katharine replied with sincere thanks for his thoughtfulness. But when she came back after seeing him out she sharply fanned up the fire with the bellows as if she were attacking someone and said, "Cut the stems indeed! I know of nothing that annoys me more than to be instructed in matters I took in with my mother's milk. The curse of being female, Andrew, is that we must pretend to be quite incapable of grasping the self-evident."

His mother smiled to herself and said, "Kate would be

bound to take exception to that. What a pity." Putting down her hairbrush she began to look at her eyebrows in a magnifying mirror. "I'm sorry you had a dull tea and I'm sorry you and Cousin Katharine don't like Dr. Codman. I, for one, wish she'd marry him. He's a very good doctor."

"Marry Dr. Codman?" His voice was a squeal. The pigeon moaned again like something sick.

"Dr. Codman or anyone!" exclaimed his mother. "Anyone at all! It has gone on too long. Her solitude has gone on far too long and year after year she has grown . . . she has grown more unpredictable."

He was indignant at the thought of Dr. Codman eating the pears at Congreve House with that blue tooth and running his hand over Minerva's helmet as he had fondled Shakespeare's beard, and he said, "If she does marry him, you can bet your boots I'll never go back to Hawthorne."

"Of course not. Cousin Katharine would have a family of her own then."

The possibility of never going back to Congreve House, of being supplanted by another boy (first of all it would be a baby and he loathed babies) so depressed him that he closed his eyes and behind them he saw small pictures of things he might very well not see again; the fruit room behind the kitchen where Mrs. Shea kept her jars of tomato preserves and grape catsup and chowchow, a room with a country coolness and a country smell where, on hot days, Beth lay at full length as limp and insensible as if she had been killed. He saw the lake and the river and the pond and the marriage elms; he smelled an early apple, freckled with pink, that he had picked up from the deep grass.

Suddenly he said, "She won't marry him, I promise you. He's a hootnanny and she knows it."

"What is he? A *hoot* what?"

There was a rapid double knock on the bedroom door and Andrew's father came in, bringing with him the chill of the street and, so Andrew thought, an echo of the smell of the room on Brimmer Street, of Cousin Katharine's unique perfume and Dr. Codman's roses and the fire on the hearth. He nodded to his son and to his wife he said, "Your match-making was a fiasco. She has sent Codman away with a flea in his ear."

Mrs. Shipley put her forefingers to her temples and closed her eyes and murmured, "It isn't natural."

"It isn't your business whether it's natural or not," her husband said brusquely. "If she marries, she'll marry."

"We shouldn't be talking this way before Andrew."

Andrew picked up his school bag and started for the door. "I'm not a child," he said. "Why did you say all that about the guest house when you were really there to make her get married?"

His father straightened up and looked in the mirror at Andrew's reflection. He smiled and winked though Andrew was in no mood to accept such an intimacy. "I was killing two birds with one stone," he said, "catching two cods with one line." He laughed at his joke, but Andrew did not. He went on, "Sorry, old man, about that thingamajig you were going to look at. A frog's gall bladder, was it?"

Andrew clenched his fists and enunciating clearly, he said, "Botany is the study of plants. If frogs have gall bladders, which I doubt, you would look at them in zoology."

"They were going to look at tap water," said his mother.

"Jove!" said his father.

When he had closed the door, he outlined on it a skull and crossbones with his finger and for a moment he listened at the keyhole. His mother said, "What is it? Oh God, John, tell me what it is!" And his father answered, "Why, 'it,' I suppose, is nothing more than the inevitable changes that are taking place in you. And in me. Nothing to get stirred up about." And in a lighter voice he continued, "I meant to call you earlier but I got jammed up. I shan't be going to the Websters' tonight. My potentate from Indiana wants to see the sights." A silence followed and Andrew went upstairs, listening briefly at Harriet's door, but she was only conjugating *fero, ferre, tuli, latum*.

That story about the guest house had been a whopper. The only thing that had been built at Congreve House this summer was Adam's doll house for his harelipped niece.

They were so flat and limp, both of them, and reconstructing that dispiriting scene, Andrew decided that while he wished Cousin Katharine were his mother, he wished someone altogether different were his father, someone he did not know, and he wondered what the drowned Mr. Smithwick had been like.

If Cousin Katharine had married him, Victor would have been his brother? But would Charles also have been his brother? Now he was rattled and he pushed aside these philosophical experiments and gazed around the room, looking for something to do.

It was an excludingly feminine room. The painted furniture was French, thin-legged and daintily furbelowed; in the recesses of the windows there were two round tables on one of which stood a figure of Minerva, on the other, Venus. On the pearl-white walls, there hung six likenesses of Cousin Katharine, by six different painters; as a shepherdess, as a horsewoman, as a bird lover, a debutante, a bibliophile, as Marie Antoinette dressed for a masked ball. On the desk that had once been a spinet, there was a double inkwell made of Sèvres and silver and there was a mountainous supply of letter paper for her huge, incessant correspondence. Here was her black record of birds and here was her big diary. And here, as in the drawing room, there were the testimonials of her restlessness: another easel, smaller than the one downstairs, with needlepoint stretched on it and beside it, a low table over which spilled from the wide maw of her knitting bag the brilliant yarns of half a dozen unfinished sweaters. Her place in *Don Quixote* was marked with a letter from the Shelbourne Hotel in Dublin, addressed in his father's hand. He would have liked to read the letter, he would have liked even better to read her diary and he touched its plump covers and lifted it up to judge its weight. He took the two thin, closely written sheets of paper out of the envelope with its Irish stamp, but as he hesitated, he saw the cat out of the corner of his eye stand up in her basket and look at him alertly. His bad conscience made him shudder as it had done earlier when he had seen Maddox's face at the window and returning the letter to its place and putting the lemon-drop box neatly on the diary so that it was encircled by the signs of the zodiac embossed in gold, he left the room, feeling the vigilant cat's eyes burning into him.

The rain had begun at last to peter out, but it was still too sopping wet to go outdoors and the house was still dark and he felt like someone going crazy in a dungeon. He must keep busy or he might begin to scream, so he went up to the big attic that ran the length of the ell and resumed his examination of other people's property. A smell of squirrels and dust came from the old beams and hornets seethed sleepily in the rafters. His footsteps made the floorboards snap and a mouse sped through the maze of rounded trunks and wicker hampers, patched with the stickers, like heraldic emblems, of the half-mythical hotels of Florence, Athens, and Madrid.

Often in the past on just such stormy days as this, he had come up here with Honor and Harriet and had dressed up in the clothes left behind by people who had died or had left them to moulder because they were no longer in vogue. Against a trunk that had belonged to Great-Uncle George leaned a pair of snowshoes that probably belonged to Maddox; he put them on, skidding clumsily over the floor and rousing every small beast in the attic. Then he opened his uncle's trunk from which arose a smell of camphor balls and wool; under the withering tissue paper lay morning coats and dinner jackets and opera capes. Uncle George had been very particular about his clothes and he had gone annually to London to confer with his tailor for three weeks. Miss Duff said of him, "Best-dressed man on God's green earth." All the fabrics were old and soft to the touch; Andrew stroked a dark red smoking jacket with velvet lapels and heavily embroidered frogs. He took out a pair of white trousers and a blazer with broad blue stripes, a crimson foulard ascot and a canvas yachting cap and when he had put them on over his own clothes (he was swallowed up and he giggled idiotically to think how he must look) he began to look for a top or a pair of Indian clubs or something, anything, to distract him for the rest of the afternoon. He found a shuffleboard set that he deduced must once have belonged on the *Empress Katharine* and a box of lotto cards and a parchesi game. And then he did find a top in a carton that contained wooden curtain rings and the ends of birthday candles. It was a bright red one and when he spun it, it seemed to have a glad life of its own; it was bursting with energy and merriment and he hated to see it slow and begin to falter and finally to keel over and become again nothing but a shape in wood. He spun it over and over, endowing it with vitality, making it a being more substantial than his twin.

Andrew was in the entrance hall spinning the top when the ladies of the house came back. He saw them through the sidelights, his smiling sisters flanking his cousin who wore a white leghorn hat, tied down with an old-fashioned motoring veil; he slipped behind the bamboo screen, meaning to give them the surprise of their lives. But the top, unfortunately, was still spinning when Honor opened the door and he could see her, through the narrow slits of the wood, glance round, a little startled, "Fee, fie, fo, fum," she said. "I smell the blood of an Englishman." He waited, breathing shallowly.

"Ignore the Englishman," said Harriet and went into the library to put down her packages. "The Englishman has knocked over the trinity of Congreve House," she called out.

The top slowed, reeled and fell, the play gone out of it.

"Harriet!" cried Honor. "We'd better go see if the Englishman has been in our rooms. Did you take the key to your Line-a-Day?" And the two girls ran laughing up the stairs. He knew that in a moment when Honor found what he had written below her forecast of her love affair with James Partridge, rage would replace her lightheartedness and the infantile frolic would be over. So he stepped out of hiding to have, at least, the pleasure of fooling Cousin Katharine. She had her back to him, looking through a sheaf of letters in her hand, but she wheeled instantly when he said, "The Empress Katharine, I presume?" She seemed, she really did, not to know who he was. She stared into the dusky depths of the hall and the letters fell right out of her hand and lay at her feet in a perfect fan.

She was taken in to such an extent that she said "John?" and could not move. It was the most successful hoax he had ever perpetrated.

Honor ruined it as he had known she would do, flying downstairs in a tantrum, spluttering unintelligibly but doing it at the top of her voice. And then, to his astonishment, he saw that Cousin Katharine was angry with him too; she looked at him frigidly, freezing him solid, and without a word she turned and went upstairs. Skinned and smarting, at the dizzy peak of his restiveness and loneliness, he shouted at her retreating figure, "I hate you! I hate you all!" and savagely hurled down the top and while it spun he snarled at his raving sister, "You shut up or I'll kill you!"

CHAPTER VI

The Child in the House

B ECAUSE HER hands shook so, ostentatiously publishing to her mirror the dishevelment of her nerves, Katharine could not undo that knot of her veil and as if this failure were a catastrophe, she sank to the floor beside a window, still hatted, and tightly locked her fingers to stop their fidgets and tried, and failed, to cry. Even in extremity, she could not seduce a single tear from her eyes. She had misplaced her rose-colored glasses which until now had taken the place of the gift of tears, and because she was herself bedeviled without them, she saw in everyone the symptoms of decay.

Andrew, masquerading clownishly in her father's clothes, looming out of the palpitant light, had seemed instinct with crime, with an active immorality that transliterated his travesty into a threat. She had felt preyed upon. This time it had been necessary, such was the increasing delicacy of her inner balance, to show him, by refusing to take part in his harmless game, that she was angry with him. Just as she had been obliged, out of self-preservation, to berate him when his eye had fallen on Mangareva, so just now she had had to throw up a smoke screen of adult displeasure to conceal her staggered utterance of his father's name. It sickened her that she had cried it out but even more she was sickened by *his* tempestuous cry that he hated her. In the course of the punishment that must follow, and in his remorse, it was possible that he would forget her aberration and remember only his own misdeed.

But it was equally possible that he would not forget. One knew as much at twelve as one was ever going to know. Even more perhaps, since at that age one was still, philosophically if not practically, in a state of nature and could cleave through the toughest tissues to the heart of the matter. Certainly she had known, known even before she was twelve, how rickety was the scaffolding of her parents' marriage; she had proceeded from just such a slip of the tongue as she had made to Andrew a little while ago, to the knowledge that her father had a mistress. It had been through some process infinitely more direct than logic, something instantaneous and unquestionable, that she had perceived that the reason her father had often seemed to prefer Maeve was that Maeve was not the daughter of his wife whom he did not love. Later, when he grew accustomed to his guilt, he had begun to lavish on Katharine the fruits of his cool heart.

She remembered how in the beginning at school in France, when both she and her cousin were languid with homesickness, her greatest joy had lain in her letters from him in which he sent impersonal messages to Maeve; even though Maeve wrote to him every day and every day, finding no envelope addressed to herself, burst into tears. She was reluctant to admit it to herself, but she was afraid that she had never really forgiven Maeve for those two or three years when she had been her father's darling. The fact was that she had never really forgiven poor Maeve for anything though she had struggled to. Bending every effort of her will and her intelligence, she had tried to love Maeve and, failing, had come at last to this ultimate betrayal. In Katharine, a grown and apparently integrated woman, there bitterly rankled still the recollections of how all the young men in her girlhood had been taken first with her and every one of them had abandoned her the moment they met Maeve, who was not more beautiful, not more alert, danced no better. This imponderable in Maeve, even now, Katharine could not define, but clearly it had been there, immediately recognizable to men and immediately alluring.

She recalled that once the two of them had fallen in love with a German who lived there in the French town, and they quivered at the sight of his great height and his blond head, in the streets and the shops when they were allowed to leave the school to make small purchases and to drink chocolate in an approved café. One day they had separated and Katharine had gone alone to the stationer's shop where she had seen the man buying a quantity of foolscap and had heard the shop-keeper address him as "M. Faust." She had stood beside him at the counter, so agitated that her French left her, so giddy that she pointed to ink when she had come for envelopes. He had smelled richly of tobacco and pomade and out of courtesy to her, he had taken off his cap, showing a sculptured, intellectual forehead. When she left, he held the door open for her and she said boldly, "Vielen dank, Meinherr," and had been transported when he smiled and bowed and paid her baby-German a compliment, "Gut gesprechen, gnädiges Fräulein." She had kept the secret of his name from Maeve and yet, on the very next excursion to town, they had met Herr Faust in the road and Maeve had greeted him, calling him by name. Katharine asked her how she had come to know it and Maeve had replied, with her disarming candour, "He told it to me. He's a novelist, you know." Katharine had not known; she had been feverish with jealousy.

Afterward, a three-cornered friendship had sprung up and they had had meetings in teashops that the girls were forbidden to enter and had taken walks together in the woods, though this was not allowed. Though the young man had listened gravely to Katharine's observations on literature (she had begun, as soon as she had learned his name, to read Goethe) his eyes were forever on Maeve. It was Maeve's elbow that was cupped when they came to a log fallen across the path, it was Maeve who was asked if she were cold, it was Maeve who was invited first to choose her pastry. But Katharine had persevered; she *would* be noticed and, seeking to flatter him by imitating him, she began to write a novel. When she had finished twenty pages of it (it had dealt with a nun who had broken her vows) she had submitted it to Herr Faust to read, and at their next meeting, returning the manuscript to her, he had said only, "You should take up the harp. Or paint ring-around-a-rosy on saucers," and to Maeve, not to her, he had explained why women should never try to write. His heavy, arrogant, Teutonic waggishness had been unendurable. As soon as they got back to the school, Katharine had written to her mother that a certain man of the town had succeeded in converting Maeve to anarchy, a yarn that could not fail to arouse the law-abiding Alma Congreve. Until some weeks later, when Sister Chrysostom had a letter from her and both girls were reprimanded for breaking rules and their permission to leave the convent grounds was suspended, Katharine had had to put up with several more meetings with the man during which he teased her about the novel which had been called "The Bright Blight." Down the years of girlhood, she had suffered these small fractures of the heart while Maeve, infrangible and unbruised, had never been aware in her tranquillity that anything was wrong.

She felt, these days, that she was living in a void and that she would continue to for the rest of time with an occasional swift trip to chaos, changing the climate from despair to dementia. For in the evening after Edmund St. Denis had witlessly held up her relationship with John to such maudlin ridicule, after she had been attended by the little doctor and her frightened maids and finally had been left alone, she had written a letter to the Shipleys in which, embedded in gossip and bulletins on the welfare and occupations of the children, she had told John that the daydream, for her, was finished.

Last winter I flirted with the notion of pulling up my stakes and leaving everything behind [she wrote], thought of going to live in Bermuda, perhaps, that blessed isle where the internal combustion machine does not intrude. If you can believe it of me, I thought of selling Congreve House or turning it over to the state for some good antiquarian cause. What possessed me, I cannot think, unless it was that usual slump that everyone falls into in February—I seem to recall that both of you were very low about that time this year—but in any case, I have come so fully to my senses that I intend to have my gravestone made in Thomas by the man who made Minerva and Papa's stone and when it's finished, to have it stored in the stable, until the solemn day when it is laid on top of me. It is a kind of insurance—however tenuous and symbolic—against my suddenly kicking over the traces and going off to a flamboyant island in my middle age. The stone will be superb, if Mr. Norman executes it as I plan. My neighbors have formed two opposing camps, one horrified, the other benedictory, and if I have done no other act of generosity, I have provided Hawthorne with a meaty subject of discussion.

Maeve's reply had been, as she had expected, filled with anxious questions and it was evident, despite the shrouding tact, that she thought Katharine was either gravely ill or mildly mad. She suggested that they come home earlier this year than usual and she proposed that if the children were a strain they be sent down to Newport to Uncle Daniel. In a postscript she added, "Our difficulties, John's and mine, do not diminish. How on earth is it going to end?"

She had expected from John a storm of anger and had, to tell the truth, looked forward to it, had in her mind written back with equal indignation, sending the letter to the business address at which he had told her to write him. There had come instead a groaning petition that she reconsider, a plea to know if he had offended her in any way and it had ended, "You must ask yourself this question: Have you the moral right to destroy me? If you are thinking of Maeve or of the children, you are being ungenerous to everyone, for the divorce is a foregone conclusion. My life is in your hands."

But Katharine was certain that he would not divorce Maeve; he would not, that is, unless another woman appeared with her hands outstretched, delighted to take his life in them. No, he would go on living with Maeve Maxwell and after half a year or perhaps a year, the talk would die down (like Maeve, the gossips imagined that he kept a dancer) and his "bit of a fling" would be forgiven and even condoned as something perfectly natural in the life of any healthy, good-looking man of forty-two. And he himself, looking back, would probably think, "That was a narrow squeak." Eventually he would even be able to console himself for his want of accomplishment by imagining that he had sacrificed his career to his family and he could die praiseworthy in his own eyes.

But none of this would he foresee now. One time she had told him that if he botched this loop-the-loop, he would hate her with far more passion than he loved her now and he had chucked her under the chin (it was hard for her to believe, just as it had been hard to believe at the moment it happened) and had said, "There will be no botching. This isn't puppy-love, you know." And puppy love, of course, was exactly what it was, but how convey that to him? How tell him: what I wanted I have now achieved, *my* desire is consummated for I have supplanted Maeve, and we would have to be born again and to live our lives up to the night of the Catherine wheels for me to pull up from my earth my intricate, tenacious roots.

She had continued to write to the two of them and had not written privately to him, and knowing what pain it must cause him, had told them of the ball she meant to have, strewing the many creamy sheets of her letter with reminiscences of their first meeting ("It was I, the bystander, that knew the two of you were done for, not you the actors in that pretty pastoral play. 'The jig is up,' said I, looking at you, for you hadn't a ghost of a chance of getting your hearts back once you'd lost them to each other") and knowing how these ambiguities would make him wince and curse lost time and tell himself, as Edmund did, that until a man is forty he doesn't know where he is at. But she wrote with her blood, for all the while that she repudiated John Shipley as he was now, she was hungry to avidity for him as he had been then, as he might have been, as he had been this very afternoon, stepping softly around the wing of the bamboo screen.

A rainbow arched across the western sky, its nearer terminus behind the canting chimney of the Smithwick house and its yonder one lost in the trees that fringed the headtide. The stone curls of the Roman notables stationed along the boundaries of the rosary were roguishly plastered with leaves from the plane trees above. And the birds that had been driven to shelter in the storm were out again, singing in the arbors, undoubtedly nettling Maddox with their cheer since he, for days now, would be cheered by nothing, now that his belles had been decapitated and their tattered petals lay in the mud at the bases of Hadrian's and Caesar's fluted columns. Katharine could see him pacing the sticky paths of the garden, his hands slack at his sides, his head disconsolately hanging forward as he surveyed his slaughtered virgins. She sometimes felt that Maddox carried his personifications too far and one time she had been disturbed when, after a heavy wind, he had had a mass burial of the ravaged blossoms (some of them stabbed by their own thorns), interring the sodden, fragrant mass in a shallow grave beside the summerhouse. She had not found the ceremony sentimental—as her friends, on hearing of it, did: "Pathetic fallacy it's called, if I'm not mistaken," Peg Duff had said—but nearly psychopathic. Thinking back on it, she was reminded of a lemon tree she had seen today, growing in a solarium of the state prison; it had produced one fruit, still green but of titanic size, and its custodian, a short and hunchbacked parricide, referred to the tree as "he" and the lemon as "his fruit," and said that he "fertilized this boy with vetch." A foul effluvium had come from a stone crock of fertilizer; the whole scene had been one of hatred and scurrility and when she turned to go, the man had said, with sarcastic piety, "I took a life so now I make a life. You know the old saying, 'A lemon a day keeps the hangman away,'" and he had tittered shrilly, squeezing his eyes between dirty wrinkles, showing huge false teeth. She had no affinity for homespun wisdom but, even so, she was repelled by this perversion of it and so had pretended not to hear (Honor and Harriet laughed and one of them said, "Jimmy will love that!") and had gone to examine a rack of trays on which were painted teapots, windmills and love birds.

An incident like this was in itself too trivial to be more than noted in passing and at another time in her life, Katharine Congreve, who believed in sweetness and light and the superfluity of all else, would have refused to remember it; if the memory had gained access in spite of her, she would certainly never have drawn a parallel between the convict in his vengeful act of penance and her gardener, an honest man whose *idée fixe*, though it was often difficult to live with, implied no unseemly motive. But "at another time in her life" she had not yet opened up Pandora's box.

The boy must get his dressing down. She stroked the cat and touched the squirming kittens and steeled herself to call to Andrew and to deliver to him a lecture on the misuse of the word "hate." But as she started across the room, it struck her that there was something wrong at her desk and she stood for a moment looking down at it. Nothing was missing, nothing was in disarray. It was several minutes before she realized that the box she kept lemon drops in had been set squarely on her diary.

She remembered that she had left it in the small guest room that morning when she had gone in to see that Mary had begun to turn the room out (there were to be several overnight guests on the occasion of the ball). She had been carrying a vase of roses that she meant to put in the hall window and now she remembered that she had forgotten them, too, having been called to the telephone in the middle of her inspection. She had gone through the drawers to make sure that there was nothing in them to distract (or interest) a visitor and in the desk she had found a photograph of herself and Maeve. It was innocuous enough except for the inscription on the back which had been childishly unkind, bearing in it a reference to a skin disorder of Maeve's which Katharine had prayed would be incurable: actually had prayed, with humble Christian words and phrases, in the Lady Chapel at Chartres while, impatient in the aisle beside her, a subaltern of the sacristan had waited, sniffling and shuffling, to guide her and Maeve up the tower, the profanity of his avarice being less despicable by far than that of her appeals to heaven. How that day, as all shameful days, came back! When they had emerged from the murk of the cold, weird winding stairs onto the lowest of the church's roofs and had leaned over the parapet looking down upon the distant little houses and the puffs of budding April trees, her muscles had tightened against the desire to fling herself off and in her desperate fear of the height, which she had never experienced before, she had been frantic, certain that she could neither go farther up nor go back down the precipitous and slippery stairs. And yet, the moment she had seen this same terror in Maeve whose breath came spastically, who clutched the solid stone for dear life and tottered when she closed her eyes to the chasm of the narrow street below, Katharine, through an act of will, regained her equilibrium, unmercifully laughed at her cousin who, really sick with fright, began to cry. She had gone on with the guide, as far up as they could go, leaving the weeping girl crumpled in the sun. When they came back, she had not moved but her rigidity was gone and she quivered and her teeth chattered as if she had a chill. The swindling little Frenchman had been, if anything, more blatant in his taunts than Katharine; their conspiring giggles, on the slow trip down, had echoed in the malign twilight. The chaperone, waiting for them in the vestibule, having admitted freely to her own phobia for heights, had hectored Maeve with smelling salts though by this time she had fully recovered and wished only that her cowardice (for that was what Katharine and the batrachian cicerone had called it) be forgotten.

No one, she told herself rationally, could possibly read all of that into the casual photograph of schoolgirls on an educational tour. But, all the same, she felt invaded, for her desk was known as sacrosanct and no servant ever touched it, even to the extent of civilly putting on it something, like this box, that she had misplaced. And if a servant had committed this pardonable transgression, she would also have put the roses where they belonged and the table in the hall window, as she

could see through her open door, was bare. So it must have
been Andrew, alone in the house, idle and restless in the rain.
What had he made of the inscription? And what else had he
done? She turned to last night's entry in her diary and read:

The boy's somnambulism has passed but his nightmares continue.
He screamed in his sleep just before dawn this morning and when I
went in to rescue him from his ogre, I found him already resting easily
again and looking, in the half-light, so like John that I was too much
drawn to him to touch him although the covering had fallen off and
the wind was cool. I mean that I had no idea what form my gesture
would take, for *he* has become the vortex of these chimeral fancies
that seek to undermine me and while I struggle to resurrect the past
by any rapacious reading of his face, I wish at the same time to efface
the face that in my own nightmares is omnipresently before me.

2

Himself again in linen trousers and a striped blue shirt, Andrew
sat on the hassock at the foot of the chaise longue, the picture of contrition, his feet in sneakers pointing, pigeon-toed,
at the tail of a golden dragon in the rug, his hands clasping
and unclasping as he admitted that he had done everything
he was accused of for no good reason except that he had had
nothing else to do since he could not find any mucilage to go
on putting together the façade of the State House, and had
therefore occupied himself with whatever had come to hand.
For no good reason, he had put the photograph of his parents
and his cousin face downward and he denied his sisters' charge
that this had been an act of disrespect to his elders; but he was
sorry. And he had written on a piece of paper that Honor was
a moron but if Cousin Katharine could see what she had written on it in the first place (he had promised, for a quarter, not
to tell) she would agree with him; for this, too, he was sorry.
Sighing, he went on with his list of misdemeanours: he *had*
dressed up in Uncle George's boating clothes and was sorry for
it, and had frightened her and was sorry and was sorry, above
all, for having said what he did for it was not true, he did not
hate them all. And he was sorry . . . but he stopped and lowered
his head. In the quiet the clock's ticks crashed.

"Maddox says it will take more than him and Adam to set off

the fireworks," Andrew said suddenly, invalidating his remorse with his exuberance and the smile that smoothed out the scowl on his forehead. "So can I help?"

"We'll talk about that later, but now I want to know what else you did this afternoon. *Did* you read your sisters' diaries?"

"They were locked," he said and lowered his head again.

"Then what else did you do? It couldn't have taken you all afternoon to turn over the picture and to write on Honor's slip of paper. I'm not really prying. I only want to know how you spent the afternoon." She tried to trap him with a friendly smile.

"Oh, you know! I walked around and looked at things. I hunted for that top. I thought."

He would admit no more; he could not or he would not say why it was that today, of all days, he had been urged to dress up in anachronistic clothes to match herself and he seemed wholly innocent when, shooting off at a tangent, he asked, "Honestly and truly, did you think I was Daddy? Just for a minute maybe?" and his disappointment seemed genuine when she told him that after her first surprise she had only played his game; she had had to appear angry with him, she quickly explained, in order not to seem to be playing favorites in Honor's eyes: it had not been kind of him to write down what he had although, the Lord knew, she said, that one could stoop to almost anything on a confining afternoon like this. She paused, waiting for his confession that he had stooped to something base, but he said nothing and tired at last of the interrogation which proceeded nowhere, she dismissed him, telling him that for having said he hated everyone, he must not speak until after dinner. His jaw set stubbornly as he turned to go; facing the door, he said, "I don't hate you, but there are some people that I do."

"You mustn't be vehement. You don't *hate* anyone."

"Oh, but I do! There are certain people that I hate so much I wish they'd die. But I *don't hate you.*" He wheeled around again and said, "When is the tombstone coming?"

"Why? Why do you want to know?" she cried.

"I'll tell you why! Because I know that the day it comes something is going to happen." He stood with his fists clenched over his head, the tip of his tongue showing slyly at the corner of his mouth, his eyes rolled upward. In her alarm at this dreadful transformation, she looked away and heard him run from the room and scramble down the stairs, heard the front door open and bang loudly to and heard the maniacal child scream at the top of his voice, "I'll talk to myself if I want to! I can talk to the trees and the snakes and the road and the houses!" She saw him running down toward the lake, calling out his own name, "Andrew! Andrew Shipley!" and she turned weakly to her desk.

She remembered having read once, in a scornful, misanthropic book that the degeneration of a society was often marked by "graphomania" when verbiage streamed from the pens of the decadent and doomed. And from that she went on to think of a friend who had gone into a nervous collapse after the birth of her child and who had written letters unceasingly to everyone she knew, covering page after page with unrelated matter, quotations from poetry, diatribes against the nurses in her sanitarium, minutely described accounts of meals and quarrels; sometimes, in the middle of a paragraph she worked out a problem in algebra. The tragedy of the letters had been that here and there in the tenebrous purgatory of them, there had been light glades of sanity and Katharine thought now of the woman's picture of the institution's dining room, "It has a hush like Sunday and there is nothing to look at except our food and a fire extinguisher that hangs beside the door. I am too near-sighted to read the words on it from where I sit and so, instead, I count the little humps in the plaster that run like a frieze around the window near my chair, but I never remember from meal to meal how many there are. My life is so reduced now to the bare necessities that I do not know what will become of me if I ever do remember how many humps there are. Still, I suppose that if this happened, I might induce them to let me change my place so that I could read the words on the fire extinguisher." The irony had then caved in and the rest of the long letter was a wandering babble.

In six weeks, Katharine's loose-leaf diary had doubled in size. She had written more in this time than she had written in the sixteen years before, since this had been her only possible confessional and she had hoped, through the articulation of her fears, to quiet them and right herself. Heretofore, it had been her custom to make one daily entry after lunch, usually as impersonal as notations in a ship's log, but now, like the corrupt graphomaniacs, she wrote in it at all hours of the day and in the dead of night when she could not sleep, drawing her shutters and her curtains so that her light would not be seen by her cordial, inquisitive neighbors. Harassed by the whippoor-wills, she would at last get up, shutting out the birds' lament with a pair of ivory ear-stopples. She seldom read over what she had written but she knew, without reviewing them, that these nocturnal outpourings, exaggerated as they were bound to be by the intensification of her loneliness in the dark and the silence, wholly revealed her. She should destroy the book, she thought, although, if the boy had read it, the damage was already done. (But he had said *I do not hate you* and he could not have said *those* words if he had read *these* words, "Is it not a sin crying to heaven for vengeance to be sometimes in love with a child and at other times, terrified of exposure, to wish him off the face of the earth?")

At times, the countless elements of her double life (it was more than double; it was a labyrinth of paths that turned back on themselves, crossing and recrossing) were as clear to her as a table of contents, and at those times the issues assumed their due proportion: she had burned no bridges and had not allowed John to burn his; she had returned from the only aberration of her life. But there were other times—and these were either in the night or when she was surprised by some fresh problem or snatched by some old misery—when she was consumed by the smallest of vexations.

One night, not long ago, she had not been able to turn her thoughts away from an absurd argument she had had with Brantley Wainright-Lowe on the subject of Cézanne. He, who "dabbled" in water colors and made dithyrambic studies of her swans and peacocks, had patronizingly patted her hand (his tactile need enraged her; he was forever touching her shoulder or her wrist as if without this physical accompaniment he could not speak), and had said of Cézanne, "There is a kind of simplicity about him that is rather charming, I admit, but he is really no great shakes. Of course I can understand how people who are in no way artistic would look on things differently from myself." Later, waking from her first light sleep, she had been beset by a hurricane of anger, no less turbulent than if the cause had been John or Maeve. Again, she had paced and fretted one whole night through over Maureen who, stupidly, was pregnant and who, trusting and devoted and naive, had put upon her mistress's shoulders the responsibility of solving her dilemma.

Her sleep could be extorted from her by word from her care-taker in Boston that a leak in the dining room had mildewed the wallpaper; or by the image of Edmund St. Denis at a picnic as he lay, rowdily spread-eagled on the sand in an unbecoming bathing suit, trying to catch her eye with a pleading, hangdog expression or to catch her ear with a cajoling whisper. Or she could spend the night calling off the roll of the men who had been in love with her as, in gentle lamplight, she gazed at herself in the mirror, drowning in her beauty; stripped of every amenity, enthroned upon her invincible self-love, she would fall forward on her arms without any warning, her realm sacked, her sovereignty dissolved and weep and weep and weep and with her wet lips pressed to the back of her hand, murmur, "They did not. Only the Humanist loved me."

She knew that it was only a question of time before the signature of her distress would be written on her face. The sleeplessness would show, staining the eyesockets, loosening the flesh from the cheekbones, and the headaches would assert themselves in lines, and the dragging weakness in her arms as if all the strata of her flesh were starving except the live, thrashing nerves. Tired to death, she could not stop the continuum of wounded-and-wounding, or of sinned-and-sinned-against (it could go on forever; if Maeve's parents had lived and Maeve had not, therefore, started it all by winning Katharine's father for those few but most important years, making it necessary from that time on for Katharine to compete with her; if Katharine's father's father had told him how to treat a daughter in that crucial situation and *his* father before him had been such-and-such—at last one came to Adam and the blame was spread out evenly upon the human race) and she could not remember when life had been anything but this, when it had been possible to enjoy, to look forward to, to want to own something or to meet someone. Now she could only take on blind faith the promise her reason made her, that there *had* to be an end to this sickness that alternated between coma and paroxysm, and that when that time came, her whole life might swing into a different course. She was not sure, she made no plans, but it occurred to her that perhaps she would no longer immolate herself to the distant August night. She, who had been constant, might change, but into what and through what means she could not yet imagine.

Her forefinger outlined the body of the gilded fish embossed on the red cover of her diary and a ceremonious plan came to mind; after the ball was over, she would assist herself in her release by burning this testimony of her years and years of frugal living upon wreckage. "After the ball was over." The tune of the song began to play and, afraid that it, like other minutiae, would go on and on like a stuck phonograph, she forcibly expelled it and turned level-headedly to making a further plan whereby to conceal her malady from everyone, for, above all, despite her outward eccentricities, she was conventional, and she did not want to have her melancholy anatomized by women at lunch and men in their clubs.

The children would stay, as always, until September and she, as always, would linger on as a denizen of Hawthorne until election day. And only then would she close Congreve House. (How hard it was to leave the country in the autumn! When the leaves had turned, flaring in the steady sun, releasing their metallic leaves to the winds that riffled over the aging grass and the dying gardens. Dogs came to play in the dunes of fallen leaves and the geese came over across the faultless sky; in the river fog at dusk the deer drank at the lake, watched by the red foxes from their lairs in the meadow. The town began to close in on itself, snuggling its houses with banking boards and storm windows. The big summer houses were bleak and out of place and the summer gentry, no longer having the upper hand, began to leave in something like embarrassment. One thing was not gone from her, she thought as she thought of the autumn, and that was her abiding love of her dominion and all the natural enchantments that surrounded it.) So, she would close Congreve House and would go back to Boston and after she had seen John once, she thought she would go away, perhaps to make a retreat at some Roman Catholic convent of a silent order, not to pray, but simply, for a time, to drop appearances.

In time, all would be well. And if the boy already knew, there was no helping it. To every child there must come some wretched, sordid foreknowledge of what it's all about and if he hated her as a result of it (his statement that he did not could have been devious and deep) and hated his father (he was bound, finally, to hate him anyhow, for John was indifferent to his children and had only a vestigial memory of what it had been like to be a boy) and if his whole life was tinged by his secret knowledge—secret, for he could never admit to his sisters or his parents that he had read a private diary, this being, thank God, in their mores, an inadmissible and heinous crime—she would not take all the blame.

"Andrew! Andrew Shipley!" Now he was running back to the house and now down the length of the lawn. At the hammock, some sound or sight arrested him. The marine light of late afternoon after a rain, and the angle from which she regarded him, enlarged him and looking as tall as a man, as she watched, he clasped his hands over the back of his long neck.

"Mercy, mercy," she softly said, stepping back from the window, and from the foot of the lawn he mocked her, calling, "Honor! Honor! Your enemy is here."

CHAPTER VII

The Leaves of the Fig Tree

A DAM AND Maddox and Andrew stood in the barn looking down at Katharine Congreve's tombstone that had come early that morning from Thomas by truck. It had taken five men, huffing and puffing and swearing, to get it into the barn. One of them had called the stone a bitch and another had called it a bastard and when they rested they marveled, using the same kind of language, at anyone who would anticipate death to such an extent in so calm a way. One of them had tapped his forehead and said, "Low tide, if you ask my opinion."

The stonecutter, Mr. Norman, an unprepossessing little old man in rimless spectacles and a square mustache, had sat on the terrace with Cousin Katharine watching the proceedings and drinking coffee with her as he accepted her compliments, bashfully denying them. He wore gray suède gloves, only one of which he removed, that exactly matched his new fedora; with his sober black suit and his old-fashioned high stiff collar and his broad black tie, he looked like a pallbearer or an undertaker and he did nothing to dispel the illusion by his conversation. At one point he said, "If you know of anyone else who contemplates this move, would you be so kind as to put in a word on my behalf? Tombstones are my forte." Honor had burst into laughter and apologized immediately but said that the phrase "contemplate this move" had been the funniest thing she had ever heard and Mr. Norman, profoundly gratified, beamed at her, shuffled his spatted feet and allowed, "My wife tells me that I turn a neat phrase every once in a while."

It was hard to associate his masterpiece with Mr. Norman and his finicking ways (his little finger had stood out at a right angle when he picked up his coffee cup and he had pursed his lips into a rosebud before each speech) and the coachman and the gardener agreed that you could never judge a man's abilities by his appearance. For the stone was as impressive as the statue of Minerva and the figure of Cousin Katharine, in marble effigy, was as heroic and as handsome. It was a likeness awesomely accurate, though Mr. Norman had made only one sketch of her on the day she came to place her order. It showed, in the piebald stone, her protuberant pompadour arising from her wide forehead and her noble nose and chin and her broad, loving lips, but it showed, even more wonderfully, her pure and vestal air; the actual person seemed to lie beneath the folds of her full sleeves and her long skirt. Between her peaceful hands she held a full-blown rose and over her head there was an intricately carved circle; seven hooked spikes curved inward from the rim pointing toward the name engraved there and the date of her birth and the empty space below that would be filled in when she died.

"Katharine Congreve, born August 30, 1898," read Adam. "Is that supposed to be a halo? Is that what you make it out to be?"

But Maddox was examining the rose; his stained, heavy fingers palpitated over the petals and he smiled, glorying in the cleverness of the stonecutter. "That's an awful wonderful thing," he said.

"Could be a rowel," said Adam, still looking at the design at the top, "except the teeth go in, not out. Is it some kind of a family dohicus, Mr. Andrew, some kind of a coat of arms?"

"It's a Catherine wheel," said Miss Congreve from the doorway. She had brought out the maids to view the stone and they stood timidly in the sunlight, hanging back, not wanting to look at all but forcing themselves to express an admiration they did not feel.

"A Catherine wheel!" exclaimed Andrew. She *did* take the cake, as Adam had said earlier. A Fourth of July thing carved on her gravestone! Why not a Christmas wreath with bells on it or an Easter basket full of painted eggs? But then he learned, somewhat to his disappointment, from Mrs. Shea who was a fount of knowledge on matters ecclesiastical, that this was the symbol of the martyr Catherine. "They tied her to a thing like that and set it spinning, but it broke before it killed her and then they chopped off her head." The little maids were even more distressed and Maureen seemed about to cry and furtively she crossed herself while the cook went on to expatiate on St. Catherine's intrepid character. The men were puzzled but they said nothing; it was all over their heads as it was over Andrew's.

By now there was a huddle of spectators in the doorway, for Miss Duff, who had seen the truck drive up, had spread the word around and all of Cousin Katharine's friends had dropped what they were doing and had come straight to Congreve House in order to be among the first to see what Brantley Wainright-Lowe called "Katy's hick-jacket." Unlike the servants, all of them at the sight of the *memento mori* were infected with an inexplicable delight and while they praised the workmanship ("an estimable performance!" said Mr. Barker and clapped his hands) and the way Mr. Norman had uncannily caught Katharine's singular look ("Damfino," said Miss Duff and slapped her jodhpurs with her riding whip, "the very spit of you"), they all agreed with old Miss Heminway that "our Katharine" was a humourist. Miss Duff and Mrs. Tyler were as gay as the others but Andrew saw them exchange a wink.

"What's that thing there?" said Mrs. Wainright-Lowe, pointing to the Catherine wheel with the handle of her butterfly net, and after Cousin Katharine had explained, in the absence of the expert, Mrs. Shea, who had returned to the house and her baking, the grass widow, whose cross she was fond of telling friends was heavier than most, chided, "Oh, now, Katharine, that's too far-fetched for words. Whoever in the world scourged you?"

"Whips tipped with metal," said Miss Duff to herself. "Interesting." The whole of Miss Duff's mind was seldom in attendance when there was a gathering of more than three.

"Far-fetched or not," said Mr. Barker defensively, "I call it a crackerjack idea. Her name's Katharine, isn't it?"

Mrs. Wainright-Lowe wagged her finger at him, made sure that the maids had gone and said, "You're going into your dotage, Rodney, if you imagine that Alma and George Congreve would ever have named her for a Popish person."

There was some discussion then over whether or not Catherine of Alexandria was included in the hierarchy of the Anglo-Catholic saints and Mrs. Wainright-Lowe, the only Presbyterian that Mrs. Tyler admitted knowing socially, was ignored. Seeking then to make amends for her blunder, she sadly said, "It's true, it's true, everyone does have a cross to bear."

Cousin Katharine smiled and said, "I'm only giving myself airs, Aunt Lowe. I fixed on this only because I thought the design was handsome. I do not really claim to have a cross." And herding them all out she asked her friends if they did not think that this was an occasion for brown sherry, the drink she said she always associated with funerals. "The most delicious sherry I ever drank was after we buried Uncle Tim who was so extraordinarily glad to die. You know he was sensitive to noise to a degree and from the time he was fifty, prayed that in his old age he would go deaf. But he never did and, in fact, his hearing seemed to get sharper. The very last words he said were 'If there is whistling in the great beyond, I'll kill myself.'"

They laughed, accepted the invitation to drink brown sherry in the library and started toward the house. "Good old Tim," said Miss Duff. "Haven't thought of him in years. We'll drink to silence in the great beyond."

Andrew lingered for a few minutes in the cool of the stable. The arrival of the gravestone had been a disappointment, for ever since he had told Cousin Katharine that it would be a sign, he had believed it. He had expected, for no reason now that he could think of, that the men who brought it would be dressed like executioners in black robes and peaked hoods and possibly even half-masks. And they had come, in harmless daylight, nothing more than ordinary workmen in dirty pants and blue shirts. He had been convinced that on this day they would learn of the end of Charles Smithwick and then all the waiting would be over, the nightmare would be done and whatever it was that had been boiling in him all summer long would quiet down. He wanted to give up his obsession, but the obsession had resolutely stayed of its own accord.

With his announcement to Cousin Katharine, it had reached a fever pitch, hotter and hotter until there was in his very heartbeat a voice that constantly said, "Charles Smithwick, die." And the worst of it was that he did not care any longer whether Charles Smithwick lived or died or became the President; he wanted only to be free, to be able to read Mark Twain and play poker with Honor and Harriet and have a little fun, for pete's sake, but the voice would not let him be. It was an undertone when he was with other people, but when he was alone, it was a roar and he had come to think that if Charles didn't die, this would go on for the rest of his life. He would never be able to study at school, he would flunk and be sent back or be subjected again to Bowman who would tutor him in that mausoleum house where his parents . . . Oh, his parents! They would be home so soon, the summer was so nearly over! At the thought of them, he turned and slapped Derek's flank; the horse disdainfully lifted his lip to show a row of grass-green teeth.

He had definitely appointed this day as the day on which Charles would die not because there was any connection between his death and Cousin Katharine's tombstone but because the fact was that he, Andrew Shipley, could stand the voice no longer. And this morning, just as the truck was coming up the drive and just as Andrew was getting out of bed, what had he seen through his window but the lanky towheaded sailor himself sauntering down the road, looking as if he had never had an ache or a pain in his life? At breakfast, which he could not eat, Cousin Katharine had come into the dining room to tell them that Charles was coming to help Maddox and Adam set off the fireworks on the next night.

It was really amazing that no one could hear the voice that made as much din in his blood and his brain as Victor's yodeling ever did; he sympathized with Uncle Tim. It was extremely loud and shrill just now and in order to modulate it, he crossed the lawn to watch the men who were putting up the stand for the orchestra beside the dancing platform. Below this, there had been pitched a red and white striped marquee for the buffet supper and some of the workmen were sitting under it, eating their lunch out of black boxes, their heads bent down in an attitude of diligence as if their very lives depended on the wedges of apple pie and the cold pork chops. When Andrew's shadow fell across their picnic ground, one of them, Congreve Smithwick, looked up. He stopped in the act of cracking a hard-boiled egg on his knee and stood up, brushing off his fingers on the seat of his pants, and came across to shake Andrew's hand in both of his. He wore Victor's knife at his belt.

"I have been meaning to write you a thank-you-kindly-ma'am letter for that knife," he said, "and partly I took this odd-time job so I could tell you in person. I said at the time it was like manna from heaven because I sorely needed that knife."

"Connie treats that knife of his like it was a baby," said another of the men through a mouthful of pie.

"It's all right," murmured Andrew. Connie unsheathed the knife and flicked his forefinger lightly over the blade and from a pocket, he brought out a small whetstone; he said that when he had nothing else to do, he spent his time sharpening it until now it was keen enough to shave with.

"There'll be no knife left when Connie gets through with it," said the man who had spoken before.

"Do you mind my asking one thing?" said Connie. Even here, miles inland, he smelled as strongly of fish as the smokehouse. "What does V.S. stand for?"

"Very Simple," said one of the men.

"Virtue and Sin," said another.

"Go on!" cried Smithwick. "My wife maintains you bought it for somebody else and those were their initials. But I maintain that you knew I needed a knife and you bought it for me."

He was in dead earnest, this credulous yokel, and Andrew thought what a simpleton he himself had been to imagine that he could ever in a million years get the knife back to give to Victor. Not that Victor deserved it or anything else except, perhaps, a swift kick.

"V.S. stands for," he began and paused, trying to hit upon a hoodwink to while away the time till lunch. He thought of the Latin words *veritas* and *semper* which together sounded like a motto, but he did not want to sound snobby and so, instead, he invented a name and told Congreve Smithwick that the man who had made the knife was called Vernon Saltonstall.

As long as he was talking, the voice was no louder than a whisper, rather like a purr, and so, sitting down among the men, he began to tell a long lie about the mythical cutler and how he had come to buy the knife, through mental telepathy, for Congreve Smithwick. Realizing that no one believed him except Connie who listened, rapt, forgetting his lunch, he gave the other men a knowing, sidelong look from time to time and imperceptibly they winked. It was a snug, club-like atmosphere there beneath the festive canvas and Andrew felt proudly popular with his audience whose connivance and buried mirth spurred him on to higher and higher flights. He said that one afternoon after school as he was going through the Common, a man had given him a leaflet about Christian Science ("C.S., you see," he said and Congreve Smithwick gaped and his companions hid their smiles with apples) and just as he sat down to read it he thought he heard a voice that spoke to him, "Do you happen to know where I can get a knife? I am a stranger here." He had turned on the bench but there was no one nearby except a fat squirrel eating peanuts on the path; this was in about January. Did that mean anything to Connie?

It certainly did! The loony flushed and fidgeted and stammered that it had been January that he had lost his old knife which, anyhow, had never been much good. The fabrication rolled on and Congreve Smithwick believed every word. The more the men showed, by nods and bogus coughs, that Andrew was a success, the softer grew the voice inside him until finally, when he hesitated once in search of some fresh improbability, he realized that it was altogether gone. He was extremely happy being the center of attention, and all the time he was spinning out his yarn, he was thinking that Victor, after all, was not the only pebble on the beach and that he was going to ask permission to join this band of workmen as an apprentice or, if they did not need one, as a jester to amuse them during lunch. He imagined himself traveling with them throughout the county, becoming famous as an entertainer, Andrew Shipley, the One-Man Show.

But before he had finished his account of Vernon Saltonstall, Honor burst out the front door crying, "Andrew! Something awful's happened!"

The men rose as a body and followed him like a herd of animals, muttering, "House on fire?" "Somebody got hurt?" Connie Smithwick said, "Lucky I got my knife along in case it's needed."

But besides the workmen, there came with Andrew the voice, more insistent than it had ever been before and it was to it and not to his sister that he shouted, "I hear you! Stop yelling at me!" When he was at the columns he panted, "How did it happen?"

"How did it happen?" she said. "How did *what* happen? Did you do it? Andrew Shipley, if you did it, I will never speak to you again in all my life and neither will Harriet or anyone else."

Harriet, the cool one, was in the hall. "Don't be ridiculous," she said. "Beth did it herself."

"Oh. The cat." He turned to face the men; he felt rather as if he were dismissing troops. "It's just about a cat," he told them and as they started back, disappointed, having hoped for an excitement, one of them said, "I'd mighty like to hear the rest of that story about Mr. Saltonstall."

"Mr. Saltonstall!" whispered Harriet harshly. "You weren't telling them about the Saltonstalls' divorce!"

"Ask me no questions and I'll tell you no lies." He had not known, until now, that the Saltonstalls were getting or had got a divorce. "What's the big idea of yelling all over the place about a cat?"

Honor was crying and it was Harriet who had to tell him what had happened. It was awful, though awful in a way so different from what he had expected, dreaded and longed for that he was not nearly as horrified as he might have been at another time. Cousin Katharine had gone upstairs to get the key to the wine closet in the library and the ancients had waited and waited and finally Mrs. Wainright-Lowe had come into the drawing room where the twins were sewing and asked them to go see if something was wrong. Honor had been the one to go and she had found Cousin Katharine in a faint again, lying on the floor of her bedroom and when Honor saw what had made her faint, she had almost fainted herself. Or died. For right in the middle of Cousin Katharine's bed, right on the lace counterpane, lay one of Beth's kittens with its head chewed off.

Cousin Katharine had been brought around with aromatic spirits of ammonia administered by Mrs. Shea but had refused to have the doctor and in spite of their protests would not hear of her friends' leaving without the sherry she had promised them. They were all in the library now and as the children entered, Miss Duff as coroner, in a visored cap, was conducting the inquest and helping herself liberally to the wine in the decanter. She looked a little tipsy or else a little thrilled. Certainly she was flinging herself wholeheartedly into what she called, from time to time, "a phenomenon of the first water."

No, said Cousin Katharine, Beth had not had an abnormal labor and Mrs. Shea, who had been with her, would bear her out. The decapitated kitten, to be sure, had been the runt of the litter but he had been well-formed and as healthy as the others; Cousin Katharine had promised him to Beulah Smithwick who for some time had wanted a black cat.

"Fitting," said Mr. Barker. "I have always said that woman was a witch."

Enthralled, they probed the possible solutions to the mystery. Why had a cat, by nature secretive, left the body of her murdered kitten in a place so public? And were the others now in danger of their lives? Had Beth gone berserk like a human being, like those mothers and fathers one was always reading about who suddenly could not put up with the crying of their infants another minute and strangled them or fractured their skulls with the first object that came to hand? Brantley Wainright-Lowe suggested that the cat's mind "had lightly turned to thoughts of death" on this particular day because the tombstone had arrived and his mother, on wondering why the creature had chosen that particular method, was told severely by Miss Duff to use her "bean," for how else could she have done it? They discussed whether or not Beth should be punished and Mr. Barker who knew a smattering of law said, parenthetically, that in ancient Greece, rocks that had fallen on people's heads and killed them had been tried and sentenced and executed although he was not just sure how.

"Pulverized," asserted the omniscient Duff who had probably never heard of the practice until now. Obviously, she said, it was impossible to punish a cat (except by putting it into a weighted gunny sack and dropping it into the lake from a boat) and this was the reason why she, personally, would never own one. "Beat a dog once or twice and he knows who's in charge but a cat, to my way of thinking, is devoid of any moral sense whatsoever."

Beth, the tribunal decided, would have to go scot-free. They clucked their tongues over the damage done to the counterpane ("which must have cost a fortune," said Mrs. Tyler who, it was rumored, had recently suffered serious losses on the stock market which she could ill afford) but said it was surprising how little blood there had been, leading them to believe that the deed had been done elsewhere and that the placing of the body on the bed had been an afterthought. They remarked, offended, the complacency of the animal when they had all gone up, the very picture of motherly love and pride, lying there in the pretty basket with her remaining kittens suckling her, purring and holding up her pansy face to have her cheeks stroked as if she had just done something bright. They talked of other cases in the lower orders in which the maternal instinct went amiss, of ewes that abandoned their ailing lambs and neurasthenic turkeys that would not take care of their eggs; but no one had ever heard of anything so gross as this, even in the order *homo sapiens*, and they did not wonder that Katharine had fainted dead away.

But it was evident that Mrs. Tyler and Miss Duff thought there was more to her fainting than met the eye, for Andrew saw how they looked alternately at her and at each other, ever so slightly inclining their heads or elevating one shoulder and Mrs. Tyler began presently to make an attempt to get the others to leave. Hadn't Mrs. Wainright-Lowe planned to catch butterflies before lunch? Didn't Mr. Barker always work up his appetite with a brisk walk? Was she wrong in her belief that Celia Heminway was under strict doctor's orders to rest, rest and rest some more and especially before meals? How well trained the Shipley children were to listen so patiently to grown-up conversation when they must be wild to be outdoors! Just a few minutes before, she had seen Andrew down with the men . . . boys did have such a jolly time around men who were working with hammers and saws.

But no one made any move at all to go and, inspired with the unusual events of the morning, they allowed their sherry glasses to be refilled and didn't mind saying that they were rather shaken, juvenile as it might be when the victim involved had only been a cat and so young a cat that it had not even developed any personality. Foiled, the diagnosticians were obliged to content themselves with a close surveillance of Cousin Katharine.

She had not touched the little green-stemmed glass of wine on the table beside her; earlier, Andrew had seen her start to pick it up but her hand was so unsteady that she could not have carried it to her lips and she put it back again. She entered into the conversation only to the extent that her role as hostess required her and did not add to the fund of parallel cases nor offer any theories. She sat in the midst of her friends, gamboling in their second childhood, as pale and unblemished as the filmy pink dimity she wore and she seemed, by her straight back and her tightly clasped hands and by the way she held her head at a slightly backward angle, to be listening for something. She was not listening to the voices of her friends but to some sound beyond the room or even beyond the house and Andrew, leaning against the door, tried to hear it too.

He could hear the drone of the lawn mowers and the erratic pounding of the hammers; he heard a motorboat's rapid snore diminishing. Nearer, he could hear someone moving about upstairs and he heard the sound of Honor's ballet slipper as she traced a parabola with her left toe on the newly waxed floor. And then his interior voice, which had been silent for some time, began clamoring. Was that what she was listening to? Could she hear it all the way across the room? His heart banged brassily and he edged backward out of the door. Just as he was about to turn, Cousin Katharine seemed to rouse herself, shaking her head a little as if she had dropped off to sleep and as he watched, the color came back to her face and she smiled and her quiet hand picked up her wineglass and said, "This is no time to be *triste* on the eve of my party!" They toasted the party and Harriet said, "Oh, yes, for heaven's sake, let's think about the party and not about that cat."

"I should have expected something of the kind," said Cousin Katharine. "It was days and days ago that Andrew told me on the day my stone arrived something awful was going to happen."

"He didn't!" cried Honor and reached out to seize him by the arm, but he flung away from her and stood just for a moment in the doorway before he ran. "You *did* do it!" she whispered but Harriet again defended him. "You are *insane*. Do you think anybody in the world would *chew* the head off a kitten? It was *gnawed*, Honor. It must have taken her hours."

"Lucky guess," said Wainright-Lowe, leering at Andrew. "If it hadn't been pussy I suppose there would have been some other little old carnage." He laughed indulgently. "Boys will be boys. I was a boy myself once, believe it or not."

They all gave Andrew a kindly, condescending look of appraisal and Mrs. Tyler, as if he were five years old, said, "He didn't want his cousin to get a tombstone, did he? Nobody wants to think that anyone close and dear is going to pass away, does he? Between you and me and the gatepost, Andy," she cupped her hand around her mouth and whispered loudly and he hated her for using a nickname that only strangers ever used and sometimes his father when he was in a falsely jocose humour, "this lady is going to live to be a hundred."

"Andrew doesn't care," said Honor but softly so that the others did not hear. "Andrew has no heart. You willed that little helpless baby cat to die."

"Honor, be quiet," said Harriet sharply. "You'll make him have a mood. Besides, he didn't do it."

Now Cousin Katharine, released from her strain, was really laughing and she said, "Will it make you all feel better if I cover it up and put a billiard table on top of it? Does that seem too bizarre or wouldn't it be rather a lark to let people play on it tomorrow night? The ones who are coming from a distance won't know what's underneath the baize."

"Kate, you're the limit!" cried Mr. Barker and laughed so hard that he had to wipe his eyes with the neatly folded ornamental handkerchief in his coat pocket. "And then you would unveil it afterward, I suppose?"

"Most gruesome thing I ever heard of," said Miss Duff, "but knowing you, I'm not going to be surprised if you do it."

"Listen!" said Cousin Katharine suddenly. Her smile was gone again and again she sat up straight. "Listen! Is that the wind? That sound?"

He ran then through the corridor and out of the house and down to the dancing platform and stood in the middle of it with all the men around him.

"Do us a jig," said one of them.

"I want to get something straight in my head about this Vernon Saltonstall," said another. "Did he know about Connie needing the knife too or did you pass that along to him?"

He had to shout over the voice to make them hear. Dizzied, he could only dimly see their faces, swimming in the hot sunlight. He shrieked that this was the last knife that Vernon Saltonstall had ever made because, with it, he had stabbed a man to death and he had given it to Andrew just before he went to the electric chair. The waving faces that had been split apart in grins began to seal themselves together and he heard someone say, "Take it easy, son." Finally, pausing for breath, his eyes focused on Congreve Smithwick whose stupid mouth was open wide and who was staring at the knife in his hands. Momentarily the men had all stopped working; an enormously tall one with a pock-marked face went over to Connie and put his arm around his shoulders, "Don't you worry about your knife, it ain't bad luck. The boy is only poetizing." The hammer began again and he knew that they had had enough of him.

"You ought to be a story writer," said the man who was consoling Connie. "Good luck, boy." With this he was dismissed and he drifted down the lawn toward the hammock. The voice, mercifully, seemed to be as tired as he was and though it was still there it was slow, like the pendulum of the grandfather clock.

As he lay down, he saw Victor and Charles meandering down the road, carrying pails and diggers. He covered his eyes with the pillow and put his fingers in his ears and he counted by fives to a hundred and fifty until he was sure they were out of sight. Out of sight and out of mind. He flopped over then and aloud he said, "You get out of my sight and out of my mind, you Smithwicks."

He began to think of the harvest of worthless mussel-pearls he had gathered once with Victor, and of a still moonlight midnight when they had stolen out of their houses and had met in the graveyard of St. James's to tell each other ghost stories; he thought of the solemn rite of the alewives and the raspberry tonic, of the parrot, and the pet vixen and Billy Bartholomew's battery radio, and the seals, and the eels, and when Maureen came down to tell him that lunch was ready, he was crying so hard that she had to call him twice before he heard her.

"But a lamb," said Miss Duff and then, embarrassed by her sentimentality, she resumed her gruffness. "Got to get ready for your shindig. Forgot to tell Maxine to press my best bib and tucker." Touching her khaki cap, she strode off across the lawn.

There had been much life within this house, thought Katharine, when the guest rooms had been occupied by long-term visitors, agreeable scholars with whom her father had all *but* talked in Greek, and feminist friends of her mother whom the men had controlled by turning upon them a bland, deaf ear. She remembered a pugnacious Mrs. Rowe who had once inquired of an English Latinist his opinion of Mary Wollstonecraft and the man had answered, "Do you mean the lady who felt it was right to expose the limbs so long as they were clad in blue stockings?" Worlds apart, the visitors, nevertheless, had not encroached upon each other's provinces; the Amazons went out to war for principles and rights while the men stayed indoors in their ivory tower. The sense of ease and holiday had made them tolerant and there were even times when they met on the common ground of play. (Was tennis not the same game it had been then? Why did it seem, today, so much faster?)

She grappled for the lost time, for the interplay of learned wit, for music as music had sounded then. She hunted, in the hollow of the present time, for the sensations that had once enlivened her on such an evening as this before a party, for those sensations that now were flittering over the skin and fevering the blood stream of the twins who were ready to cry, ready to laugh hysterically, equally ready to fall in love and to spoil all their chances by gabbling nonsense. She had seen them a little while ago in Honor's room, fresh and pink and fragrant from their baths, wearing lacy slips, pinning up their hair; breathless and intent, they had been sitting side by side before the dressing table, making braids with which to crown and age themselves and they had not known that she was watching them. Honor's blue dress lay on the bed with its morning-glory skirt spread out and beside it was a pair of brand-new silver dancing slippers. The party, after all, thought Katharine, was not for her and the cremation of her regrets, but it was for these flower-like, simple, punctiliously feminine girls, devoutly putting all their eggs in one basket. Their pantomime was as graceful and as fundamental and as revealing as the dances of birds, and Katharine tiptoed away.

For the point of the ball, except for Honor and Harriet, was gone. While she intended still to burn her diary after the guests were gone and the lanterns had been extinguished, she did not expect to arise from the ashes of it; the act was far more expedient than symbolic (but because she died hard and gave up her habits of thought grudgingly, she could not relinquish the two small rituals of time and place; she would destroy it after the commemorative ball and in her father's study). And the act necessary rather than elective. It was an act and not a gesture for, uncertain of the course her life was now to take, she did not want to leave behind these lares to be rummaged through. If they had not been already rummaged through!

Her fear of Andrew was inescapable. What he knew, she could not guess, nor could she guess the terms by which he scrutinized his knowledge, but yesterday in the library when she had asked the others if they heard a sound and they had not, he had turned at once and run from the house; in the split second before he took to his heels, he had given her a look that she had construed as unspeakable hatred. He had looked at her through half-closed eyes and his lips parted in contempt.

It had been the fear of him that had made her faint earlier when she found the mangled kitten. Before she lost consciousness, she had attributed to Andrew the sophisticated blackmail of this desecration of her bed, and she remembered that as she began to fall, she had vainly tried to call him in the intention, as she now supposed, of finally ferreting out of him the reason for his preoccupation, unbroken since the day he had arrived. She had been alarmed when Maureen had found him crying in the hammock, so passionately and convulsively that the maid had had to take him by the hand and lead him, stumbling, blind with his tears.

And still, he had allowed himself, like a much younger and much more pliant child, to be consoled with promises. He was to help set off the fireworks and if the carpenters agreed, he was to watch them move a house from Thomas to Hawthorne; his requests had been so normal and so boyish that for a while she had been reassured. He had even nestled against her for a pitiful moment and the shudder of his final sobs, running the length of his body, had been copied in her own nerves and muscles. But she had not been convinced that the freshet of his tears had been released, as he said it had, by a bee sting, for he was a Spartan child (all Congreves, Shipleys, Maxwells were physically courageous if that was any virtue) who would never admit to fatigue or aches.

"It's the excitement of the party," said Maureen to her privately and, having no wish to analyze her cousin with anyone, she agreed. "It's the gravestone that makes him sad if you'll pardon me for saying so, Miss Congreve," said Mrs. Shea and Katharine nodded her head. Mary said he had had too little breakfast and too much sun and Harriet accused Honor of badgering him into this collapse. But the proud boy stuck to his story of the bee and even asked for baking soda which he took up to his room, saying, with an attempt at a smirk, that he would have to make the application himself because the "scurvy bee" had stung him in the belly button.

All afternoon he had mooned in the hammock, and all of this day he had been invisible except at breakfast and lunch. It was almost four o'clock when he had come up from the direction of the lake with a string of fish, the very last thing on earth anyone wanted today, and when Mrs. Shea, who was on the verge of tears with worry over the success of her meringues, ordered him to take his reptiles back where they came from, he had savagely flung them into the garbage pail beside the door, thrown his rod into the lettuce bed and thudded upstairs to his room from which presently there came to the ears of the edgy household the sound of his jew's-harp squeaking through the opening bars of "Jerusalem, the Golden." But then, a little later, he had knocked on her door and had asked to see Beth and had shown only a natural curiosity to know, as Peg Duff had wanted to know, if Beth was sorry for what she had done. Thoughtfully, using the terms of the newspapers as glibly as if this were his ordinary speech, he said, "I think it was a mercy killing. I think there was something wrong with the kitten that the cat would know and we wouldn't. It may have fallen down and sustained injuries, in which case she ought to be shown clemency."

Katharine dressed slowly, taking a long time before her mirror to brush her hair into a Psyche knot and plait it with a string of baroque pearls; with silver hairpins she arranged in it two rosebuds, doled out grudgingly by Maddox who hated parties because they meant that his gardens were stripped to fill the vases; he had once, in all seriousness, suggested that she keep artificial flowers in the house.

Her dress was a masterpiece. Beulah had outdone herself. The yards and yards of *mousseline de soie*, cloud-white and gossamer, cascaded over a ridge of crinoline at the waist and fell to the floor, showing through its mobile folds a full and pale blue rustling petticoat; the dead-white satin bodice was cut low at the shoulders, smooth and unornamented, for she had refused Beulah's suggestion of a frill of starched lace at the neck. No matter how gifted they were, these diamonds-in-the-rough, they could not leave well enough alone but wanted always to add extras to their work. It had required consummate diplomacy to keep Mr. Norman from carving a bed of roses for her to lie on, and one year she had disputed a full afternoon with a carpenter who had come to repair the capital of one of the columns and who had implored her to let him make a connecting molding across the front of the house, looping a wooden ribbon from pillar to pillar. Or let him, even better, take down these useless "fence posts" and build for her a porch on which, protected from the bugs and damp, she could far more comfortably watch the world go by than she could on her terrace. He had advocated, she shuddered to remember, screens. She had withstood Beulah Smithwick's further suggestion that she wear a high Spanish comb like a battlement upon her castled hair.

It was dusk. Maddox was lighting the candles in the lanterns with a taper longer than himself and the small orchestra were tuning their fiddles and a cello. They were five old German brothers with faded brown faces like withered apples who had arrived that afternoon from Boston, overwhelmed with happiness to leave the city's heat and to find a landscape that reminded them of the Tauber valley. The sweet and sour scraping of the violins and the swaying of the lanterns at the touch of the taper and the smell of the coffee that was being brewed in the dining room in the immense urn made her tremble with expectation and suddenly she wished she had invited an escort for herself; even Jack Codman, who was a simpleton, could have been metamorphosed through her party eyes.

She envied the twins who came in to ask her if they "looked all right" perfectly knowing and preening themselves on the knowledge that nothing could have improved upon their looks. They pirouetted before her long glass and boldly sprayed themselves with her perfume and exclaimed rhapsodically as they leaned out the windows to look at the lanterns and at all the other finery of the lawn.

A regiment of servants recruited from the kitchens of her friends were stationing the punch bowls on the long tables under the marquee and covered platters of salmon mousse and lobster salad and partridge in aspic and *daube glacé*.

From Honor's windows, they had earlier seen wine coolers and bottles of burgundy and magnums of champagne being taken to the summerhouse. Could they have champagne? They knew they would be too excited to eat a bite, would Cousin Katharine be able to? Was she *sure* that this way of doing their hair was becoming? Their skirts were not too long? Were the seams of their stockings straight? Would she not grant that their shoes were absolutely the last word in chic? They were not interested in the answers to any of their questions, for the ecstasy of their anticipation was their sole concern. They did not even notice Katharine's dress and she was shocked to realize that their failure to do so wounded her; she was cast into a shadow by their conflagration, for they were so very young! And their hearts were so very simple and their minds were so clear and shallow, their ambitions so modest and direct that she was certain they would never come to grief. Theirs, in the end, was the supreme talent: they had the talent for happiness and it radiated from them even in their perpetration of these addled, adolescent idiocies; it was their one depth and it amazed her for they had had neither the help of heredity or environment to bring about its cultivation.

The first car to come up the drive was James Partridge's yellow roadster and, beside themselves, the girls froze at their post and in the end had to be urged and all but pushed downstairs to receive the boys. Katharine heard them, refusing to acknowledge the ague of their lovesickness, talking matter-of-factly about the headmistress of their school as if she were a subject of pressing interest.

Now Edmund's car came in between the maple trees and when she saw him get out, his plumpness seeming everywhere to push at his clothes, a momentary disenchantment chilled her; the evening lost its dimension of romance and the violins grated and the lanterns appeared sleazy and absurd. Edmund's temerity had been put to flight at once as soon as she had fainted and he kept a nervous distance from her now even while he continued, out of habit, to cast lovelorn glances at her and endeavoured at large gatherings to be alone with her to pay her some proprietary compliment. She had awakened that day in the drawing room to hear him say, "I'm staggered. I thought Katharine was made of iron." The violence of her reaction to his profession—for he would have no way of knowing that a far greater weight had crushed her down—had flattered him a little but far more had dismayed him and he had sent her an apologetic note, typewritten and noncommittal and signed only with the letter "E" in which he implied that he had thought she knew all along that he had only been joking. His need for her, now that he saw she was in need, was gone.

The house was lighted tonight only with candles and, by accident, with the green flashing of fireflies, and as she went down the stairs, hearing her sibilant petticoat, she thought it had never been more magnificent. Always immaculate, it had been washed and polished and burnished from the cellars to the attics for this occasion so that glass glittered and metal burned and wood gleamed like hide. Perfect and plenteous, Congreve House was the locus but was also the extension of herself; not the events that had taken place in it which she had clung to out of her stubborn self-destruction, but the very pan-eled walls themselves and the wide random boards of the floors and the marble mantels and, above all, the ironic spirit of the house, mature (as she must learn to be) and indestructible (as she was despite all her efforts to destroy herself).

It was her father who had imbued the house with its spirit of acceptance; she looked back up the stairs at his portrait and was ashamed, meeting the face in which judgement and resignation were balanced equally. As if he were there and had held her up to friendly ridicule, had said all this emotion was infantile and unattractive, she felt her broken structure begin to mend, begin to move articulately, and whole, mistress of Congreve House, she emerged from the embrace of it into the summer evening.

2

For the first time, Andrew had a close look at Charles Smithwick. He had come into the stable where Adam was teaching Andrew to play pool on Cousin Katharine's tombstone (she really had done it and Adam had told him what Billy Bartholomew had said when he had heard of it. He had said, "She has bats in her belfry as big as my old white horse") and began at once to correct Adam, saying, "Your form's all haywire. Here, lemme show you how." He wore a pin-striped business suit, much too small, so that his knobby wrists hung long below the sleeves and the tops of his white socks were visible below his trouser cuffs; he wore a proper white, starched shirt, a red bow tie and squeaky ox-blood shoes. He looked dressed for a business interview, and he was so brash and toplofty that Andrew wanted to ask him if that suit was left over from highschool graduation or if it belonged to Victor. Popping his gum loudly, he said, "Who's getting the twenty-one gun salute?" And when Adam asked him what he meant by that, he said, "Who's the blow-out for? The king of Canada? Or the Jewish postmaster general?"

He sneered at everything though Adam tried to shush him because of Andrew. He said, "Oh, stow it. It's a free country, ain't it?" He said he had never seen anything on land or sea to beat the paper moon and he would like to know just who she thought she was kidding, the kindergarten? Was *that* the band? That bunch of dried-up hardware salesmen-looking shrimps? He had bright tumid lips and stupid, glassy eyes, and the smell of his Juicy Fruit gum was sickening.

"How come the pool hall's here?" he asked, and immediately leaped back, sending the cue ball lolloping down the felt. "Oh, hey, Billy told me. Jesus, that gives me the creeps!" Serious for a moment, he looked around uneasily and started when Pegasus gave forth a muted whinny. But seeing Adam start to make a shot, his egotism overrode his uneasiness and he came back to the table to offer advice.

"When are you going back to your ship?" asked Andrew and Charles, intent on pocketing the red ball said, "One of these days if I feel like it."

"How *do* you feel?" Andrew watched him from the foot of the table and hoped he would miss the shot, but he did not. The ball rolled smoothly and surely into the pocket and Charles gave himself a warm handshake.

"How do I feel? Well, I'll tell you. Some days I feel like a million and some days I feel as good for nothing as one red cent. I'm up and then I'm down, if you follow my meaning."

"On the days you're 'up' do you do things with Victor? You know, like fishing? I mean do you dig clams and things like that?"

"Oh, sure," he said. "Yeah, I play nursemaid to the kid brother."

"Missed!" crowed Adam for Charles's ball had sailed past the pocket. The sailor snapped his fingers. "You joggled my elbow, dammit," he said. It was not true; Adam had not been anywhere near him. Andrew was delighted to find that besides being a braggart Charles was a liar and a bad loser.

"Well, on the days you're 'down,'" he pursued, "what do you do?"

"Lie around the house and wish I was dead."

"Do you really wish you were dead?"

"You betcha I do. And you would too if you felt like you had a buzz saw in your bread-basket." He stopped in the act of taking his stance for another shot and addressing Adam he mused, "You know about that wishing you were dead, it's a funny thing. Once or twice, I've gotten to feel so god-awful that if somebody came along and offered to shoot me, I swear I think I'd take them up on it. I never would go and do it myself because in my opinion people that commit suicide are cowards and I don't care what reasons they give or how they try to whitewash it. But if some one of these traveling nomad gypsies came up in the yard and offered to kill me I swear I think I'd say 'hop to it' if I was feeling the way I sometimes do."

The voice began again and Andrew lurched backward into a shadow.

"What's that?" said Charles Smithwick. "Is that a musical saw?"

Andrew's throat constricted suddenly. The air seemed shut off by a thin membrane.

"That's one of the twin girls singing," said Adam. "Miss Honor or Miss Harriet, I can't tell them apart unless they're standing side by side and then I know that one of them is on the east and the other is on the west."

Through the roars of his own voice, Andrew could hear Harriet, somewhere close by, singing James Partridge's favorite song, his favorite because his name was in it, "On the first day of Christmas, my true love brought to me a partridge in a pear tree."

"No kidding, I mean it," said Charles reverently. "It's like a lady I heard playing the musical saw in Tokyo."

Her voice diminished with distance and then it stopped as the orchestra began to play the first waltz. Charles Smithwick, reminded of Japan, began to talk in man-to-man innuendoes of geisha girls. Andrew left the barn, driven by the voice that clashed and clanged like a brass band and boomed like kettle-drums, although he did not *care*. Charles was stuck on himself and rude and unlikeable, but Andrew did not *care*. Between clenched teeth, he said furiously to the voice, "Shut *up*. I say, *shut up*."

He felt no part of this festival gathering. He watched the dancers on the platform, circling and dipping in the waltz, his sisters' blue skirts whirling out as round and round the outer edges they danced with Raoul and James. Cousin Katharine was dancing with Mr. St. Denis who looked like a porpoise and wore the kind of mess-jacket Mr. Barker's butler wore. If Andrew had to dance, he thought, that would be the very end. He moved down toward the pond where a group of older people were sitting, hoping that their conversation would be interesting enough to drown out the voice, but they were only telling each other, as if it were news, that the face of the man in the moon was accounted for by craters. He wondered con-temptuously if anyone had told them about the Easter rabbit. There followed some dispute over the identity of the man in Katharine's artificial moon but it was agreed, at length, that it looked the most like Theodore Roosevelt.

"The Rough Rider," explained Miss Duff, who had also posited the original statement about the craters of the moon. "Invented the word *mollycoddle*."

She was ignored though several people smiled politely at her. "The only things left out of this picture," said a dreamy-eyed old lady Andrew had never seen before, "are John Shipley and Maeve. Do they never come to Hawthorne now?"

"Sometimes they come to take the young fry back, that's all," said Miss Duff. "They're city people. City people don't know what they're missing by not getting on the land."

"Is Katharine quite well again?" asked the same woman. "We heard in some very roundabout way that she hadn't been well this summer."

The talk was diverted then to the fainting fit of yesterday and what had brought it on and Miss Duff went through the whole post-mortem again while Mr. Barker implored her not to go on, seeming to feel that she was somehow blackening the name of Hawthorne and of Congreve House.

"I don't see how she can stand to have the cat in the house after what happened," she concluded. "I'd be reminded of that mess every time I looked at a cat."

Mr. Barker said, "That's nonsense, Peg. One must rise above such things. Else would we not quail at the sight of the Atlantic because the *Lusitania* went down? At oil lamps because Mrs. O'Leary's cow kicked one over?"

"Always wanted to see Chicago," said Miss Duff. This message was followed immediately by another, "First dance over. Katharine coming this way, no more talk of you-know-what."

She spoke in telegrams but Mr. Barker, Cousin Katharine said, sounded frequently like a greeting card. He got up and said, "Hail to the mistress of ceremonies! Methought I had wandered into Arcadia."

"You all must go and dance," cried Cousin Katharine.

"Too old to dance," said Miss Duff, but Mr. St. Denis bullied her to her feet, laughing noisily, and in her surprise she permitted herself to be propelled across the lawn and up to the platform; she danced like a bundle of sticks.

"The very picture of carefree youth," said Mrs. Tyler peevishly. "I mean, of course, the Shipley girls and their swains."

"Oh, surely you don't think that youth is carefree," said the woman who missed John and Maeve. "At their age—perhaps a bit older, I was wretched. Growing up for me was like coming out of purdah. To be relieved at last of those awful jealousies! Those dashed hopes!"

Except for Mrs. Tyler who held out a little longer for the reality of joy she was sure lay within the girls' appearance of it, the elders on the terrace agreed that they would not for anything be under thirty-five again.

They complimented Cousin Katharine on the music and though they would not agree to dance, for all her urging, they would agree to eat and drink. In pairs and threes they drifted away from the terrace in the direction of the buffet and of Minerva's temple. When they had gone, Cousin Katharine loitered, picking up the petals of a shattered flower that lay on the stones. She came to the edge of the pond, so close to Andrew that he could have reached out from the shadow that hid him and touched her dress. He saw her toss the petals onto the black water and watch the swans move slowly toward them. She seemed, again, to be listening. He looked at her and then looked up at the stable where Charles Smithwick was standing to one side of the door to let two of the men guests by.

"Can you hear it, Cousin Katharine?" Andrew said softly.

She put both her hands over her heart but she turned her head very slowly and when she spoke, her voice was even. "Do you mean the pump, dear? Or do you mean the music?"

Picking up her skirts so that the grass would not stain them, she went back to her party to mingle with her fifty happy guests, pretending that she had not heard the voice. Always pretending! He would have to go somewhere to drown it out by screaming; sometimes it stopped for a while if he ran fast. He ran now across the meadow and when he was deep in the pine-woods, near the Indian burying ground, he hallooed to himself, "Androoo! Yoo-hooooo! Androoooo Shiii-pley!"

It was the longest party Andrew had ever been to or ever heard of. The first people had come before six o'clock and at midnight they behaved as if they had just arrived. There was a steady parade of servants bringing fresh platters of food down from the kitchen and stacks of clean plates and pitchers of punch to fill up the bowls. In the summerhouse the grownups were drinking wine from George Congreve's cellar and champagne that Mr. Barker had brought. The orchestra, barely pausing between waltzes, went on like a perpetual motion machine without a sign of fatigue.

Down in the meadow, Andrew waited with Adam and Maddox and Charles for the signal to begin shooting off the fireworks. They stood at the four corners of the square they had sickled down that afternoon and all of their hands itched to get at the flares and skyrockets in their bright Chinese wrappings.

The road in front of Congreve House was crowded with the townspeople standing on the running boards of cars and even, in the case of children, sitting on the tops of them. "The rabble waits without," Andrew had heard Mr. Barker say to Cousin Katharine and Miss Duff had growled, "Typical. Always after something free gratis for nothing." But Cousin Katharine defended them, said she had let it be known that everyone was welcome and that, in fact, she would have been offended if they had not come.

She was flushed with high spirits and to three different people, he had heard her say, "I have never been happier in my whole life!" and Edmund St. Denis, quite drunk and trouty, remarked to no one in particular, "She doesn't look a day over sixteen. I say Katharine Congreve is nonpareil," and as if someone were about to deny it, he tentatively put up his hands for a fist-fight.

Everyone was there except Em Bugtown who was down with summer complaint. Billy Bartholomew was there on Carrie Nation who wore an old Western saddle with the pommel broken off; he sat in it as if he were sitting in a chair and tilting it back on two legs. "First we'll see her ladyship's pyrotechnical to-do and then every able-bodied man in the county will spend the rest of the mortal night in a bucket brigade putting out the forest fire," he declared in a voice of doom and his wife, a safe distance from him and from his horse, told him to dry up. Poor Hollis was there and so was his mother; she was very small and withered but she had her arm around her son as if he were an infant. They were near the gate and Andrew had seen how, when Billy's angry voice frightened Poor Hollis, his mother tugged him closer to her and he heard her say, "There, now, let me hear you ring your pretty bell." Jasper, the epileptic, was treading an erratic path up and down the road and Billy said, "He'll be going in circles, sure as shooting. Somebody'd better go get the paddywagon for the inevitable event of our fair city."

They had been waiting an eternity when Andrew saw someone coming up from the lower edge of the meadow. In a moment, as the figure came closer, he recognized Victor Smithwick's lope, a wasteful gait in which the arms and the head participated far more than necessary. He went directly to his brother without so much as nodding to Andrew. "Do you know what the five-letter word for 'legal excuse' was? Alibi!"

"I'll be damned," said Charles. "I didn't know alibi was a *legal* excuse. I thought it was just the opposite. I mean I thought an alibi was an *illegal* excuse."

"Hello, Victor," said Andrew.

Victor peered across at him. "Oh, hello, there, Shipshape. I didn't recognize you with your hat on," and the brothers burst into laughter.

"Did you shoot pool? You know where I mean?" Victor's voice shook with giggles. They held a conversation, Victor and Charles, showing off the security of their brotherhood as Honor and Harriet often did, laughing madly at allusions no one could understand except themselves, speaking in a kind of code so that a listener felt himself to be the butt of jokes, pilloried and hooted at. What had happened to Victor's admiration of Cousin Katharine that he would make fun of her tombstone, not kindly as he used to do of her horse-drawn whatsis but meanly, like Billy Bartholomew? What was the matter with him that he had spent this whole evening at home doing a crossword puzzle when he might have been here where everyone else was? Everyone including his brother? There was only one possible answer, that he could not bear the sight of Andrew.

"Anchors aweigh!" cried Charles, breaking off in the middle of an exposition on the differences between billiards and pool and those between real pool and the kind of pool that Adam played.

"We're off," said Maddox, for the signal had been given. The orchestra had stopped playing and through a megaphone, James Partridge, elected because both the twins were in love with him and were under the impression, therefore, that the party was in his honor, announced that the fireworks display was now to take place and that his "gracious hostess" had asked him to say that the dancing would continue when it was over.

Adam and Andrew set off the first two girandoles. They went in opposite directions, one toward the lake and one toward the river, bursting five times. From the dying shower of scarlet, there shot a higher spray of violet from which sprang blue, then green and the far, last opening cone was brilliant gold. When the last of the sparks had perished, applause came gustily from the road and the lawn and then everyone fell silent, waiting as if for the curtain to rise in the theater on the next act.

In the south sky they saw a blood-red waterfall and in the north a silver rain. An ephemeral sun, hissed into existence, hung in the summer firmament, blotting out the Pleiades. They saw serpents coiling upward to dissolve at the highest point of their path into radiant green stars. The tourbillion fires ascended, spiraling straight into the sky and beneath them, like a ballet chorus, the small pastilles spun themselves quickly to nothing. Two of the skyrockets were delinquent and ploughed through the timothy to fizzle out, but all the others, the blazing, blasting garnitures and galaxies, rose triumphantly to the sky.

The finale was to be five Catherine wheels, set in the clearing, four of them revolving simultaneously and the fifth coming a little later as the *premiere danseuse.* Andrew was watching a curving rain of gold falling, gently like snow and dying in the air above the pine trees by the lake when he heard Cousin Katharine's voice behind him. "I have come to superintend the final outburst," she was saying to Maddox. "It has been stupendous."

Respectful of the men, she stood aside and Andrew saw Victor move toward her and heard her say, "Victor Smithwick! You're a total stranger these days. Why didn't you come earlier to stand on your head? Your mother tells me you have got a whole book of crossword puzzles. I'll tell you one thing, 'slave' is always 'esne.'" Victor started to reply but she silenced him, "We'll talk about ers and ems another day. The Catherine wheels are going off."

Andrew and Maddox and Charles and Adam, at Victor's count of three, struck their matches to set off the fuses and leaped back into the tall grass. In a moment, Charles ran forward again to light the fifth. There was a flare too low and everyone at the same time realized that the Catherine wheel was a dud.

He heard Adam say, "Too bad to spoil the grand march," and then he saw fire illumine Charles's face as he knelt, still trying to make the wheel go off. His high white hair was on fire! Charles Smithwick's head was blazing like a torch! It had been bending over, the head with its shock of coarse hay-hair, and the gunpowder had set it on fire! It was a Catherine wheel that was killing Victor's brother, it was beloved Cousin Katharine's quick, ravishing wheel that would burn him up as it burned itself up, while in the stable her other one, motionless in stone, was as cool and as permanent as the sky. Andrew had been right, after all: her tombstone was a sign.

He stood where he was, assailed by the voice, bending with it and resisting it. He was a tree and this was the wind and he could not move a step forward because his obstinate roots were in the ground. He saw the other four of them, his cousin first, rush to pound and stamp Charles with their hands. The fire eddied like a thin, roiled liquid at their feet, burning the bodies of the used matches and the seepings from the rocket cases, and the sailor, turned into a candle, squawled.

"*Now* do you hear it, Cousin Katharine? You hear the voice inside my head, don't you?" roared Andrew above all the other cries from the startled bystanders in the road and on the lawn.

But she was busy. She was beating the sailor's head to save his life and her white skirt was on fire at the hem. He watched, fascinated, as it ate scallops into the filmy cloth.

"Katharine!" Mr. St. Denis came scrambling down the lawn and into the field and after him came a phalanx of men and behind them came Honor and Harriet. The gardener was the first of the men below to see that her skirt was burning and, leaving Charles, he seized her by the arm and pulled her down into the higher grass, but then, insane with terror and confusion, she evaded him and ran by herself in a widening circle, fanning the fire until it reached her waist; she screamed unceasingly.

A battalion of her guests closed in upon her, like dogs on a fox, and someone managed at last to fling her to the ground and roll her, as if she were inanimate, until the ravenous flames stopped eating her. For a minute, there was a vast, unnatural silence and in it, as soft as an insect sound, Andrew heard the tinkle of Poor Hollis's bell. He turned a little in the direction of that soft, affectionate noise and as he did so he saw Charles Smithwick standing where his rescuers had abandoned him for Cousin Katharine. He was holding his hands on top of his head but he was already beginning to relax from his surprise; in a moment, unhurt, he went to join the others.

After they had taken her up to the house and after all had been done that could be done, it was Andrew that she asked to see. At the sight of her hideous black face and the intolerable, sickening suffering in her eyes, his misery pushed before it a tide of tears. Her arms were swathed in bandages and there was a turban of gauze wound round and round her head. But her voice, though it was weak and hesitant, was almost her own when she said, "I heard it, Andrew. I heard it when you heard it."

He swayed against the bedpost, sightless with his tears; it seemed a sacrilege to make these gulping, baby sounds but he could not stop. The pain must have driven her out of her head for when she spoke again she said, "I heard the Catherine wheel swinging low to get me . . . only it swung high, it swung, it swung, it swung . . ." She tried to move her hands to imitate the revolving lights, but the least motion was agony and she moaned. Across the bed from him the doctor nodded his head in some signal that Andrew could not understand at first and then he indicated that the boy should move closer to his cousin. Reluctantly, he edged along the bed until he was looking directly down on her dying, unrecognizable face.

"Is that boy all right? Charles Smithwick?"

Before Andrew was obliged to answer, the doctor said, "Don't trouble yourself on that score. His hair was singed, that's all. He's home asleep by now, resting up to go back to his ship next week."

Her voice grew slower and slower as if she were going to

sleep and long pauses came after each word. "Andrew," she said, "do this for me. Take my big red diary and burn it. And forgive me my trespasses if you love me."

The last thing she said, she said to herself. "He was not worth it."

Oh, no, no, he had not been worth it! Victor Smithwick's friendship had not been worth the shortest moment of Cousin Katharine's love. When at last he found it and could use it again, his voice came out in a questioning plea, "Cousin Katharine? You're the only person I ever loved, ever, ever, ever!"

He could tell that she was trying to smile but her lips barely moved and her eyes seemed not to focus. The doctor, bringing the diary to Andrew, put it into his hands and told him to leave. He took the heavy book down to the kitchen where the fire was banked in the coal stove and leaf by leaf, without reading a word of them, he fed the pages to it, his big tears hissing and skittering away in minute bubbles on the iron lids.

The thin leaves curled and disintegrated into cracking char. The voice in Andrew was silenced now but in its place there was a swishing, sibilant swirl and the eyes in his mind saw four bright Catherine wheels perishing in glory. Wheels wheeled within the wheels and Cousin Katharine wheeled with them until the last page of her history was black ash. He put the stove lid back and after that he heard nothing but the sound of her faithful servants weeping.

APPENDIX

"Author's Note" to the 1972
Farrar, Straus and Giroux
printing of The Mountain Lion

T HE LAST sentence of *The Mountain Lion* was written on a misty April day in 1946 in Damariscotta Mills, Maine, while a local carpenter was screwing handles on the drawers of a desk he had made for me. He had lived in Maine for most of his life, but originally he was "from away" and was not graced with the autochthonous Down East taciturnity. He was the gabbiest workman I have ever had on any premises anywhere. But he was an excellent artisan, so I put up with his homespun wisdom ("Like the feller says, never rains but it pours." "Can't count on only two things in this life, them being death and taxes") and his disgraceful politics and his totally incomprehensible jokes (I either laughed too soon or failed to laugh at all and, thinking I had been listening to a misfortune, would say, "Oh, what a pity!"). His head was just below my typewriter and his breath was strong (he chewed, but mercifully forebore to do so in his clients' houses; I *did* own a cuspidor but it was small and made of milk glass and I kept straw flowers and bittersweet in it) and as usual he was twaddling on, sixteen to the dozen.

But I was so deep in my remorse for what I had done to my heroine, Molly Fawcett, that I heard not a word he said and cared not a pin that he was there.

The desk has been moved ten times. At it, I wrote another novel and a great many short stories and essays and reviews. It is too big for my present study, but it is up in the attic and in its well is the Royal portable on which I wrote *The Mountain Lion*. I bought that typewriter, paying for it in installments, in 1937 when I had a salary of $100 a month for teaching Freshman English to pretty, featherheaded girls in Missouri. The typewriter has long since been replaced by a series of standards which reach obsolescence in early nonage. It antedates the desk by eight years, but it is still in working order (it is stiff in the joints from disuse and its touch is heavy, but I can limber it up with a little workout) and it served me valiantly until its retirement: on it I wrote several novels that weren't any good and abide, yellow and crumbling, in my files; and on it I wrote all three of my published novels. Every now and again, I go up to the attic on a cool day and, removing the Royal's shabby cover, I write what I always write when I am trying out a new typewriter or a new pen: "This is the day when no man living may 'scape away."

Good Deeds says that in *Everyman*. I can't remember when this announcement of Doomsday is made—probably toward the end of the play when the grim reaper lets it be known that Everyman's number has come up—but I should know, because I used to have that particular Morality by heart. At least I knew by heart what Good Deeds had to say because I played the role one time when I was a student at the University of Colorado. Good Deeds is one of Everyman's men friends, and I was a girl at the time—now I am an old lady with a crocheted hug-me-tight around my shoulders and a tatted cap upon my nodding head—but I was chosen for the part; I suppose it could be argued that out there, in those olden, golden days, we were already on to the treacheries deriving from Male Chauvinism and this was a little bitty protest. I think it is more likely, however, that I spoke his lines because I had (and have) the voice of an undertaker. And Good Deeds, while well-intentioned (he is, in fact, a real brick and goes, as you recall, along with Every-man to the hereafter when all his other fair-weather friends have ditched him), is melancholy.

And up there in the attic, amongst the hornets and the cob-webs, in my house at the eastern end of Long Island, across the continent from the Pacific Seaboard where Molly was born (and, by curious coincidence, so was I) and far from the Rocky Mountains where she died (and I was stage-struck for a couple of weeks), I grow as melancholy as Good Deeds. Poor old Molly! I loved her dearly and I hope she rests in peace.

JEAN STAFFORD

The Springs
Long Island
September 21, 1971

CHRONOLOGY

NOTE ON THE TEXTS

NOTES

Chronology

<table>
<tr><td>1915</td><td>Born Jean Wilson Stafford on July 1 in Covina, California, the fourth child of John Richard Stafford and Ethel McKillop Stafford. (Father, born 1874 in Atchison County, Missouri, was the son of a successful cattle rancher. After graduating from Amity College in College Springs, Iowa, he worked as a journalist in Chicago and New York City and for the telephone company in Tarkio, Missouri. Mother, born 1876 in Rock Port, Missouri, was the daughter of an attorney. She attended Tarkio College and taught school in Rock Port and Salida, Colorado. Parents married in Tarkio in 1907 and had three children: Mary Lee, born 1908, Marjorie, born 1909, and Richard (Dick), born 1911. Father published novel *When Cattle Kingdom Fell* in 1910 and later wrote Western stories for pulp magazines under the names Jack Wonder, Ben Delight, and O. B. Miles. Family moved in 1912 to Covina, where father used his inheritance to purchase a ten-acre walnut ranch and build an eight-room house at 831 Lark Ellen Avenue.)</td></tr>
</table>

1920   Father sells walnut ranch and moves family to San Diego, where he speculates in stocks. Stafford enters kindergarten.

1921   Father loses proceeds from sale of the Covina ranch along with much of his inheritance in the stock market. Family travels by car to Colorado in summer and moves into rented house in Ivywild neighborhood of Colorado Springs. Stafford enters first grade. Father borrows money from his mother and continues writing.

1923   Family moves to Stratton Park area of Colorado Springs.

1925   Family moves to house on Arapahoe Street in Boulder so that Mary Lee can live at home while attending the University of Colorado. Stafford begins attending University Hill school.

1928   Family moves to house at 1112 University Avenue. Mother begins taking in female students as boarders. Father remains unemployed while working on treatise on government finance and debt (book is never completed).

1929   Mary Lee graduates from University of Colorado and
            begins teaching in Hayden, Colorado. Stafford enters
            State Preparatory School as sophomore.

1930   Marjorie graduates from University of Colorado. Stafford
            begins working during summers as a waitress and maid
            at a dude ranch in Ward, Colorado.

1931–32   Wins statewide student essay contest for "Disenchant-
            ment," account of her family's move from California to
            Colorado. Marjorie begins teaching in Tahlequah, Okla-
            homa. Stafford becomes features editor of *Prep Owl*, her
            high school newspaper. Family moves to house at 631
            University Avenue. Stafford graduates from high school
            in June 1932.

1932–34   Enters University of Colorado on scholarship that covers
            her tuition fees. Studies philosophy, Latin, and the his-
            tory of science. Majors in English and takes courses in
            Victorian literature, Middle English, and Anglo-Saxon
            taught by Professor Irene McKeehan, who becomes
            her academic mentor. Writes stories and short plays for
            creative writing course taught by John McLucas. Dick
            graduates from Colorado A&M in Fort Collins in 1933
            and becomes forest ranger in Oregon. Stafford earns
            money for expenses in series of campus jobs, including
            posing as nude model for art classes.

1934–35   Leaves home and moves into boardinghouse at 1001
            Tenth Street. Becomes friends with Lucy McKee Cooke
            and Andrew Cooke, married law students at the center
            of social circle known for heavy drinking and sexual
            experimentation. Moves in with the Cookes.

1935–36   Becomes friends with Robert Hightower, a premed stu-
            dent with literary interests. On the evening of November
            9, 1935, Lucy McKee Cooke returns home in an agitated
            state, quarrels with her husband, and then fatally shoots
            herself while Stafford is telephoning a physician for assis-
            tance. Stafford's parents move to Denver. Forms lifelong
            friendship with Paul Thompson, an instructor in the
            English department, and Dorothy Thompson, his wife.
            Writes senior thesis "Profane and Divine Love in English
            Literature of the Thirteenth Century." Awarded scholar-
            ship to study Anglo-Saxon at the University of Heidel-
            berg for one year; Hightower also receives a scholarship

at Heidelberg. Writes one-act play about the death of Beethoven, *Tomorrow in Vienna*, that is performed by the University of Colorado drama club in April 1936. Awarded BA and MA degrees in English in June. Attends summer writers' conference at the University, where she meets Whit Burnett and Martha Foley, editors of *Story* magazine and the Story Press, and Robert Penn Warren. Lands in Cuxhaven, Germany, on September 18 and joins Hightower in Heidelberg. Struggles with spoken German and stops attending lectures in November.

1937   Visits Munich and Paris before returning to the United States in April. Falls ill with infection caused by ovarian cysts and is hospitalized for three weeks in Brooklyn and Manhattan. (Stafford will suffer from ill health for much of her adult life, exacerbated by heavy drinking, heavy smoking, and poor eating.) Spends much of the summer on ranch in Hayden owned by Mary Lee and her husband, Harry Frichtel. Attends the University of Colorado writers' conference, where she meets the novelists Ford Madox Ford, Evelyn Scott, and Caroline Gordon, the poet and critic Allen Tate (who is married to Gordon), and Robert Lowell (born 1917), an aspiring poet from a socially prominent Boston family. Begins teaching composition at Stephens College, a women's college in Columbia, Missouri, in the fall, but quickly comes to dislike the college and her students. Works on novel "Which No Vicissitude" and corresponds with both Hightower, who is studying East Asian languages at Harvard, and Lowell, an undergraduate at Kenyon College.

1938   Whit Burnett of the Story Press rejects "Which No Vicissitude." Begins writing "Neville," novel inspired by her experiences at Stephens. College declines to renew her contract. Meets Hightower in Albany, New York, in June, and travels with him to Colorado before going to Oswego, Oregon, where her parents now live. Begins teaching composition at the University of Iowa in September. Leaves Iowa City in November and travels to Cambridge, where she moves in with Hightower. Sees Lowell when he visits Boston at Thanksgiving. Moves to rented room in house at 2 Monument Street in Concord. Atlantic Monthly Press rejects "Neville" but pays her $250 for an option on her new novel "Autumn Festival," about an affair between an American student in Germany and a Nazi aviator. On December 21 Stafford and an intoxicated Lowell are driving through Cambridge when Lowell turns down a dead-end lane and hits a wall. Stafford suffers a smashed nose and fractures to her jaw, right cheekbone, and skull that keep her in the hospital for almost a month.

1939   Undergoes five facial operations from late winter through early spring (will have breathing problems and suffer from headaches for the rest of her life). Sues Lowell's insurance company for $25,000. Submits "Autumn Festival" to Atlantic Monthly Press in late summer. Spends two months in fall at Mary Lee's ranch in Hayden. Atlantic Monthly Press rejects "Autumn Festival." Short story "And Lots of Solid Color" published in November *American Prefaces* magazine. Moves into Cambridge apartment with two roommates. Receives $4,000 settlement from Lowell's insurance company, which she uses to pay debts. Writes to Hightower in December that she is engaged to Lowell.

1940   Marries Lowell at St. Mark's Episcopal Church in New York City, April 2. Spends spring at ranch in Hayden while Lowell finishes senior year at Kenyon. Hightower marries Florence (Bunny) Cole, one of Stafford's Cambridge roommates. (After surviving Japanese internment in China, Hightower becomes a professor of Chinese literature at Harvard.) Attends Lowell's graduation from Kenyon on June 9. Stafford and Lowell spend several weeks in Memphis at home of Lowell's classmate, the writer Peter Taylor, who becomes her lifelong friend. In the summer they move to Baton Rouge, where Lowell has a fellowship at Louisiana State University. Stafford becomes office manager of the *Southern Review*, literary magazine edited by Cleanth Brooks and Robert Penn Warren. During trip to New Orleans in October Lowell strikes Stafford during a quarrel and breaks her nose.

1941   Lowell is received into the Roman Catholic Church in late March. Stafford also joins the Church, and at Lowell's insistence, they are remarried in Catholic ceremony. Suffering from recurring fevers and respiratory problems, she spends most of the spring at her sister's ranch in Hayden. Moves in the summer with Lowell to New

York City, where they rent apartment at 63 West 11th Street. Becomes part-time secretary to Frank Sheed of the Catholic publishing firm Sheed & Ward. Works on new novel "The Outskirts."

1942   Meets Robert Giroux, an editor at Harcourt, Brace and Company, after he reads manuscript of "The Outskirts." Signs contract with Giroux on April 30 for its publication by Harcourt, Brace in return for $500 advance. In the summer Stafford and Lowell move to Monteagle, Tennessee, where they live in a large house with Allen Tate and Caroline Gordon.

1943   Sends manuscript of "The Outskirts" to Harcourt, Brace in February. Begins cutting and revising the novel in response to comments by editor Lambert Davis (Giroux is serving in the navy) as well as criticism from Tate and Gordon. Spends July and August at the Yaddo artists' colony in Saratoga Springs, New York. Joins Lowell in New York City in early September and learns that he has decided to resist induction into the armed services. Lowell sends public letter to President Franklin Roosevelt on September 7, refusing to serve as a protest against the Allied bombing of Germany and the policy of unconditional surrender; on October 13 he is sentenced to serve one year and one day in prison. Stafford rents apartment on East 17th Street. Visits Lowell in federal prison at Danbury, Connecticut. Becomes friends with writer Delmore Schwartz.

1944   Submits revised version of manuscript to Harcourt, Brace in January (the novel is retitled *Boston Adventure* by the publisher). Story "The Darkening Moon" published in January *Harper's Bazaar*. After Lowell is paroled in March and assigned to work as a hospital janitor in Bridgeport, Connecticut, Stafford finds apartment for them in the Black Rock district of Bridgeport. Story "The Lippia Lawn" appears in Spring *Kenyon Review*. Stafford is visited in July by her brother Dick, now a second lieutenant in the 95th Infantry Division. *Land of Unlikeness*, Lowell's first book of poetry, is published September 18 in edition of 250 copies. *Boston Adventure* published September 21 in first printing of 22,000 copies. It receives favorable reviews and becomes a best seller (Harcourt, Brace edition sells 35,000 copies by

May 1945, in addition to 199,000 copies sold by the
Book League of America and 144,000 copies of a condensed Armed Services edition). Learns in October that
Dick was killed on September 18 in a jeep accident shortly
after his division landed in France. Visits parents and
sisters in Oregon. Moves with Lowell to rented house on
nine acres of land in rural area of Westport, Connecticut.
Story "A Reunion" published in Fall *Partisan Review*.

1945   Commutes to New York one day a week to teach course
in short story writing at Queens College. Hires Marian
Ives as her literary agent. Awarded Guggenheim Fellow-
ship in April. Works on novella that becomes novel *The
Mountain Lion*. Story "The Home Front" published in
Spring *Partisan Review*; "Between the Porch and the
Altar" appears in June *Harper's*. After Westport house
is sold by its owner, Stafford uses earnings from *Boston
Adventure* to buy house in Damariscotta Mills, Maine,
and moves there with Lowell in August.

1946   Signs contract with Harcourt, Brace for publication of
The Mountain Lion. Stafford and Lowell leave Dam-
ariscotta Mills in late January and stay with Delmore
Schwartz in Cambridge for several weeks. Story "The
Present" (later retitled "The Captain's Gift") published
in April *Sewanee Review*. Completes final version of
The Mountain Lion in Damariscotta Mills in late April.
Hosts series of visitors, June–August, including John
Berryman and Eileen Simpson, Peter Taylor, Robert
Hightower, Robert Giroux, Philip and Nathalie Rahv,
and the painter Frank Parker. In September Stafford
and Lowell go to New York City, where they soon sepa-
rate. Stafford drinks heavily. On a psychiatrist's advice
she enters a sanitarium in Detroit, but soon leaves and
goes to Denver, where she sees Mary Lee for a few days
before returning to New York. Stays in series of hotels
in New York and Connecticut and continues to drink
while rarely eating. Learns that Lowell has abandoned
Catholicism and is seeking a divorce. In late November
Stafford enters the Payne Whitney Psychiatric Clinic at
New York Hospital, where she is treated by Dr. Mary
Jane Sherfey. Story "The Interior Castle" is published in
the November–December *Partisan Review*.

1947   Story "The Hope Chest" is published in January *Harper's* and "A Slight Maneuver" appears in the February *Mademoiselle*. Stafford learns that her mother is dying of malignant melanoma and is granted emergency leave from the hospital. Arrives in Oregon after her mother's death on February 3. *The Mountain Lion* is published by Harcourt, Brace on March 1; it receives enthusiastic reviews but sells poorly. *Lord Weary's Castle*, Lowell's second volume of poetry, is awarded Pulitzer Prize in May. Stafford sells house in Damariscotta Mills. "My Sleep Grew Shy of Me," essay about her insomnia, published in *Vogue*, October 15. Released from Payne Whitney in November. Continues to see Dr. Sherfey (will remain in therapy with her until the late 1950s). Rents apartment at 27 West 75th Street. Delivers lecture on "The Psychological Novel" at Bard College literary conference (published in *Kenyon Review*, Spring 1948). Signs contract with Harcourt, Brace in late November for novel "In the Snowfall," inspired by her friendship with Lucy McKee Cooke, and receives $4,000 advance. Fires Marian Ives as her agent (will represent herself for the next seven years).

1948   Story "Children Are Bored on Sundays" appears in the February 21 issue of *The New Yorker*, the first of twenty-two stories Stafford will publish in the magazine. Becomes friends with Katharine White, her fiction editor at *The New Yorker*. Meets President Harry S. Truman in Washington, D.C., when she receives National Press Club award on April 3. Awarded second Guggenheim Fellowship. Spends six weeks in U.S. Virgin Islands obtaining divorce from Lowell. Forms lasting friendship with the writers Nancy and Robert Gibney, who own a home on St. John. Stafford receives onetime payment of $6,500 when divorce becomes final on June 14. "Profiles: American Town," article about Newport, Rhode Island, appears in August 28 issue of *The New Yorker*. Story "The Bleeding Heart" published in the September *Partisan Review*, and "A Summer Day" appears in the September 11 issue of *The New Yorker*.

1949   Three of her stories appear in *The New Yorker* during the year: "The Cavalier" (February 12), "Pax Vobiscum" (later retitled "A Modest Proposal," July 23), and

"Polite Conversation" (August 20). Learns in April that Lowell has suffered a severe mental collapse and has been hospitalized. (Stafford and Lowell will occasionally see each other until his death.) Visits Great Britain, Ireland, France, and Germany during summer. Publishes articles in *The New Yorker* about the Edinburgh Festival (September 17) and returning to Heidelberg (December 3). Meets Oliver Jensen (born 1914), an editor at *Life*, in the fall.

1950   Marries Oliver Jensen on January 28 at Christ Church Methodist in New York City. They honeymoon in Haiti and Jamaica, then move into Jensen's apartment at 222 East 71st Street. Delivers lecture "Observations on the Use of Autobiography in Fiction" at Wellesley College on April 17 (published as "Truth and the Novelist" in *Harper's Bazaar*, August 1951). Article "Enchanted Island," written in Jamaica, appears in May *Mademoiselle*. Publishes three stories in *The New Yorker*, "A Country Love Story" (May 6), "The Maiden" (July 29), and "The Nemesis" (later retitled "The Echo and the Nemesis," December 16), as well as "Old Flaming Youth," which appears in the December *Harper's Bazaar*. Moves with Jensen into house on Long Lots Road in Westport, Connecticut. Sets aside "In the Snowfall" in December and begins novel *The Catherine Wheel*.

1951   Becomes friends with the writer Peter De Vries, a neighbor in Westport. Story "The Healthiest Girl in Town" published in *The New Yorker* April 7. Visits Mary Lee in Colorado during summer and sees father for the last time. Completes *The Catherine Wheel* in the fall. Article "Home for Christmas" appears in December *Mademoiselle*.

1952   *The Catherine Wheel* is published by Harcourt, Brace on January 14 and receives mixed reviews; it sells 12,000 copies in three months. Serves on jury that gives the National Book Award for Fiction to James Jones for *From Here to Eternity*. Drinks heavily as marriage to Jensen becomes increasingly strained. During the year publishes articles "The Art of Accepting Oneself" (*Vogue*, February 1) and "It's Good to Be Back" (*Mademoiselle*, July) and stories "The Violet Rock" (*The New Yorker*, April 26), "Life Is No Abyss" (*Sewanee Review*, July), "I Love

Someone" (*Colorado Quarterly*, Summer), and "The Connoisseurs" (*Harper's Bazaar*, October). Attends University of Colorado writers' conference in Boulder, where she delivers lecture "An Etiquette for Writers" on July 22. Leaves Westport home in early November and moves to Hotel Irving on Gramercy Park South in New York City. Undergoes hysterectomy to remove fibroid tumors at New York Hospital. Travels to U.S. Virgin Islands in late December to obtain divorce.

1953   Publishes three stories in *The New Yorker* during the year: "The Shorn Lamb" (later retitled "Cops and Robbers," January 24), "The Liberation" (May 30), and "In the Zoo" (September 19). Divorce from Jensen granted on February 20. Elected to the Cosmopolitan Club, New York City club for professional women. *Children Are Bored on Sunday*, collection of ten stories, published by Harcourt, Brace in May. Stafford breaks with Harcourt, Brace in dispute over publication of the English edition of the story collection. Signs contract with Random House on October 23, receiving $7,000 advance for a novel and volume of short stories. Moves to apartment in house at 24 Elm Street in Westport.

1954   Novella *A Winter's Tale*, adapted from her unfinished novel "Autumn Festival," is included in *New Short Novels*, edited by Mary Louise Aswell and published in paperback by Ballantine in February. "New England Winter" appears in February issue of travel magazine *Holiday*. Story "Bad Characters" published in *The New Yorker*, December 4.

1955   Publishes three stories in *The New Yorker* during the year: "Beatrice Trueblood's Story" (February 26), "Maggie Meriwether's Rich Experience" (June 25), and "The Warlock" (December 24). Travels to England in late summer, but cuts trip short and returns home because of financial worries.

1956   During the year Stafford publishes three stories in *The New Yorker*, "The End of a Career" (January 21), "A Reading Problem" (June 30), and "The Mountain Day" (August 18), as well as "The Matchmaker" (later retitled "Caveat Emptor") in *Mademoiselle* (May). Hires James Oliver Brown as her new literary agent. Sails to England in June and rents flat at 20 Chesham Place in the Belgravia district of London. Begins friendship with Eve Auchincloss, an editor at *Harper's Bazaar*, who will help her obtain magazine writing assignments. Meets and begins affair with A. J. (Joe) Liebling (born 1904), a writer for *The New Yorker* since 1935 who is separated from his second wife and living in Europe for tax reasons. Visits Belgium in September after Liebling goes to Algeria on assignment. Returns to Westport in early autumn.

1957 Sees Liebling when he visits New York City for two weeks in January. Moves to apartment at 18 East 80th Street. Publishes stories "My Blithe, Sad Bird" (April 6) and "A Reasonable Facsimile" (August 3) in *The New Yorker*. Travels to England in early September to see Liebling. They visit Paris together before returning in November to New York, where they move into separate rooms at the Fifth Avenue Hotel in Greenwich Village.

1958 Finds it difficult to sell stories to *The New Yorker* after Katharine White retires as a fiction editor. Story "The Reluctant Gambler" appears in *Saturday Evening Post*, October 4. Publishes two articles in *Harper's Bazaar*: "Divorce: Journey Through Crisis" (November) and "New York Is a Daisy" (December).

1959 Interviews Isak Dinesen for *Horizon* magazine (article appears in September). Liebling reaches divorce settlement with his wife, Lucille Spectorsky. Stafford and Liebling marry at New York City Hall on April 3 and move into apartment at 43 Fifth Avenue; they also spend time at house Liebling owns at 929 Fireplace Road in the Springs section of East Hampton, New York. Story "The Scarlet Letter" appears in July *Mademoiselle*. Travels in July to Louisiana, where Liebling covers election campaign of Governor Earl Long (Stafford had suggested that he write about Long). Sails to England in late August. Visits Isle of Arran off the west coast of Scotland, the ancestral home of her mother's family, while Liebling covers British general election. In October they travel to Greece and the Aegean and then go on Mediterranean cruise before returning to New York in late November.

1960   "Souvenirs of Survival: The Thirties Revisited," memoir of her college years, appears in *Mademoiselle* in February. Sent by *Harper's Bazaar* to Reno, Nevada, to cover production of the film *The Misfits*, starring Marilyn Monroe, directed by John Huston and written by Arthur Miller. Writes article that is rejected by the magazine. Publishes six film reviews in *Horizon*, September 1960–May 1961, including pieces on Satyajit Ray, Italian neorealism, and Akira Kurosawa.

1961   "The Ardent Quintessences," article on whiskey and cocktails, appears in April *Harper's Bazaar*. Moves with Liebling in fall to apartment at 45 West 10th Street.

1962   Serves on jury that gives National Book Award in fiction to Walker Percy for *The Moviegoer*. Leaves Random House and signs contract with Robert Giroux, now an editor at Farrar, Straus and Cudahy, for a novel, a collection of stories, and a book about Arran and the Greek island of Samothrace. Receives $12,000, of which $7,000 is used to repay her Random House advance. *The Lion and the Carpenter and Other Tales from the Arabian Nights* published by Macmillan as part of its "Marvelous Tales" series of children's books. *Elephi, the Cat with the High IQ*, children's book about one of the many cats Stafford kept during her lifetime, published in September by Farrar, Straus and Cudahy.

1963   Travels with Liebling to Normandy, the Loire Valley, and Paris in July and August. Visits American military cemetery above Omaha Beach where her brother Dick is buried, but is unable to find his grave. Visits London before returning to New York in September. Begins seeing internist Dr. Thomas Roberts, who will be her primary physician for the rest of her life. Liebling is hospitalized with viral pneumonia on December 21 and dies from heart and renal failure on December 28.

1964   Collapses from heavy drinking in January and spends sixteen days recovering in New York Hospital. Begins writing book reviews for *The New York Review of Books* and for *Vogue* (will publish fifty-two reviews in the magazine from January 1964 to March 1974). Story "The Tea Time of Stouthearted Ladies" published in the Winter *Kenyon Review*. Suffers heart attack in early April and is hospitalized for five weeks, but does not quit smoking. Moves to Long Island country house in the Springs, which sits on thirty acres of meadowland. Maintains active social life despite not knowing how to drive. Story "The Ordeal of Conrad Pardee" appears in the July *Ladies' Home Journal*. Spends 1964–65 academic year as Fellow at the Center for Advanced Studies at Wesleyan University. *Bad Characters*, collecting nine stories and novella "A Winter's Tale," published by Farrar, Straus and Co., October 12. Resumes heavy drinking by the end of the year.

1965   Travels to Fort Worth, Texas, in May to interview Marguerite Oswald, mother of Lee Harvey Oswald, the accused assassin of President John F. Kennedy. Receives $6,000 grant from the Rockefeller Foundation to work on her novel. Article "The Strange World of Marguerite Oswald" published in the October *McCall's*.

1966   Father dies on January 9 in Lake Oswego, Oregon. *A Mother in History*, expanded version of her profile of Marguerite Oswald, published February 25 by Farrar, Straus and Giroux; it receives mixed reviews and sells 10,000 copies in three months. Article "Truth in Fiction," a revised version of "Truth and the Novelist," published in the October 1 *Library Journal*.

1967   Accepts two-year appointment as adjunct professor in the writing program of Columbia University's School of the Arts. Rents apartment at 11 East 87th Street and teaches class on the short story that meets once a week.

1968   Dislikes students and is unhappy with political turmoil on campus. Signs new contract with Farrar, Straus and Giroux on June 27 for volume of collected stories and her novel in progress, now titled "The Parliament of Women." Story "The Philosophy Lesson" appears in *The New Yorker*, November 16. Resigns teaching position after fall semester.

1969   *The Collected Stories of Jean Stafford* is published February 17 by Farrar, Straus and Giroux and receives favorable reviews. Stafford becomes regular contributor to the *Washington Post Book World* (publishes forty-four reviews in the newspaper from March 1969 through October 1976). Writes lengthy Christmas roundup of children's books for *The New Yorker* (continues to write this feature annually through 1975).

1970   Stafford is elected to the American Academy and Institute of Arts and Letters in January. Serves as writer in residence for two weeks at Pennsylvania State University. Publishes articles "My (Ugh!) Sensitivity Training" in *Horizon* (Spring) and "Love Among the Rattlesnakes," about Charles Manson and his followers, in *McCall's* (March). *The Collected Stories of Jean Stafford* awarded Pulitzer Prize for Fiction on May 4.

1971   Delivers series of five lectures on "Tradition and Dissent" at Barnard College in March. Writes introduction for *The American Coast*, picture book published by Scribner's. Publishes articles "Suffering Summering Houseguests" in *Vogue* (August 15) and "Intimation of Hope" in *McCall's* (December).

1972   *The Mountain Lion* is reissued in hardcover by Farrar, Straus and Giroux in April with a new preface by Stafford. Awarded honorary LittD degree by the University of Colorado at Boulder on May 24. Gives talk at Norlin Library in which she pays tribute to her mentor Irene McKeehan (published as "Miss McKeehan's Pocketbook" in Spring 1976 *Colorado Quarterly*). Suffers from worsening respiratory problems. Becomes regular contributor to *Vogue* (will publish nine feature articles in the magazine through June 1975, including profiles of newspaper publisher Katharine Graham and Representative Millicent Fenwick). Receives additional $3,000 advance for "The Parliament of Women."

1973–74   Delivers commencement address at Southampton College in June. Continues to support herself through freelance journalism, publishing reviews and articles in *The New York Times*, *The New York Times Book Review*, *McCall's*, and *Esquire*.

1975   Fires James Oliver Brown as her literary agent and replaces him with Timothy Seldes of Russell & Volkening. Serves on jury that awards Pulitzer Prize for Fiction to Michael Shaara for *The Killer Angels*. Diagnosed with chronic obstructive pulmonary disease. Begins writing monthly book review column for *Esquire* in October (last review appears in October 1976).

1976   Suffers ischemic stroke on November 8, which causes severe aphasia and leaves her unable to write or speak intelligibly.

1977   Robert Lowell dies of heart attack on September 12. Stafford lessens her financial worries by selling her thirty acres of meadowland for $114,000 in December.

1978   "An Influx of Poets," story extracted by Giroux from the manuscript for "The Parliament of Women," published in *The New Yorker* on November 6. ("Woden's Day," another extract from "The Parliament of Women," is published posthumously in *Shenandoah* in Autumn 1979.) Makes new will that leaves most of her estate to Josephine Monsell, her longtime cleaning woman in Springs.

1979   Admitted to New York Hospital February 20 with advanced pulmonary disease. Transferred on March 20 to Burke Rehabilitation Center in White Plains, New York, where she dies from cardiac arrest March 26. Her ashes are interred next to Liebling on April 10 after graveside service in the Green River Cemetery, East Hampton, New York.

Note on the Texts

This volume contains three novels by Jean Stafford: *Boston Adventure* (1944), *The Mountain Lion* (1947), and *The Catherine Wheel* (1952), along with the "Author's Note" Stafford wrote for the 1972 reissue of *The Mountain Lion*.

Stafford recalled that she began writing *Boston Adventure* soon after she moved in the summer of 1940 to Baton Rouge, Louisiana. In the spring of 1941, she wrote a 175-page outline of the novel while staying with her sister, Mary Lee Stafford Frichtel, on her ranch in Hayden, Colorado. Stafford sent the outline to the Houghton, Mifflin publishing firm, which failed to express interest in acquiring the novel. She continued to work on the manuscript after moving to New York City in the summer of 1941, using the title "The Outskirts." In early 1942 she sent the first third of the novel to Harcourt, Brace and Company, where it was read by Frank V. Morley, the editor-in-chief of the trade division. Morley passed the manuscript on to Robert Giroux, a junior editor at the firm, with a note asking: "I found that it kept holding me; but will it keep hold of a public?" Giroux later wrote that he was so "enthralled" while reading the manuscript on a commuter train that he missed several stops. Stafford and Giroux signed a contract on April 30, 1942, for the novel's publication by Harcourt, Brace, with Stafford receiving a $500 advance. In the summer of 1942 Stafford and her first husband, the poet Robert Lowell, moved to Monteagle, Tennessee, where they shared a house with the novelist Caroline Gordon and her husband, the poet and critic Allen Tate. On February 1, 1943, Stafford submitted a manuscript to Lambert Davis at Harcourt, Brace (Giroux was now serving in the navy). Davis responded in March, praising the novel while raising questions about its style. Stafford also received critical comments from Gordon and Tate and began making extensive revisions and cuts. She continued to revise and cut the manuscript while staying at the Yaddo artists' colony in the summer of 1943 and submitted a final version to Harcourt, Brace in January 1944. Two excerpts from the novel, which had been retitled *Boston Adventure* at the suggestion of the publisher, appeared before publication: "The Wedding—Beacon Hill" in the June 1944 number of *Harper's Bazaar*, and "Hotel Barstow" in the Summer 1944 number of *Partisan Review*.

Boston Adventure was published in New York by Harcourt, Brace and Company on September 21, 1944, in a first printing of 22,000 copies. By May 1945 the Harcourt, Brace edition had sold a total of 35,000 copies, while another 199,000 copies had been sold through the mail by the Book League of America. (The novel was also published in a condensed paperback Armed Services Edition that sold 144,000 copies.) An English edition was published in London by Faber & Faber in October 1946. Harcourt, Brace subsequently included *Boston Adventure*, along with *The Mountain Lion* and Stafford's collection of short stories *Children Are Bored on Sunday*, in *The Interior Castle*, an omnibus volume published in 1953. Stafford did not revise the novel after its initial American publication. This volume prints the text of the 1944 Harcourt, Brace edition of *Boston Adventure*, but corrects a typesetting error that appeared in that edition: at 394.8, 413.32, and 474.40–475.1, "*Der Traum den Rote Kammer*" becomes "*Der Traum der Roten Kammer*."

Stafford may have begun *The Mountain Lion* in February 1945, not long after the death of her older brother Dick, who was killed in a jeep accident while serving with the army in France. She completed 105 manuscript pages by July and sent a draft of the novel to Lambert Davis in December 1945. Stafford signed a contract for its publication with Harcourt, Brace on January 17, 1946, receiving a $2,000 advance against a 15 percent royalty. She sent a revised manuscript to Robert Giroux (who had returned from the navy) in April 1946. An excerpt from the novel appeared in the January 1947 number of *Harper's Bazaar* under the title "The Tunnel with No End." *The Mountain Lion* was published in New York by Harcourt, Brace and Company on March 1, 1947, in a printing of 10,000 copies. An English edition was published in London by Faber & Faber in February 1948. Harcourt, Brace included the novel in the 1953 omnibus volume *The Interior Castle*, and it was reissued by Farrar, Straus and Giroux in 1972 with a new "Author's Note." Stafford made no revisions to the novel after its first publication. This volume prints the text of the 1947 Harcourt, Brace edition of *The Mountain Lion*.

In November 1947 Stafford signed a contract with Harcourt, Brace for "In the Snowfall," a novel inspired by her college friendship with Lucy McKee Cooke, a law student at the University of Colorado who had committed suicide in 1935. Stafford worked on "In the Snowfall" for several years before setting it aside in December 1950 and beginning a new novel. She made rapid progress on the manuscript and submitted a final version in the fall of 1951. *The Catherine Wheel* was published in New York by Harcourt, Brace and Company on January 14, 1952. An English edition was published in London later that year by Eyre & Spottiswoode. Stafford did not revise the novel after its initial publication. The text printed here is of the 1952 Harcourt, Brace edition.

Stafford wrote a short "Author's Note" that appeared as a preface in the 1972 reissue of *The Mountain Lion*. It is presented in this volume as an appendix, and the text printed here is taken from the 1972 Farrar, Straus and Giroux printing.

This volume presents the texts of the original printings chosen for inclusion here, but it does not attempt to reproduce nontextual features of their typographic design. The texts are presented without change, except for the correction of typographical errors. Spelling, punctuation, and capitalization are often expressive features and are not altered, even when inconsistent or irregular. The following is a list of typographical errors corrected, cited by page and line number: 40.16, *zwansig*; 136.1, *gansbart*; 151.37, steeds paw; 181.25, coincidence I; 212.3, intentions" had; 225.34, perigrinations; 235.37, evening.; 246.27, exigesis; 253.37, *tulipes noire*; 261.37, Winetka; 265.13–14, excrutiating; 273.5, up I'm; 282.30, Gardiner's; 294.9, Happle; 324.35, them.); 350.3, sheath; 361.15, exigesis; 367.7, last; 383.25, other's; 393.7, clam-bake; 394.29, practiticed; 401.28, mornning; 408.18, Walter; 410.6, *Imensee*; 413.4, perigrinations; 418.39, *marveilleuse*; 431.26, forbears; 441.27, it's; 446.18, veiw; 450.37, Aggasiz; 452.38, Katherine; 463.14, Britanny; 492.27, connossieur; 534.1, saying.; 539.24, stereoptican; 572.2, L. L.; 601.31, Freudenburg's; 606.31, soundlessly.); 628.8, creaming; 650.31, if it; 655.8, wastless; 714.19, man; 735.23, vicarous; 840.22, said.

Notes

In the notes below, the reference numbers denote page and line of this volume (the line count includes headings). No note is made for material included in the eleventh edition of *Merriam-Webster's Collegiate Dictionary*. Biblical quotations are keyed to the King James Version. Quotations from Shakespeare are keyed to *The Riverside Shakespeare*, ed. G. Blakemore Evans (Boston: Houghton Mifflin, 1974). For further biographical background and references to other studies, see David Roberts, *Jean Stafford: A Biography* (Boston: Little, Brown, 1988); Charlotte Margolis Goodman, *Jean Stafford: The Savage Heart* (Austin: University of Texas Press, 1990); and Ann Hulbert, *The Interior Castle: The Art and Life of Jean Stafford* (New York: Alfred A. Knopf, 1992).

BOSTON ADVENTURE

2.1   *For Frank Parker*] A classmate of Robert Lowell at St. Mark's School, Parker (1916–2005) left Harvard College to study art in Paris and served as a volunteer ambulance driver during the fall of France in 1940. He returned to the United States, enlisted in the Black Watch of Canada, and was captured in the Dieppe raid in 1942. Parker was a prisoner of war at the time *Boston Adventure* was published and did not return to the U.S. until 1945. (His father, an American volunteer officer serving with the Royal Navy, was killed in the North Atlantic in 1941, while his younger brother was killed on Okinawa in 1945.) Parker's art appeared on the covers of several of Lowell's volumes of poetry. He remained friends with Jean Stafford after she and Lowell were divorced in 1948.

6.30   *pokhlyobka*] Thick Russian soup, usually made with grains and cabbage or potatoes.

8.21   *mein herr*] Sir.

10.8–13   Till with age . . . a pretty girl!] From "The Troika," a song included in the Russian chapter of *A Treasury of the World's Finest Folk Song* (1942), collected and arranged by Leonhard Deutsch, explanatory text by Claude Simpson, lyrics versified by Willard Trask.

14.1–2   *Riders of the Purple Sage*] Western novel (1912) by Zane Grey (1872–1939).

14.21   *ni't wahr?*] Isn't it?

21.5–6   Chilton Club] A Boston women's club, founded in 1910.

21.28   E. P. Roe] Edward Payson Roe (1838–1888), American Presbyterian minister who published seventeen popular novels, including *Barriers Burned*

Away (1872), a story of spiritual conversion set in Chicago at the time of the 1871 fire.

21.29 Elsie Dinsmore books] Series of twenty-eight children's books (1867–1905) about a pious young girl in the American South, written by Martha Finley (1828–1909) under the name Martha Farquharson.

21.36 *Bob, Son of Battle*] American title of *Owd Bob, The Grey Dog of Kenmuir* (1898), children's book about a sheepdog by English novelist Alfred Ollivant (1874–1927).

22.7–8 English Speaking Union] An international organization founded in Great Britain in 1918 for the purpose of promoting closer relations among English-speaking countries.

31.25–26 "The Stag at Eve"] Common name for the first lines of canto I of *The Lady in the Lake* (1810) by Sir Walter Scott (1771–1832).

31.26–27 Kipling's "If"] The poem was first published in 1910.

32.23 *Das Gesetz der Mormonen*] "The Law of the Mormons."

32.40 *"Lieber Gott!"*] "Dear God!"

33.29–30 *Monstruosum . . . activam*] A monstrous state between the contemplative and the active life.

35.3 *"Verzeihung!"*] "Forgive me!"

37.18 *muchacha*] Girl.

39.24 *Messbuch*] Missal.

40.16 *zwei und zwanzig?*] Twenty-two.

44.31 *Frances and the . . . Buena Vista Farm*] Children's book (1905) by American writer Frances Trego Montgomery (1858–1925).

46.3–4 *"Confiteor Deo . . . semper Virgini*] "I confess to Almighty God, to Blessed Mary, ever Virgin": the opening lines of the confessional prayer recited at the beginning of the traditional Latin Mass.

46.6–7 *"Gott! Gott! . . . mir verlassen?*] "God! God! Why have you forsaken me?" Cf. Mathew 27:46

48.11 *Mädchen*] Girl.

48.21 *"Jawohl!"*] Yes!

50.25–26 *Die wunderschöne Augen! Die magische Augen!*] The beautiful eyes! The magical eyes!

56.28 *lebkuchen.*] Gingerbread cookies.

67.33–34 "Comin' through the Rye"] Scottish song from the eighteenth century, often sung with lyrics (1782) by the poet Robert Burns (1759–1796).

68.31–32 "*Bitte, sprechen Sie Deutsch, gnädiges Fräulein?*"] "Please, speak German, young lady?"

73.6 sired by Kaiser Bill] Wilhelm II (1859–1941) was rumored to have fathered several children out of wedlock in addition to the seven children he had with the Empress Augusta Victoria (1858–1921).

73.9 "*Stille Nacht, Heilige Nacht*"] "Silent Night, Holy Night," (1818) Austrian Christmas carol, with words by Joseph Mohr (1792–1848) and music by Franz Xaver Gruber (1787–1863).

75.20 Liederkranz] An American version of German Limburger cheese.

76.23 *Motor Boat Boys*] A series of seven adventure stories for boys published from 1912 to 1915, beginning with *Motor Boat Boys Mississippi Cruise, or The Dash for Dixie.* They were written by Louis Arundel, one of many pseudonyms used by St. George Rathborne (1854–1938), a prolific writer of juvenile fiction.

76.24 Waverley novels] Series of twenty-seven historical novels published by Sir Walter Scott from 1814 to 1831 that included *Waverley* (1814), *Rob Roy* (1817), and *Ivanhoe* (1819).

76.29 *Quo Vadis*] Historical novel (1896) set during the reign of the Emperor Nero by the Polish writer Henryk Sienkiewicz (1846–1916).

77.30–78.8 Far from where . . . Woman's sad lot] From "Woman's Sad Lot," a song included in the Russian chapter of *A Treasury of the World's Finest Folk Song* (1942), collected and arranged by Leonhard Deutsch, explanatory text by Claude Simpson, lyrics versified by Willard Trask.

79.9–10 "Roses of Picardy," . . . Blue Danube."] "Roses of Picardy," song (1916) with music by Hadyn Wood (1882–1959) and lyrics by Frederick Weatherly (1848–1929); "The Bells of Saint Mary's," song (1917) with music by A. Emmett Adams (1890–1938) and lyrics by Douglas Furber (1885–1961); "The Blue Danube," waltz (1866) by the younger Johann Strauss (1825–1899).

79.22 "the spreading chestnut tree] The "spreading chestnut-tree" mentioned in the first line of Henry Wadsworth Longfellow's poem "The Village Blacksmith" (1841) was chopped down in the 1870s as part of the widening of Brattle Street in Cambridge, Massachusetts.

79.23 that old bridge . . . the British."] The North Bridge in Concord, where Massachusetts militia repulsed British troops on April 19, 1775.

79.29 *Lariat, West*] *Lariat* (1925–51) and *West* (1926–53) were Western pulp magazines.

81.25–26 Bebe Daniels . . . Richard Barthelmess] Bebe Daniels (1901–1971), Clara Bow (1905–1965), Ramon Navarro (1899–1968), Janet Gaynor (1906–1984), and Richard Barthelmess (1895–1963) were Hollywood film stars in the silent era.

85.10   *effroyable*] Frightful.

92.11   *tsvetiki*] Flowers.

94.8   The Uffizi] An art museum in Florence, Italy.

94.15   State Street argot] State Street was the center of the Boston financial district.

94.31   *The Awkward Age*, by Henry James] The novel was first published in 1899.

106.5   *Black Beauty*] Children's novel (1877) by Anna Sewell (1820–1878) about the life of a horse in nineteenth-century England.

112.1–2   *Wilhelm Meister* and *Werthers Leiden*] Novels by Johann Wolfgang von Goethe (1749–1832): *Wilhelm Meisters Lehrjahre* (*Wilhelm Meister's Apprenticeship*, 1795–96) and *Die Leiden des jungen Werthers* (*The Sorrows of Young Werther*, 1774).

112.5–6   "*Ach, der Abendstern!*"] "Oh, the evening star!"

112.9   *Confessions of a Young Man*] Novel (1888) by the Anglo-Irish writer George Moore (1852–1933).

112.15   Nouvelle Athènes] A café in the Place Pigalle in the ninth arrondissement of Paris.

117.25–26   *Literature and Life*] *Literature and Life*, Book Four (1924), a secondary-school textbook edited by Dudley Miles, Robert C. Pooley, and Edwin Greenlaw.

125.37–126.12   Well they know . . . while we may.] See note 10.8–13.

127.35–38   Till with age . . . a pretty girl!] See note 10.8–13.

133.25   judge . . . Rastus] Minstrel shows often featured a character named Rastus appearing before a judge.

135.35   Dr. Joachim's Hungarian Concerto] Violin Concerto No. 2 in D Minor "in the Hungarian Manner" (1861) by the Hungarian violinist and composer Joseph Joachim (1831–1907). Joachim was awarded an honorary doctorate by Cambridge University in 1877.

136.1   *gamsbart*] A tuft of hair used for decoration on traditional men's hats in the Bavarian and Austrian Alps.

139.11   *Ethan Frome*] Novella (1911) by Edith Wharton.

144.8–11   the Point . . . lights of Boston] The geographic location of the fictitious town of Chichester corresponds with the town of Nahant northeast of Boston.

147.18   *Ars longa est*] "Art is long," from *Ars longa est, vita brevis est*: Art is long, life is short.

151.27   Devitschiepol convent] The Novodevichy convent in Moscow, founded in 1524.

151.36–152.6   They shout . . . pass the Don.] From *The Empire of the Czar*, volume III (1843), an English translation of *La Russie en 1839* (1843) by Astolphe-Louis-Léonor, Marquis de Custine (1790–1857). In *The Empire of the Czar* the "air" is described as "the national song of the Don Cossacks."

162.11   *Verzeihung*] Forgive me.

163.29–30   one in Concord . . . authors were buried.] Sleepy Hollow Cemetery in Concord, where Henry David Thoreau (1817–1862), Nathaniel Hawthorne (1804–1864), Ralph Waldo Emerson (1803–1882), and Louisa May Alcott (1832–1888) are buried.

164.12   Revere or Otis] Paul Revere (1735–1818) and James Otis (1725–1783) are interred in the Granary Burial Ground in Boston.

164.20–21   Cabot . . . Windsor] John Cabot (1680–1742) emigrated to New England in 1700, sixty years after John Prescott (1604–1681), who arrived in 1640. The Howard family has held the dukedom of Norfolk since 1483, while the House of Windsor, created in 1917, is descended from the House of Hannover, the dynasty that ascended to the British throne in 1714.

168.13–14   *The Boston Evening Transcript*] Daily newspaper (except Sunday) published in Boston, 1830–1941.

168.15   author of its contumely] T. S. Eliot (1888–1965). His comic poem "The Boston Evening Transcript" ("The readers of the *Boston Evening Transcript* / Sway in the wind like a field of ripe corn") was first published in *Poetry* in 1915 and later included in his collection *Poems* (1920).

168.30   the Athenaeum] The Boston Athenæum, an independent library and cultural institution founded in 1807.

168.38   Holy Sonnets of John Donne] A series of nineteen devotional sonnets by John Donne (1572–1631) that were first published posthumously in 1633.

169.3–4   Except you' . . . ravish me.] Lines 13–14 of Holy Sonnet 14, "Batter my heart, three person'd God."

169.11   Groton] An Episcopal boarding school for boys, founded in Groton, Massachusetts, in 1884.

169.19   Porcellian Club] An exclusive social club for Harvard College students, founded in 1791.

172.19–21   Apthorp . . . *Henry Adams*] In chapter V of *The Education* Adams recounts meeting Robert E. Apthorp (1811–1882) in Berlin, where Apthorp spent the winter of 1858–59 "for the sake of the music."

172.22 *The Americanization of Edward Bok*] Autobiography (1920) by Edward Bok (1863–1930), a Dutch-American magazine editor and social reformer.

181.22–23 *The Deserted Village*] Poem (1770) by Oliver Goldsmith (1728–1774), included in *Literature and Life,* Book Four (see note 117.25–26).

183.25–26 *Ode on Intimations of Immortality*] Poem (1807) by William Wadsworth (1770–1850).

183.32–34 *In medio ramos . . . Somnia vulgo*] Virgil, *Aeneid,* book VI, lines 282–83. In the translation by Henry Rushton Fairclough (1862–1938) for the Loeb Classics (1916): "In the midst an elm, shadowy and vast, spreads her boughs and aged arms, the home which, men say, false Dreams hold, clinging under every leaf."

193.13–14 "Die 28 Apr . . . a Cruce,"] April 28 was the feast day of St. Paul of the Cross (1694–1775), founder of the Passionist order.

205.34–35 Lady-of-the-Lake voyage] Ellen Douglas rows a skiff across Loch Katrine in canto I of Sir Walter Scott's poem *The Lady in the Lake* (1810).

213.5–6 Little Sister of the Poor] A member of the Little Sisters of the Poor, a Roman Catholic religious institute founded in France in 1839.

214.3 Fox sisters . . . Mr. Slipfoot] In 1848 Maggie Fox (1833–1893) and her sister Kate (1837–1892) began giving demonstrations at their home in Hydesville, New York, of their supposed ability to communicate with the dead through rapping sounds. They initially addressed the spirit allegedly haunting their home as "Mr. Splitfoot," a nickname for the Devil, but later claimed that it was the ghost of a murdered peddler. Their sister Leah Fox Fish (1814–1890) became the family impresario, arranging séances for paying audiences in cities across the United States. In 1888 Maggie Fox confessed that she and Kate had made the rapping sounds themselves; she recanted her admission the following year.

225.36–37 consistency . . . little minds.] In his essay "Self-Reliance" (1841), Emerson wrote: "A foolish consistency is the hobgoblin of little minds, adored by little statesmen and philosophers and divines."

225.39 Harriet Martineau's peregrinations] The English political economist Harriet Martineau (1802–1876) visited the United States in 1834–36. She wrote favorably about Emerson and the Unitarian clergyman and essayist William Ellery Channing (1780–1842) in her *Retrospect of Western Travel* (1838).

227.21–22 Shreve, Crump, and Low . . . Mark Cross case.] Shreve, Crump, and Low, Boston jewelry store founded in 1796; Mark Cross, Boston luxury leather goods store founded in 1845.

233.29 *Ladies' Home Journal*] American women's magazine that was published monthly from 1883 to 2014.

235.33 *lebkuchen*] Gingerbread cookies.

241.37 *The Rise of Silas Lapham*] Novel (1885) by William Dean Howells (1837–1920).

245.30 *Arma virumque cano*] "Arms and the man I sing," the first line of book I of the *Aeneid*.

245.37–38 Shall I compare . . . more temperate.] William Shakespeare, Sonnet 18, lines 1–2.

246.6–7 When in disgrace . . . outcast state.] Sonnet 29, lines 1–2.

246.12–13 That time of . . . few do hang.] Sonnet 73, lines 1–2.

246.18–23 She shall be . . . insensate things.] William Wordsworth, "Three Years She Grew" (1800), lines 13–18.

246.28 *The Prelude*] Autobiographical poem in blank verse by William Wordsworth, published posthumously in 1850.

246.32 those Lucy poems] Name given to five poems by Wordsworth, including "Three Years She Grew," that were first published from 1800 to 1807.

249.26–27 'east is east . . . twain shall meet.'] Rudyard Kipling (1865–1936), "The Ballad of East and West" (1887).

249.31 Bartlett's] *Bartlett's Familiar Quotations*, reference work first published in 1855 by American writer and bookseller John Bartlett (1820–1905).

250.4 the Country Club] Founded in Brookline, Massachusetts, in 1882, the Country Club was the first of its kind in the United States.

250.13–14 Chilton Club . . . St. Botolph] Chilton Club, see note 21.5–6; St. Botolph, Boston men's club founded in 1880.

253.7 *tulipe noire*] Black tulip.

255.7 T Wharf] A wharf in Boston Harbor that adjoined the north side of the Long Wharf. Built in the early eighteenth century, it was removed in the 1960s.

257.17 Winsor School] A private school for girls founded in Boston in 1886.

258.15 Pierce's] A Boston grocery store founded in 1831.

262.34 post-Versailles] Under the terms of the peace treaty signed at Versailles on June 28, 1919, Germany lost 10 percent of its population and 13 percent of its territory. The treaty also severely restricted the size of the German army and navy.

265.10   Badger] Boston portrait painter Joseph Badger (1708–1765) or his grandson, painter Thomas Badger (1792–1868).

271.20   St. George] An Episcopal boarding school for boys in Middletown, Rhode Island, founded in 1896.

272.4   Saint-Simon] Louis de Rouvroy, duc de Saint-Simon (1675–1755), French statesman whose memoirs of the court of Versailles were first published posthumously in 1829–30.

274.19–20   Far from the . . . ignoble strife] Thomas Gray (1716–1771), "Elegy Written in a Country Church-Yard" (1751), line 73.

276.18   Vanzetti's sister] Luigia Vanzetti (d. 1950), who came to the United States from Italy in 1927 to visit her brother Bartolomeo Vanzetti (1888–1927) in prison. In 1921 Vanzetti and Nicola Sacco (1891–1927) were convicted of murdering two men during a payroll robbery in South Braintree, Massachusetts, the previous year. Their case became an international cause célèbre, with their defenders arguing that the two men had been unfairly convicted because of their Italian immigrant backgrounds and anarchist beliefs.

276.22–23   the Committee's decision] On June 1, 1927, Massachusetts governor Alvan T. Fuller (1878–1958) appointed a three-man committee headed by A. Lawrence Lowell (1856–1943), the president of Harvard, to review the Sacco-Vanzetti case. The Lowell committee reported on July 27 that the defendants had received a fair trial and were guilty beyond a reasonable doubt. Fuller then denied their request for clemency, and Sacco and Vanzetti were electrocuted on August 23, 1927.

279.15   *anima mundi*] World soul.

279.30–31   'When Lilacs . . . Bloom'd'] Title of poem (1865) by Walt Whitman (1819–1892), written as an elegy for President Abraham Lincoln.

280.16–17   Empress Augusta Victoria] Augusta Victoria (1858–1921), empress consort of Germany, 1888–1918, was married to Wilhelm II from 1881 until her death.

281.6–7   "*Der Tannenbaum* . . . Thine Eyes"] "The Fir-tree," song (1875) by Richard Wagner (1813–1883), with lyrics from a poem by Georg Scheurlin (1802–1872) that was also set to music (1891) by Alfred Tofft (1865–1931); "I Love You," song (1803) by Ludwig van Beethoven (1770–1827) with lyrics taken from the poem "Zärtliche Liebe" ("Tender Love") by Karl Friedrich Herrosee (1754–1821). "Ich Liebe Dich" is also the title of a song by Edvard Grieg (1843–1907), with German lyrics by Franz von Holstein (1826–1878). "Drink to Me Only with Thine Eyes," song (1790) with music by John Wall Callcott (1766–1821) and words taken from a poem (1616) by Ben Jonson (1552–1637).

282.28   Barrons] Weekly financial newspaper founded by Dow Jones & Company in 1921.

282.29–30   Stearn's . . . Mrs. Gardner's palace] R.H. Stearn, Boston department store founded in 1845 that closed in 1978; museum modeled after a Venetian palace that was built (1899–1903) by Isabella Stewart Gardner (1840–1924) to house and display her personal art collection.

292.8   *malentendu*] Misunderstood, mistaken.

292.12–13   General Hooker . . . Loew's Orpheum] The equestrian statue by Daniel Chester French (1850–1931) of Union Civil War general Joseph Hooker (1814–1879) outside the Massachusetts State House, dedicated in 1903; Goodspeed's Book Shop, founded in 1898; Loew's Orpheum, a vaudeville theater that had previously served as a concert hall.

293.4–9   *"Doch, ist's so . . . auch deutsche."*] "Is it really so late?" / "No, it's early, I think" / "Why then . . . ?" / "I'm a German girl, too."

294.3–4   *"Ein Regenpfeifer! Still!"*] "A plover! Quiet!"

298.19   *Sammlung*] Collection.

301.19   *Japanerin*] Japanese.

302.36   Koussevitsky] Serge Koussevitsky (1874–1951), Russian-born music director of the Boston Symphony Orchestra, 1924–49.

302.40–303.1   Fine Arts Museum . . . Luxembourg] The Boston Museum of Fine Arts and the Musée de Luxembourg in Paris.

304.18   *démodé*] Old-fashioned.

304.19   *Père Goriot*] Novel (1834) by Honoré Balzac (1799–1850).

323.24–25   Priscilla Alden . . . Margaret Winthrop] Priscilla Mullins Alden (c. 1602–c. 1685) and Mary Chilton (1607–1679) were passengers on the *Mayflower*; Margaret Winthrop (c. 1591–1647) was the wife of John Winthrop, the first governor of the Massachusetts Bay colony.

324.20   palmer] Pilgrim.

325.11   *Harvard Advocate*] The Harvard College literary magazine.

330.26   *Weltschmerz*] World-weariness.

330.33   the Lincolnshire] A residential hotel in Boston.

330.40   Amiel's *Journal*] *Fragments d'un Journal intime*, posthumously published (1883–87) private journal of the Swiss critic and philosopher Henri-Frédéric Amiel (1821–1881).

333.24–25   La Grande Mademoiselle . . . Madame de Maintenon] Anne Marie Louise d'Orléans, duchess of Montpensier (1627–1693), known as the "Grande Mademoiselle," a leading figure at the court of Louis XIV, and Françoise d'Aubigné, marquise de Maintenon (1635–1719), the second wife (1683–1715) of Louis XIV.

343.12   "Enfant Perdu"] Poem (1851) by Heinrich Heine (1797–1856).

344.11   Radcliffe] Harvard undergraduate college for women, founded in 1879 as the Harvard Annex and chartered as Radcliffe College in 1894.

344.34   *Faerie Queen*] Epic poem (1590–96) by Edmund Spenser (c. 1552–1599).

344.35   *La Grande Jatte*] *A Sunday Afternoon on the Island of La Grande Jatte*, painting (1884–86) by Georges Seurat (1859–1891).

348.37   the North Shore] The Massachusetts coast from Boston north to New Hampshire.

368.38   Somerset Club] Boston men's social club, founded in 1852.

374.35   Niersteiner] A white wine produced in the region around Nierstein in the Rhineland-Palatinate.

374.38   *daube glacé*] A jellied beef stew made with beef stock.

392.26–27   Elmer Tuggle and Gasoline Alley] Elmer Tuggle was the main character in *Elmer*, a newspaper comic strip written and illustrated (1926–56) by Charles H. (Doc) Winer (1885–1956). *Gasoline Alley* was a newspaper comic written and illustrated (1918–59) by Frank King (1883–1969).

394.8   *Der Traum der Roten Kammer*] German translation (1932) by Franz Kuhn (1884–1961) of the classic eighteenth-century Chinese novel *Dream of the Red Chamber* by Cao Xueqin.

402.15–16   Gertrude or her king . . . villainy played out.] See *Hamlet*, III.ii.

407.5–6   the Fifth Commandment] See Exodus 20:12, Deuteronomy 5:16.

408.4   Bernard de Ventadour] A Provençal troubadour (fl. 1140–1180).

408.17   *Mittelhochdeutsch*] Middle High German, the form of German spoken from 1050 to 1350.

408.18   Walther von der Vogelweide] A German minnesinger (c. 1170–c. 1230).

408.22   *Alte Gebäude*] Old buildings.

409.25   *The Agenbyte of Inwyt*] "Remorse of Conscience," a religious work written in the Kentish dialect of Middle English in 1340 by the Benedictine monk Dan Michel of Northgate. It is a translation of the French moral tract *La somme des vices et des vertues* (*The Book of Vices and Virtues*) written in 1279.

410.4   Metro Goldwyn Mayer] Hollywood motion picture studio formed in 1924.

410.6   *Immensee*] Novella (1851) by Theodor Woldsen Storm (1817–1888).

417.14–15   Lilly Daché, Mainbocher] Lilly Daché (c. 1904–1989), French-born American milliner; Main Rousseau Bocher (1890–1976), American couturier.

418.12 Adrian] Professional name of Adrian Adolph Greenburg (1903–1959), American fashion designer who was the head costume designer for Metro-Goldwyn-Mayer, 1928–41.

418.21 *vieille furie*] Old fury.

418.39 *chose merveilleuse*] Wonderful thing.

419.21 *renarde*] Vixen.

419.24 *mariage de convenance*] Marriage of convenience.

419.34 *enceinte, ne c'est pas*] Pregnant, isn't it so?

432.7–8 Al Smith . . . president] Governor Al Smith (1873–1944) of New York was the Democratic nominee in 1928 and the first Catholic to run for president on a major party ticket. Smith was defeated in a landslide by Herbert Hoover.

433.40–434.1 Sacco and Vanzetti] See notes 276.18 and 276.22–23.

436.10 march from *Lohengrin*] The bridal chorus from act three, scene one of the opera *Lohengrin* (1850) by Richard Wagner.

443.12 Faneuil Hall] Boston meeting hall that opened in 1743, known as the "Cradle of Liberty" for its role in the American Revolution.

444.15 Parker House] Boston hotel founded in 1855.

445.37 Rebels in Spain] The Nationalists, led by General Francisco Franco (1892–1975), had rebelled against the elected left-wing government of the Spanish Republic in July 1936.

446.5 Loyalist] A defender of the Republic in the Spanish Civil War, which ended in a Nationalist victory in March 1939.

446.15 *echt deutsch*] Real German, true German.

450.28 Best's] Best & Co., a chain of stores specializing in clothing for women and children.

450.37 Agassiz! . . . glass flowers] The Harvard natural history museums were often referred to as the Agassiz, after Louis Agassiz (1807–1873), the founder of the Museum of Comparative Zoology. From 1886 to 1936 the Harvard Botanical Museum acquired more than 800 glass models of flowers made in Dresden, Germany, by Leopold Blaschka (1822–1895) and his son Rudolf (1857–1939).

451.14 *dämmerung*] Twilight.

452.37 Mae West] An American actress, singer, playwright, and screenwriter with a successful career in vaudeville and film, West (1893–1980) became famous for her risqué wisecracks.

457.27   Paolo and Francesca] In canto V of Dante's *Inferno*, where they are condemned to the Second Circle of Hell.

459.5   *tsubaki*] Japanese camellia, a flowering evergreen shrub.

466.6   *locum tenens*] Substitute for, placeholder.

466.7   Eliot House] A Harvard residence for undergraduates.

466.20   *Doch, ist's so spät*] "Is it really so late?"

473.34   'By their fruits shall ye know them,'] Matthew 7:20.

475.17   *The Well-Tempered Clavichord*] *The Well-Tempered Clavier*, collection (book I, 1722; book II, 1742) of keyboard preludes and fugues by Johann Sebastian Bach (1685–1750).

478.37   the Old Manse . . . Howard Johnson] House in Concord, Massachusetts, built in 1770, that was the residence of Ralph Waldo Emerson, 1834–35, and of Nathaniel Hawthorne, 1842–45. The Howard Johnson restaurant chain was founded in Quincy, Massachusetts, in 1925.

483.20   *wanderlustig*] Desiring to wander.

489.22–23   *arbiter bibendi*] Master of drinking.

494.37–495.2   "One thing have . . . rock of stone."] Cf. Psalm 27:4–5.

495.21   St. Marks] Episcopal boarding school for boys in Southborough, Massachusetts, founded in 1865.

495.28   the Tuileries] The Tuileries Garden in Paris.

497.28   "*Ulalume!*"] "Ulalume," poem (1847) by Edgar Allan Poe (1809–1849).

THE MOUNTAIN LION

500.1   *To Cal and to Dick*] "Cal" was the nickname of the poet Robert Lowell (1917–1977), Stafford's husband from 1940 to 1948; "Dick" was her older brother Richard Stafford (1911–1944), who was killed in a jeep accident in France on September 18, 1944, while serving with the 95th Infantry Division.

503.28   Palmer Method] A method of penmanship developed by Austin Palmer (1860–1927).

503.32   Willys Knight] An automobile built in Ohio from 1914 to 1933 by the Willys-Overland Company.

504.19   Huns had done to the Belgians] In 1914 invading German troops executed some 5,500 Belgian civilians and burned the university town of Louvain. The actual atrocities committed by the Germans were then exaggerated and sensationalized by Allied propaganda.

504.32   *The American Boy*] A monthly magazine published from 1899 to 1941.

507.29   Dr. Kellogg] John Harvey Kellogg (1852–1943), the superintendent of the Battle Creek sanitarium in Michigan who developed dry breakfast cereals in collaboration with his brother Will Keith Kellogg (1860–1951), the founder of the W. K. Kellogg food company.

507.37   Elmer Tuggle] See note 392.26–27.

507.37–38   Happy Hooligan] The main character in a newspaper comic strip (1900–32) written and drawn by Frederick Burr Opper (1857–1937), Happy Hooligan was an unlucky but good-natured hobo.

508.4   *McCall's*] A monthly women's magazine published from 1897 to 2002.

512.16   Schmierkäse] Cheese spread.

512.40   Schöneshund] Beautiful dog.

513.34–35   Marshall Field's] Chicago department store (1881–2006).

515.24   Fatty Arbuckle] Roscoe "Fatty" Arbuckle (1887–1933), a highly successful star and director of silent film comedies, was charged with manslaughter in September 1921 after Virginia Rappe (1891–1921), an actress whom he had allegedly assaulted in a San Francisco hotel suite, died of peritonitis caused by a ruptured bladder. He was acquitted in April 1922 after two earlier trials had ended in hung juries. Although Arbuckle continued to direct films under the name William Goodrich, the scandal effectively ended his acting career.

516.18   E. P. Roe] See note 21.28.

516.35–36   Boswell's . . . *the Hebrides*] Narrative (1785) by James Boswell (1740–1795) of his journey through Scotland in 1773 with Samuel Johnson (1709–1784). Johnson published his own account of the tour, *A Journey to the Western Islands of Scotland*, in 1775.

521.4   the Sorosis] An independent women's club with local chapters across the United States, originally founded in New York City in 1868 by the journalist Jane Cunningham Croly (1829–1901).

522.21   Howard Pyle] Pyle (1853–1911), a writer and illustrator of children's books whose works included *The Merry Adventures of Robin Hood* (1883) and *Men of Iron* (1892).

523.36–39   Gravel, gravel . . . no head?"] Eileen Simpson (1918–2002) wrote in *Poets in Their Youth: A Memoir* (1982) that Stafford told her in 1946 that she had composed this poem at the age of six.

524.19–20   "O Beautiful for Spacious Guys"] Cf. "O beautiful for spacious skies," the first line of "America the Beautiful" (1911) by Katharine Lee Bates (1859–1929).

527.7   "A Capital Ship . . . Trip,"] Poem (1885) by Charles Edward Carryl (1841–1920), sung to the melody of the sea shanty "Ten Thousand Miles Away."

528.6–7   Volstead Act] Common name for the National Prohibition Act, after its sponsor, Minnesota Republican congressman Andrew J. Volstead (1860–1947). Passed over President Wilson's veto on October 28, 1919, the act enforced the Eighteenth Amendment by making illegal the manufacture, transport, and sale (but not the possession) of intoxicating liquor.

534.23–24   Marthas as well . . . Marys] See Luke 10:38–42.

536.32   Venus de Milo] An armless ancient Greek statue of the goddess Aphrodite (Venus) found on the Aegean island of Melos in 1820 and later acquired by the Louvre Museum in Paris.

537.18   "Break, Break, Break"] Elegy (1842) by Alfred, Lord Tennyson (1809–1892).

538.13   "at the crossing of the bar."] Cf. "Crossing the Bar," (1889) poem by Tennyson.

538.19–20   "When You . . . Maggie."] Poem (1864) by Canadian school-teacher George W. Johnson (1839–1917), set to music (1866) by American composer James Austin Butterfield (1837–1891).

541.11   Barney Oldfield] Oldfield (1878–1946) was an American race car driver (1902–18) who set a world speed record of 131 mph at Daytona Beach, Florida, in 1910.

546.13   *Lorna Doone*] Historical romance (1869) by Richard Doddridge Blackmore (1825–1900), set in southwest England during the seventeenth century.

546.16–17   *The Idylls of the King*] Cycle of twelve poems (1859–85) by Tennyson about the rise and fall of King Arthur.

546.27   Gaboriau] Émile Gaboriau (1832–1873) wrote more than a dozen detective novels, including *L'Affaire Lerouge* (1866) and *Monsieur Lecoq* (1869), and is regarded as the creator of the genre in France.

555.30–31   "Comin' Through the Rye"] See note 67.33–34.

555.33   Snap] A card game.

558.16–17   *The Little Shepherd . . . Curiosity Shop*] *The Little Shepherd of Kingdom Come* (1903), novel by John Fox Jr. (1862–1919) set in Kentucky during the Civil War; *Sevenoaks* (1875), novel by Josiah Gilbert Holland (1819–1881) about an unscrupulous New York financier; *The Old Curiosity Shop* (1841), novel by Charles Dickens (1812–1870).

558.20–21   "All Through . . . Marble Halls."] "All Through the Night," Welsh folk song; "Old Black Joe" (1853), song by Stephen Foster (1826–1864);

"I Dreamt That I Dwelt in Marble Halls," aria from *The Bohemian Girl* (1843), opera with music by Irish composer Michael William Balfe (1808–1870) and libretto by English theatrical manager Alfred Bunn (1796–1860).

558.22–23 "The Brook" . . . Chambered Nautilus,"] "The Brook" (1855), poem by Tennyson; "The Chambered Nautilus" (1858), poem by Oliver Wendell Holmes (1809–1894).

569.18–19 false Armistice?"] An inaccurate report sent from Brest, France, to the United Press in New York City on November 7, 1918, caused newspapers across the country to report that an armistice had been signed with Germany.

574.34–35 "O Mistress . . . Deck the Sky?"] "O Mistress Mine," song from *Twelfth Night*, II.iii.39–52, that has been set to music by numerous composers; "Why Does Azure Deck the Sky?," song (1801) by Sir Thomas Moore (1779–1852) that also has several musical settings.

575.1 Van Briggle] Van Briggle Art Pottery, company established in Colorado Springs in 1899 by Artus Van Briggle (1869–1904) and Anne Lawrence Van Briggle (1868–1929), his wife.

575.2 Garden of the Gods] Public park in Colorado Springs famous for its red sandstone formations.

580.28 pom-pom-pull-away] A tag game.

582.2–4 towns in Oklahoma . . . sundown."] More than fifty towns were founded by African Americans in Oklahoma from 1865 to 1920, but there is no record that white visitors were threatened with violence in any of them for not leaving before nightfall.

587.37 package of Luckies . . . ammonia coke.] A pack of Lucky Strike cigarettes and a Coca-Cola with added aromatic spirits of ammonia.

590.5 Baron von Munchausen] Karl Friedrich Hieronymus von Münchausen (1720–1797), German soldier and hunter famous for telling implausible and absurd tales of his exploits. A number of stories attributed to him were compiled and embellished by Rudolph Erich Raspe (1737–1794) in *Baron Munchausen's Narrative of his Marvellous Travels and Campaigns in Russia*, published in London in 1785.

594.38 "Out Our Way"] Newspaper comic (1922–77) created by James R. Williams (1888–1957) that appeared as a single panel daily and as a strip on Sundays.

595.17 *Dr. Jekyll and Mr. Hyde*] *The Strange Case of Dr. Jekyll and Mr. Hyde* (1886), novel by Robert Louis Stevenson (1850–1894).

595.34 H_2SO_4] The chemical formula for sulfuric acid.

597.1 Epworth League] A Methodist organization for young adults aged eighteen to thirty-five, founded in 1889.

598.39   *Bleak House*] Novel (1852–53) by Charles Dickens.

606.14   Mary Pickford."] A highly successful star of silent films, Pickford (1892–1979) became known as "America's Sweetheart."

606.38   "The Sweetheart of Sigma Chi"] Song (1911) with music by F. Dudleigh Vernor (1892–1974) and lyrics by Byron D. Stokes (1886–1974).

609.31   moth-miller] Term used in Colorado for any type of moth commonly found in or around houses.

610.4   *Les Misérables*] Novel (1862) by Victor Hugo (1802–1885).

610.30   Hutchinson's teeth] A sign of congenital syphilis, Hutchinson's teeth are shorter and more widely spaced than normal and have notches on the biting surfaces.

611.26   *The Girl of the Limberlost*] Novel (1909) by the writer and naturalist Gene Stratton-Porter (1863–1924) set in the Limberlost swamp in northeastern Indiana.

611.31–32   "Glow Worm," . . . Four Leaf Clover."] "Glow Worm," song from operetta *Lysistrata* (1902) with music by Paul Lincke (1866–1946), German lyrics by Heinrich Bolton-Baeckers (1871–1938), and English adaptation by Lilla Cayley Robinson; "Sleepy-Time Gal," song (1925) with music by Richard A. Whiting (1891–1938) and Ange Lorenzo (1894–1971) and lyrics by Joseph Alden and Raymond Egan (1890–1952); "I'm Looking Over a Four Leaf Clover," song (1927) with music by Harry M. Woods (1896–1970) and words by Mort Dixon (1892–1956).

612.3   Lily cups] A brand of paper cup.

618.18   Bull Durham] A brand of loose-leaf smoking tobacco.

619.25–26   *The Scarlet Pimpernel*] *The Triumph of the Scarlet Pimpernel* (1928), British silent costume drama adapted from the novel (1922) by Baroness Orczy, directed by T. Hayes Hunter, with screenplay by Angus McPhail and starring Matheson Lang, Juliette Compton, and Nelson Keys.

623.19   faunched up] Attacked in a rage.

625.37   Model A roadster] Two-door automobile manufactured by Ford, 1928–31.

627.35   Boston bag] A traveling bag with two carrying handles.

629.17–18   "The Little Swiss Twins"] *The Swiss Twins* (1922), one in a series of children's books written and illustrated by Lucy Fitch Perkins (1865–1937) that began with *The Dutch Twins* (1911).

630.11   Elsie Dinsmores."] See note 21.29.

637.8   salesman for the *Book of Knowledge*] Multivolume children's encyclopedia published by the Grolier Society (1912–66) that was sold door-to-door.

642.13 have a t.l.] A trade-last, i.e., a compliment to be exchanged for another compliment.

642.18 *The Pathfinder*] Novel (1840) by James Fenimore Cooper (1789–1851), one of the Leatherstocking Tales.

648.4 Reo] An automobile manufactured (1905–36) by the Michigan-based Reo Motor Car Company.

654.6 Brownie] One of a series of simple and inexpensive film cameras manufactured by Eastman Kodak, 1900–86, including the No. 2 Brownie (1901–35).

658.5 *bas bleu*."] Bluestocking.

659.11 elephant . . . the Broadmoor] The Cheyenne Mountain Zoo was founded in Colorado Springs in 1926 to house the exotic animals formerly exhibited at the nearby Broadmoor hotel and resort.

662.15–16 *Frater Ave Atque Vale*] Poem (1885) by Tennyson; the title means "brother, hail and farewell."

663.28–29 *The Count of . . . Beau Ideal*] *The Count of Monte Cristo* (1844–45), novel by the elder Alexandre Dumas (1802–1870); *Graustark: The Story of a Love Behind a Throne* (1901), novel by George Barr McCutcheon (1866–1928) set in an imaginary Eastern European country; *Beau Ideal* (1928), novel by Percival Christopher Wren (1875–1941) set in the French Foreign Legion.

666.35–38 Oh, we'll sit . . . blaws bare.] From the Scottish folk song "The Twa Corbies."

666.36 hause bane] Collarbone.

666.38 theek] Thatch.

THE CATHERINE WHEEL

672.1 *To My Father . . . My Mother*] John Richard Stafford (1874–1966) and Ethel McKillop Stafford (1876–1947).

674.1–9 *Man's life . . . to unreality*] From Part I of Eliot's verse drama (1935).

675.3 marriage elms] Term used in Maine for a pair of elm trees planted by a newly married couple outside their home.

676.27 "Scattergood Baines"] Collection of stories (1921) by Clarence Budington Kelland (1881–1964) about a shrewd hardware store owner in a small Vermont town.

677.3–4 *The Saturday Evening Post*] Weekly magazine (1821–1963) published in Philadelphia that achieved its greatest success under the ownership of Curtis Publishing, 1897–1969.

679.35 T Wharf] See note 255.7.

684.4–5   Hitler Jugend] Hitler Youth, Nazi youth organization established in 1926. It had almost 5.5 million members by 1936, representing more than 60 percent of the German population age ten to eighteen.

684.11   *Hakenkreuz*] Swastika (literally, "hook cross").

686.30–31   John Drew . . . Maude Adams] American actor John Drew (1853–1927); American actress Maude Adams (1872–1953), the first performer to play Peter Pan on Broadway.

686.32   Bridge of Sighs] Bridge across the Rio di Palazzo canal in Venice connecting the Doge's Palace with the New Prison.

689.14–15   Olympics . . . Berlin] The 1936 Summer Olympics.

691.8   phrenetic] Frenetic.

697.37   Prince of Wales] Edward VIII (1894–1972) was Prince of Wales, 1910–36. He ascended to the throne in January 1936 following the death of George V, but abdicated in December 1936 in order to marry Wallis Simpson (1896–1986), a divorced American woman.

711.5   *nymphaea*] Water lily.

714.18–20   "when many that feared . . . not of monuments."] From *Hydriotaphia, Urne-Buriall, or, A Discourse of the Sepulchrall Urnes lately found in Norfolk* (1658) by the physician and writer Thomas Browne (1605–1682).

716.25   *The Georgics*] Poem (36–29 B.C.E.) by Virgil (70–19 B.C.E.) about rural life.

717.7–8   for God's sake . . . deaths of kings.] *Richard II*, III.ii.155–56.

718.13   *Bowle*] Punch.

722.24   Ponce de Leon] Juan Ponce de León (1460–1521), Spanish explorer who, according to tradition, searched for the Fountain of Youth in Florida and the Bahamas.

724.36   golfing in Ballybunion] Town in Ireland on the Atlantic coast of County Kerry, the site of a golf club founded in 1893.

725.2   the North Shore] See note 348.37.

725.7–8   Brimmer Street] Street in the Beacon Hill area of Boston.

729.1–2   "Who is Kath'rine . . . commend her?"] Cf. *The Two Gentlemen of Verona*, IV.ii.39–40: "Who is Silvia? What is she, / That all our swains commend her?"

736.18   *Gone with the Wind*] Best-selling novel (1936) by Margaret Mitchell (1900–1949).

737.19   Musterole] Trade name of mustard ointment manufactured and sold by the Musterole Company of Cleveland, Ohio, 1907–56.

739.37   black-hand letters] Extortion letters.

740.40   *ma bonne*] My housemaid.

742.5   snipsnapsnorum] A card game for three or more players.

742.30–31   "Something is . . . of Denmark,"] *Hamlet*, I.iv.90.

743.27   *The Decline . . . Roman Empire*] History (six volumes, 1776–88) by Edward Gibbon (1737–1794).

743.34   *The Harvard Advocate*] See note 325.11.

746.5   Mayor Curley] James Michael Curley (1874–1958), a Democrat, was a Massachusetts congressman, 1911–14 and 1943–47, governor of Massachusetts, 1935–37, and mayor of Boston, 1914–18, 1922–26, 1930–34, and 1946–50.

746.19   Lizzie Borden] Borden (1860–1927) was accused in 1892 of murdering her father and stepmother with an axe inside the family home in Fall River, Massachusetts. She was tried and acquitted in 1893.

750.25   *Life on the Mississippi*] Autobiographical narrative (1883) by Mark Twain (1835–1910).

750.31–34   "I sent thee late . . . not withered be,"] Cf. "Song: to Celia" (1616) by Ben Jonson (1572–1637).

755.19   Mothersills] A popular remedy for seasickness, manufactured by the Canadian Mothersill Remedy Company, that used hyoscine as its main ingredient.

755.28   Albert Payson Terhune] Terhune (1872–1942) was a popular writer of fiction about dogs, including *Lad: A Dog* (1919) and *Lad of Sunnybrook* (1928).

757.1   Scollay Square] A square in downtown Boston, now the site of the Government Center.

757.9–10   Poor Richard . . . *Breakfast Table*] *Poor Richard's Almanack*, published from 1733 to 1758 by Benjamin Franklin (1706–1790); *The Autocrat of the Breakfast-Table* (1858), collection of essays by Oliver Wendell Holmes (1809–1894).

762.35–36   "On the Sunny . . . the Street"] Song (1930) with music by Jimmy McHugh (1894–1969) and lyrics by Dorothy Fields (1904–1974).

762.37   "Santa Lucia"] A traditional Neapolitan song that is also sung with Italian and English lyrics.

764.15–16   those dolls . . . *the Native*] *The Return of the Native* (1878), novel by Thomas Hardy (1840–1928) in which the superstitious Susan Nunsuch makes a wax doll of her enemy Eustacia Vye, sticks it with pins, and then burns it.

766.14   St. Stephen's Green] A park in central Dublin.

770.4 the Phillips Brooks calendar] An appointment calendar that featured daily quotations from the sermons and lectures of the Episcopal clergyman Phillips Brooks (1835–1893), who served as the rector of Trinity Church in Boston, 1869–91, and as bishop of Massachusetts, 1891–93.

772.36 *fin amour*] Fine love, i.e., courtly love, chivalric love.

773.21–28 Michael Henchard . . . Jude] Michael Henchard, protagonist of *The Mayor of Castlebridge* (1886); Eustachia Vye, character in *The Return of the Native* (1878); Tess Durbeyfield, protagonist of *Tess of the D'Urbervilles* (1891); Jude Fawley, protagonist of *Jude the Obscure* (1895).

774.4 Dr. Johnson's dictionary] *A Dictionary of the English Language*, published in 1755 by Samuel Johnson (1709–1784).

776.30 Murad] An American brand of cigarette made from Turkish tobacco.

782.24 "Lord Randal"] A traditional Scottish ballad.

787.17 *Old Ironsides*] Poem (1830) by Oliver Wendell Holmes about the frigate USS *Constitution*.

790.37 "The Volga Boatmen"] A Russian folk song.

792.2 Loch Katrine] A freshwater loch in the Scottish Highlands.

792.13–14 *Henry Esmond . . . Illustrated London News*] *The History of Henry Esmond, Esquire* (1852), novel by William Makepeace Thackery (1811–1863); *The Age of Fable* (1855) by Thomas Bulfinch (1796–1867); *The Illustrated London News*, weekly magazine (1842–1971).

792.18 Canfield] A solitaire card game.

793.34–35 *The Language of Flowers*] The book was "arranged" by the American journalist Caroline Matilda Kirkland (1801–1864) and published circa 1848.

794.28–29 Godey's ladies] *Godey's Lady's Book*, monthly magazine (1830–98) known for its hand-tinted illustrations depicting the latest women's fashions.

795.2–3 Lear's *Nonsense Rhymes . . . Green Hat.*] *A Book of Nonsense* (1846) by Edward Lear (1812–1888); *Memoirs of a Midget* (1921), novel by Walter de la Mare (1873–1956); *The Green Hat* (1924), novel by Michael Arlen (1895–1956).

801.32 conjugating *fero, ferre, tuli, latum*] Conjugating the irregular verb for "to carry, to bear."

807.2 "Vielen dank, Meinherr"] "Many thanks, sir."

807.4 "Gut gesprechen, gnädiges Fräulein] "You speak well, young lady."

808.16–17 Bermuda . . . combustion machine] Automobile ownership was prohibited on the island from 1908 to 1946.

821.33 martyr Catherine] Catherine of Alexandria, who according to tradition was martyred during the reign (306–12) of the Emperor Maxentius.

825.28 *veritas* and *semper*] "Truth" and "always."

836.30 "Jerusalem, the Golden"] Hymn with words (1851) by John Mason Neale (1818–1866), based on a twelfth-century Latin poem by Bernard of Cluny, and music (1853) by Alexander Ewing (1830–1895).

837.37 Tauber valley] In the Franconia region of Germany.

838.16 *daube glacé*] See note 374.38.

843.24–25 *Lusitania* . . . Mrs. Leary's cow] A German submarine sank the British liner *Lusitania* off the coast of Ireland on May 7, 1915, killing 1,198 people. The conflagration that devastated Chicago, October 8–10, 1871, destroying 17,500 buildings and killing as many as 300 people, began in a barn owned by Catherine and Patrick O'Leary, although there is no evidence supporting the story that the fire began when a cow kicked over a lantern.

APPENDIX

854.7 *Everyman*] *The Somonynge of Everyman*, a late fifteenth-century English morality play.

854.34 *The Springs*] The northern section of East Hampton, New York.

THE LIBRARY OF AMERICA SERIES

Library of America fosters appreciation of America's literary heritage by publishing, and keeping permanently in print, authoritative editions of America's best and most significant writing. An independent nonprofit organization, it was founded in 1979 with seed funding from the National Endowment for the Humanities and the Ford Foundation.